SURVIVOR

STUART HARVEY

Printed in the United States of America

ISBN: Softcover   979-8-88622-473-3
             eBook   979-8-88622-475-7
             Hardcover   979-8-88622-476-4
Republished by: PageTurner Press and Media LLC
Publication Date: 07/21/2022

To order copies of this book, contact:
PageTurner Press and Media
Phone: 1-888-447-9651
info@pageturner.us
www.pageturner.us

TABLE OF CONTENTS

CHAPTER ONE

The Nearly Ordinary Girl

Time; in a sense when your young, goes very; very slowly. Free, wild and innocent, are usually words that are used to describe the young of a modern world. Many young lives would thrive in a modern world, with technology, world class healthcare and an ever-adapting social scene, which is as diverse as it's ever been throughout history. In most cases, right at their fingertips; and always there when it's needed. Planet Earth, as we know it, has never had anything like it. Even so, there is always an ever-present danger which threatens all life on Earth. A presence so powerful, that it has shaped everything since the Earth was formed; that force; is the mighty, mother nature. Mother nature is the most powerful force of all. It decides our weather and climate, what survives and what doesn't, and can even shape the very fabric of time itself.

Everyday lives, countries, events and history have all been determined on the whim of mother nature; and mother nature, always wins. No matter how fast you run or how far you travel, mother nature always gets you in the end. The January of 2020 had come around that year as very cold and very dark. The branches on the trees were covered in frost, with a dampness in the air from the low hanging fog, which rolled in off the many fields surrounding the small town of Lillington, which was situated right on the very edge of the Hertfordshire border with the county of Essex in the British Isles. This was the scene that greeted the residences of the town of Lillington, on this particular Monday January morning. Lillington, with its small square red and grey bricked houses and accompanying lush green lawns, looked the same as any other ordinary English town would look.

This was the same on the outer edge of Lillington, down the cul-de-sac named Edgeware Gardens. At number 14 Edgeware Gardens, was the home of the lovely and charming Bonham family. Eldest of them all, was Richard Bonham, a fifty-six-year-old Engineer, with short cropped hair that was so thin, you'd think he was almost bald. He was clean shaven, and very well built for his age, having spent many years as the rank of Warrant Officer class one, in the British Army's Royal Engineers battalion, fixing and repairing all of its equipment and machinery on a daily basis. Also in the house, was fifty-four-year-old Yvette Bonham, who had been married to Richard for over thirty years. Yvette was a little shorter than Richard, only standing at five feet, eight inches tall, with shoulder length black hair, which was nearly always tied back in a tight bun at the back of her head.

This she did, because she worked as the towns Librarian at the local library, and always maintained that she had to look as professional as possible, at all times, due to the nature of her work, keeping the proud and noble shelves of Lillington library in alphabetical and category order. The last member of the Bonham household, was Richard and Yvette's only child, by the name of Samantha. Samantha Bonham, commonly known by many as Sam, was just as she liked to see herself; but not quite, all of the same. For one thing, Samantha was very free in her life; she was, as put by her parents, 'the nearly ordinary girl'. Samantha herself, was quite proud of one thing in particular though, above all else; and that were her looks. She adored them wholeheartedly, and always spent every spare moment that she had being photographed as a model, in everything from a Hawaiian beach bikini, to full length prom and evening gowns of all shapes and sizes.

Her naturally flowing shoulder length brunette hair was a little curly, but still fell gracefully and gently around her head and face. Her father Richard, always said that Samantha was his tough little angel. Whereas Samantha's mother Yvette, always said that Samantha was her wonderful baby princess, due to her wonderful heart shaped face, meaning she seen as quite the attractive type amongst the local guys within the town. Samantha always wanted people to know about her wonderful kindness too, which her family had always praised her for, and made her one of the most popular people among the neighbours. She was a lady who always swore to never turn her back on people who needed help, even if they had done wrong, as she always believed in second chances for people in the world.

Maybe it was this wonderful particular personality trait, that had caused her to go into the career that she had. As much as any stereotypical person would make assumptions, but charming, intelligent, bubbly, pretty Samantha Bonham, wasn't a newspaper page three model, glamour queen or even fancy blogger. No, she had chosen and followed through in her dream to become a long-distance lorry driver. Her ultimate dream, even from earliest childhood days, had been to own her own truck, but she'd sadly never been able to afford one, owing to their expensively high one hundred thousand pounds starting price, just for the basis of model trucks. So, she had been forced to settle for a company lorry instead, which she had christened 'Betsie', on her very first day when she had started at the haulage company that she worked for in Lillington.

The residences of number 14 Edgeware Gardens however, were all about to be woken with a start, with the alarm clock, which promptly shrilled out loud, before falling to the floor and smashing into a half dozen pieces, as it would often do in funny cartoons on the television.

As they were all still in bed, this being around 6:30am in the morning, it made for mixed results. Richard Bonham immediately snapped upright as a soldier would do on a parade ground, and began to dress at top speed, knowing he was on duty at 7:30am that day, and he certainly didn't want to be court martial for being late onto duty, as those were the rules of military life. Yvette Bonham got up a little more slowly than her husband, rubbing her eyes, but still with a brisk snappiness, like her husband Richard had done.

The only one who didn't snap out of bed at the sound of the alarm clock, was Samantha, but it wasn't because she couldn't be asked; but because of the fact that it was her day off today, and she was having a well-earned rest from doing many long shifts at the wheel of her wonderful steed, Betsie. There was a sharp knocking sound on Samantha's bedroom door, as Yvette walked in half dressed, whilst holding a piece of toast in her hand. "You can't stay in bed all day young lady, just because it's your day off today, doesn't mean you can laze around" said Yvette, her voice muffled slightly, due to the effect of a mouthful of toast, as she walked back out of the room. Samantha, who had only been half listening, peered her head above the duvet, her hair sticking to her face and her eyes only half open, as she had not been expecting her mother to just burst in on her unexpectantly as she had done so.

"I'm not lazing around mum, I'm meeting Greg this morning, and then I'm out with the girls later tonight" replied Samantha, as she caught a glimpse of Yvette's retreating back, as Yvette was walking away down the stairs from Samantha now open bedroom door. Greg was Samantha's boyfriend, as they'd both met at their place of work, which was the small logistics haulage firm of Travis Transport Limited, based in Lillington's small industrial estate on the other side of the town from Edgeware Gardens. Greg was also a lorry driver at Travis Transport Limited, and they had both planned to have the day off together, which at Travis Transport Limited, was quite a skill to do. If Greg hadn't been the boss's son however, then it might have a bit more difficult to do so, but he just said to his father that he and Samantha wanted a bit of quiet time to

4

themselves for once.

Samantha had also planned to meet up with her friends, or 'the girls' as she knew them, later that night; and had even been shopping the previous week to get a brand-new dress for the night ahead, which was hanging up in her wardrobe since she had brought it back from the shops the previous week. Samantha had sat up in bed by now, running a hand through her hair, to brush it backwards across her head and out of her face. Yawning and stretching, she reached across to her bedside table, and took a sip from the glass of water that she always kept by the side of her bed. She then pushed the bed clothes back to the foot of the bed, before checking the time on her smartphone positioned on the bedside table. The time on the screen showed that it was 6:35am; but this wasn't a problem, as Samantha was a get up and go girl anyway.

In honest truth, this was really on work days, as she did like to have a lie in if that was something she could do. Samantha then pulled herself upright onto her feet, walking out of the bedroom and onto the landing, pulling a dressing gown on over her pyjamas. After a short trip down the small staircase, Samantha arrived in the downstairs kitchen, where she found Richard tucking into a bowl of porridge, whilst Yvette was pouring some milk into her cup of tea. This was quite a skill of Yvette's it had to be said, as she was trying to pull her hair back into the tight bun at the back and clip it into place with a hairpin, whilst also making a cup of tea. "Ah there she is, how are you this morning Sam my angel" asked Richard, as he spotted Samantha entering the kitchen, with a spoonful of porridge halfway to his lips.

"Aww, bit sleepy dad, but looking forward to seeing Greg and the girls later" replied Samantha, as she gave Richard a big hug, narrowly missing Richard's outstretched spoon of porridge as she went. "Ah yes of course, this illusive Greg character that you keep telling us about; well, all I will say is that I hope he's going to take good care of you today" replied Richard, smiling slightly as he saw the look of happiness on Samantha's face, as she broke away from hugging her father, heading instead for the nearest cupboard where the cereals were located. As the family were an overall generally healthy bunch, things like porridge oats, corn flakes, and other healthy brands of cereal and food packages, littered the inside of the kitchen cupboards, alongside the boxes of teabags and coffee beans that were also present on the kitchen worktop.

"I'm sure he will grace us with his presence soon enough darling" said Yvette, who had just seated herself down at the kitchen table with her usual morning cup of tea. "Ah mum" replied Samantha, who was starting to blush slightly, as Yvette finished speaking. "He sounds like a nice boy that one, I wouldn't knock it you know; I know you said you've always wanted a church wedding" replied Richard, through a mouthful of porridge. "Ah yes, well we do want to see some grandkids at some point Sam" said Yvette, following on from Richard's last comment. This latest comment from Yvette had made Samantha go, if it was possible, even redder than before, as she blushed again. "Ah mum, dad, please, don't rush me, Greg's cute and everything, but I don't want to rush into things too quickly" replied Samantha, as Richard looked down at the military grade wristwatch, strapped onto his hairy left arm.

"Best be off you know, I think I'm going to be late tonight darling; as I've been told the RAF are flying back some of our jeeps and things from Afghanistan today, so I'm probably going to be working over time getting them all processed; I'll try and call later if I can if anything changes" replied Richard, as he stood up and returned his now empty porridge bowl over to the sink, and placing it on the kitchen sideboard, after rinsing it off in the sink dishwater. "Of course, have a good day darling" replied Yvette, giving Richard a kiss, as Richard stopped just before the kitchen door into the hallway. "Have a good time today Sam" said Richard, as he picked up his royal army engineers beret from the sideboard, before fitting it smartly onto his head as he went. "Aww, thanks dad, have a good day at work" replied Samantha, giving Richard another teddy bear type hug, before pulling away from him again.

Richard gave Samantha a smile in return, before picking up his keys and walking straight out of the front door, as it clicked shut behind him. Samantha then walked around to the cupboard and began to pour out some cereal into a bowl, as the unmistakeable sounds of an army jeep engine starting up and backing out of the driveway reached their ears. Richard being the rank that he was within the Army, allowed him certain perks of the job, one of them enabled him to bring an Army jeep home to be used as his mode of transport to and from work every day. "What time are you meeting Greg" asked Yvette, as Samantha sat down at the table with her bowl of cereal. "Not till ten o clock, he's picking me up in his new car from the garage this morning as well; think he wants to show it off or something" replied Samantha, grinning slightly at that moment, in the same way that a small child would do, if they were being presented with a very large toy.

Amongst her other things, Samantha was also a bit of a petrol head too, and had always wanted to own a large collection of vehicles, including a number of cars and motorcycles. Her father Richard had ridden one in his early twenties, but had sadly been involved in a crash with it, and so Yvette wasn't keen on letting Samantha own and ride one, because of her father's crash many years earlier. After breakfast, Samantha had disappeared back upstairs to her bedroom, as Yvette had left for work calling upstairs as she left through the front door, "remember to lock up when you go out", as the front door clicked shut. Samantha meanwhile had opened up her wardrobe and began going through the clothes that she would wear that day. As she wasn't sure what Greg had got planned for her that day, she decided on going with some casual clothes, as this usually delivered the best results, when she was in doubt about these things.

All that Samantha really knew of course, was to meet Greg in the local park at 10am that morning. And so, at exactly 9:50am that morning, Samantha found herself sitting on one of the local park benches, waiting for Greg to arrive in his new car from the garage. The local park in Lillington was quite small compared to most parks around the country. There was a line of trees by the roadside on one side of the park, and a block of flats on the other, with the river running through the centre of it. Samantha had gone for a plain and casual look today wearing jeans and a top, whilst wearing her black leather jacket as well to keep her warm, as this was still January time, when the temperature dropped below freezing at times. The weatherman had said earlier that day on the forecast, that it was supposed to warm up that day, but that didn't stop Samantha's breath to swirl and gather in front of her in clouds of warm steam vapour.

Almost instinctively, Samantha suddenly looked to her right, and saw a family with their young kids standing on the river bridge, throwing bits of bread into the river to feed the half a dozen swans, that had congregated there since she had arrived and sat on the park bench. Samantha grinned to herself, remembering a memory from her own childhood, where she was feeding the ducks with her family using a loaf of bread. Right on que; at exactly 10am; the unmistakable sounds of a high-powered car reached Samantha's ears; the sound itself becoming louder and louder as it got closer to her. The engine sound swelled to a roar, as at that very moment, a bright yellow Lamborghini Aventador came into view before Samantha, slowing to a stop by the kerbside on the road, close to where Samantha was sitting, which made Samantha nearly jump backwards in alarm.

Sat at the wheel of the Lamborghini Aventador was Samantha's boyfriend, Greg Stent, who grinned from ear to ear when he saw Samantha sat on the bench. Samantha's jaw dropped, when she saw what Greg had brought, before getting to her feet and walking slowly over towards the car. "Hey hey, how's it going babes" said Greg, opening the driver's side door, and then proceeding to walk up to Samantha, who had just closed her mouth, so as not to let dribble come out of it, where she had been gapping at the sight of the bright yellow Lamborghini. In traditional noble fashion, he kissed Samantha on the lips, and then proceeded to take her hand, and lead her over to the car. "What do you think eh babes, cool isn't it" said Greg, still smiling broadly at the site of his girlfriend, gazing at the £200,000 super car, as if she had never seen one before in her entire life.

Greg was around a year older than Samantha was, standing in at around six foot in height, with a muscular six pack underneath his shirt, along with arms that looked like battleship guns. Samantha was a bit shorter than he was, and was now regretting not wearing high heels; as she would have needed them just to come up to Greg's skyscraper height. "How, how did you get this" stammered Samantha, as she took in the yellow Lamborghini's over shinny paint and bodywork in front of her. The Lamborghini Aventador seemed to look shinier, not just because of its freshness, but also because of the fact that the sun was out, which gleamed off the paintwork, blinding anyone who looked at it. "Well, there are advantages to being the boss's son" replied Greg, which was true of course. Greg was indeed the boss's son at Travis Transport Limited, and had been allowed to get away with a lot more than most at the company over the years he had worked there.

"Come on, there's something I want to show you, hop in" replied Greg, as he allowed Samantha to climb in to the passenger seat, before closing the door for her, which didn't open and close like a normal car door would. Instead, the Lamborghini's doors opened and closed vertically, rise straight up into the air when they were opened. Once Samantha was inside, Greg climbed into the driver's seat, closing his driver's door behind him as he went. Greg inserted the small blocked key into the ignition, as the Lamborghini seemed to come to life around him, as he started up the engine again. The engine roared into life after a second or so, as Greg pushed the gear lever into the forwards position, as it was an automatic gearbox. Knowing that Samantha got a little nervous as a passenger sometimes, Greg drove off a little more slowly than he would usually have done.

Had he been alone in the driver's seat, Greg would have most certainly have opened the taps, as Greg was a bit of a fan of Formula One, and did have a bit of need for speed gene in his blood. "I still can't believe that this is your new car" replied Samantha, afraid to even put her feet out in front of her all the way forwards, so as not to put dirt in the footwell. "Ways and means babes, ways and means" replied Greg, giving his nose a quick tap with his finger. Samantha couldn't help at that point but allow herself a grin. "Where are we even going, it feels like a right mystery tour" asked Samantha, as she clipped on her seatbelt, still amazed that Greg had managed to get himself a car that was worth so much money. "You'll see" replied Greg, turning his head slightly to look at her, a small smile breaking out across his face.

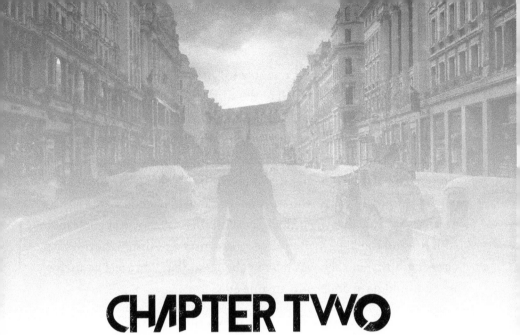

CHAPTER TWO

Friends and Surprises

Greg drove for around five minutes or so, before pulling up in a free parking space on one of the many side streets in Lillington. Samantha immediately recognised where she was from the surrounding buildings and parade of shops. It was the closest side street away from the town centre, as she could see people and traffic rumbling by on the main road leading into it. "Ok, you've brought me into town" replied Samantha, sounding a little put out, as she had thought Greg was taking her on a mystery tour somewhere. "You'll see; the trip isn't over yet; come on" replied Greg, opening his door and stepping out of the car. 'Thank god I didn't wear heels' thought Samantha, as she too opened her door and stepped out of the car, feeling that whatever Greg had planned for her, having blisters by the time she got there, wasn't what she had in mind for that day.

Greg had started to walk away, beckoning Samantha to follow him, so Samantha broke into a jog to catch up to him, as Greg had longer leg's than what she did, and was able to cover twice as much ground as Samantha could with only half of the stride from his own legs. "I'm still at a loss as to where you're taking me you know babe" said Samantha, as she caught up to Greg, panting slightly from having to work harder to catch up. When Samantha had finally caught her breath back, Greg held out his arm, allowing Samantha to take it in her own. "You'll see soon, it's a surprise" said Greg, who was now starting to make Samantha a little nervous. She was always a little concuss of what she allowed people to do with her and the like when it came to surprises and things; but this was Greg her boyfriend she was talking about, so she didn't feel as anxious as she would have done with anyone else.

They both walked a short way down the high street, which was packed full of busy shoppers, all trying to get the latest deals in the post-Christmas January sales. Greg suddenly stopped outside of the local town centre newsagents, nearly making Samantha trip over in shock, as she was not expecting Greg to suddenly stop beside her. "Woah, what was that for" exclaimed Samantha suddenly, as Greg turned to face her, taking both of Samantha's hands in his own. "Do you trust me babe" asked Greg in a calm voice, as Samantha felt a little chill go up her spine. It wasn't a bad spine chill though, but instead, a feeling that butterflies were rising slowly inside her stomach.

"Of course I do Greg, what is it" replied Samantha, in what she hoped was a questioning voice, as Greg looked directly into Samantha's eyes. The busy shoppers passing them by, didn't seem to be paying to much attention, as Samantha stood nervously awaiting what Greg was going to do next. "I'm going to need to ask if you can close your eyes, and let me lead you" said Greg, as Samantha's nerves hit the roof. It sounded as if Greg had led her into the town centre, just to ask her to dance with him. "Erm, you want me to close my eyes, can't I just see what you want me to see here and now" asked Samantha, feeling that if ballroom dancing was what Greg wanted, he could have done that in the local town dance hall? "Trust me, I need you to do this for me" replied Greg, as he was starting to wonder whether Samantha would comply or not to his request.

Fortunately, Samantha did as she was told, and closed her eyes, allowing Greg to suddenly pull her to the right. Samantha cautiously walked forwards with anticipation, allowing Greg to lead her where he wanted her to go. It must have looked strange to other people who were passing, seeing Greg lead Samantha around with her eyes closed, hoping that she wouldn't bang into anything as she went. There was a tinkle of a shop bell, and the sound of a door opening, as the coldness of the outside air was suddenly replaced with a wall of warm air. Samantha jumped slightly as she heard the shop bell, as she wasn't expecting to hear it, as she still had her eyes closed, as per Greg's instructions. She also began to sweat a little as well, because she was wearing her leather jacket, and this shop was warmer than it was outside in the high street. "You can open them now" said Greg, as Samantha opened her eyes, and what greeted her, made her jaw drop in shock.

She was standing in a wedding shop, with comfy red chairs and a sofa, and matching carpets on the floor, made out of the same red velvet material, that could be seen being used by celebrities at a high function event. Hanging up down one aisle, was row after row of stunning bridal gowns, each one coming attached with the designer's label and price tag. On another row, were just as many bridesmaid's dresses, and further down towards the back of the shop, were the evening and prom gowns, again, each with a designer and price label attached to them. "Surprise" exclaimed Greg, throwing his hands up in the air and then back down again, smiling broadly at Samantha as he did so. Samantha stood there for a second with her mouth wide open in a perfect gapping gesture, whilst simultaneously bringing her hands up to her mouth, hardly daring to believe where she was standing at that very moment.

"What do you think then babes, I arranged it all with your family for you to come here today and have a fitting done" replied Greg, as realisation hit Samantha with the force of a speeding train. "O.M.G, did you just propose to me" exclaimed Samantha, finally closing her mouth and lowering her hands away from her face? Before Greg could answer Samantha's question however, the shop owner came through from the back of the shop. She was quite a young-looking woman, around Samantha's own age and height, also with short brunette hair, and with a broad smile on her face. "Ah, you must be the bride to be then" said the shop owner, as she rushed forward and grabbed Samantha's arm. Samantha looked back at Greg, with a look of half admiration, and half shock on her face; as Greg just returned it with a simple smile, allowing Samantha to be towed away by the shop owner, into the depths of the shop.

"Have fun babes, you earned this; I'll be waiting in the car for you when you've finished in here" replied Greg, before he turned on his heels, and was straight out of the door without a backwards glance. "Ok my dear, I think we can start over here" said the shop owner, as Samantha clearly wasn't thinking straight as she was pulled along through the rows of hangers, feeling as if she some kind of motor vehicle's trailer, and had just been hitched up by an exceptionally powerful road car. The rest of the morning, and even a good half of the afternoon, seemed to flash past at lightning speed, as if someone had tampered with the clocks, to make them tick by at twice their usual speed. Samantha couldn't deny, that it was one of the happiest days in her life, and it had all started with the moment that Greg had turned around in the shop entrance, and presented an engagement ring to Samantha, before she had been whisked away from him.

All that Samantha could really properly remember from that day, were seeing all sorts of different styles of bridal gowns flashing through the air, as one by one, she would try one on, only for it to get pulled off of her, and another one slid on in its place. But with each one she tried, the happier she seemed to become. By three' o clock that afternoon, Samantha had managed to select the dress that she wanted, out of all of the dresses she had tried on that day; but then came the most interesting question of all; how exactly was she going to pay for it? She wasn't exactly carrying her bank account with her, or her debit card for that matter, and the dress itself had been worth well in excess of £700, being that of a designer one too boot. The wedding gown Samantha had chosen, looked exactly as she had always pictured how she would look walked down the aisle.

It was a strapless design, but with lace sleeves down either side, and a nice hooped skirt, with lace pattern decoration all over the chest and breast area. Almost as if by using an invisible psychic skill, the shop owner had seemed to read Samantha's face, as she quickly responded, "don't worry about the payment sweetie, your Fiancée has already sorted that out for you, and paid up in advance". If anything, up until this point hadn't shocked Samantha already that day, then this piece of news, practically sent her soaring upwards in delight. First Greg had brought a new car, which had cost him, heavens only knew, many hundreds of thousands of pounds. Then taken Samantha surprise wedding dress shopping, because he had proposed to her, without her even knowing she was being proposed to. As promised hours earlier, Greg was sitting in the bright yellow Lamborghini Avantador, exactly where they had parked earlier that day.

Greg nervously drumming his fingers on the steering wheel, hoping against hope, that Samantha hadn't got too carried away, and not been rushed to hospital due to overexcitement. As Greg sat inside the Lamborghini, his hand twitched slightly, as he kept glancing all around him, as if he was in fear of the fact, that person or persons unknown were watching him, as he sat there in the driver's seat. At that exact moment, Samantha rounded the corner to the side street, carrying a bulky dress bag, which she was desperately fighting against, trying to keep the dress bag straight, not wanting to crease it in any way. Seeing Samantha approaching the Lamborghini in the rear-view mirror with the rather bulky dress bag, Greg waited until Samantha had drawn level to him, before he quickly hopped out of the car, throwing open the boot lid, so as to carefully lay the bulky dress bag down gently inside of it.

Closing the Lamborghini's boot lid very carefully with a small click,

Samantha waited until they had both clambered back into the car, before launching herself over at Greg and kissing him, whilst simultaneously locking him in an arm breaking hug. "Wow, what's all this about then" exclaimed Greg, as he managed to wriggle free of Samantha, but Samantha pressed a finger on his lips before he could say anymore. "You are the most sexist, kindest and selfless guy I will ever meet; and that was for today; I loved trying on all those gowns, I felt like a princess" replied Samantha, pulling away from Greg to sit back in her seat, as Greg turned bright red, a little abashed. "Well, you are my princess babes, I always told you that" replied Greg, who pulled a small scarlet red box out of his pocket. "I think this belongs to you" he said, as he opened it in front of Samantha.

Samantha was almost prepared for what was inside it, but still couldn't help letting out a small whimper and grin broadly, when she saw the diamond engagement ring gleaming inside it. "Aww" couped Samantha, as she gently pulled the ring from the small scarlet red box, and slid the ring onto her finger, holding it up to the light, examining it as she went. "I only want the best for my bride to be" replied Greg, as he closed the boxes lid, and placed it inside the glove box, just to the left of the centre console. As Greg's hand retreated back from closing the glove box door however, Samantha's attention was suddenly taken by what looked like a small laminated postcard pamphlet, sitting in the centre console, among Greg's sunglasses case, and a bag of toffees. At first, it looked like a flyer for a travel company, as Greg had always been a keen travelling, and had expressed a wish to tour the world during his lifetime.

The words, 'The Future Start Here', were emblazed across the top on the back of the card, while on the front meanwhile, was a picture of a coastline that Samantha didn't recognise. "What's that babe" asked Samantha, pointing down at the pamphlet in the centre consol. Greg looked down at it, and then his eyes darted back to Samantha, a look of puzzlement on his face. Greg's look of puzzlement however, immediately changed to understanding when he saw it, remembering what it was all of a sudden, as the memory of it came back to him in an instant. "Oh yeah; I'd forgotten I'd had that with me; it was delivered to my house this morning with my name on it" replied Greg, pulling it out and opening it. Samantha glanced at it seeing a series of numbers in three rows, which looked like dates of some kind. "Must be some kind of junk mail" said Samantha, as Greg handed it to her; but as he did so, he was suddenly struck with a mad idea.

"Here you go Sam; tell you what; if you work it out; I'll even pay for the honeymoon in Hawaii as well" replied Greg, as Samantha's face lite up again, realising what Greg was saying to her. "No way, you're planning on sending us both to Hawaii for a honeymoon; alright, you're on" exclaimed Samantha, taking the pamphlet from Greg and pocketing it, determined to work out what the pamphlet was all about, even if it killed her. "Or gave me a mental nervous breakdown" thought Samantha, allowing herself a broad grin as she thought about that very subject. "That's the spirit babes, I'd better get you home, as your out with the girls tonight eh" replied Greg, as Samantha smiled at him again, before starting to play with her hair a little, curling it around her finger as she went, to see what would happen to it. Samantha didn't quite know it, but she could have sworn that Greg wasn't being as clear about the pamphlet, as maybe he should have been.

Greg started up the engine, as it roared into life, leaving a squeal of tyres, and a quick puff of white smoke from the tyres, as it sped away, leaving a few people looking after them at the impressive style that the bright yellow Lamborghini Aventador had on them, both physically and mentally. Once back in her bedroom at home, Samantha hung up her brand-new wedding dress with pride, making sure that it did not clash with anything that she already had up hanging up around the room. Samantha would have dearly loved to try it on again; but fearing that she would ruin it before the big day, so rather sadly decided against it. Besides, that night was the girl's night out, and she needed that time to start getting ready, knowing how important a night on the town was to her. Samantha sadly never got much of a chance to socialise due to work and the like, so anytime that she did get to do it, was always very sacred to her.

As Samantha wasn't having dinner until later on that evening, she decided to have the full works as she called it. This involved having a shower, washing her hair, and even straightening it, which wasn't what she usually did, as Samantha always liked her hair slightly wavey like in appearance. She did however decide on a few curls at the front, for a little bit of a dramatic and beautiful effect, just to show off a little to her friends. Doing her makeup was fairly easy for her, as she was so used to doing it day after day, plus with the added bonus of not having to do as much, due to her skin and the fact that she was in a rugged line of work, rather than working in an enclosed environment. But the one thing she was most proud of, was the dress she had brought. An off the shoulder knee length dress, made of silk fabric and royal blue in colour, along with matching three-inch high heeled shoes.

She'd finished off the whole look, by adding a pair of diamond earrings to her ears, which had been sent to her as a birthday present a few years ago. Samantha grinned slightly, as she admired herself in the mirror, turning on the spot to admire her looks in the mirror. Samantha subconsciously ran a hand down her dress to flatten it down, thinking of what her friends would say when they saw her engagement ring, and saw pictures of her wedding dress when Samantha got around to showing them off. Samantha had agreed to meet the girls at a local restaurant in the town centre at 7pm that night; and sure enough, when the taxi that Samantha had ordered to take her there, dropped her off at 7pm on the dot, she could clearly see the girls sitting at a round benched booth in the corner of the room, beside the window with an open view out onto the main high street itself.

Samantha thanked the taxi driver for bringing her into the town centre, and then paid the taxi driver with a few twenty-pound notes that she had in her pocket with her, before proceeding up to the restaurant door, her high heeled shoes making the usual clicking sounds on the pavement as she walked. A group of lads came up to the restaurant door on their way out, and in gentlemen style fashion, they kindly held it open for Samantha as she approached. Samantha thanked them as they passed, but even though they were being friendly towards her, Samantha couldn't help but clearly hear a couple of them wolf whistle as the door closed behind her. Samantha's friends immediately saw her when she entered, proceeding to beckon her over to them, as they all sat at the table by the window, admiring Samantha as she approached them, grinning broadly.

"Ah wow, you look stunning babes" was the general response from them all, as Samantha sat down at the table with them, in the only vacant chair which had been set aside especially for her. Samantha grinned broadly at the sign of her best friends, as she always did when she was in the best of company. "Aww, thanks peeps" replied Samantha, as a waiter came over to their table, notebook in hand, ready to take their orders for the meals. "Are you ready to order" asked the waiter, as they all placed their orders, Samantha only quickly flicking through the menu, to find out what she liked, and whether it was still being served or not. Samantha managed to make up her mind quite quickly however, as the waiter collected up their menus and strolled away, leaving them all to chat amongst themselves, as the girls went back to admiring Samantha again, loving every inch of her as they always did so at times like this.

The girls, as Samantha always knew them, consisted of three of her best friends from her school days, alongside Samantha herself. Rachel Stevens, Emily Forrester and Diana Gibbs, were three intelligent and very charming ladies, just like Samantha was, and had all been the best of friends, ever since their school days. They were all around the same height as each other, which was about five foot, nine inches tall, without the sometimes monster high heels they sometimes wore. Rachel Stevens had long blonde hair, and a slight long pointed face, with thin eyebrows, which she always tried to make thicker using an eyebrow pencil, as he always felt that they were too thin for her. Emily Forrester had shoulder length black hair, just like Yvette Bonham had, and her face and eyebrows were more heart-shaped in appearance; a fact which she was constantly reminded, suited her very well.

The last member of the group was the charming Diana Gibbs, who also just happened to be the brightest out of the four of them. Diana had the shortish hair length of them all, with her brunette hair only reaching down to chin; but she had always liked it that way, as she had explained to the rest of them when they had all said about why it wasn't as long as theirs were. They were all very thin as well; just like Samantha was, most of them not going bigger than a dress size ten. But even so, Rachel, Emily and Diana, were always amazed at how skinny Samantha could be, despite being a lorry driver by trade, spending most of her day sat around on her backside, not moving as much. "OMG, did I get so stitched up today peeps" exclaimed Samantha with a giggle, as all three of them looked surprised and shocked. "Why; what happened Sam" asked Emily, as she took a sip of her cocktail that she'd ordered earlier on.

"It was Greg, I'd agreed to meet him you see, and I was completely in the dark this morning; then, if would you believe it; he turns up with this brand-new Lamborghini; then he took me into town, told me to shut my eyes, and then promptly walked me into the bridal shop, and told me to try on as many as I liked, before then proposing to me in the car, after he'd paid for a stunning gown" replied Samantha, as she told her story, watching the looks on her friends faces begin to grow in surprise, as Samantha got further and further into telling them the story of that day. Their looks didn't seem to be as shocked as Samantha would have expected from her friends, and Samantha did partly suspect that her friends must have known that she was bound to be proposed to, at some point in her lifetime. "Well; come on then; let see the dress Sam" replied Rachel, in response to Samantha's story.

Maybe it was the room; or what had happened in the space of twenty-four hours; but Samantha had a funny feeling in her gut, that she still felt that they weren't acting the way that they should have been. Her friends would have usually been jumping with joy if they were told the news that Samantha had been given, rather than sitting around smiling away at Samantha, like a Cheshire cat which has swallowed a bottle full of anti-depressant pills. Turning her attention back to what

Rachel had said, Samantha quickly obliged, pulling her smartphone out and opening up the photo folder on the screen, where she quickly had the brief idea earlier that day, to take half a dozen pictures or so of her brand-new wedding dress, thinking her friends were bound to ask for them, Samantha being the bride to be and all. Predictably, and as all the ladies did at a time like this one, they all naturally started to compliment Samantha on her choice of dress for her big day.

"You guys will have to come bridesmaid shopping at some point you know, need to get your dresses sorted as well" said Samantha, once the stream of compliments had died down. It was at that point that Rachel, Emily and Diana all shifted very suspiciously, as if suddenly caught in the act of wrongdoing. "We all have a bit of a confession to make on that front Sam" said Rachel, as Samantha's face took on a surprised look, not quite understanding where Rachel was coming from, in her last comment. "We all went there yesterday, while you were at work, going through the collection in the shop, selecting the bridesmaid's dresses for you already" replied Rachel, as Samantha's jaw draw dropped, at the sound of the fact that her friends had almost gone behind her back, for her big day with Greg. "It was all Diana's idea, don't blame us" said Emily, as Diana laughed, getting the jokey sarcasm in Emily's voice as she went.

"Pick on the small one, why don't you" replied Diana, with a slight giggle, as the others followed suit, being the bunch of happy go lucky ladies that they were. "Ok, I forgive you; what do they look like anyhow, seeing as if you'll all going to be standing around me wearing them on the big day" replied Samantha, as her words were followed by multiple clicking sounds, as Rachel, Emily and Diana all pulled their phones out of their handbags, before showing Samantha the pictures of the bridesmaid dresses on the screen in front of them. They'd gone for a strapless floor length maxi dress design, which were made of flowing satin, in a nice peach colour. It was a crafty move on her friend's part, it had to be said; but Samantha felt that she could forgive them, all the same; especially after they had managed to keep the whole a secret from Samantha for a good couple of weeks, maybe longer.

"Peach; guys, you read my mind, they look lovely" was Samantha's reply, as the four of them began to titter again, much to the looks of the elderly couple sat on the table next to them, who seemed a little put out at what they considered child like behaviour from four adult ladies. "Oh, you should have seen this one babe; Rachel decided to model them for us, you should see these pictures" replied Diana, as she showed Samantha the images of Rachel trying on the peach-coloured bridesmaid dress. Rachel, whether by accident, or on purpose, had managed to select a dress which was far too big for her, and was having to hold it up, so as not to show more than she had intended. "Ah, you had to go and tell the bride to be about that little wardrobe malfunction didn't you" said Rachel, in a bit of a giggly voice; but her words were lost a little, as the others just fell about laughing all the same.

It turns out that this outburst had come just in time, as the old couple on the table next to them decided to leave a few minutes beforehand, and therefore hadn't seen the image on Diana's phone, showing Rachel's wardrobe malfunction. The rest of the evening passed with a blur of laughing, telling funny stories, and drinking late into the night. It almost felt like a hen do, with the way they all went about partying and the like at a few bars and clubs, following after the sit-down meal in the restaurant earlier in the evening. By the time the taxi dropped Samantha at home at just after 3am, it was hardly surprising that her parents had left a quick hand scribbled note on the kitchen sideboard, which said quite clearly, that if she came home drunk, she would be clearing up any mess that was made as a result of it. Samantha's memory suddenly recalled a night out with the girls, where she had managed to vomit all over the doormat, after she'd had a few shots.

The shots had certainly not agreed with her stomach it had to be said, and so, Samantha made a mental note to herself after that particular incident, to never drink more than half a glass of anything acholic ever again. Even though Samantha was feeling a little light headed than she was when she had left the house hours earlier, she still managed to find her bedroom without turning on any of the lights, or waking her parents up for that matter. This was a specialist skill in of itself, as her father may have been used to sleeping with noise going on around him, but Yvette's hearing was very sensitive, when it came to detecting noise things, especially as she worked in the local library, where the decibel level was never usually above a whisper. Crossing the landing in near total silence, Samantha closed her bedroom door behind her, and promptly collapsed onto her bed, still fully clothed, and feel asleep, almost as soon as her head touched the bedsheet.

She didn't even have time to listen to the snoring coming from the next room along, where Richard and Yvette lay snoring fast asleep. It was amazing how loudly they snored, considering that their bedroom door was closed at night time, and the walls were not as thick as Samantha thought that they would be. But what was making Samantha grin as she fell asleep, was that day, had been one of days of her life. Greg, Diana, Emily and Rachel, all rolled into one; Greg showing up with his swanky new Lamborghini, which was shock number one. Then taking her to the wedding shop, where she'd spent most the next few hours being treated like a princess; that had been shock number two, and by far the biggest one out of them all. And then finally, to the third and final shock of the day, where Samantha had found out that her friends had already selected and purchased the bridesmaid dresses behind her back.

"I'll get you back for that one girl's, I know I will" jokingly thought Samantha to herself, as her dreams became ones of memories of the day's events. But there was a small mystery to end the day on as well, as that day's memories, wasn't the only thing which was going through her mind. It had been earlier on in the evening, when the four of them had been leaving the restaurant in town, heading for the nearby clubs and bars. Diana had been acting a little strangely since then, telling the others that she suspected that the four of them were being watched and followed by a tall dark male stranger, wearing a smart navy-blue coloured business suit and matching tie, who was leaning up against a streetlamp around twenty yards away or so. This tall dark stranger sadly wasn't close enough to have his face identified by any of them sadly, but they all reassured each other that they would be vigil all the same.

After all, Lillington was a nice enough area to live in, compared to other areas around Hertfordshire; but it wasn't completely crime free either. They never saw the tall dark stranger again after that, so they just shrugged it off, putting it down to a late-night reveller, who just happened to have chosen that moment to look in their direction, minding his own business, just like everyone else was doing. And so, they just forgot all about it, and moved on, thinking about the coming days ahead, and their busy work and social lives to go with it. But what none of them could have possibly known, was that this wasn't going to be the last time that this stranger, would be in their lives for a few more times, yet to come.

CHAPTER THREE

Collision

A few days had passed since the girl's night out in town, and Samantha found herself waking up with the same old alarm clock, which predicably, and as normal, gave a loud shrill ringing sound, before falling to the floor and smashing into a half dozen pieces. The one good thing about this, was that it kept her father Richard quiet for a while, as he would often sit at the kitchen table after a full day at work, repairing the broken alarm clock. Samantha even thought to herself on a daily basis, "as long as my family are happy, I'm happy"; picturing a man like her father, as he repaired whatever was placed in front of him, always with a smile on his face, and a spring in his step. That day had started a little overcast, cold and dull, as it was still January after all, and the temperature during the day barely got above around five degrees centigrade, owing to the weather outside.

"Hurry up Sam, you'll be late for work if you don't get up now and have your breakfast" came Yvette's voice from downstairs, as Samantha pulled herself up, pushing the bed clothes back to foot of the bed. Pulling herself onto her feet with a yawn, Samantha pulled open her wardrobe and began to dress slowly, picking out her usual work gear, which consisted of a pair of jeans, and a top, with the company logo embryoid in the top right-hand corner. As this was Samantha's first day back at work after a few days holiday, she wasn't aiming to be smartly dressed, as her boss wasn't too worried about how she looked, so as long as she did a good honesty days work for the company. After pulling on her jeans and top, Samantha turned her attention to her makeup, which in retrospect, never took Samantha as long as it would have on her friends, as she knew that her working environment wasn't the cleanest of ones to work in.

As she applied a thin layer of foundation, and skipped over wearing her mascara, she took a second or so to look in the mirror, observing her bedroom all around her. Like any other bedroom, it always reflected what interested that person the most. Samantha's bedroom walls however were painted a royal blue colour, her favourite colour by far; but there was hardly any free space to see that colour, as most of the space was made up of posters and pictures, of everything from pictures of friends, cars, motorcycles and even lorries. A few books even sat on a few shelves around her room, containing car manuals and even a copy of a history of Formula One racing. Samantha's passion was of course driving; but she had other skills as well, like for example, she was quite an adept outdoor camper, having learnt a lot of survival skills from her father Richard, and his military training from being in the Army for many years.

But as Samantha was back at work that day, it wasn't going to be her bedroom that was getting her full attention that day. It would in fact be her eighteen wheeled pride and joy, Betsie; in her opinion, the finest diesel drinking wagon in the west, as she quoted to anyone who would listen. When Samantha had finally finishing getting herself ready for that day's work, she skidded down the stairs and into the kitchen a few minutes later, grabbing some bread off the side as she went. "You are going to toast and put that on a plate aren't you Sam" said Yvette in a questioning like voice, as she waved the butter dish knife in Samantha's direction, watching Samantha look as if she was rushing slightly with her breakfast routine. Yvette was always someone who believed in sticking to the rules, so at times, she did sound like she was being very strict; but Samantha always knew, that she did it for a good reason, and not a bad one.

"Of course I am mum" replied Samantha, dropping the slices of bread into the toaster, before switching it on with a small click. "Ah Sam's doing fine I'm sure, ready for another day on the highways and byways I suspect" said Richard jovially, who had just walked in, dressed in his camouflage Army work uniform. "I'm always happy to be back dad" replied Samantha, as the toaster popped, ejecting Samantha's toast out with enough force, that it flew around a foot into the air, before landing on her plate with a slight rattle and dislodging a few crumbs in the process. "Excellent, the toaster modification has worked perfectly, thanks for testing it for me Sam" said Richard, with a slight chuckle as Yvette gave a slight twitch at the sound and sight of Richard's toaster modifications. At this sudden action of the rocket propelled piece of toast, Samantha gave a small scream and jumped backwards, not expecting it to happen so violently.

"What the hell was that" exclaimed Yvette, after Samantha's small scream had finished echoing around the kitchen. "Ah yes, did a bit of tinkering around with the toaster after I kept nearly burning my fingers trying to get the toast out of it; so, I tightened the spring up inside it, and now it shoots the toast out rather than just resting below the top of the outside of it" explained Richard, but Yvette at least got the joke, as she let out a stifled giggle. "Boys and their toys" she chuckled, as her and Samantha exchanged smiles. Samantha was strongly reminded at that very moment, of a cartoon she had seen on the television as a child, where an inventor had invented a hostile toaster, which fired out pieces of toast at people as they passed; this was also alongside a homicidal kettle, that went berserk and squirted boiling water at people when they tried to pour hot water out of it.

Samantha had strongly hoped that her father Richard would never go as far as to create those sorts of inventions, as inventing was one of his hobbies that he did in his spare time. However, as Richard had never built anything as wacky as a homicidal kettle, or a hostile toaster, Samantha was hopeful that the crazy gene had passed her family by. Ten minutes later, after Samantha had eaten her single slice of toast, she soon found herself by the front door, gathering her work kit bag up from the coat hangers that hung beside the door, before hoisting it onto her shoulder and leaving out of the front door, closing it behind her with a hurried 'see you later' to her parents. Luckily for Samantha, Travis Transport Limited where she worked, was only around a mile or so from her house, so she was easily able to walk it in no time at all, without having to rely on a motor vehicle, train or bus.

After all, it was important to Samantha to stay as fit and healthy as possible, as Samantha would often have to drive long distances without doing much moving around in between deliveries. Samantha wrapped her coat around her as she walked, as she could see that the grass was very damp on the verges, and there had also been a weather warning in place for ice for the rest of the day. As a result, Samantha was a little more careful underfoot than she would usually have been, but she was still confident that her work boots had plenty of grip, and would help her in any slippery situation. Samantha's hair blew around in the chill wind now coming from down over the river, where she crossed over to get into the local Lillington town industrial estate, where the humdrum of another working day was beginning to come to life all around her. Every so often, a pushbike would go wising past her, as another worker made their way towards their workplace.

Owing to remarkably good hearing, Samantha had managed to get out of the way of the cyclists just in time, therefore avoiding a collision with any of them. After crossing over the river, Samantha followed a rout iron metal fence, topped with barbed wire at the top, as she rounded the corner, and directly ahead of her she saw the main gates into the Travis Transport Limited yard, which were wide open, and already serving the first trucks of the day as they were parked in the yard. The sign advertising the company's location, was at the entrance to the driveway into the yard, on a large billboard sign, held up by two large wooden posts.

As Samantha walked into the gate, she was passed by one of the company's lorries, which tooted its horn at Samantha in a friendly manor, as it drove pass in the opposite direction, heading out onto the highway. Samantha gave a quick wave at the driver, before turning her head back towards the main office building. A second or two later, she reached the main reception building, pulling the door open with a quick gust of cold air behind her, as struggled slightly with the door because of the wind outside. Predicably and as normal, Samantha's nose began to run with wet snot, as it always did when she went from a cold to a warm environment very quickly. However, Samantha was always prepared for this, as she quickly went straight for her coat pocket, where a packet of tissues always remained on standby, for such an eventuality as the one she was in at that very moment.

"Morning Sam, runny nose again" said one of the drivers, as Samantha passed them heading towards the reception desk. "Tell me about it" joked Samantha, as she drew level with the reception desk. There was a sudden blast of cold air again, as the other driver exited through the reception front door, followed by a click as the door shut properly on its latch. "Morning Sam, keys and paperwork are here and ready to go, plus the forklifts are just loading your pallets on for you now" replied the lady behind the desk, as she slid the folder containing that day's manifests, and Betsie's truck keys over the counter to Samantha. Samantha thanked her, whilst simultaneously picking up the folder and her keys, before making straight out of the front door again, across the bustling yard now full of the sounds of shunting trucks, and forklifts loading pallets onto trailers, before finishing up in front of Betsie, her faithful iron horse and one true road going hero.

Betsie the truck, was a dark green coloured M.A.N TGX Lion class

H.G.V tractor unit; the very latest truck model of 2020, which had been delivered only a matter of weeks earlier. Its halogen headlamps were so bright, that even people driving in bright sunlight were almost blinded by them. From the moment Betsie had arrived however, Samantha had immediately fallen in love with her, and had made the cab her very home from home. It was decorated inside with soft pink fabric seats, and a pink throwover blanket on the bunk in the back. Samantha's boss had brought them for her as a birthday present, which Samantha had accepted, but only with a small smile, as she could tolerate it in small quantities, but not in huge amounts, as male banter always seemed to be in a workplace such as the haulage and transport industry. But Samantha had to be given credit for at least trying to blend in with this incredibly fluctuating environment.

After all; being a female HGV driver in of itself was rare enough, as statistics showed that only two percent of all HGV drivers were female, so Samantha was always aware of being in a male dominating environment ninety eight percent of the time. Although it was fair to say that her charm was always put to good use, when she was feeling the heat from a troublesome day on the road. The driver's seat dropped downwards slightly as Samantha sat on it, and then rose steadily back upwards again, as Samantha climbed into the cab, looking around her at the many different features in the cab. Placing the keys into the ignition, she gave the steering wheel a quick wobble, as the dashboard powered into life, flashing up all of the different warning lights and gauges that proceeded an ignition start up procedure. The M.A.N logo flashed for a second on the dashboard screen, before it was replaced with all of the relevant driving information.

While this had been happening on the dashboard, Samantha had pulled out a pen and her log sheets, and began to fill in the sheets with that day's driving data, including the miles and damage status of Betsie. As Samantha saw Betsie as her pride and joy, should could safely say that Betsie the truck, was easily the cleanest and in show room condition. As if Samantha was on some sort of autopilot, she mentally completed all of the checks in her head, whilst putting in her digital tacho driver's card into the tachograph machine, right above where her head was. Afterwards, it was a quick walkaround check, making sure the trailer was connected to the tractor unit, and then she would be off on another wonderful day on the busy UK road network, with all its stretches of motorways, A-roads, B-roads, dirt tracks, and the any other kind of vehicle trials that could be considered as a road.

Fifteen minutes later, Samantha was given the green light to depart, which came in the form of a shout from the yard supervisor. This was it; the yard loading was complete; the trailer was loaded; and now, she was ready to set off. Starting up the engine, and with a great hiss of air from the brake cylinders, the mighty truck Betsie began to roll slowing forwards, pulling off of the warehouse bay door, moving slowly out of the main gates marking the entrance to the yard, towards the main industrial estate road. "Another day in paradise" thought Samantha, picturing the Phil Collins song by the same name in her head as she went. At the main gate, Samantha slowed down slightly, as a car was coming around the bend towards her. Samantha waited patiently for the car to pass, before swinging her articulated lorry onto the main road, towards a set of traffic lights, which lead to another road out of Lillington, and down towards the motorway.

Silence in the cab never really suited Samantha too much, as she was always a bit of a fan of having some sort of background noise of some description. As it was the daytime, the radio was always the best form of media and entertainment for her; so, she switched it on, and allowed the latest music and chat to come pouring out of it as she drove along, helping her to relax slightly, as she knew that multiple driving challenges lay ahead. The drivers of Lillington, were sadly never renowned for their safe and consensus driving, but sadly in a lot of cases, quite the opposite. For countless times in the past, Samantha had been forced to lower her window, and vent her anger at fellow motorists, who seemed to think that her presence on the roads was a curse upon humanity, rather than an essential and vital worker for the economy of the country as a whole.

But there were always upsides to working in a road going environment, as Samantha had found out when she had first started driving HGV's many years beforehand. For one thing, the isolation and freedom of being her own boss, but not having to worry about leading, was always a comfort. Yeah sure, she was expected to stay in contact with the company, but whenever things got tough, all she had to do was hit the off switch on her mobile phone, and it was peace and quiet for however long she wanted. Betsie the truck did have a tracking device on it for security reasons of course, but Samantha was always confident that she was never being spied upon by her own boss, using this state-of-the-art system. As Samantha was cruising along the motorway, around ten minutes after she had left Lillington, the jingle for the latest news and weather came over the radio, it's usual amount of death and destruction always making the main headlines.

The first line was of a strike by French workers in the French town of Calais, where protestors had gathered to argue for fairer pair and working conditions. Then to a pair of planes, which had narrowly missed one another in mid-air over the skies of Canada; followed by the third article, which stated that a famous singer was getting divorced with his wife. But it was the fourth article that came over the radio, that seemed to perk up Samantha concentration out of all of the others that had been on beforehand. Samantha narrowed her eyes a little in curiosity, as she turned the volume up slightly to listen more carefully. The newsreader reading the articles, appeared to have a slight fear in his voice, which immediately made Samantha curious. Newsreaders, as Samantha had always known them to be, were always supposed to be cool and calm, with a slight hint of humour at times, depending on the article in question.

"In other news today, a passenger cruise liner crossing the Pacific Ocean, has been forced to way anchor in Japanese territorial waters, after a passenger onboard came down with a mystery illness. Some experts are putting it down to the new pathogen called Coronavirus, and if so, it will undoubtably be the first confirmed case of the pathogen, outside of the city of Wuhan, in China. The rest of the passengers onboard include at least five British tourists, who are still trapped onboard along with the other passengers, isolating inside their cabins. The Chinese and British government are denying that Coronavirus has made its way into Britain, although some government departments, including the world health organisation and public health for England, are saying that measures need to start being taken, to avoid Coronavirus becoming a pandemic. And now, it's time for the weather, where you are".

The opening music to the next show came over the airwaves, as Samantha turned the volume back down again, feeling a little sorry for the people stuck onboard the cruise liner stuck off of the coast of Japan at that very moment. Samantha shook herself slightly, as she thought, "there can't be a pandemic in this century with today's health care, can there?". The last time there had been a health scare like this, was during the foot and mouth disease outbreak of the early 2000s. Even so, Samantha couldn't help but feel a slight chill go up her spine as she thought about it, wondering what life would be like, if Coronavirus ever did get into the country, and start killing people off with impunity; like some invisible grim reaper with a scythe, or a scare chemical or biological weapon would. It was a good thing that Samantha had a road to focus on, rather than scary images of grim reapers with scythes.

Considering the time in the morning, Samantha had managed to make good time on her route, as she was due into Coventry for her first delivery by 10am, as her dashboard clock read just after 8am in the morning, sitting alongside the rev counter and speedometer. The traffic was flowing very freely, as Betsie cruised along at top speed, the speedometer needle pointing straight at the fifty-six miles per hour position on the gauge. Samantha could have gone faster if she wanted to, but these trucks were limited to that speed under UK law, and breaking that speed would have meant very serious trouble, not just from her boss, but also from the renowned highway's agency as well. Samantha hummed cheerfully, drumming her fingers on the steering wheel in a rhythmical still fashion, to a song which was playing out of the radio at that very moment in time.

Being behind the wheel of a forty-four tonne HGV, Samantha couldn't afford to take her eyes off the job, but she still couldn't have foreseen what was going to happen next. A midnight black Toyota Hilux pickup came swerving across her path, nearly crashing into Betsie as it did so. Samantha gave a short sharp blast on Betsie's horn, and had been forced to apply the brakes with some considerable pressure, causing the car who was illegally tailgating her to swerve out of the way, nearly colliding with another lorry that was coming alongside Samantha at the time. The midnight black Toyota Hilux pickup truck that had just cut up Samantha and the other lorry, seemed to be unable to control itself, as by the looks of what Samantha and her fellow motorists could see, it was being driven by an overexcited toddler which had just been gifted with a pedal car.

It served from one lane to the next, with its driver looking as if they were under the influence of something like drink, or drugs. The midnight black pickup truck suddenly slammed into the hard shoulder crash barrier, only a matter of yards in front of Samantha, who was forced to slow right down to a crawl to avoid a collision with the now stricken and badly smoking picking truck. Betsie's brakes squealed slightly as she came to a complete stop only a matter of feet away from the Toyota Hilux pickup truck. A rapid hiss of air from underneath Betsie, alerted everyone in the immediate vicinity, that the hand brake had been applied. The hazard warning lights began to flash away like mad, as Samantha opened up her cab door, before climbing down the cab steps onto the ground, closing the cab door behind her. Without pausing to think, Samantha world class truck driver training instantly kicked in, working out what to do next.

Firstly, Samantha looked all around her, in the direction of collection of the stunned motorists nearby who had witnessed the crash. Secondly, towards the pickup truck, where no sounds or movement could be heard from inside it, as Samantha feared that maybe the driver of the pickup had been killed in the collision. And then thirdly, all around her, to make sure that she hadn't missed an emergency vehicle, which could have been trying to get through the now building up clot of traffic along the motorway behind Betsie. Whether through fear, or a desire to help whoever she came across, Samantha approached the pickup truck with caution, looking around for any signs that she or other people could still be in danger; thankfully, Samantha quickly worked out that no-one else was in any danger, so proceeded on as she had planned. The stricken pickup truck, wasn't the prettiest of sights, that Samantha had ever seen.

Its front end had been completely smashed in, although the cabin seemed to have survived the impact, as the doors were not warped or bent too badly from the force of the impact. Steam was pouring out from under the crushed bonnet, as if someone had just a fire underneath it, and Samantha feared very much that fuel might have been leaking as a result of the impact. "Everything ok love" came a sudden voice from Samantha's right, as Samantha jumped about a foot in the air. She spun around, to see the driver of the second lorry standing beside her with a mobile phone in his hand. Samantha hadn't heard the other driver come up next to her, but that would have been due to her concentration levels at the time. "Err, yeah, I'm ok; I think you better call an Ambulance, I think the driver maybe injured, as I haven't seen any movement from inside yet" replied Samantha, as the other driver turned on the spot and walked back towards the other truck.

Considering that a matter of minutes earlier, Samantha had been angry at being cut up by the pickup, she had managed to remain calm and collected the whole time since the collision, she seemed to be taking things in very well; it was almost as if Samantha had an automatic pilot system that meant that she went into a controlled resolve due to this sort of situation. Approaching the still smoking pickup truck, she noticed that there was a man seated in the driver's seat, but was very badly injured, as she could see that the man was unconcise, with streaks of blood down his face, from the multiple cuts that he had picked up from the impact. At a best guess, Samantha would have put him in at around the mid-forties mark, in terms of his age, along with jet black hair, which had some greys in places. This mystery man, was of medium build, around six feet tall in height, but he was still a considerably more well-built in the body, than Samantha was.

He'd obviously sustained a head injury of some kind, as he murmured incoherently to himself, whilst there was blood dripping from a nasty wound on his jaw and his cheek. The airbag had also deployed, and there were shards of broken glass littering the inside of the cabin, where the windscreen, front driver and passenger windows had all shattered due to the force of the impact with the hard shoulder crash barrier. "Hello, can you hear me" asked Samantha, as she reached into the smashed window, to see if she could help the injured pickup truck driver. The driver's eyes were only barely open, but because he was murmuring to himself, Samantha knew that at least he was still alive and breathing. The injured pickup truck driver, must have had plenty of strength despite his injuries, as suddenly and without warning, he suddenly turned his head towards Samantha, and his speech at that point, become concise and clear.

"Get away from me you bitch" he screamed in a complete rage, as the other truck driver returned back around from calling the police using his mobile phone. Samantha tried to back out, but the man's hands had risen up from his side, and attempted to grab Samantha's throat. "I'll kill you, you manic bitch, I'll kill you" screamed the man, who out of Samantha's vision, had managed to locate the door handle, kicking the door open as he went. The driver's door itself flew off its mountings, landing a few away, as the man dislodged himself from the midnight black pickup truck, staggering like a drunken Zombie, making every effort that he could to strike out at Samantha, to hurt her in any way he could. Samantha screamed and ran backwards, as the man advanced on her teeth bared, as the other truck driver seemed to be struck dumb, wondering what was going on in front of them.

Samantha could see several fillings from the state of his teeth, and his breath had smelled incredibly of alcohol when Samantha had leaned in to check to see if he was ok. As if something had snapped in the other lorry driver, who's truck had pulled up alongside Betsie, the other lorry driver intervened, coming between them both, shielding Samantha from harm. "Wow, steady on mate" replied the other lorry driver, as he held out a hand, to stop the pickup truck driver in his path from causing any more harm to Samantha. Samantha couldn't help but feel a wave of gratitude towards the other lorry driver for coming between them, as Samantha herself was quite petite, and wasn't able to easily defend herself against the pickup truck driver. "Get out of my way mate, I want that bitch's neck" shouted the pickup truck man, as he took another lunching swing at the other truck driver, in an attempt to get to Samantha.

But before any more action could take place between the three of them, there was a blaze of noise and lights, as an Ambulance came screaming around the second truck, slowly coming to a stop in front of the stricken pickup truck, as a male and female paramedic climbed out of either side, making their way quickly towards, Samantha, the other truck driver, and the pickup truck driver. On catching sight of the Ambulance, the pickup truck driver quickly staggered to a halt, as two paramedics drew level with them all. "Hold still sir, we're going to take care of you now" said the female paramedic, as the male paramedic set the medical bag down that he was carrying, and began to bring out bandages, a pair of scissors, and other assorted medical appliances. "You ok love, what was that all about" asked the other truck driver, as he turned around to check to see if Samantha was alright, as Samantha had been shaking slightly in shock.

"Yeah, yeah, I think I'm ok; I've no idea, he just came at me suddenly without warning, but I think he's under the influence of alcohol" replied Samantha, as the other truck driver seemed to have a look of understanding on his face. As if someone had suddenly flicked a switch in the pickup truck driver's brain, he suddenly went back again to blabbering what sounded like gibberish, rather than the rage he had displayed less than thirty seconds earlier. The female paramedic told the pickup truck driver to remain as still as possible while she cleaned up his wounds, as the male paramedic turned his attention to the other truck driver and Samantha in turn. "It doesn't surprise me, he was all over the road back there" said the other truck driver, as Samantha tried to recover a little from nearly being mauled to death by an irate man, who clearly through that she was the cause of the road traffic collision.

Of course, in reality, it was the pickup truck driver who had caused the crash, and not Samantha herself, which is the recollection of the other truck driver as well. "Her you are love, let's get this on you" said the male paramedic, as he threw a tin foil blanket around Samantha, so that Samantha tried to recovered from her shock of the incident that had just taken place. Samantha was a little out of breath due to shock, but otherwise seemed to be recovering quite well. As Samantha was advised to sit down by the male paramedic, she decided to follow his advice, sitting down on the hard shoulder crash barrier, as the other truck driver filled the male paramedic in on what had happened. Samantha sat there on the crash barrier, watching the other vehicles pass slowly by, gazing in amazement at the collision to the left of them. One thing was for certain however; Samantha wasn't going to make her next delivery on time that day.

There was a second blaze of noise and lights, as a police patrol vehicle arrived, which pulled up behind the two trucks, it's blue lights flashing away, closing off three lanes, out of the four laned motorway, forcing the other vehicles on the motorway down to a single lane of traffic, as a large clout of congestion had now formed in the wake of the collision scene. From behind then, a motorway traffic officer vehicle, and a road works van had also come to secure the scene, so as to assure the safety of those at the scene. Two female police officers, who were both wearing bright high visibility jackets over their police uniforms, were now walking from around the back of the two articulated trucks, as they came into view, standing there for a second or so, analysing the crash scene before them. "Can anyone tell us what happened here" said the first police officer, who seemed to be the older of the two, in around her mid-thirties in age.

The second female police officer however, was around Samantha's own age, and she pulled out a notebook and started to make notes with it, including that of the number plates, and the positions of the vehicles. The first police officer immediately approached the other truck driver, as asked the other truck driver what had happened, as the other truck driver began to explain about what had happened at the scene. The second police officer however suddenly approached Samantha, who was still sat on the hard shoulder crash barrier with the tin foil blanket around her. "Are you alright miss" asked the second police officer, as she came over to Samantha, crouching down to look into Samantha's eyes. "Yeah, I'm sorry, it's just" began Samantha, but she broke off, as she looked at the pickup truck driver, who was still being treated by the paramedics, as they shone a torch into either of his pupils, to see if there was a reaction.

Every time they did so however, the pickup truck driver would try and look away, cringing his eyes at the brightness of the light. "Are you ok miss, we just need to find out what has happened" replied the second police officer, as she looked over to where Samantha was looking. "Thank you constable" said Samantha with a slight croak in her voice, as the second police officer took out a notebook, and turned back to Samantha. "I'm Police Constable Julie Guard from Hertfordshire Constabulary, can you tell me your name miss" asked the second police officer, as she began to write down notes in her notepad, keeping one eye on Samantha, and another eye on what was going on around her. Despite the situation going on around them, the second police officer had a calm, well-spoken voice about her, which was making Samantha feel very relaxed, as she felt some of the shook of the crash start to eb out of her body slightly.

Samantha did give a slight shiver however, as it was still January, and the temperature wasn't very warm outside, and she wasn't close enough to Betsie to get any warmer from the still cooling engine, which Samantha had switched off earlier on after the crash had happened. "Well, I was driving along here, and the smashed black pickup truck over there, cut up me and this other truck, trying to get through the traffic" began Samantha, as her attention was once again focused back towards the pickup truck driver. "Ok, so the black pickup swerved in and out of traffic; and then what happened" asked PC Guard, as Samantha turned her head back to face PC Guard. "Yeah, then it smashed against the crash barrier here; I had to brake pretty hard to avoid it, you can probably see the skid marks from back there" replied Samantha, as she pointed her right hand back in the direction of where the police car was parked behind the two lorries.

"So, the black pickup was the cause of the crash; do you know if any other parties were involved in the collision" asked PC Guard, making notes in her notepad as she went. "No not as far as I know, although I stopped and went up to the pickup driver's side window to see if the driver was ok" replied Samantha, seeing a glimpse flashback of what had happened suddenly flash in front of her eyes, like a sped-up piece of film. "Was the driver injured" asked PC Guard, making another note in her notepad. Samantha took a deep breath, as she remembered the attack, before she spoke again. "He was, there was a series of nasty cuts on his chin and cheek, which were bleeding, and I could smell alcohol on his breath as I reached in to see if he was ok; he was mumbling too, I couldn't really understand what he was saying". "I presume he must have been concussed" said PC Guard as Samantha nodded, but then she blurted out, "that's when he come at me".

"Sorry I don't understand, who come at you; the driver of the pickup you mean" said PC Guard a little confused, as she gestured with her pen that she was holding, in the direction of the pickup truck driver. "Yeah, as I'm leaning in the window to see if he's ok, he just suddenly snaps, and lunges at me saying, 'I'm going to kill you bitch' over and over again; then he kicked the door out, and started to advance on me, it's only thanks to the other driver that he didn't physically hurt me" replied Samantha, trying to beat back a feeling of fear that was starting to creep up her body. PC Guard seemed to recognise this, as she perched herself down on the crash barrier beside Samantha. "Thank you for telling me this miss; I never asked your name you know" asked PC Guard, as Samantha suddenly jumped, and went all flustered, as if it was her fault that she hadn't given this crucial piece of information sooner.

"Oh yeah; I'm Samantha; Samantha Bonham" replied Samantha, as PC Guard made another note on her notepad. "Good to meet you Samantha, I'm Julie; I shouldn't really be telling you this, but this man is known to us; the evidence you've provided for us today is very helpful, and we can make an arrest and have him charged with dangerous driving and driving whilst under the influence" replied PC Guard as Samantha smiled slightly, glad to hear that she had helped another fellow human being. "That's good to know, who is he anyway" asked Samantha, as if the pair of them were discussing the matter over a cup of tea. "Well, I shouldn't be telling you this strictly speaking, but his name is Edward Fitzgerald, 45 years old, and he's been arrested for a few things before now" said PC Guard as she stood up, looking a little uncomfortable as she told Samantha who the pickup truck driver was.

PC Guard soon recovered herself however, as she stopped writing in her notepad, before closing it and tucking it away on her police stab jacket. "I'll have the paramedics look you over before you go, and then I'll let you get on your way" said PC Guard, speaking again with her soothing calming voice. "Thank you Constable Guard" replied Samantha, as PC Guard gave Samantha a small smile, before walking away back towards the Police patrol car. Samantha got back to her feet, taking off the tin foil blanket, and folding it up into a neat square. Once Samantha had handed it back to the paramedics, she headed back the opposite way towards Betsie, just in time to see the first police officer arresting Edward Fitzgerald for driving whilst under the influence and dangerous driving. "What a psycho ah; makes you wonder why they let people like that drive" said the other truck driver, approaching Samantha, as she was about to climb back into Betsie's cab.

"Tell me about it, well, that's my day thrown out of line" replied Samantha, as she tried to make light of the situation, seeing the annoyed look on the other truck driver's face. "Same here, it's just typical isn't it, it's almost as if some people just think they own the road" replied the other truck driver, with a short sharp sigh, as he shook his head slightly. Before Samantha could reply however, the first police officer came up to them both, having just finished speaking to the police control room on their police radio. "There's a rolling road block being put in place in the next ten minutes or so, so we will be recovering the pickup truck and letting you two go on your way" said the first police officer, gesturing to the scene as a whole, as Samantha and the other truck driver nodded to show that they had understood the first police officer. PC Julie Guard had disappeared out of view, but then Samantha spotted her beside the police patrol car, directing traffic.

As Edward Fitzgerald was being loaded into the back of the police van wearing handcuffs ten minutes later, Samantha could very clearly see Edward mouthing the words, 'I'm coming for you bitch', knowing that only Samantha would be able to see him mouth the words. The other police officers seemed to be distracted dealing with other motorists, and also by making sure that the recovery vehicle was able to load the smashed pickup truck onto the back of it. The metal doors were closed on the back of the police van, as the other police officers who had come with the van climbed into the van's cab, before driving it away with it's blue lights flashing and sirens wailing. If this particular scene didn't stand out in Samantha's memory, then she would have sworn she had dementia. As per instructions, the scene was cleared after another police vehicle had come along to support them get back on the road again.

The rest of the day seemed to pass without incident, with only a few other hold ups along the way, so Samantha was able to make it back to the Travis Transport yard, and then back home again in a reasonable amount of time, so she wasn't too late home like she would have been on an overtime shift. Samantha's boss of course had been very sympathetic about the whole collision incident, and had offered Samantha the opportunity to have a day's leave off of work, should she need to recuperate from quite a traumatic incident as Edward's attack on her. Samantha naturally thanked her boss for this gesture, but said that her best form of therapy was to be out driving on the road, which naturally she did anyway, and with great skill to her name. "It's just another day at the officer" thought Samantha, as she tucked herself into bed that night, whilst thoughts and images chased themselves around her brain, like overexcited ant's in an ant's nest.

But the look on Edward's face as the police had taken him away in the back of the police van, hadn't been that of anger; it had been of a sheer determination, and pure hatred. Edward had also spent that night sitting the police cell, while he cracked his knuckles, thinking of how he would get his revenge on the woman who had cost him his pickup truck. Even though, Edward had been the one who had smashed up his pickup truck, and not poor Samantha, who had taken the brunt of Edward's rage at the collision scene. Little did Samantha know it; but that wouldn't be the last time, she would encounter, Edward Fitzgerald.

CHAPTER FOUR

The Great Pandemic, COVID-19

January faded out with some snow on the ground, and a chill still in the air, but this wasn't too last long. By the time March rolled around, this sort of weather had warmed up slightly, to temperatures that sat between ten to fifteen degrees centigrade. It was days and day of clear skies, and a sign that things would start to improve, as the world breathed a sigh of relief, that the months of cold and darkness were finally at an end. If things on the weather front were improving, they certainly weren't inside the halls of power on the street of Whitehall in London. At the British Home Office headquarters in London for example, things seemed to be going from bad to worse. Everyone was flat out, working out the complicated matters of the day, and hoping that nothing major would come up while they sat there beavering away on the important affairs of state.

For one lady in particular, the small matter of Covid-19 popping up in the Pacific Ocean, was going to soon become a considerably problem for everyone. The cruise liner moored in the Pacific Ocean, had now been there for over eight weeks, and both cabin crew and passengers had all suffered the effects of Covid-19. Out of over two thousand people who had started onboard at the start of its voyage, over twelve hundred people onboard had got infected, and then died as a result of the Covid-19 pathogen. As far as the public were aware, the cruiser liner had been moored out to sea, and that people were marooned onboard, having to deal with Covid-19. But no-one had said anything about any deaths, or been allowed to publish anything in the newspapers. For shadow home secretary Helen Dukes, the cruiser liner conundrum as she had come to know it, was giving her a considerably headache to say the least.

She was in constant contact with the foreign secretary, who in turn was speaking with the Japenese foreign secretary; but they were still being a pain in the backside when it came to releasing information regarding this new serious pathogenic threat. Helen Dukes working conditions hadn't exactly been helped by the fact that not only was she supposed to be on a conference meeting with the prime minister later that day, to discuss the pull out of military forces home Afghanistan, but she now also had to contend with potentially bringing home large numbers of British nationals from Japan. With the treasury wanting to make large cut backs on their cards as well, the cost for such a large-scale evacuation from Japan would be going on their budget, as number ten Downing Street had refused to let them have more money until the situation in Japan had all died down.

It had been 'damaging enough with relations with China' were the prime minister's words to her, earlier that day, as the prime minister had tried to keep a calm and level head, while keeping Helen and his other cabinet members on their side at the same time. Helen, in her almost ghost like role, was the shadow home secretary, and spent most of her time running around after the main home secretary, who she thought was a complete pompous pig, who was nothing more than just a yes man to the prime minister, and never cared about anyone but himself. Helen was quite tall and slim, as she did tend to like to wear some very high heeled court shoes, which she always kept polished and clean as much as she could. Her hair was strawberry blonde in colour, which she always had tied back in a tight bun at the back of her head, so as to stay looking official in the offices around Houses of Parliament and Westminster Palace.

This was usually topped off by a very posh looking satin blouse and pencil skirt. Just the sort of outfit you'd expect an office secretary would wear, even though Helen was certainly a far higher rank than that of your regular office secretary would be. Today however, Helen could be found behind her desk at the home office, as the home secretary had taken a day off due to sickness. The very strange thing was, that the home secretary hadn't said what was making him unwell, but this was hardly the most pressing thing on Helen's mind at the present moment. Helen had summoned her aid into her office, and was dictating a memo, which was to be forwarded to her other departments. "It's paramount that we get British citizens out of Japan as soon as possible; pass on the instructions that they are to be flown home from Tokyo, and then keep in isolation for at least fifteen days once they land, otherwise this could spread throughout the population".

"Yes ma'am, what shall I tell the press office" asked the aid, as Helen sat back and placed her fingers together, doing some very quick thinking. "Tell them; tell them that we are doing everything we can to bring these people home; that's all we can tell them for now; we've nothing more to go on for the time" replied Helen, as the office door was suddenly flung open, and a second aid stuck her head around the corner. "Sorry to disturb you ma'am, but we've just received reports of the first confirmed Covid-19 case in the country" said the second aid, as Helen closed her eyes for a second, and run a hand through her hair, realising that her worse nightmares had been confirmed. Helen running her hand through her hair, was more out of frustration than anything else, as if it taken around three weeks to spread throughout and then kill three quarters of a cruise liner's crew.

"Where is the first case" asked Helen, as she sat dead upright, making an attempt to try and look as if she was still in control of the situation, even though every passing second made her feel like that she wasn't in control at all. "Milton Keynes" said the second aid, as the second air closed the office door and went back to their work. Helen nodded to the first aid, who left the room at the moment, leaving Helen alone in her office, as she began to turn over theories and solutions in her mind. Picking up a remote beside her desk, she turned on the television in her office, to find it broadcasting on the daily news, where she was pleased to hear and see, that the news about the Covid-19 case, wasn't being broadcast on the news. Immediately, the news reader read out the story about the stranded holiday makers trying to get back from the cruise ship moored off the coast of Tokyo in Japan, in the Pacific Ocean.

But Helen wasn't the only person, that had spent that day having to deal with the Covid story, as events across the London border, was about to change everything for the Bonham family, alongside Helen Dukes. At the Lillington army base in Hertfordshire, Richard Bonham, had just overseen the arrival of his batch of Army jeeps, which had been driven into the base, after arriving back into the country earlier that day onboard a Royal Air Force transport plane, which had returned from Afghanistan after the big pull out announced on the national news. Richard strolled up and down the rows of jeeps inside the garage complex, occasionally inquiring with some of his mechanics on how the maintenance work was coming along, when suddenly he was approached by one of his soldiers, carrying a clipboard, and looking a bit peaky, as if the soldier was trying to fight off a bad head cold.

"Excuse me sir, sorry to both you, but I need you to sign this service parts order for me" said the soldier, as he offered a salute, and then handed over the clipboard to Richard. "Ah yes, of course" replied Richard, as he returned the salute, before placing his signature on the piece of paper clipped on the clipboard which had been handed to him. "Thank you sir" said the soldier as Richard handed him back the clipboard, giving the soldier a good looking over. The soldier suddenly gave a sudden loud sniffle from his nose, and some snot ran down into his mouth. "Are you quite alright Stebbs, you look like you have a nasty cold coming on" said Richard, as the soldier called Stebbs, placed a hand to his face. Stebbs himself was a young soldier, who was only around twenty years of age, with short cropped hair and very small in size and stature, with a little beard stubble on his chin.

Immediately as Stebbs put a hand to his face, he could feel the snot sticking to his hand, as it felt warm and runny on his hand. "Oh, I'm so sorry sir, it won't happen again" replied Stebbs, as Richard pulled out a handkerchief, and handed it to Stebbs. "It's quite alright Stebbs; I'd have the medics check you over right away, you're looking a bit peaky" said Richard, as Stebbs accepted the handkerchief, and blew his nose with it. When Stebbs tried to hand the handkerchief back to Richard, he waved it away, realising that he didn't want to catch whatever was draining Stebbs strength. "Thank you, sir, I'll go over to the medical wing right away" replied Stebbs, as he turned on the spot and walked away, blowing his nose again as he went. Richard watching him out of sight, before resuming his pacing up and down the rows, making sure that everything was running according to the base commander's orders.

Little did Richard know it, but Stebbs, like the unnamed first case person reported in the Milton Keynes hospital, had the early stages of Covid-19, and had inadvertently spread it around the Lillington base as he went on his day's duties. Richard of course had noticed this, but had not yet made the connection between Stebbs, and five other soldiers in his unit, all of whom had gone down with the same ailment as Stebbs had; and the ongoing Covid-19 virus, which was about to tear across the world, in a vicious and systematic way, unlike anything that not one single human being had ever seen before. Within a week of Richard's encounter however, it had been leaked to the press that Covid-19 had in fact made its way into Britain. By the middle of March, the Covid-19 virus had infected over a million people inside Britain, with around a thousand people out of that million having died as a result of contracting Covid-19.

So far, everyone from the Prime Minister downwards, were still trying to play down the Covid-19 virus, saying that it was a bad head cold. But after it had infected over a million people in the space of just one week, even the politicians couldn't help but admit that something had to be done. Helen Dukes the shadow home secretary, had been one of these people, who had managed to play down a lot of rumours about Covid-19, just saying things like, "it's just a nasty cold, we'll be fine", or a statement like, "scientists around the world were working on vaccinations to combat the spread of the coronavirus". Helen and her department naturally knew that this was only partly true, and had been stretching the truth by quite a considerable margin. Yes, it was true that scientists around the world, were research as much about Covid-19 as they could, as well as starting to work on a vaccine to combat it.

But everything they had tried so far, didn't appear to be working in curing Covid-19. A sudden rush in flu jab production had been authorised by the British government, in a way to combat Covid-19, but instead of slowly it down, it had seemed to accelerate the speed of the virus. After this little government cock up, Helen found herself sat in a meeting with some of her top medical advisors, and the home secretary themselves phoning by video link from his home. Helen had certainly looked better in the past, but now looked just as peaky as Stebbs had been, when Richard had authorised him to go to the medical wing to get checked out. Even the home secretary wasn't looking entirely well, as he too had a nasty cold, so his voice was a little distorted through the video call. "So, what options have we got left" demanded the home secretary, as Helen took a deep breath, thinking about how to answer the home secretary's question.

"All of our treatments so far haven't worked" replied Helen, as she was very much aware of every single pair of eyes in the room looking directly at her, listening to her ever word. "The flu jab has not cured covid, but instead has supercharged it, so that it now stands at over one million infections, and it continues to rise, with another ten thousand cases being discovered every day" finished Helen, as the medical expects sat around the table all nodded in agreement at Helen's word. "This information is classified top secret" said the home secretary, as he leaned back in his chair before continuing. "The prime minister returned from his trip to India, and was immediately rushed into quarantine on arrival; it is confirmed; he has Covid-19". The faces around the room all looked stunned, as they learned that their countries leader had contracted the so far uncurable Covid-19.

"Good heavens" said some of the doctors and professors seated around the table. "I can confirm it today, which means as of now, as the Prime Minister is now in intensive care and unable to make decisions, I have been uploaded to acting Prime Minister with immediate effect, and Helen here is appointed as my number two" replied the home secretary, in response to the looks on the faces of all those present in the room. "I'm also now decreeing that as of today, a state of emergency is now in effect, and the UK will go into a full-scale lockdown to prevent a further spread of Covid-19; Helen, I'm leaving you in charge of this operation; carry on" finished the home secretary, as the TV screen with them on it went out, fading into blackness, as the home secretary had signed off from the video call. There was a stunned silence in the room for a few seconds, before one of the doctors piped up, "a full-scale lockdown, is that even possible"?

"Not without mass panic, or even causing a serious amount of damage to the economy" said the second expect sat next to Helen. "We have to do what we're told, and the acting prime minister has spoken; the country will have to lock down" replied Helen. "But how ma'am, how exactly are we supposed to do that; supply chains still need to be kept open, emergency services still need to staffed, and from my last figures the emergency phone lines were all jammed with calls" replied the third expect who was sat a few chairs down from where Helen was. "There would need to be some sort of payment scheme, a way to keep people employed while they are stick in their homes". This latest suggestion from another expert, had made Helen sat at the top of the table, shaking her head in alarm. The reality of the situation was only just starting to dawn on everyone sat around the table, as was the mountain of problems Covid-19 would cause as a result.

"The economy wouldn't survive this; we would be looking at another financial crash along the lines of the Wall Street Crash of 1929" came one voice from around the table. "The government would have to furlough workers, and pay the wages of all non-essential workers within the country infrastructure" came another voice, but this suggestion sounded just as absurd as the last prediction of facing a modern-day version of the Wall Street Crash. "The government can't pay people's wages for them; it would bankrupt the country" replied Helen, as the some of the expects closed their eyes and rubbed their heads in frustration. "What about drafting in the armed forces to fill in essential roles, plugging the gaps where the other services can't cope" asked Helen, after a short pause to the room at large, when no other suggestions came her way from the rest of the advisors gathered around the table.

"The Ministry of Defence is still bringing back troops and equipment from Afghanistan ma'am, and those troops who return will need to quarantine for at least fourteen days before being allowed to be deployed onto other duties" replied one of the expect advisors. "There are ways and means of setting up temporary field hospitals within the military bases, where all of our current Covid-19 patients can go; at least they can be isolated away from those who are not infected". This suggestion from a fourth expect, had managed to achieve a few to perk themselves up around the room, as even Helen couldn't hide the fact that she thought that this was by the best idea so far. "How soon could these field hospitals be set up, and how many people could we hold inside of these field hospitals" replied Helen, as the expects began flicking through some paperwork on the table in front of them.

"According to the calculations, if we were to requisition all the current land spaces inside all former and currently serving military installations, we can isolate all of the Covid patients inside of them, so that it should quarantine and hopefully curve infection rates" replied another expect. This latest statement, seemed to have settled the matter, as they sank into silence, awaiting Helen's decision on what she wanted to do next. "It's settled then, the military are now to begin moving covid patience's out of the hospitals, and onto their nearest military base for immediate quarantine" replied Helen, as she nodded her head and stood up, pushing her chair backwards as she went. The whole room followed suit, as Helen walked out of the office, straight back into the corridor, where the sounds of multiple voices and the dozens of desk phones were ringing away, keeping communications open for the rest of the country.

For the rest of that day, radio stations, news centres and the like, were all putting out the news that had been decided in the Home Office that morning. At midnight that night, a state of emergency had been declared, in which a national lockdown would come into effect the following day. Police officers had been given instructions, that they were to patrol the streets, making sure that all residences returned to their homes, and then remain at their homes, until the Government announced that the Covid-19 pandemic had passed. To many people, this was seen as a great inconvenience, and some even refused to be locked in their homes, with the police out in force making many arrests within the first twenty-four hours, after the national emergency lockdown had been declared through the media. This of course, had only made the problem worse, as more police officers then begun to become infected with Covid-19 as well.

Struggling the most with the Covid-19 surge, was the military; the army barracks, air bases, and Navy dockyards had all suddenly become flooded with Covid patience's, all being kept in quarantine behind high security fences, patrolled by armed guards. For those left on the front lines, it was a day-to-day challenge on a scale which had never been seen before. Outside of the military bases however, life was a little different than the normal day to day activities that usually went on. All essential workers had been issued with passes, which were to be showed to patrolling police officers or military personnel, if that worker was stopped going to and from work. For Samantha Bonham and her family, the day-to-day life under Covid seemed to be as normal as normal could get, with a few different things under the new lockdown regulations that had been put in place under the emergency measures plan.

Richard Bonham was now second in command at the Lillington Army base, where Covid-19 patients were being held in isolation there, so he was going to and from his house and the base every single day. Samantha Bonham had been put on a government rota, which meant that her and Greg, along with their fellow drivers, were expected to do whatever the government told them to move, according to the latest data. Yvette was the only person who wasn't having to go into work, as all of the libraries in the country had been closed under the new lockdown measures. But Yvette had signed up with the local Red Cross service, so as not to be stuck at home day in and day out. After around a month or so, even these new measures weren't working, as even the government had to admit. By the time April rolled around, well over three quarters of the population had been infected, and over three million people had died.

Every time a new case was found, a whole establishment had to be shut down, and whoever had been there, were immediately deported to a military base, for immediate isolation and quarantine, along with every other person that they had come into contact with. This should have been illegal under European law, but because of the martial law that had been declared, these sorts of measures could be taken without fear of resistance or any court injunctions of any kind. In most of the military bases, it looked like scenes from a wartime ghetto, with people living, breathing and dying, all held up together inside of the bases, only being able to rely on the resources being given to them by the government. The Ministry of Defence had placed a rush order for thousands of tents to be made and shipped to the bases, to house those who had been moved onto the bases.

But many of those forced to stay in the rapidly produced tents, quickly complained about the conditions they were being forced to live in, and how the government was failing the country badly. One morning had even seen news pictures being beamed into people's homes right across the country, of riots taking place inside of the military bases, only for them to be beaten back by the base guards, who had been forced to open fire on some of the protestors. After this particular incident, those living on the base were bought into line, as it was a choice between protesting and getting shot, or staying in line, and at least hopefully surviving and getting out of the situation alive. To the now Home Secretary Helen Dukes, this news only made her even more annoyed and frustrated than she had been before then. After all, she hadn't asked for Covid-19, anymore than the rest of the population had.

"What do they expect, we can't just let them back out onto the streets when they are infected with covid" exclaimed Helen, during one particularly heated meeting between herself and her top advisors one afternoon, around a month after the lockdown had been declared. "We understand the position ma'am, but we will need to start to relieve pressure somewhere soon" said the first advisor, who was reading off some paperwork in front of him. "Arrest rates have skyrocketed since we introduced lockdown measures a month ago, according to the latest statistics" said a second advisor. "And covid is continuing to spread, even though we have quarantined it on the military bases" exclaimed Helen, to the room at large. "That's correct ma'am" said a third advisor, as there was a sudden knock on the door. "Come in" snapped Helen, as one of her office juniors entered, carrying a piece of paper in her hands.

"Sorry to both you ma'am, but this just came through from number ten, it's marked urgent and for your eyes only" said the office junior, as she placed it down on the table in front of Helen. "Thank you, Claire," said Helen, a little less snappish than the voice that she had used before, as the office junior walked out again, closing the door behind her. Helen picked up the peace of paper and read it through to the bottom of the page, as her eyes continued to get wider and wider, as she read further down the piece of paper, until eventually after a few minutes reading, she looked up slowly, and placed the piece of paper down on the desk in front of her, her face white as a sheet. The faces of the advisors around the room seemed to be a little confused at the sight of Helens facial expression, as they all seemed to be confused at what had just happened. But they were soon to find out, as Helen cleared her throat, and started to speak.

"I regret to inform you all, that the prime minister, and acting prime minister both died a few minutes ago of Covid-19". Helen finished speaking and leant back in her chair, looking stunned at the news. The advisors all looked stunned at this sudden ground breaking news, and none of them said a word as Helen continued. "This also means, that as of now, I have been promoted to fill the post of Prime Minister with immediate effect" finished Helen, as she leant back forwards again in her chair, straightening a few papers on her desk. "Well, I suppose this means; congratulations Minister, and our condolences on the loss of our countries past leaders, who passed away a short while ago" replied the first advisor, as Helen composed herself, realising the pressure she was now under, and this sudden rise up the ladder that she least expected to be thrust upon her at a time like this.

"Thank you everyone; I will wish to make a statement to the nation, and tell them of the demise of our late prime minister and home secretary; and to advise the public of our next steps forward" replied Helen, as she stood up out of her chair. The rest of the room followed suit, as Helen walked out of the room, flanked by two bodyguards, which she had inherited because of her status as the prime minister. Just as with a few months earlier, every television and radio began to buzz away, awaiting the response from the home office and number ten Downing Street on the Covid-19 situation. Over the last few months, the media coverage on Covid-19 had been up to date, with every fact and figure being beamed through every media it was possible to beam it through, as the country held its breath, wondering what the following days, week and even months had in store for them all.

As the sun began to set later that day, Helen stood behind the famous black door of number ten Downing Street, ready to step out of it for her speech to the nation. Helen twisted her hands slightly in nervousness, as if she was back at school, and had been asked a very difficult question in order to pass an all-important exam paper. "Ready for you now Minister" said one of her bodyguards, as Helen nodded to the bodyguard. The bodyguard opened the door, and allowed Helen to step right out into the street, outside Number Ten Downing Street. Immediately, there was an explosion of lights, as the press and media tried to capture as much of this fast passed action as they could, along with shouting all sorts of questions towards Helen, as she walked out to the Prime Ministers podium, trying her best not to look nervous. Helen cleared her throat slightly, and held up a hand, waiting for the questions to stop being asked.

As she did this, the crowd in front of her immediately fell silent. It was a silence so intense, that you could have heard a penny drop, with the sound of it echoing off the dark brick houses of Downing Street around them all. It was a mark of how serious the situation was, too how long it was between when Helen had stepped out of the front of Number Ten Downing Street, to the moment that she started to speak. In fact, it was hard to tell who was more scared, Helen Dukes, or the dozens of reporters, who had been given Covid clearance by the government to be stationed in places of importance to bring the general public the very latest in the news of what everyone was doing to combat Covid-19. Heads seemed to be glued to televisions and radio's all over the country, as the silence was broken by Helen, who straightened a few of the papers in front of her; took a deep breath; and started to speak.

"Ladies and Gentlemen; family and friends; citizens of all ages; we regret to inform you at this time, that the prime minister and home secretary have passed away this morning. They had been overcome by Covid-19, and their deaths will be felt deeply by us all, as a result of this deadly pandemic. I urge each and every one of you, to stay in your homes. I urge the public to remain vigilant, for those who may have Covid-19, to keep themselves away from others, so as to stop the spread of the pandemic. I also urge the public to remain strong, as we begin to rebuild after the loss of so many; our friends; our family; our nearest and dearest, who have suffered during this time. We mourn the loss of so many, and promise you, that salvation can be found, in the darkest of times. I therefore please ask, that you treat each other with respect. Be kind, thoughtful humans, and do not descend into animals, your government as always; remains strong".

Helen finished speaking with a gesture of thanks to the crowd of reporters, before she turned on the spot, and walked quickly away, seeing the reflections of the flashes of the cameras in the Downing Street windows, and hearing the shouts from the crowd of reporters, firing questions at her, as she walked through the open door of Downing Street, before hearing it click shut behind her. The moment it had shut, Helen breathed a sigh of relief, as she felt a lonely tear running down her face, feeling emotional from the situation. Helen's first term of leadership at Number Ten Downing Street, wasn't what she had in mind at all, as she proceeded to walk up the stairs to her office on the second floor. Once inside, she closed the door, and slid down onto the floor, uncontrollable tears now streaming down her face.

She knew it was no good; Covid had won; the world was being choked under the weight of far too many sick and dying people. Helen managed to pull herself to her feet, just in time to watch the reporter's spotlights click off outside the window. Helen didn't know it, but she was facing her final week as the Prime Minister of Great Britain, as the death toll continued to mount over the next few weeks. The essential services still carried on doing their duties to the best of their abilities, but even they couldn't help but notice, that the other services and resources were failing. A week after Helen's broadcast, the communications system broke down, which meant that people were cut off from everyone. All of the internet servers had also crashed, owing to the major number of people who were trying to use it. Back in Hertfordshire, Samantha had been struggling with an ever-increasing workload, but couldn't help but notice strange things.

Samantha was finally told not to come into work two weeks after Helen's news announcing the death of the prime minister. The news about not coming into work, had certainly confused Samantha a great deal, as she was classed as an essential worker, and was therefore needed to supply the country with whatever it needed. But even this was up for debate, as Samantha had another mystery which she was trying to figure out. Strangely, Greg had not been in touch for a few days, and with no means to communicate with him, or being allowed to go around and see him in person because of the government's lockdown rules, Samantha had steadily gone insane, wondering what to do. But with the daily broadcasts making frequent references to the fact that anyone caught breaking lockdown rules would face immediate prison time, Samantha didn't dare venture out to go and find Greg, to see if he was alright.

Only Richard, protected by his Army status, was the only member of the Bonham family now allowed out of the house every day, in order to go to work, where even Samantha was worried about him, having to be in close proximity to all of the people who were infected with Covid-19. It was hardly surprising that the air around them, felt so much easier to breath. The silence as well was also something that everyone was getting used to, having been used to hearing trains flying past on the local railway lines, airplanes passing over above their heads; and even once of twice, catching the rare sounds of birds in the trees. Despite everything that the country seemed to throw at it, the national grid still appeared to be working, despite more and more power demanding power, being stuck at home all day because of the government's lockdowns, and having to listen to the reports coming in of the latest Covid-19 figures.

As the days crept by, people started to become more and more desperate, in order to get what they needed. Every week, food parcels had been delivered to the front doors of those who were being forced to isolate in their homes, but even these parcels hadn't been enough, so some families had been sneaking out at night to loot from the nearby shops, all with mixed results. It was also a scene out of a scary film, as Samantha observed an entire family go missing off of the street one day, when an Army lorry turned up, carting the whole family away in the back of the Army lorry. "They broke the rules, it's the law now" were Richard's words to Samantha, when she questioned him about it. "But surely they can't do that, it's barbaric" was Samantha's response, as Richard looked at her in despair. "It's the way of life now, Covid doesn't discriminate, so you have to presume everyone is a threat" was Richard's supply.

Samantha loved her father dearly, but couldn't help but think that Richard was being a little cold hearted about this. They were still people after all, not farmyard animals that could just be horded into their own homes, and then told that they had to stay there, going hungry and thirsty every day, just so Covid could die out. It seemed that's Covid's mission in the world was too do just that, and wipe out society as they knew it, and even Samantha had to admit, that it was doing the perfect job of doing it. Everywhere was failing, society was collapsing, the world as they knew it, was about to disappear, forever. Mother nature yet again; had won.

CHAPTER FIVE

Aftermath

The final week of a civilised world on Planet Earth had affected everyone everywhere, and a silence, not seen since the days of the dawn of time, fell across the Earth. For the Bonham family, up until this point, they had all been hands on deck. Yvette Bonham had been volunteering as a red cross volunteer nurse, helping out at the nearby hospitals, who were dealing with the non-Covid patience's. Richard Bonham had of course been kept busy at the local army base, looking after those with Covid, alongside his regular mechanical duties. Whilst Samantha, had been drafted into doing army haulage work, moving vital goods around the country. Out of the whole family, Samantha was the one who had seen the most of the country under the new lock down rules. She had seen the desperate attempts of those to sneak out between police patrols to get supplies, and at the same time, complete isolation of the country that had come to a standstill.

Samantha was still driving during the day, so her routine hadn't been affected that much during the pandemic. However, she was still nervous about catching Covid and bringing it to her family, as was everyone else that she came into contact with. Well, some people thought that way anyhow; others just saw it as a way for the government to control them, as was the many other conspiracy theories that were starting to fly around all over the place, including on the social media websites. It felt just like any other morning on Edgeware Gardens, which had dawned bright and mild for the time of year. The early morning sunshine poured in through the open bedroom window where Samantha lay sleeping on her bed. She'd gone to bed fully clothed the night beforehand, having worked so many hours over the last few months due to the Covid-19 pandemic.

Samantha stirred ever so slightly, sitting up a little, and looking over at her bedside table as she went. The first thing that Samantha noticed that was strange, was the lack of an alarm clock, that should have been sitting on it. This was the very same one that regularly fell to the floor when it was ringing, and smashed into around a half a dozen pieces as it went. Samantha looked down at the floor, and was surprised to see that it lay there, smashed as usual, like it always did, rattling itself off the table and smashing into the many pieces that it did. What was even stranger still, was the fact that Yvette hadn't shouted up the stairs to tell Samantha to get herself ready to go to work. Samantha frowned slightly in confusion; there was clearly something strange going on, as this wasn't the usual regular routine that happened inside of the household every single morning.

She pulled herself out of bed, and immediately strolled downstairs into the kitchen, where she was surprised to see that her parents weren't there. Opening up the fridge to get out the milk carton, she was immediately overcome by a strong smell of gone off food, which came wafting out of the fridge as she stood there, quickly throwing her hand up to her mouth in order to mask the smell. Using her free hand, Samantha pulled out the milk, opened the lid, and took a quick sniff. One whiff told her quite clearly, that it had gone off, but this didn't surprise her too much, considering the smell which had preceded it. There had been problems with the mains power, as power cuts had been happening more and more often since there had been shortages of staff at the power stations due to Covid. The food and drink that had gone out of date inside the fridge however, had still failed to answer Samantha's question; where were her parents, Richard and Yvette?

As if overcome by a sudden thought, Samantha closed the fridge door, and proceeded back upstairs, opening her parent's bedroom door. She could see the bedsheet across the bed, and what appeared to be her parents sleeping under the duvet. "Aww, you two had a long day of things too I see" couped Samantha, as she walked into the room, opening the closed curtains by their bedroom window. "Come on guys, up you get, the electricity has gone out again, so it looks like we're having dry cereals again" replied Samantha, as Richard and Yvette didn't move of stir from underneath the duvet on the bed. "Er, guys" said Samantha, as she started to sound a little concerned, as her parents had never slept in like this before. There was nothing else for it; direct action was needed, as Samantha had made up her mind of what she was going to do next; the series of events had frightened her slightly, and she needed answers rather than more questions.

Grabbing hold of the duvet, Samantha pulled it with all of her strength, as the duvet went flying backwards off of the bed, onto the floor. The sight that greeted her however was so horrific, that Samantha immediately began to scream, uncontrollably. She screamed; and screamed; until it felt like her voice was so horse, that she felt like that she could have drunk the River Thames dry. Lying on the bed, hunched together in what looked like a hug, were her parents, Richard and Yvette; their eyes were wide open, but they were unmistakably dead. Samantha ran from the room, straight into hers, where she snatched up her smartphone from the bedside table, and immediately began dialling the emergency number. When Samantha she pressed the green telephone button to call however, something rather strange happened. Instead of the usual dialling tone that preceded a phone call, there was no sound at all.

Samantha tried dialling the emergency number again, only for it to happen for a second time, with no sound coming out of the speakerphone. Over and over again she tried, with the same result every time; in shock, and slightly panicking owing to the situation of finding her parents dead in their bedroom. Samantha ran back downstairs, and straight out of the front door into the street, not paying attention to the fact that she wasn't wearing anything, except for her dressing gown. There was no one in sight, but that didn't stop Samantha running up and down the street, banging on all of the windows of the neighbour's houses, trying to get people's attention, but no one came to her aid. Having tried and failed to get any help at all, she ran back into the house, slamming the door behind her. Taking her phone out of her dressing gown pocket, she immediately began to dial Greg's number, hoping that he would be able to help her.

But yet again, just like when she had tried to call for an Ambulance, the phone line was completely dead, with no sound coming out of it at all. Samantha now started taking slow deep breaths, remembering what her father Richard always told her about remaining calm in an emergency situation. "Never panic, remain calm, and keep yourself alive", Richard would always say to her, from his days of army training, as Samantha shook herself after hearing her father's voice inside of her head. "Of course, you must think rationally in these situations" thought Samantha, as she put her phone back in her dressing gown pocket, and began to pace up and down thinking hard. She'd woken up, and her parents were dead; and so was everyone else in the street, from what she had seen and heard, trying to draw attention to the fact that Samantha had two dead bodies in her house, that hours earlier had been her alive and well parents.

She'd tried to call for an Ambulance, and call Greg as well; but neither had worked, because there was no power going to the phone lines to make calls on. So that must mean; Samantha didn't want to think it, but after everything else that she had seen and heard, it all seemed likely. Covid had finally finished off humanity; was she Samantha, really the last human being on earth. If she was indeed the last human being on earth, then it was a daunting prospect, and not one that she wanted to believe was true. After giving her current situation a great deal of thought, Samantha came to the conclusion, that she needed to know who else was out there. Disappearing back upstairs again, Samantha slipped off her dressing gown, and slipped on a pair of jeans and a top, whilst slotting her smartphone into her jeans pocket as she went, as Samantha flew back down the stairs again, into the living room.

Samantha snatched up her car keys, closing the front door behind her as she went, before walking quickly straight down the driveway, to where the yellow Lamborghini Aventador was parked. This was the very same car, that Greg had been driving on that faithful day, that he had taken Samantha to the bridal shop, to try on all of the wedding dresses ahead of her wedding to Greg. Greg being the kind and caring gentlemen that he was, had allowed Samantha to drive the Lamborghini, and have it parked at her house as an early wedding present to the pair of them. Unlocking the Lamborghini, Samantha opened the door, easily sliding herself into the tiny sized racing seat that the Lamborghini had, before closing the door behind her with a small muffled banging sound. Starting up the engine with its usual roaring sound, the Lamborghini tore out of the driveway, making the tyres squeal slightly as it went.

Samantha knew full well, that if she had got caught out of her house without permission, it meant being sent immediately to a Covid camp inside of the nearest military base, which just happened to be the one in Lillington, where her father Richard had worked at before he'd died. Samantha drove up one street, then another, but didn't see signs of anyone else that was alive, nor any police patrols either. After five minutes of driving, Samantha rolled up to the outside of Greg's house, which was located on the far side of Lillington. From the front of the house, it appeared to be deserted, as there were no cars parked in the driveway, nor were there any lights on inside of the rooms, or signs of movement from behind the net curtains hanging up in the windows. Samantha however, wasn't going to give up that easily though, as she stepped out of the Lamborghini, slamming the door behind her.

Approaching the front door to Greg's house, she tried the door handle and amazingly it opened first time, letting herself into the hallway, looking around as she went, for any signs of movement that there were people inside the house. "Greg, it's me Sam, are you in" called Samantha through the house, as she went from room to room, opening cupboard and wardrobe doors, as well as going out into the back garden, to see if Greg was relaxing on one of his deck chairs on the garden patio. No matter how hard Samantha tried, there was no reply, and no sign of anyone in the house; all except for Greg's parents, who just happened to include her boss at Travis Transport Limited, lying dead in their living room chairs, with a number of black flies buzzing around them, which showed that they had clearly been dead for at least a few days at the bare minimum.

Having seen her own parents like this earlier on, the shock of seeing dead bodies again had worn off somewhat; however, as a mark of respect to Greg's parents, and for Greg as well, Samantha found a few towels in the bathroom, and threw them over Greg's parents heads, covering their faces. Once this was complete, Samantha now turned her attention to her next great mystery which was confusing her. Greg it would appear, was not there; where had he gone? Looking around the room, Samantha saw photographs on the walls of Greg as a child, his family on holiday, and even a picture of her boss, Greg's father, standing next to his first ever HGV, which he had purchased many years previously. On catching sight of this picture on the mantlepiece, Samantha was suddenly hit with a brilliant idea. She knew that she had to survive somehow in the world, so she would need to get provisions and the like.

It was almost as if someone had flicked a light on in her brain. Samantha knew where she needed to go now, and what to do next, in order to survive. As if following orders, like a soldier on a parade ground, Samantha walked straight out of the house, closing the front door behind her as she went, more out of respect for the dead, rather than to keep out would be burglars, who might have attempted to try and strip the house of all of its valuables. After leaving Greg's house, Samantha climbed back into the Lamborghini, and consolidated on her situation. Greg was missing, and both her and Greg's parents were dead; there was no signs of any police patrols anywhere, and it seemed that there was no-one else alive in the town. Instead of answering Samantha's questions, the current situation had only generated more questions, on top of the ones that Samantha already had.

Making up her mind, Samantha closed the Lamborghini's door, and turned the keys in the ignition, firing up the engine for the second time that day. Soon afterwards, the Lamborghini was speeding towards her next port of call. Samantha was going to gather up her friends, gather some previsions, then drive them down to the Travis Transport Limited yard, before taking Betsie out with a trailer, travelling around the country and living on the road, in her mission to find Greg and survive in this new post-apocalyptic world. The Lamborghini handled so well while on the road, that within a short time she had reached Rachel's house, to find her deceased along with her parents. Then onto Emily's house, only to find the same thing again, as Emily and her family were just the same as everyone else, their bodies been subjected to the effects of Covid-19, as it had gone through the family, wiping them all out.

Tears began to leak down Samantha's face when she finally arrived at her last friend's house, which was home of Diana and her family. However, at Diana's house, Samantha found Diana's parents and older brother dead at the kitchen table, but strangely, there was no sign of Diana. Had Diana somehow survived, and was out in the town somewhere; "maybe Greg was out there with her perhaps? After all, the pair of them only lived a few streets apart, rather than Samantha, who lived on the far side of Lillington, around a mile distance between both houses. When Samantha had finally emerged from Diana's house, after giving the same treatment to the bodies in the house as she had done at Greg's parent's house, Samantha at least could make one question. Greg and Diana were obviously alive at there, otherwise they would have been inside the houses along with the other members of their families.

Samantha had done all she could for her friends, so it was now time to commence the next stage of her daring new operation. Climbing back into the Lamborghini, as she had done so multiple times that day, Samantha drove straight back to her house, jumping out of the Lamborghini on the driveway when she arrived home, before racing back into the house, leaving the door wide open as she came flying in through the doorway. Flying up the staircase at top speed, she grabbed a suitcase from under her parent's bed, and began to pack things into it. This she had to very carefully, as Samantha didn't know what she would be coming up against in the times ahead. This theory was tested a bit however, as when she finally got to the wardrobe, one item of clothing made her break her rule very slightly. The wedding gown Greg had paid for was still hanging in the wardrobe, where it had been placed months beforehand by Samantha herself.

Deciding that she needed good memories as well, Samantha folded the dress bag containing the wedding gown inside it very carefully into the suitcase, before zipping the suitcase shut. Taking one last look at her bedroom, making sure that she had not missed anything out that she wanted to take with her, Samantha closed her bedroom door, and then proceeded along the landing, carrying the suitcase behind her, until she reached her parent's bedroom. Richard and Yvette's bodies were still as Samantha had left them less than an hour earlier, but she could see a few flies starting to gather around their bodies on the bed. They buzzed in through their open bedroom window, the sound strangely magnified by the silence outside of the house. The fly population was certainly going to explode in this new world, what with all the new dead human bodies lying everywhere to feast on.

Samantha felt new fresh tears running down her face now, as she wept slightly at the sight of her now deceased parents, knowing that they had joined so many in the world that had died because of Covid-19. As

Samantha had never seen her parent's wills, it was difficult to say what they would have wanted to happen to their property when they died. To be buried with a tombstone perhaps, or even just to be cremated and have their ashes scattered somewhere. Then a sudden thought occurred to Samantha, as she stood there in the doorway, allowing the sunlight to hit her face through the bedroom window. Richard her father, had served in the Army when he was alive; there were certainly such a thing as military funerals. Yes, that is what she would do, a military funeral for them both. Although Samantha would have to cremate the bodies, otherwise they could spread diseases like typhoid, and by feasted on by swarms of hungry flies.

Thinking ahead, Samantha carried the suitcase full of her things to take with her down the stairs, walking it out of the front door and loading into the back of Richard army jeep, which was also parked on the driveway alongside the Lamborghini. Samantha had decided against using the Lamborghini to get around, as it was many things, but it certainly wasn't the ideal survival machine. Richard's army jeep on the other hand, was far better suited to operations like that, with all of its many different types of survival and fighting equipment onboard. Samantha also managed to find Richard's spare army backpack as well, which was leaning up against the wall in the cupboard under the stairs. It was empty, so Samantha quickly whipped around the kitchen, gathering up any food and liquid that was still useable as she could, before proceeding around the rest of the house gathering up medical supplies, batteries, and much more.

By the time she'd finished gathering everything that she needed to survive out in the wild around fifteen minutes later, the army backpack was defiantly bulging. This was saying something, as these backpacks were some of the toughest and finest rucksacks in the world, that could hold all sorts of things. Samantha hauled the rucksack outside, before loading it into the back of the army jeep, closing the army jeep's rear door with a snap as she went. Looking carefully around the house to make sure she hadn't forgotten anything, Samantha immediately found a length of rubber hose in the garage, feeding one end into the Lamborghini's fuel tank, and held the other against a metal jerry can, which was attached to the side of the army jeep. Samantha immediately began to suck on one end of the rubber hosepipe, and within seconds, the fresh petrol began to pour straight into the jerry can, filling it all the way to the top.

This fuel was vital to her, so it was no good leaving it in the Lamborghini's fuel tank. Samantha hadn't spoken in the whole time that she was carrying out these tasks, but every now and then, she would mutter to herself to make sure she'd collected up everything that she would need to take with her, before then carrying out the task that she'd just muttered to herself. Eventually, Samantha closed the back door on the army jeep, ready to leave the house; but there was just one more thing left to do. Going back into the house, she went again into the cupboard under the stairs, and found Richard's army service revolver. Samantha knew it was there, after Richard had told her about it, in case she would have to defend herself if the house was burgled and the like. Proceeding back up the stairs with the revolver in her hand, she walked into her parent's bedroom, and stood at the foot of their bed, looking directly at them both on the bed.

"I know it's not the way you would want to go guys, but I think you'd respect the gesture, and hope I will see you again someday" said Samantha, as she raised the revolver into the air and pulled the trigger three times in slow succession. With each pull of the trigger, came a loud bang, as each bullet was discharged out of the pistols barrel. Three perfect round small holes also appeared in the ceiling as she pulled the trigger on the service revolver, but as the house was now no longer occupied, it wouldn't have mattered anyway; nor that no-one would be coming along to investigate what the loud bangs were. Samantha then placed the service revolver on the bed next to Richard as a sort of 'farewell to arms' type gesture, before taking a step backwards away from the bed. In traditional military fashion, Samantha than raised her right hand in an army style salute for a few seconds, before bring her arm back down to her side.

Samantha then turned on the spot and walked out of the bedroom, closing the bedroom door behind her, feeling that a well written and very long chapter of her life had just closed behind her for good. Yet again, she let out a small cry and slid slowly down the closed door, crying her eyes out as she went. Her life up until this point, had always been so mundane and routine; now, it would be full of mystery; unknown; and potentially dangerous, not knowing who she was going to be coming into contact with, or how friendly or hostile they were going to be. Samantha didn't know how long she sat huddled at the foot of her parent's bedroom door, whether it was minutes, hours, or even days; what Samantha did know for certain, was that she had to get on the move, as quickly as possible. Greg and Diana were still missing, and this was now the quest which Samantha had been burdened with, as this was the way of the new post Covid world.

Picking herself up from the floor, Samantha wiped away her tears, before making her way back downstairs into the hallway, as she picked up a milk bottle which was full of an amber like liquid on the table, which had a lump of rag stuffed in the end. This was the home-made fire bomb which Samantha had prepared earlier, to burn down the house behind her, so that her parent's bodies wouldn't be left to the fate of the flies, which had begun to form all over the place. Samantha had just about enough time for a quick look back at the house, before she threw the home-made fire bomb into the kitchen, as it exploded, sending the kitchen into walls of flames. Samantha quickly exited through the front door, closing it behind her, as climbed into the army jeep, firing up the engine with the ignition keys. Samantha looked straight forward out of the windscreen, just in time to see the flames licking at the front door.

The army jeeps engine sounded a lot lighter and less throaty than the Lamborghini's had been, as Samantha put the army jeep into reverse gear, and backed out of the driveway. Clunking the army jeep into first gear, Samantha headed straight up the road, leaving Edgeware Gardens behind her for good. An ear defending loud explosion behind her, told her that the home-made petrol bomb had reached the gas lines inside the oven.

Samantha gazed into the rear-view mirror as she drove off up the street, just in time to see a fiery mushroom cloud flying up into the air, as a total unprecedented level of destruction was left in its wake. The army jeep had been almost blown sideways with a sharp jolt, as the shockwave from the explosion hit it, as Samantha was thrusted forwards in the driver's seat, her seatbelt cutting into her neck slightly. "At least you're at peace now guys" said Samantha, more to herself than anyone else.

Ten minutes later, Samantha, still at the wheel of the army jeep, rolled up outside the gates to the Travis Transport Limited yard, situated in the local industrial estate, near to the Lillington town centre. On a normal day, Samantha would have expected this part of the town to be busy, and bustling full of freight traffic and cars, with their occupants on their way to their various workplaces. But now, in the post Covid times, it was as silent and as quiet as the grave. The main gates to the Travis Transport yard were locked, as Samantha's boss would have locked them on their last night within the warehouse, when he went home from work. 'Perhaps Greg was in there, and had barricaded himself in to protect himself from Covid' thought Samantha, as she had a quick look around her, to see if there was anyone else in sight. There was only one way to find out; as Samantha didn't have a key, she would have to ram the gates open using the army jeep instead.

Reversing up a little, she engaged first gear, and revved the engine hard, releasing the hand brake at exactly the same moment. There was a squeal of the tyres as the army jeep shot forwards, smashing into the gates, which flew off their hinges with such force, that they were catapulted through the air, landing several feet away with a loud crashing noise. Samantha quickly hopped out, dragging the now smashed gates out of the way of the entrance, before she got back into the army jeep, and drove it forwards until it was parked in front of the main reception area, just in view of the main transport building. Samantha jumped out of the army jeep, walking up to the reception door, and giving it a pull. Naturally and as Samantha had predicted, she found it locked; but that was not a problem, as the army jeep would make short work of it, like it had done with the main gates.

Fortunately for Samantha, and by army specifications no doubt, the army jeep had been fitted with military grade bull bars, so it could withstand and break through a lot more things, than a lot of other vehicles could not. "Glad I didn't bring the Lamborghini along" said Samantha, as she climbed back into the army jeep, and drove it with some force at the locked reception doors. Just like with the main yard gates beforehand, the reception doors proved to be no match for the army jeep, as they crashed open with the sound of breaking masonry and smashing glass. Reversing slowly out of the now smashed and destroyed reception area, which resembled the scene of a bombsite, rather than a transport company reception area, Samantha parked the army jeep, applied the hand brake, and switched off the engine, climbing out and locking the driver's door behind her.

"Did seem a bit silly, locking a door now, but then again, you never knew these days" thought Samantha, as she climbed over the now wrecked doors and the destroyed counter, and managed to locate the key cupboard inside the main transport office, remembering where it was in the days when she used to work there as a driver for the company. Samantha quickly found the keys to her truck Betsie, located on one of the hooks inside the secure lockbox, which weirdly, was unlocked and not secured. After a quick rummage around, Samantha located the keys to Betsie, and made for the door to the warehouse area, which with one strong kick, gave way, so that Samantha could let herself in to the gigantic inside warehouse area. The vast inside of the Travis Transport warehouse stored aisle upon aisle of shelves and racking, which went right up to the ceiling, which in of itself, looked large enough to house an aircraft hangar, and several large aircraft to boot.

To Samantha's great delight, she spotted Betsie parked up in a line with the other trucks, right in front of one of the warehouse shutter doors, leading out into the yard. Strolling over, Samantha located the metal chain, which hung from the ceiling, connected to the main shutter door via a lever and pulley system. Samantha pulled down hard on the chain, as the chain began to rattle and the shutter door began to slowly open, creaking as it went, flooding the warehouse with the bright sunlight from outside, which bounced off the walls and ceiling. When the door had been fully opened, Samantha pulled Betsie's keys out of her pocket, and as she did so, a piece of paper, which looked like a pamphlet of some kind, fell out and landed on the floor beside her. The pamphlet had been folded neatly into quarters, so as to fit inside the average coat pocket, hence maybe why Samantha hadn't noticed it fall out of her pocket.

It was only because the pamphlet had made a slight flapping sound when it had hit the ground, that Samantha had noticed it at all. Samantha bent over and picked it up, opening it as she went, now able to read it clearly in the warehouse shutter doorway. It was the pamphlet which Greg had given to her many months beforehand; the one with the image of the coastline on it, and the numbers that looked like a series of dates on it. "Here you go, tell you what, if you work it out, I'll even pay for the honeymoon in Hawaii as well" came Greg's voice from inside Samantha's head, as if it was a distance memory from many years ago, but in reality, it had only been a matter of months ago back in January, when Greg had taken her on that faithful trip into Lillington, to go wedding dress shopping. Samantha let out a little whimper, which seemed to echo and bounce off the walls, racking and vehicles worse than ever, in the large silent warehouse.

CH∧PTER SIX

Ghost Plane

A crazy thought had suddenly hit Samantha, as crazy thoughts always did when the vast majority of humanity had been wiped out by a deadly uncurable pandemic virus such as Covid-19 had. What if this pamphlet had been sent to Greg on purpose? What if, these dates, were some sort of code, that only Greg understood. Had Greg in fact been working for some sort of secret government organisation like Military Intelligence, or something similar. Or even, maybe Greg was part of some secret cult, who's numbers on this pamphlet meant a time and meeting place for a ritual. Perhaps even Diana was part of it as well, as she had not been at home with her family when Samantha had gone round to her house earlier on that day. Or perhaps they were both survivors of Covid, like Samantha was, and had decided to go their own way, although this theory did seem a bit farfetched, considering that her and Greg had been due to be married.

Even Diana wouldn't have just Samantha to be out here on her own, being the caring considerate person that she was. One thing was for certain though, she would find out what this pamphlet and its information meant, even if it killed her. "Samantha Bonham P.I" joked Samantha in her head, as she had a fleeting image of her standing there in front of her Lamborghini, whilst wearing aviator sunglasses, like the ones in the television series Magnum P.I. Boyed up with this new determination Samantha had picked up, she folded up the pamphlet and placed it carefully back inside her pocket, being careful to be gentle with it, so as not to erase any vital evidence that would be needed for later on when the real puzzle solving and investigation work began in earnest. Samantha proceeded over to Betsie, opening the cab door with one flick and click of the key, before climbing the stairs into the cab.

Once inside the cab, Samantha turned the keys in the ignition, as the engine started up and made a slow steady rumbling noise whilst its engine was on tick over. Looking down at the fuel gauge, Samantha was pleased to see that the yard staff had filled Betsie full of fuel, so this gave her a good eight hundred to a thousand miles worth of fuel, before Samantha would need to look at fuelling up again. Finding the gear lever, Samantha slid Betsie into gear, and began to move her slowly forwards out of the warehouse door, into the brightly lit yard. Samantha knew there was a diesel fuel tank on the site, so she would use the spare jerry cans on the jeep to fill them up with diesel, and then take them with her, just for an added bit of range for Betsie. Sure enough, when Samantha took the spare jerry cans over to the diesel fuel pumps in the yard a few minutes later, she was pleased and amazed that there was still spare diesel in the tanks.

This was quite surprising, despite the news outlets and many industry leaders pointing out about fuel shortage warnings before Covid had struck. Samantha had about four spare jerry cans attached on the army jeep, but yet there was still more than enough diesel to be able to fill all of them right to the brim. She did struggle lifting them up again to get them back to Betsie, but soon managed to find a way of securing them to Betsie's outside cab, near to where the airline and electrical cables were. This in of itself would have been a health and safety nightmare, as keeping anything explosive next to live electrical lines, was a pretty stupid thing to do. Fortunately for Samantha, the passenger side footwell was more than big enough to house the spare jerry cans full of fuel, so it was decided, that the jerry cans could live there for the time being, until a more permanent home could be found.

By the time Samantha had loaded her suitcases into the cab as well, she had worked up quite a sweat, and an appetite to match. The little food and water that she had managed to scrounge from her family's kitchen, wasn't going to keep her going for long, so she'd have to find the nearest shop and stock up, which also gave her another idea. Samantha did after all have an HGV tractor unit, which could tow a trailer, so why not load up a trailer, and keep her supplies in said trailer. After all, her employment before Covid had been logistics, transport and deliveries; so why not do that now. "There must be other people out there who survived as well, so supply for them too" thought Samantha, as she felt the wonderful ideas brush over her, like waves on a beach. As Samantha sat there thinking this all up, and deciding what to do next, something directly ahead of her up in the sky, suddenly caught her eye.

As it was a clear sunny day, Samantha could see the object quite clearly. Placing her hand up to her forehead to shield her eyes from the sun, Samantha squinted at it, wondering what it could be. Samantha's first thought was of U.F.O, having seen enough programmes about them on the television over the years; but then thought that it was moving far too slowly to be anything like that. Whatever the object was, it did seem to be coming in her direction, and as she looked on examining it further, Samantha was suddenly aware that it seemed to be losing height at an alarming rate, almost as if the object in the sky was on some sort of crash dive collision course. "No; that's not possible; can it be" exclaimed Samantha, in a questioning voice; but her question was soon answered, as the unmistakable sounds of a racing jet engine reached her ears, gathering speed as it went.

The sound was getting louder and louder, and with horror, Samantha realised that the spec in the sky, was in fact a Boeing 747 jet airliner, that was gliding downwards towards where Samantha stood, at rapid speed, it's wings seeming to glow slightly as it descended, in the same way that a meteorite would when it entered the Earth's atmosphere at supersonic speeds. There was nothing else for it; Samantha would have to run; now! Sprinting back to Betsie, Samantha launched herself into the cab, turning on the ignition, trying to get the engine to start. "Come on, come on, come on old girl, don't let me down now" shouted Samantha, a slight air of panic in her voice, as she banged the steering wheel repeatedly in frustration. The engine roared into life a second later, as Samantha planted her foot hard on the accelerator, making the engine roar slightly because of the revs now being pumped into it.

Betsie shot forwards, straight out of the open gateway; narrowly avoiding the army jeep; past the smashed gate; and eventually bringing it to a stop when Samantha was at a safe enough distance away, the sound of the jet engines getting louder and louder with every second. Samantha looked around just in time, to see the white underbelly of the Boeing 747 sore less than fifty feet above her head, before it slammed into the ground, leaving a trail of sparks behind it as it went. It slid for a few seconds on its belly, before ploughing nose first into the industrial units behind where the Travis Transport Limited building was. The force of the explosion that followed, was enough to blow Betsie forwards by a good six feet, as her tyres squealed slightly from the friction of the shockwave, as the cab rocked from side to side, like the rocking motion of a ship would do, far out to sea.

Samantha, who had dived onto the floor of the cab for protection, felt the force of the explosion, as a piece of flaming metal debris came flying past the cab, missing it by inches, skidding to a stop on the road in front of Betsie. Samantha lay on the floor in shock for a few seconds, trying to take in what had just happened, as a strong smell of burning aviation fuel reached her noses, as it hung around in the air and from where it had been splattered on the nearby industrial estate buildings that were still standing after the blast. "No one could have survived that" thought Samantha, as she slowly and gingerly reached for the driver's cab door handle, and pulled it. The driver's side cab door swung slowly open, as Samantha carefully climbed down the cab steps, completely transfixed by the scene in front of her; but very much still aware that there might be other resulting explosions as a direct result of the first one.

The front nose and cockpit of the aircraft were completely intact, minus a considerable number of scratches and dents in many places, where it had scrapped along the ground, generating a number of sparks as it went along the ground. The middle fuselage section had been blasted away, as Samantha could see right inside of the main passenger area itself. Samantha began to walk back towards the wreckage, which was on fire in some places, and when she had finally got up close to the 747's wreckage a minute or so later, she could see that the impact had completely annihilated the Travis Transport Limited warehouse and other buildings around it. By the looks of things, there had been no passengers alive on the plane when it had crashed, as they all looked perfectly fine, apart from the fact that they were all dead. Samantha couldn't know for sure, but she had a good theory of what had happened.

This was a very clear and sure sign, that they had come from another country somewhere, trying to escape from Covid and the like, thinking there would be refuge and shelter elsewhere in the world. The aircraft had probably run out of fuel, and promptly crash landed after gliding for miles on just the wind and its own mechanical systems. From a personal point of view, Samantha couldn't have possibly imagined what the final moments on that aircraft must have been like. Samantha shook herself slightly, and pulled her phone out of her pocket to report the crash to the emergency services. Then quickly realising a split second later, that there were no emergency services to call. The plane would just have to sit there forever more, smoking and flaming away, like some lost abandoned machine, that no one knew or cared about;

like so many other things in this new world, right around the planet.

The one thing Samantha knew that she would have to leave behind, was Richard's army jeep, as when she looked around for it, she could see it still parked where she'd left it just minutes earlier. The only drawback was, that there was now a large jet engine turbine fan blade sticking out of the bonnet, which was smoking heavily; whilst another engine fan blade had split the army jeep cleanly in half, like a knife would go through butter. "Well; farewell my friend; you were a faithful and mighty steed, and served my family and your country with pride" said Samantha, placing her hands on her hips, looking directly at the now destroyed army jeep, looking also unrecognisable as it had done only minutes earlier, when it had been a fully working vehicle. But little did Samantha know, that she wasn't out of danger yet, as a strong smell of petrol reached her nostrils, mixed with the kerosine that was already in the air.

Samantha swore loudly, and began to sprint away from the wreckage at top speed, with only seconds to spare. There was another loud bang, followed by another loud explosion, as the army jeep's fuel tank exploded, sending flying debris in all directions. The force of the explosion knocked Samantha off her feet, as she cried out in pain, hitting the hard road tarmac beneath her as she was knocked to the floor by the force of the explosion. Thankfully, Samantha hadn't suffered any broken bones, or many major injuries during the fall, but her face and clothes were now filthy and dirty, and smelled strongly of bonfire smoke. Samantha took short, sharp slow breaths, as she steadied herself on her hands, sitting up slightly, as the smell of bonfire smoke reached her nostrils for the first time. Samantha's first thought when confronted with this smelly situation, would have been to take a bath, or a shower.

But would any of that work now, with the national gird off line, and water pumps which were bound to have stopped working since Covid. One thing was for certain; Samantha may now be living in a new apocalyptic post Covid world, but she still insisted on some things; and that was not to walk around smelling like a bonfire, thank you very much. Knowing that there was a good chance that no-one was going to come around the corner at that very moment and see her, Samantha began to strip off out of her old clothes, until she was done to her underwear, and with her trucker work boots on her feet. Grabbing up the bonfire smelling clothes, Samantha walked forwards, and then dumped them on the now burning army jeep, thinking that at least she could make use of the fire which had sprung up in front of her. Having completed this smelly and rather unpleasant exercise, she then climbed back into Betsie's cab, and closed the door.

It felt weird sitting in Betsie cab, half naked, whilst only wearing her underwear and trucker boots. "But then what's normal anymore" thought Samantha, as she began pulling a fresh pair of jeans and a top out of her suitcase, slipping them over her head, and up her legs as she went, removing her boots as she did so, because the jeans wouldn't slip on, if she had still been wearing them. As Samantha knew she would most likely be facing all weathers and rough terrain, Samantha had only packed jeans and tops, rather than any of the usual summer dresses that she usually liked to wear when the sun was high in the sky, warming the ground around her. The thoughts of her childhood, playing with parents in the back garden, kept her sane for a short while, as she slipped her trucker boots back on, before climbing back into the driver's seat, as a slight smile and a lonely tear came across her face.

This wasn't the time for self-pity however, as Samantha was very much aware that if anyone had heard the explosion from the plane crash, they would have definitely been on their way over to the crash site, as it would now be a prime location for looters and the like, to steal whatever they could, from wherever they could onboard the parts of the plane that were left. Starting the engine back up again, Samantha drove Betsie slowly away, thinking that she would have to pick a trailer up from somewhere else. For now, Samantha could more than happily run with just an HGV tractor unit on its own. Samantha drove Betsie into Lillington's town centre, which was just as deserted as everywhere else that she had been too that day. There would have usually been a great amount of hustle and bustle, as the towns residences went about their shopping, on the colourful and stocked up high street.

But now; it was a ghost town; a scene from a Zombie apocalypse film, with quiet shops, which were still stacked full of everything you could possibly need. Samantha proceeded straight for the nearest shop, which just happened to be a newsagent's store, where she managed to grab half a dozen items that could only just fit into Betsie already overcrowded cab. Samantha then proceeded to the local swimming pool, where she was able to enjoy a short while of calm, as she washed herself down in the shower cubicles, making sure to run as much soap and shampoo over her as was possible in a short period of time. Samantha then grabbed a towel from an open locker, and dried herself down, putting her hair back into a ponytail with the spare black hair band that she had stashed in her bag, hoping that it would dry naturally, as there was no power to work the hair dryers in the locker rooms.

It all seemed so surreal to be walking around these places, expecting another human being to pop up at any moment; but none ever did. It wasn't until later that day that Samantha finally got around to being stocked up on her essential supplies, with Betsie carrying as much as her cab would permit, the overhead lockers fit to bursting with all of the provisions that Samantha had managed to precure throughout the day. By this point in the day, Samantha had gone around most of Lillington, finding everything that she needed as she went; but there was one thing that wasn't a compulsory item, but was still worth trying to get hold of anyhow. Samantha had never really been a big believer in guns and other weapons of sorts, which seemed quite ironic considering her father's military background. However, Samantha did have a very strong belief that defending herself, was an absolute must; so, Samantha decided she needed to get some pepper spray.

A substance which was used by the police forces around the

country, as an anti-deterrent to criminals, if they became too aggressive towards police officers whilst on duty. Samantha planned to use it in case she was attacked by another survivor of any kind, or even against wild dogs, if they proved to be attacking her in any way. One place where Samantha knew that she could easily get hold of some pepper spray, was at Lillington's local police station, where there would be a store room of some kind, housing all of the equipment that was used by the police on their day-to-day patrols. As Samantha approached the Lillington police station, she couldn't see anyone around; so, Samantha thought that getting access to the station would be a piece of cake; and to her great surprise, it was. Betsie the truck stopped outside the gates, as Samantha jumped down from the cab and switching the engine off, locking the cab doors behind her as she went.

All of the gates to the police station car park and offices, were wide open, and so was the front door as well. "Wait, this is too easy, why is everything open" thought Samantha to herself, as she gingerly walked forwards, looking all around her, in case she saw signs of movement from behind the glass windows. "Hello, anyone in" called Samantha, as she slowly stuck her head inside of the front door, looking around the main reception area, taking in the deserted Sergeants desk and the blanket computer and television screens, which would have showed the CCTV cameras located inside the prison cells. From what Samantha could see and hear, it appeared to be deserted; so, Samantha began looking all around the police station, trying to find out where the supplies area was. Eventually Samantha found it, located in a cupboard at the far reach of the station, down a corridor which was lined with different offices and cubicles.

This was the only cupboard which Samantha had found locked inside of the police station, so Samantha grabbed a big iron ramraid door key up from the corner, and threw it with all of her strength at the cupboard's lock. The lock smashed open with one hit, as Samantha wrenched the doors open, to see a full stash of police equipment, including that of dozens upon dozens of bottles of pepper spray.

Samantha grabbed around a dozen bottles of pepper spray, carefully placing them in a clear plastic evidence bag that she had found lying on a desk a few feet away. As Samantha was turning to leave however, she suddenly heard a small noise from behind her. Samantha spun around, expecting to see someone standing there; but there was no one there. Thinking she had imaged things, Samantha exited the room, and made her way back downstairs, out of the front door, making straight for Betsie, who was still parked up by the front gates.

Samantha had her hand in her pocket, ready to pull out Betsie's keys to open the passenger door, when she suddenly felt a vice like grip seize her arm, before slamming her whole body against the side of Betsie, taking Samantha completely by surprise. "Get off me, what are you" screamed Samantha, struggling against the grip; but Samantha had the chance to finish her sentence, when a familiar voice came from behind her, but it sounded very stern and controlled from the one that she had heard before. "Remain still madam, you're under arrest on suspicion of theft; you do not have to say anything, but it may harm your defence when mentioned something you later rely on court; anything you do say will be taken down and used as evidence against you". As the familiar voice finished speaking, Samantha felt the handcuffs being snapped onto her wrists.

The handcuffs felt tight, painful, and very cold, as if someone had just dropped an ice block from the freezer onto her hands. Samantha felt herself being turned around, before then being slammed back up against Betsie, as the face of the person who had manhandled her came into view for the first time. Samantha suddenly realised who it was, right at the same time as the other person did as well. It was PC Julie Guard; the very same police officer who had attended the road traffic collision that Samantha had been involved in with Edward Fitzgerald back in January that year. Julie's face suddenly changed from a look of sternness, to that of surprise. "Hold on; I know you don't I" replied Julie, as she backed away slightly in surprise. "Oh my god; your PC Julie Guard aren't you; don't you remember me; you were the officer on the scene at the collision I was at months ago" asked Samantha, suddenly recognising Julie for the first time in months.

Police Constable Julie Guard was certainly looking a lot wilder, than what Samantha could remember seeing her on that faithful day, when Edward Fitzgerald had smashed his pickup truck into the crash barrier, before then attempting to physically assault Samantha in a drunken rage. Rather than being held up at the back, Julie's hair was hanging downwards, and looked more ragged, as if she hadn't put a comb through it in days. Julie's face too looked a little gaunter than before, but that might have been to do with the lack of makeup on her face that she'd been wearing, the last time they had met back in January. Julie wasn't wearing her police uniform either; but instead, was wearing a light green top, and black jeans, similar to the fashion that Samantha was showing. "My god; your Samantha Bonham; I remember you now" replied Julie, as her face seemed to relax a little, as she realised who it was.

"I'm really sorry if I took your stuff, here, you can have it back" said Samantha, and she tried to give the carrier bag back to Julie. But all that Samantha felt as she did so, was sharp stab of pain, as the metal handcuffs cut into his wrists a little, as they were still very tightly fixed onto her wrists. "Ouch, did you have to handcuff me like that; is there any chance you can take these things off" exclaimed Samantha, a little put out by the fact that she had been manhandled in this very aggressive way, and then thrust up against the side of her own truck Betsie. Julie's face suddenly changed from that of seriousness to understanding, as Julie understood what Samantha was going on about. "Oh yeah; sorry about that; hold still Samantha" said Julie, as she turned Samantha back around slowly, and unlocked the hand cuffs, as Samantha took slow deep breaths, keeping herself calm as Julie released her.

The handcuffs fell away into Julie hands with a small clicking sound, as Samantha pulled away a little, rubbing her hands slightly where the hand cuffs had cut into them. Small red marks had formed on her hands where the handcuffs had dug in, but Samantha knew from experience, that these would be gone within a short period of time. Samantha's hands did feel a little numb however, but she knew that the feeling would return to them within a short period of time. Julie was about to reply with an apology, but before she could do so, without warning, Samantha had launched herself at Julie, not to attack her, but to hug her.

CHAPTER SEVEN

Royal Air Force Station, North Lakes

Before Julie could stop her however, Samantha was sobbing her eyes out into Julie's shoulder, feeling a great weight lifting from around her shoulders, as if a bolder had been sitting there for some time. "I knew I couldn't be the only one left, I knew there had to be others still out there somewhere" cried Samantha, through great sobs. Julie, who looked a little confused at why Samantha was hugging her, returned the hug by putting her arms around Samantha. "Police college certainly never trained me in this scenario" thought Julie, as Samantha broke away, wiping her eyes on her hands. "I'm sorry, I know that was probably a little impromptu" began Samantha, but Julie cut her off mid-sentence. "No, no it's fine honestly, it's been quite traumatic on all of us". Samantha regained herself a little, as Julie handed over the carrier bag full of the pepper sprays to Samantha.

"Here, I think you should have these, you're going to need them" replied Julie, as Samantha took them looking puzzled. "But you just said, I was under arrest for theft; aren't you going to take me into custody" said Samantha, in a puzzled voice, as Julie seemed to register what Samantha was telling her. "What custody; there isn't even a police service anymore to arrest you; Covid has seen to that" replied Julie, looking sad, as she knew her career was well and truly down the toilet by now, due to Covid. "Has nothing survived at all" asked Samantha, looking a little scared, thinking that maybe even a scrap of the old infrastructure remained in place to help the Covid survivors. "Not in the society we used to know; it's a rumour that's been going around for weeks now" replied Julie, as she had been given access to far more information than Samantha or anyone else had been.

"There must be something left; anything; anyone; I mean, not even the basic services" replied Samantha, now starting to feel that her future, and even her very existence, hung in the balance. It really did look like Samantha, and now Julie, like so many unknown others, would be forging a new life somewhere else, other than where they had been for some many years previously. It became very clear to Samantha now, that choosing to start out with Betsie, rounding up supplies and things, wasn't that bad of an idea after all. "Not as far as I know, our last instructions from headquarters were to maintain the basic structure and keep moral up; that was forty-eight hours ago; and we've heard nothing since then" replied Julie, as Samantha let out a low slow breath, trying to hold her nerves. "So, I guess that's it; we're all on our own now" replied Samantha, in a voice which clearly said, 'goodbye old life'.

"Looks that way, do you know what you'll do now" asked Julie? "Well, I figured that if I found a trailer for old Betsie here, then I could gather up supplies and be a sort of travelling sales person" replied Samantha, leaning up against Betsie and giving her a little tap with her right hand, as her left was tucked in her jeans pocket. "Ah of course, I keep forgetting truckers name their trucks; great idea though" replied Julie, as she gave a small smile. "What about you Julie, what do you plan to do" asked

Samantha, as Julie's face sprang into what looked like an interested look. "Me, well; I have always wanted to live on a farm, out in the countryside; I'd always planned to go there when I retired, but I guess I can go there now I suppose" replied Julie, as Samantha smiled, thinking that living on a farm would be a wonderful idea, with the wide-open green spaces and fields, whilst living off the land at the same time.

"That would be fantastic; you'd probably make a great farmer" replied Samantha, having a sudden fleeting image of Julie carrying a pitchfork over her shoulder, moving hail bails around, whilst driving a tractor across a field. "Me, hardly; I've never even picked up a spade before" joked Julie, as they both looked at each other stunned, as Samantha could tell that Julie had never really been the manual labour type, but being better suited to a pen pushing line of work instead. "I'm sure you can learn on the job; why don't you come with me for a bit, until you find a place that you like to stay at" replied Samantha, as Julie's face lit up with happiness, feeling as if she had just been promised a real treat. "Can I, aww thank you Samantha, I really appreciate that" replied Julie, as Samantha opened the passenger side cab door on Betsie, as Julie caught site of all of the jerry cans, crammed into the passenger footwell area.

"You do realise that transporting unsecured flammable liquids in any class of vehicle is a criminal offence" replied Julie, her face suddenly turning a little stiff again, as if someone had flicked a switch inside of her brain from cool girl, to stern police officer. Then Julie's face suddenly fell again, and a grin came across it, as she realised that she could stand there quoting the law at people until the cows came home, but it made no difference, as those laws were from before Covid, not for the world after it. Samantha looked at her, as they both started laughing. They laughed and laughed until their sides hurt, and when Samantha suggested that their best course of action was to get back on the road, Julie couldn't help but agree, thinking that they needed to find somewhere to park up for the night. It seemed incredible that the pair had started the day wondering what was happening all around them; now however, they had a full formed plan in their heads.

With difficulty, Julie climbed into the passenger seat, and then swung herself onto the bunk in the back of the cab, being careful not to knock the jerry cans full of fuel as she went. Samantha fired up Betsie's engine again, as they set off up the road, making their way towards a local truck park, which Samantha had known from the days before Covid as a secure parking place for overnight truckers, passing through on their way up and down the country. When Betsie reached the truck park half an hour or so later, they were pleased to see that it was deserted, and it didn't look like anyone had been there for some time. As the passenger footwell and passenger seat with all crammed full of Samantha's things, she offered Julie the bunk in the cab to sleep on for the night, whilst Samantha herself went and found a nice bench to sleep on, whilst borrowing a blanket from within the truck stop store room.

As the sun began to set, Samantha had to started to think that maybe Covid, however destructive it looked on the surface, had been a good thing for the planet. Maybe the human race could start all over again; maybe it wasn't curtains for everyone after all. Even though, Samantha still didn't feel completely safe, with only a set of locked doors to protect her, she still managed to drift off to sleep that night, thinking about the day's ahead of them. Julie finding herself a nice farm to settle down on, whilst Samantha would become a travelling salesman, helping people out all over the country as she went. Samantha wasn't entirely sure if she'd drifted off to sleep or not, because she suddenly became aware of the fact that there were a pair of headlights, lighting up her section of the building. Samantha was suddenly wide away; there were others, there were others still alive out there in the world, apart from herself and Julie obviously.

Although the voice that suddenly came drifting in through the open window, was not one that sounded friendly at all. In fact, Samantha could have sworn blind that she had heard that voice before now. It was a deep voice, which immediately told Samantha that it was a man who was speaking; and it seemed to be moving away, and then getting louder again, as if it was methodically moving around the truck park. "There's nothing here Ed, looks like it's been deserted for ages" said a second voice, this too, belonging to a man. This was a new person that Samantha didn't recognise, although she felt the same level of fear creep up her back as she listened to it, as if this was a nightmare situation. Samantha had brought a bottle of pepper spray in with her to the service area, but this bottle was only enough to stun someone temporary, and not stop them completely.

"Come on Pat, let's go, there's other places we can go and scope out tonight" said the first man's voice, as there came the sound of footsteps on gravel, before the sound of a set of car doors slamming. This was followed by the sound of a vehicle's engine, as the unknown vehicle outside the service building that Samantha was in moved away slowly, making the building dark again, as its headlights moved away off down the road at speed. Even though Samantha knew they were gone, she didn't dare move, just in case there were others around, through fear of alerting them. Julie at least, had Betsie's warm secure cab locks to protect her. But there were plenty of windows that could be smashed on the truck service building, so anyone could just walk in and attack Samantha as she slept. After what felt an age, Samantha managed to drift back off to sleep again, with her brain still spinning, as if she had just got off of a fairground ride.

The first voice the she had heard when the vehicle had arrived, was someone that Samantha could have sworn blind to herself that she heard before now, but where? Samantha racked her brains, trying hard to think about where she had heard the voice before, but couldn't come up with anything at all. But even so, the fear had been very real, and that was what mattered to Sam. If there was no law and order anymore to stop bad people, who knew how bad it could get for everyone who had survived. That question for now remained unanswered, but if Samantha and Julie were to survive in this world, they would need to adapt, and fast. "Samantha; Sam; wake up Sam" came Julie's voice from somewhere above her head. Samantha woke with a start, sitting bolt upright, looking around for Julie. Julie was seated just to the right of Samantha, holding a set of knifes and folks out to Samantha.

"Alright; take it easy; I've made you some breakfast, seeing as if you're doing all the driving at the moment" replied Julie, as Samantha looked a little flustered, still breathing quite heavily from her shocking encounter of being woken up by Julie. On catching site of Julie and the full English breakfast that she'd managed to cook up, Samantha calmed herself down and rolled over, letting the blanket fall away from her onto the floor. As Samantha didn't know what she was going to encounter, she had remained fully clothed while she had slept. "Aww, thanks Julie, I'm starving" said Samantha, as Julie allowed Samantha to tuck into her breakfast, with a little added salt, pepper and tomato ketchup on the side. It was incredible to see that the service area had so much food stocked up, although there did seem to a bit of a nasty smell coming from the back room, which turned out to be the service station owner, who had sadly died as a result of Covid-19.

"So, what are we doing today then Captain" said Julie in a slightly jokey voice, pulling an A-to-Z road atlas map book forwards towards her, flicking open its pages until she found the grid reference that showed the town of Lillington and the rest of Hertfordshire. "I worked out last night, that we're about here; and there are a few truck yards dotted around the place where we can get ourselves a working trailer to use for storage, and to set up as a mobile base if need be" continued Julie, pointing her finger to a spot on the map a short way outside of the Hertfordshire boarder, which was near to the junction for the M1 motorway, sounding as if she was giving a briefing to a room full of police officers on a drugs raid. Samantha sat and listened, while tucking away to her full English breakfast, thinking that bringing Julie along on a trip like this, wasn't as bad of an idea after all, as Julie knew exactly how to plan and work in a hostile environment.

"Sounds like a plan; and I'm hoping I can work out this little mystery as well" replied Samantha, pulling out of her pocket, the pamphlet with the picture of the coastline on it that Greg had given to her months earlier. "What's that" asked Julie, who quickly glanced at the pamphlet with the words 'The Future Start Here' written on it. "That's what I'm trying to work out, it was sent to my fiancée Greg before Covid hit, and I've been trying to work it out ever since" said Samantha in a curious voice, as Julie looked more closely at the numbers that look like dates on the back of the pamphlet. "How strange; you know; this kind of looks familiar" replied Julie frowning slightly, racking her brains, wondering where she had seen the pamphlet before. "You've seen it before" asked Samantha, suddenly looking more alert and interested, as if Julie might be able to answer the mystery?

"I have; there was one on my chief superintendent's desk when I went into his office one day to give him a report on a case that CID was working on; I honestly thought it was something to do with a case so, I ignored it" replied Julie, but her last comment had put an idea into Samantha's head, as she'd had a strange lightbulb moment inside of her head. "Maybe it's some sort of calling card, like a Noah's Ark list of some such; given out to some, but not everyone" said Samantha, more to herself, than anyone else. Julie widened her eyes in shock when Samantha had said this, but then took on a more puzzling look. "But even if that were the case, why not hand them out to everyone, and only a select few" asked Julie, putting this question directly at Samantha? "I don't know, but I have a feeling that someone in authority might be able to work out what these numbers mean" replied Samantha, as Julie looked a little affronted at this latest statement.

"I'm someone in a position of authority" replied Julie, a little put out, as after all, Julie had spent many years as a police officer; easily someone in a position of authority. "No, no I meant like someone from the government or the military maybe; this is obviously a code of some kind; one that would be made up by the likes of MI5, MI6 or GCHQ even" said Samantha, as Julie's face relaxed a little, realising what Samantha had meant, knowing now that Samantha wasn't insulting her interiority as a police officer. "Ah I get you, I see; if that be the case, then we need to be going around the military bases, to find out if anyone from the armed forces is still alive who can help us with it" replied Julie, as Samantha nodded in agreement, thinking that having some sort of a plan, was a lot better than having no plan at all. It almost sounded like Julie was planning a sort of school trip for them both, with the element of an apocalypse about it for good measure.

"My father Richard was an engineer in the Army, he could have told me what this meant" said Samantha, suddenly looking a little downcast, remembering that her own family had links to the military themselves. "Did he; you know" replied Julie slowly, looking a little nervous; however, Samantha seemed to cotton on to what Julie was trying to say almost at once. "He did, him and my mother; they both died from Covid" said Samantha slowly, as Julie suddenly looked very sombre, as if she had just come from a funeral. "Oh; I'm really sorry for your loss Sam" replied Julie, but Samantha seemed to be ok about it now, as she realised that her parents had led good lives, alongside raising Samantha as best as they could into the woman that she had become. "It's ok, they led good lives, and I know they'd be proud of me for trying to help others survive in the new world" replied Samantha, as Julie cracked a smile, making her cheeks ache slightly.

"I am too you know; you're serving the country with pride" replied Julie, as Samantha pushed her plate away, the plate a lot emptier than it was beforehand, as Samantha knew that leaving any food scraps behind was now seen as a crime, where food and drink would start to become scarcer by the day. "That was a rather yummy meal; thank you Julie" replied Samantha, as Julie smiled again, but without the ache this time, as Julie started to get used to being out of a job where you needed to remain professional at all times. "Your welcome Sam" replied Julie, as the pair of them stood up and made their way back outside towards Betsie, who was still where they had left her the night beforehand. "Were you not hungry" asked Samantha, as she realised that she hadn't seen Julie eat anything at all, since they had both stopped for the night at the Lillington truck stop.

"I ate mine before I woke you, it was important you had the most to eat, as you needed your strength to drive" replied Julie, as Samantha thanked her for her wonderful service, not being able to think that maybe Julie was more of an honourable human being that what was prepared to let on. After making sure that it looked as if no one had been inside the truck stop at all, Samantha and Julie got back on the road, Betsie clanking and clicking due to the number of items which filled the inside of the cab many spaces, including the overhead lockers and floor cupboards.

According to Julie's maps, Hertfordshire was full of many wide-open country lanes, which would provide them both with plenty of nice fields to park up in, should they have needed to stop at all. After a while of driving along the lanes, the memory of the night visitors had gone slightly to the back of Samantha's head; but it would soon start to creep back up again as time went on.

Samantha had ultimately decided that she would trust Julie with the navigational duties, providing that is, that Julie didn't get them lost, as their fuel supply was limited, and mistakes could cost them dearly in the long run. As Betsie was running with no trailer on the back of her, she did start to become a little bumpy after a while, even with all of the provisions that Samantha had stocked up on back in Lillington's town centre. Samantha of course was used to the ride quality of heavy goods vehicles like Betsie, but poor Julie ended up being bruised and bashed all over, as the day went on, wincing slightly from time to time, as she felt every bump and jolt of the cab, as Betsie moved down the country roads. Samantha felt a little guilty as she heard Julie wincing slightly as Betsie bounced in and out of the potholes, but then again, it was a catch twenty-two situation, as Samantha couldn't do anything about it, even though she felt Julie's pain.

"Do you know where the nearest base is from here" asked Julie to Samantha, as Samantha leaned over from the driver's seat, and placed her finger on the map, where there was a large blank square. "Here, it's called Royal Air Force North Lakes; it's a transport aircraft base as far as I know; so, it will be littered with military equipment and all sorts" replied Samantha, as Julie placed the map back in front of her, ready to resume her navigation duties. "I hope we can have a bit of a break when we're there, this truck isn't the most comfortable of places" replied Julie, as Samantha looked over at her and grinned, realising that Julie maybe a competent police officer, but was certainly not built for life as a lorry driver. "You'll get used to her eventually, it just takes a little skill to guess when it will rock and jolt" replied Samantha, as Julie winced again when Betsie went over another pothole in the road, making the cab sway rapidly from side to side.

95

And sure enough, a short way up the road from where Samantha had pointed to on the map, was the main gate to the Royal Air Force airfield called North Lakes. Betsie turned into the driveway leading up to the gates, as Samantha and Julie caught sight of the signs to reduce their speed to a crawl for an inspection by the guard at the guard post. It would have been common place to usually have seen a guard or two posted on the entrance to these sorts of facilities; but like everywhere else they had passed that day and the previous day, it was completely deserted with no signs of life at all. The electronic security gate which ran either side of the main guard post was open, so Samantha drove on, heading straight for the main office buildings, housing who knew what sorts of secrets. Samantha reduced their speed to only that above walking speed, as her and Julie began looking around for any signs of life.

A few dead bodies lay here and there as they drove through the maze of buildings on the air base; some of the bodies were wearing camouflage military uniform, others were in normal civilian clothing, but all of them with a swarm of flies either above, or landed on them, making them look liked they had some black spotted plague all over them. A strong smell of rotting flesh began to waft its way in through the cab windows, which would have been smelt for miles around, the smell being far stronger than that of the fertilisers and manure on the nearby farms. Naturally with so many dead bodies located in one place, the smell was going to be overpowering to the point that whoever was nearby would have easily become very weak and faint exceptionally quickly. Even Julie, with her many years of police work, having attended crime scenes with bodies and corpses, was feeling overpowered by the site and smell of some many who had died.

"We need to find some masks, or a cloth of some kind, and tie it around our mouths and faces to stop the smell from overpowering us" said Julie in a hurried voice, Samantha gagging slightly, feeling a lump coming up in her throat. Betsie rounded a corner onto an open flat aircraft taxiway, as the site that greeted Samantha and Julie was so horrific, that it nearly made the pair of them pass out in shock. Laying out in front of them, spread across the green spaces of grass around the taxiways and main runway, was a sea of tents, that seemed to go on for miles and miles. Most of the tents were painted in army green colours, but many others were in different colours, shapes and sizes, as if tens of thousands of people had just suddenly decided to rack up there, at a sort of strange, end of the world type rock concert. The tents stretched as far as the eye could see, right up to the perimeter fences that marked the boundaries to the airfield itself.

Hovering above each of the tents, were what looked like half the world's population of flies, which also was making a hell of a din, because of the sheer volume of so many flies in flight, all at the same time as each other. They almost looked like great black balls of fire, hoovering just a few inches above each tent, buzzing with a menacing force, that made both Samantha and Julie feel like they were standing inside of a nest full of them, pinned in on all sides. As suddenly as Samantha and Julie had arrived, there attention was suddenly taken up by what looked like an RAF jeep, fitted with a flame thrower, which was driving slowly up and down the runway, spraying each tent with a burst of flame as it went. The moment each tent was sprayed with flames, it immediately began to melt and smoulder under the heat, looking as if several thousand bonfires were all being set off all at once, just like on Guy Fawkes night.

Before long however, each tent and all of its contents, soon become a smouldering pile of ashes and soot, which smoked away on the ground, turning the once green smooth grass, into a number of chard black patches, littering the airfield, as someone had come along and dumped truckload after truckload of human ashes out onto the ground in a heap. The smoke cloud that had risen up into the sky was also just as big and impressive, but had very swiftly dissipated after the tents had stopped burning. The smell of corpses had certainly not gone away completely, but had reduced considerably, so that Samantha and Julie could breathe properly again. Feeling that it was safe to proceed, both Julie and Samantha climbed down from the cab and began walking towards the nearest hanger. "That is just horrible, and barbaric" said Samantha in complete shock, as she tried to mentally erase the images of the tents from her mind.

97

"I know, this was part of the protocol that we had to stick to during the lockdowns; the moment anyone come down with Covid symptoms, they had to brought to the nearest military base; I guess the bigger the base, the more it was housing" replied Julie, as she too shook her head in disbelief to what she was seeing, not quite being able to get her head around the sheer impact that Covid-19 had taken upon the world as they knew it. Samantha and Julie were so preoccupied with thinking about the tents, that they hadn't been attention to the fact, that there was certainly another person alive, who was on the base, and driving the RAF jeep. The flame throwing RAF jeep had come to a stop just inside of the doorway of the nearest hanger, after driving back down the main runway and along the taxiway to get there, drawing level with Samantha and Julie, as its suspension creaked slightly as it slowed to a halt.

As the RAF jeep it drew level with Samantha and Julie, a man wearing a fully protective hazmat suit and topped off with a gas mask, climbed out of the driver's seat, before walking around the jeep to where there was a stack of red canisters, each one with a flammable warning sticker on them. Samantha and Julie looked at each other in complete amazement, as the hazmat suited man seemed to have not seen them at all, but had instead proceeded in his tasks of burning the tents out on airfields green spaces. "Hello" said Julie cautiously, as she slowly crept forwards towards the hazmat suited man. The man in the hazmat suit suddenly caught sight of Samantha and Julie both walking in his direction, as he snatched up his machine gun weapon in a rush, raising it to shoulder height at both of them, brandishing the weapon at them both, shouting through his gas mask, which sounded muffled and distorted through the thick rubber casing.

Even though Samantha and Julie were only a few metres away, they had to strain their ears, to make sure they had heard the man correctly; although the site of the hazmat suited brandishing his weapon at them both, had caused the pair of them to scream and jump backwards in alarm. "Stay there; on your knees; hands above your head, both of you do it, now" shouted the hazmat suited man through his gas mask, as he creped slowly towards Samantha and Julie, machine gun still drawn, pointing straight at them both, making Samantha and Julie cry out in terror. Seeing as if Samantha and Julie had no choice in the matter, they quickly did what they were told, getting down on their knees and placing their hands behind their heads, hoping against hope, that the hazmat suited man wasn't about to gun them down where they were crouching on their knees, looking terrified and powerless to do anything.

"Who are you; what are you doing here" demanded the hazmat suited man, as he pointed his machine gun into Julie's face, who was the closest to the hazmat suited man. "I'm Julie Guard, I'm a police officer in the Hertfordshire Constabulary; and this is Samantha Bonham; we're here looking for your help, and to find out what happened to everyone" replied Julie in the most authoritarian type voice that she could muster. This fact that Julie saying that she was a police officer was stretching the truth a little, as that only applied to the world before Covid, as Covid it seemed had completely destroyed the country's entire infrastructure. "It's obvious isn't it; everyone's dead; there all dead" exclaimed the hazmat suited man, sounding a little angry, as if he thought that Samantha and Julie were somehow trespassing on private property. In the days before Covid, it would have been near impossible to get to where they were now, due to the top rate security.

Now in the new world however, the once great security forces that would have guarded the property of her majesty the Queen, were reduced to nothing more than a skeleton, with no more of the privileges it had once had at its disposal. "We can see that much, but we need to talk to someone in the military, we think that we have something which may be of use to all of us" replied Samantha, trying to stay as calm as she could, knowing that this hazmat suited man was a highly trained soldier, who was trained to kill on command, and would most likely see Samantha and Julie's actions as nothing more than espionage. Samantha did have a good reason to be nervous; even though Samantha's father Richard had been in the Army, she'd never really got used to the idea of firearms; preferring instead, to sort everything out in a diplomatic fashion, rather than by force at gunpoint.

This was obviously a thought that Julie shared, as she turned to the hazmat suited man and said, "I don't work very well with a gun in my face, so maybe you can put it down, and we can talk some more about this like civilised human beings". This did nothing more than to enrage the hazmat suited man, as he responded to Julie's remarks by jabbing the machine gun into Julie's and responding with; "are you contaminated; have you got Covid". "We can't have Covid, otherwise we'd be dead wouldn't we" responded Samantha, feeling that this was a bit of a stupid question to ask, as Covid had certainly killed off everyone who wasn't immune to it. It was a tense few moments, as the hazmat suited man stood there, weapon drawn, with Samantha and Julie on their knees and their hands above their heads in a position of surrender. The hazmat suited man's head lowered slightly, as if a sudden unseen realisation had flashed across his mind.

He slowly lowered the weapon until it was almost pointing at the floor, before taking a step back, still keeping his eyes on Samantha and Julie as he went. After a second or so, he placed his machine gun down onto the floor, and raised both of his hands towards his face, to pull off the gas mask covering his face. After a quick tug, the gas mask fell away, showing the face of a young man, around Samantha and Julie's own age; although his facial expression looked worried and frightened, as he seemed to have lost the air of bravery and invincibility that those within the armed forces always seemed to have about them. He was around five foot eleven inches tall, clean shaven and of medium build, with short brown hair which flicked up into a small quiff at the front. "Is it true miss; is it really all gone out there" asked the young airman, still wearing the hazmat suit, as he spoke with a slight south London accent?

"I'm afraid so sir; we've come all the way up from Lillington in Hertfordshire, and we've not encountered a single soul on the way here" replied Julie, as Samantha fidgeted a little, as she had yet to tell Julie about the encounter back at the truck stop on the outskirts of Lillington. Samantha knew full well that this last statement wasn't completely accurate, but she would tell Julie about the night visitors at the truck stop soon enough. "I suspected something must have happened" replied the young airman, as he began to strip out of the hazmat suit, his voice starting to come back to some sort of normality as he did so. It fell away to the ground, as Samantha and Julie could now see that the young man was wearing a Royal Air Force engineer's mechanical uniform underneath the hazmat suit. A pair of Corporal's stripes could clearly be seen on both of his shoulders, showing that he was a non-commissioned officer within the ranks of the Royal Air Force.

"Sorry; but can we get up now; my knees are starting to hurt" asked Julie, which was true, as they had been kneeling on the floor with their hands above their heads for a while now. Samantha's knees had also started to feel sore, as the hanger floor was made of solid concrete, and wasn't the most comfortable of surfaces to kneel on. "Oh yeah sorry, you can stand up and relax now; I know you're not the enemy" replied the young airman, as he finished getting out of the hazmat suit, putting his black military grade boots back on his feet, as he he'd had to take them off, so as to slide the suit off the bottom of his feet. Samantha and Julie both stood up, bring their arms down to their sides as they went, listening very carefully to what the young airman had to say, as they were interested to hear what had been happening elsewhere in the world, owing to the fact that they had both been limited on where they could go during the Covid lockdowns.

"You're an engineer, my father was in the Royal Army engineering corps" said Samantha, as the young airman looked surprised. "I'm glad to hear it miss; I'm Corporal Fredrick Loose; I'm based here at RAF North Lakes; well, was based here I guess" replied the young airman, as the young man offered his hand to Samantha and Julie, as Samantha and Julie shook Fredricks hand in turn. "So, you said I could help you with something, what do you need from me; as long as it doesn't breech the official secrets act of course" said Fredrick, as Samantha pulled the pamphlet out of her pocket, and handed it to Fredrick. "This was sent to my fiancée before Covid hit; I'm trying to make sense of this numbers here, and why it was sent to him" explained Samantha, as Fredrick took one look at the pamphlet and smiled, realising that he knew exactly what he was looking at with the information on the pamphlet.

"Well, I've no idea about what the words mean, or where that picture was taken, or who sent it to your fiancée; but I can tell you is that I've got a strong suspicion that those numbers aren't dates, they look very much like map coordinates to me" said Fredrick, as Samantha secretly kicked herself, wondering that there had to be a simple explanation for the numbers. She'd been silly into thinking that the numbers were some sort of secret spy code, but in truth, more like map coordinates and reference points. "Come with me, I think I have a piece of equipment here which might be able to help you" replied Fredrick, as he beckoned them forward into another building, next to the very hanger that they were standing in. Fredrick led them both into a room which was a lot smaller than the hanger had been, which contained all of the radar and tracking equipment that was used on military operations.

Fredrick walked over to one piece of equipment, and switched it on, as it flashed into life showing a picture of the United Kingdom on it. It was amazing to see that it had power going to it, as the national grid must have easily gone down by now. "All the military systems have backup batteries powering them, so it can generate power in the field" replied Fredrick, in response to Samantha and Julie's surprised faces at seeing a piece of electrical equipment that was still working. Holding the pamphlet in his left hand, Fredrick used his right hand to punch in the numbers on the pamphlet, the keys making a clicking noise, as he pressed on the numbers on the keyboard. When Fredrick had finished imputing the information on the strange looking radar machine, it began to make beeping and whirring noises, sounding like a mix between an old-fashioned typewriter, and an early dial up internet connection.

After a few moments, a small clicking sound came from it, as the strange looking machine printed out an A4 sheet of paper, which showed a map of a length of coastline near the town of Clyde in Scotland. Fredrick took it from the out tray on the strange looking machine, before then handing it to Samantha and Julie to read, as Samantha and Julie leaned in to look at the sheet of paper in front of them. "There you go, those numbers there are coordinates; according to your pamphlet, that is a pickup or drop off point for a series of pickup dates at that location" explained Fredrick, showing Samantha and Julie how the pamphlet's information, all seemed to fit together like giant jigsaw pieces. "Thanks so much Fredrick, that's really helped us out; we would have been sat there for ages otherwise trying to work it out" said Julie, as Samantha nodded vigorously in agreement, as her words seemed to have failed her at that exact moment.

Samantha, for the first time in days, felt relief; she now had a good idea of where Greg could be heading, and maybe even Diana could be going the same way as well, as Greg could had told her about the pamphlet as well. Samantha did seem a little put out that Greg or Diana hadn't told her about this course of action before going; but then again, they could have been forced to leave in a hurry because of Covid, or maybe thought that Samantha had died of Covid. "Can we do anything to repay you Fredrick; this has been a really great help to us, it really has" asked Samantha, but Fredrick waved a hand in front of her face in response to Samantha's remark. "That's very kind of you Samantha, but I don't think you can help me with anything to be honest; I've already got things worked out here now, and what I'm going to do next" replied Fredrick, as Samantha and Julie both looked surprised.

"What do you plan to do next Fredrick" asked Julie, as Fredrick took a deep breath in and replied, "well, there's a Chinook transport helicopter in that hanger over there; I've been servicing it for weeks now, but I know it can still fly". "Can you fly one" asked Samantha, as the three of them made their way back into the main hanger building. "Fly one, hah; the engineers know more about these aircraft than the pilots do; I can practically fly one of those with my eyes shut" replied Fredrick, laughing slightly at Samantha's last question, as Samantha realised that Fredrick was right. It would seem a bit silly if an aircraft engineer didn't know how to fly the aircraft and helicopter; almost like having a car mechanic that didn't know how to drive a car. "So, where will you fly to, Clyde in Scotland where the pamphlet says" asked Julie, who was asking the question more out of curiosity than anything all?

"Nah I'm not sadly, otherwise I'd give you a lift up there; I'm thinking of going to the Isle of White on the south coast, I can set up a camp there; a whole island where I can relax and live-in peace, not have to rely on modern technology or any of the other things we've taken for granted in the twenty first century" replied Fredrick, as both Julie and Samantha looked mildly interested. Considering that Fredrick had spent his RAF career fixing and maintaining equipment and machinery, it seemed logical that he would want to spend his new days not having to worry about any of it. "That sounds like a good idea Fredrick; can I ask, are we ok to take whatever we need from here" asked Samantha, fearing that Fredrick would say that everything had either been taken already. To Samantha and Julie's great surprise however, Fredrick didn't seem to be fazed by Samantha's request at all.

"Nah, help yourselves; I don't need any of it anymore; besides, there's some quite nice trailers knocking around here that you can use, plus a handy fuel tanker as well" replied Fredrick, gesturing around at the airfield, as Samantha's face lit up with delight, as she had been thinking about Betsie, and how Betsie would need a trailer to tow. "That's fantastic, can you help us modify them to work on Betsie; Betsie is my truck" replied Samantha, as Fredrick looked a little puzzled, wondering what Betsie was. "Sorry, who's Betsie" asked Fredrick, as Samantha pointed at Betsie the truck, sitting on the taxiway outside of the hanger the three of them were standing in. "Ah I see, Betsie is the name of the truck; nice truck I have to say" replied Fredrick, as Samantha nodded at him, and then grinned, as she was quite attached to the plucky M.A.N that had seen so much in the time that Samantha had driven her.

Fredrick's face however had suddenly split into a grin, as he quickly understood what Samantha was asking for. "I might have just the thing for you two; follow me" said Fredrick, as he gave them a wink of his eye, and beckoned for them both to follow him. Exactly what was on Fredrick's mind became clear as they strolled along the taxiway, and into the hanger next door. As they all rounded the corner through the hanger doorway, they all saw parked up against one wall, a forty-foot-long triaxled articulated trailer, which was painted dark green and had a military grade shipping container sitting on it, which was also painted a dark green colour. Sitting next to it, was a fuel tanker trailer; but this one was painted silver, and looked like an ordinary road going fuel tanker trailer rather than a military one. This trailer however had been modified, so that it carried a set of dolly wheels, and an A-frame.

Although Samantha knew from her years of truck driving on the roads, that these sorts of trailers still carried what were known as fifth wheel pins, fitted as standard to all road going articulated lorries. "So, what do you think, do you reckon you could use it" asked Fredrick, as Julie looked at them non plussed, as her experience of trucks and truck driving was virtually non-existent. "Well, all I know is that I'm looking at some sort of trailer, and that they connect up behind trucks; this is defiantly more of Samantha's department than mine" replied Julie, in what she hoped was a sensible voice, as Samantha gave a little giggle of laughter, understanding what Julie was trying to say. Although secretly in the back of Samantha's brain, the many cogs of imagination had begun to turn, spinning out an idea inside of her head, which Fredrick and Julie couldn't see clearly, but yet made perfect sense too Samantha.

Samantha's brilliant plan that she was thinking of, was to have both trailers towed behind Betsie, although there would be have to be serious modification completed first, in order to bring her brainwave into reality. "Ah it's perfect, but I'm only going to be able to take the container and it's trailer I'm afraid Fredrick, as I can't tow both behind Betsie" replied Samantha, her voice faltering slightly, realising that her wonderful plan wasn't going to work as well as she had been thinking it would. Fredrick, it seemed, had been thinking along the same lines, as he too raised a hand to his chin, thinking hard about what Samantha had just suggested about both the container and tanker trailers. "Ah that's no bother, both can be hooked to each other, see the A-frame on that" explained Fredrick, pointing to the tanker trailer dolly wheels on its front before he started speaking again.

"We modified it as a bit of an experiment for long distance deployment overseas, so the tanker using the dolly wheel and A-frame can connect to the back on the container trailer via the coupling link on the back". Samantha suddenly felt as if Fredrick could read her mind, as Fredrick lead both her and Julie across the hanger, to where the pair of trailers both sat gathering dust in the corner. Fredrick led them both around to the back of the trailers, where sure enough, there was a drawbar coupling located on the rear of the container trailer, so that the tanker trailer could be hooked up to it. Samantha suddenly had a fleeting image of the Australian road trains, which would thunder across the remote outback wilderness many thousands of miles away from where they were now in England; if it was surely possible for the road trains to work out in the outback, then Betsie could surely manage these two trailers.

"That's amazing Fredrick, military technology at its best; but it still doesn't solve the power problem though; I mean, Betsie can only pull up to fifty tonnes" replied Julie, as Samantha was taken aback slightly by Julie's sudden statement, as Samantha considered Julie's knowledge of trucking negligible. However, Julie had still made a valid point; Betsie was a fine truck indeed, but she was still a very low powered machine for a truck of her size and weight.

CHAPTER EIGHT

The Green Goddess

Fredrick stood there for a second or two after Julie had spoken, putting a hand up to his chin and scratching his short beard stubble, pondering Julie's point of interest. "I suppose it is possible, theoretically, to give this Betsie of yours a complete overhaul" replied Fredrick, as Samantha looked appalled at the thought of her beloved Betsie being vandalised in this way. "But she's a civilian truck, not a military one" replied Samantha, a little surprised and amazed that Fredrick was still being incredibly positive about of all of this. Samantha couldn't help standing there thinking about the size of the problem at hand. Betsie after all, was not a specially built recovery truck, which packed a far greater horse power capacity than a standard lorry would have. But even Samantha thought that an HGV recovery truck, would be nowhere near powerful enough to pull two full loaded articulated trailers.

The overall combined weight of both trailers would have been nearly one hundred tonnes, as Samantha thought to herself that she would need a railway locomotive, to be able to pull that sort of weight. "What make and model of truck is it again" asked Fredrick, who had been standing in the same place with his hand on his face for the duration of time that Samantha had been thinking. "It's an M.A.N T.G.X; it's the latest 2020 model; she's less than six months old" replied Samantha, as Fredrick's face brightened up straight away after Samantha had said this. "Oh, I've got spare parts for those in the stores here, and I can even get a few modifications done too; give her a bit of a tune up, if you get my drift" replied Fredrick with another wink of his eye. "What exactly do you mean by a tune up" asked Samantha, as she was still very much still protective of her pride and joy.

"Don't worry, just bring Betsie round into the hanger next door to this one, and I'll show you" replied Fredrick, as they all walked back out through the hanger door, Fredrick making for the next hanger along the taxiway, and Samantha and Julie for Betsie, who was still parked where they'd left her, outside the original hanger where the RAF jeep had come in and parked. Fredrick's idea of a tune up, was certainly like nothing that neither Samantha or Julie had seen before in their lives. Despite the fact that Samantha had been brought up around mechanics and engineering because of her father's background, it was still quite a sight to see what Fredrick could do with Betsie. "Mind you, if you want the best, just to the military" thought Samantha, as her and Julie watched in amazement, as Fredrick rolled in what looked like half the world's tool box, inside the back of a crystal white Ford Transit van.

The third hanger on the airfield that they had all stepped into, looked more like a mechanics workshop, rather than a storage area for aircraft. There were aircraft parts everywhere, in the hundreds of crates and boxes lining the walls, along with vehicle parts and accessories in all shapes and sizes. As the sun began to go down later that day, Betsie had been hauled into the third hanger, which was full of the spare parts and mechanical equipment, as Fredrick set to work, with Samantha and Julie looking in as interested spectators, who were taking part in a car mechanical programme. After a short time however, Samantha and Julie were begging Fredrick if they could help him, as boredom had started to set in very rapidly, having done nothing all afternoon except watch Fredrick take apart Betsie, until she was completely unrecognisable to the truck that had rolled onto RAF North Lakes earlier that day.

Fredrick as it transpired, had been working on an experimental engine, which he was now helping Samantha guide in using a heavy-duty chain and pulley crane, attached to the ceiling on a large iron roof supporting join, which according to Fredrick, was powerful enough to lift and hold an aircraft engine in the air for long periods of time. Betsie's standard engine, a twelve litre straight six which had been made by M.A.N themselves, sat on a few blocks of wood on the other side of the hanger, after being carefully removed a few hours earlier. Every now and again, Fredrick would take parts off of it, and fit them to the new engine, that had now been secured into place on Betsie's chassis. "The gearbox might struggle a little under the new engine, but as long as your careful, it shouldn't blow out of there" explained Fredrick, as Julie looked suddenly horrified, at the thought of an exploding truck engine.

"Blow out; is that likely" asked Julie in a shocked voice? "Well, this is a military grade engine we're putting in here Julie, and it's having to work with a civilian gearbox; so, with the amount of power it's producing, if the engine is revved too hard, it will either shatter the clutch plate, or burn out the axle splines" replied Fredrick, in answer to Julie's question, as he popped his head up from underneath the chassis on Betsie. Fredricks face was a little dirty from where he had been cleaning and working on Betsie, and he certainly looked like he was in his element, having one final project to sink his teeth into. Julie on the other hand, who's mechanical knowledge was a bit limited, did look a bit non plussed after Fredrick's explanation. "In order words, if I don't drive it carefully, it will blow up the truck" replied Samantha, as Julie's face broke into a sudden understanding.

Samantha herself, who was a little more mechanically minded, had donned a boiler suit and tied her hair back, in order to help Fredrick out with the modifications. "If all goes well, this should all be done within a few days, and you'll be back on the road again" came Fredrick's voice from underneath Betsie, as it sounded a little distorted, as it bounced around in the echoey chassis framed underside of Betsie. "That sounds great guys; but I'm sorry to be a pain, but is there anything I can do to help" asked Julie, who was still leaning up against one of Betsie's mudguards, looking down into where Samantha and Fredrick had been working away? It was true; Julie had indeed been standing around for nearly the whole day, watching both Fredrick and Samantha working away, but because she didn't know much about mechanics or engineering as much as Samantha and Fredrick did, she wasn't really able to help as much as she'd like.

"Tell you what Julie, there's some ration packs in the stores next door, and I've got a bonfire bin and an iron grill in there as well; if you want to start a fire in that, you can use the fire to cook up the meals in the ration packs if need be" replied Fredrick, in answer to Julie's question. "Right, thanks" replied Julie, sounding a little put out, that she'd essentially been given the job of a dinner lady. "Quite a come down" thought Julie, as only a matter of days earlier, she would have been patrolling the streets of Lillington, as the friendly local bobby on the beat, who was now being made to make dinners on a bonfire bin, as if she was on a camping trip. Then again, this was a post Covid world; everything that everyone had even known, was now gone forever, so Julie would have to adapt quickly to the new world, or it would be curtains for them all, as they tried to survive day to day.

Even though Julie wasn't any good at camping, she had still managed to start a fire in the bonfire bin, using old bits of newspaper, and whatever else was going spare that Julie could find knocking around in the nearby hangers and buildings. The bonfire crackled and hissed away, as Julie found the iron grill to go over the top of it, before placing a round cooper cooking pot on it, dropping in some packets of rise, and even boiling a mess tin full of water which Julie would use to make tea and coffee for them all. The fire in the bonfire bin was so warm, that Julie could even feel the heat coming from it standing a good five to six metres away, which was quite an achievement for her, considering that this was the first time she had ever lit a fire before. "You learn something new every day" thought Julie to herself, as she watched the packets of rice expand and then cool down, as the hot water was removed from the cooking pot.

"Just the pipes and cables to connect now, then we can add the bull bars on the front; once that's done, old Betsie will be up and ready to go" said Fredrick, as they all tucked into Julie's rice dinner an hour or so later, seated on some very nice mobile collapsible chairs that Julie had managed to find in the store room next to the small mountain of ration packs. The fire seemed to be the brightest thing in the hanger now, as a light breeze whipped inside the hanger, blowing around some of the dust particles that had started to gather on the floor. The sun had nearly set now, as all three of them sat around the bonfire bin, trying to catch some of the warmth that was emanating from it. Samantha had a look on her face which told everyone else in the group that she was thinking about something. "I know that look all too well; what are you thinking about Sam" asked Fredrick, as Samantha turned towards Fredrick, still with the same look upon her face.

"I think I'd like Betsie to have a new paint job; and; possibly a new name too" replied Samantha in a modest voice, in answer to Fredrick's question. Samantha half expected Fredrick to say that he didn't have any spray tools to do the job, but was surprised to see the grin on his face, as if the wonderful wheels of inspiration had hit him once again. "I had a feeling it was that; don't you worry Samantha, we've got tools here for practically any job you can name" replied Fredrick, as Julie looked stunned. "Is there anything you can't do" replied Julie, sounding a little sarcastic, but Fredrick and Samantha only laughed at this latest remark from Julie; even Julie couldn't help but crack a smile at her own sarcasm. "Julie, the man is a military engineer; there probably isn't a single job in the world he can't do" replied Samantha, as Fredrick grinned at her appreciably, feeling that he was being presented with a lifetime achievement award.

Samantha couldn't help but grin back, thinking that she could have sworn she saw Fredrick look back at her in a passionate way. "You're wearing an engagement ring, don't do it Sam; you'd be letting Greg down if you passed off passionate feelings for another" thought Samantha, as she quickly turned away, pretending to be filling her mess tin full of more rice from the cooking pot. "What was you thinking about as a name then Sam" asked Julie, as she too, went in for second helpings of rice. "Well, as I'm thinking she could be painted military green, like the same colour as the trailer and tanker are; and the name; well; I was thinking about maybe calling her, 'The Green Goddess'; or something like that" replied Samantha. "The Green Goddess you say, we have fire engines and water tenders here called those; but those are just nicknames for them really" replied Fredrick in a positive voice, considering Samantha's last comment for a second or to.

"I think it's a great name Sam, The Green Goddess" said Julie, waving her arms in the air, as if pretending the name 'Green Goddess' was up in lights on a fairground ride. "Green Goddess it is" said Fredrick, as he finished his meal of rice, placing the mess tin down on the floor beside him. "Do you really think that humanity will ever be the same again, I mean considering how many never survived Covid" asked Julie to the group at large. It was such a sudden question, that Fredrick and Samantha both looked surprised that Julie had even mentioned it, but they could tell it had been playing on Julie's mind for some time. Fredrick however seemed to have the answer to that particular question ready, as he said; "Well, from what I had last heard from headquarters, it seems that the mortality rate from the number of Covid victims was over ninety five percent of the world's population".

"Ninety five percent" replied Samantha and Julie together, both in shock at the mortality rate, as Julie handed Fredrick a cup of tea, that Julie had managed to scrounge from what was left of that day's ration pack. Fredrick thanked Julie for the cup of tea, before continuing with his explanation. "You see, while Covid was going on, the government had decreed that all of the Covid victims were to be moved from the hospitals, to all of the military bases around the country, to keep them isolated from everyone else, hence why you had all of this lot". Fredrick gestured to all of the cremated remains outside, which only hours earlier had been hundreds of tents containing the bodies of the Covid victims.

"That's what I was doing when you both arrived earlier today; all of the bodies had to be cremated, in case they started a second wave of Covid" finished Fredrick, draining the rest of his tea in one gulp, and placing his mug back on the floor.

If coming across a whole airfield of rotting corpses wasn't bad enough for Samantha and Julie, then hearing this piece of news was even more devastating still. Ninety five percent of the world's population; that had to mean that the United Kingdom must have had one of the smallest amounts of people still left alive inside of it, from what Fredrick had said to them earlier on that afternoon. Samantha thought for a second about the other countries around the world, and what some of their populations must have suffered during Covid, and what it must be like now in the new world, as the United Kingdom wasn't the only country that had been affected. According to the news broadcasts, which had been coming in daily through the television sets during the country's nationwide lockdown, the Covid-19 virus had originated in the city of Wuhan in China, on the continent of Asia.

China's human population itself, was near enough a billion people, in terms of population. The same too could be said with the country of India, with its population of over a billion people as well. Even some of the western countries like America, Canada and even the likes of Brazil, must have been hit hard too, suffering the most fatalities around the planet. Samantha suddenly felt a hot surge of anger at that moment, at the way things had been handled in the world, and at the way that the British government had handled the Covid situation, when they had learned that it had been inside the country. How the way that the authorities had been granted emergency powers to drag random people off the streets, and imprison them on the military bases, like the Nazi German regime had done with their enemies in the concentration camps during the second world war.

How the very same people, who had been dragged off the streets because of Covid, had been forced to then live in tents, where dysentery and disease would have run rife; where sanitary conditions would have been near appalling to downright alarming. It was because of Covid, that Samantha, Fredrick, Julie, and so many other survivors, now had futures which were bleak and completely unknown. It was due to the way that the government hadn't tried to stop Covid crossing over the UK boarders, that Samantha might have still had friends and family alive today. But Samantha then shook herself, trying to clear her head of these sorts of thoughts. Even when Covid had been discovered inside of the United Kingdom, because the symptoms took so long to show themselves, that mounting any form of defence against it, would have been a useless and pointless effort.

It wasn't the most pleasant of thoughts that Samantha was thinking about, as she drifted off to sleep that night, curled up in a blanket on the hanger floor, as the fire crackled away, slowly burning further and further down, until it had burnt itself out completely. It was the smell of freshly cooked porridge, that woke Samantha from her slumber the following morning. Her mess tin was lying beside her when she woke up, as Samantha caught site of Julie standing a few feet away next to the bonfire bin, where Julie had managed to start a brand-new fire within it, cooking a few mess tins on the metal grill above the flames, filled to the near brim with lovely yummy porridge oats. Samantha sat up, propping herself up with her hands on the floor, as her blanket fell away slightly onto the floor. Samantha wasn't too worried about this, as she had slept fully clothed through the night, and didn't need to worry about covering herself up.

"Morning sleepy head, breakfast is on the floor, and when you've finished eating, I think Fredrick might have something to show you" replied Julie, who looked wide awake and fresh. "Thanks Julie, what time is it" asked Samantha, feeling a little drowsy. "Just after 10am, but don't worry; I let you sleep as you had a busy day yesterday, and we will have another busy one today" replied Julie, but as she finished talking, Samantha looked over at where they'd been working on Betsie the previous day, and her jaw, dropped. She was looking at Betsie, but somehow, it didn't look like Betsie at all. The company livery of Travis Transport Limited had gone, and instead was now painted exactly the same military green colour as what the trailer, container and tanker were. On the front was a mounted set of giant stainless steel ball bars, also the same military green colour as the rest of the vehicle was.

The usual large chrome M.A.N logo on the front, was now jet black in colour, but seemed to look just as impressive as the rest of the vehicle was. And most impressive of all, were the words 'The Green Goddess', stamped in black stencil type letters between the windscreen and the radiator grill. Samantha scrambled to her feet, a huge smile spread broadly across her face, as Fredrick appeared from around the other side of the truck. "Ta-da, well, what do you think; worked on her all night to get her finished; the only one of her kind" said Fredrick, throwing both of his arms open in mock surprise. Samantha ran forward and hugged him Fredrick so tightly, that Fredrick thought that his ribs might break. "Ok, you can let go now" replied Fredrick, in a strained voice, as Samantha let go of him, fearing that she may have just gone a little far in thanking Fredrick for his amazing work on Betsie, that was now the legendary Green Goddess.

"Aww, it's perfect, how can I ever thank you Fredrick" couped Samantha, as Fredrick brushed himself down, and waved a hand in front of Samantha. "Oh, it was nothing really; I just love engineering, and you're a sweet lady, so it made the perfect fit" replied Fredrick, as Samantha blushed such a deep red colour, that it wouldn't have been surprising if rose petals would have started blossoming out of her face. "I knew you'd like it" said Julie, who had walked over to them both, holding Samantha's mess tin in her hand. "Thanks Julie, you're a star" said Samantha, as she took the mess tin and started to eat the porridge using the spoon that was resting up against the side of the mess tin. "I've upgraded all of the tyres to multi-terrain ones, including on the trailers; given the cab a bit of an overhaul inside too, where I've put in a bunk bed, so you can both sleep inside the cab" explained Fredrick, as he gestured with his hands in front of him.

As Fredrick spoke, he pointed out all of the new improvements and upgrades that he'd made to make Betsie the new Green Goddess that she was. "And naturally she's designed to run off road as well as on the tarmac, and I've added a snorkel in case she's travelling through deep water, and the exhausts now go out through the top of the cab through these stacks I've run down the sides to give her more ground clearance". As Fredrick finished speaking, Samantha managed to close her mouth, and even found time through amazement, to finish the rest of her porridge. "So, is she fit for a highway princess" asked Fredrick, looking at Samantha, hoping that she would like it. Samantha blushed ever so slightly, and responded with, "Aww, of course it is, thank you so much Fredrick, she's perfect". Julie was almost smiling behind both of their backs, as packed away the breakfast bits, washing them in a barrel of water just outside of the door.

Very helpfully, there had been a spot of rain come down over the airfield as they had all been sleeping, so Fredrick had left an open topped barrel outside, so as to collect rainwater for them to use. Julie had managed to then heat the water collected over the fire, so they could use it to wash out the mess tins and everything else that had been used for cooking. "How can we ever repay you" asked Samantha, as Fredrick looked a little taken aback at Samantha sudden remark. "Repay me, you don't need to that Samantha; I'm on my way out now anyway; just going to load up the Chinook with some basic supplies, and then I'm flying south, to set up home somewhere peaceful" replied Fredrick, pointing across the airfield, to another hanger that stood with its door opened wide. Sitting inside the hanger, was an RAF Chinook twin rotor blade transport helicopter, which was prepared for take-off.

"I've emptied out the tanker as well, it had aviation fuel inside of it, so that would have been useless to you guys, so I emptied into the Chinook's tanks instead, so there now full" explained Fredrick, as he gestured to the fuel tanker trailer hitched up at the back behind the container trailer on the Green Goddess. "Are you sure we can't help you" asked Julie, who like Samantha was most grateful for all of Fredrick's help. "I'll be fine, just some help with these supplies and then I'll be on my way; you ladies help yourself to whatever you like in here" replied Fredrick in a casual way, as he waved another hand in the air. It was easily around lunchtime before the Chinook had been packed full of supplies, and was ready for take-off. Fredrick had banded them both goodbye and good luck for their journey ahead, and hoped that they might meet again one day in the future.

After this, Fredrick had given Samantha and Julie a big hug, before closing the door on the Chinook, and waiting until Samantha and Julie were at a safe distance before starting up the engines. As Samantha and Julie had only seen Chinook helicopters flying in the air over their houses, it was fascinating watching one powering up on the ground. Fredrick had warned them to keep their distance as he powered the Chinook's engines up, because of the force of the downwind draft from the rotor blades. The Chinooks engine fired up, getting loud and loud, as the rota blades spun faster and faster, until they were eventually blurs, due to the speed that they were spinning at. The great green mass of the Chinook helicopter began to lift slowly into the air off the taxiway, where Fredrick had positioned it too for take-off, Fredrick keeping it in a steady hovering position, as if he had been flying helicopters for years.

From the open glass cockpit windows, Fredrick waved to Samantha and Julie, as the Chinook pitched forwards, and began to climb straight up into the sky, banking towards the south as it went. Samantha and Julie waved after the Chinook, until it had vanished from view, as they both sighed, and retreated back inside the hanger to where the Green Goddess stood, waiting longingly to be driven for the first time. "Well, time to go I think; and I know that you've been dying to try out that new engine" said Julie, as Samantha looked at Julie with a 'you read my mind' sort of look. Walking back inside the hanger to where the Green Goddess was parked, they both climbed into the cab, Samantha into the driver's seat, and Julie into the passenger's seat, picking the map up from where it had been sitting on the front dashboard section next to the front windscreen.

"According to the coordinates that Fredrick gave us from the pamphlet, we're heading for the town of Clyde in Scotland" replied Julie, as Samantha took in the newly designed cab, with its brand-new rear bunk beds, which allowed Samantha and Julie to sleep comfortably inside of the cab from then on. Julie spoke with a very matter of fact style voice, as she pointed to a little word on the map saying 'Clyde', showing the far reaches of Scotland, where the town of Clyde sat on the coastline, as remote as the furthest reaches of the British Isles could take them. By Samantha's mental calculations, the town of Clyde was at least five to six hundred miles from where they were sitting at that very moment, on the RAF North Lakes airfield. "Right you are navigator; prepare for take-off; main engine start" said Samantha, in the same way that an airline Captain would brief their passengers on that day's flight.

The Green Goddess's engine sputtered for a second or two, and then rumbled into life, not in the same way as a normal truck engine would, but with a lot more might and authority in its growls, as the pistons on the new mighty experimental engine pumped up and down inside their cylinder mountings. Samantha and Julie exchanged excited looks, as Samantha selected first gear, and pressed her foot gingerly onto the accelerator pedal. Samantha didn't have to press it too hard to get a response out of the Green Goddess, as there was a hiss of air, and the Green Goddess began to roll slowly forwards, the cab not even moving, due to the weight of the trailers behind the tractor unit. Samantha let out a small giggle, as a child would do when there told they are going to a sweet shop, or too somewhere that brought them great pleasure. "Easy dear, you don't want to get too excited now" replied Julie, as Samantha brought herself back under control, thinking ahead.

"We're on the move again, rolling down the highway" said Samantha, as she sat back in her chair, feeling the full power, weight and length of the Green Goddess for the first time. Julie grinned at Samantha in agreement, as she sat with the road atlas on her lap, ready to take up her usual role of navigator. They managed to get out of the hanger, and even around the airfield buildings with ease, although it did seem strange to Samantha that she was now driving a vehicle, which was in excess of over one hundred feet long, and weighed just under one hundred tonnes. Even a standard everyday articulated lorry would have at least five or even six axles to help it on the road. The Green Goddess on the other hand, had a grand total of ten separate axles; four on the tanker trailer at the back, three on the container trailer, and three axles on the unit, all of them needed to stabilise the bulk of the vehicle as a whole.

The power of the Green Goddess was almost overwhelming, as Fredrick had stripped out the regular twelve litre straight six, and instead fitted it with an experimental six litre 'W' sixteen engine, which was well over twice the size, and three times the power of the original engine. Because of the extra weight however, it would mean that the Green Goddess would burn more fuel than her predecessor Betsie, and be able to pull the two trailers behind her with ease. Even though Fredrick had said that her top speed would be limited, the Green Goddess was still able to thunder along at fifty-six miles per hour, which was the old top speed of Betsie. Even Julie for the first, didn't have anything to complain about being in the passenger's seat of the Green Goddess. Beforehand, Julie had been bounced around all over the cab, as Betsie was running on her own as a single tractor unit, and no trailer.

This made it incredibly bumpy to ride in, because of the lack of weight behind it; so now having two fully loaded trailers behind the tractor unit, made an incredible difference when it came to ride comfort. This was just proved only a few miles outside of RAF North Lakes airfield, as the Green Goddess hit its first pot hole in the road, and Julie didn't even wince as they went over it, so smooth was the ride coming from the suspension and the wheels. Naturally, it would have been normal with a vehicle as big as the Green Goddess to stick to the main roads, as those would be the only roads big enough to take her. However, Samantha had easily pointed out that if there had been other survivors of Covid out there, then they would most likely stay locally to their homes at first, and then begin to branch out as they went along. This point had certainly been proved, as Samantha had heard the two men hanging around the Lillington truck stop, a few nights ago.

By the time Samantha and Julie had both decided to come off the road and stop for the night at six o clock that evening, they had travelled through half a dozen villages throughout Hertfordshire, and across the border into Bedfordshire, where they were greeted with more open fields and a couple of empty shops, still with their shelves stacked with everyday items. "Fifty miles today and restocked with supplies, can't be too bad eh" said Samantha, as her and Julie tucked into some tins of pears and baked beans. They'd decided to stop in a lay-by on the side of an A-road, in the Bedfordshire countryside. On the side closest to them, was a six-foot-high hedge; but on the other side, were completely open fields, all full of freshly growing wheat and sunflower seeds, which blew around slightly in the small gentle breeze that came in off the fields, making Samantha and Julie shiver slightly, as the temperature had only just crept above ten degrees centigrade.

Just along the road from them was the entrance to a small hamlet, where they could see a post office shop and a few houses, all of them completely deserted, as if their owners had just popped out, and were coming back to them in a short while. "You'd be able to get a nice farm around here you know to live on, I'm sure there deserted now" said Samantha to Julie, who was now toasting some bread on the mobile gas hob that they had brought with them, as part of the camping gear that they had managed to scrounge from the stores at RAF North Lakes. Julie did seem to ponder this for a moment, before she gave a response to Samantha's comment. "I was thinking maybe in Yorkshire, or maybe in the Lake District if I wanted a farm, far more of a remote location than Bedfordshire; it's still really close to home to be honest" replied Julie, as she finished toasting her bread and took a bite out of it.

"Yeah, I guess so" replied Samantha, taking a mouthful of beans; swallowing them, and then continuing. "Back before Covid, I remember doing a delivery of fertiliser to this farm building complex up in the countryside around Sheffield; as I was coming down and going up, some of the scenery in that part of the world was just stunning, just fabulous I tell you; some of the best I've seen in my life". Julie pondered this, before taking another bite out of her toast. "I thought you'd want me to travel with you all the time" said Julie, as Samantha turned to her and smiled.

"Your free to go wherever you like honey, you're not bound by borders, or jobs, or places anymore; you can live anywhere, anytime, or go with whoever you please" replied Samantha in an understanding and reassuring voice. "You know, I wish I was like you, free spirited and all that" said Julie, as Samantha looked puzzled, wondering what Julie meant by that.

"How do you mean Julie" asked Samantha in a curious voice, as Julie put down her baked bean tin and spoon. "Well, I mean to say; I've had to be strict with myself for years, being a police officer and everything; but you just strike me as this rugged lady who can just deal with anything life throws at her" replied Julie, as Samantha giggled slightly. "Aww, you are a sweetie, but you have to remember, I had a father who was in the Royal Army Engineers, so I wasn't your typical girly girl from birth really" explained Samantha, as Julie seemed to understand what Samantha was saying to her. Samantha placed her baked bean tin to one side, and got up out of her chair she had been sitting in, strolling across the road to stand on the opposite pavement, looking across the fields full of wheat and sunflower seeds. Samantha then walked back across the road, and seated herself back in her collapsible deck chair beside the Green Goddess.

Julie still seemed to look a little downtrodden, but Samantha soon took Julie's hand, as Julie looked Samantha straight in the eye as she did this. "Listen, Julie, honey; what you have to remember is your old life, my old life, the world is gone; everything we ever knew, loved and cared about has been taken from us forever; what matters now is that we survive and start anew, like this" said Samantha, as she pulled out the pamphlet from her pocket, which showed the picture of the Scottish coastline on it, and it's coordinates and dates for the town of Clyde. "You're hoping Greg will be there I'm guessing" replied Julie, who sounded a little more positive than she had been before, as Samantha smiled again at the mention of Greg's name. Samantha almost did it without thinking; then again, Samantha and Greg had been due to get married, and she had no proof that Greg and Diana were dead, so she was still very hopeful that they would be found.

"Yes, I do; Greg and a lady called Diana, who was a friend of mine since my school days; she wasn't at home when I first called after Covid had struck, so maybe they might have both escaped away from it all" replied Samantha, as she spoke these words in a confident voice. It then suddenly dawned on Samantha, that she still had her wedding dress, tucked away in the suitcase she'd brought with her from Lillington, which was stored right at the back of the shipping container sitting on the first trailer directly behind where the main cab was on the Green Goddess. "Your right, your absolutely right, I'm being silly; I need to pull myself together if I want to survive" replied Julie, with an also sheer determination in her voice. "You'll be fine, you've done well so far; who says you can't survive in this new world" said Samantha, in a reassuring voice, feeling that Julie was just on a bit of a downer, as they were reminded of the new world and its ways.

Julie smiled at Samantha, as they finished tucking into their meals, allowing their conversations to be on times gone by, Julie having some wonderful and awe-inspiring stories to tell from her days as police officer in Lillington's police service. The sun slowly sank lower and lower in the sky, as Samantha and Julie sat chatting away about times gone past, until it was only just about light enough to see. When the sun had finally disappeared below the horizon a few hours later, they'd both decided that it was time for bed. So, they packed away all of the dinner things and the camping equipment, and settled themselves in for the first night sleeping inside the new Green Goddesses cab, Samantha taking the bottom bunk, while Julie had volunteered to sleep on the top one. However, as they both said good night to each and turned out the cab lights, for one of them; the nights activities weren't over; just yet.

CH/\PTER NINE

The Stalkers

Julie fell asleep quickly that night, feeling the comfort of her new bunk, as if she was lying on her usual soft feather mattress back at her old house. Samantha also fell asleep quickly that night, however in the early hours of the morning, she was suddenly awoken by what looked like a flash of light in the wingmirror. The curtains were of course closed around the cab windows, but from where Samantha was laying on the lower bunk, her eyes could see through a narrow gap in the curtains onto the road outside. She shook herself slightly; thinking that it must have just been a trick of the moon light; or was it a trick of the moon light? Samantha sat up a little, to look more closely through the crack in the curtain, and sure enough, there it was again, only this time, the lights stayed on, and it seemed to belong to a vehicle of some kind that was coming down the road, through the little hamlet ahead of where the Green Goddess was parked.

At first, Samantha assumed that the vehicle contained other survivors, who were scavenging for food, drink and other essential supplies. It was only when the light got close enough, that Samantha could make out the outline of what looked like a pickup truck, which drove slowly past the post office shop on the edge of the hamlet, and came to a stop about ten yards from where the Green Goddess was parked. Samantha immediately realised in horror, that the Green Goddess wasn't your normal everyday vehicle, and if these scavengers in this pickup truck found the supplies in the back, they would have a field day with it all. The occupants of the pickup truck couldn't see Samantha or Julie inside the Green Goddesses cab, but then she could suddenly hear quite clearly, that these voices were most certainly the same ones that she had heard before, and they were coming closer by the second.

They were the same two voices that Samantha had heard less than two nights earlier, when both herself and Julie, had been parked up at the truck stop on the outskirts of Lillington. That was too farfetched to be a coincidence; they couldn't have run into them twice within the space of two separate counties, and especially down the same road that both Samantha and Julie happened to be camping on at the same time. Samantha strained her hearing as hard as she could, hoping that she could hear what was being said. "Might be worth casing the joint, it doesn't look like anyone is around" said the first voice, as it sounded gleeful and hopeful at the same time. "Are you nuts Ed, that's a military wagon, and the curtains are closed, so there must be someone inside of it right now" said a second voice, again, also a familiar one, as Samantha recognised it from the night at the Lillington truck stop.

"Do you think there armed" replied the first voice, sounding like he was putting this question directly to the second person in the vehicle. "Don't want to risk it, and there could be two of them, that cab looks big enough to house two people" said the second voice, sounding a little apprehension, not knowing that neither Samantha or Julie, were not armed, or from the military. "Good thing I choose to paint her green" thought Samantha to herself, as she carried on straining her eyes to listen to the mystery stalkers. "Fine, have it your way then" said the first voice, a little put out, as there was a sudden rumbling of an engine noise, as the pickup moved off down the road, moving slowly at first, and then gathering speed into the night. Samantha stood still for a second, not daring to move or breath, as if she feared that she wasn't out of danger just at that very moment.

That was now the second time that Samantha had heard those voices, and that was now the second time that these strange men had shown up in exactly the same place as she and Julie both were. That could not have been a coincidence; this jet-black pickup truck was clearly some sort of reconnaissance vehicle of some kind, and maybe the two people in it were part of a bigger group who went around finding and bringing together other Covid survivors somehow. No; something in Samantha's guts told her that this probably wasn't the answer somehow. "Then what could it possibly be" thought Samantha; but at that point, a very sinister theory flashed in front of her, like a flicking movie trailer, followed closely by a single word; stalker. But who would be stalking her and Julie; or was it just Samantha, or just Julie perhaps? After all, these men had only appeared in their pickup truck, since Samantha and Julie had joined and began travelling together.

Samantha suddenly had too flash back, to what felt like an almost previous life, to all of the memories she had made with past boyfriends, and those who had dumped her cruelly over the years. But that was a stupid thought to have anyway, and even if those boyfriends had survived Covid, why would they want to waste their time and energy hunting down Samantha, what would have been the point of it all. "Maybe this has got something to with the pamphlet" Samantha thought, thinking back to the conversation that she and Julie had been having over it, on the first day they had met back in Lillington. "Yes, we're dealing with a stalker here; one that is clearly prepared to do anything to get their hands on us, or this pamphlet" thought Samantha, as she climbed back onto her bunk, and did her best to fall asleep again, despite fearing that she would start dreaming about strange men breaking into the Green Goddess and robbing them blind, or worse.

Samantha must have had what felt like the worlds shortest amount of sleep, but she was being shaken out of her slubber by Julie, who told her very cheerfully, that a mess tin full of porridge was waiting for her at the breakfast table. "Breakfast table" replied Samantha in a confused voice, but she would soon find out what Julie meant. As part of the camping gear that they had managed to find along the way, was a couple of chairs, and a small fold up table, which was now sitting on the road. In normal circumstances, setting up a pop-up table on the white line of an A-road, would have been a very silly thing to do indeed; it would have meant that they would be run over by faster moving traffic for a start. But there was a very slim chance of something like that occurring on a day like today, or indeed any time in the near distance future, so Samantha felt confident enough to sit down in one of the chairs, and begin tucking into her breakfast.

The morning breakfast contained a bit of a surprise, as while Samantha slept, Julie had raided the little post office shop, and had found it to be more of a mini supermarket, rather than a post office. She'd come back with a considerable number of items like packets of bacon, eggs, flour, bread, cheese and even some tomatoes, which looked like they were going over a bit. "You should really stop cooking breakfast from time to time and let me do it, I should pull my weight a bit more" replied Samantha, but Julie cut her short as she spoke. "I'd told you before, you're driving all day every day, all I do is read the stupid map" blurted out Julie, but Samantha got what she meant. "Reading the map is crucial to what we're doing, it's by far the most important job; if you didn't tell me where to go, I would probably end up driving into a lake or something" replied Samantha, as Julie let out a laugh, picturing the Green Goddess in a lake somewhere.

"How could you drive into a lake, you'd see it coming wouldn't you" laughed Julie, but Samantha was too busy tucking into her breakfast to answer Julie's rhetorical question. Samantha had good reason to give her whole attention to her cooked breakfast, as it contained a bacon and egg sandwich, with a few slices of cheese on the side; a small luxury that could still be cooked up, even in the new world. When Samantha had finished her breakfast however, the memory of the night's events came back to her, as if it was being played on a roll of film in the cinema. Samantha would have to say something to Julie at some point, she'd just have to; Julie was bound to work it out eventually, as she had been a police officer after all, and was very likely trained on how to spot if people were hiding things. Samantha helped Julie pack away the breakfast things, washing them down with some hot water that Julie had boiled up in one of the mess tins.

The morning had dawned fine and dry, with a few scattered white clouds high up in the sky, meaning that the early morning sunshine shown off the cab windows, making things look brighter than what they appeared in the surrounding countryside. The light breeze was once again blowing across the fields, making the leaves on the hedge rustle in the wind. It felt weird looking up into the sky and see no helicopters or aeroplanes flying above them, as Samantha and Julie's current location would have been on a flight path to a major UK airport. It made them both think about Fredrick, and whether he had managed to reach the Isle of Wight or not, to set up a brand-new life there. It made Samantha and Julie both think about their lives ahead, as at some point, that they may have been forced to separate from each other, if Julie found her perfect farm to live on, and Samantha living on the road in her new ambition to be a travelling salesman.

As they were both making their way back to the Green Goddess cab however, Samantha suddenly stopped, making Julie nearly walk into the back of her. Julie managed to stop herself just in time however, as Samantha turned to face Julie, bracing herself up for the open confession that she was about to make to Julie. "I need to come clean with you about something Julie" said Samantha, in the sort of voice that would have been used if her and Julie were sat in an interview room in a police station. "Ok Sam; well; just remember you can tell me anything, I was a police officer after all" replied Julie, as Samantha grinned a little. Samantha's grin soon vanished though, as she took a deep breath in, and then exhaled very slowly, gathering herself for her explanation. "Do you remember when we were back at RAF North Lakes, and Fredrick asked us if we had seen any other people" said Samantha, as Julie looked surprised.

"Yeah, I do, I can't really forget it can I; he had us both on our knees and our hands above our heads at gunpoint" said Julie in a jokey like voice, as Samantha suddenly blurted out very quickly, "I think we're being stalked". "Sorry" replied Julie, looking a little puzzled, having not quite caught all what Samantha had said. "I think we're being stalked Julie" repeated Samantha, a little slower this time, as Julie suddenly looked horrified. "What; how are we being stalked; I haven't seen anyone except you and Fredrick since the first day after Covid" replied Julie, who was now looking at Samantha in a confused sort of way. Samantha swallowed and then continued. "That first night on the road when we stayed at that truck stop outside of Lillington, while I was sleeping in the service area, I heard a vehicle pull up outside; I remember it, because it's headlights lit up my part of the building".

Julie leaned up the container trailer, as Samantha continued speaking. "Then last night, while you were asleep, I heard a car pull up outside, just here in fact". Samantha gestured to the strip of the A-road where they had been sat having breakfast minutes earlier. "Could it have possibly been two sets of people, there must be others out there after all" asked Julie, who didn't seem to be fazed by what Samantha had told her? "Not unless these two guys have identical twins, each who sound exactly the same as the truck stop pair, and I can swear blind, I've heard one of their voices before now" replied Samantha, as Julie's face changed again; this time she looked interested, feeling that she would have to do a bit of investigation work, just like from her police days. Fortunately for Samantha, Julie had brought her police notebook with her, which she now pulled out of her jacket pocket, and began to scribe in it with a small pencil.

"Was it just the voices you heard" asked Julie, as Samantha replied, "Better than that, I heard names too". Julie's face lit up, as if she was working back at Lillington's police station, and had just made a major breakthrough in an investigation. "That's fantastic, what were they" replied Julie in an excited voice, as she started scribbling like mad in her notebook. Samantha looked stunned for a second, that Julie still had such equipment like that with her, but couldn't help thinking that Julie was going the right way about things. In response to Samantha's expression, Julie replied, "police officers are never off duty Sam; so, what were these names". "Well, I heard one voice that said Ed, and other voice said Pat" replied Samantha, as Julie made another note in her notebook. "You're doing really well Sam; now, these voices; how old would you say they were" asked Julie?

"They both sounded like they very deep voices, hence why I knew they were both males; and at a guess, I'd say that they were both in their forties" replied Samantha, as Julie finished writing, having taken down everything that Samantha had told her. Samantha was only guessing on the men's ages, as she hadn't seen there faces clearly, due to surrounding darkness. "Did you happen to see what sort of car they were driving" asked Julie, pencil at the ready for Samantha's response. "It was a bit hard to tell what make and model it was, as it was dark with no streetlights, but from the outline I guess it was black, and a pickup truck" replied Samantha, as Julie made another note in her pocket notebook. "I'm glad you've told me Sam, thank you; we'll just need to be more careful from now on; if this vehicle and its occupants really are stalking us, then there must be a reason why" replied Julie in a careful voice, as she could understand Samantha's position.

Julie closed her notebook and then slipped the notepad and the pencil she'd been writing with back inside a pocket in her leather jacket, giving it a quick tap, just to check that she had put it in their securely. "So, where are we taking ourselves today then Captain" asked Julie, as Samantha seemed to come back to her senses. She'd finally got her worries off of her chest about the strange night time stalker, as Samantha felt a slight weight lift off her shoulders through telling Julie about her worries. Julie looked at Samantha in anticipation, wondering what path their adventure would take them too next. "Well, I was wondering if maybe, you'd like to take the wheel today Julie" replied Samantha, as Julie looked a little taken aback at this odd request from Samantha. Julie had to admit to herself, that she had never thought about being asked to drive the Green Goddess, but still felt that she would have to at some point.

"But I'm not qualified too, under the road traffic act" began Julie, but she quickly stopped at the sight of Samantha's face. Samantha had raised her eyebrows, and was looking at Julie in a way as if to say 'there is no highway code now remember'. Julie quickly changed tack at the speed of light. "But then I suppose as you're a skilled qualified driver yourself Sam, you can teach me" finished Julie, as Samantha beamed at her. "That's the spirit Julie" replied Samantha, as they both climbed into the Green Goddess's cab; Samantha on the passenger's side, and Julie into the driver's seat, with Julie still looking a little nervous. "Hey, chill out Julie, you'll be fine, just think of it as a big car" said Samantha, as Julie's hands shook a little on the steering wheel. "I've driven patrol cars and van before, but never anything as big as this" said Julie, as Samantha reached over and patted her arm.

"You'll be fine honey; look on the bright side, at least you won't have to worry about traffic" replied Samantha, as Julie giggled slightly, thinking back in time too when the road would have been jam packed full of cars, buses, trucks and many other types of vehicles. "Ah well, start her up number one" said Samantha, as she pulled the map towards her, and placed it on her lap, as Julie nervously turned the key in the ignition. The engine fired into life, with its deep throaty slow roar of a noise echoing around the nearby fields. "Select forwards gear, and then gently press down on the accelerator until the handbrake releases" said Samantha, as Julie did what she was told, selecting forwards gear, and pressing her foot down on the accelerator. As the Green Goddess had an automatic gearbox, this certainly helped matters considerably when it came to judging the amount of power and torque that was required for each gear.

There was a hiss of air as the hand brake was released, and the Green Goddess began to roll slowly forwards. "That's it, perfect; you're doing it Julie; now don't forget to turn the wheel towards the road, but not too tightly" said Samantha in an encouraging voice, as Julie let out a small whimper, as the Green Goddess changed up a gear and began to pick up a little more speed. The Green Goddess, with Julie at the wheel, passed through the small hamlet with no problems at all, as most of the houses in the street had driveways, so there were no cars parked on the roads, but instead, stood alone and abandoned in their driveways, in the knowledge that they would never being driven again. After passing through the small hamlet, Samantha and Julie passed through village after village, and even passed another RAF air base, where there were forced to wind the windows up, due to the smell of rotting corpses, riddled with Covid-19.

Samantha and Julie certainly breathed more freely again, after they had passed by, as the smell became weaker and weaker as they drove further and further away from the Bedfordshire RAF air base. The Green Goddess coped with every bump and pothole with little or no effect on its part, and even managed to prune a few trees and hedges as it went, as the container trailer hit the overhanging branches, shearing them clean off, as they fell onto the road surface behind the tanker trailer as it went.

CHAPTER TEN

Mile End Farm and the Flintstone Community

B y that afternoon, Samantha and Julie had crossed over the Bedfordshire border, into the county of Northamptonshire, occasionally having to slow to a near crawl, so as to navigate the Green Goddess's two large trailers through the tightest of gaps. But most impressive of all, was Julie mastering the Green Goddess's controls by that afternoon, and by the time Samantha announced that she was fit and well enough to start driving again, Julie was a little sad that she had to give up the driver's seat. "I really appreciate you allowing me to drive today, Sam; I'm not entirely sure what I was nervous about now" replied Julie as Samantha smiled at her; although there had been one nasty point that morning, when Samantha been forced to nearly grab the steering wheel out of Julie's hands, when Julie had strayed the Green Goddess a little too close to an approaching hedge than Samantha thought was safe.

"Not at all Julie, you've got to learn somehow" replied Samantha, in a happy cheerful voice, as Samantha knew that their greatest challenge that day was coming up that afternoon. There route took them straight through the centre of Northampton, where they saw some wild dogs tearing at a cow carcass which was lying on a village green, and dustbins which now lay scattered all over the place, as if they'd been blown over in a high wind. Ragged pieces of newspaper and empty plastic wrappers, lay all over the road and up onto the pavements. Samantha had decided that she would not stop in the towns or cities, but stay as rural as possible, so as to avoid any nasty unpleasantness. Julie also agreed, saying that the towns would house more survivors, trying to scavenge food, drink, and even medical supplies, although Samantha thought that if they did come across any other survivors on their trip, they would try and help them as best as they could.

"I came to a caravan park near here on holiday once when I was a child" said Samantha, as the Green Goddess ploughed slowly down the main road, barely moving above fifteen miles per hour, which Samantha thought was the best top speed to have, so that they wouldn't get struck between the parked cars on either side of the road. "It just doesn't look like the same town does it" replied Julie, as she surveyed the scene all around her through the cab windows. There wasn't a single shop, house or building, that didn't look like it was broken or smashed in some way shape or form. Since the lockdown had come into force many months earlier, many of the usual services that would have kept and maintained these buildings, had been denied access to work. Any grass that could be seen in the parks and front lawns, was well over a foot in height, due to the council's lack of care for it.

Clean brick buildings were now covered in dirt and grim, and even moss appeared to be growing out of the manhole covers by the kerbs. Every so often, they saw a building which was on fire, and others that were burnt out shells. Samantha and Julie both remembered seeing Fredrick burning the tents back at RAF North Lakes, and wondered if maybe some of the survivors had burned other things as well, having seen the burnt-out buildings. One building, which they were surprised to see that wasn't on fire, was the hospital; but even so, maybe no one had been around to sterilise it properly before Covid had passed through, and seen off most, if not all of the town's population. The tree's branches which lined some roads were smacking against the side of the Green Goddess, but would soon fall away to the ground as her mighty bodywork snapped them in half, due to months of neglect and the weathering effect getting into the inner twigs.

Even the police station, with its fine-looking building and white washed walls, looked more ghostlike than ever. "There would have been dozens of police officers working in their before Covid" said Julie almost in a dreamlike voice, as she stared at the police station building, as they passed by it slowly. "Hang on, I've had an idea, can we stop here quickly please" asked Julie, as Samantha was so shocked, she stamped the brakes on in alarm. There was a loud hiss of air, and the bedclothing on the bunk slid forward sharply, as the top bunk duvet nearly fell out, nearly landing on top of Samantha's head. "Are you nuts, we can't stop here, it's far too dangerous" exclaimed Samantha, but Julie had already unlocked the cab door. "Trust me, lock the cab doors behind me, and don't open them again until I come back; I'll be right back" replied Julie, as she leapt down from the cab, slamming the door behind her and sprinting across the road into the police station.

Samantha did as she was told, locking the whole cab down with a simple push of a button on the centre console, as it went with a click, and she saw the indicators flash once as it did so, showing that the cab had locked itself. "Fine time to play cops and robbers Julie" said Samantha, a little put out, as she started to feel nervous at the same time. The fear of being attacked was always one that had been at the back of their minds, and if there were any placed where that was likely to happen, it would be in the towns and the cities around the country. If a single car or any other vehicle came up the main road now, and blocked them off by parking directly in front or behind the Green Goddess, it wouldn't have been able to pick up enough speed to get away, or even ram the hostile vehicle out of the way using the military grade bull bars fitted to the front of the Green

Goddess.

As Samantha sat there pondering this thought however, something directly ahead and further up the road caught her eye. Samantha could have been imagining things, maybe being isolated with so few other human beings, had finally driven her mad; but she could have sworn, she'd just seen the highway's agency traffic direction sign in front of her flicker. Samantha stared at it, and yet again, it flickered on for a second, and then went off again. Before Samantha even had a chance to think about what to make of this sudden strange phenomenon, Julie had returned, banging on the passenger side cab door. "It's me, I'm back, open up" called Julie from outside. Samantha opened the door for her, as Julie thanked Samantha and climbed back into the passenger seat, carrying what looked like a police uniform, and two long cases. "What the hell did you go in there for a police uniform for, and what the hell are those" exclaimed Samantha.

As Samantha said this, she waved her hand at the two long metal boxes that Julie had just lifted up into the cab and onto the lower cab bunk. "Think they might come in handy someday; are you alright; you look like you've just seen a ghost or something" replied Julie, in response to Samantha's question. "I think I may well have done" said Samantha, pointing out the window to the now un-flickering highway's agency sign. Julie looked in the direction that Samantha was pointing, and then looked back at Samantha confused. "Are you feeling ok Sam, you're not going senile on me are you" asked Julie, with a slight humour to her voice, feeling that Samantha's years of driving large vehicles might have finally gone to her head. "I hope I'm not, because I've just seen that sign up their flicker, as if it had an electrical supply going to it" said Samantha, as Julie turned to look at the sign, thinking it was flickering.

"It must have been a trick of the light or something, the power grid has been offline for ages now" replied Julie, as Samantha continued to look at the sign, almost transfixed by it. Even Julie was starting to feel a little freaked out now, fearing that Samantha was finally cracking up under the strain of living in the new post-apocalyptic world. "Err, Sam; we need to keep moving" said Julie in a concerned voice, but with a little hint of fear in it, as Samantha suddenly snapped out of her daze, like coming out of a mildly interesting daydream. "Oh yeah, of course, let's get out of here" replied Samantha, as the Green Goddess moved off slowly, heading for the edge of town, where they could blend in well with the farm buildings, green fields and woodland that surround Northampton. "One of the unfortunate drawbacks of driving a limited-edition super truck" thought Samantha, as her and Julie watched the scenery change outside of the cab windows.

Around twenty minutes or so later, the Green Goddess was back on the winding country lanes again, when suddenly, Samantha saw it again. A red triangle warning sign around fifty yards in front of where the Green Goddess was, had a light on it, as clear as day; and the light was on, it was most certainly switched on, and working. Samantha stamped on the Green Goddesses brakes, making the tyres squeal, as the solid rubber made hard contact with the road surface. Fresh black skid marks could now be seen on the road behind them, as Julie screamed out in shock, as she was nearly flung through the windscreen, such was the force of the braking power on the Green Goddess. "What, what it is" yelled Julie in shock, as she picked herself up off the cab floor, where she had been flung into the passenger footwell a second or so earlier, due to the force of Samantha's sudden braking.

Julie had narrowly avoided hitting her head on the windscreen, but still looked flustered all the same, wondered what had caused Samantha to take such evasive action. "Look, just look" exclaimed Samantha, pointing in surprise at the sign with the light on it. Even Julie's eyes widened in shock, at the sight of the sign that was lit up like a Christmas tree, beaming away, as if someone had just fixed a car battery to the back of it. "That's mains power, that's got to be the national grid surely" exclaimed Julie, as both her and Samantha just sat there for a second or so, mesmerised by the miracle sign, which stood there, as clear as day. "Maybe it's a solar powered one, I'm pretty sure there's a solar farm near here somewhere" said Samantha, still in a shocked voice, wondering if this was some sort of supernatural paranormal activity possessing the sign.

"Come on, we need to see if there are more of them that are lit up" replied Julie, urging Samantha on, as Samantha drove the Green Goddess forwards more carefully, not wanting to miss any more of these wonder miracle signs, that seemed to be able to defy all the known laws of science. After a minute or so the Green Goddess rounded another bend, and crossed over a fine-looking river bridge, where there was another corner at the end of it. The Green Goddess crossed over the bridge slowly, where they could hear the flowing water gushing underneath it, the sound strangely magnified because of the ever presence silence of an emptier planet than before the worldwide pandemic. There was a sharp left-hand corner on the other side of the bridge, which the Green Goddess only just managed to get clear with scrapping anything, before the road opened out into an open expanse of fields, all with different colours crops growing in them.

Around three hundred yards or so to the left-hand side of where they were, lay a series of farm buildings, and as the Green Goddess drew level with the driveway gate that led up to what they presumed was a farm complex, Samantha and Julie could both very clearly see that the gateway lights were most defiantly switched on, and working. The gateway looked quite wide, as if big heavy vehicles often passed up and down the driveway leading up to the farm buildings. The farm buildings themselves looked like they were in an excellent condition; however, there was a strong smell of silage coming from where the farm buildings were, as if someone was spreading fertiliser on the fields all around them. "What do you reckon, worth checking out don't you think" asked Julie, as Samantha looked around her, having the exception strange feeling that they were being watched.

The road was completely empty, but before they could both do any more listening out for things, a sudden shrill, almost like the sound of a steam whistle, came from within where the farm buildings were. There was nothing for it, this was an unusual sound in of itself before Covid, and any sounds like that had to mean that there were people nearby. Samantha and Julie looked at each for a second, smiled, and made up their minds without speaking. Even with the wider driveway, the Green Goddess with its twin trailers, only just about made the turning, not hitting any of the gates of gateposts on its way up the driveway. The sign hanging on the low dry-stone wall besides the entrance read, 'Mile End Farm, B Fields and Family'. Underneath this sign, was another sign; which read; 'the Flintstone Community'. The Flintstone community sign looked a lot newer and cleaner than the Mile End Farm sign did, as if it had only been put up quite recently.

"The Flintstone Community" said Samantha in a curious voice, as Julie shrugged slightly, just as interested and intrigued as Samantha was about it. It suddenly occurred to Samantha, that driving up this driveway with a one-hundred-foot-long articulated vehicle without checking what was ahead first, now seemed like quite a silly thing to have done, but it was too late now. They'd need not have worried about this little drawback however, as when the Green Goddess pulled into the farmyard, they could see it was very large, and easily big enough to be able to turn around a vehicle of the Green Goddesses size and weight. There were several sheds and barns that they could see around them, and a cloud of black smoke came from over the top of one of the buildings, moving upwards in cloud like formations, as if there was some sort of bonfire alight in the field on the other side of the buildings.

In the fairly oversized whitewashed farmhouse directly ahead of them, they could both clearly see there was a light on in one of the downstairs windows, and a man wearing a dark blue boiler suit and jet-black farmers wellington boots, was leaning over and tampering with a what looked like an electrical mains fuse box, which was located in the next farm building along from the farmhouse. The man wearing the dark blue boiler suit and jet-black farmers wellington boots, suddenly jumped up and looked surprised when he saw the Green Goddess roll to a stop in the yard. There was a hiss of air, as the Green Goddesses engine shut down, as Samantha and Julie jumped down from the cab, closing the cab doors behind them as they went. "Intruder alert, all hands, battle stations" shouted the man in the dark blue boiler suit, as before either Samantha or Julie could even say hello, they were surrounded on all sides by other people.

The members of the group all seemed to be carrying and pointing some sort of weapons at Samantha and Julie, from a twelve-bore shot gun, right down to a set of bows and arrows. Immediately, Samantha and Julie reacted instinctively, throwing their hands skywards into the air at the sight of all of these people suddenly appeared from out of nowhere. One member of the group was even brandishing a pitch folk into Samantha's face, as Samantha was reminded of the television series Dad's Army, where the Home Guard would use makeshift weapons to fight with. "Who are you; where have you come from; and what in the name of all that's holly is that" exclaimed the man in the dark blue boiler suit and jet-black wellington boots, gesturing at Samantha and Julie, and then behind them to the Green Goddess. The man in the dark blue boiler suit appeared to be the oldest of the group, and also the one who was brandishing the twelve-bore shot gun.

He was going slightly bald, with grey hairs around the sides of his head, making him look more like a medieval monk than anything else, and spoke with a very broad Northamptonshire accent. This man was obviously a local, and very territorial by the sound of his voice that he used at Samantha and Julie. "I'll ask you again, and if you don't respond within fifteen seconds, I'll be forced to take your head off with this" said the man in an angry voice, as Samantha let out a scream of panic when the man cocked the firing pin on the shot gun, making the sound echo around the farmyard. "My name is Julie Guard, I am a police officer, and I am travelling with this lady beside me" replied Julie, speaking again in her authoritarian style type voice, as she could have sworn blind that moment, some of the members of the group who were pointing the weapons at them, seemed to faulter slightly.

"A police officer ah, and what about you then sweetheart, who are you" demand the man in the dark blue boiler suit, still looking a little menacing with the twelve-bore shotgun. "My name is Samantha Bonham, I'm a truck driver; we saw lights on at the entrance to your driveway, and came up here to investigate it" said Samantha, feeling her voice cracking a little, as she was still a little nervous that this man might still decide to shoot her. At the moment that Samantha had mentioned about the lights being on however, the man in the dark blue boiler suit seemed to faulter a little, and lowered the shot gun slightly in surprise. "You saw the lights on" the man in the boiler suit said in surprise. "Yes, we both did, and we saw a sign flickering in town, and a road sign with a light on the other side of the river bridge" said Julie, in response to the man's question, as a murmur seemed to go around the rest of the group, brandishing the weapons at them.

"Well, I'll be dammed" came the voice of man in the dark blue boiler suit, who lowered his shot gun right the way down in surprise at this latest comment from Julie. "They don't look like Foxes too me Brian, and they don't look like there carrying weapons" came a man's voice from within the group, as the man in the dark blue boiler suit looked at him. The new man who had spoken had lowered his bow and arrow, so that Samantha and Julie could see his face more clearly. He was in around his mid-thirties, with a clean-shaven face, and had a head full of brown hair, which put Samantha and Julie in mind of a beech surfer. He was very thin as well, and as Julie looked at him, Samantha could have sworn blind that Julie had just smiled at him. "True, they not kids Trev; where have you come from you two" asked the man in the blue boiler suit, as the groups attention turned back to Samantha and Julie.

"The town's called Lillington in Hertfordshire, we've been travelling from there for a few days now; you're only the second group of human beings that we've seen since then" replied Samantha, as Julie had explained who they were a second or so earlier. The group seemed to ponder Samantha and Julie for a second, until the man in the blue suit spoke again. "Where are you heading"? "Clyde in Scotland; I'm searching for my fiancée" replied Samantha, as she felt her arms starting to ache slightly from having to hold them above her head for a little while now. "They must have seen the smoke from the steam engine Brian, and heard the whistle too" said another member of the group, this time an older man, who looked a few years younger than the man in the boiler suit did. "Please, we don't want any trouble, we just came here to investigate what was going on; it's practically dead out there" replied Julie, as she too, felt her arms starting to go numb.

"Give them a chance Brian, for crying out loud, there not the Foxes" replied another voice, this time a woman's, who looked as if she was in her early forties. "There's that word again, Foxes" thought Julie, as she made a mental note of it, thinking it was some sort of code that these people were using to describe something or someone. "Come on girls, I think this deserves a celebration" said the man in the dark blue boiler suit, who didn't look angry any more, but ecstatic, as if he'd had someone had suddenly flicked a personality switch inside of his brain. Not knowing what to think of what had just been said, Samantha and Julie both lowered their arms down, and looked around at the group as a whole. "We've got power everyone; we've got power" said the man in the dark blue boiler suit, as the rest of the group lowered their weapons downwards, before erupting into cheering and clapping.

If this whole situation wasn't confusing enough to Samantha and Julie already, then nothing else would be. Firstly, Samantha had seen a flickering light on a highway's agency sign; then both and Julie had seen a light that was on along the road; before they had finally been threatened at gunpoint, and now looked like they were in the centre of a party, rather than a hostage situation. Samantha and Julie both looked around at the applauding group of people, wondering what they should do next. Even the man in the dark blue boiler suit had put his hands together and was clapping. "Welcome friends, welcome one and all; hands down you two, you're our friends, not our enemies" replied the man in the dark blue boiler suit, as Samantha and Julie slowly lowered their hands, trying not to look traumatised. The rest of the group now approached Samantha and Julie, holding out their hands in a gesture of welcome.

"Welcome Samantha and Julie; I'm Brian Fields, owner of Mile End Farm" replied the man in the dark blue boiler suit, as he was the one who reached Samantha and Julie first, being the closest to them. Julie suddenly sniggered, as if something had amused her; Samantha looked a little surprised that Julie found the situation funny, as everything up until this point hadn't been worth laughing about. "Yes, I saw that snigger young lady; yes, I know, quite the name you would say for someone who was a farmer by trade, before Covid came along of course" replied Brian in response to Julie's snigger, as he gave Julie a small wink and a smile. Samantha cottoned on too what Julie had sniggered about, and couldn't help but crack a smile herself, the muscles in her face aching slightly, as if they had been tightly wrapped in cotton wool. Brian now stepped back to allow the rest of the group to close in around Samantha and Julie, shaking their hands as they went.

"I'm Trever Hull; I was a lawyer back in the old days" said a man with a round face, looking like he was in his mid-thirties, with short brown hair, who had just shaken Julie's hand, after following Brian over from the rest of the group. Samantha was surprised to see that Julie blushed ever so slightly when Trever did this, and could have sworn Trever did the same in return. "The doctor will you see now" joked a middle-aged man, who had quite a pointy face, and sunken dark eyes. "This is Doctor Stuart Victor, he's the farm's doctor; although still quite a good hand in the field I have to say" said Brian, as the man called Doctor Stuart Victor shook Samantha and Julie's hands, smiling as he did so, making his eyes look less sucken than they had been beforehand. Doctor Victor backed away, as a very slim middle-aged woman came bustling up to them, beaming from ear to ear as she did so.

"I am Melissia Gomez, hairdressers and wonder woman of hair and makeup" said Melissa, doing a little gig as she said this. Melissa spoke with a very broad Spanish accent, as Samantha had to stifle a small giggle as Melissa did her little jig, as if she was a ballerina on a well-lit stage. The last person to step forward was a very well-built black man, who spoke with a higher pitched and timid South African accent, which took both Samantha and Julie by surprise. "I am Misim Ugarte, I repair clothes and make new ones here, as I was a Tailor and Seamstress back before Covid" said Misim, who shook both Samantha and Julie's hand as he spoke. Julie quickly made the deduction that Misim's hands were used to making and repairing clothes, because they were almost as soft and delicate as their own hands were, minus the fact that Julie and Samantha had been washing their own hands using stream water from doing stops in the countryside.

It took several minutes for them all to be introduced, but Brian was soon calling for silence, as any leader would be to a community of people. Brian reminded Samantha and Julie of a town mayor, the sort of person who would know how to lead, without having the need to shout or threaten anyone. "Ok everyone, back to work, there's still plenty to be done before we finish for the day" called Brian to the crowd at large. They group of people in the farmyard now broke apart, heading back to their separate work stations, while Brian walked forward with Samantha and Julie to examine the Green Goddess. "I can't say I've ever seen a machine quite like this one before, what is it exactly; some sort of military experimental vehicle" asked Brian, as Samantha launched into an explanation about the Green Goddess, as Julie hoovered close by, still looking around her at the many buildings and farm house around Mile End Farm.

Samantha began to explain to Brian how the Green Goddess had started life as the truck called Betsie, and then been converted at RAF North Lakes into an all-terrain go anywhere articulated supply vehicle. "We carry supplies and try to help out as many people as we can, that's what we've decided to do in the post Covid world" explained Julie, as Brian's face lit up, being very interested in the line that Samantha and Julie had chosen to take up. "If you have anything that we need, we can easily barter for it; everyone here does like their own little niceties from the old world" replied Brian, as he looked longingly at the container trailer, thinking that all sorts of goodies and wonders would suddenly spill out of the back of it like sweets from a party goody bag. All three of them walked around to the back of the container trailer, and helped Samantha open the double doors, where inside sat all of the supplies that anyone could ask for.

"I guess the mobile shop of Guard and Bonham is now officially open for business" replied Julie grinning from ear to ear like an eager school girl.

144

Samantha climbed up the steps which hung from the back of the container trailer, strolling up and down inside the container, checking all of the items in the three layers of racking, which easily went from the floor to the ceiling inside the container, mounted to the floor by solid metal bolts. The distance between the two sets of racking on either side was only just about wide enough to walk down, but could still be done at a squeeze. At the very front of the container up against the bulkhead, where the remaining ration packs that Fredrick had given them before they had departed from RAF North Lakes. These were stacked right to the ceiling, and came forward a good five or six feet deep, all of them well within date.

The many compartments and shelves within the containers metal racking contained many different products, from that of toiletries, to cosmetics and medical supplies, plus a few home comfort products on the side as well. "Well strike me down" said Brian in shock, taking a look into the back of the container, while at the same time, trying not to admit that he was shocked at the many numbers of different items that was stretched out before them. "It's good isn't it" replied Julie, seeing the look on Brian's face, which had just gone from that of shock, too that of major delight. There were even a number of motor vehicle spare parts in some of the trays inside the racking, which included most of the popular and well-known car manufactures. "If the foxes knew that this lot was here, they'd have a field day" replied Brian in amazement, as Samantha and Julie both looked sympathetic, wondering what Brian meant.

"Must be a right pain here with foxes, although I've no idea why foxes and their cubs would want all of this lot; I thought foxes went after water, and meat, chicken and the like" replied Samantha to Brian's comment, as Brian realised that he hadn't explained himself to them. "Oh, sorry Samantha love, maybe I should have explained more; when I say foxes, I mean other people, from outside the farm, you know" replied Brian, as Samantha and Julie suddenly looked puzzled. "Why's that Brian, have you been raided by other people before" asked Julie, looking curiously at Brian as she spoke. Samantha almost expected Julie to dig out her notebook and pencil again and start making notes on this latest revelation; but this time, it seemed that Julie was not as interested as before, or maybe felt that this was a matter that you couldn't report or write down to investigate further.

"Afraid we have, hence why we were a bit jumpy when you arrived; we thought you'd showed up with this container here to take everything that we have here on the farm; not to mention that you could be infected with Covid" replied Brian, as he stepped away from the container, to allow Samantha and Julie to close the container doors, before then locking them by clipping the twin door handles into place. "That's true that, I thought exactly the same of Samantha when we first met after Covid had hit" replied Julie, as Brian laughed at Julie's outburst, making Samantha go a little red as Julie spoke. "I honestly thought you two were sisters by the way you acted when we first saw you" replied Brian, with another slight chuckle. "Oh, we're not sisters, but we lived and worked in the same town, Lillington in Hertfordshire" said Samantha, as Julie blushed and giggled again, thinking that Brian had a funny sense of humour.

The idea that Brian thought Samantha and Julie were sisters, was obviously quite amusing to Julie, as Brian quickly looked around to make sure there were no problems around him from the farm. "Lillington ah, can't say I've heard of that place, but then again I've been here all my life, so I haven't travelled too much; these guys on the other hand, have been stumbling in here from all over the country" replied Brian, gesturing around him to the farm buildings, but in fact meaning the people inside of them, doing all of the important jobs within them and around the rest of the farm. "How have you kept yourself supplied; I suppose you've lived off the land here I guess" asked Samantha suddenly, as Brian turned to look at her, thinking that this sort of the question was bound to be asked sooner rather than later, as after all, supplies didn't just land on their doorstep by magic.

"Ah well you see, most of the supplies we can get from here, but every now and again, I send the gang out on a foraging trip in the Land Rover over there down into the city to get supplies of things that we need" replied Brian in answer to Samantha's question, as he gestured to a four-wheel drive Land Rover Defender, parked up in an open shed near to the farm yard entrance. "We came up through Northampton on the way here, we didn't see anyone while we we're driving through" replied Julie, as Brian snorted in disgust. "Ah well you two were lucky then, every time we go down there into Northampton, we always have to go in armed, because the light-fingered sods try and nick stuff" said Brian in an annoyed sounding voice, as if this was a common problem that he wanted to fix, but couldn't do anything about because of a lack of support or help in the new world.

Brian gestured at the Green Goddess before he continued on by saying; "Oh there's people down in their in the town alright; the reason they didn't come up to you two with this thing is because it looks like it could be military, and they know that to attack something like this on their own would be tantamount to suicide". It really did look like that Samantha and Julie had made a lucky escape, if things were as bad as Brian was describing in his speech. "But that's your basics really, I'll give you the full tour and orientation in the morning, but I'll let you girls rest for now, and wake you at 7am sharp to start work" replied Brian, as he shouldered his twelve-bore shot gun, and walked back into the farm house, closing the door behind him as he went. Samantha let out a long slow breath, throwing her head back, and placing her hand behind her head, as if a great weight had been lifted from around her shoulders.

"I really honestly thought we were for the chop then" said Samantha, as Julie gave her that 'you read my mind' sort of look. "I think it's fair to say we're part of the team now; I mean, it looks like they want us to stay doesn't it" replied Julie, as Samantha nodded slightly in agreement, thinking that they shouldn't stay at Mile End Farm for too long, as Greg and Diana could still be out there somewhere. "Personally, remaining here for the time being would be the best option, as it will help us to not go completely mad, with the lack of humans and all that" replied Julie, as if she had almost guessed what Samantha was thinking in her mind at the time. Samantha nodded, wondering what had made her do it, thinking that they had maybe stumbled on some sort of island paradise in the middle of the Northamptonshire countryside. Mile End Farm certainly seemed to look and sound like it, from what Samantha and Julie had found out so far about them all.

As it was now the middle of March that year, the sun had started to linger around in the sky a lot longer now than it had done at the start of the year. At around six o clock that evening, Samantha and Julie sat in their camping chairs beside the Green Goddess, watching the sun set over the open fields, with the crops growing in them and the farm animals grazing in the other grass fields, which lay all around them on the farm. It later transpired that the shrill whistle Samantha and Julie had heard earlier on that day, had come from an old fashion steam traction engine, which was powering a hail bailing machine and running a flywheel, which in turn powered the workshop machinery and generated electricity and heat for the main farmhouse. Julie, who had very rarely travelled anywhere in her life, was completely fascinated by all of the farm machinery and other assorted equipment around Mile End farm.

As Julie had expressed an ambition to go and live on a farm, Samantha couldn't help thinking that Julie had finally found her new home, and that Samantha would be pressing north without her from now on. After the rest of the crew had finished work for the day, Samantha and Julie had gone to socialise with the other residents of Mile End Farm, as they too had come outside to admire the Green Goddess, and her uniqueness in this new world where anything and everything could happen. Brian Fields, had apparently grown up on Mile End farm for the whole of his life, having inherited the farm from his father, who had passed away some ten years previously. As each member of the group had travelled across the country, coming across Mile End Farm as they went, Brian had utilised their skills to help build the farm up into a thriving community which was commonly known as 'The Flintstone Community'.

The Flintstones had apparently been a favourite TV show of Brian's when he had been growing up as a kid, and so the name had sort of stuck from then on. This also happened to be the first night that Samantha hadn't seen the stalkers that she claimed had been following both her and

Julie since leaving Lillington. This certainly seemed to cheer Julie up, as she was worried that they might attack them while they were all asleep; but Samantha had banked on the fact that maybe it was the number of people on Mile End Farm that could be keeping the stalkers at bay, rather than the fact that they hadn't followed them, and were probably hold up in one of the houses in a village nearby, or even within Northampton itself. At 7am sharp the following morning, there was a loud wrapping sound on the Green Goddesses cab door, which seemed to echo slightly on the inside of the cab.

"Rise and shine Flintstones, breakfast is being served, and then into the fields for another day's work" came the voice of Brian from outside, sounding buoyant and positive. Samantha, who was the closest to the door, quickly put a thumbs up through the closed cab curtain, to show that she and Julie had heard and understood Brian. Footsteps outside, told Samantha and Julie, that Brian was making his way back to the farm house, where the smell of a cooked breakfast met their nostrils. As Samantha reached forward to put on her day clothes, she saw Julie move above her in the upper bunk, as the cab rocked slightly as Julie sat up. The clothes that Samantha was wearing were pretty smelly by now, as they were the same set of clothes, she'd been wearing for three days straight now; and Samantha had made a wild guess that Julie had been wearing hers for the same period of time as well, if not longer.

Not to mention they were both starting to smell as well, owing to the fact that neither of them had washed in days, due to the lack of shower or washing facilities. It was surprising how useless some of Samantha and Julie's supplies were, without any water to support them in using them. As both Samantha and Julie traipsed into the kitchen five minutes later for breakfast, they were met in the doorway by Brian, who wrinkled his nose slightly as they approached. "Don't worry Brian, we know we smell, we've had no way of cleaning ourselves for the past three days" replied Julie, in the response to Brian's reaction. Brian then suddenly smiled a second later however, and held an arm out, showing them the way up the stairs and into the bathroom, which to Samantha and Julie seemed like the most welcome sight in the world, having caught a whiff of themselves, which made their noses wrinkle as well as Brian's had done a moment earlier.

"Not to worry you two; the bathroom is straight upstairs and on the far end of the landing; give yourselves a good clean up before breakfast; then after breakfast, I can give you the guided tour" responded Brian, as both Samantha and Julie climbed the stairs, before walking along the landing into the bathroom, Julie allowing Samantha to go first, as she waited outside for Samantha to finish. As Brian had a continuous supply of electricity from the generator the day beforehand, it now meant that the electric shower in the bathroom was working perfectly. The warm flowing water felt like bliss against Samantha's skin as she stood there in the shower, cleaning out three day's worth of muck and grim from her hair and skin, giving her much needed body the freshness that it needed. There came a sudden wrapping sound on the bathroom door, which made Samantha jump slightly, nearly knocking the shower head off its mounting as she did so.

"Hurry up Sam, leave some water for me you know" came Julie's voice from the other side of the door, feeling that Samantha was taking a little longer than was necessary. Samantha giggled slightly, understanding Julie's line of humour, as Samantha switched off the shower, and then proceeded to change into some fresh new clothes, and a light blue boiler suit, which Brian had left out for her in the form of a work uniform. The boiler suit felt crisp and clean, as Samantha slipped it on, and finished it off by tying her hair back in a pony tail, ready for that day's work. When Samantha had made it back downstairs again after leaving the bathroom, she saw that everyone else had seated themselves around the table, tucking into the freshly made delicious full English breakfasts, courtesy of the gas cooker powered by the gas bottles stacked up outside.

They all greeted Samantha with a 'good morning', and did the same with Julie, who came bouncing down the stairs ten minutes later, looking the same as Samantha in a matching light blue boiler suit. Brian's way of running the Flintstone Community, was in hindsight, actually quite a fair system to work under. Brian who had made the rules within the community, had made them as the most basic of rules to follow, which even in themselves sounded fairly reasonable. They were that everyone on the farm was equal, and got the same regardless of what job they did, or however long they worked for. That if they wanted to eat, they had to do a full day's work for it; and that anyone could leave the farm at any time, as long as they had benefited the farm in some way shape or form. For a man who had spent most of his life on a farm, it was quite incredible how Brian had managed to master politics so well, as Julie pointed out to Samantha over breakfast.

Brian always started the day with a briefing of who was going to be where, and when. Everyone had their usual jobs, like Misim for example; as Misim was in charge of repairs and servicing their works uniforms and the like, as that had been what his job had been before, and now after Covid. However, for people like Julie, Trever, Doctor Victor and Melissia, who had all had jobs outside of farm work before Covid, there work changed daily, and they would be given a different job every day, depending on what needed doing and when. When Samantha had mentioned to Brian about her lorry driving connection however, Brian had immediately placed her on ploughing the fields behind the wheel of the farm's tractor. This had certainly put a smile on Samantha's face, as she had worked with cutting edge machinery through her work at Travis Transport Limited back before Covid had struck.

"Good work everyone, keep yourself safe in your work today; and remember, keep an eye out for those pesky foxes; we had another breech in the fence again last night, and I reckon they were trying to get into the farm house as well to steal from us" said Brian, as the others around the main kitchen table looked shocked and alarmed. Before anyone could respond however, Brian had reassured them that he would be on patrol around the farm perimeter, making sure that no-one was breeching it that day. Samantha did think that this was a bit of a pointless effort, as these foxes as Brian called them, clearly struck at night, and not during the day, when everyone was awake and alert to them. But then again, Samantha and Julie had only been at Mile End Farm for less than twenty-four hours, so couldn't really question Brian's, or anyone else judgement at that time.

Plus, it seemed very inadvisable to argue with someone who regularly walked around with a loaded twelve bore shotgun slung over their shoulder, as Julie had been kind enough to point out to Samantha the previous evening before they had joined the others inside the farm house. "What happens if we do catch sight of one of the foxes" asked Samantha, who was very curious to know what Brian did to thieves on his farm, as Julie's ear seemed to pick up as well. "Well, if you see one of them trying to take anything, jump on them, and shout for the nearest person; once you do that, they can get a message to everyone around the farm, which filters back to me, and then I lock them in the shed for a bit" said Brian, as Julie let out a cry of surprise. "You can't do that Brian, that's false imprisonment, under section" began Julie, but stopped herself at the look on Brian's face.

"I know where you're coming from Julie, but seeing as if calling the police is not an option anymore, we have to make our own justice here; these foxes are thieves, and they don't care who they hurt to get what they want" replied Brian, as Julie's face went from that of surprise, to that of understanding. Although, Julie had to admit that if justice was now something that was determined by Brian, she would certainly only comply with it, when it was done fairly and did not involve doing anything which was out of the pre Covid world laws.

CHAPTER ELEVEN

The Foxes

After that day's briefing had been concluded, they all got up from the table, and headed outside into the farmyard, where they all set about their daily tasks. Samantha headed off to the barn, to find the rather oversized scarlet red coloured CASE C.E.T farm tractor, which in reality looked more like a battle tank rather than any piece of farm machinery. Stuart Victor, the friendly doctor, had been assigned to keeping the farm's steam traction engine going, which was powering the hay bailing machine, and charging the generator keeping the farm house night batteries topped up, for when that's days work had finished, and they had all retreated back into the farm house. This in itself, was hard hot work, so Doctor Victor always spent the longest in the bathroom every night, keeping his hair free of soot and muck, as well as having a continuous change of clothes due to the smoke, which hung around on them like the smell of a bonfire did.

Trever the barrister, as he had come to be known, had the task of collected the eggs from the hen house, and then had to put a new fence up on one of the farm's outer fields, as it was a fence that had needed replacing for some time now. This was where, according to Brian, 'the foxes' as they were known, had apparently broken through it, and stolen some of the eggs out of the hen house during the night. Melissia and Julie had been set the jobs of bailing the hay, by feeding it into the hay bailing machine, as this was to be used to keep the horses happy in the stables. Julie was certainly not used to this amount of manual laboured work, and even after an hour or so, felt her back aching slightly because of the weight of the hay bails and speed in which the hay came out of the hay bailer, where it had been wrapped up with strong blue rope, where the fibres from it made Julie itch all over from where they were sticking to her like glue.

Brian went out into the fields as well, manning his usual job as the farm's patrolman, walking around the farm's boundary fence with his loaded twelve bore shot gun, ensuring that those 'blasted foxes' as he always said, couldn't and didn't get in. Even though Samantha had been used to HGVs for many years now, she still found the CASE C.E.T tractor to be a complete mind boggle, when it came to the many different buttons and controls. But with a quick crash course from Brian, Samantha managed to get it up and running fairly quickly. Coupling the plough to the tractor for Samantha was a doddle, and she was soon underway, heading up to one of the fields in the centre of the farm, where the tractor and plough began turning over the soil in nice straight lines, ready to plant that year's crops. Brian's intentions for the year ahead, was to try and grow a wheat crop, as this would be the perfect crop for turning into flour for making bread.

Brian had already managed to plough and seed a few fields with the same wheat crop in them, which were coming on quite nicely, there short yellow stalks blowing around in the gentle breeze which whipped across the farm's fields. "It just seemed so peaceful and tranquil" thought Samantha, as the day wore on, lulling herself into thinking that she was on a sort of field trip, or a weekend away somewhere. Samantha did have to confess that the field ploughing looked like easy work, but in reality, it wasn't. It seemed that keeping a straight line in a field, was actually a lot harder, than what it looked. Samantha always remembered how easy it was travelling down the motorway in a straight line, sitting between the white lines in her lane, and was almost taken back to those memories for whole minutes at a time, while she sat there, carving out straight lines in the newly ploughed field.

"Wow, that is some fantastic ploughing there Sam, I'm impressed" exclaimed Brian in a jovial voice, suddenly bringing Samantha out of a day dream that she had been having, whilst cutting out a plough line half way across the field. Samantha had remembered to tell Brian over breakfast that morning, that most people called her Sam, just to make names easier to remember. "Aww, thanks Brian, I really appreciate that; I think I'm getting the hang of it" replied Samantha, as Brian smiled at her, his twelve-bore shotgun slung over his left arm as he went, looking like every local rosy faced farmer would do. "Ah your welcome Sam, keep it up, you're a natural at it; time for a spot of well-earned lunch I think" said Brian, as Samantha brought the tractor to a stop, shutting down the engine and climbing out of the cab, following Brian back across the fields towards the farm house.

"Crickey Julie, what happened to you" giggled Samantha, as she saw the state that Julie was in. Julie, who had been bailing hay all morning, had hay sticking to her boiler suit, and some of it had ended up stuck in her hair. "I only cleaned my hair this morning, and now look at it" replied Julie, sounding a little sad, as she pointed up at her hair, which was now partly covered with straw. "Come here, let me help" said Samantha, as she brushed the top of Julie's hair, to make some of the straw pieces fall out and onto the floor, where Trevor had broken out a broom and begun to sweep it up. It did seem to do the trick, as they headed inside the farm house, where a ploughman's lunch had been prepared, complete with a loaf of fresh bread from the oven, and a fresh batch of homemade cheese, alongside a basket full of apples. Julie couldn't help but hear her stomach rumble, as she was confronted with fresh food, having not eaten for a good several hours.

"You know the drill, one slice of bread and cheese each, and one apple each as well" said Brian, as they gathered in the small kitchen to collect their individual ploughman's. "Did you know, that Apples contain acidic acid, which has been known to rot teeth" said Doctor Victor, who according to Trever, always wanted to give them a fun health tip of the day whilst they sat there eating their food. For most of the group, growing up in towns and cities, these sorts of tips came in quite handy for living on a farm in the countryside, and was always a way of connecting with some form of the outside world. "I'm going to do something about your hair, it's in need of some good old-fashioned makeover styling I think" said Melissia, who had been making comments to Julie, and now Samantha when she was sat in the kitchen, about the state of their hair.

This was true, as Samantha and Julie had always managed to keep their hair cleaned, trimmed and looking presentable before Covid; and it certainly didn't seem to look that way now. "I shall give it an excellent and well-deserved trim tonight, and a dam good comb through to make it look fresh again" replied Melissia, to the looks of delight on Julie and Samantha's faces. Samantha was just about to respond, when there was a sudden disturbance out in the farm yard, and they could clearly hear the sound of a group of people running away, followed by what sounded like screams of pain and fright coming from out in the farm yard. Immediately, everyone was on their feet and racing out into the farm yard, where they saw Brian clearly pointing his shot gun at a group of what looked like teenage boys, and then down to the floor, where a boy, who looked no older than the age of thirteen, was struggling to get free from Brian's farm wellies.

"What's going on here" asked Trevor, who had the longest legs out of all of them, having managed to get out into the yard first to investigate the commotion. "Foxes, trying to steal the flour bags in the store room; the rest got away, but I managed to get this little rat as he tried to escape" replied Brian angrily, pinning the boy to the floor with his farmers wellies, whilst brandishing his shot gun directly into the boy's face. "What in the name of all that's holly, are you doing" exclaimed Julie, as she saw the scene of the boy crying on the floor, and Brian standing over him, teeth bared, brandishing his shot gun at the boy on the ground. Brian looked around at Julie for a second before he responded, "Ridding this world of thieving little rats like him, that's what I'm doing" snarled Brian, as he cocked the shot gun, ready to fire it. "No" shouted Samantha, as Brian attention now turned to Samantha, who's face had gone pure white with horror.

Samantha and Julie had been the only ones who had reacted, as the rest of the group didn't seem to be any more non plussed about it; even Doctor Victor seemed to be caught between frustration and exasperation. It was interesting seeing what the friendly doctor thought about all of this, as he had after all, sworn a Socratic oath to help and preserve life, rather than allow it to be taken. All the same, Doctor Victor didn't seem to be stepping in to stop Brian from using his shot gun on the teenage boy. "Brian, look at him, he's just a kid" said Julie, with a pleading note in her voice, feeling that defending the boy was the best course of action, as if this was a hostage siege, and that Brian was the hostage taker. "That's one of my primary pet hates Julie; people who steal; and this little rat is proof of it" shouted back Brian, as Julie took a very brave step forward, pointing down at the boy on the floor.

"If you kill this boy, you will have committed a very serious criminal offence Brian" replied Julie, looking Brian dead in the eye as she said this. "There's no law anymore Julie, just a need to survive" retorted Brian snarling a little again, as he turned back to the boy, who was still whimpering and crying slightly on the ground. "Don't get me wrong Julie, I am a kind and caring man, but I don't tolerate stealing, or people betraying their own kind" said Brian, as Samantha let out a little whimper, feeling that this boy was about to be killed right in front of them all. "Don't kill him, he's just a boy" whimpered Samantha, as her whimper seemed to spur on Julie to protest more. In a brave step, Julie appeared to come between Brian and the young teenage boy on the ground, looking a lot braver and calmer than what she was letting onto everyone else around her.

"Brian, you don't have to do this, just let him go; he's probably starving, you've seen what conditions are like elsewhere; if you kill him, then you kill him in cold blood; and that would make you a very evil man indeed Brian" replied Julie, as the others seemed to join suit in what Julie's words. "Julie's right Brian, he really is just a boy, I'd let him go, just this once" said Melissia, also fearing that Brian may turn on her at any moment for even suggesting such a thing. "Same here Brian" replied Doctor Victor, as the same word went around everyone; "same; same; same". Feeling the general vibe of the group, and fearing what would happen if he really did shoot the boy, Brian lowered his shot gun, and nodded to the boy. The boy quickly scrambled to his feet, and went to run off, but as he did so, he caught Samantha's eye. Almost without speaking, the boy guessed the question that Samantha was going to ask, and answered it out loud.

"Charlie, my name is Charlie miss; thank you" said the boy, as he ran off down the driveway, leading back to the main road. Brian turned on his heels, and marched away back into the farm house, slamming the door behind him. This latest scene, caused the biggest silence yet; a silence that could have very easily been cut with a knife. Misim, Melissia, Doctor Victor, and Trevor, were all looking amazingly at Julie, as if she had just been presented with a bravery medal. "Can I just say Julie, that was amazing, you must have done negotiation training in the past or something" replied Trevor, as Julie blushed slightly. "Hendon police college was where I was trained; I came second in the class, only by one point during the exam" replied Julie, who even now, looked quite taken by the striking appearance of Trevor, with his trim appearance, and smartly combed back hair.

And there it was again, that look that Julie had in her eye, along with Trever, almost as if; "but no, she can't be, surely not" thought Samantha, as she watched Trevor and Julie go back into the farm house together, chatting about Julie's police training days on the force. All of a sudden without warning, Julie and Trevor held each other's hands, and put their heads together. "Oh, don't you worry, I saw it in those two before now as well you know Sam my darling" came Melissia's voice to Samantha's right. Samantha jumped about a foot in the air, as she realised Melissia was there, as she hadn't gone back into the farm house like the others had.

"I think those two will make a great married couple" said Melissia, as she too walked back towards the farm house to finish her lunch, pondering the same thoughts as what Samantha had felt, when she had caught sight of Julie and Trevor together.

Samantha let Melissia walk a little ahead of her, then followed Melissia into the farmhouse to finish off her lunch, thinking that the day's dramas would have certainly make a good plot line on any of the soap programmes on the television before Covid. Considering that early afternoon's drama, Brian's temper had subsided somewhat, and he seemed to be back to his normal everyday self again. Samantha, to Brian's great delight, had managed to finish all of the ploughing in the field, where the seed would be planted the following day. This greatly cheered Samantha up, and when she had finished working at six o clock that evening, both her and Julie were gifted with a real treat. After both Samantha and Julie had both consumed their dinner, Melissia treated them both to a complete hair styling, showing off her wonderfully talented skills as the skilled hairdresser that she was.

Melissia did everything right, including trimming the split hairs, giving their hair a dam good shampoo job, and then finished it all off by combing their hair so well, that Samantha and Julie both believed that their hair would never be curly ever again. "Thank god for electric hair tongs" thought Samantha, as both her and Julie went to sleep that night, both still buzzing from the wonderful experience of being groomed properly since leaving their homes after Covid. Julie fell asleep very quickly, having been tired out from the day's workout, but Samantha lay awake, thinking how she may have just found a new way of life on Mile End Farm. Now that the electricity was flowing into the farm, thanks to the steam traction engine powering the night batteries as they were known, Brian had expressed an ambition to run an electric fence around the farm, to stop any more of the pesky foxes from breaking in and stealing anything else from around the farm.

But this was a job which would be done the following day, as Brian had told them all over dinner that night, so at least they had a bit of free time for some sleep. As Samantha and Julie slept in the Green Goddess cab however, it would slowly come to pass, that they were not alone that night. In the early hours of the morning, Samantha was suddenly aware of the sound of a vehicle's engine coming towards them up the farm's driveway. Samantha knew this, as she could see through the tiny gap in the cab curtains, as the light's reflected on the wing mirror. Samantha was suddenly wide awake; this wasn't normal behaviour, even for the days before Covid, and she now knew exactly what to do. It looked as if the stalkers had returned, or even caught up with them yet again, and Julie had given Samantha exact instructions of what to do if they ever returned.

"Julie; Julie, wake up" said Samantha in a nervous whisper, shaking Julie slightly in the top cab bunk, as Julie stirred from her slumber. "What is it Sam" asked Julie, who yawned widely, still very tired from the day's work. "There back" whispered Samantha, as Julie went from being tired, to wide awake. "Stay very still, do not move" whispered Julie in an urgent voice, as her and Samantha remained perfectly still, trying to listen to what was happening outside. From what Samantha could see through the small gap in her cab curtain, the headlights outside the window had suddenly gone out, and they heard a pair of car doors opening and then closing quietly. The car door sounds were then followed by the same familiar voices as Samantha had heard before, although Julie had not. "Hey Ed, wasn't that the same army truck that we saw outside of that hamlet in Bedfordshire" said the voice belonging to the man calling himself 'Pat'.

"Yeah, your right, it was, what's it doing here" asked a second voice, this one belonging to Ed, who spoke with puzzlement in his voice. Inside the Green Goddesses cab however, Julie had suddenly gone stock still, her eyes as wide as dinner plates. "What is it" whispered Samantha, as she noticed the look on Julie's face in the semi darkness. "Samantha, that's the voice of Edward Fitzgerald, the man who made threats on your life at the collision scene on the motorway months ago" whispered Julie, as Samantha had to clap her hand over her mouth to stop herself from screaming out. "And I recognise the other voice too, I think that is Patrick Devises; I brought him in on a sexual assault charge once" whispered Julie, as she recognised both voices at once, which Samantha now felt a little silly at, having heard at least one of them shouting at her after crashing his pickup truck, making threats on Samantha's life.

"We'll to watch this property, alert the top that we may be in possession of the suspects" came Edward's voice from outside, as there was a sudden snapping sound of car doors, followed by the sound of a car reversing out of the driveway, until the sound faded into nothing. There was then a distant screech of tyres, as they heard Edward and Patrick's vehicle roar off down the road at breakneck speed. Back in the Green Goddesses cab, Samantha let out a small whimper, her hands shaking slightly; meanwhile Julie had sat up in her bunk in horror. "We have to tell the others, first thing in the morning" said Julie, a worried and frightened look upon her face. "Why, why do we have to tell the others, it's clearly me and you that their after, not everyone else" said Samantha, taking her hands away from her mouth since trying not to scream a few moments beforehand.

"Trust me, Edward Fitzgerald and Patrick Devises were known to us in the police service, but that's not the most worrying point of all" replied Julie, as Samantha looked confused, wondering what Julie meant by her last comment. "What is" replied Samantha, in the same curious voice as before. "In the police, military and secret service lingo, 'the top', is radio shorthand for the top brass, aka the government" replied Julie, as she made an emphasis on the words 'the top' as she finished off by saying; "I think Devises and Fitzgerald have been recruited as some sort of agents for a higher power; perhaps even someone who has clout, and used to work for the government". Julie's latest statement made Samantha let out a gasp of shock. "What can we do, if there watching the property, they could be armed and everything, and we can't possibly defend ourselves" replied Samantha, as Julie put a hand on her shoulder in a comforting sort of way.

"Get some sleep Sam, and then in the morning during the breakfast briefing, we can tell the others then about it all" replied Julie in a calm and caring voice; the sort of voice she would have used when she was back on the beat as a police officer of the law, and there was a vulnerable person in

161

need of her help. Samantha did as she was told, trying to get back off to sleep again, but when she closed her eyes, images of Fitzgerald screaming at her "I'm going to kill you bitch", kept flashing through her mind, haunting her as she slept through the rest of the night. When Brian's wakeup call came through at 7am, they couldn't have longed for it to come any sooner, as Julie and Samantha got themselves ready, and then headed into the farm house for breakfast, and the morning briefing. They were both desperate to tell Brian and the others what they had discovered, and felt that a group decision was the only way forward to solve the problem.

However, Samantha couldn't help but feel a slight pang of dread rising up inside of her, wondering what the others would say, when Samantha and Julie told their story over that morning's breakfast. "Morning all, lovely day as always" said Brian in a cheerful voice, as they were all sat around the breakfast table, tucking into freshly toasted bread, eggs, bacon and other assorted foods. There was a general round of, 'morning Brian', in return, as Brian sat down at the table, helping himself to breakfast as he went. "So, I wanted to start by saying a big congratulations to Samantha and Julie for completing their first day here on Mill End Farm" said Brian, as there was a small round of applause from everyone at the table. Samantha and Julie grinned in appreciation to the round of applause, as Brian continued on with his speech, once the applause had died down.

"So, today we are going to focus most of our efforts on putting up the new electric fence, which we run right around the perimeter", but Brian suddenly stopped speaking, as Julie had shot her hand into the air. It felt weird for Julie to do this, as she felt like she was back in school and the teacher had just asked her a question that she knew the answer too. It was even stranger for everyone to then suddenly look at Julie, every face fixed with a confused look upon it. "Oh, we always leave the questions until the end Julie" responded Brian, as he smiled at Julie in a respectful sort of way, making Julie feel a little embarrassed by the situation. "Sorry Brian, what I need to say, hasn't got anything to do with the farm" replied Julie, as she lowered her hand back to her plate on the table. Brian looked a bit surprised, as no-one had ever done this at his morning briefings before now.

"Ah I see, well we always do important things first, if it's personal and important to you Julie, fire away" replied Brian, as every eye around the table fixed themselves on Julie. "Well, there's no really easy way to do this, but I believe the farm maybe in danger" said Julie, as calmly as her voice would allow her in that exactly moment in time. Immediately at Julie's words, there was a sudden murmur that went right around the room, as everyone on the breakfast table looked alarmed and worried. "I see, is it to do with the foxes" asked Brian, as Julie shook her head slightly. "No, it's just, myself and Samantha you see, we think that we may have been followed here by some very dangerous men" replied Julie, as another murmur went around the room. Brian's expression didn't change or faulter at all, but instead he remained calm and collected, pondering what to say next in response to Julie's answer.

"I'm very grateful that you have raised this with us Julie, what is your evidence for this" asked Brian, as Samantha pipped up, "we ran into a black pickup truck three times in a row while on the way to the farm". Everyone's attention turned to Samantha as she pressed on; "The first time we saw the pickup truck was on the first night after leaving home, just after I met Julie here". Samantha waved a hand at Julie, and then carried on speaking; "This was in a truck stop outside Lillington; the second time was in a layby outside a small hamlet in Bedfordshire". Samantha took a deep breath trying to hold her nerves, but Julie came to the rescue by finishing off Samantha's speech by saying, "and the third time was last night; they even came right up into the farm yard itself". At the mention of the farmyard, there were some stunned looks that flashed across everyone's faces, including Brian's, as he had believed that Mile End Farm was a safe place.

"That's impossible, how could they have tracked you down to three separate independent locations without both of you knowing how they were doing it" said Trevor, who was sitting at the far end of the small kitchen table. "They could have been using that number plate system that

163

the police use to track down vehicles and things" said Misim, but Julie shook her head, knowing this system wasn't being used to track them at all. "The system is called A.N.P.R, automatic number plate recognition; and it only works if there was electricity, which up until around five miles from this place, nether Samantha or I have seen" replied Julie, as Misim put his hand on his chin scratching it in thought. "What about some sort of tracking device, looking at the size of the Green Goddess out there, you could easily hide a tracker anywhere on that, and no one would ever know it was there" said Doctor Victor, who suddenly piped up from the middle of the table.

"It's possible I suppose, we didn't see what they were doing, just heard voices" replied Samantha, who had to think back to that first night in the truck stop outside of Lillington. "Do you have any idea who these people might be, names, faces, activities; anything at all that might help us keep them at bay" asked Brian from the top of the table, where he had remained silent, listening to what Samantha and Julie had to say about their night time visitors. "Yes, we know names, and a little history too" replied Julie, as all of the eyes around the table fixed back on Julie once again. "They're called Edward Fitzgerald and Patrick Devises, and we think they may have links to the government as well" replied Julie, as even Brian raised an eyebrow this time. "But how can they have links to the government, there is no government now, it was all destroyed by Covid" said Brian, as even he now looked worried by this revelation.

"It all boils down to the same, these men are clearly after Samantha and Julie for something, but what I don't understand is why these men have not tried to kidnap, kill, or do anything else to you before now" came Melissia's voice from opposite to where Doctor Victor was sitting deep in thought, as Samantha could have sworn blind that at the mention of Patrick Devises name, he had looked a little uneasy. Melissia was one of the few people who hadn't spoken up until now, and a few heads nodded and murmured around the table, as they thought that Melissia had made an excellent point. Even Samantha and Julie thought that this particular question still remained to be answered out of all of the question that had been asked so far. Why hadn't they made their move on Samantha and Julie yet; surely Samantha and Julie would be easy pickings for two men who had clout behind them?

They must have known that they could easily over power them if they needed too, so why had they just been skulking behind, never showing their faces too them, or even as Mellissa had said, attempted to kidnap or kill them both before now. Samantha's thought dwelled on the pamphlet, and then thought that must have been the reason why they were both being stalked. Either that, or this was some deranged vendetta that Edward had on Samantha because of the collision on the motorway. A collision which after all, Edward had caused himself by being drunk, and that Samantha was just some innocent bystander in all of it. Could it really be all because of that? And where did this Patrick character fit into all of this? Maybe he was after Julie for arresting him on that sexual harassment charge, Julie had told Samantha about earlier that morning while they lay half sleep inside the Green Goddesses cab.

"It comes down to this" said Brian, bringing Samantha out of her thoughts with a bang, as he continued, "I don't blame Samantha or Julie for bringing them here, it sounds like they are some nasty twisted evil bits of filth to me anyway". "They are, I arrested one of them for an accusation of sexual assault; and the other caused a road traffic collision which Samantha was at earlier this year" replied Julie after Brian had said his piece. "All the same, I'm glad you have shared this information with us you two; otherwise, it could have been a lot worse for us; at least now we can make preparations to stop these people dead in their tracks, or bringing danger to this community" replied Brian, as he stood up from the table and finished off that morning's briefing, doing his usual drill of handing out jobs to the group as a whole, making sure that all of the lists were ticked off, and everyone had been assigned for that day's work.

"Samantha and Julie, I want you two on the fence as far from the farm entrance as possible, fitting the new electric fence up at the far end of the farm; if these two stalkers of yours are watching the farm, then they will have a harder time getting at you from the main road pass the farm". After that statement, Brian nodded his head in approval, as they all trooped out of the farm house, to go about their normal daily tasks. Samantha, Julie and Melissia, all making for the far top field, where the new electric fence would mark the boundary between Mile End Farm, and the following fields beyond it. "You shouldn't think too harshly of Brian you know, after this morning and yesterday lunchtime, he really is a genuinely nice man really; he took me in, even though I had no farming experience at all" said Melissia, as the three of them worked away putting the new electric fence up.

Considering how complex Brian had made putting an electric fence up would be, it was surprising how easy it was. It involved driving in the wood stakes into the ground using a pile driver, which was a long iron tube, open at one end and closed at the other. Samantha, who seemed to have more upper body strength despite her petite size, was doing the actual driving of the stakes with the pile drive, whilst Mellissa held the stakes in place and Julie wound the metal cable around the stakes as they went along. "I did honestly think he was going to kill that young teenage boy Charlie yesterday, I really did" said Julie, as Samantha looked scared at the mention of it, wondering what Brian would have done if they hadn't of intervened to stop him. Brian could have quite easily shot and killed Charlie, but Brian seemed to have short fuse at times, and Samantha had wondered whether Brian had maybe been diagnosed with a mental health condition in the past.

"I think he wanted to send a clear message to the other foxes that stealing was never going to be tolerated by the community, so that's probably why he let the kid go, to tell them to never come back again" replied Melissia as she gave a thumbs up to Samantha, to start hammering the stake in with the pile driver. "I like him, he's a nice enough guy, just not when he's carrying a shot gun" said Samantha, as she too remembered the incident with Charlie the teenage boy. At that moment, they were interrupted by Misim, who had come walking across the field carrying a tea tray in front of him. "Tea is served my lovelies" said Misim in a cheerful voice, as all three took cups of tea each from the tray. "Aww Misim, you're an angel, thank you so much" said Mellissa, as the others spoke words of thanks to Misim for the cups of tea. The three of them slowly drank their tea, as Misim walked away back towards the farm house across the open fields.

As the three of them stood there, Samantha suddenly let out a small giggle, looking in Misim's general direction. This sudden giggle from Samantha caused Julie and Melissia to look around at Samantha in curiosity. "What's so funny Sam" asked Julie, as she took another sip of her tea, feeling the warmth of the teacup radiate through her hands. "He's really cute isn't he, I mean I know he's gay and everything, but still really cute" replied Samantha, as even Julie and Melissia smiled in a girly sort of way. "Oh of course, he admitted it to us that he was homosexual when we first met him; he was such a sweaty, and we all accepted him straight away" replied Melissia, as she took another sip of her tea. "So, tell us about your work before Covid then Melissia, we're both dying to know" said Julie, as Melissia's face broke into a wide grin and she waved her hand in a feminine sort of way.

"Oh, my shop and my hairdresser's salon, was a place of wonder and amazement; ladies and sometimes men, would come in to be styled in the most lavish ways; my favourites were always the ladies going to the lavish parties, proms and even weddings" replied Melissia, as she recounted her days working in her hairdresser's salon before Covid. Samantha and Julie had leaned themselves up against the fence, listening to Melissa, as she continued. "By far my favourites were always the brides, who would come in and show me the wonderful photos of the gowns they had ordered for the big day". As Melissa spoke, Samantha was reminded back to the time when she had been taken to the wedding shop by Greg, and had spent a whole afternoon trying on the many wedding gowns that the shop had to offer. The very same gown which even now, was packed away neatly in the suitcase inside the container on the trailer onboard the Green Goddess.

Something in Samantha's face seemed to show this, as Melissa suddenly said "I know that look Samantha my darling". "What look" asked Samantha, who couldn't help but blush slightly at Melissia. "That look my dear, the look of a lady who is dreaming of days gone by" replied Melissia, as she made the connection between Samantha's face, and perhaps what she had been thinking. Julie looked confused, as the realisation of what Melissia had said suddenly hit her with a bang. "No way, was you married or something Sam" said Julie, but her face suddenly changed, as she realised that maybe that wasn't the case. "No not quite Julie my darling, Samantha here was due to be married, but Covid stopped it" replied Melissia, as they both saw that Samantha's eyes were full of tears. "Oh, I'm so sorry Sam" said Julie in a compassionate voice, as she realised what had happened, fearing that she might well have accidently put her foot in it.

Samantha began to cry, as Melissia and Julie both put an arm around Samantha. "I'm so sorry my darling, did your fiancée die of Covid" asked Melissia in a soothing voice. "His name is Greg, and I don't want to think he's dead; I think he's still out there somewhere, and that's what me and Julie were doing when we found the community; we were trying to find him" sobbed Samantha through a fresh wave of tears. "I'm really sorry my dear, please forgive us for talking about weddings in front of you" said Melissia, as she rubbed Samantha's back with her free hand. It was hardly surprising that Melissia and Julie looked a little sheepish at that point, as they clearly hadn't been in a position where they were going to be married to someone who was still missing. As Samantha sobbed with her head bowed, Brian came walking up the field, shot gun over his shoulder, smiling slightly as he drew level to the three of them a few moments later.

CHAPTER TWELVE

Julie and Trevor

"Come on ladies, back to work; I don't feed you to stand around you know" chuckled Brian, but he suddenly stopped chuckling as he saw Samantha crying. "Sorry Brian, Samantha was just having a little trip down memory lane, and it just overpowered her a second, that's all" replied Julie, as Melissia continued to comfort Samantha, who was still weeping slightly. "Oh, I see; I'm sorry to hear that Samantha; well in that case, take as long as you need, it's coming on great ladies, it really is" said Brian looking a little abashed, but he was soon on his way again, walking up the field alongside the perimeter, keeping an eye out for any foxes that might have been trying to sneak their way in through the incomplete sections of the new electric fence. Samantha composed herself after a few moments, rubbing her eyes slightly, which were slightly red from where she had been crying.

"I'm sorry I never told you before guys, I really should have" said Samantha, but she immediately waved down by both Melissia and Julie, who were both being sympathetic towards Samantha. "Don't be silly dear, just remember, life in the community means no secrets, we are after all, here to help each other" said Melissia, as Samantha nodded, still a little red around the eyes from where she had been crying. "Your right, I'm sorry, Brian's right you know, we should get back to work, otherwise we probably won't get any supper tonight" replied Samantha, as the three of them returned to work, knocking in the fence stakes which hadn't yet been put in to complete the electric fence. Samantha and Julie spent the rest of the afternoon filling Melissia in about the rest of what they knew about the outside world, and the mystery pamphlet that had been delivered to Greg before Covid, and Samantha's mission to work out the mystery of it, and its origins.

How the pamphlets numbers had actually been coordinates, and how they made a reference to the town of Clyde and its coastline in Scotland. By the evening, the entire new electric fence was complete, and Brian had gathered them all together in the farm yard for the grand switching on of the new completed fence. It wasn't like watching the Blackpool or Brighton lights, thought Samantha, but it was still interesting that they each had to go up to each corner of it, and throw a stick at it the wires on the fence, to see if there was an electric current flowing through it or not. And sure enough, when each stick was thrown at each section of the fence, it was followed by a collection of blue and white sparks, to show that the fence was live and working all around the farm. It made it all feel very real somehow, that during the times before Covid, this sort of fence would have been completely illegal, due to the twenty thousand plus volts running through it.

"Those stalkers and blasted foxes will think twice before coming here again" said Brian triumphantly, as they all sat round the kitchen table that evening over dinner, which tonight included a nicely made steak and kidney pie, cooked up by Misim, who had admitted to being a bit of a dab hand with a cook book in his youth. After dinner, they all sat around chatting, as the topic of interest that night had been their previous lives before Covid, which after all, seemed to be the only things they could talk about, as nothing new ever seemed to happen whilst at Mile End Farm. Samantha suspected that perhaps Melissia had filled the others in about Samantha's past, as none of them had mentioned to Samantha about Greg, or her quest to find him. Instead, Samantha spent the evening telling them all about her time working on the HGVs, and how she'd always dreamed of doing truck driving work since she was a child.

The conversation did slowly slide in the direction of the mystery pamphlet that Greg had given to Samantha, so Samantha decided not to fight it, and instead brought it out, laying it on the table for everyone to see. "It's a lovely view, always wanted to go there" piped up Misim, over a round of evening coffee. "Have you tried scanning it under ultra violet light" asked Doctor Victor, as Samantha shook her head, wondering why Doctor Victor would have suggested such a thing. "Err, I haven't done that no doc" replied Samantha, as Doctor Victor picked up the pamphlet, and held it up to the light. "Sometimes, when you shine something under ultra violet light, it shows up hidden details which maybe invisible to the naked eye; it's a technique we had back in the olden days before Covid in forensic science; an incredible field of science I have to say" replied Doctor Victor, as Samantha was fascinated by Doctor Victors days in forensic science.

Samantha did have to confess to herself, that she wasn't really paying full attention, as her gaze kept drifting over to the far corner of the living room, where Julie and Trevor appeared to be chatting happily. "Those two seem to be getting quite close" thought Samantha, as it did look like Julie and Trevor seemed to be enjoying each other's company a lot more than everyone else did. "But then again, when you live in such a small community, you can't really keep any secrets at all, and you are bound to notice more things" thought Samantha, thinking back to Melissia's advice earlier that day. Samantha had certainly noticed that Julie and Trevor seemed to be enjoying each other's company more and more often these days. Even when Samantha had even mentioned Trevor's name to Julie, just in passing, Julie seemed to have that look on her face which told Samantha that something was going on between them.

"So, would you like me to examine it for you" asked Doctor Victor, snapping Samantha back to the conversation that they'd been having, as Samantha had been looking at Julie and Trevor seated together in the corner of the room. "Oh yes, of course" replied Samantha, handing over the pamphlet to Doctor Victor, who took the pamphlet and then proceeded over to the kitchen table, where Brian sat cleaning his twelve-bore shot gun. On catching site of Doctor Victor, Brian quickly moved over slightly, so Doctor Victor could lay the pamphlet on the table, in order to conduct a more in-depth examination of the pamphlet. Samantha was glad that the friendly doctor had decided to do this, not just to try and find out more answers about the pamphlet, but also so that her attention could be diverted back to Julie and Trevor again. To Samantha's great surprise however that Julie and Trevor had both vanished from the corner of the room.

Little did Samantha know, when her attention had been taken by Doctor Victor offering to examine the pamphlet, Julie and Trevor had gone outside, through the farmhouse back door, and into the small garden behind the farm house. As it was now springtime across the country, it was a little lighter outside then it would have been at any other time of the year. "I think Samantha is onto us you know" said Julie, outside in the small garden behind the farm house, as she and Trever perched themselves on the chicken coup fence, which was the only part of the farm fence that wasn't electrified. "So what if she is, it's a free country isn't it" replied Trevor with a slight grin, as Julie moved in closer towards Trevor, so that the pair of them were sat together. It was true, Samantha did have a very keen eye for detail, and tended to notice certain things that maybe other people might have missed.

Maybe this was the reason why Samantha seemed to be more adapted to living in this new world, then maybe she had been in the old non Covid one. Julie, with her life of structure, discipline and order had brought her so far, but she was still very far from openly surviving in this new world. "Samantha has been there for me since I met her" replied Julie, as Trevor looked a little surprised. "I thought you two had only known each other less than a week" asked Trevor, in a curious voice? "Well, we sort of have, but it feels so much longer than that now, because of what's been happening and everything; I mean, we actually first met at a road traffic collision back in January" explained Julie, as Trevor's face went from that of confusion, to understanding. "Ah, so you staid in contact from then on" said Trevor, as Julie replied, "oh no, it was actually chance how me and Samantha met really".

"How so" asked Trevor, as if he was directing questions at a witness during a court room cross examination. Julie seemed to recognise this, having been in a court room plenty of times before now, on many different cases in the past. "Well, your honour; we actually ran into each other at my local police station in Lillington, as Samantha had come in scrounging for pepper spray and the like to defend herself with in the future" said Julie, as Trevor let out a slight chuckle on hearing the jokiness in Julie's voice when she had said the words, 'your honour'. "So, you agreed to come with her and travel together" asked Trevor as Julie let out a short laugh. "That and the fact that I'd also arrested her first for theft, before realising that there were no theft laws anymore" replied Julie, remembering the dramatic scene outside of the Lillington police station, where Julie had slammed Samantha up against Betsie's cab, and then proceeding to snap some handcuffs on her.

Although Julie had made it clear to Trevor that this was before Julie had realised who it was, and then removed the handcuffs from Samantha's wrists. "Good heavens, so that is how you met; a story worthy of your autobiography I must say" replied Trevor with a slight chuckle. Julie giggled slightly at Trevor's words before falling silent, staring up at the early evening clear blue sky, not yet being able to see any stars up above them. A small breeze suddenly whipped through Julie's hair into her face, blowing into Trevor's face at the same time. "Oh, I'm so sorry" replied Julie apologetically, suddenly raising a hand upwards, to brush her hair out of their faces; but then realised that Trevor was smiling and leaning in closer towards her. Before they both knew it, they were embracing and kissing each other, little caring who came out and saw them at it.

"What if someone sees us" Julie said suddenly, pulling away from Trevor a little nervously. "Oh stop it, now come here you" said Trevor, who launched straight back in again, kissing Julie all over. Julie giggled slightly, as the pair of them embraced and kissed each other, whilst the chickens behind them pecked and squawked away in the chicken coup. Julie had planned to do many things in her life; travelling the world and having kids being the top two ambitions on her bucket list. But even Julie had to admit, she never would have expected in a million years to be snogging an ex-lawyer next to a chicken coup, on a farm in the Northamptonshire countryside. Back inside the farmhouse however, it hadn't escaped everyone's attention that Julie and Trevor had disappeared into the night, as it was a very small community of people after all; if you could call half a dozen people living on a farm as a community that is.

"What do you reckon then, do you think those two are enjoying themselves" said Misim, who had just come back downstairs after using the bathroom to have a wash and a shave. "As long as the chickens are happy about it" replied Brian in a jokey voice, as they all laughed at Brian's laughable comment. As the laughter died away however, there came a sudden exclamation from the kitchen table, where Doctor Victor sat, still closely examining the mystery pamphlet that Samantha had given to him. "Yes, I think I have found it; the wonders of ultra violet light and good old-fashioned finger rubbing" exclaimed Doctor Victor in a cheerful voice. "What have you found Doc" asked Brian, as Samantha leapt up from her living room chair, walking quickly through from the living room and into the kitchen. "What is it doctor" asked Samantha, as Doctor Victor beckoned Samantha over to the kitchen table.

Doctor Victor held his ultraviolet torch up, before shinning it down onto the pamphlet, lighting up the whole area of the pamphlet within its beams. "See here, the ultra violet has shown up what looks like a logo of some kind, and these letters here; T.C" said Doctor Victor, answering both Brian's and Samantha's question simultaneously. Doctor Victor was right; the pamphlet was lit up under ultra violet light, but it defiantly seemed to be some sort of logo of some kind. It consisted of a triangle background, and within the centre of the triangle, was a picture of a scientific test tube, with a few drops coming out of the top of it. The letters 'TC', could now be clearly seen across the centre of the test tube, and underneath the test tube, across the bottom of the triangle were the words, 'the company'. "The company; I can't say I've heard of them before" said Samantha, a little confused, as she scratched her head in deep thought as too what 'the company' meant.

But Doctor Victor's face had suddenly lit up with a smile, which made him look as if his eyes were about to pop out of their skull. "Of course, I should have known it would be from them" replied Doctor Victor, who was now running his hands through his hair, his smile suddenly disappearing at this moment of understanding, which only Doctor Victor seemed to see. "Do you know these guys then doc, from the olden days I mean" asked Brian, as the whole kitchen had suddenly gone very quiet, looking directly at Doctor Victor. Doctor Victor suddenly looked very sheepish, as this sudden look was not missed by the others. "Yes, but it's worse than that" replied Doctor Victor, as he placed his hands back on the table, and looked around at Samantha and Brian before responding; "I used to work for them". There was a stunned silence that went around the kitchen, as if someone had suddenly turned off the sound.

"I can explain" said Doctor Victor, as everyone seemed to move a little closer to Doctor Victor, intent to know the friendly doctor's backstory. Doctor Victor took a deep breath, and began to explain. "I qualified as a doctor in 1991, and started working as a GP; one day, I'm at work, and I get offered this job out of the blue to go and work for these guys, but they weren't called the company at that point; there actual name is Grey's Pharmaceuticals when they started up in the 1960s; but a part of their operations was to focus on virus control, and also working alongside Porton Down, in order to counteract chemical and biological weapons". Samantha looked ready to kiss Doctor Victor, as she now realised that she had yet again stumbled across a vital clue in finding out where Greg may have gone. Doctor Victor took a death breath before continuing with his speech.

"One day, when working at their head office near Leicester, I came across this file on the mainframe codenamed, Covid-19; when I looked into it, it seemed that Gray's Pharmaceuticals had actually been in a pact to make weapons for China and North Korea". There was a collective gasp and widening of eyes around the table as Doctor Victor continued talking. "Yeah, I know; I'm not proud of it". Doctor Victor suddenly looked frightened, as if he thought every person in the room was about to jump on him and attack him. "If what you're saying is true doc, these people are responsible for wiping out ninety five percent of the world's population" said Samantha, as everyone looked at her in horror. "Ninety five percent" they all said in unison. "How did you come about that information Sam" asked Doctor Victor, who's expression had gone from that of shock, to curiosity.

"On my way up here, myself and Julie stopped at an airbase called RAF North Lakes; we met a man there called Corporal Fredrick Loose, and he told us that Covid-19 had killed an estimated ninety-five to ninety eight percent of the world's population" explained Samantha, as the others expressions seem to reflect that, as they now seemed to understand this fact. "Corporal Loose was very well informed, as that was what the figures were projecting on this report I saw" replied Doctor Victor, as Brian suddenly pipped up. "Hang on Doc, wasn't there a law that was created to stop human experimentation like this", as everyone turned to look at Brian, and then back at Doctor Victor again, waiting for his answer. It then suddenly occurred to Samantha, that this was one of those government-like secrets, that people in higher positions within the country's management, attempted to keep this sort of activities classified by any means necessary.

"There was, it was called the Nuremberg code, it was created in

176

the aftermath of the Nuremberg war trials after the truth came to light about the Nazi and Japanese concentration camps, and the Russian Gulag system; it meant that any human experimentation done by a person or state was now consider a crime against humanity and could be punishable by death" replied Doctor Victor in answer to Brian's question. "But that law could be violated, I mean cosmetic companies used people to test their products all the time, and I don't see any of their company executives swinging from the rafters" replied Misim, who in truth knew the least about science matters than anyone else who was present in the room at the time. "That is true Misim yes, if those people gave consent to be tested on of course" replied Doctor Victor, as he then carried on with his explanatory tale.

"Back in the 1950s, Porton Down ran what they called a test to cure the common cold; but what they were really doing, was testing a nerve agent called Sarin on people; one serviceman even died as a result of the tests; I even read the case file on it, name of Ronald Maddison". "But surely the government knew about Grey's Pharmaceuticals and what they were doing" replied Melissia, who had just voiced what everyone was thinking at that exactly moment in time. "You'd like to think so, but they were clearly up to no good behind the scenes; by the time the news hit about the breakout of Covid in Wuhan, I knew it was already too late; so, I gathered as much information as I could, and made a run for it" replied Doctor Victor, as the others were responding to Doctor Victor's words with mixed feelings on their faces. Some looked stony faced, as if they believed Doctor Victor was somehow responsible for what had happened.

But not everyone saw the friendly doctor as a bad person however; some saw it differently. Brian for one, had not shifted in his position for the whole time Doctor Victor had been talking, but he suddenly spoke into the silence. "Doctor, if I was the Queen, I'd give you a bloody medal". Nearly everyone in the room looked around at Brian, who stood up and held his hand out to the friendly doctor. "Thanks Brian, but I don't deserve it, I was too slow to alert the government to the problem, and now all human life is dead because I failed" replied Doctor Victor. "No, it's not, of course it's not; every single person in this room maybe immune to Covid, but by god, in the end, you did the right thing; you didn't stand by the company, you stood up to them and even tried to whistle blow on their operations to the rest of the world" replied Brian, in an understanding and welcoming voice.

Samantha started to clap, as the others followed suit, showing their respect towards the friendly doctor, who was at that moment, the hero of the hour. "A toast, to the friendly doctor" said Brian, who hoisted his cup of tea into the air, as the others stopped clapping and followed suit, toasting Doctor Victor and his efforts in attempting to stop Grey's Pharmaceuticals from destroying the world. Doctor Victor managed to pull a weak smile on his face, but Brian then said, "you know more don't you doc". "I do, the C.E.O is a man by the name of Patrick Devises, although I suspect there maybe another person pulling his strings further up the chain, as Grey's Pharmaceuticals was just one of many companies" replied Doctor Victor, as Samantha felt as if a led weight had just plummeted from the sky, and smacked her hard on the head. Samantha had heard that name once before, a few nights ago, when her and Julie had laid half-awake in the Green Goddess cab.

Patrick Devises, the man Samantha and Julie believed to be the one who was travelling with Edward Fitzgerald and stalking them both wherever they went since leaving Lillington. "That's the man who was here a few nights ago under the cover of darkness, along with Edward Fitzgerald" said Samantha, as Doctor Victor started. "Devises can't know I'm here, if he does, we're all in danger" replied Doctor Victor in a scared voice, as he made to get up and leave the kitchen. "You better not be thinking of leaving us Doc, it's a dangerous world out there you know" said Brian, as Doctor Victor looked back at him, wondering what to say or do next. "It's ok doc, we'll protect you, we're all family here" said Melissia, as Doctor Victor looked a little more relieved to hear this latest statement from Melissia. "I think it's time we were all in bed, I'll do a patrol around the farm to make sure we're not being watched, and then we'll discuss this more tomorrow".

Brian's final words seem to act as a good conversation finisher for everyone, as they all disappeared to their sleeping locations, and Samantha headed outside to the cab of the Green Goddess, where she had been sleeping every night alongside Julie. As she went, Samantha caught sight of Trevor and Julie chatting over by the chicken coup. "At least there happy and contented" thought Samantha, as she unlocked the Green Goddess's cab driver's door, and climbed inside, shutting the door behind her with a click. Samantha knew not to lock the cab door, as Julie would be coming into the cab herself to go to bed whenever she felt ready to do so. To Samantha's surprise however, when she woke up the next morning, she found that the upper bunk was deserted, with the duvet and pillow untouched from the night beforehand. "Julie and Trevor defiantly had a good time last night" thought Samantha, as she stared up at the upper empty bunk bed.

Samantha herself had started to get used to Brian's wakeup calls now, and she was steadily starting to get the hang of life at Mill End Farm. "Morning Sam, hope you slept well; Melissia is doing breakfast this morning, so I think we'll escape having food poisoning" said Brian, chuckling slightly as his own joke. "Morning Brian, yeah I think she'll be fine" replied Samantha, as she smiled slightly at Brian's joke, wondering how Melissia would have reacted after hearing Brian's comments about her cooking. Brian had told them all the story of a few days ago, when Melissia had attempted to cook them all a roast Sunday meal, which had resulted in her cremating the turkey, and nearly setting fire to the kitchen. But Melissia had been practicing on her evening's off, and she'd started to get quite good at it, as nobody had complained about Melissia's cooking ever since.

Even Samantha had joined in at times, creating some fantastic dishes out of some of the many types of produce that Mile End Farm could grow. It was the usual routine, breakfast around the table, then followed by the briefing, and then out into the day, working all over the farm as they went. Julie and Trevor were sat next to each other at the table, and Samantha could have sworn she saw the pair of them exchange a kiss earlier on, when they didn't think anyone was watching. Samantha sadly didn't really have a chance to prove this theory however, as Brian had told her that she was needed in one of the top fields on the outskirts of the farm, which needed to be ploughed ready for another batch of crops. Julie, Trevor and Misim meanwhile, had been sent on what was known as a 'hazard run'. The 'hazard run', as Brian often referred to them as, was usually what it said on the tin, in what it involved.

This was where two or more people would go out into Northampton itself, or to the nearby towns and villages, to collect as many different types of supplies as possible, from different types of foods, to bottled water, and even a few non-essential items, which nearly always managed to find their way into the shopping bags as well. As Brian had told them to take the farm's horse box trailer behind the Land Rover Defender as well, it meant that there would be more than enough supplies to keep them going for weeks on end. "Good luck" said the others, as they watched Julie, Trevor and Misim, all climb into Brian's Land Rover Defender, before it rolled out of the farm yard, rattling slightly, as the horse box was being towed behind it. The others then broke off, heading for their different places and jobs around the farm. Doctor Victor could be seen as always in his usual position as stoking and maintaining the fire onboard the steam traction engine.

His usual blue boiler suit was completely caked in ash and soot, as if it hadn't been washed for weeks. But he didn't seem to mind this, as a fresh batch of soot flew out of the chimney and came to lay in a circle around him, with everyone who was left on the farm, trying their best to stay out of the line of fire, every single time this happened. After driving the very large scarlet red CASE C.E.T tractor a few days earlier, Samantha was hoping that Brian would give her something a little smaller to work with from now on. Something in Samantha's however seemed to show this, as Brian steered her in the direction of a smaller shed, where an old 1950s built light grey Ferguson tractor sat, looking very shinny and new considering that it was nearly seventy years old. Samantha had no trouble trying to start it, as it's little four-cylinder engine chugged away, making light pale coloured fumes flow out of the exhaust silencer box as it went along.

As Samantha drove past on the farm's small grey Ferguson tractor, she waved to Doctor Victor up on the steam traction engine, who waved back, as he had finished brushing the last of the soot out of his hair, strolling up and down the wooden running boards, squirting oil lubricant into the stream traction engines many gears, and pistons, as it sat billowing smoke and hissing out steam from its pistons. It was almost quite therapeutic, listening to the sounds of the steam traction engine powering the work shop machines and charging the night batteries which providing power, light and warmth to the entire farm. It sounds seemed to fade away into nothing, as the small grey Ferguson tractor bounced along a little, moving further and further away from the farm buildings as it went. As Samantha drove it along one of the many farm tracks to the top end far field, it's plough behind clinking slightly as swayed slowly from side to side.

As Samantha had done this before a few days earlier, she always switched off slightly in her work, allowing her brain to go into an almost autopilot type state, as the small grey Ferguson tractor began to drive up and down, creating perfectly straight plough lines, where the ground soil and earth was turned over in order to plant the seeds. Brian had realised that the diesel and petrol fuel required to power the farm machinery wasn't going to last forever, and the fuel stations in and around the area, would have likely been drained already by those panic buying before Covid hit. So, Brian's master plan, had been to grow some petrol and diesel biofuel in the field that Samantha was now ploughing. "If anyone can plough that field to the way it will be needed, that would be you Sam; you've got a great eye for detail, and did a fantastic job last time" were the words of Brian at that morning's briefing on the day's jobs.

As Samantha loved driving anyway, it was a win-win situation as far as she was concerned, as Brian's word rang in her ears, making Samantha beam with pride at the sound of them. Not to mention the fact, that she really starting to feel like she was fitting in well at Mile End Farm and within the Flintstone Community. The little grey Ferguson tractor wasn't the fastest of machines in the world, so Samantha was able to watch the sun rise up into the sky, in order to pass the time as she sat there, trundling up and down the field, turning the soil over with the plough. She'd had a small break from ploughing that day to go for some lunch, where it was a quickly knocked together sandwich, with a few Lettice leaves and some strawberry jam. Then back on the little grey Ferguson tractor, to finish off ploughing the field before the sun went down later that day, and it would be harder to see anything, as the Ferguson tractor had no lights on it.

Considering it was now nearly the month of April, where rainfall was likely to increase, and the ground to become more saturated, this would make ploughing a field a little more difficult than it would have been at any other time of the year. At least one advantage in the environment, was that the sun wouldn't take long to start to set again, as the summer time was a little way ahead yet, and didn't kick in until May time, where the changes in season would mean harder work, and more crops that would need to be grown in advance of the winter to come.

CHAPTER THIRTEEN

Fox Troubles

Samantha had just finished the second to last row of ploughing in the field, when something in the thick line of trees to her left suddenly caught her eye. Samantha knew not to go to close and touch the fence, as it was now electrified, and would certainly give her a lethal shock if she touched it. Shutting down the engine on the tractor, she leapt down and starred into the line of trees, swearing blind that less than a second earlier, she had seen something move in amongst the treeline. It was quite difficult to see through the trees, as they cast great dark shadows beneath them, and as it was quite a sunny day, they were even darker still from where Samantha was standing. At first, Samantha thought it might have been a dog, or a cat, or maybe even a fox cub. But as she started to walk slowly forwards over to the fence, she heard the bushes rustle slightly, and it was too much of a movement for it to be caused by the wind.

"Hello, is there someone there" called Samantha, as she reached the fence, making sure not to trip and fall onto it. The fence itself was around six feet in height, but had no barbed wire at the top, due to the fact that the electric shock off of it would have been enough to paralyse, or even kill anyone who tried to climb up it. Even trying to stick fingers through it would have been difficult, as the wire mess was so closely packed together, sealing off the field from the trees on the other side of it. From where Samantha now stood closer to the fence, she could see that the darkness between the trees had thinned a little, as there appeared to be what looked like a pile of leaves, just on the other side of the fence from where she stood. Samantha suddenly realised what it was, and let out a small scream, nearly falling over backwards because of the freshly turned over soil, as she clapped her hands over her mouth in shock.

Lying just on the other side of the fence, was the dead body of what looked like a human child, probably no older than eleven, who's clothes were dirty, with tears in the fabrics in some places all over his body. The child's body didn't look like it had been there for very long, as flies could be seen and heard buzzing in and around it. As Samantha sat there examining the child's body, she saw and heard the trees rustling again, and thought that maybe a stray dog or even young fox cub was lurking in the undergrowth, ready to drag the body off for its next meal. "Is anyone there" called Samantha again, as there was a sudden movement on the other side of the fence, and a teenage boy straighten up, staring Samantha dead in the eyes, pointing a long sharp pole in Samantha's direction. It looked almost like a wooden broom handle, but the end had been sharpened, so it now looked like a very spiking point, almost like a hunter's spear.

"Halt, are you a witch" said the boy, as Samantha looked startled, and held her hands out in from of her, in an attempt to at least try and defend herself. If the boy chose to suddenly try and jab at her from the other side of the fence, he would be killed as well, as it would get stuck in the fence, and end up sending an electric shock through the teenage boy. The teenage boy had jet black hair which was untidy and a face which looked as if it was a lot older than it was, which looked as if it hadn't been groomed or looked after himself in years. His clothes were slightly torn, just like the child's body on the ground was, as the teenage boy stood behind the body of the small child in front of him, trying to hide a lonely tear, which was fighting to flow out of his eyes, and down his cheek. "A witch, no, are you here for your friend" replied Samantha, as the boy brandishing the speer, gave it a small jab in her direction.

The boy looked almost as old as Samantha was, although his sunken and dishevelled appearance might have clouded her judgement somewhat on his age, as well as the fact that people of her age didn't tend to brandish broom handles, and then refer to other people as witches. "You're a witch, you've killed him" demanded the teenage boy, gesturing downwards at the small body at his feet, not taking his eyes off of Samantha as he said this. "I didn't kill your friend, I swear I didn't kill him; please just be careful, that fence is still live" pleaded Samantha, with a slight air of worry in her voice, as her natural caring persona seemed to take over at that moment in time. Even though she was older than this teenage boy was, he still looked as if he could hurt Samantha quite badly if he chose too, or worse, even manage to kill himself on the electric fence, which Samantha knew was still flowing full of electricity.

A sudden thought occurred to Samantha, as sudden thoughts always do when you're standing on one side of an electric fence, and there is another human being on the other side of it, pointing a homemade spear at you. The teenage boy kept saying the word, 'witch'; was this perhaps some sort of a code, that this boy, and maybe others, had come up with to describe those who lived in this post Covid world. After all, Brian always referred to the people trying to steal his produce as 'foxes'; perhaps maybe 'witch', was the opposite meaning to those outside of Mile End Farm who viewed the Flintstone Community. "I'm really sorry about your friend, he must have been killed when he tried to climb the fence" said Samantha, trying to stay calm. Even though Samantha had never been a fan of guns, she couldn't help but think that Brian with his twelve-bore shotgun at the ready, could have resolved this situation in a heartbeat.

Not by shooting the boy, but by making him surrender the spear and place it on the floor out of harm's way from everyone else. "What's your name" asked Samantha, as if she was trying to make light conversation with the boy, so that he would calm down and not do anything rash or silly to hurt either Samantha or himself. Samantha had never seen herself as a trained police negotiator, that was more of Julie's department than hers; but Samantha still felt that she would have to improvise all the same in the current situation. "My name is Isaac, I am the leader" replied the teenage boy, who lowered the spear slightly, trying to keep himself posed to strike at Samantha, if he felt that he had to. "It's nice to meet you Isaac, my name is Samantha, but most people call me Sam" said Samantha, who despite the situation, was starting to relax a little, as she started to think that there was a good chance that Isaac didn't plan to do Samantha any harm.

Samantha could hear the local Northamptonshire accent in Isaac's voice as he spoke again. "I am the leader of the gang, my gang; we are the Foxes Gang" proclaimed Isaac, as Samantha was briefly reminded of the Scottish and Celtic clans, who would run into battle with a war cry, brandishing swords and shields at the enemy. Samantha gave a slight giggle and grinned slightly, as Isaac's face became a little put out, feeling that there was nothing funny about being in the presence of someone who he felt was the enemy to the Foxes gang. "What's so funny, do you mock me and my gang" said Isaac questioningly, as Samantha looked surprised. "No of course not, it's just, that's what we know outsiders to be, or that's what Brian our manager calls them" replied Samantha, having a sudden thought. Samantha hadn't thought about it up until now, but Brian was a farm manager before Covid, and he was now the leader of their community.

Isaac suddenly had a look of understanding on his face, as if he had somehow physically read Samantha's mind at that moment. "We took our name from that, we were just a gang back then, but now we call ourselves the Foxes Gang, because we heard the term by one of your people" explained Isaac, as a recent memory came back to Samantha of Brian brandishing a twelve-bore shot gun in a young boy's face; as Julie had pleaded with Brian not to kill the boy, and instead set him free. "That little boy down there, that's not Charlie is it" asked Samantha, hoping against hope, that the small dead body by the fence wasn't Charlie's. "No, it is not Charlie; that boy down there was our youngest fox; his name was Peter, and he was just eight years old" said Isaac, feeling his voice cracking slightly as he spoke, feeling that it was such a terrible thing for someone so young to become an innocent fatal victim of the new world.

Samantha too had tears in her eyes, as she realised that eight was no age to meet an end like that, as even she still felt a little young herself, despite being nearly three times Peter's own age. "I'm so sorry Isaac, we should bury him here on the farm, with a proper grave and things, a true send off for a wonderful young boy" replied Samantha, now fighting the urge to break down and cry herself. "You are kind Samantha; you are not like the others; we will remember this kindness" replied Isaac, but as he went to turn away from Samantha, some other voices came out of the bushes from just behind where he stood. "Isaac, what's going on, have you got Peter" said a squeaky voice, which Samantha guessed was from a young girl. "It's safe everyone, this is Samantha, she's friendly to our cause" replied back Isaac, taking a step back, placing the spear down on the ground next to Peter's body.

There was a general rustling of leaves, as what looked like two other teenage boys and a small blonde-haired girl, came crawling out of the bushes and then stood up so that Samantha could see them quite clearly. Samantha recognised Charlie, the boy who Brian had spared, standing on Isaac's left, as Samantha gave him a small wave and a grin, which Charlie returned, smiling slightly through slightly yellow teeth, as if he had not brushed them in weeks. The other boy had jet black hair, with darker coloured skin, looking no older than around fifteen years old, as Samantha guessed that this teenage boy was from a middle eastern country by his looks, as she could see a slight beard stubble on his face from where he was standing. Whilst the small blonde haired-girl looked tiny in comparison to the rest, and didn't look any older than eleven, with her hair untidy, which looked as if it hadn't been combed in weeks.

The three children standing before Samantha were all wearing clothes that were shabby, dirty, and in some places, ripped and torn, like they'd all been doing a lot of living in the wilderness with them, or even living as tramps on the streets. "Wow, you all look like a mess, how long have you been living rough" asked Samantha, as she gazed at them all, with her mouth slightly open at the way the kids were all dressed. "We've been living rough since Covid struck; we were all living in Northampton quite happily, and then the pandemic took our families from us" explained Isaac, as Samantha bent down slightly, so as to be at the same eye level as the teenage boys and the small girl. Isaac began to gesture around at the others around him, as he began to explain who they were. "This is Suresh, he's originally from India" said Isaac, pointing at the dark-skinned teenage boy behind him.

"Hi Sam" said Suresh, waving slightly, as Samantha returned the wave with a smile, and a small wave of her own. Isaac pressed on; "Charlie you know of course; and this is Charlotte, she's from Northampton as well". The small blonde-haired girl standing to Isaac's right, waved slightly when her name was spoken out by Isaac. Samantha quickly returned it, still with the same smile on her face that she had used for the others, not being able to help thinking about the fact that Charlotte looked sweet, and not the sort of person who should be having to live rough in this uncertain new world. "Peter was one of us too, until he was sadly killed" said Isaac, as Samantha could tell he was putting on a brave face for the others, trying to fight back tears. Samantha was very surprised to see, that the other kids didn't seem to be frightened by the fact that Peter's dead body lay close by too them, with flies landing and circling above his body.

But then again, the whole city must have been full of dead and decaying bodies, so the shock of seeing them lying around everywhere must have worn off somewhat. It certainly had for Samantha, who's nose suddenly began to pick up the smell of old unclean clothes and body odours. "You all need looking after that's all, you should all be able to have a home here; Brian is a nice man, he's just misunderstood sometimes; I will try to speak to him if I can" said Samantha, as Isaac smiled slightly, realising that maybe calling Samantha a witch, wasn't the best way to begin a first conversation with a stranger that he didn't know very well. "Thanks Sam, we must go now to bury Peter our friend" said Isaac as Charlie, Suresh and Charlotte all disappeared into the bushes. "Good bye, and good luck" called back Samantha sympathetically, as Isaac reached down and picked up Peter's body, cradling it in his arms as he went.

"I'm sure we will see each other again in the future Sam" said Isaac, as he smiled and turned away, walking back into the undergrowth around the trees after the others. Thinking that she would be missed if she stayed out in the field too long, Samantha hoped back on the tractor and finished off the rest of the field, ploughing the rest of the rows that needed doing, before heading back down the fields, into the main farm yard. As Samantha rolled to a stop in the main farm yard, she could see that Julie, Trevor and Melissia, had all returned from their days shopping trip, with the Land Rover and horse box trailer packed to bursting with supplies. It was surprising to see how many supplies there were still left out there, as Julie, Melissia and Trevor all recounted their experiences from that day's gatherings, as they got to work in the farm yard, moving the appropriate supplies into the correct sheds and barns around the farm.

"We managed to get right down into Northampton itself, where we went to the garden centre, and found bags and bags of seeds still just lying there from before Covid" said Trevor, who was explaining it all to Brian, who was directing everybody on where to put everything. "And the shops too, they were the biggest surprise, most of the shops that we saw had broken windows and open doors and things, but most of them still had full shelves full of things, you would have thought that they would be ransacked" said Julie, who was speaking to the group as a whole, not being able to believe their luck. "And I managed to get us some goodies as well, as I think we have all deserved some relaxation time I think" replied Melissia, as she pulled out what looked like a flour sack from the back of the Land Rover, packed to bursting with cakes, sweets, chocolate bars, and all other sorts of things from the shops they had been too.

The prospect of everyone getting one of these things from the flour sack certainly put a smile on everyone's faces, as they hadn't been able to properly enjoy such luxuries since the days before Covid. "Now now everyone, we need to make sure those are stored for a rainy day, before we start diving in to far" replied Brian in a jolly voice, but even he couldn't help back crack a smile at the prospect of some goodies from days gone by. "Do you see any other survivors then guys" asked Samantha, as she directed this question at Trevor, Julie and Melissia. "We saw a few people out while in Northampton, but they all seemed to hurry away when they saw us; one was brave enough and tried to attack us by throwing a brick at the windscreen, but it didn't break" replied Julie, as she expected Brian to be annoyed that the farm's Land Rover had been damaged, but instead, Brian looked calm and collected, as if he wasn't worried by this news in the slightest.

"Ah good old fashioned anti-shatter proof glass that stuff, I was involved in a crash with the old Land Rover a few years back now, and had it fitted by the garage afterwards" explained Brian, giving the Land Rover a little knock was his hand. "Well, it certainly helped, as we swerved to avoid this guy who'd thrown the brick, he managed to grab hold of the back of the trailer as we passed, but he fell off after a few seconds, so we weren't sure whether he was dead or not" replied Trevor, as Melissia took up the story, with the others all wrapped up with their attention, listening to her speak. "Don't worry, we think he was alright, as we saw him get up and stagger away into a nearby building looking a bit drunk; but something tells me he won't try and mess with us again for a while" finished Melissia, as everyone tittered when she'd said about the man getting up and staggering away.

"I bet he'd had a bit of a head ache after that" replied Misim with a slight chuckle, wondering how he would feel grabbing onto a trailer as it moved off down the road, before falling off onto the road surface. It was incredible how much stuff could be fitted into a horse box and Land Rover, but even though it was packed to bursting, it was soon completely empty, as 'many hands made light work', as Brian always seemed to quote at them, at every available opportunity. As Brian had just finished putting the horse box trailer away, a sudden commotion at the farm yard entrance made them all look round to see what was happening. As the entire Flintstone community were all out in the farm yard at that very moment, everyone could see very clearly what was happening, and what they saw made them all gasp in horror. Isaac and the other fox gang members, were walking slowly towards them, as Isaac was still carrying Peter's body in his arms.

They must have walked all the way around the electric perimeter fence, and then up the farm driveway from where Samantha had spoken to them earlier on that day. Everyone seemed to be completely dumbstruck to move at all from where they were standing; all except Brian of course, who suddenly made a violent move forward, swinging his twelve-bore shotgun from around his shoulder, brandishing it directly into Isaac's face. If anyone had seen Brian angrier than this before, then they could not remember it. Brian's face was incandescent with rage, and there appeared to be a slight twitch going in his cheek, which throbbed and pulsated as he stood their teeth bared, staring directly at Isaac, who hadn't moved or flinched from Brian's reaction towards him. Everyone began looking backwards and forwards between Brian and Isaac, as if they were watching a tennis match, as the silence between them all could have been cut with a knife.

"I warned you what would happen if I ever saw you here again, what the hell is all of this" exclaimed Brian with a snarl in his voice, as he looked directly into Isaac's face, taking in his downtrodden appearance and Peter's dead body in his arms. "Brian, stop" shouted Julie, as Brian was so shocked, he looked around at Julie in alarm. They had all only heard Julie shout like that once before, and that was when she had told Brian off the first time, when he had tried to shoot Charlie from the fox's gang. Brian rounded now rounded on Julie, "you support thieves do you

Julie, I thought you were a police officer, I expected better of you then to defend thieves" snarled Brian, with an air of wanting justice about him. Some of the others shifted uncomfortably, as it was obvious that they looked as if Brian had a point about stealing, but still looked frightened to say so all the same.

"I was a police officer Brian, and I told you before, the old way of life maybe gone forever, but murder is still murder, and it's far worse than stealing" replied Julie, but Brian changed tack at the speed of light. "So, you'd rather stave than help others then Julie" retorted Brian, trying to argue his point, but Julie being the trained police officer, knew how to respond back straight away. "Yes; rather me than see these children starve; there the future of this world Brian, and you want to just shoot them for just trying to stay alive" argued Julie, as she stood her ground, looking a lot braver than she felt. Brian seemed to faulter slighter, as Charlie, Suresh and Charlotte all began to sob, tears flowing down their faces. "Your electric fence killed my friend, his name was Peter, and he was just eight years old" said Isaac, who had managed to stay calm and collected all throughout Brian's rage.

There was a collective gasp from everyone, as they all clasped their hands over their mouths, hearing the news about Peter. At this last statement, Brian lowered his twelve-bore shotgun, as even he felt that this was something that no child should ever have to endure. "He was obviously trying to steal from here then wasn't he" snapped Brian, who had stopped shouting, but still looked a little intimidating. "No, he wasn't trying to steal anything; Peter ran away from our gang when he told us he wanted his mum and dad; we suspected where he had gone, and came up here to find him" explained Isaac, as even Julie's face seemed to go from that of reasoning, to understanding. "That woman over there, Samantha, she spared us, and didn't turn us in" said Isaac, as everyone turned to look at Samantha. If Samantha had chosen any situation in the world not to be in at that very moment, it would have certainly been this one.

Fearing what other people would think about their encounter up by the fence in the far field, Samantha had been hoping that she could have kept quiet about it all for the time being; but as she didn't know what Isaac was going to do in that moment, her hand had been forced into quite a difficult position. "They came up to the other side of the fence to where Peter's body was, while I was ploughing the field earlier on; they weren't trying to steal anything Brian, they just wanted to bring their friend Peter's body back and give it a proper send-off" replied Samantha, as Brian looked shocked to think that a fellow community member, would stoop to such a basic level of treachery such as this. "Look at them Brian, there just kids, what chance have they got in this world now; they probably had bright future's ahead of them, and that has now been torn away from them" said Julie sympathetically, as Brian pointed a finger at Isaac.

"This one stole from here five years ago, thought he'd take the old jeep out for a joyride" blurted up Brian, as Isaac lowered his head in shame, looking like a small child caught in wrongdoing. "I'm not proud of it sir, I was stupid and silly, and was only trying to impress my friends by proving myself to them; you can imagine, that I regret doing that now" replied Isaac, who sounded very apologetic, fighting back the tears himself now. "Was you ever charged with the offence of stealing Isaac" asked Julie, as Isaac shook his head at Julie, as a look of understanding came across Julie's face. "They issued me with a caution instead" said Isaac, as Brian turned away, rubbing his eyes a little, as even they had gone a little red themselves. "What did you want to be when you grew up Isaac" asked Julie a slight smile coming over her face, as if she was speaking to a far younger child than Isaac was himself.

"My parents wanted me to study media at university, but then I thought I would become a lorry driver" replied Isaac, as Samantha gave a slight smile, knowing full well that Isaac was unaware of the fact that Samantha could drive lorries, and had done so regularly before Covid. Julie then looked at Suresh, with same expression that she had used with Isaac a few moments earlier. "I wanted to be a builder, like my father" replied Suresh, who had come across as a little shy, due to being around so many unknown strangers standing nearby. "I've always wanted to be a fire fighter" said Charlie, who appeared to be the bravest, aside from Isaac. Julie then finally looked at Charlotte, who grinned slightly as Charlotte blurted out, "I wanted to be a princess". Everyone seemed to titter in response to Charlottes words, all except Samantha, Julie and Melissia who all went 'aww' after Charlotte had spoken.

"I'm sure that can be arranged sweetheart" said Melissia from the back of the group, as Julie turned back to Brian, who still facing Isaac and the other kids, his head hung downwards slightly as he listened to them all speak. There was a silence following this latest action, as Brian turned slowly around to face them all again, his eyes looking a little red, so as a dead giveaway that he had been crying silently. "I had a family here, wife, daughter; and then they were taken from me by Covid" said Brian, as the others all listened with rapt interest, as they had never heard Brian talk about his family before now. "I never got the chance to give them the send-off that they deserved, because I had to cremate them because of the risk of infection" explained Brian, as Julie approached Brian slowly, and then embraced him in a hug, feeling Brian's pain all over her body as she did so.

"Let them stay Brian; they need feeding, clothing, real people to take care of them and show them the way forward" replied Julie, as she broke away from Brian, hoping that she had finally managed to get through to him about what was happening. Brian sighed heavily and then nodded slowly, seeming to make up his mind about the matter. "We must bury Peter, it's only right that we do that; and then we can give these kids new lives here" replied Brian, as Isaac lowered Peter's body down onto the ground, before standing back up, and stretching out his hand to shake Brian's. "We owe you our lives sir" said Isaac, as Brian stood up straight, faced Isaac, and then shook his hand in businessman like fashion. Everyone began to clap, as Isaac and Brian smiled at each other, realising that a new peace could exist between them from now, in the Flintstone community at Mile End Farm.

"Your friend deserves our respects; you all seem like hard working kids, so I think you can be fitted in here with no problem at all" replied Brian, as he carefully picked up Peter's body and walked slowly across the farm yard with it, until they were in the stretch of green lawn around the back of the farmhouse, the others following Brian as he went, looking sad and upset by the site of Peter's body in Brian's arms. "Peter should be buried here; he would like the view out over the farm from here" said Brian, as he gently laid Peter's body down on the ground, next to the spot where the grave would be dug. No one said a word in response to this, so Brian took that to mean, that everyone agreed with his decision to bury Peter in the spot that Brian had picked out. As the next few hours ticked by, Isaac steadily dug a suitable sized grave, before laying Peter's body at the bottom of it, before then being helped to climb out and fill in the grave with the topsoil.

While Isaac had been doing this rather delicate task, Brian and the others had been making a small wooden cross, in which they had carved Peter's name, the date of death, and the letters 'R.I.P'. The rest of the community stood back a little, as they watched Isaac, Charlie, Suresh and Charlotte all carry the wooden cross over to the freshly dug grave, and stand it up at the end of it, so that the grave looked a little simple, but yet marked the respect for the person now decaying under the freshly dug up earth. The foxes gang then took a step back, and bowed their heads, and silent tears began to flow down everyone's faces, as they all stood in silence, in a mark of respect to Peter. Even though none of them, with the exception of the fox's gang kids of course who had known Peter the most, they all seemed to share a sense of sadness from the situation all the same.

Even just months earlier, a young child like Peter would have been opening presents on a Christmas day, before Covid had reared its ugly head, and had parents caring and looking after him; not knowing that months later, they would be lying at the bottom of a grave, having been electrocuted by an electric fence for simply the crime of being in the wrong place at the wrong time. It was a very sombre group in the farmhouse's kitchen that night; but by the following morning, it seemed that everyone was ready to move on from the events of the previous afternoon. Julie for one, found this the most difficult to comprehend, and usual bereavements went on for more than one day normally, feeling that this sort of forgetful behaviour was tantamount to gross negligence or even borderline psychopathic. However, it was the friendly Doctor Victor, who was the voice of reason and common sense, as any self-respecting medical professional would be.

"I always say every day is a gift here; you just never know what's going to happen next, so things get forgotten about quite quickly really" explained Doctor Victor to the others, as they all sat having breakfast the following morning. Over the morning briefing, Brian explained what jobs the newly instated, Charlie, Suresh, Charlotte and Isaac could all do around the farm. Despite living city lives before Covid, the foxes gang members all seemed to be quite enthusiastic about their new lives at Mile End Farm. Although they suspected that there upswing in moral might have been done to Brian suggesting that most of their day would be devoted to playing and looking after each other. Isaac and Suresh however only seemed to want to go along with this, because it would have meant getting out of doing some of the more heavy-duty manual labour tasks around the farm.

Charlotte had in fact spent most of the day with Misim, as Misim had spoken out that he wanted a little helper in his small workshop that day, helping him to do uniform repairs and assorted other clothing duties. Once the younger ones had been put to bed that evening however, it seemed to dawn on everyone that not all of the habitancies of Mile End Farm were as sleepy as they should be. It later turned out, that Samantha wasn't the only one who had noticed Julie and Trevor becoming close friends over the last few days. Whilst they were all in the living room, Julie suddenly got to her feet, and spoke to the room at large, clearing her throat in a professional manner, as the room went very quiet. "I need to tell you all something" said Julie, as they all looked up from their evening activities with curious looks on their faces, wondering what Julie was going to say next.

"As I'm sure you know, me and Trevor have been, well, seeing a lot of each other over the last few days" began Julie, but she seemed to faulter slightly, as if her nerves were failing her somehow. Something about the smile, now starting to grow across Samantha's face, must have helped, as that seemed to be egging Julie on. "We're engaged, we want to get married" suddenly blurted out Trevor, as the room at large realised with was going on, and fell into complete sympathy. There was a collective, 'aww', that went around the room, as everyone began to clap, then suddenly stopped, as they realised that their clapping downstairs in the living room, would wake up the kids upstairs where they were laying fast asleep in their bedrooms. Julie blushed so deeply with embracement, that her face went as red as a set of traffic lights, as she quickly held up her hands to her face, so as not show her fresh embarrassment to everyone else.

Samantha and Melissia both made joyful giggling sounds, whilst Brian, Misim and Doctor Victor, all stood up and walked over to Trevor to shake his hand, and give Julie a hug. "I never thought I would be hosting a wedding on this farm" replied Brian chuckling slightly, as Julie went up to him. "Thanks Brian, there's a lot of work to do I know, but I'm hoping we can do it here" said Julie, as Brian waved his hand in the air. "Oh don't be silly Julie; if you and Trevor want it here, then here is where we will do it; just need to find a vicar now" replied Brian, as Julie laughed slightly, but she suddenly realised that Brian had a point. Where exactly were they going to get a vicar to marry them at the ceremony, seeing as the small matter of getting married, was something that had happened before Covid, where they could have both gone to a church or a registry office to carry out the act of marriage.

"Me and Julie have already thought about that Brian, seeing as if you're the farm's owner and sort of the leader around here, we thought you could do it" said Trevor, as Brian's face looked shocked, at being presented with this highest of honourable deeds. Brian wasn't alone in being shocked, as everyone else had gone wide eyed at Trevor's suggestion as well, imagining Brian in a white dog collar and black suit, as most vicars tended to wear during such a ceremony. "Well, that's very gracious of you Trevor, but I suppose it should be right of me to do it, if that is what you want" replied Brian, as the whole room started clapping again, this time not worried if they woke up the kids upstairs or not. "That's the spirit Brian" said Misim, who had come through from the kitchen, carrying a tray full of teacups and a teapot, which clinked and clanked as he walked, making the usual sounds that a tea service would.

Misim placed the tea tray down on the coffee table in the centre of the room, as everyone began to help themselves to tea and coffee, still in awe of Julie and Trevor, who had chosen to tie the knot on Mile End Farm. "To the happy couple" said Doctor Victor, as they all toasted Julie and Trevor on their engagement, feeling that a great surge of uplifting vibes had gone through them all like butterflies in the stomach. Julie and Trevor spent the rest of that evening moving around the room, speaking to different people in turn, finding out what they could do in terms of preparations skills for the upcoming wedding. Most of all, Misim and Melissia were in their element, as this was defiantly an area for which they were both familiar with before Covid had struck, having run shops and businesses where clothing alterations and hair styles would have been performed on a daily basis.

"We shall have to see about hair styles Julie my darling, that is an absolute must" said Melissia excitedly, tilting her head from side to side, examining Julie like she was a wax figure on display at a museum. "And I will have to get to work making outfits, especially a lovely ball gown dress for you Julie" said Misim in his most excited of voices, as Julie placed a hand on Misim's leg, feeling that she being treated like royalty by them both. "You're all very kind, you really are; and I'd always love a great dress Misim, I'd never say no to one of those" replied Julie, as Misim hurried away to fetch his tape measure from his haberdashery, skipping slightly as he went. Now with Misim gone temporarily, and Melissia distracted with a woman's weekly magazine, Samantha was finally able to get to Julie and Trevor to talk to them, feeling both happy and sad at the same time.

"Aww, Congratulations you two" said Samantha, as she managed to sit down next to Julie and Trevor by the open fireplace. "Thanks Sam, we really appreciate it" said Trevor, as Julie smiled at Samantha in appreciation, unable to think of any words to say at that moment. "I thought something was up with you two for the last few days" replied Samantha, as Julie looked a little sheepish, and grinned again. "You would have made a great copper Sam, yes, I sort of felt a little romantic towards Trevor when I first met him here" said Julie in a jokey voice. "We were even saying about how you might be our chief bridesmaid Sam, I mean, that's only if you wanted too of course" replied Trevor, who seemed a little nervous at this point, but Samantha's face had immediately lit up at the mention of this suggestion. "Aww, thanks guys, I'd be honoured too, I really would" said Samantha, grinning from ear to ear as she spoke.

"I bet you never thought you'd be a chief bridesmaid to me would you" said Julie cheerfully, as Samantha laughed, secretly believing that if it hadn't been for Covid, none of them would have met at all. "Not to you Julie no, I had friends before Covid, but I would have expected to a bridesmaid at their weddings instead; how times change eh" replied Samantha, as Julie grinned in an understanding sort of way, feeling that Samantha had made a very valid point about the Covid situation. It then suddenly dawned on Samantha, that not all of her friends were dead and gone. Greg was still out there somewhere, as was Diana; but there had been no sign of anyone at all, especially not from these two. Samantha had a rough idea that Greg may have tried to travel to Scotland with what the pamphlet had said, but as for the disappearance of Diana, there was no trace of her whatsoever.

Maybe Diana had decided to do exactly what Samantha had done, found a community like this one, and chosen to settle down with it. Samantha would never believe for one second that Greg, or Diana, would abandon her in any way, as even a little thing like Covid couldn't have driven a wedge between their relationship. Maybe they had believed

Samantha was dead along with the rest of the Covid victims, and simply decided to go their own way. As Samantha sat there thinking this, Misim returned with his tap measure, and so Julie was ushered away into one of the other rooms, where Misim worked and kept his needles, pins and other assorted tools which were used in his tailoring and seamstress work. The others sat talking to Trevor for a while, until Samantha suddenly had a wild thought; so she got up out of her chair and walked across the room, exiting first into the kitchen, and then out of the front door.

As everyone seemed to be distracted talking and congratulating Trevor about his engagement to Julie, they didn't notice Samantha leaving. Samantha now crossed the semi dark farm yard across to where the Green Goddess was parked, and then proceeded to the back of the container sitting on the trailer. The container door squeaked slightly as Samantha opened it, and then climbed inside, flicking on the light that had been installed inside the container. Samantha immediately found what she was looking for just behind the door, which was the black suit case Samantha had packed before she had left her home back in Lillington. Unzipping it carefully, so as not to damage anything inside the suitcase, Samantha immediately found what she was looking for, folded nearly inside of it. It was Samantha's very own wedding gown, that Greg had paid for when she had gone dress shopping a few months earlier.

It was still in the same pristine condition as before, having been protected by the dress bag that it was now stored in. Samantha lifted out the dress bag, and as she did so, a corner of an item of clothing which was royal blue in colour flashed before her eyes. Curious as to what this sudden flash of royal blue might have been, Samantha hung the dress bag up on the open door so as not to lay it down on the floor, and began to rummage through the suitcase, moving a few clothes out of the way, until she could clearly see what it was. It was the very same off the shoulder royal blue satin dress that Samantha had been wearing out to dinner that faithful night after going wedding dress shopping in Lillington, out with her friends before Covid had struck. "I wonder" said Samantha to herself, thinking out loud, as she took out the royal blue coloured dress, folded it carefully, before slipping into a spare bag, which she had found inside the container.

Jumping down to the ground, Samantha grabbed the two dress bags containing both items of clothing, and made her way back to the farm house, closing and locking the container door behind her. It later turned out that Samantha stealthy departure out of the living room, hadn't gone completely unnoticed, as Brian stood at the door way, watching Samantha coming back towards the farm house. "Wow, what have you got there then Sam" asked Brian, looking directly at Samantha, as she reached the farmhouses doorway. "I've got an idea for Julie's wedding, but I need to get this into Misim's workshop" replied Samantha, as Brian suddenly had a look on his face, as if he had worked out what Samantha had in the dress bags, and what she was going to do with them. "Where the hell did you get one of those so fast" asked Brian in amazement, but Samantha made flapping moments at him with her free hand.

"I'll explain later, please, I need to get this through" said Samantha, as Brian stopped her from proceeding through the farmhouse. "Don't go through here, everyone will see; I'll distract people and you can get into Misim's workshop through the back door round the side of the farm house" replied Brian, as Samantha thanked him, before proceeding back out of the front door and around the side of the farm house, to a small wooden green painted door. Samantha knocked on it, and then pushed it open, to suddenly be greeted by quite a comical scene. Misim was holding a tape measure around Julie breasts, and Julie was only wearing her underwear. Julie quickly let out a small scream, before trying to cover herself up with her hands, but then relaxed a little when she saw that it was Samantha who was standing in the doorway, holding the dress bags in one hand, and the other hand on the doorhandle.

Even Misim seemed to jump about a foot in the air at the sound of Julie's small scream, as even he didn't expect anyone to come in through that door, especially holding what looked like a dress bag. "It's alright

Julie, it's only Sam" said Misim, as Julie relaxed a little from her scare a few moments earlier, her heart racing a little in her chest, as if she had just run a mile. "Sam; you gave us such a fright; is everything ok" asked Julie, as Samantha apologised for bursting in on them both, and then promptly hung the dress bags up on a couple of clothes pegs nearby. Misim's workshop looked the same as any other tailors and seamstress's shop would look, except that it was inside what looked like a farmhouse outbuilding with half a dozen pegs around the walls, and piles of what looked like used rags in the corner. From the outside, it looked a bit old and dingy looking; but on the upside however, Misim had managed to install a few home comforts, like a soft carpet, and smooth white washed painted walls all around them, giving the room a slight glow about it from the outside farm buildings and open fields.

CHAPTER FOURTEEN

The Wedding

Both Misim and Julie suddenly looked confused, at the sight of Samantha bringing the dress bags inside the workshop; but like Brian before them, they both seemed to realise what Samantha had brought in, and immediately as Samantha had done so, both of their faces had lit up with happiness. "Yeah, everything's fine Julie; I just thought that this might be of use to you" replied Samantha, pointing at the largest dress bag, as Misim walked over to it and opened it slowly and carefully. Even in the brightly lit workshop, the gleaming white wedding gown inside the dress bag radiated outwards, casting everything else into darkness. "Oh my" said Misim, placing a hand to his chest in shock, as he caught site of the wedding gown in the dress bag; as Julie meanwhile, had clapped her hands over her mouth in shock at the sight of the wedding gown that Samantha had brought into the workshop.

"It's mine; it was going to be my wedding gown that I would be wearing at my wedding to Greg; but I think it would serve you better

Julie, I really do" replied Samantha, in answer to both Misim and Julie's reactions, feeling that she at least owed Misim and Julie the truth of where the wedding gown had come from in the first place. Julie seemed to be temporarily stunned, as there were quite a few seconds of silence between them that followed Samantha's latest statement. However, it would be Misim who broke the awkward silence first, as he hadn't moved his gaze once, staring at the wedding gown as if it was an undiscovered long-lost treasure. "My my, this is something else Samantha, what a fabulous piece of embroidery and needle work" replied Misim, as even he was taken aback at the pure beauty that Samantha's wedding gown was showing them all.

Julie, by this time, had taken her hand away from her mouth and said, "Sam; I don't know what to say". "You don't have to say anything at all; I wouldn't be able to live with myself if I didn't help" replied Samantha, as Misim began running the wedding gown through his hands, almost in the same way that a historian would pick up an ancient artifact, and study it more carefully for signs of imperfections. "Hmm, expensive for sure this is; I would say this gown didn't cost anything less than about seven hundred pounds" said Misim, fixing Samantha with a curious look, hoping that Samantha would solve his question by filling in the blanks for him. "Yeah, bang on Misim, that's how much Greg paid for it" replied Samantha, as Julie gasped again, her hands going straight up to her mouth, like they had done before when Samantha had brought in the dress bags.

"I can't possibly accept it" replied Julie, thinking that this proposition was too good to be true, whether in this new world, or the pre-covid one. "I insist Julie; I brought it with me from home, as I thought it would be a good memory for me; but I've realised now, that it would do better serving you in your wedding to Trevor" replied Samantha, resolution in her voice, prepared to fight her corner on this with every breath that she had. Misim was still frozen in mid-air, wondering what to do next; but Julie beat him too it. Without pausing to think, Julie rushed straight round Misim, and flung herself around Samantha, tears of joy forming in her eyes as she hugged Samantha. "You don't know what this means to me, you really don't Sam, thank you so much for this" replied Julie, as Samantha felt like Julie could have easily suffocated Samantha if she wasn't careful.

"It's ok Julie honey, I know it will be perfect for you" said Samantha, as Julie broke away from hugging Samantha, rubbing her eyes slightly to clear away the tears. Misim looked delighted as well, as if he had just been gifted with a massive treat. "I never thought I would ever see ladies hugging each other, where one of them was in her underwear" said Misim, as Samantha and Julie both laughed out loud at Misim's comment, cottoning on to what Misim was talking about. It then suddenly dawned on Julie, that she was indeed standing in front of them both, wearing only her underwear, but it didn't seem to bother her as much as it would do normally. Misim now took Samantha's wedding gown fully out of its bag, examining it more carefully, muttering to himself as he went, making Samantha and Julie look at each, thinking that Misim was going mad.

"I think it could do with a little alteration around the busts, and maybe flare out the skirt a little more to make up the difference in the front; but other than that, it could fit you like a glove Julie" replied Misim out loud, addressing Julie as he finished examining the wedding gown. Misim then proceeded to move the wedding gown from the hook beside the door, to another peg further along the wall, so as not to crease or damage it in any way. "Well, I must work on this now, so I shall need to be with Julie alone now please" replied Misim, as Samantha realised what he meant; which was the polite way of telling Samantha to remove herself from his workshop, so that he could continue taking Julie's measurements and have her fitted up for the now nearly delivered stunning wedding gown. Getting the message, Samantha quickly exited through the same green door she had come in by, closing the door behind her as she went, with a small click.

But even as Samantha crossed back over the farm yard towards the farmhouse, she couldn't help but smile broadly, as the look on Julie's face when she had been told she could have Samantha's wedding gown, was a memory that would stay with Samantha for a very long time to come. As Julie and Trevor were now sleeping together in the same room, Samantha had suddenly found that she was alone sleeping in the Green Goddesses cab, but this didn't dampen her spirits in any way. Life on Mile End Farm, had certainly seemed to take a defiant upswing, since Julie and Trevor had announced their engagement. It was incredible how quickly things seemed to move in the Flintstone community on Mile End Farm, despite there being a wedding to plan, and jobs on the farm that still needed to be completed and checked off of the many lists that hang around the farm, like persistent bucket and to do lists.

Before Covid, weddings would often take months to prepare, including wedding videos, a cake to make, guest lists to write up, invites to send out, and even a DJ to do the evening music and disco. So doing a wedding post Covid style, was even stranger still, as the Flintstone community would have to try and do all of those things, without the usual help they would get. As everyone on Mile End Farm was getting a custom too, there was no good asking the internet, yellow pages telephone directory, or any other self help guide for that matter; but that wasn't through lack of trying. For one thing, the venue had already been sorted, the cake was going to have to be made by those within the Flintstone community, as there was no outside help to have it made for them. As for a DJ, none of them possessed any form of musical ability at all, although they had worked out that it wasn't as simple as just putting on a load of music and leaving the DJ decks too it.

For one thing, they didn't have any disc jockey decks, although Brian had kindly and thoughtfully decided to rig up an old stereo that he had in the farmhouse, which came complete with a CD player and MP3 and Bluetooth connectivity. Weirdly though, Brian didn't have that many CDs on him, and even those that he did have were of music from forty or so years ago, claiming them to the choice of his wife's, who was a few years older than he was, and had sadly been killed as a result of contracting Covid. Brian did however show them a collection of vinyl records, which was so large, that he had stored them all within an entire room inside the farmhouse, which had been hurriedly converted into the children's bedroom, when the fox's gang had come to live on Mile End Farm. It was an amazing wonder that the bedroom floorboards hadn't caved in under the weight of some money vinyl records, so it made them all tread very carefully in the room itself.

Brian's whole vinyl collection could be played on an old-fashioned gramophone, which had a winding handle on its side, and which made everyone roll about laughing when it got stuck on a particular bit of the song on a record which it was playing at the time. "Well, I'm not exactly a DJ in a night club you know, how would I know about these things" joked Brian in a comical voice, trying to fix the gramophone one afternoon, as it once again got stuck on a particular part of the record, making the same note play out over and over again, the children laughing away at it, thinking the old-fashioned gramophone to be a comical joke compared to the modern technology the pre-covid world had to offer. Once the music had been sorted out, by far the second most important job, was making the three-tier wedding cake for the reception party after the service.

Melissia had very much volunteered herself for this particular task, and had been given the extra challenge of keeping the younger children, Suresh, Charlie and Charlotte among them, from sticking their fingers in the cake mixture while Melissia had been making it in the farm house kitchen. Isaac had joined Doctor Victor, in maintaining and running the steam traction engine out in the yard, but in order to keep the other children at bay, Melissia had come up with the idea of letting them decorate the cake once she had made it. This certainly seemed to do the trick, as they stopped trying to stick their fingers in the cake mixture after they'd been given this important of jobs, as they all knew that the future happiness of Julie and Trevor partly depending on this most important of tasks. Given their age and previous lives before Covid, Suresh, Charlie and Charlotte all seemed to do rather well at the cake decorating, working seamlessly as a team.

By far the busiest out of all of the Flintstone community, was Misim, who not only was doing the alterations to Samantha's wedding dress so that it would fit perfectly onto Julie, but had also been expected to make everyone else's outfits for the wedding as well. However, as with all great minds and skilled workers, Misim had cheated slightly on this task, as he had given Samantha and Julie the job of going down to the nearest wedding shop that they could find, and bring back as much readymade clothing as they could find, so as to make alterations, rather than Misim having to start completely from scratch trying to make so many outfits for so many different people. It was a fortune thing that Melissia had not been in ear shot when Misim had suggested this action, as she would have most likely tried to come on a shopping trip along with Samantha and Julie, having been taken in by the chance to do a very girly type task.

As Misim had instructed, Julie and Samantha had disappeared shortly after breakfast the following day, and not returned until nearer to dinner time the same day, as they had both become a little bit too distracted on the bridesmaid's dresses front, hanging up on the many rails inside of one wedding shop that they had seen in the centre of Northampton itself. "You ladies and your dresses, a mystery I will never know the answer too" joked Brian, as Samantha and Julie giggled slightly at this remark, after they had returned from their shopping trip with all of the outfits that Misim had requested them to get for his workshop. As Brian was going to be conducting the ceremony as a stand-in, would-be vicar, Trevor had chosen Doctor Victor as his best man, with Charlie, Suresh and Charlotte being his ushers. The chief bridesmaid role had of course fallen to Samantha, but Samantha and Julie had attempted to stick to the usual wedding theme from before Covid.

For one thing, Samantha had decided to wear her royal blue satin dress that she had with her, and so had tried to get a colour and style of dress as close to it for everyone else. Julie had found by far the cutest of them all to be young Charlotte, who at only eleven years old would be the youngest there. As she only came up to just above Julie waist, and could have quite easily disappeared under Julie's enormous wedding dress, and never be seen again, as that would have been fairly easy owing to the six-foot diameter hoop on it. "How times have changed" thought Samantha, as the deadline that had been set for the wedding, drew closer and closer as the days went by. Melissia had only just about managed to make the one-week deadline with the wedding cake, as she had needed to bake each tier individually, owing to the size of Brian's kitchen oven, which wasn't the largest in the world it had to be said.

The Flintstone Community had probably set a Guinness world record when it came to planning and executing a wedding in the period of just a week, but it had still been a great journey and task well down all the same. It seemed to be the right thing to be doing in all of these troubled times, just to lift people's spirits, as there was no getting away from the fact, that nearly all of humanity had been wiped out by this super bug that was called Covid-19. The day of the wedding dawned bright and early, as Brian wasn't doing his usual wakeup call, like he always did on the farm, as he felt that it was a day of celebration, and not of work. The hum of activity was starting to come to life all over the farm; well, all the girls and Misim were buzzing with activity at any rate, but Brian, Trevor, Doctor Victor and Isaac along with Charlie and Suresh all remained asleep in bed, feeling that they had earned an extra hour or so in bed.

The only man who wasn't still asleep, was Misim; having missed out on the role of best man, Misim had instead been told that he was to give Julie away to Trevor. "I have to confess; I did secretly want the job of giving away the bride all along" replied Misim to Julie, as he helped Julie into a bathroom robe, before pushing Julie down into her chair by the large dressing room table mirror. Melissia had decided to pull out all of the stops for this event, as she knew that it was probably one of her last ever wedding's that she was ever going to be doing hair and makeup for. Julie had kept it a secret from practically everyone, except Melissia, what her chosen hairstyle was going to be that day. "I'm not saying what it is, you will just have to wait and see" replied Melissia with a cheeky grin, as Samantha and Charlotte had tried to get it out of her, as they sat in chairs in Melissia's bedroom, waiting to have their hair styled and makeup applied.

"Now Charlotte my darling, your hair is perfect as it is, I love it so much; but Samantha dear, I was thinking of having yours in a sixties beehive sort of style, rather than having it in its usual straight and downwards style" explained Melissia an hour or so later, as Samantha stared into the mirror in front of her, watching Melissia flick her hair around, wondering what to do with it. Charlotte, who's hair was quite short anyway, had opted to just have it as it usually was, with a good comb through of course. Melissia's hair had already been twisted into a nice elegant bun at the back of her head, aided slightly by Charlotte, who had wanted to comb it for her. By the time Melissia had finished Samantha's sixties beehive hair style however, the early afternoon sunlight was streaming in through the farmhouse windows, as the sounds of birds singing in the nearby trees and hedges reached their ears.

Julie, being the all-important bride, had been rushed off to Misim's workshop, so she was out of sight of everyone else before the ceremony. Trevor and the other boys had only just appeared, as they had tried to have as close to a stag do as possible the previous night, which had culminated in many of them, except for Isaac, Charlie and Suresh, all having strong headaches. The wedding itself was to take place in the main barn, which usually housed Brian's mighty farm machinery, including the combine harvester and CASE and small grey Ferguson tractors; but they had been cleared out a few days beforehand, so as to make room for the wedding party and the tables, which they would be having their wedding feast on later that day. Samantha, Melissia and Charlotte were the first to reach the barn, staring around inside it, up at the rafters which had been cleared of cobwebs and other assorted muck and grim, so it looks crisp and clean.

"Wow, looking lovely you three" said Brian, who appeared a few minutes in the doorway, carrying a bible and wearing a very smart black suit, with a brown tie. If they didn't know any better, they would have almost assumed that Brian was going to a funeral rather than a wedding. Samantha stood there, wearing her satin royal blue dress with matching heels, her hair back in its sixty's beehive effect. Melissia also wearing as close to a royal blue coloured dress as Samantha was wearing, showing off her almost school ruler straight legs as she did so. Where as Charlotte had looked like Samantha and Mellissa in miniature, with a small navy-blue dress. Trevor appeared next, flanked by Doctor Victor, with Suresh and Charlie bringing up the rear, all in smart suits and ties, all with flowers in their button holes, looking a little strange with combed hair, as they all usually looked a little rough in their work clothes, not having time for personal appearance.

Trevor looked a little blurry eyed, but that might have due to the amount of drink he had consumed the night before. "Looking great girls" replied Trevor, as Doctor Victor in gentlemen style fashion, kissed Melissia and Samantha's hands, and even gave a warm sweet smile in Charlotte's direction. As there was so few of them, it didn't take long for everyone to be seated, and ready for Julie's entrance in the barn's open doorway. The seats themselves weren't in rows, but instead in a semicircle surrounding the makeshift altar, that Brian had quickly erected earlier on that day. It felt weird to Samantha, seeing the young kids looking so clean and healthy, as when she had first met them, they were almost like tramps living on the streets. Isaac walked in at that moment, seating himself next to Samantha, before leaning closer to her and saying, "you look lovely Sam".

"Aww, thank you" couped Samantha, as she turned her head away from Isaac, to suddenly see that Brian was gesturing to them all to stand up. They all got to their feet, as a sudden shadow fell in the doorway. They all looked around, and to their delight saw Julie the bride, with Misim holding her arm, walking slowly towards them, between the row of seats where they were all sat. There was a collective sigh from the room as a whole, as Julie beamed around at them all, welling up with total happiness as she went. Misim really had done a fantastic job with Samantha's wedding gown, as Julie seemed to radiate and light up the whole room as she drew level with them all. As they were unable to find the wedding march soundtrack on any of Brian's old music records, Melissia had instead offered to sing the anthem instead, as Julie had walked towards them all in the barn.

Melissia as it turned out, had such an amazing singing voice, as Julie felt a slight tear come to her eye drawing level to Trevor and Brian at the altar, Misim standing slightly behind her as she came to a stop beside Trevor. Melissia stopped singing, and sat down along with the others, except for Julie, Trevor and Brian, as Brian cleared his throat. "Well, I'm not a real vicar you see" explained Brian, as everyone laughed at Brian's joke, before Brian spoke again. "Dearly beloved, or however it goes", everyone laughed again at this last part that Brian had said. "We are gathered here today, in the site of all those present, and that includes the very nice man upstairs" said Brian, as everyone tittered slightly, as even Julie and Trevor found it hard to try and not laugh. Brian, it seemed, had a great number of skills up his sleeve, asides from being a farmer, as they could all tell that he been practicing this speech in front of a mirror for days beforehand.

"Julie and Trevor, you are here today because you are both happy for each other, and have made it your wish to be together for the rest of your days; please hold hands and both swear after me" replied Brian, as Trevor and Julie turned to face each other, and took each-others hands. "You both swear that for the duration of your lives, you will cherish, nurture and guard each other against what life may throw at you" said Brian, as both Julie and Trevor said "I do" in unison. "Then by the power vested in me, by Flintstone law, I hereby declare you both married for life; you may kiss each other" exclaimed Brian in a jovial voice, as Julie and Trevor kissed each other, as a round of applause erupted from everyone seated around them. Julie and Trevor broke apart, Julie throwing her flowers into the crowd, which Misim caught, as everyone laughed, realising the flower throwing was a tradition reserved for the bridesmaids.

In truth, the one person who should have caught the bouquet, was Samantha, as it was still her intention to find Greg, and then marry him as they had been planning to before Covid, with Diana or Julie as her chief bridesmaid. "Thanks Brian, I never expected that kind of a speech" responded Julie ten minutes later, as they all sat around the table inside the barn, tucking into a wonderful and marvellous feast, collated together by Brian, who had littered it with all sorts of wonderful goodies. The main course meal, was a nicely oven baked roast turkey, which Brian had stashed away in the back of his home powered fridge for a rainy day; but even Brian admitted that hosting a wedding on Mile End Farm, had to be classed as more important than a rainy day. "Ah it was nothing really Julie, you and Trevor are going to be happy together, I know you are" replied Brian, as they all listened to the sounds of the old-fashioned gramophone playing in the background.

Charlotte, Suresh, Charlie and Isaac were all grouped up one end of the table, as Charlotte was showing them all how to make a daisy chain, which was a clear sign that spring had mostly arrived on Mile End Farm. Brian and Julie gazed down the table at them all, not being able to help but muster a small smile for what they were doing at the other end of the table. "We really are the future here aren't we" asked Julie in a rhetorical type voice, as Brian looked round at her, thinking that maybe Julie was having an epiphany? "If you're on about the kids, then yeah, I guess you are; some of the older ones, like me, the doc, even Melissia, we're had our day really; but I think you, Trevor, Sam, Misim, and the kids, have all got a fighting chance" said Brian, who had just been tapped on the shoulder by Charlotte, who was holding a freshly made daisy chain in her small outstretched hands.

"I made you a daisy chain" explained Charlotte in her small squeaky voice, as Brian smiled at her, hoping to look like the usual rosy faced farmer that he was. "Aw that is very kind of Charlotte, thank you so much" said Brian, as he excepted the daisy chain that Charlotte gave him, before laying it on the table in front of him, realising that maybe Charlotte may have made a slight miscalculation on the size of the daisy chain. Charlotte hurried away, as Brian attempted to put the daisy chain that Charlotte had made for him around his neck. It sadly wouldn't fit, as Julie gave a slight giggle before jokingly saying, "I'm not Charlotte, but I'm sure she designed it to fit on you Brian; still, it would have been very pretty on you". Brian merely looked at Julie, laughing slightly at Julie's joke, as Samantha came and sat down in the chair opposite Julie and Trevor at the table.

"Can you believe that this dress still fits me; mind you, I can't believe that's my dress right there" responded Samantha, as she pointed a finger at Julie, looking her up and down, feeling a little envious inside that her new best friend was wearing her wedding dress, brough for her by Samantha's boyfriend Greg of course. "I know darling, you look super stunning today" said Misim, as Julie blushed deeply red again, feeling fresh embarrassment wash over her, like the tide on a beach would do. "Stop it guys; I'm supposed to look this way; it's my wedding day after all" replied Julie, letting out a small giggle, not being able to help the fact that all of the women on Mile End Farm had gone into full blown giggle mode. "Even so, I'm so proud of you, we all are" said Misim, as Julie sat back in her chair, placing her hands in her lap, making a light imprint in the skirt.

"Keep it up Misim, it will be you I'll be asking to have the first dance with, rather than Trevor" said Julie almost a little sarcastically, so that Misim immediately pulled a face and then laughed. "I think it might be time for you to do just that you know, care to take to the floor you two" inquired Brian, as he held out a hand to help Julie stand upright, as this was a little trickier for Julie to do, owing to what she was wearing at the time. "Let's hear it for the happy couple, and their first dance" called Brian to the room at large, as everyone started clapping. Brian managed to find a good up beat tune on his gramophone records, and pretty soon was watching Julie and Trevor dance themselves in time to the music coming from the gramophone. Samantha was immediately reminded of some of the dances she had seen on the TV as a kid, and even sometimes to the day's where she would go out clubbing with her friends in the local nightclubs back in Lillington.

Watching Julie and Trevor dance around on the dancefloor, made Samantha think of how it would have been for her, wearing the same dress, dancing to a tune that her and Greg had picked out for their wedding day. "How times change" thought Samantha, as she clapped along with everyone else when Julie and Trevor had finished their first dance. Samantha was quite surprised however, as immediately after Julie and Trevor had finished their first dance, Julie came straight over towards Samantha, her white coloured heeled shoes clicking slightly on the concrete barn floor as Julie went. "Come on Sam, come and dance with me, I owe you one for letting me have this fabulous gown for the day" said Julie giggling like mad, as Samantha grinned and allowed Julie to lead her over to the dancefloor, where most of them had now got up onto their feet and were now bouncing away to another tune, this time one more pop like in nature.

Julie, as Samantha could see, was in her element, and even Trevor had managed to steal Samantha for a little while, making Samantha dance around with Trevor in her high heels. This culminated after an hour or so, with Samantha having to conceive defeat, as she was able to do quite a bit physically wise, but dancing for a long time in high heels, was certainly not one of them. As it was now the beginning of the spring season in the month of April, there was always going to be a chance of a downpour, or rain of any kind all over the place. It also meant that the temperature inside the barn seemed to go up and down rapidly, meaning that Samantha soon felt that sweat was starting to build up on her face and body from dancing, but would then feel like she was shivering from the low temperature. This was also to add from the fact that Samantha had picked up a nasty sharp pain in her feet, as it had been a while since she had worn shoes like that.

Samantha grabbed her glass of wine that she'd been drinking from, poured a little extra wine into the glass, and then promptly sank into a chair, in an attempt to try and take some of the weight off of her feet.

215

Samantha could feel a slight band of sweat starting to build up on her forehead, but this would have been nothing compared to Julie, who would have been sweating buckets in her wedding dress, with its many layers. "I know that look young lady" said Misim, who had suddenly dropped into the chair beside Samantha, making her jump about around a foot into the air, as she was not expecting Misim to suddenly appear next to her. "What look" replied Samantha, a little confused, trying to keep her breath steady, and her heartbeat under control. Misim stood up, turning the chair around, before sitting back down again, so that he and Samantha were facing each other.

"That look of a lady who is missing her fiancée; and also wondering how much sweat you can lose in a multi layered wedding gown on a day like this" replied Misim, as he spoke very quickly, but with the air of a man who seemed to understand the female mind. If Samantha hadn't been amazed before, she certainly was now, as looked Misim directly in the eye. "How on earth did you know what I was thinking" replied Samantha in amazement. "Because I've seen that look in a lady's eye a hundred times before; the look of always being the bridesmaid, but never the blushing bride" replied Misim, as he recounted the lyrics from a song a long time ago. Samantha gave Misim a very admiring look, as Misim returned it with a smile, as Samantha was suddenly hit with a thought. "You're not trying to chat me up are you" asked Samantha, with a slightly tipsy giggle, as the wine was starting to take effect in Samantha's blood stream.

"Samantha my darling, I certainly would never dream of that, as that would be a great insult to my community; and besides, Greg would probably have me assassinated for even chatting to a princess like you" replied Misim, as Samantha let out a giggle and a snort, as she had heard what Misim had just said, finding it quite amusing. Samantha had to quickly stop however, as other Misim would have thought that Samantha was making fun of his homosexuality, which she would never do in a million years, having known many people over the years from all sorts of different backgrounds. "I did suspect you were a homosexual

216

Misim honey; but it's really sweet of you to do these things for us" said Samantha, but Misim waved a hand in front of her. "Think nothing of it Sam my darling, you're always fabulous, always have been, and always will be" replied Misim, as Samantha went bright red, grinning broadly from ear to ear.

Misim may have said that he wasn't chatting up Samantha, but it certainly sounded and felt that way from where Samantha was sitting. But then again, he could have been joking with her, and not trying to get sexual in any way shape or form. It did, for some strange reason, seem to be a lot harder to tell these things in the modern day and age, as Samantha was used to the workplace banter of a truck yard, rather than office-based politics. Without warning, Misim suddenly sneezed into his hand, but. It was such a small sneeze, that if Samantha hadn't been looking at the time, then chances are, she would have missed it. "Bless you; oh dear, touch of the hay fever there Misim" joked Samantha, as Misim pulled out a pocket handkerchief, then quickly whipping his nose with it. Misim folded up the handkerchief, and slid it into his suit blazer pocket, thinking that he would dispose of it in the firebox on the steam traction engine in the near future.

"Yeah, been having it over the last few days now, nearly ruined Julie's dress when I started feeling a bit bunged up; maybe it's just hay fever; I've never had hay fever before now, nor been on a farm, so it might be just a reaction to the environment" replied Misim, in answer to Samantha's statement, as Samantha herself looking quite interested, whilst subconsciously feeling slightly nervous, as she didn't think it was hay fever somehow, remembering that this was a post-covid world where anything and everything could come along. "I think you might want to have an early night there Misim, you don't look well" said Samantha, as Misim nodded in agreement, before he hurried away out of the open barn door, a hand held to his nose to try and catch another sneeze again. The rest of the evening seemed to hurry by, as moths and other small insects began to zoom around inside the barn, settling by the ceiling lights, casting small shadows below them.

In fact, it was nearly midnight by the time Julie and Trevor found themselves alone in the barn, revolving slowly on the spot to a slow tune from the gramophone. As Brian had not got a bridal suite of any kind in the farm house, like there usually would be in a hotel or a wedding reception of some kind, he had suggested that the barn itself become the bridal suite for Julie and Trevor to spend the night in, giving them some privacy as well away from everyone else. It wasn't exactly what you'd call a five-star hotel, or what any normal married couple would stay in on their wedding night; but as Brian had said to them earlier on that evening, "tell me what's normal about any of this". Everyone could tell how much Julie and Trevor enjoyed their night's stay, as they didn't emerge out of the barn until nearly 11am in the morning. Brian had again skipped the usual wakeup call, as he knew most on the farm would be nursing hangovers of some kind.

In fact, it seemed that the only ones who were fully awake were Isaac, Charlotte, Suresh and Charlie, who had all decided to go into the hen houses to collect some eggs, ahead of that morning's late breakfast. The hen coup, just happened to be nearby to where Misim's workshop was, because when Isaac had gone past it to collect the eggs from inside the hen coup, he could hear strange sounds coming from inside Misim's workshop, as if he was suffering from some sort of cold. Misim was coughing quietly, but it sounded like he was coughing up a hairball of some kind, almost the same as a cat would. Fearing something maybe up, Isaac and the other children raced back into the farmhouse, and called for Doctor Victor, who immediately abandoned his breakfast and headed straight for Misim's workshop, making sure to take his medical bag with him as he went.

For good measure, and as a good standard of medical procedure, Doctor Victor had chosen to enter Misim's workshop wearing a face mask, and some latex gloves. This was something that Doctor Victor insisted on doing, as he managed to bring a whole stockpile of gloves and face masks with him to Mile End Farm from before Covid, fearing that someday they would be needed. "Misim, can you hear me, it's Doctor

Victor, is everything alright in their" asked Doctor Victor, as he wrapped smartly on Misim's workshop door, everyone else staying as far back as they could, having been instructed to do so by Doctor Victor a few moments earlier. Misim didn't answer, so Doctor Victor pushed the door handle, as the door opened slowly, creaking slightly on its hinges as it went. Doctor Victor could see Misim lying on his camp bed in the corner of his workshop, coughing, with sweat running down his forehead and soaking the upper half of his body.

It was only thanks to the fact that Misim was wearing his suit trousers and no shirt, that Doctor Victor could see very clearly what was going on, and what was in front of Doctor Victor, nearly made him slam the door and bolt it shut behind him. Doctor Victor's eyes widen in horror, and then swore very loudly, as he realised what he was looking at inside Misim's workshop. "Quarantine the farm right now, no one in, no one out; get back now" exclaimed Doctor Victor, as backed out of the doorway, slamming the door behind him, suddenly noticing Isaac and the other kids standing closer than what he had instructed originally. "What's happened doctor" asked Isaac, but Doctor Victor didn't appear to have heard what Isaac had said, as he was already barking orders at the others standing at the safe distance that he had recommended for them all to do while undergoing an inspection of Misim's workshop.

"This door is now being locked, and it will stay locked until I say otherwise, there is some anti-viral wipes and a cloth in my secondary medical bag; go and get for me, right now" commanded Doctor Victor, as the other kids carried out what he'd told them to do, and within a few minutes, they had returned bringing the anti-viral wipes with them. Doctor Victor thanked them, and then proceeded to wipe down the doorhandle into Misim's workshop. He then marched straight over to the steam traction engine, before disposing of the medical anti-viral wipes and the latex gloves into the firebox, where a roaring fire soon burnt them to a crisp, killing off any chance of germs or infection, whilst Isaac and the other children looked on. "Gather everyone together in the farm yard, go" said Doctor Victor, in his most severe style voice he

219

could muster, sounding more like an army general commanding troops on a battlefield.

Within minutes, everyone was in the farm yard, yawning slightly, and still looking very tired from the night before. "What's going on doc, the kids said Misim was ill or something" said Brian, who immediately froze mid speech, cottoning on to the situation that was happening in front of him. "I'm sorry to gather you this morning everyone, but as of now, I'm placing this farm into an immediate quarantine zone; Misim has Covid-19, he's been infected with it" said Doctor Victor, trying to stay as calm as he could, even if the faces around the group were suddenly alert, shocked and surprised all at the same time. "That's not possible, is it doc; I mean, Covid killed everyone who wasn't immune didn't it" replied Brian, a little unsure of what to think of Doctor Victor's latest statement. There were mummers coming from the group, as panicked thoughts began to run through their minds.

"Even I'm out of my depth here, but until I can find out where it's come from and when, no-one can go anywhere near Misim, the workshop, or come and go from the farm" replied Doctor Victor, as Brian turned to the group as a whole. "Ok everyone, from now on, unless stated otherwise, Doctor Victor is in charge; he knows best" replied Brian, as everyone all turned back to Doctor Victor, expecting him to fill them in on what he knew, or even suspected. Doctor Victor took a deep breath, exhaled, and then proceeded to walk up and down for a few seconds scratching his head, trying to think of what to do.

CHAPTER FIFTEEN

The Second Wave Begins

After a few seconds, Doctor Victor stopped pacing, and turned to look at them all, a look of grim unrest on his face. "Misim is showing very clear symptoms of Covid-19; these sorts of symptoms only start to show there themselves after two weeks, which means that he would have been infected at a bare minimum from two weeks ago; does anyone know where he was two weeks ago" asked Doctor Victor, posing this question to the group as a whole. "I sent him on a scouting run into Northampton and the nearby villages to get supplies two weeks ago" said Brian, as he tracked back through his memory of where everyone had been and when over the last few weeks. "Thanks Brian, that may be of help, but I shall have to try and find some way of communicating with Misim, without going near him" replied Doctor Victor, putting his hands together in thought, feeling that he was now in a predicament.

Everyone now mirrored Doctor Victor, thinking hard on what to do about the problem of communication; how were they going to communicate with Misim, without going anywhere near him, as that would have meant certain contamination for sure. "You could try the cups" pipped up Samantha suddenly, thinking back to her school days in a science lesson she had attended once, where the teacher had been talking about early forms of communication. "What do you mean Sam" asked Doctor Victor, who was curious to know what Samantha was talking about. "You know, the cup trick; take a pair of plastic cups, put a hole in the bottom of each cup, tie two knots in a length of string through each cup, and then tension the cable" explained Samantha, as if she a science teacher, teaching a room full of school children about basic science. Doctor Victor's face suddenly lit up, as did everyone else's, as they all realised what Samantha was implying.

"Samantha Bonham, you are a genius, why didn't I think of that" replied Doctor Victor, as he seemed pleased, but then a little put out with himself, as after all, he had done a science degree at university, so in theory should have come up with that idea himself. "Well, in your defence doc, you're a man of medicine rather than a scientist as such" said Trevor, who still looked a little bleary eyed from the night beforehand. "Alas Trevor that is very true, but even so, I must say well done to Sam for coming up with that though" replied Doctor Victor, as Samantha blushed slightly from being paid a compliment by the friendly doctor. "I have some cups upstairs somewhere; I use them to sometimes place my tools in them" said Melissia, as she quickly hurried away, thinking of her barbers shop upstairs in the farm house. Brian now stepped forward, so that he was level with Doctor Victor.

"Ok everyone, jobs as normal, except Sam, who I want working with Doctor Victor today, and Julie and Trevor, I'd like you two on the steam traction engine, keeping the power going" commanded Brian, as everyone spit up, following Brian's orders, going about their daily tasks. "I'm really sorry to have to make you two do work on your honeymoon break" began Brian, speaking directly to Julie and Trevor, but Julie cut across his. "No, we understand Brian, this changes things". "We're a community here Brian, you've helped us celebrate the perfect day for us, now we must help you by helping keep the farm going" said Trevor, as Brian smiled in appreciation of Trevor's words, before striding away up the fields, shotgun over his shoulder, doing his usual patrol of the farm's perimeter fences. Back outside Misim's workshop, Doctor Victor had been attempting to slip into a protective bio hazard suit.

This was part of the large stockpile that the others had managed to gather from in and around the local area, plus Samantha had been able to get a few from RAF North Lakes, which had been stored in the container pulled behind the Green Goddess. Very helpfully as well, Samantha had managed to construct a decontamination chamber, using a large camping tent with plastic sides. This would enable Doctor Victor to be decontaminated as he entered and exited Misim's workshop, using high pressure water from the huge water bowser, which was currently being used to feed water into the steam traction engine. "Here you are doctor, we've attached the plastic cups on each end of the string, so that we can open up communication between Misim, and the rest of us" said Melissia, as Doctor Victor nodded in acknowledgment, and took the plastic cup in his gloved hands.

It was a bit difficult to speak, what with all the decontamination gear on, hence why Doctor Victor had not spoken since putting on the suit, but was instead making sign language at them, in order to communicate his instructions to them all. "Good luck" said Samantha, in a nervous voice, as Doctor Victor, now fully kitted up in the hazmat suit, oxygen mask and goggles, turned and walked towards Misim's workshop door, through the decontamination chambers, and into the workshop itself, closing the workshop door behind him. The workshop looked the same as it always had been, but Doctor Victor realised that now everything in here was a lethal weapon, that could kill him with Covid if he touched anything. Misim himself, was lying on the camp bed in the corner, coughing slightly, his skin a chalk white colour, and looking as if he'd lost a lot of weight in a short period of time.

"Misim, it's Doctor Victor; can you hear me" asked Doctor Victor, as he knelt down beside the camp bed, putting a hand to Misim's face, before pulling back one of his eyelids, to check to see if Misim was able to hear him. Doctor Victor's voice was strangely muffled, due to all of the protective gear he was wearing, as if he was speaking into a plastic bag. "Yes" replied Misim, who's voice sounded very faint, as if he hadn't used it in years. "You've been infected with Covid Misim, but I'm going to install a cable in here which will allow you to chat with everyone outside of here, to save coming into contact and infecting anyone else" replied Doctor Victor, as he stepped away, and began to run the string cable with the cups on either end through the workshop and out into the farm yard. Doctor Victor finished securing the cables to the workshop, and headed back outside, closing the door behind him.

Immediately as Doctor Victor stepped outside, the decontamination chamber sprang into life, as he felt a strong jet of warm soapy water spraying him from head to toe. "Melissia and Samantha have really done their homework here" thought Doctor Victor, as he unzipped the decontamination chamber door flap, and stepped through it, zipping it back up behind him, giving a quick thumbs up to Samantha and Melissia who were standing several feet away. On seeing the thumbs up signal, both Melissa and Samantha immediately came forward and began to help Doctor Victor strip out of his hazmat gear that he was wearing. "It should all now be working and be able to speak with Misim directly" said Doctor Victor, when the oxygen mask had finally been removed. "How is Misim, is he ok" asked Brian, who had just come walking around the farm yard to see them, having completed his first single patrol of the farm's perimeter fence.

"It's as I thought, he's got a sore throat through coughing, white as a sheet and considerable weight loss; but this must be a new type of strain of Covid, as the weight loss doesn't usually start until later on down the line" explained Doctor Victor, as if he was back in his GP surgery and was speaking directly to a patient. Brian, Samantha and Melissia all looked confused, as they didn't believe that a second strain of Covid was even possible, the first strain having taken out most of the planet's population. "I don't understand, what does that mean exactly doc" asked Brian, posing the question that had to be said? "It means that Misim could have picked it up from another covid survivor out there somewhere, and that would mean he is not the first case, or patient zero as you might put it" explained Doctor Victor, as he gestured with his hand into the surrounding countryside.

"Is he going to die doc" asked Melissia, who sounded very worried now, as she had come to respect Misim since had arrived on Mile End Farm. "I honestly don't know Melissia, the early symptoms of Covid that we saw took weeks to come out into the open, and sometimes people could take weeks before they died; now, this seems to be more aggressive, and attacks faster than ever before" explained Doctor Victor, as they all now looked very scared, thinking the worst. If Misim really had been infected with a new strain of the Covid-19 virus, then the others within the community could possibly get very ill, very quickly. "Hello, is anyone there" came Misim voice, through the newly installed cup phone system. Everyone jumped, as they all scrambled to get nearer to the cup, which was now hanging on the side of the farm house. Doctor Victor was the first to reach the system, as he placed himself as close to the cup as possible.

"Misim, are you alright, it's Doctor Victor here" replied Doctor Victor, as the others strained their ears to listen. "Yes, I'm feeling a little light headed, and my stomach is hurting" replied Misim, as Doctor Victor took a deep breath, as if he was bracing himself for telling bad news to one of his patients. "Yes, I'm afraid we have to keep you isolated Misim, this isn't going to be easy to tell you, but you've been infected with Covid-19" replied Doctor Victor, as they heard Misim let out a little whimper. After a few seconds of silence, Misim spoke again; "Is it fatal doc, can I be saved"? "I can't be sure Misim, it appears to be a more violent strain this time as you've lost a lot of weight by the look of things" said Doctor Victor, as the others egged him on, feeling that encouragement was better than just giving Misim the facts. "But whatever you need, we will do our absolute best to help you".

"Well, I think it's time I confess, and ask for a request" replied Misim, as the others exchanged surprised looks. "I understand Misim, do you wish to speak alone, as Sam, Melissia and Brian are here with me; I can send them away if need be" asked Doctor Victor, but Misim quickly replied, "No, no I want them all to hear, you are all my friends, and you all have a right to know". Misim spoke with great determination in his voice, as he started to come to terms with his reality. Misim was certainly never going to be able to leave his workshop again, that was a fact that he had to accept. "We understand Misim, we'll listen to you, whatever you've got to say to us" said Samantha in a friendly voice, as Doctor Victor nodded in agreement, with Brian and Melissia both doing the same. Misim took a long slow deep breath, and then continued speaking, with the air of man dictating his obituary to a journalist.

"It may have been noticed by you all that I am gay; I had a boyfriend, but he died of Covid". "We're really sorry to hear that Misim, please carry on, get it all off your chest" replied Melissia in a smooth gentle voice, as Misim pressed on. "Well, I had suspected for some time now, that I may not be gay at all; I think, I might be transgender instead" replied Misim, as the others looked around at each other. "Aww Misim, it may be a new world, but you can still be whatever you like" replied Samantha, in the same style of voice as Mellissa. "What is that you need from us Misim, we can try and get you whatever you want" replied Doctor Victor, as they could hear Misim's breathing echoing into the plastic cup phone system. "Doc, if I am a dying man, then I would like one final request" asked Misim. "Of course, name whatever it is you desire Misim" replied Doctor Victor, as they stood in curiosity, wondering what Misim would want on his near deathbed.

There was a slight pause, and then Misim softly spoke, "I want to undergo Gender Reassignment Surgery; I want to become female". This latest statement from Misim was met with the longest silence yet, as everyone didn't know what to make of this information. Doctor

Victor, Samantha and Melissia all looked around at each in turn, all with exasperated looks on their faces, wondering what to do next. Out of all of the tasks they were expected to do up until this point, not a single one would be as hard as this one. For one thing, none of them, with the possible exception of Doctor Victor, knew anything about surgical procedures; and for another, how exactly we're they going to perform surgery on Misim without being able to touch him, or go anywhere near him without becoming infected, with what Doctor Victor believed, was a new far deadlier strain of the Covid-19 virus pathogen.

Not to mention, the lack of medical tools and equipment that they had on the farm itself, which were designed for first aid efforts, and not professional surgical procedures. Doctor Victor had come along with a small medical bag when he had first settled on Mile End Farm, but none of that equipment was geared up for a surgical procedure of that nature, with Doctor Victor thinking that he might as well use a swiss arm knife for a surgical procedure, for all the good it would have done. "Of course, Misim, we shall do whatever it takes to make that dream possible" replied Doctor Victor, as Samantha and Melissia looked at him in shock, wondering how Doctor Victor could have made such a silly empty head promise at a time like this. "We'll let you sleep now Misim; you must get your rest, and we can see how you are tomorrow" said Melissia, as she beckoned to the other two to follow her.

"Thank you, you all mean the world to me" replied Misim, his voice sounding a little faint again, as the others trudged back to the farm house, concerned and saddened looks on their faces, wondering if it was even possible that they could really do, what Misim had asked of them. "You told him he could have what" exclaimed Brian, back in the farm houses living room later that evening, as the others sat around him in the comfy armchairs, just as shocked as Samantha and Melissia had been, when Doctor Victor had made him the promise to do the surgery on him. "Misim wants gender reassignment surgery, to those who don't know what that is, it means a sex change" explained Doctor

227

Victor, as most of the adults had heard of one, but the kids were not as well educated as the adults were and so required enlightening on this rather delicate of medical subjects.

"Honestly, are they not teaching anything medical to kids these days" exclaimed Doctor Victor, a little put out at the lack of medical knowledge that was reflected back to him in every face around the room. "With all due respects doc, me and Samantha, and even Trevor were all educated under section twenty-eight; LGBT matters weren't even discussed when we were at school, so gender reassignment wasn't something I knew about until my police college days" explained Julie, as Samantha and Trevor nodded in agreement, remembering the very clear lack of anything gender related in their school days. "Well, I for one, think it's excellent; the man is expressing his true self; and we should honour that, seeing as if it's his dying wish" said Melissia, who spoke in a proud speechlike way, feeling like she was the leader of a world-famous political party as she spoke.

"No one is doubting that Melissia, not at all; but it still doesn't get around the problem of how it would be done" replied Brian, who still looked exasperated, wondering how they were supposed to perform surgery on a man who they couldn't even touch without becoming incredibly sick. "I do see Brian's point; yes, Misim is now very much contaminated with Covid-19; even a so much as slightly brushing against his skin, touching any objects he's touched, or even any spit particles that would come from his mouth by speaking, would be enough to get us all infected" explained Doctor Victor, as if he was standing in front of a crowd of students in a lecture hall in a university campus. They all sat in silence for a little while, pondering Doctor Victor's explanation of the situation they were facing. In a normal situation, Misim would have been put on a waiting list and then be seen by a specialist surgeon, but there was certainly none of that now.

"But we've all been exposed to him doc; I mean he's been breathing the same air as us, eating at the same table, working in the same environment; he was even in close proximity to Julie when he was making adjustments to her wedding dress for crying out loud, and none of us are showing any symptoms at all" exclaimed Trevor, who got a weak smile off of Julie as she had a fleeting memory of what Trevor had just described. "I'm not denying that Trevor, but we do still need to keep an eye on the situation, as if this is a new strain, then this whole farm could be out of limits for everyone for weeks, if not permanently, and we would never be able to leave here every again" explained Doctor Victor, a serious air to his voice as he spoke, thinking to himself that maybe the others in the community weren't taking him as seriously as he would have hoped.

"Well, usually on this occasion it would be my call, I am the head of the Flintstone community after all; however, under the circumstances, I have to default to a higher power; it's all down to you now doc" explained Brian, who sounded exhausted from the day's activities, as he looked at Doctor Victor. Doctor Victor put his hands together, and pressed his fingers to his face, thinking hard. After a few seconds, he lowered his hands away from his face and spoke, "it can be done, that much I should be able to do". "That's fantastic doc" began Samantha, but Doctor Victor quickly waved her down to silence her. "However, I swore a Socratic oath to protect and heal anyone and everyone who came to me for help; as long as we use precautions, and as long as it is done properly, there is no reason why any of us should have to fear anything" said Doctor Victor, as Brian put his hands together too, to show that he was thinking as well.

"Ok, I think that settles it, we're going for surgery" replied Brian, as the others seemed to brighten up a little at the sound of it, thinking that maybe Misim's hopes of living the rest of his life in happiness were greater than they had first thought. "Well said" chimed Julie and Melissia in unison. "Here here" said Samantha, sounding more like a parliamentary Politian as she said this. "Asking a very silly question doc, but I presume you've done a gender reassignment surgical procedure before now" asked Trevor, as Doctor Victor looked a little sheepish at this point. "To tell you the truth Trevor, no I haven't; but I did study anatomy after all, so it can't be too difficult to pick up" replied Doctor Victor, sounding a little more confident as he spoke, as Trevor smiled at him in a positive way. "Always do what the doctor orders" thought Samantha, as she remembered back in her childhood, when she had been afraid about going to the doctors for anything.

"So, what do you need then doc, we should be able to rustle some bits up for you, or improvise with anything if need be" said Brian, as Doctor Victor began to explain what would be needed for Misim's surgery. "The local hospital in Northampton will have all of the tools, scalpels, needles and the like; they will all need to be soaked in boiling water to sterilise them before the surgery; as for the place to do the surgery itself, it will need to be a flat surface, well lit, and with a way of keeping the patient subdued, while we do the surgery itself" explained Doctor Victor, as he listed the items and tasks off on his fingers. "There's quite a bit of kit in the back of the goddess, so feel free to have a look doc if you like" said Samantha, as Doctor Victor thanked her for mentioning the equipment stored in the container onboard the Green Goddess.

"Not sure about any drugs and gas or anything doc, might be worth a trip down to Northampton General Hospital to see if you can find any" replied Brian, who was thinking quickly about what stocks of things there were stored in the many barns and sheds dotted around the farm. "I'd bring back whatever you can; you'll need a rota of who watches over Misim between now and the surgery, just to make sure there is no change in his vital signs" explained Doctor Victor. "I can do that if you like" piped up Samantha, who put her hand slightly into the air, as if she was answering a question in a school classroom. "Well volunteered Sam, I will need to know immediately if his condition changes in any way" said Doctor Victor, as Brian began delegating other duties out to everyone else, feeling that the Flintstone community was really starting to work properly as a team for the first time.

And so, the following morning, they were all awake very early, as the sun had only just started to rise, so that it was just about light enough to see what they were all doing, seeing to the tasks that they had all been set. Melissia, Julie and Charlotte had all volunteered to go into Northampton with the Land Rover, attempting to bring back all of the equipment Doctor Victor had requested on a hurriedly scribbled list the evening beforehand. The list had been pinned to the Land Rover's windscreen, and was surprisingly filled with every single item when they returned to Mile End Farm a few hours later. A point had been made that none of them were to leave the farm owing to the risk of contamination. However, this problem had soon been fixed, as Melissia, Julie, and even Charlotte, had all left wearing protective gear, so as not to come into contact with anyone, or anything else, outside of Mile End Farm.

Brian was a little put out that Julie had been forced to ram the Land Rover into the hospitals main sliding doors in order to get them to open, but at least he seemed to forget about it fairly quickly. "There rugged old things Land Rovers, it'll survive, never fear" said Brian, as he surveyed the damage with a closer look, seeing a dent or two in the bull bars and chipped paintwork. But if anyone was to be given points for ingenuity, it would have been young Charlotte, who according to Melissia, had managed to climb in through a partially open, air-conditioning duct, before then clambering down into a locked store room, where the required gas canisters that Doctor Victor had requested were being housed, before then opening the locked door from the other side. Thanks to Charlotte's wonderfully small size, she was able to perform this with ease, something sadly that Julie and Melissia could not.

It came as no surprise therefore, that Charlotte was pleased to hear that for her actions that day, she was to be given extra rations of food that night. After all, Charlotte had just performed a task that none of the others could do. Elsewhere on the farm, Doctor Victor had managed to find a suitable place from where to conduct the main surgical procedure itself, which was to be done in the same barn where Julie and Trevor's wedding had been held only days earlier. It's residents, which included the combine harvester, tractor and assorted other equipment linked to them, were temporarily moved out, so as to make room for the lights and operating table which would be required by Doctor Victor and the others. Isaac, Suresh and Charlie had been kept busy mucking out all of the dirt, that had made its way in through the open barn doors, as Doctor Victor had instructed, needing the surgery room to be as clean as they could make it.

Isaac, Charlie, Suresh and Charlotte, though being children living a modern life before Covid, had adapted very well to life on Mile End Farm, as Brian was kind enough to point out after they had finished that day's work. "Many hands make light work" said Brian cheerfully, as Samantha debriefed the group from her medical watch that day. "Misim has been given some food today, and should have his main strength up and running for the surgery tomorrow" explained Samantha, as Doctor Victor tapped her on the shoulder to congratulate her on a good day's work. "Sam has done well, but I will need to select my surgical team for tomorrow" said Doctor Victor as he paced around the room. "Who have you chosen doc" asked Trevor, as Doctor Victor continued. "I want Samantha, Julie and Melissia in the surgery room with me; this frees up everyone else for farm yard duties elsewhere".

There was a collective gulping sound from Samantha, Julie and Melissia, as comprehension dawned on them about what Doctor Victor was expecting them to do. "You three should follow my lead, I did do surgery in the past; not as much as I'd liked to do, but still enough for me to learn the basics" replied Doctor Victor, gesturing with his finger around at Samantha, Julie and Melissia, in a way which told them of the seriousness of what they were about to do the following day. All three of them slept a little less comfortably as they liked that night, fearing of the task ahead of them the following day. For one thing, none of them had been anywhere near a hospital surgery before, let alone handled surgical equipment. Samantha was more used to the steering wheel of a lorry, and even Julie admitted that she was far more used to handling sharp objects wrapped inside evidence bags, than handling surgical scapples.

Only Melissia, with her years of working with barber's scissors and combs, could possibly even begin to understand what Doctor Victor could need from them all. The following morning dawned, sending a chill for the first time over the Flintstone community since they had been formed. They had all slept a little less comfortably that night then what they would have liked, many of them being very nervous about the surgery ahead of them. "Without electricity and power, I would not be able to do this; we'll have to almost comatose Misim in order to get him ready" explained Doctor Victor, as he, along with Samantha, Julie and Melissia, all geared themselves up into military grade bio hazmat suits, with thick boots and gloves, all part of the stockpile of equipment that Samantha had been given by Fredrick back at RAF North Lakes, which all resided inside the container behind the Green Goddess.

All four of them looked very strange as they stood there, wearing heavily protective biohazard gear, as they stood facing each other, their faces slightly squashed inside the suits. "Coming in with the tape now" said Isaac, as he, Charlie and Suresh walked slowly around, gaffer tapping up all of the gaps in the gloves, boots and zips on the hazmat suits. It did feel very strange, as if all four of them were being tapped into giant supermarket plastic bags, feeling like they were being slowly suffocated as they went. "Ok, all ready to go everyone" said Suresh a second or so later, as Doctor Victor gave them the thumbs up, as Isaac, Suresh and Charlie all retreated to a safe distance. "When we come out, start spraying inside the tent immediately" said Doctor Victor, his voice sounding a little distorted through his suit, as all three boys nodded to show that they had understood Doctor Victor's instructions, taking up their positions, manning the water hoses.

The four-hazmat suited team, slowly started to walk forwards into the tent, as Melissia zipped up the plastic door as she went.

"When we go in, don't worry too much about what is touched, as we will decontaminate when we are back in this tent; we will begin to administer the anastatic once we have made sure Misim is breathing well, and we can then move him into theatre to operate" said Doctor Victor, as he placed his hand on Misim's workshop door handle. "Ready when you are doc" said Samantha, her voice too a little distorted, as Doctor Victor pushed down on the door handle, as it swung slowly open, creaking slightly as it went.

CHAPTER SIXTEEN

The Surgery

The workshop looked the same as it had done the first time that they had discovered Misim had Covid, however, the temperature inside the workshop had certainly dropped since the last time that they were all inside of it several days ago, where Julie was being fitted up for her wedding dress. "The temperature is reading twelve degrees doc" said Julie, her voice also distorted, as she read off of an old-fashioned thermometer, which was gaffer tapped to her right arm, the red mercury liquid inside of it suddenly dropping sharply as they all entered the workshop. Julie had after all, volunteered to be the equipment carrier for the team, with the outside of her hazmat suit looked more like a human Swiss army knife, carrying all the equipment in the utility belt that she was wearing around her waist, whilst other gauges hung around the suit, giving the others something to keep an eye on.

Misim was lying on his camp bed, looking a little tired, with a small sweat patch breaking out on his forehead, his eyes appearing to go in and out of focus as he took long slow breaths. "It's alright Misim, it's Melissia, we're going to prep you for surgery" explained Melissia, as Misim made to jump up at them, but Samantha held Misim back to stop him from touching any of them. "Everything is going to be fine Misim, we're going to administer the anastatic now, so you need to stay as still as you can" replied Doctor Victor. Julie moved forward at that moment, and inserted a very small needle into his arm, which was connected to a syringe, full of same strange clear liquid. "I've administered the anastatic doc" said Julie, as she stood back up again, keeping her eyes fixed solely on Misim as she did so. Within seconds of Julie stepping backwards, Misim's body began to convulse and shake, as if he was being electrocuted.

Samantha, Melissia and Julie all stepped backwards in alarm, as Doctor Victor stepped forward, keeping a close eye on Misim as he went. "It's alright, I did a little work on the formula last night, so it's a bit more powerful than any other types of anastatic" explained Doctor Victor, who had not jumped backwards, or looked shocked. In fact, he had that sort of look on his face that clearly stated 'I was expecting this to happen'. Immediately after Misim had begun to convulse, he stopped moving, and lay quite motionless on the camp bed, his breathing steady and in time with his heartbeat. "Alright everyone, let's move him out of here into the theatre" said Doctor Victor, as Julie, Samantha and Melissia all moved forward very slowly, their suits rustling slightly as they walked, knocking things aside as they went if it blocked or impeded their journey in any way.

Julie positioned herself behind Misim's head, whilst Samantha had grabbed hold of Misim's feet, with Melissia and Doctor Victor both supporting Misim on either side, so it almost looked like Misim was being carried in a blanket after jumping from a burning building. They only just made it out of the open doorway, straight into the decontamination tent outside, as immediately after Doctor Victor had closed the door to Misim's workshop, a shower of water gushed down from the ceiling, as the shower hoses sprang into action, operated by Isaac, Charlie and Suresh. They all ducted slightly, as not only was the water very hot, but it was also coming out with tremendous force, nearly knocking them off their feet. At least the four of them were wearing protective clothes, but Misim who wasn't protected by any type of suits whatsoever, was soaked through, and getting a face full of water at the same time.

After around five seconds or so, Doctor Victor signalled to the boys outside to turn off the water supply, and then signalled at them to stand clear, as they were coming out from the decontamination tent. Isaac, Charlie and Suresh all did what they were told, retreating to where the others were all standing around seven metres away or so, as this is what Doctor Victor had ordered for them to do during that morning's farm briefing. Using her free hand, Melissia managed to bend down, and unzip the plastic tent flap curtain, as they all moved slowly across the yard, carrying Misim between them, only just been kept clear of the ground by a few inches or so. The rest of the community all looked on, all with worried looks on their faces, as they watched Doctor Victor, Julie, Samantha and Melissia supporting Misim, slowly crossing the farm yard, heading for the main barn, where the theatre had been set up for the operation.

"I do hope he's going to be ok, and that it all works out for him" said Brian, as the others nodded in agreement, praying to themselves that everything was going to be alright, and that Misim was going to pull through it all. They all heard a creak and a snap, as the huge barn doors were closed shut, locking Misim and the others inside the barn for the surgery. "Well, back to work everyone, there's nothing more we can do now" called Brian to everyone around him, as they went about their business on the farm, still hoping that it would be a success. Inside the barn meanwhile, lights flickered on, making the dark barn suddenly ablaze with artificial light. Misim lay on the makeshift operating table, head laying softly on a pillow, with a tube inserted into his mouth and nose, following a steady beeping noise, in time with his heartbeat, as the sounds emitted from the small life support machine stationed just behind Misim's head.

"The patient is stable, and ready for surgery, please bring forward the scapples" said Doctor Victor, as the others gathered around the operating table, following through Doctor Victor's instructions. "Pulse and heartbeat are steady doc" replied Melissia, as she stood up near to Misim's head, keeping her eyes on the heartrate monitor screen. "Very good, scapple please Samantha" replied Doctor Victor, as Samantha handed Doctor Victor one of the scapples from the tray, where they had been sterilised earlier on that day. Doctor Victor's hands shook slightly, as he stood there, holding the scapple in his gloved hands. He'd even begun to sweat inside of his suit, as droplets could be seen building up on the plastic screen in front of his face. Samantha, Julie and Melissia all seemed to notice this, as Melissia leaned forward and gently took Doctor Victor's free hand, before giving it a friendly squeeze.

"You can do this doc; I know you can; we're all behind you" said Samantha, in a reassuring voice, as the others nodded in agreement, there suits making rustling sounds as they moved. "Thank you Melissia, it's been a while since I was doing this" replied Doctor Victor. "At least you know more about this than we all do doc; I never thought in a million years I'd be doing gender reassignment surgery wearing a military grade hazmat suit" said Samantha in a jokey voice, as the other chuckled slightly. Even Doctor Victor couldn't help but crack a smile at Samantha's words, feeling that if Samantha and the others were being positive about this, then he should be as well. "Very well, I see what you mean Sam; let's get this over and done with" replied Doctor Victor, as he moved in to create the first incision with the scapple, Misim giving the odd occasional twitch of the eye as each minute ticked by.

The hours went by slowly, with Doctor Victor making incision after incision, first asking for one scapple, then a needle, then for other tools along the way. The clock that the others had placed on the wall a few days earlier, ticked slowly away, only just being audible over the heart rate monitor and life support machines that were beeping away in the background. Under normal circumstances, there would usually be a whole room full of surgeons, able to assist Doctor Victor, but that wasn't the case now. This surgery was being performed by a forensic pathologist, a police officer, a lorry driver and a hairdresser; if anyone had been joking at this point, they would have said that it was the makings of a bad nursery rhyme, and something very much reserved for the whelms of fiction. As they worked, Misim continued to remain stationary, with the odd occasional twitch from his eyes as they all worked away.

Even though Julie, who everyone had believed would be the best when it came to seeing blood, turned a nasty shade of green, and even turned away, when Doctor Victor began to open up a cavity where Misim's genitals would have been, in order to create a channel for the Urethra. It later transpired that although Julie had gone to murder scenes and the like as part of her role as a police officer, it turns out that she had not been able to hold her nerve at times. "Believe me, the first time I was called to a scene involving a dead body, I went outside and threw up in a nearby drain" said Julie, as she winced slightly, seeing Doctor Victor conducting the surgery. "But surely you got used to it as time went on Julie" replied Samantha, as Julie turned to look at Samantha, a little shocked, as Julie was under the impression that Samantha knew about Julie's squeamishness when it came to the sight of blood.

"Well, I sort of did, and I didn't; my Superintendent didn't reprimand me for throwing up in a drain while on the job, but it was still pretty nasty what had happened at the scene" replied Julie, as even Doctor Victor paused slightly. "It's never nice Julie, I should know and I feel your pain; I spent years as a forensic pathologist before Covid, and some of the bodies they brought in were pretty nasty at times" replied Doctor Victor, as none of them looked surprised to hear this. "Jack of all trades then doc" replied Samantha in a casual voice. "You could say that Sam, seen a lot of death in my time, so was always used to it; but I want to give Misim this chance to be who he wants to be, before he's gone from this world" said Doctor Victor, with such determination in his voice, it stopped any other conversations stone dead. None of them had ever heard Doctor Victor speak like this before, and they didn't sound like they wanted to question him.

Quite out of the blue however, Julie spoke up. "My first ever crime scene I went to, it was a murder of a middle-aged Asian man, but he'd clearly been held in the house against his will for some time, as when we found the body, it was tied to a chair and had slash wounds all over it, as if it was a racially motivated crime". "That's barbaric" replied Melissia in response to Julie's statement. "That's what I told myself, but my inspector told me, that was the nature of the job, finding and having to deal with stuff like that, maybe not all the time, but still on occasions" replied Julie, as she recounted memories from her police days of dealing with all kinds of criminals and criminality. This latest statement from Julie had even made Samantha and Mellissa go a bit green, as they wouldn't have been used to seeing scenes like the one Julie had described on a daily basis.

"We're almost done, a couple more stitches and the surgery is complete" said Doctor Victor, as he threaded a needle and length of cotton thread down between Misim legs. Misim's new Urethra was certainly impressive, as even Samantha could help but comment to Doctor Victor that it looked better than her own one. This latest comment from Samantha caused a great amount of muffled giggling from Melissia and Julie, as they turned a little pink with embarrassment. Doctor Victor hadn't seen or heard this however, having the same suit on as they all did, it had somewhat blunted his hearing; but it may have also been to do with the fact that he was monitoring Misim as Samantha had spoken. Misim seemed to have come through the surgery, with no problems to speak of, only that they had all seen Misim's eyes flicker a number of times, but then soon relaxed when he was pumped with a little more anastatic.

"We can remove the breathing tube now, and retreat to a safe distance, allowing Misim to wake up naturally" said Doctor Victor, as he turned to face the others, going back into senior practitioner mode. "Ok doc" they all said in unison, as all four of them walked slowly outside, opening and then closing the barn door as they went. Once they had stepped through it, they were suddenly being soaked in steaming hot water, which made them all recall, as the same decontamination tent which had washed them earlier, now did so again, as it had been moved into the new position by everyone outside of the barn. Just as before, the shower heads positioned above them, stopped pouring water, as Doctor Victor unzipped the plastic tent flap and the four of them stepped slowly outside. Immediately as they did so, they were greeted with a round of applause, as everyone in the community had come to welcome them back outside.

"I don't ever want to go through that ever again" Melissia was heard to exclaim, as she was aided out of her hazmat suit by Brian and the others. Julie and Samantha had already removed their suits, and was helping Doctor Victor with his, using a Stanley knife to cut through the industrial strength gaffer tape which lined the cracks and spaces in the suits where the gloves would be. "Well, I'm going to lie, that was certainly the most nerve-racking thing I have ever done in my life, and that includes my first ever post mortem" remarked Doctor Victor, once his suit had been removed, and he was able to breath and speak more properly again. "You were amazing in their doc, I knew you could do it" said Julie, as she, Samantha and Melissia all clapped him on the back. Despite being quite a strong man, Doctor Victor couldn't help but sway a little, as the others clapped him on the back as well.

"You all did really well in there, how is Misim, is he stable" asked Brian, who had just come level to them, having watched the surgery team come out of the barn, and gone through decontamination. "He is, but we must keep him isolated and let him wake up naturally, he's going to be weak for a few days, but as long as we keep him supplied with food and water, he'll stay in a stable condition; in the meantime, we keep an eye on him, just in case anything changes" replied Doctor Victor in answer to Brian's question. Julie had gone to re-join Trevor, as they both walked away sharing a kiss and a cuddle, Trevor doing to his best not to pry Julie for details of what had happened during the surgery. Melissia was also now talking to everyone else about what had gone on within the barn during the surgery, feeling like a bit of a modern-day celebrity. Samantha on the other hand, felt like she didn't want to talk to anyone,

241

or do anything social at the moment.

It was now the early evening time, and Samantha had decided that she wanted to go for a walk around the farm, so while everyone was distracted, Samantha slipped away unnoticed. The sun was beginning to drop in the sky, and she could see moths, bats and even small insects begin to fly low all around her. Samantha stood in the mild spring evening air, having taken a walk up to one of the far fields on the farm, to gaze out across the horizon. From Samantha's viewpoint, she could see some of the high buildings of Northampton spreading before her in the background, and even the wind farm fields, all them tall and white, but without moving, as their parts would have seized through lack of service and maintenance. Without realising she was doing it, Samantha had sunken to her knees in the field, and began to cry her eyes out, having become overcome with shock and pressure of what she had just done.

Samantha must have sobbed out the equivalent of the River Thames in tears, as she allowed her emotions to come pouring out of her, without stopping to think for even a second whether anyone could see or hear her. As Samantha sobbed, thoughts of all of the people who she had seen killed by Covid, friends, family; and even Greg and Diana's faces swam in front of her. "I'll always be there for you babes, always" came Greg's voice from inside her head. "You're the best friend Sam, the best" came Diana's voice, after Greg's voice had faded away into obscurity. After what felt like an age, Samantha pulled herself up onto her feet, and just casually stood there, her hands on her hips, sniffling slightly as she felt her eyes watering and stinging slightly. Life on Mile End Farm within the Flintstone Community, was certainly turning out to be far more interesting, than Samantha could have ever imagined it would be.

What with one thing and another, Samantha felt very much that if she written all of this down in a non-fiction book, that no one would read it, as it would sound too far-fetched and unbelievable for words. "I wondered whether I'd find you up here" came Brian's voice from behind her, as Samantha jumped out of her skin and span around in shock so violently, that she felt as if Brian had just shot her with a taser stun gun. Feeling a little embarrassed by this, Samantha quickly wiped away the tears from her eyes, and tried to look pleased to see Brian, her hair blowing around slightly in the gentle breeze now whipping their faces. Brian was indeed standing there, twelve bore farmers shot gun slung over his shoulder, smiling at the site of Samantha, who felt a little abashed to see him, still wanting secretly to be left alone. "Brian, I'm sorry, you scared me" replied Samantha, as Brian chuckled slightly.

"I was a little worried that you might have accidently tripped the fence and got a shock off it, you've been up here for ages now" replied Brian, as he came and stood beside Samantha, looking out over the fields towards the outskirts of Northampton. "I just needed a walk, I wasn't expecting what I was going to see with Misim and everything" replied Samantha, as Brian placed an arm around her shoulder, before giving it a quick squeeze. "You've got nothing to fear, believe me, we've all had trauma that we will never be able to shake off" replied Brian, speaking to Samantha in the same way that a father and daughter would converse together, as if it was a personal issue of theirs. "I take it you didn't come up here to gaze at Northampton" responded Brian, who seemed to have read Samantha's mind, as Brian always gave off that orea of a man who knew far more about other people than what he was prepared to let on.

Samantha had indeed come up to this point on the farm to think over a plan that she was hatching, but hadn't had a lot of time to think about it, owing to the demanding nature of working on Mile End Farm. Samantha had certainly come to the reality, that she couldn't stay on Mile End Farm forever, however peaceful the Flintstone community seemed to be towards her and Julie since they had arrived. Samantha knew that Greg and Diana were still out there somewhere, maybe even trying to find her themselves, although any chances of finding Samantha on a farm surrounded by an electric fence where very slim, if not non-existent. And there was even the mystery of the pamphlet, which had pointed in the direction of this Grey's Pharmaceuticals company. "How did you know what I'm thinking" asked Samantha, completely in shock, wondering

243

how Brian had pulled off this act of sixth sense magic.

"Because I've stood in a place exactly like where you are now, and thought about leaving too" replied Brian, who winked slightly at Samantha. "Ok, I want to know now; how the hell did you know I was thinking about leaving" demanded Samantha, as she was so shocked, she took a step backwards from Brian in alarm. "Samantha my darling, I have been around for over sixty years now; I have gained many life experiences in my time and I can tell what a person is thinking just from their facial expressions, and other assorted body language" replied Brian, as Samantha giggled slightly, realising that Brian after all was well over twice her own age. "You still sound like a mind reader to me, it gives me the shivers" replied Samantha, as Brian laughed at Samantha sarcasm, having come to terms with the fact that Samantha was still classed as a young person in the world's eyes.

"Well, I have been known for that too" replied Brian, in a jokey style voice, before he then finished, "if you want to leave Samantha, I can't stop you, and you'd be welcomed back here at any time, you know that". Samantha couldn't help but crack a weak smile when she heard this, wiping her eyes with her hands as Brian spoke. "Thanks Brian, I want to stay here of course, but I need to find my friends; Greg, Diana, their still out there somewhere, maybe expecting me to find them; and the company that the doc found on the pamphlet, could have some answers to everything that's going on" replied Samantha, as Brian slowly nodded in agreement as Samantha spoke, understanding Samantha's position. "You know we would always help you Sam, whatever may happen" said Brian, as Samantha flicked her hair out of her eyes due to the small breeze blowing it into them.

"Come on, I wouldn't stand up here to long into the evening, the midges and other things will eat you alive with their bites" replied Brian, as Samantha let out a small laugh, and then walked with Brian back across the fields towards the farm house. It slowly dawned on Samantha, that she had been a bit silly; she should have consulted the others after all, rather than coming up here to the top field, and breaking down. "So, I know some of you will be shocked to hear this, but I'm leaving the Flintstone community" explained Samantha, back in the farm house kitchen an hour or so later. It was about ten o clock in the evening by this time, as darkness had now completely fallen outside, as the night time generators had kicked in to power the farm houses power systems. The looks on the others faces had been quite surprised, as they had all expected them all to stick together for the rest of time.

"Blimey", was the response that came from Trevor, Isaac, Suresh, Charlie and Melissia. Charlotte had gone to bed as she had been quite tired from that day's work. Julie looked on with understanding in her eyes, as she had been with Samantha from the start, but it was only Doctor Victor that had that facial expression which showed understanding. "I know where you want to go" replied Doctor Victor, as the others turned to look at him, wondering if Doctor Victor had the same sixth sense for emotions as Brian did. "Where would Sam go doc" was the reply of Trevor, who'd only been practically listening to the events of what had happened to Samantha since she had found out about the pamphlet. "Samantha is going to Grey's Pharmaceuticals" replied Doctor Victor, as there was a stunned silence that went around the room after Doctor Victor had finished speaking.

"Why the hell would you want to go there for" replied Melissia, after a few seconds, but it was Julie who responded before Samantha could. "Because Sam believes that Grey's Pharmaceuticals, aka the company, potentially knows what happened to her friends, and they may even know what is really going on with the pamphlet that was sent to her boyfriend before Covid broke out" replied Julie, as everyone looked back at Samantha, now with sympathy on their faces. "Aww Sam, of course you should go, if these people know what happened to your friends, then you should get answers" replied Melissia, as Samantha gave them all a respectful look, feeling a wave of gratitude towards them all for understanding her need to leave Mile End Farm in order to find Greg, and even Diana if she was still alive as well. It had never occurred to

245

Samantha for even a second, that either of them could be dead already, but Samantha always said she would sense it.

But even so, the task ahead was incredibly daunting, as Samantha would be putting herself out into the new world again for the first time since leaving Lillington, away from the protection of Mile End Farm. It was time to commence, Operation, Infiltration.

CHAPTER SEVENTEEN

Operation Infiltration

"The real problem is getting inside; the main building complex in its time had top level security, and there were at least four levels to the building, three above and one below; plus, there's a series of science labs and clean rooms towards the centre and at the back of the building" explained Doctor Victor, as he found a pen and a piece of paper, and began to sketch the layout to the Grey's Pharmaceuticals complex. This was about the most useful information as Samantha could get, as she knew full well that she couldn't just Google it on a computer or on her phone, as there was no internet anymore. "I'm going to need to know as much as I can about the surrounding countryside doc, as I can keep the Green Goddess in a field somewhere, using her as a base of operations, doing scouting trips to and from the main complex, monitoring things from a distance" explained Samantha, sounding just like the military general that she had imagined in her mind.

This sudden thought of a military general commanding troops in battle, gave Samantha a sudden rush of gratitude towards her now late father, who had shown her tricks and tips of how to stay alive during the camping trips that they had done while on holiday when Samantha was a teenager. "If memory serves, there is a farm which backs onto the building, depending on whether the farm was occupied or not, you could park the Green Goddess in the fields, and then work from there" replied Doctor Victor, quickly drawing a box off of his original 2D sketch, showing the farm and where it was in relation to the Grey's Pharmaceuticals building. "Can you see the farm from the windows on the main building doc" asked Brian who had a pondering look on his face, as if something was bugging him somehow, but no one knew what it was, as Brian did seem to do quite a bit of thinking these days.

"Not that I know of; but I do remember seeing a lot of hedges around those fields at the back, so that would be a good cover for the Green Goddess, should you be able to go to that farm and park in the fields" replied Doctor Victor, as Samantha pondered all of the information before her. "I hope you all understand why I'm having to do this" said Samantha, as everyone immediately came to Samantha's aid, making Samantha feel suddenly overwhelmed by the support. "We do understand you Sam, it's important to you, and we respect that one hundred percent" said Trevor, as the others nodded in agreement. They all continued to plan Operation Infiltration for the rest of the evening, as the clock on the wall ticked slowly by, getting later and later, although no one felt remotely tired. Samantha sat at the kitchen table late into the night, as the others around her drifted off to bed, wishing her all the best for the following day.

Samantha was so absorbed in her own thoughts, that she hadn't noticed that Julie had come over to her, and sat down in the opposite chair at the kitchen table. Samantha jumped when she saw Julie was there, but soon recovered, as Julie seemed a little startled that she had scared Samantha. "I just wanted you to know Sam, that I'm staying here; I know I've been coming with you up until this point, but I've found my life here now with Trevor and the others" explained Julie, as Samantha looked confused, wondering why Julie was telling her this. "Don't worry Julie, I already knew that; when we first met, we said we'd travel together until you'd found a nice farm to settle on, and now you've found it" replied Samantha in a sooth calm voice, as she took Julie's hand and gave it a squeeze. Julie fell silent for a few seconds, as Samantha continued to look at her, as if she was a long-lost friend who had come back to her after so many years.

"No, I did suspect that, it was just that we'd become such good friends and I thought you'd want to stay here, rather than trying to find Greg and Diana, as they could be anywhere, if there even still alive" replied Julie, as if she too was secretly thinking what Samantha was thinking about whether it was worth chasing after two people, that Samantha didn't even know were still alive or not. "I know they are; I would feel something if I knew they weren't" replied Samantha, with conviction in her voice, sheerly determined to not give up, no matter what. After all, Greg and Diana weren't in Lillington, so if they weren't there, then they had to be still alive. Julie looked a little sheepish, but Samantha soon replied with, "oh I'm coming back, I'm just leaving to find Greg and Diana; once I've found them, I'll bring them back here to the community and the farm, and we can live out the rest of our lives in peace away from the rest of the world".

"I get that Sam, what I'm worried about is the stalkers; they must still be watching the farm after all" said Julie, as Samantha suddenly looked surprised, and a little abashed at this. Samantha after all, had been so busy planning on how to get Grey's Pharmaceuticals and set up an observation point nearby to the company, that'd she completely forgotten about their stalkers, who even now, after a few weeks of being on Mile End Farm, could still be sitting out there, waiting for them to emerge from their place of sanctuary. But then, Samantha was struck by an idea, as Julie seemed to clock this sudden change in facial expression on Samantha's face. "What's up Sam" asked Julie, as Samantha suddenly spoke up. "If Devises is the C.E.O, he will be expecting me to come up to Grey's anyway" replied Samantha, as Julie suddenly looked shocked, realising what Samantha meant.

"But they would be working on the basis that you wouldn't have worked out that the pamphlet was the company's property, or some sort of calling card for it" said Julie, as Samantha run a hand through her hair, breathing in and out slowly as she did so, sounding as if she was hyperventilating in slow motion into a giant brown paper bag. "Well, whatever happens, there's only one way to find out; I have to go there" replied Samantha, in an also determined voice, as if there was no other choice in the matter. Julie didn't say anything, but gave Samantha a weak smile, stood up, and then walked around the table until she was level with Samantha's shoulder. "I know you'll do what's right, and I'll always support you whatever that may be" replied Julie, giving Samantha's shoulder a little squeeze as she did, acting like the reassuring parent in a child's difficult situation.

"Thanks Julie, you're the best" said Samantha, as Julie bid her goodnight, proceeding towards the staircase in the hallway, as her feet echoed slightly on the stairs as Julie climbed them, heading towards hers and Trevor's bedroom. In fact, Julie was standing in the farm yard, as Edward Fitzgerald held a small pistol to the back of Julie's head. Samantha stood there, with her hands held in front of her, trying to reason with Edward Fitzgerald, who looked manic and deranged, like the psychopath that he was, teeth bared, as if he felt as if the whole world was against him, but still with the satisfaction of a hunter who has just cornered their prey. "This is my revenge bitch, for you smashing up my truck" shouted Edward, as Julie began to cry in fear, as she could feel the cold metal of Edward's pistol on the back of her head, feeling that her life was about to end in the empty and lonely farm yard before her.

"Don't shoot Edward, she's my friend, you're not a killer" pleaded Samantha, sounding terrified as she spoke, fearing that her words would do nothing to stop Edward from ending Julie's life in one swift stroke. "You think that's going to stop me, say goodbye, Bonham" snarled

Edward, as he thrust his hand forwards, shoving Julie to the ground, whilst at the same time taking aim straight at Samantha's forehead. There was a sudden bang like a gunshot, as Samantha heard a whizzing sound cut rapidly through the air, as if the bullet that was meant for Julie, was now streaming straight towards her instead. Samantha looked down, and had only just about enough time to hear the scream that came from Julie, who had rolled over on the floor, surveying the scene in front of her. Samantha looked down, and could see a clean round hole in her chest, and knew that Edward had shot her at point blank range.

Blood began to ooze out of the clean round hole in Samantha's chest, as she felt herself start to feel weaker and weaker, Julie's screams echoing in her ears. Samantha woke with a start, as she suddenly found that her plan that was drawn for her by Doctor Victor, was stuck to her face, her head resting on the kitchen table, where Samantha had fallen asleep the night beforehand. "Thank god it was only a dream, but it seemed so real" thought Samantha, as she heard the sounds of Brian coming down the stairs. "Morning Sam, I'm surprised you chose the table to sleep on, it would be much more comfortable on the cab bunk bed I would have thought" said Brian, as Samantha seemed to start slightly at the sound of his voice, not being as fully awake as she had liked. "Oh yes, sorry about that Brian" replied Samantha, a little more slowly than normal, still a little sleepy, looking down at her chest, as if she was expecting to see a gaping bullet wound there.

"So, today's the day eh, you getting back on the road after weeks being here; hope the Green Goddess can still work" said Brian, as Samantha gave him a weak smile, feeling pleased that she was not nursing an injury, or had blood pouring out of her chest. "Yeah, and I wanted to thank you for being there for me Brian, and for taking me and Julie in" replied Samantha, as Brian waved a hand around in front of Samantha, busying himself with the kettle and teabags as he went. "Oh, it was no bother at all Sam, but I know you're coming back, and you'll be bringing others with you, so the more the merrier, so it's not good bye after all" replied Brian, as Samantha perked up a bit, realising that Brian was the unopposed leader of the Flintstone community, so if he agreed to have more people within the Flintstone community at Mile End Farm, than that should have good enough for everyone else.

"That's true, and I will probably come back with other equipment and supplies too that I didn't have before" replied Samantha, as Brian was pulling down plates from the cupboard, and starting to line them up along the worktop, ready for that morning's breakfast. "We'd all miss you, but at the same time, you could give us an insight as to what's going on out there in the rest of the world" replied Brian, who had now turned on the cooker, as blue flames erupted from the hobs, while Brian placed a frying pan on hob, whilst laying strips of bacon and cracking some eggs, which begin to sizzle as they cooked. "I know one thing I'll miss, and that's these fry ups" replied Samantha with a slight chuckle, as even Brian smiled broadly. "Well, it should remind you of the days sitting in the laybys, having whatever the burger van could dish out" said Brian, as Samantha laughed, remembering her lorry driving colleagues and their burger van escapades.

"I did try to avoid that when and where I could; had to try and watch my weight and my figure" said Samantha, but she appreciated Brian's gesture all the same, having been one to tell her family that she wasn't prepared to have to go up a dress size just because of her working life. It was indeed true, Samantha had always prided herself on her almost barbie doll type figure, which had always granted her a lot of compliments and the like from her friends, family and work colleagues. They both sat talking for a little while, until it was time for Brian to bang the wake-up gong, which when it was hit, echoed right around the house, chiming as loudly as the Big Ben bell tower would do in London. In twos and threes, the others trooped down the stairs, all looking a little tired themselves, as if they had slept like Samantha had done, head against a kitchen table.

It seemed to Samantha, that she hadn't been the only one to sleep roughly from the previous night. Now there were so many of them, it was hard for them all to squeeze around the farm's kitchen table, even though the kitchen was quite a sizeable one. This was no problem when it came to getting everyone's attention though, as Brian smartly wrapped his knuckles on the table, calling for order as he usually did at the start of every day. There was a collective sound of knives and forks being placed onto plates, as everyone stopped eating for a second to listen. "Morning everyone" said Brian, as there was a general cheerful morning greeting from everyone in return, as they all turned to look at Brian, as they always did during a morning's briefing session. Samantha seemed to have switched off temporarily, allowing her gaze to wander wherever it liked, until it was snapped back again by Brian, who was always the first to speak.

Brian cleared his throat before he continued; "now, as we all know, today, Samantha embarks on her new adventure from here, to find her fiancée Greg, and her best friend Diana, who are still considered missing since Covid struck". Brian cleared his throat again, and took a sip of water before continuing; "I'm sure I speak for all of us here Sam when I say, good luck, and god speed; a toast". Brian and everyone else raised their glasses and toasted Samantha. Samantha felt her face going slightly red, as she stood up from the table, and thanked Brian and the rest of the Flintstone community for their wonderful gesture to her. After breakfast, Samantha headed out into the farm yard, where she was preparing the Green Goddess for its departure from Mile End Farm in a few short hours, having made sure everything was packed and secured, ready for travelling.

As Samantha walked around doing her checks, she was reminded of back in the days before Covid, when she would do her pre drive checks, to make sure that the vehicles were ready for use on the road. The sounds of hissing air, slow moving lorries, and even the beeping noises of a reversing forklift filled Samantha's head, as she went around touching cables, checking if the doors were closed, and lastly checking the lights. "Not that I would need lights anyway" thought Samantha, as it was the spring time after all, and the days were lighter for a while longer than they would be at any other time of year. After about thirty minutes or so however, Samantha had finished all of the checks that she had needed to do, and was now giving the all-clear signal to the others, who had temporarily stopped work to come and say goodbye to her, whilst still taking the might and size of the Green Goddess into their minds eye.

Samantha had of course gone to say farewell to Misim first when she had finished her checks on the Green Goddess, who was still being made to stay in isolation by Doctor Victor, his condition having improved slightly since they had last spoken to him. Misim had seemed to recover from the surgery quite well, but was still infected with Covid, and was still being fed with plates of food, being pushed through a makeshift cat flap which had been installed before Misim had been moved into the barn. "I wish you all the best Sam, and I'm looking forward to seeing Greg and Diana when you find them and bring them back here" said Misim cheerfully, as he and Samantha communicated through the same cat flap used to get food inside the barn to Misim. Samantha wished she have gone inside and given Misim a hug, but she knew that was out of the question, owing to the nature of reinfection of the others.

So instead, Samantha thanked him for his kind words, and then walked away, hoping that Misim was going to be ok in the future, and not go the same way as the vast majority of the human population. "Good bye Sam, I managed to pack everything you'd need for the journey, and hopefully you should be able to work with some of the things we've given you" said Brian, after Samantha had returned from saying good bye to Misim, as Brian pointed out some of the kit that he and the others had packed onboard the Green Goddess for Samantha's trip. These included two large spare gas bottles for working the camping stove that was already onboard. A set of large solar panels, around a metre square, which were exceptionally lightweight, and could be erected anywhere, acting as a mobile power station. There were also two large water office coolers, both filled with pure drinking water from Mile End Farm's stock supply.

But most impressively of all, was finding a brand-new military style backpack, which was full of all sorts of survival gear, including a brand-new set of jet-black boots, and a giant camouflage net, which was big enough to cover the whole of the Green Goddess in what could only be described as a large green blanket. "Aww thanks Brian, that's fantastic, I could stay in the field for weeks or even months with this lot" said Samantha, as Brian gave Samantha a friendly pat on the back. "That's the general idea, and the green net can be used to hide the Goddess away from the rest of the world; if it was in a field, and this was over it, from a distance, it would just look like a giant pile of leaves, so no one would take any notice of it" explained Brian, as he pointed out the different patches of colour on it, representing the many different types of woodland and undergrowth that the UK countryside was full of.

Without warning, Brian suddenly hugged Samantha, making Samantha feel as if she was being suffocated in the process. "Oh" replied Samantha in surprise, as Brian let go of her, a little abashed, hoping that he hadn't done Samantha an injury. "Sorry, just a friendly way of saying good bye" replied Brian, who smiled and stepped away, allowing Melissia to step forward. "Good bye Sam, bring me back a stick of rock if you can" said Melissia, as Samantha laughed, understanding the joke. Doctor Victor now came forward, holding out his hand in a professional like manner. "Good luck Sam, and please take care" said Doctor Victor, as Samantha shook his hand, almost feeling like she was shaking hands with a town mayor. While Samantha was doing this, she hadn't noticed little Charlotte, who had come between Melissia and Doctor Victor, as they both moved aside to let her through.

Being nearly twice Charlotte's height, Samantha had to kneel down to look at her, as Charlotte smiled her most cheesy of smiles. "I'm going to miss you as well Princess" said Samantha, as Charlotte held her hands forward, on which she was carrying a small home-made daisy chain, which she had found and made up for Samantha in the fields around Mile End Farm. "Aww, is that for me" asked Samantha, as Charlotte nodded, and then tilted her head slightly, looking a little shy. "I made it for you Sam" replied Charlotte very quietly, so that only she and

Samantha could hear her speaking, as Samantha felt as if her heart was going to melt with the sweetness of Charlotte's present. "Aww, that is sweet of you darling, I'll treasure it" replied Samantha, as she gave Charlotte's shoulder a little squeeze. Charlotte then suddenly without warning, dived forwards and threw her arms around Samantha, almost knocking Samantha off of her feet.

There was a collective "aww" from everyone else, as Charlotte released Samantha, turned around and ran back towards the others. Julie and Trevor now walked up, holding each other's hand in married couple style fashion. "Good luck Sam, we will miss you" said Trevor, as he gave Samantha a little kiss on the side of the cheek, not wanting to do it too much, in case Julie thought she was being cheated on. "Oi, behave you" said Julie a little embarrassed, as she gave Trevor a little jokey style smack on his shoulder with the back of her hand. "Oh yes, sorry dear" replied Trevor, as Julie and Samantha giggled slightly at Trevor's behaviour. Trevor turned away smiling slightly, and headed back towards the others, who were all still looking at Samantha. "Alright everyone, back to work, nothing to see here now" called Brian to everyone at large, in an official type voice; but he couldn't help giving Samantha a small wink as he turned away.

"Ah men, always slave drivers" said Samantha, as Julie giggled again, realising that she would have to get back to work as well. "I guess I'll see you again soon Sam, but it's been a great adventure so far" replied Julie, as she too leaned in for a hug. "True, so true Julie; I'll come back, I promise, once I've found Greg and Diana" replied Samantha, as Julie leaned back after giving Samantha a bear like hug. Julie then stood back and waved, as she knew that Samantha would need all of the room that she could get to turn the huge one hundred foot long Green Goddess around in the farm yard. Before long, Samantha had opened the cab door, and swung herself inside, closing it behind her with a slamming sound. The usual start up messages and warning lights flicked into life on the dashboard, as Samantha turned on the ignition, before then turning the key all the way forwards, firing the cylinders inside of the might internal combustion engine.

The mighty Green Goddesses engine roared into life, as Samantha engaged forward gear, and pressed down slowly on the accelerator, whilst at the same time turning the steering wheel slowly, in order to go into a wide arc to then be pointing back in the direction of the farm driveway. Samantha tooted the air horn, and waved out of the window, as the Green Goddess moved down the farm driveway towards the gate, reached it, and then swung left out of the farm gateway, which began to close slowly behind her as the mighty Green Goddess moved onto the main road, now picking up a little speed as it went. As her next destination was the outskirts of Leicester, Samantha felt it was now safe to use the motorways, as the chances were that people would have either gone to ground, or be unwilling to show their faces to any strangers, should Covid try and take them off.

Samantha decided to stick to using the motorway service stations, which were the ones bound to have fuel in their storage tanks, owing to the fact that hardly anyone would be taking the fuel from them since the Covid lockdowns, so she was hoping for good stock to still be laying around. The Green Goddess wound its way slowly up the twisting and turning lanes, passing silent house after silent house, their owners most likely deceased from Covid, as Samantha could see no signs of life from behind the net curtains and closed windows. Or even, that its residents were at that very moment hunkering down inside them, afraid to step outside, in case they were attacked by wild dogs, or other people. Samantha did indeed see a few wild dogs, tearing away at a horse carcass, that lay in a field that she was passing, thinking that these wild dogs were once loveable household pets, groomed and cared for by their owners.

It seemed that the dogs didn't fear anything these days, as none of them scattered at the site of the Green Goddess as it drove past, with its deep throaty engine rumbling along. Samantha even expected the dogs to suddenly turn away from the horse carcass and attack the Green Goddess, but none of them did. Instead, the wild dogs continued to tear away at the rotting flesh of the horse carcass, looking more like ferocious lions than loveable household pets. Samantha switched on the radio, hoping to have some background music to pass the time, but then remembered that none of the radio stations worked or even had any staff in them anymore, owing to Covid. All that came back instead was a steady crackling static noise, which only reminded Samantha how depopulated the world really was. Samantha had almost expected that maybe someone would have got hold of a radio station by now, broadcasting a help signal of some kind.

But even if that was the case, who exactly would these people be hoping was listening in? Maybe the government might have broadcast some sort of emergency message of some kind, in case they had things to say, but then again, if there was no power going to people's homes, then who would be able to listen in anyway. Feeling that waiting around for imaginary hope was pointless, Samantha switched the onboard radio system over to the CD player, as it fired up the CD inside the disk player. A sudden low tune came out of the cabs speaker system, which was the soundtrack to the driving tune 'on the road again, by Willie Nelson'. Samantha listened to this for a while, singing along to it, which is something she hadn't done since the days before Covid. This kept Samantha going until she joined the M1 motorway a little while later, as she was reminded of how empty the world really was, used to seeing traffic thundering up and down.

The memories of her time back on Mile End Farm seemed now to feel like a distance memory, but they kept her entertained for a while along with the music coming from the cab speakers from the album entitled, 'the greatest driving music ever'. When Samantha had joined onto the motorway, there was a section of the carriageway, where major road works had been going on back before Covid. It all seemed too sad that these road cones, signs and even plant machinery all laid out before her, would never be used ever again, as it's army of road workers were all gone. Twenty miles or so later, Samantha found a motorway service centre, turning off the motorway into the service area, remembering to steer a little more carefully than usual, as she knew that the Green

258

Goddess was just that little bit longer than the other vehicles that had once traversed the millions of miles of UK roads.

Thanks to the hoses on the tanker trailer, Samantha was able to pump diesel and petrol into the many separate compartment tanks, and was surprised to find, that she was able to fill up all of the tanks on the trailer right to the brim, along with the Green Goddesses own fuel tank as well, with fuel going spare after all of that. "This is bizarre, I thought this place would be drained" thought Samantha, as she placed and secured the hoses safely back on the trailer, before diving into the small shop in the petrol station for a light snack. There was a nasty smell coming from the back room, and also from the freezers lining the wall, but Samantha soon located the source of the smell, as there was the half rotting body of who she presumed was the shop owner, slumped on the floor. Out of respect, Samantha quickly found a high visibility jacket, carefully placed it over the shop owners head and face.

Samantha was careful not to make contact with any rotting bodies these days, in case they were carrying any underlying diseases like chorea, tuberculosis, typhoid or even still riddled with Covid. Samantha then retreated out of the shop, after picking up a few items of food and drink, before heading back to the Green Goddess, careful to make sure that the items were still within date. To Samantha's great relief, they were, as she set out again, towards the motorway, in higher spirits than before, as having food inside of her was always going to put a smile on anyone's face, especially in a world where supplies were bound to be depleted. Throughout the rest of that day, the Green Goddess made its way up the motorway, Samantha at the controls, drumming her fingers against the steering wheel, humming and even sometimes, singing along to some of the tunes coming out of the cab's speakers from her driving tunes CD.

Samantha felt a small pang of fear, as she didn't pass anyone at all on her way up towards the outskirts of Leicester, again wondering whether people were out there, but avoiding her, or whether she really was the only human being for miles, stuck in this strange apocalyptic world, which she and others like her, had found themselves in. As Samantha had no one to talk to, or no other human beings hanging around at the road side, her thoughts began to wander back to days gone by with her friends and family. Their faces swam in front of her mind, until she was forced to give her head a violent shake, wondering if she was steadily descending into madness. "There dead, there all dead; and listening to their voices in your head won't bring them back, you better get a grip on yourself if you want to start getting answers to things" thought Samantha, in a determined sort of way.

At one point, Samantha had even brought out the pamphlet, laying it on the dashboard in front of her, starting to thinking about her destination, and hopefully the answers that she would be able to get from the files at Grey's Pharmaceuticals. Samantha even wondered at one point whether Devises and Fitzgerald were following her right that second, somehow staying out of sight on the long stretches of road that lay before and ahead of Samantha. The thought of it made Samantha shiver slightly, as if she ran into either of these men, she would have been in grave danger, as even though she knew a few self-defence techniques, they wouldn't have been much use if Devises and Fitzgerald were armed with guns. Eventually Samantha turned off the motorway up a slip road, onto another main A-road, which lead to the industrial estate on the edge of Leicester, where Samantha knew the Grey's Pharmaceuticals was located.

Not wanting to be seen or detected, Samantha worked out a route which took her around the outside of the industrial estate, and then into an open field, which in turn, gained access to the farm that Doctor Victor had pointed out on the map the night beforehand. "Best to keep your head down if you can avoid it, the place should be deserted, but always best if you stay out of the way to start off with, in case survivors may be camping out inside the building" came Doctor Victor's words from a memory that Samantha recalled from the night beforehand. Locating the farm that Doctor Victor had pointed out on his map, Samantha rolled slowly into the deserted farmyard, as there was a squeak of the brakes and a hiss of air as the airbrakes were applied. The low rumbling engine sound slowed to a stop, as Samantha switched off the engine and jumped down from the cab.

Samantha carefully made sure to close the driver's cab door very quietly, thinking that maybe a whole group of people were suddenly going to rush out and attack her. Samantha was half expecting a dog to come running out at her, or even the owner to come out brandishing a shot gun, like Brian had done on her and Julie's first day at Mile End Farm. When neither of these things happened, Samantha automatically assumed that the dog and owner must have been sadly killed by Covid. All the same, she pressed her head to the glass, and couldn't see any signs of life inside of the farmhouse. When Samantha prised open a downstairs window however, a strong smell of decaying bodies reached her nose, which made her recall, coughing slightly, closing the window with a snap behind her. "Yeah, defiantly not going in there" said Samantha out loud to herself, making a mental note, not to touch the farm house at all from that point onwards.

Fortunately for Samantha, the Grey's Pharmaceuticals main building complex, wasn't visible from where she was parked, so at least Samantha could be guaranteed some privacy. This had been Samantha's grand plan after all, as Samantha didn't want to alert the rest of the world to the fact that the Green Goddess was where it was. Instead, Samantha would have to trek around a mile or so over the fields, to reach the back door of the building, where according to the rough map that Doctor Victor had drawn, was where the back door was located. It put Samantha in mind of what her father and his army colleagues would have been trained to do, where they sneaked around, doing reconnaissance missions, gathering intel on enemy positions and troop strengths. However, in the here and now, this was something that Samantha could put off for the time being, as it was time to start setting up camp for the night.

Samantha folded up the rough piece of paper showing the map of Grey's Pharmaceuticals and surrounding area, before proceeding to open the container doors, where Samantha began to pull out the camouflage sheet, throwing it as best as she could over one side of the Green Goddess, as there was a high hedge opposite her, which was helping as a natural camouflage barrier. Being such a large camouflage sheet, it took Samantha the best part of three attempts to get the camouflage sheet into position and fixed down, but once it was completed, it filled Samantha with great satisfaction, knowing that the Green Goddess was parked up there, hidden away from the world. The rest of the equipment didn't take very long to set out, but Samantha quickly found her new set of jet-black boots, and the survival belt which had come as part of the backpack that Brian had given to her back on Mile End Farm.

Having been on camping holidays with her parents as a child, Samantha found being outdoors again wasn't as much of a bother as she thought it would be. Samantha had rations packs, accommodation, and equipment which was more than up to the job of keeping her alive while she conducted observation and investigation trips on Grey's Pharmaceuticals. It put Samantha in mind of the explorers in the years gone by, when they had been observing fascinating animals and environments around the world. One thing that Samantha said to herself that she would do before the sun went down, was try to find a local library, as this was a place where Samantha hoped to find some blueprints to the industrial estate that she was going to observing. To Samantha's great surprise, the local town a few miles away had a library, so Samantha broke into the library through a down stairs window, quickly locating the section marked 'maps and ordinate survey'.

Snatching a few atlases from the shelves of the local area, Samantha then found the section containing history books, and even to her great delight, a locked cabinet, which she managed to smash open using a screwdriver in a tool box, before finding a complete set of blueprints to the Grey's Pharmaceuticals building complex. Samantha made sure to fold these very carefully, before stealing them away in her backpack that she had brought with her. Exiting through the same window that she had come in from, Samantha walked down the now deserted high street, where she saw rubbish all over the street, windows closed, and the slight whiff on the air of decomposing corpses. Samantha walked slowly down the middle of the road, looking left and right as she went, thinking back to when this street would be a bustling busy high street, with shoppers, traders and maybe even a fair ground ride or two.

Samantha managed to snatch a few packets of biscuits and a loaf of bread from a corner shop at the end of the street, which surprisingly still tasted quite good, even having been left on the shelves for at least a few weeks. After this, Samantha made her way back to the farm and the Green Goddess, which had now become her base of operations, in which to conduct covert observations on Grey's Pharmaceuticals. She sat beside the Green Goddess that night, eating the supplies in one of the ration packs that she had, and after she'd finished, took the box back inside the container, hoping to recycle it for carrying other things at a later date. It was at this point in the evening, that something caught Samantha's eye, sat between all of the racks of shelves inside the container. Two sturdy large black rectangular boxes sat one on top of the other, both with bull dog suitcase type metal clips holding them shut.

Samantha could see that a message had been written on one of the boxes, in military stencil type letters, as if what was in the box was somehow official-like in nature, being the property of some government organisation. 'Emergency use only' read the message, making Samantha think about where it had come from, suddenly remembering that Julie had got hold of them in the Northampton police station, before they had stumbled upon Mile End Farm. What exactly was classed as an emergency these days, was anyone's guess; but Samantha made a mental note to herself not to open the boxes, unless she came under attack, or was discovered where she was by anyone who wasn't friendly. "Those two things would be classed an emergency" thought Samantha, as she turned around and jumped down out of the container, closing the door behind her and locking the doors with a slight creaking sound.

The following morning, Samantha woke suddenly, as she was half expecting to hear a wake-up call from Brian, by means of a sharp wrap on the cab door. Releasing that Brian wasn't there any more, Samantha took no rush in getting up, pulling on her clothes and boots a little slower than usual. In fact, it was five whole minutes after waking up before she moved at all. It was a stunning warm morning, as a gentle breeze rustled the leaves on the trees and the hedges. Samantha's backpack stood ready by the passenger's seat inside the cab, for her first trip out that day, to investigate Grey's Pharmaceuticals and the mystery of the pamphlet. After consuming a hurriedly made breakfast, consisting of a tin of porridge oats, Samantha slung the backpack onto over her shoulders and began to make her way across the farmland, making sure to keep to the edges of the fields, where the trees lining them granted her some cover away from prying eyes.

After crossing two whole fields, Samantha pulled out her makeshift hand drawn map, looking it all over to determine where her position was. Making up her mind, Samantha stowed the map away again and continued walking along the line of trees, until she reached the edge of the field. It was at that point, that she had to duck very quickly behind a hedge, as she had suddenly seen a big white building with a curved slopping roof come into view. It was by far the cleanest building that she could see, and so came to the conclusion, that this building had to be the Grey's Pharmaceuticals one. Remember the training that her father had given her from his Army days, Samantha was able to make her way around another field, using the border hedge between herself and the industrial estate fence as a cover, until she was level with the Grey's Pharmaceuticals building.

Samantha wasn't entirely sure in her own mind about why she was sneaking around, as there were no other human beings in sight, but thought that keeping hidden was her best line of attack until she had done at least one reconnaissance trip on Grey's Pharmaceuticals. Samantha suddenly froze, as out of nowhere came a pair of voices, which were deep, and had a slight toughness to them, not sounding friendly at all. "Do you see anything" asked the first voice, sounding as if they were standing at some sort of guard post, keeping watch over the surrounding countryside. "Nah, must have been a trick of the light, come on, let's get back on patrol" said the second voice, as there was a crunching of footsteps, as if heavy boots were making contact with gravel stones and chippings. "Yeah, you don't want to get the sack now do you, this world is hard enough as it is to live in" replied the first voice, as the sound of their footfalls got fainter and fainter.

It was clear to Samantha now, that the building was indeed occupied, and the people inside of it, may not be as friendly as she would have first hoped. Thinking that the two voices were now at a safe enough distance away, and still hidden by the field's perimeter hedge, Samantha made her way further around the perimeter hedge, to see if there was a way through or over the hedge into the back of the building. This turned out to be a bit of a dead end for Samantha, as there was nowhere in the hedge for a kissing gate, turnstile or any other entrance at all which would get her over the hedge and into the grounds itself. Samantha wasn't easily defeated however, as she doubled back on herself, and managed to find a point somewhere in the long grass in the field opposite, which had a clear view across the car park, to the front door of the Grey Pharmaceuticals complex.

As Samantha had donned camouflage clothing before leaving her base of operations by the Green Goddess in the farmyard, she could very easily blend into the background, and not be seen by those inside the complex, as she carried out observations on them, watching the day to day running of the place. And so, it went on, day after day, Samantha would wake up, cross over the fields, sit watching the complex all day until it was dark, then head back to the Green Goddess and go to bed. For two whole days, there was no movement at all; three days went past, with the same results; by day five, there was still no activity going on. Samantha steadily started to get bored of doing this same ritual day after day, preying that something would happen, but realised that these people would have to show themselves eventually. After all, all that she had seen so far, was a few armed guards walking around the perimeter on some sort of a daily patrol.

At one point, one of the patrolling guards had come within a few meters of where Samantha lay watching them, and even had to clap a hand over her mouth, so as to muffle her breathing. The camouflage disguise must have been working however, as the guard soon walked away, leaving Samantha shaking slightly at nearly being discovered. On the sixth day, Samantha suddenly saw movement in the car park, as a silver Jaguar saloon car came slowly into the car park, making Samantha snap into full awareness mode, feeling that now more than ever was the time to be paying attention. A man wearing a smart suit, tie and sunglasses, climbed out of the Jaguar saloon car, and made his way into the Grey's Pharmaceuticals building. Samantha raised the binoculars to her eyes that she had with her, and to her horror, recognised the man walking into the building's main reception area.

It was none other than Edward Fitzgerald, the man who had been stalking Samantha all of this time, swagging along as he walked, looking as if he owned the place. Samantha's eyes widened in shock; so, Edward Fitzgerald was working for Grey's Pharmaceuticals, aka, the Company. As Samantha lay there on her front, taking it all in, she saw another official looking car arrive, and this time, the driver was a woman, wearing a silver satin blouse and black pencil skirt, with matching black heeled court shoes. Samantha was dimly aware, that she had seen this woman before now, as the mystery woman was flanked by two men, both wearing black suits. Samantha decided she would spend the night in her position, as if there was any movement now, she was bound to see it, where she lay hidden by the long grass and bushes. Samantha watched as the mystery woman walked into the main reception area, flanked by the two men in dark suits.

Samantha was just hoping that Fitzgerald and this mystery woman would show themselves again before long, so that Samantha could get a clearer view of them together and maybe identity what they were both doing there, wondering whether anyone else would show themselves in the coming days. As the sun began to go down on the sixth day watching the complex, Samantha felt her eyelids begin to droop with tiredness. It turned out that doing observations like this was very draining, as Samantha's attention couldn't fade at any point, nor could she drop her concentration for even a second. She was strongly reminded at that point of military sharpshooters, who would be expected to maintain a vigil eye at all times while they were on a stakeout, or watching an enemy target. Samantha's eyelids felt heavier and heavier, as her head sank slowly down onto the ground, drifting slowly off to sleep, feeling confident that she was protected by the hedge.

Samantha had no idea how long she had been asleep for, because when she slowly opened her eyes, the sun had risen into the sky. A sudden rustle of clothing from behind her, made her snap awake, jerking slightly upwards as she went. Samantha gulped heavily, as the rustling clothes sound was followed by the sounds of heavy breathing, as if someone was standing behind her wearing a gas mask. Samantha was suddenly aware of a tall male like figure, who was wearing a hazmat suit and gas mask, standing over her, as she lay on her front, hoping that if she didn't move a muscle, whoever was there, would think that she was recently deceased from Covid, and walk away. Samantha tactic of playing dead, had not been as successful as she would have liked, nor had her camouflage worked either in hiding her. Before Samantha had time to react to this new threat, she heard a familiar snide voice, coming from just out of her line of sight.

"Hello Samantha; we meet again" came the voice of Edward Fitzgerald, who sounded triumphant, as if Samantha was some poor animal that Edward had been hunting in a forest. As Edward said this, two vice like hands came straight down, turning Samantha over on the ground, so that she was looking straight into the eyes of her stalker, who had tracked her over many miles of the countryside. "You, what do you want, get off me" cried out Samantha, as she tried to get free, struggling slightly against the hazmat suited figure, who's hands were now locked around Samantha's arms, pinning her to the floor. "Suspect secured sir" came the distorted voice of the hazmat suited man, who had Samantha pinned to the ground. Samantha struggled so much that the hazmat suited man cried out, "for gods sack, do something before she has our eyes out or something".

Edward must have been enjoying watching Samantha and the hazmat suited man struggling away on the floor, but soon the struggle to an end, because at that very moment, Edward directed his shot gun straight into Samantha's face, making her freeze where she stood. This was the end now, Samantha's life was going to end here and now, she just seemed to know that somehow. Samantha slammed her eyes shut, fearing about what was going to happen, but soon realised that Edward hadn't fired his shotgun. "Oh, don't you worry Sam; you're coming with me, into custody; on terrorism charges" explained Edward, still in the same snide voice, suiting the psychopathic personality that he possessed in his dark and wicked ways. Samantha seemed to stop breathing, as she tried to take in what Edward had just said, wondering how on earth Samantha was supposed to be guilty of terrorism charges.

"You're sick, you're just sick" said Samantha, as Edward let out a derisive laugh. "Oh, and I think I will add insulting a member of parliament to that list as well" replied Edward, as Samantha now looked doubly shocked. "You monster, what do you want from me" cried out Samantha, as Edward kicking her sharply in the stomach. Samantha screamed out a little from the pain of it, as tears came into her eyes, as she was not as tough body wise as she would have liked to be. "Call me a monster again and it will be the worse for you" exclaimed Edward, but Samantha didn't care. New world or no new world, she wasn't going to become a victim of this psychopath. "Get away from me" screamed Samantha, as she tried to wriggle free, but she couldn't, as the hazmat suited figure was pinning her down to the ground, doing his best to prevent Samantha from getting loose.

"Shut her up will you" exclaimed Edward, a little impatiently, as the hazmat suited figure, struck Samantha across the face with the butt of his machine gun that he was holding. As it was made of metal, Samantha felt herself feel the blow across her face, as first she could see stars popping in front of her eyes, followed by blackness, as she was knocked out, falling down; down; down.

CHAPTER EIGHTEEN
Grey's Pharmaceuticals

The next thing Samantha knew, she was regaining consciences inside what looked a dark prison cell, where a small window of sunlight filled the room from a high up bared window near the ceiling. It was near impossible to tell where Samantha was, or how long she had been out for, but as Samantha came around from being knocked out, she found that she couldn't move her hands, which were locked together above her head. She had clearly been handcuffed to a length of rope fixed to the ceiling, and it felt as if she was restrained by the legs as well, so that her body was being held in a bolt upright position, like a medieval prisoner would be before they were tortured. Samantha winced slightly as she felt the handcuffs cutting into her wrists, but this was hardly the most worrying concern for her at that present moment, as she stared around the room, trying to take in as much of her surroundings as she could.

Samantha had no idea where she was, but soon took a rough guess at the fact that maybe she had been taken inside the Grey's Pharmaceuticals building complex, thinking that perhaps this cell was some sort of underground bunker system that ran underneath the building. It was a pretty feeble guess at that; but considering that Samantha had virtually nothing to look at except a semi dark grey prison cell with a narrow window up near the ceiling and a steel door with no hatch in it, it wasn't really a lot to go on to determine her exact location at that present moment. Samantha had seen the movies, where the damsel in distress would have been kidnapped and held hostage, screaming their heads off in these places, but Samantha knew that screaming out was not a sensible idea, as it would only aggravate her captors, and cause them to perhaps gag her just to shut her up.

Little did Samantha's captors know though, that Samantha had a small but very handy ace up her sleeve, for if she ever found herself in this position. Her father Richard, had taught Samantha a few tricks about resisting torture, for which Samantha now released, was going to come in very handy in the present-day climate. "Try to avoid a confrontation; be polite, and treat your captors with respect" came Richard's voice from inside her head, as Samantha recalled the moment in her memory that she had heard Richard tell her this vital lifesaving knowledge. As soon as Samantha had thought of her father's torture training memory however, there was a loud bang which echoed around the small prison cell, as the handle was pushed down on the door. Samantha jumped slightly at the noise, but then braced herself for what could be coming next, realising that by showing fear at that moment, was not an option.

This was certainly the moment that Samantha would find out, how brave she really was, relying on the world class training her father had given her throughout her lifetime. Edward Fitzgerald stood there in the open doorway, machine gun slung over his shoulder, like he was trying to like cool and impressive, but in Samantha's opinion, only made him look more terrifying than ever before. "So, what sort of play thing have I got today" said Edward with a smirk, as he walked slowly into the cell, closing the door behind him with another small banging sound. Edward seemed to be speaking more to himself, rather than at Samantha directly, but he kept a hungry eye on her all the same, like a shark circling a blood-soaked carcass. Samantha said nothing in response to Edward's words, but instead fixed Edward with a look that clearly stated, 'touch me and I will break you'.

"Oh, you read my mind, of course I'm going to break you" replied Edward, who had almost guessed what Samantha was thinking, as if he possessed some sort of psychopathic mind reading technic, being able to see into Samantha's mind and thought process. "Yes; you see, I think you'll do very nicely" said Edward, in the same voice as before, but this time, the smile of evil began to curl around his mouth. It took every nerve in Samantha's body not to scream out, as she knew that this was exactly what complete psychopaths like Edward fed on, in their sick and twisted power play games. As Edward had walked around behind her field of vision, Samantha stood stock still, making sure not to make any sudden movements, in case Edward came in for an attack. This didn't stop Samantha from flinching a second later however, as Edward run a finger down her back, through the curve of her spine, as Samantha bit her lip, in an attempt not to scream out loud.

Edwards's hand felt cold and horrible, and it certainly felt like torture to Samantha, as she could guess what was coming next, as Edwards's left hand had found its way down to her backside, giving it a good hard squeeze. "Supper time I think" whispered Edward, as he leaned into Samantha's right ear, as sweat began to run down Samantha's forehead into her eyes, through the strain of holding her nerves against Edward's monstrous ways. Samantha tried to scream, but at that exact moment, Edward had clamped his free right hand over Samantha's mouth, as she struggled slightly, unable to make a sound. Edward's right hand however, had slipped itself inside Samantha's jeans, and had made its way around her legs, to grope her from the front, with Samantha powerless to stop it. "Any minute now, he's going to rape me" thought Samantha, as she half struggled, half resisted against Edward's vice like grip.

Edward's hand that was clamped tightly across her mouth, was making Samantha's eyes water, as it smelled horribly like stail cigarettes and felt as if it hadn't been washed in days. If it was Edward's intentions to knock her out, then just the smell of his hands would have been enough, rather than needing any drugs or gases to do the job. "Don't struggle bitch, it will only make matters worse for you" sneered Edward, adopting the same tone that he had used when Samantha had been captured in the bushes outside of the Grey's Pharmaceuticals building. "What's going on; Edward, what are you doing" asked a stern sounding female voice, as Edward immediately removed his hand from inside Samantha's jeans and tried to look innocent, as if nothing was happening. "Interrogating the suspect ma'am" replied Edward, as he spoke in a way like he was answering a higher authority figure.

"I don't recall an interrogation of a terror suspect requiring the interrogator to have their hand in the suspects trousers" replied the stern female voice, as Samantha's head dropped, so that she was now looking directly at the floor. After the adrenaline of the moment had stopped flowing, Samantha suddenly felt very weak, as her stomach gave a very quiet rumble, as if she had not had any food inside her for hours, or even days. From Samantha's new position however, she could see that the woman with a stern voice, was wearing jet black court heeled shoes, that were very smartly polished. This immediately put Samantha in mind of a woman who would have worked in a very clean environment, like the office of a company director or an embassy of some kind. Considering that everything else in the room seemed to be so dirty and slightly smelly, these shoes certainly looked very out of place compared to everything else.

It was almost as if they were to clean to be allowed. It then suddenly dawned on Samantha who this woman was, but before she had time to look up, a pair of vice like hands had grabbed her arms, and was releasing Samantha from the handcuffs that held her to the ceiling. "Take her to the interview room" said the same stern female voice, as Samantha was half carried, head still bowed downwards, out of the prison cell and along the corridor, to a second room, which looked a considerably lot cleaner than the prison cell beforehand. Samantha was roughly thrown down onto a chair by the desk, and then both of hands were held behind her back, as she restrained again in the chair, so that she sat facing the stern voiced woman, who had now taken a seat, and was flicking through a file in front of her. This was the first time that Samantha had been given the chance to get a better look at this mystery woman, as Samantha looked up from the floor.

With a small start, Samantha immediately recognised who the woman was. "Close the door Edward, I will call you when it is time to return the suspect to their cell" said the woman, as Edward, without speaking, walked out of the room and closed the door behind him. "Hello Samantha, I'm glad you could join us" said Helen Dukes, who had now leaned forward and placed both of her arms on the desk, facing Samantha as she did so, being as calm and as friendly as if the pair of them were sat outside a café drinking tea on a warm summer's day. Helen Dukes, the former Prime Minister of the United Kingdom, didn't seem to look like she was struggling in this new world at all. Her hair was still as neat and tidy as it had been on the news broadcasts she had made as Prime Minister. Her satin blouse and pencil skirt were clean, shiny and highly professional, and she was wearing a perfume which was so strong, that it made Samantha's eyes water.

"You look tired Samantha, here, have some water" said Helen, pouring Samantha a glass of water, before holding it up, and allowing Samantha to drink from it. It felt so good to taste the water, but Samantha was ashamed to drink it, as it could have contained a truth drug to make Samantha say and do things that she would have no control over at all. "You're a thug" was Samantha's response, as Helen looked surprised at Samantha's outburst. "I'm sorry" replied Helen a little confused, as Samantha looked her dead in the eye, feeling a sudden surge of anger towards Helen. "You're a thug, and that monster you call a henchman out there in the corridor" replied Samantha, as Helen's face relaxed a little, realising what Samantha was talking about. "It's not what you think Sam; I can call you Sam can't I" asked Helen, as Samantha glared at her, wishing her nothing but ill.

"I've been kidnapped; held hostage; sexually molested and nearly rapped in that prison cell, and been wrongly accused of being a terror suspect; I'm pretty sure there are laws against all of those things" replied Samantha in an angry voice, but then remembered what Richard had told her. "Don't lose your temper, keep calm and keep your head" came Richard's voice echoing once again in Samantha's head. Helen seemed to look a little taken aback after Samantha has finished speaking, but carried on with her statement none the less. "You're being accused of terrorism charges because you were known to be carrying sensitive classified government information". Samantha was so taken aback by this piece of shocking news, that she widened her eyes to their fullest extent, thinking that they would pop out of her skull if she opened them any wider than what they already were.

"What sensitive government information, I came here because of a pamphlet that was given to me before Covid-19 struck the world" replied Samantha in a calm voice, as she knew that these people obviously needed her alive for something. "We know about the pamphlet, that is what the sensitive government information is" replied Helen, as it dawned on Samantha that she had been right about the pamphlet all along. This was obviously the very reason why Edward and Patrick had been stalking her and Julie since the beginning, ever since the pair of them had left Lillington. "You know who I am don't you" replied Helen suddenly, making Samantha jump slightly at the sudden change in the tone of Helen's voice. "Yeah, your Helen Dukes; you're the Prime Minister" said Samantha, again keeping her voice calm, but with a note of distaste in it.

This was hardly surprising, as Helen clearly had no idea that the men who supported her, were nothing short of thugs, bullies and psychopaths. "I was, or what is left of the government; you don't need to fear me Samantha, I'm your friend, I'm here to help" replied Helen, but Samantha had a look on her face which clearly told Helen, that Samantha didn't believe a word of what Helen had just said. "The information which was sent to you is important, or I should say, was sent to Greg" replied Helen, as Samantha gave an involuntary sob, as she felt a tear begin to run down her face at the mention of Greg's name. "He was close to you wasn't he" said Helen in a sympathetic voice, as she leaned forward to give Samantha's shoulder a small squeeze, in what Helen thought was a compassionate way, but Samantha immediately knew that this was a seduction trick to get into Samantha's mind.

Samantha tried to lean backwards to avoid Helen's hand, nearly unseating her off of her chair, as she tried to hide the fact that Helen had touch a nerve in Samantha's mind. Helen thought better of it, as she could see that Samantha was not warming to her presence within the room; so, she tried a different angle instead by saying. "Your Fiancée Greg, was aiding Grey's Pharmaceuticals in a vaccine programme to protect people against Covid-19; he was sent an invitation, came here, but then escaped a few weeks ago, and he's not been seen since". This last statement couldn't help but arouse Samantha slightly to where Greg might have gone too, but at least she was now sure of one thing; Greg, was alive. Had Greg in fact, worked out what was on the pamphlet given to Samantha by him, and even now, making his way up to Clyde in Scotland for whatever was happening there.

One thing for certain however, was that Helen was clearly doing some sort of good cop, bad cop routine on Samantha, and Samantha wasn't going to give in that easily. Samantha worked out that Edward would be posing as the bad cop of course, by the way he had attempted to sexually assault her whilst in the prison cell, which in truth, had certainly been lived up to in his sick and twisted personality. Then again, Edward Fitzgerald was a psychopath anyway, so being the bad corrupt cop character wasn't too difficult for him to pull off. "Judging by the way this place is laid out, I'm guessing this is a makeshift holding facility for torture and interrogation" replied Samantha, as Helen smiled slightly, in a way that Samantha hadn't recognised up until now. It was a smile which told Samantha, that she was somehow correct on what she had said about Grey's Pharmaceuticals being a holding place for illegal human experimentation.

"You've been watching too many films Samantha; this is research laboratory, not a dungeon" replied Helen, as Samantha retorted; "and how many others have you got in this building Helen; are they being restrained and held here against their will like me, or am I just a special case". Helen appeared to look downright alarmed, as if Samantha was referring to Grey's Pharmaceuticals, not as a building full of doctor's and scientist's intent on doing good by humanity, but instead more like a concentration camp, where gruesome human experiments took place within its walls. Samantha even strained her ears in an attempt to see if she could hear any screams of pain from anyone else, but no other sounds reached her ears from outside of the room. From what Samantha had seen of the outside however, the Grey's Pharmaceuticals complex had looked very large, and covered many acres of land.

Then again, Samantha was basing all of her theories and ideas on the fact that she was defiantly inside the Grey's Pharmaceuticals building. As Samantha had been knocked out for an unknown length of time, it was hard to tell if she had been moved meters or even miles from where she had hidden in the bushes around the Grey's Pharmaceuticals building. Samantha had a crude idea that this room had been sound proofed, as when she had walked in, the room had been set up in exactly the same way as a police interview suite would look, as there was a sort of strange deadness of air inside of it, where the walls were somehow absorbing the sound. If only Julie had been there at that exact moment; being a former police officer herself, she would have known how to deal with a room like this, having spent enough time interviewing suspects inside of them back in the Lillington police station.

Helen had been looking directly at Samantha in the whole time that they had been talking together, but at the mention of the concentration camps, Helen changed her tune, becoming sterner again like she had been with Edward back in the prison cell, rather than the motherly voice

276

that she had used before. "I'm sure you will come round to my way of thinking soon enough; Edward, take her back to the cell" said Helen, as Edward came back in through the closed door, hoisting Samantha out of the chair onto her feet, before frogmarching Samantha back down the corridor towards her cell. Once back inside the cell, Edward forced Samantha down onto the ground, but this time released the handcuffs from her hands behind her back, and then exited the cell, closing the door behind him with a bang as it was followed by metallic clicks as the door was locked behind him.

Samantha lay there, curling slowly up on the floor, as she heard Edward walking away down the corridor, whistling slightly as he went. Once Samantha thought that Edward was out of earshot, she began to sob uncontrollably, as if she somehow knew, that she wasn't going to get out of there alive. Samantha could only but guess what was going to happen next, as the hours ticked slowly past, with the light getting fainter and fainter outside of the narrow small barred window up near the ceiling. Helen and her two thugs Edward and Patrick, were most likely going to use Samantha for some kind of human experiments by the sound of it to cure Covid, which in Samantha's opinion would have been fine in the hands of doctors and other medical professionals. But in reality, Samantha felt that in the hands of Helen and her gang of thugs, this was not the best way forwards, or the right or even moral way of doing things, despite the new world order.

For one thing, human trials took years, the person's consent, and mountains of red tape paperwork to undergo in the old world. It certainly didn't involve keeping those who participated in medical trials as prisoners during said trials, and allowing them to be exposed to complete monsters like Edward. Samantha remembered the next line of what her father Richard had taught her, his voice once again filling Samantha's head, like listening to long lost memories gone by. "Listen and make mental notes on everything; hear all, see all; build up as much of a picture of your kidnapers routine as you can; and always keep track of their movements, whatever they maybe". Samantha tried to control her breathing, as she wiped her eyes, trying to brush away the tears which had built up in them. Even though there was no mirror within the locked prison cell, Samantha could tell that her eyes would be very red and sore.

Samantha began to feel tired again, as after all, she had not been fed for some time, but before she had time to think on this point too much, there was a lock clicking sound, and the door swung open, as a man wearing a hazmat suit and gas mask walked in, laying a plate of food down beside the wall. The hazmat suited man then retreated back out of the room, closing the door with a snap, before locking it behind him with the usual clicking sounds. Immediately after the door had closed, Samantha pounced on the food, which consisted of a pair of ham sandwiches, and a slice of cheese. The cheese tasted slightly off a bit, and the sandwiches were a little dry, but Samantha didn't complain about it, as it was food after all, and she had no idea when she would be fed again. Samantha's mind was now fixed completely on one thing; escape; and how she was going to get away once she had escaped from her location.

Once she had finished eating, Samantha lay back on the floor, crawling up into a ball to try and stay warm, as the prison cell wasn't the warmest of places to be in, and her jeans and top were not thick items of clothing to keep warm in. Samantha had no idea how much time had passed, but she was suddenly aware of multiple footsteps coming towards her from outside in the corridor. She sat up a little, just in time for the footsteps to stop dead outside of the prison cell door. "Get off me, how dare you manhandle me like this" came a very familiar voice from outside the cell door, as there was a lock clicking sound, and the door swung open with a squeak from its hinges. Edward stood there in the doorway, attempting to push a struggling young woman forward into the cell, who's hands were pinned down by her side by Edward's muscular arms.

The young woman stumbled forward into the ceil, as Edward pushed her inside, but not before the young woman had screamed; "go to hell you oversized bully". Edward only laughed at this outburst and slammed the door in her face, before locking it, and moving away laughing with an evil grin on his face. This was the first time that the two women had looked each other in the eyes, as the young woman had turned to look at Samantha, and had almost jumped backwards in shock. "Oh my god, it can't be; Samantha" exclaimed the young woman, who was looking on at Samantha in shock. "Diana" exclaimed Samantha, as the two ladies launched themselves forward, locking each other in chest breaking hugs. It was indeed Diana Gibbs, Samantha's lifelong school friend, who Samantha had gone looking for after Covid had struck, as Samantha believed her to be travelling with Greg.

Diana didn't seem to look the same as she had done before Covid had struck, in the time were personal hygiene and appearance were taken for granted. Diana's hair was a complete mess, and had gone wild, rather than the sleek shinny appearance it usually showed when she was at work or on a night out. The Diana before Covid had been as skinny and as beautiful as Samantha was. Now however, she appeared to look like she had put weight on, which seemed very strange seeing as food supplies were bound to be dwindling by now. That being said, Diana did seem to look a little pale, and drained of strength from where it looked like she had been living rough for some time. Diana winced slightly as she and Samantha had both hugged each other, and as Diana pulled away, Samantha could now see Diana's solid stomach bulge more clearly, even in the now failing light outside the prison cells barred window.

The truth hit Samantha with the force of a speeding train; Diana had put weight on, but certainly not the fatty kind of weight. "No, you're not, but how did you" spluttered Samantha in complete shock, taking in Diana's appearance, as the entire situation was becoming more and more bizarre for every second that it was going on for. Not only was the fact that Samantha's best friend was still alive and in the same building as she was, but also because of the fact that she was very clearly. Samantha backed against the wall in shock, placing her hands over her mouth to prevent a scream from issuing out of it, as what greeted her, was more than enough to make her scream out in shock, and strangely despite the situation, in excitement as well. "I know what you're thinking Sam, and

279

your right; I'm pregnant; please, let me explain, it's a long story" replied Diana, as she sat herself down on the floor beside where Samantha stood.

Samantha slid down the wall, so she came to rest next to Diana, who was now looking at her with longing eyes, wanting to know as many details as possible about how one of her best friends had ended up to be carrying an unborn child inside of her. "When did this all happen, the last time I saw you was before the lockdown came in, and we were stuck in Lillington" began Samantha, but Diana had placed a hand on Samantha's shoulder, and smiled. "Please, let me tell my story, I promise I will answer your questions afterwards" said Diana, as Samantha fell silent in order to listen more carefully to what Diana had to say next. "I'm nearly eight months gone, and I suspect the baby may come any time soon" replied Diana, who had responded to the look of joy that had suddenly come across Samantha's face. It was still incredible to think that in dark times such as these, little things like babies could still be brought into the world.

"I'm so happy for you, congratulations babes" couped Samantha in a slightly higher pitched voice than normal, as she gave Diana's stomach a light rub with her hand. "You'll be Auntie Samantha when it's born you know" replied Diana, who's smile faded slightly when Samantha looked slightly worried. The prospect of becoming an Auntie in all but name to Diana's unborn child was certainly a daunting one, as Samantha had always focused on her career, rather than allowing her mind to wander in the world of childcare. Diana suddenly shivered, as there was no form of heating in the prison cell, and the window high above them was clearly open to the elements. But in the fading light however, Diana was prepared to tell Samantha everything, as after all, they had both been on quite an adventure to get here. One burning question seemed to be playing on Samantha's mind however, so she chose to blurt it out without warning.

"Who's the father" asked Samantha, as Diana turned to look at Samantha again, having temporarily looked down at her bump to rub her hand on it in a comforting manner. "Well, that's where the story starts really" replied Diana, as Samantha snuggled closer towards Diana, in an attempt to keep her warm. This was a trick that Samantha had learned from her father through doing survival training back in the days before Covid had struck. By using her own body heat, Samantha hoped to give Diana and her unborn baby as much warmth as possible, keeping them alive during the night time, where the temperature was bound to drop considerably without the sunlight to warm them. Samantha did try her best to explain to Diana about what she was doing with her, as Diana looked at Samantha wondering if she had gone slightly mad, but agreed all the same, realising that her unborn baby needed just as much protection as Diana did.

Diana issued a hurried thanks to Samantha, as Samantha and Diana lay down together on the floor, huddling close to keep each other, in order to keep warm. If anyone had walked into the cell at that exact moment, it would have been a very strange site, as everyone would have thought that perhaps Samantha and Diana were both lesbians, by the way they were huddling together. Diana starred straight into Samantha's eyes, and Samantha did so in return, desperate to hear what had happened with Diana since they had last spoken, which was before all of the Covid lockdowns. "Doesn't look like we're going anywhere in a hurry, why don't you tell me all; I'll promise I won't interrupt" replied Samantha, as Diana grinned in appreciation. "Well, seeing as if you asked so nicely babes" replied Diana, as she launched into her story.

CHAPTER NINETEEN

Diana's Tale

Nearly nine months earlier, life for Diana and indeed everyone else in the world was as usual as it had been for decades and even centuries beforehand. It was in fact the night of Diana's birthday celebration party, and the four of them which included Diana, Samantha, Rachel and Emily, were all enjoying a night out in Lillington's town centre, taking advantage of a real opportunity to celebrate. The sounds of the sirens from nearby Ambulances and police cars, as well as late night shoppers and party goers reached their ears, as the four of them walked along the high street, talking happily, and occasionally giggling when a group of young men in their late teens wolf whistled at them as they walked past. The four of them being the ladies who they were, with their near perfect hourglass figures and soft beautiful complexions, that this sort of behaviour of men towards them was an understanding that they had all grown up with throughout their lives.

Diana, it transpired, also had another reason to be celebrating out on the town that night. Diana had also recently started at a new job the week beforehand, and her first week at work had gone very well indeed. Diana's position was a work from home one, where she worked as a science technician for a major pharmaceuticals company based in Leicester. In short, Diana didn't know it at the time, but she herself was working for Grey's Pharmaceuticals, but had yet to get properly introduced to everyone on the management team. Diana after all, had been the brainiest out of all of them, after receiving top marks in all of her GCSEs and A-levels at secondary school. The four of them walked down the high street, their heeled shoes making the usual clip clopping sounds on the concrete pavement as they went, handbags swinging slightly on their arms, looking around for their destination.

After walking a short distance, they all found what they were looking for, as they all turned left into a restaurant, near enough to the very wedding shop where Greg had taken Samantha wedding dress shopping. It was that time of the year, when it was warm outside during the day, but then dropped rapidly in temperature at night, almost the same as being stuck in the middle of the African Sahara Desert. It was no surprise that the four of them shivered slightly as they went, before felling the warmth of the restaurant hit them as they walked in through the door. "Evening, dinner reservation for 8pm please, name of Stevens" said Rachel, who had booked the table for the four of them earlier that day. "I know we're a bit early sorry about that" said Emily, as the doorman who had opened the door for them waved a hand at them in recognition, showing that it wasn't a problem about the group's early arrival.

"Not at all madam, we have prepared a table for you, as another customer was here earlier than expected" replied the doorman, as a waiter came over to them. "Right this way madam, your table is ready" said the waiter, as the four of them were led over to the table, and ordered their drinks for the meal ahead. Samantha was the only one still on her feet, as everyone else had all sat down at the table, talking happily and laughing. "I'd like a bottle of Champagne please, perhaps two depending on what we drink first" asked Samantha to the waiter, who had finishing seating everyone. "Of course, madam, I shall get those for you right away" replied the waiter, as Samantha thanked the waiter, and then sat down with the others. None of them had noticed Samantha ordering two bottles of Champagne right under their noses, so Samantha's plan of planning a surprise for Diana's birthday was working perfectly.

"Now Diana, I have to confess this right here, right now, that I'm paying for the meal tonight, and I don't want any arguments on that one" said Samantha, waving a stern finger at Diana, who giggled, and then pulled an amusing face. The others giggled in unison as she did so, finding Diana's amusing face towards Samantha very comical. "Ooh, well that's us put in our place isn't it" couped Diana, Rachel and Emily all at once, as Samantha grinned widely. "I feel it's only fair, after all, you are my best friend, and we all love you" replied Samantha, as if this settled the matter. "Lorry driving paying you well then Sam" asked Emily, as the others turned to look at her. "Money can never replace friendship, not this friendship at any rate; cheers" replied Samantha in a speech like fashion, as if she was reading out a quote or a speech, whilst the others toasted her and Diana with their wine glasses.

Samantha, realising what Emily had just said, waved a hand in appreciation; but couldn't really reply, as she was still taking a swig from her wine glass at the exact moment. "Oh come on babes, we can all take credit to being successful; do you remember what we nicknamed ourselves in school" said Rachel as the others all giggled. "The spice girls" they all said in unison, as a waiter came over to top up their wine glasses with fresh sparkling wine. They were all occupied so much, that none of them had noticed the smartly dressed middle aged man, who had just walked in through the main restaurant door. It was Patrick Devises, C.E.O of Grey's Pharmaceuticals, wearing a smart silk light grey suit with a red tie, and carrying a bunch of flowers in his right hand, with what looked like a birthday card stuck between his fingers of his left hand.

Patrick then flagged down a waiter who was passing, briefly engaging the waiter in conversation, asking the waiter where Samantha and the others were sat at the table, as the restaurant was starting to fill up with customers. The waiter kindly pointed them out at the table, as Patrick thanked the waiter, and moved slowly across the room, as Rachel let out a small giggle. "Hey, check out the George Clooney lookalike that's coming this way" tittered Rachel, as the others looked in the direction of Patrick. To everyone's complete surprise, Diana's eyes had suddenly widened in shock as she had seen Patrick coming over towards them. "Who's that" asked Samantha, as Patrick drew level to their table, looking quite pleased with himself that he had managed to catch them before the meals had arrived. "That's my boss, Patrick Devises" replied Diana, as Patrick looked directly at Diana, with the others looking on in wonder.

"I'm really sorry to intrude ladies, but I heard from the girls in the office that it was your birthday today Diana and I thought I would drop by with these for you; so, happy birthday I suppose" said Patrick, looking a little embarrassed, but giving a weak smile none the less. "Aww, thanks so much for these sir" couped Diana, as she placed a hand on her chest, being so taken aback at Patrick's sudden arrival, and then joy at seeing the lengths he had gone to on her birthday. "You really didn't have to you know" replied Diana, with a slight giggle as even Patrick cracked a smile, realising that this was Diana's strange way of saying thank you to her company director. "Yes, I'm sorry this is a little impromptu, but I thought it was best to get them to you on your birthday rather than when you were back at work on Monday" explained Patrick, as it was a Saturday night, so Diana had been able to properly enjoy her birthday without worrying about working.

"I best leave you all alone I guess, good evening to you ladies" said Patrick, giving a short quick nod of the head to the group, before walking away, fastening the button of his suit blazer jacket as he went. Samantha, Rachel and Emily, who had all managed to keep straight faces while this was all going on, fell about giggling after Patrick had exited through the door. "Oh stop it" replied Diana, who always couldn't help blushing at the same time as the others had begun to giggle, feeling fresh embarrassment flood up to the surface once again. "Wish my boss was as fit as that, and as nice" replied Rachel in a jokey sarcastic style type voice, who waved her hands in front of her face to beat off the tears of laughter that had begun to stream down it. "You'll need to find a vase for those now you know Diana" said Emily, as Diana finally looked around at them all, as the giggles slowly died away.

"I can't believe he'd do that, I mean, I'm just a technician after all" replied Diana, as Samantha spoke up. "You'd better be careful you know babes, looks like you might have an admirer on your hands". "It could be worse I suppose" replied Diana in a throwaway voice, as she opened the card that Patrick had brought in with the bouquet of flowers. The card itself was a very fancy looking one, with a picture of a hand painted rose on the front, and golden slanting letters inside that read, 'Dearest Diana, wishing you a very happy birthday, from Patrick'. "Ok, that is not at all creepy in any way" joked Diana, as the others tittered, but Diana couldn't help but feel a small shiver go down her spine at that moment. It was almost as if this birthday card was trying to tell her something, but she couldn't think what it was, with her head so full of other things at that very moment.

"You must be doing something right ah babes, looks like you'll be employee of the month before you know it" replied Samantha, as the others raised a glass to Diana again, to celebrate her birthday. When the food they had ordered arrived a few minutes later, the waiter serving them had offered to take the flowers that Patrick had brought for Diana and place them in a vase of water until she was ready to take them home with her. Diana thanked the waiter, as he bustled off with them to water them, as the others tucked into their meals. "He sounds like a decent bloke your boss" said Samantha reassuringly towards Diana, as they both sat together on a bench in Lillington's local recreational park, whilst Rachel and Emily had both gone across the busy main road to order some taxies to take them back to their houses, which in their minds, was the best thing in the world at that moment.

As much as they all loved keeping their barbie doll figures in check, walking miles in high heels, wasn't exactly a way to go about it, hence why they had opted for a taxi approach to take them home from the town centre. This being a Saturday night, the main road bustled with cars, all taking people clubbing, out to local attractions, or else just seeing friends and family. "Yeah, I suppose he is, bit of a massive shock seeing him here mind" replied Diana, as Samantha looked suddenly around, as if having the sudden impression that they were being watched. "Where did you say he lived again" asked Samantha, turning her attention back to Diana, feeling that her sudden feeling of being watched was a trick of her mind. "Er, outskirts of Leicester I think, it's where my companies head office is based" replied Diana looking a little confused as to why Samantha had just looked around behind her.

"You ok Sam" asked Diana, as Samantha snapped back to her normal self again. "Sorry babes, I thought I could feel someone watching us you know, just felt it suddenly" replied Samantha, as Diana gave a little shiver, not from fright it would seem, but from the chill light breeze blowing around them. But before Diana could enquire further into Samantha's point, Rachel and Emily had crossed back from over the road and into the recreation park, up to the bench where Diana and Samantha were sitting. "The taxi is going to be about an hour's wait tonight, it's crazy" exclaimed Rachel, as she and Emily both sat down alongside Diana and Samantha on the bench, sliding their high heeled shoes off of their feet, in complete disbelieve of how long they were going to have to wait for the earliest taxis to arrive. This piece of news came as no surprise to Samantha, knowing all about driving and the attitudes of the population when it came to the road network.

"Well, it is a Saturday night, probably quicker to walk home" replied Samantha, who was used to having to walk up and down her lorry and trailer every day when making deliveries. "In these heels, are you nuts Sam; we haven't all got your cross-country trekking skills you know" replied Rachel in a jokey voice, as Emily nodded her head in agreement, knowing of Samantha's agile rugged abilities. "I'm glad it's a warmer night at any rate, otherwise we'd be frozen stiff" replied Emily, as there was a sudden beeping sound coming from Diana's handbag. Diana reached inside her hand bag and pulled out her mobile phone, to see that she had received a text message. Diana opened up the message, and saw that it was from her mother, inviting her over when she had five minutes. "Sorry guys, you'll have to go on without me, I need to go and see my mum" replied Diana, as the others smiled slightly in response.

"That's ok, she's probably only wanting to wish you a happy birthday; we'll probably see you later" replied Samantha, as Diana issued everyone with a hurried apology, before rushing away, going as far as her heels would allow her to go. "Are you sure you don't want to wait for the taxi" shouted Emily after Diana, but Diana politely refused Emily's offer. "It's only a few streets away, I can walk it" called back Diana to the others, as she crossed the road, waving to a car which had slowed down to allowed her to cross safely. Diana did indeed now feel a slight chill down her back, as the streets were dark and the street lamps were only few and far between to help the cars along the road, rather than the more vulnerable pedestrians. Diana rounded a corner, and was within sight of her own front door, where she lived with her mother, when a figure stepped out of the shadow from between the nearest streetlamp and the front door of Diana's mothers house.

It was Patrick, who looked like he'd been sitting in his car outside waiting for her, which was parked in the dark space between the two lampposts on the street, almost hiding him in complete darkness. "Diana, sorry, I know this is a little out of the blue, but I wanted to quickly give you this" said Patrick, as he attempted to hand over a brown A4 paper sized envelope. This was done with great difficulty however, as at the moment that Patrick had appeared, Diana had jumped about a foot in the air and issued a small scream, whilst nearly falling over the dustbin which sat at the garden wall at the end of the driveway. "Patrick, what are you doing here, you almost gave a heart attack" gasped Diana, who clutched at her chest in shock. "I'm really sorry, I was just heading back to the hotel, when I remembered to give you this" said Patrick, as Diana took the envelope from Patrick, trying to hold it steady in her trembling hands.

Patrick smiled slightly, as Diana's breathing slowed down to a more normal speed, but she couldn't help but think that it was suspicious all the same. The nearest hotel from where her house was only around the corner from there, but Patrick would have had to have driven past it in order to get to Diana's house. So why was he sitting outside of her house late at night waiting for her, when he could have just dropped the envelope through the front door. There was something funny going on here, and Diana's senses had begun to tingle, as if they were somehow warning Diana that some sort of grave danger was fast approaching her. "Thanks Patrick, I'll have a look at it later, I'll see you on Monday" replied Diana, in what Diana hoped was a wood-be-casual voice, as Patrick bad her good night, proceeding to climb back into his high-end sports car, before driving away with a slight screech of the tyres.

Diana watched Patrick go, and then proceeded up the driveway, letting herself into the semi dark house, feeling that the night couldn't possibly have any more dramas in stall for her. To Diana's great delight, no more dramas presented themselves, and she spent the rest of the evening with her mother, wishing that she was still out on the town with the other girls. Monday morning rolled around, as Diana found herself on the morning commuter train travelling up to Grey's Pharmaceuticals for that day's work, where Diana had been called to be at head office for a day, owing to a new project which Patrick had called, 'most urgent to discuss'. The train journey itself was always a good one in Diana's opinion, as she was always able to get some work in while on it, making up for the fact that she would have to do many hours that day if there was no way of accessing her e-mails, or other important files.

This was down to a brand-new company laptop, as well as having her train fairs paid for her by the accounts department on the company's expenses bill. "One of the many wonderful perks of the job" thought Diana, as she busied herself with her work on the laptop, allowing the train to speed up the line from Lillington station, to the outskirts of Leicester.

In the recent weeks that Diana had worked at Grey's Pharmaceuticals, the company had begun to experiment with government contracts, part of this being that a small detachment of staff had been sent from the UK's secret facility known as Porton Down, to oversee vaccine work against chemical weapons. As Diana wasn't in the military directly, she was relatively free to work outside of their control, but was still expected to never speak about her work to anyone, due to the nature of the information being sent and handled by her.

Anthrax, Sarin, Ricin, Ebola, Foot and Mouth and many others, were all being researched and having vaccines developed by Grey's Pharmaceuticals at one time or another, so Diana felt pleased in herself that her work included making a better world for the future. The other passengers on the train paid no attention to Diana, as she sat working through the many pieces of red tape paperwork that she had to oversee as part of her work. The slight gentle swaying of the train even helped some of the passengers to fall asleep on their journey, as the sun had only just started to climb above the horizon, making the whole train compartment glow a golden-brown colour. As Diana worked away, a file popped up on her main frame e-mails with a sudden bleeping noise. The word 'Coronavirus' could clearly be seen in the subject title, as Diana clicked on the email link, to open up the e-mail on her laptop screen.

Immediately after Diana opened the e-mail, she could see that it had a number of attachments on it, one of them was a short video which showed a patient in a hospital bed. As Diana watched, a doctor on the video described the symptoms that the patient was suffering from, and what antibiotics had been given to the patient over the past few days. The patient was being helped to breath by a tube which was inserted down their throat, and the machine nearby which beeped accordingly along with their heartbeat. Patrick had added a side note on the bottom which read, 'Diana, this needs to be investigated ASAP, can you do as much as you can to find out if this is a chemical or biological weapons attack'? After reading through the e-mail very carefully to make sure that she hadn't missed anything, Diana had fired off a quick reply, telling Patrick that she would

291

investigate it immediately.

A few hours later, Diana's train that she was travelling on rolled into Leicester station, where Patrick had sent a company car for Diana to take her to the Grey's Pharmaceuticals building on the outskirts of the city. "Morning everyone" said Diana as she strolled into the office, being greeted by her colleagues with a general 'morning' in return. As Diana suspected that she maybe in meetings for the whole of that day, she had opted for a smart approach, wearing a satin blouse and pencil skirt, with black heels, which made her look more like a company executive, rather than a science lab technician. "Morning Diana, did you get the e-mail that I'd sent you this morning" asked Patrick, who had just come over to Diana, as she sat down at her desk, whilst her desktop computer switched itself on in front of her, showing the start-up screen requesting a username and password.

"I did, it's not a chemical or biological weapons attack as far as I can see, although the symptoms are unlike anything I've seen before" replied Diana, as Patrick sat down in the chair next to her, leaning on one of the chair arms as he went. "It's pretty vicious, I'll give you that; we've received reports from Wuhan in China that's it's already infected the patient's lungs, and there trying to stop it developing into bronchitis" explained Patrick, as Diana looked at him curiously, as that had been the one thing that hadn't been mentioned in the email that Diana had read. "It attacks the lungs, that is interesting indeed; why are we investigating it" asked Diana, who was thinking that it may have been a serious reaction to some sort of new hair care product or something silly like that, as Diana did regularly get messages asking for assistance on these subjects.

But these were more often than not quite minor medical complaints, and was never seen as a major threat to anyone, as most of these things were curable with the right treatment. "The patient in question is a UK citizen, so according to international law, we have to investigate it; alongside the Chinese Government of course" replied Patrick, as Diana managed to find the files on her computer, by logging into the Grey's Pharmaceuticals system. "Did you have a good birthday" asked Patrick, as Diana turned to face Patrick and smiled. "I did, it was a real surprise to see you in Lillington, must have been one hell of a drive down" replied Diana, as Patrick gave his usual jolly smile and chuckle. "Quite easy to do in a sports car that can do one hundred miles per hour plus, nippy bit of kit as you can probably tell" replied Patrick, as he leaned forward slightly to lower his voice.

"Don't suppose you fancy a spot of dinner tonight after work, would love to get to know you a bit better being the new girl and all that" asked Patrick, so that everyone else around them couldn't hear them over the noise of the phones ringing, and the other workers at their desks chatting to their clients down the phone lines. "Ok, yeah, I'll meet you after I've clocked off" replied Diana, not really thinking clearly, as Patrick gave her a double thumbs up, before getting up out of the chair and walking away, leaving Diana to answer the phone to a company client. It then suddenly dawned on Diana that maybe this was a bit of a new thing that the company did to its latest employees, even though that in reality, Patrick was old enough to be Diana's father. After all, the other new girl in the office by the name of Susan, had also been asked out to dinner by Patrick as a 'welcome to the company' type of gesture.

"There's nothing creepy about that at all, is there" thought Diana, as she worked away on the Coronavirus case, watching a strange group of people walk backwards and forwards from Patrick's office as the day went on. As this was a building where they were working on government contracts, it was hardly surprising that all sorts of people were walking past Diana as she worked away, only catching quick glimpses of them in the corner of her eye. There were several gentlemen, who were all wearing different kinds of uniform, from police to military ones. Then there was a woman who looked like a beauty cosmetics model. But the strangest of all, was a man who in Diana's memory, looked very familiar indeed. "I could have sworn blind that man who just walked past looked like Greg, Samantha's boyfriend" thought Diana, as the man Diana was thinking about walked past, accompanied by Patrick, who offering him a drink as he entered the office.

This exceptionally unusual activity carried on right throughout the day, as the office slowly emptied around Diana, as her colleagues clocked off from their working day, heading for their homes, bidding each other a good evening as they went. "Ready to go Diana" asked Patrick, who suddenly appearing behind Diana, making her jump about a foot in the air again, as she had been preoccupied with the work on her computer screen. "Yes, of course" replied Diana, who was breathing heavily again, trying not to freak out too much from where her boss had accidently made her jump. "Shall we" said Patrick, as he gestured his hand towards the open office door, which lead down to the reception area on the ground floor, who seemed to have missed the fact that he had almost given Diana a heart attack. Patrick's idea of a sit-down dinner turned out to be in a hotel bar, which apparently Patrick had booked earlier that day.

"If this is the sort of treatment that I'm going to get by working for this company, I should have come here years ago" joked Diana to Patrick, as they sat down at the hotel bar table over their meals of lasagne and pasta. Patrick laughed slightly, as he replied, "well, you came to us with flying colours, and you're a real loyal worker Diana". Diana smiled and raised her glass to him, as they sat talking about the new Coronavirus project for a while between their meals. Considering that this was supposed to be a top-secret research project, Patrick didn't exactly seem to be worried too much if people passing their table heard about it or not, despite the fact that he was the C.E.O of Grey's Pharmaceuticals, and would have been bound by a lot of confidentiality agreements. Diana did have to look a little worried from time to time when Patrick did this, but he always seemed to stop himself just in time, before something sensitive slipped out by accident.

"What gets me, is that this can't be an isolated case; if it attacks the lungs, then it must be something in the air, so lots more people must have got it, but maybe aren't showing symptoms yet" replied Diana, as Patrick had just given her a 'so, what do you think of covid' sort of look. "I wanted to ask you actually, who were all those people you were seeing today; they looked a bit random if you don't mind me saying" asked Diana, feeling a lot braver than she felt, asking such as a question of her boss at such an early stage in her working career. When Diana had finished speaking, Patrick leaned forwards in his chair, and spoke in a lower voice than normal, so as not to be overheard by anyone. "Let's just say, it's a bit of a side project I'm working on; they all had similar blood groups you see, and we needed people like that for medical trials and things; all volunteers of course" replied Patrick, as Diana nodded in agreement to show that she understood Patrick.

But Diana couldn't help but feel a small shiver go down her spine. It was strange that she had suddenly felt cold, as it was warm inside the hotel bar, but Diana couldn't help but feel that Patrick hadn't been entirely trueful with her about what was really going on with all of the unusual people going to and from his office that day. "Sorry to ask boss, but I couldn't help but see that I might have recognised one of the people that you saw today in your office" replied Diana, as Patrick raised his eyebrows in surprise. "Really, you should have said Diana, that will help the programme for sure; who did you think it was just as a matter of interest" asked Patrick, as Diana relaxed slightly. "I think he's the boyfriend of one of my best friends, a man by the name of Greg Stent" replied Diana, in an enquiring voice, as Patrick took another mouthful of lasagne from his plate, only just about getting it inside his mouth, as he began to chew it.

"Stent you stay, Greg Stent; oh yes, I remember now; he was a young chap who came up on our radar" replied Patrick, in a matter-of-fact style voice, peeking Diana's interest so high, that she was afraid that she may have levitated off of her chair. It had amazed Diana considerably of how Patrick had managed to answer her question with such a large amount of food in his mouth, but he still managed to succeed in this task all the same. "Willing volunteer from what I could tell, but we put out the flyers anyway, and he responded" explained Patrick, as Diana relaxed a little, but was still very curious in her mind about the new mystery programme that Patrick was running. "What a coincidence though, Greg being a part of the programme" replied Diana, but Patrick seemed now to be trying to change the subject, as if he felt Diana had asked a few too many questions.

"Shall we go to your hotel room, it's much more private if you want to talk business and work" asked Patrick, as Diana looked suddenly concerned, wondering what was going on. "Oh, I thought I was going back home on the train tonight, my mother is expecting me after all" replied Diana, but Patrick waved a hand in front of her. "Don't worry, I booked a hotel room for you, it will be easier for you to get to work tomorrow without having to take that train ride of yours" replied Patrick, as Diana smiled slightly, but still getting that shiver down her spin, feeling that something was up. "Oh, ok then, thanks Patrick" replied Diana, as Patrick told Diana that it was no problem at all, and allowed her to go up to the hotel room, while Patrick carried her bag behind her. Diana let herself into the hotel room, closely followed by Patrick, who placed her handbag down on the small table beside the bed.

"Thanks so much Patrick, I appreciate this, there must be a lot on if you want me staying up in Leicester for the night" joked Diana, then without warning, Patrick kissed her on the cheek, making Diana go bright red with shock. But Diana did appear to forget who she was, and that she a lot younger than Patrick was, as without even pausing to think, Diana kissed Patrick in return. Before they both knew it, they were both going at each other, both of them forgetting who they were and what they were doing. But things would soon suddenly take a different turn, as within minutes, Patrick's hand had found its way up Diana's leg, as he hoisted her onto the bed with surprising fitness, considering his age. "What are you doing" cried out Diana, suddenly coming to her senses, as Patrick went in again, reaching a hand under her pencil skirt to have a slight grope.

Diana tried to beat him away, but Patrick had a hungry look on his face, and Diana felt a hand close over her mouth, so that she was unable to scream out. "New girls to the team always get the Patrick treatment" replied Patrick in a sickly dark voice, as Diana attempted to scream out, the sound strangely muffled from behind Patrick's hand. Diana clamped her eyes tight shut, and struggled as much as she could to try and get free from underneath Patrick, but she sudden felt herself begin to lose feeling throughout her body, as if she had been given some kind of sedative drug.

It was clear now that Patrick had drugged Diana with some sort of date rape substance, as she was still awake and breathing, but here memory from that point onwards however had become a big blur. But Diana didn't have to be a detective to work out what was happening to her; she was being raped by Patrick Devises, and nothing and no-one was there to help her.

Diana soon stopped struggling, as the effects of the date rape drug started to take effect, paralyzing her on the bed where she lay as Patrick leaned over her, committing the horrible act that he was now doing. "I can make your life very uncomfortable if you ever speak out about this; I have connections, influence and power beyond what you know" leered Patrick, who after he'd finished raping Diana, stood inches from Diana's terrified figure as she sobbed silently in fear, tears rolling down her face. "See you at work tomorrow" said Patrick, as he picked up his jacket, and exited the room, closing the door behind him. Diana slid down off the bed huddling on the floor, as she cried her eyes out, realising what had just happened to her. It took hours for the effect of the drugs to wear off, but when they finally did, the pain that followed only felt ten times worse than what it already was.

"Oh my god, he just raped you like that, no warning or anything" replied Samantha, back in the present-day prison holding cell at the Grey's Pharmaceuticals building, as Diana nodded, having still been traumatised by what she had been through in the hotel room nine months earlier. "I didn't stand a chance babe, I really didn't; it was beyond words what he did too me, and now I have to live with his baby" explained Diana, as she looked down at the bump in her stomach. "The dirty" began Samantha, but held herself just in time, as she was about to say a word that Diana certainly wouldn't have approved of. "I went to the police in the end and they arrested and charged him, but before they got a chance to take it to court, Covid came along and everything was just wiped out, so he walked away a free man; but he is free in here now to do it again if he wants" finished Diana, as she felt fresh tears rolling down her face at the very thought of it.

"Ah babes, that's just horrific" replied Samantha in disgust who had got up onto her feet, pacing the prison cell as she went. "It is, but I've always wanted to have a baby, just never like this" replied Diana, as Samantha felt a tear coming to her eye as well. "But babes, you don't seem to realise that Patrick raped you, and you could have aborted the baby in the early stages when you found out that you were pregnant" argued back Samantha, who felt anger at the fact that Patrick had done a monstrous act on her best friend. "I know that Sam, but I always wanted a child and I had to lie to my mother and everyone else about who the father was, so that they wouldn't know I was rapped" replied Diana, as Samantha couldn't believe what she was hearing, but then realised that she had no right to be angry with Diana, as it was Diana who had been raped, and not Samantha.

"I'm a scientist, a medical person; I may not be a doctor, but I swore to protect life, not to destroy it" replied Diana, in a calmer voice than the one she had used a few minutes earlier. "But I've seen you these last few months and you certainly didn't look as big as you are now" replied Samantha, who was curious to know how Diana had pulled off this level of camouflage right under the nose of her entire friends and family network. "I wore pregnancy pants and had a girdle to hide the early belly fat, but only when I was around you and the girls; when I was around my family, I didn't bother with it" replied Diana, as Samantha's face looked shocked and surprised. Up until this point, Samantha had thought that having to work during Covid was bad enough, but at least Samantha hadn't tried to hide the fact that she had been raising a child inside of her, right under the noses of everyone she knew and loved.

"But you could have been killed; you could have caught Covid and it could have killed you and the baby at the same time" replied Samantha exasperated, as Diana sat up on the prison cell floor, propping herself up on her hands as she did so. "I know, but I must have been immune, as I survived just like you did" replied Diana, as Samantha looked back at Diana, feeling that this was one fight that she wasn't going to win. "But one thing I can be sure about is that Greg was there that day, I swear it; if he wasn't, then it was his identical twin" replied Diana, as Samantha's ears definitely perked up at that very moment when the word 'Greg' had been mentioned. "Greg was there that day, but why was he there; why did he not tell me about this programme he was on" exclaimed Samantha, making Diana start slightly, as Samantha and Greg had always been known to share every little thing that they knew about each other.

"I, I never really found out too much, after that, the sub managers that took over after Patrick was arrested had me doing other work apart from his programme, and I was still terrified about what had happened" replied Diana, as Samantha rubbed her forehead with her hand in frustration. "I just can't believe he was here back then, and never said anything; maybe he's here right now, and we don't even know it yet" said Samantha a little shaken, as Diana replied. "Sam, the project was top secret; for all you know, he could have signed some sort of confidentiality agreement to prevent him from speaking out about it". Samantha continued to pace the prison cell again, trying to think hard about the situation. "These other people, they must have had some sort of connection to the company, or even been a part of their programme; who was on the meeting list again" asked Samantha, as Diana ticking them off on her fingers.

"There were half a dozen military personnel, a senior police officer, the chap who looked like Greg and half a dozen others who were all in regular daytime clothing" replied Diana, as Samantha stopped her pacing, taking in everything that Diana was saying with wrapped interest. "These people must have something in common; they must have" said Samantha a little confused by Diana's words, as Diana replied, "the senior management told me that my Covid research had indicated that it had something to do with blood groups in one of the e-mails that had been sent to me during". "Greg was A positive blood group, same as I am, I remember we always joked about it saying we could keep each other alive if either of us were involved in an accident or such like" replied Samantha, thinking back to her medical records kept by her doctor during the days before Covid.

"I'm A positive too" replied Diana, as Samantha suddenly smacked herself across her forehead. It was so obvious now, what the very thing was that these unknown people on Patrick's programme all had in common. "You idiot Sam, why didn't you think of that before" thought Samantha, as even Diana looked puzzled at Samantha, wondering what was happening. "That's it, those with A positive blood types must have survived Covid-19; it all fits, and I bet you anything that all of those people that Patrick was meeting with, were A positive blood types as well" exclaimed Samantha, as Diana, now cottoning on to what Samantha meant, continued on Samantha's trail of thought. "Yeah, and what if, Patrick had somehow been in on the spread of Covid in Wuhan, so that's when the government came asking him about it, he already knew" said Diana, feeling that new blisters of truth were suddenly popping in front of their eyes.

"Of course, the future start here; oh, that's clever, that's so clever; and no government in their right mind would suspect a thing" replied Samantha, as Diana looked at her, whilst Samantha pressed on, new avenues of truth and understanding flying through her head like electrically charged eels in a pond. "Think about it, climate change, world powers, expanding populations, it would be the perfect cover to save the planet and start humanity afresh; if you're a foreign power now, and you wanted to save the planet, end conflict and stop a population boom, what would you do"? Samantha posed this question to Diana, who just sat there for a few seconds, looking incredibly non plussed at Samantha, as if Samantha wasn't making any sense whatsoever. When Diana just shrugged her shoulders a few seconds later however, Samantha pressed on again, using the sort of voice that a person would use when explaining that one plus one equalled two.

"Well, isn't it obvious, you'd put out a deadly virus, one that would attack our bodies, but make it look like a normal pathogen, like the common cold and flu for example; billions are killed off, but each country would have a programme, which would round up survivors, and have them transported elsewhere; those coordinates that were on the pamphlet must be the meeting point for the survivors". "But it still doesn't explain what it's all been for, humanity was advancing with technology and science and all sorts; we were even making progress with climate change, so why kill off the human race now in 2020" retorted Diana, as Samantha paused to think, thinking that Diana had just raised a very interesting point in their discussion. It was certainly true that any government body would have been prepared to take a massive backlash, should any information like that ever come to light.

"Well, to save the planet, or gain a domination over those of us who were left in the world after Covid had flushed through the population" replied Samantha, but before either of them could carry on the discussion, there came the sound of the keys turning in the lock, and a bang of the door handle, as the cell door swung open with a squeaking sound. "Well, well, well, the bitches figured it out after all" sneered Edward Fitzgerald, who had just come in through the open prison cell door, a machine gun slung over his shoulder, along with his usual wicked grin. Both Samantha and Diana hadn't realised how long they had been talking for, as there was now a glint of sunlight starting to come through the prison cell barred window telling them that it must now be morning time. "That's enough Edward; Samantha, Diana, you're both coming with me" said Helen Dukes, who had appeared over Edward's shoulder as Edward had finished speaking.

Edward looked a little downtrodden, as if he had been denied a real treat; but he proceeded forward, and snapped handcuffs on Samantha and Diana's wrists, before two men wearing hazmat suits and gas masks entered the prison cell, and hauled them both to their feet. "Take it easy will you, can't you see she pregnant" retorted Samantha, as they were both manhandled out of the prison cell and along the corridor, where Samantha and Diana were pushed into a lift, where the doors juddered open with a slight creaking sound. There was clearly some sort of an electrical power source keeping the building going, as there was a constant flow of electricity powering everything from the lights above their heads, to the heaters along the walls. The lift's lights flickered slightly as they got in, making it look reminisce of a horror movie, or something out of an apocalypse.

It certainly felt like a horror movie at any rate, as the lift doors closed, the pair of gas masked and hazmat suited men held on so tightly to

Samantha and Diana's arms, that Diana felt herself start to go blue from the compression, and Samantha began to see her veins in her arm become clear as day. Even despite this sudden pain, neither of them dared speak, as the lift juddered slowly upwards, presuming taking them from the basement, to the upper floors. Even as they all stood there in silence, Samantha was already formulating a plan to escape from this hell hole of a building. But when the doors opened a second later, they found themselves looking out at a clean white lab, where Bunsen burners sat flaming away heating up strange coloured liquids, and the sounds of screeches and squawking came from the many cages around the brightly lit lab where animals were being held, no doubt being experimented on by Grey's Pharmaceuticals.

Around half a dozen men and women in white science lab coats, were moving around slowly, all wearing face masks and safety goggles, examining the animals in the cages, and making notes on clipboards as they went. The two hazmat suited men who had hold of Samantha and Diana, now forced them forwards out of the lift, dragging them down into two chairs in the centre of the room. The other scientists looked on, as Helen, Edward and Patrick, all came out of the lift a few minutes later, having climbed inside it after Samantha and Diana had been brought upwards inside it to this strange laboratory type environment. Samantha and Diana felt the bright light burning their eyes, as if they were looking directly into the sun, as they held their arms up with difficulty, whilst being handcuffed to shield their eyes from the light. As their eyesight began to recover slightly, they could hear the sounds of clicking heels on the floor, as Helen leaned in to speak to them both.

CHAPTER TWENTY

The Escape

"As you're both guilty of crimes against the government" began Helen, but Diana cut across her, a look of utter shock on her face. "What, I've done nothing wrong, nothing" screamed Diana, as Samantha just glared into Helen's eyes; but Helen ploughed on, regardless of Diana's outburst. "You're sentence for such a crime, is to be a part of the clinical trial to find a Covid vaccine, this you will do for the rest of your life". Helen smiled slightly as she spoke, leering in the same way as Edward did, as Diana began to scream out. "You're going to kill us all, I'm pregnant you evil cow" screamed back Diana, as Helen turned and walked away, flanked by her two thugs, Edward and Patrick, who both leered and smiled their evil smiles, stepping back into the lift as the doors closed slowly behind them. Diana began to struggle against the hazmat suited man who was holding her down, as they both witnessed a pair of white lab-coated scientists approaching them.

"Don't worry, we're only taking some blood samples" said the first of the white lab-coated scientists, as they drew level with Samantha and Diana, syringes outstretched, looking more like zombies on a blood lusting quest as they approached Samantha and Diana, both with face masks across their faces, so that only their eyes were visible behind plastic goggles. "Don't struggle Diana, it will only make it worse" said Samantha, in a surprisingly calm voice for the situation that they found themselves in. Diana meanwhile had started to scream, but a blue latex glove on the hazmat suited man holding her down, had suddenly snapped across Diana's mouth, silencing her, as she continued to struggle. As the first scientist leaned in with the hyperendemic needle however ready to take a blood sample from Samantha, she was suddenly aware that the scientist above her, had just given her a small wink, and released their grip very slightly.

It clearly hadn't been noticed by the others, but Samantha couldn't help but notice that the eyes behind the goggles were more friendly looking than all of the others. "Well, what are you waiting for, take the samples" retorted the first white lab-coated scientist in an annoyed voice, as the other scientist standing over Samantha had stopped what they were doing. "Sorry doc, these two aren't compatible with the programme" said an all too familiar voice from the second white-lab coated scientist. This statement was such a shock to everyone, that even Diana stopped struggling in confusion about what was going on. "What are you talking about" said the first white lab-coated scientist, who was now looking directly at the scientists who'd winked at Samantha. But before any of them could even move an inch further, the white lab-coated scientist holding the hyperaemic needle suddenly lunged sideways, plunging the needle into the other scientist's arm.

The first white lab-coated scientist screamed out in pain, as everything seemed to happen all at once. The first white lab-coated scientist fell backwards onto the floor, still screaming in agony, as they could all clearly see that the needle was sticking out of their arm, as blood began to squirt from the wound, only stemmed slightly by the fact that they had clamped their hand over it. Both of the men in the hazmat suit and gas mask who was holding down Diana and Samantha, both reacted at the same time. The one holding Diana, attempted to come around the chair where Diana was sitting, but was impeded slightly as Diana had stuck out her leg making him trip up and faceplant straight onto the floor. Diana in her haste to get up, had accidently knocked into the side of the worktop, causing a Bunsen burner and a beaker to become dislodged from the worktop.

The strange amber liquid inside of the beaker splattered itself onto the hazmat suited man, which burned a hole in his suit as it made contact with his clothes. The man screamed out in pain as next to them, Samantha had suddenly flown out of her chair at speed, as her hazmat suited guard, who had dived at the second white lab-coated scientist, punched him full on in his mask, making him fall backwards in shock, hitting into another work station, which made the computer screen topple off and land on his face. They heard a muffled grunt from the man, followed by a smashing sound, as the computer screen landed on his head, knocking him out cold from the impact of it. There came screams and shouts from the cages, as the animals inside of them started with alarm at the sound of all of the noise that was going on, plus a great deal of shouts from the other scientists, who had started in alarm at the sight of the commotion happening in front of them.

The other scientists scattered throughout the lab, all seemed to want to attack and defend themselves against this sudden piece of action that was occurring right in front of them, but then they decided to think better of it, as the second white lab-coated scientist suddenly grabbed a beaker with another amber coloured liquid inside of it, and launched it with all of their strength against the opposite wall. The beaker hit the wall, knocking over another Bunsen burner on its way to the wall. "Get down" shouted the second white lab-coated figure, as they, Samantha and Diana, all divided down behind a work bench, as the beaker hit the wall, and shattered into a thousand pieces. The resulting explosion that followed was so powerful, that it blasted the opposite wall out of existence, sending bricks and mortar flying everywhere, the sound making them all clap their hands over their ears as a result.

Two out of the half a dozen scientists who had been running for cover at the time, were also caught in the blast, as they were thrown backwards off their feet onto the floor, screaming as they went. It was hardly surprising that they didn't move or get back up again, as Samantha and Diana both suspected that they had either been knocked out, or were sadly dead as a result of the explosion. Sunlight now poured in through the open wall space, making the already bright lab look even brighter than the prison cell had been. The other scientists had all escaped through another door at the far end of the lab, as Samantha and Diana finally began to breath normally again, picking themselves up off the floor. "Are you alright" said the second white lab-coated scientist, as they offered their hand down to help Diana up, as she was the one who was struggling the most from what had just happened.

"Yeah, I think I'm ok" replied Diana, breathing heavily as her hands shock slightly, owing to all of the action that had just taken place. "Thank you; we owe you our lives, just who exactly are you" asked Samantha, as she lent up against a work top, breathing just as heavily as Diana was. The second white lab-coated scientist now reached up to their face and removed their goggles, which had steamed up slightly due to their heavy breathing. "Police Constable Julie Guard, Hertfordshire Constabulary" said Julie, who's face had now become visible, as she threw away the goggles, lab coat and face mask onto the ground. On hearing Julie voice, Samantha spun around, to stare into the face of her friend, Julie Guard, who was now fully visible to them, as Samantha brain went numb. Julie was indeed standing there in front of them, broad smile on her face, grateful to see Samantha once again.

Samantha's face lit up, as she ran at Julie and embraced her in a hug that was so tight, that even Julie felt her rib cage begin to crack under the strain. "Wow, don't kill me after I've only just saved you" said Julie in a jokey voice, as Samantha released her with a hurried apology. "It's so good to see you again Julie, what are you doing here" asked Samantha, as her breath returned to normal. "Erm, I don't want to be a massive pain in the backside or anything Sam, but aren't you going to introduce me" replied Diana, who had been pulled to her feet by Julie, and was looking backwards and forwards between them both with surprising interest. "Oh yeah, sorry about that; Diana, this is my good friend, Julie Guard; we meet at a road traffic collision earlier this year; Julie, this is Diana, one of my best friends from my school days" replied Samantha, as Diana and Julie shook hands, Diana feeling a complete wave of gratitude towards Julie as she did so.

"Pleasure to meet you Julie, I always knew you were a badass Sam; how did you get into a traffic collision" asked Diana, as Julie replied, "she didn't, it was Edward Fitzgerald that caused the crash, Samantha just happened to be on the road when it happened, and was caught up in it". Diana suddenly seemed to understand what Julie was telling her, but they didn't have long to digest this information, before all hell seemed to break lose again. At that exact moment, an alarm began to ring out, with a female voice saying, "intruder alert, intruder alert, all guards to the labs, all guard to the labs". Red lights began to flash all around the walls, as if they were caught up in a fire drill of some kind. "We're in trouble now, I hate to think how many laws we just violated" replied Julie, who seemed to be on a bit of an adrenaline high at that exact moment in time.

"Time and a place Julie, come on" said Samantha, a little exasperated, as Julie suddenly snapped into a serious state, realising that this wasn't the time to be discussing potential crimes that the three of them had just committed. Without speaking, Julie suddenly ran across the room, to what looked like a desk with a computer on it, and pulled open a draw. Both Diana and Samantha went wide eyed in shock, as Julie returned from the desk a moment later with a jet-black coloured machine gun, whilst simultaneously clipping a magazine fully loaded with bullets into it. "Where the hell did you get one of them" demanded Samantha, as Julie replied with a hurried, "in the armoury, this place is loaded, plus I did firearms training back in my police days, but was never attached to the armed response unit; just as well really, as I was never any good with them anyhow".

Samantha and Diana were temporarily stunned at that moment wondering what was more impressive, the fact that Julie was trained in firearms, but yet hadn't been comfortable with them; or the fact that she had saved them all from inside Grey's Pharmaceuticals itself. Pulling back the firing pin, Julie raised the weapon to shoulder height, pointing it at the open door, as the lift behind them suddenly whirred into life, rattling downwards towards them. "They're coming down, what are we going to do" screamed Diana in a panicked voice, but her voice seemed to clear Julie and Samantha's heads. "Cover" shouted Julie, as she swung the machine gun around, which was followed by two loud bangs, as Julie fired two bullets into the lift controls, which sparked as the bullets hit them. Samantha and Diana ducked instinctively, as they cover their eyes due to the noise.

The lift whirring sound suddenly stopped, as Julie turned back to face the others, lowering the machine gun down, so that it pointed at the floor out of harm's way. "That should slow them up for a while, so, how do we get out again" said Julie, more to herself than the others. "Ask him" said Samantha, as she pointed down at the first white lab-coated scientist, who had still been moaning and groaning all of that time, where the needle was still sticking out of his arm, his hands sticky and wet with blood. Without pausing to think, Julie leaned down, and yanked the needle out of their arm. The scientist screamed in agony, as Julie grabbed hold of his neck. "Now you listen to me Doctor Death, how do we get out" snarled Julie, who looked so menacing at that moment, that even Samantha and Diana backed away slightly in alarm. "Go to hell" retorted the scientist, as Julie hit him across the face with all of her strength, snarling as she did so.

It was a mark of how desperate they all were to get to safety, that Julie was prepared to act and show her emotions in the way that she was doing at that moment in time and certainly not in the manner befitting a police officer of the law. "I won't ask you again scumbag, how do we get out" snarled Julie again, as the scientist pointed, using his good hand, as his other was covered in blood, out through the open hole in the wall. "Out there, along the side of the building, as it leads to the front car park" replied the scientist, gathering up all of their strength to answer Julie's question as best as they could. "Thank you kindly dear" said Julie in a sweet girly voice, as she was clearly enjoying being seen as the hero of the hour. Julie stood up again, a newly formed plan hatching in her mind as she stood there thinking hard. "I hate to think how many police protocols you just broke there Julie" joked Samantha, as Julie couldn't help but grin.

"Times change Sam, times change" replied Julie, as Diana still looked shocked, clutching a hand to her stomach again, looking as if her unborn baby had just given her a sharp kick. "I don't want to be a kill joy or anything, but I'm pregnant, and there's a load of bad people with weapons about to break in through that door" exclaimed Diana, gesturing to the door where the other scientists had escaped out of earlier on during the action. "You're not wrong there Diana, follow me everyone" replied Julie, as she slung the machine gun over her shoulder. Samantha was reminded a little of one of those action movies, where the heroine of the story would be a bikini clad woman, who looked like Lara Croft or someone similar, wielding a weapon and saving the day at the same time. Maybe Julie felt the same way, as her police career before this would have most likely been pencil pushing and paperwork, rather than this sort of action.

"Ok team, let's move out" replied Julie in an encouraging voice, bringing the machine gun into a stance position ready to fire it again, in case anyone attempted to stop them leaving. Samantha volunteered to go first, as she gingerly stuck her head out of the hole in the wall, which was wide enough for them all to climb through. After sticking her head out and looking up and down the sides of the building to see if anyone was coming, Samantha then retreated her head back inside again. The sounds of muffled running footsteps could be heard coming from the other side of the door, getting louder and louder as they all stood there. "Their coming, their coming" said Diana, over and over again in a panicking voice, as Julie stepped forward. "Stay close to me Diana, you'll be fine; Samantha, I need you to go ahead to the end of the building to see if anyone is in the main car park" said Julie in a calm, but stable voice.

Diana gingerly walked beside Julie, as the three of them climbed through the whole in the wall, just as they heard the hurried footsteps stop outside of the closed lab door. It was lucky that the hole in the wall was facing the hedges of the farms field that Samantha had crossed what felt like days earlier now, as Julie took the lead, Diana closely behind her, supporting her stomach and wincing as she went. "I didn't ever think that my birthing plan would involve being chased by a load of bad guys at my former place of employment" said Diana, who was puffing slightly at the amount of physical exercise she was being expected to do, whilst being heavily pregnant. "At least your baby will be proud of its mother when it comes ah babes" replied Samantha, as Julie came to a halt at the corner of the building, holding up her hand to stop and Samantha and Diana from progressing any further forwards.

Looking careful around the corner, Julie could see the car park which was deserted, all except for Patrick's, Edward's and Helen's cars, but no sign of any guards. "We may have to make a break for it; they suspect that you came in across the fields, so we'll need to skirt around the building, and through a hole in the hedge I found a few weeks ago, so you can back to the Green Goddess without being seen by anyone" said Julie, as she pointed out the situation and her plan in turn, as Samantha and Diana stood listening carefully, slightly out of breath. "Your amazing Julie, where did you learn your firearms skills from" said Samantha, as Julie turned back to her. "I went on a firearms course, never passed first time, but how hard can it be ah" replied Julie, as she peered back around the corner again, checking to see if any movement had occurred since she had last looked around at the scene before her.

"There has to be a vehicle or some such somewhere, how did you get here Julie" asked Diana, as Julie smiled slightly, knowing that it was time to reveal the very large ace up her sleeve. "Let's just say, I got a bit of a helping hand from the wonderful boys and girls at Northamptonshire Constabulary Diana" replied Julie, as she gestured to a point just off to her right, where it looked like a blue and yellow colour zebra stood motionless behind the hedge. "Tell me that is not transport" said Diana, as the three of them gingerly crossed over the small wasteland area, looking left and right as they went, to the point where the blue and yellow zebra stood. But it wasn't a Zebra at all; it was in fact a BMW four-wheel drive police car, with slightly faded paintwork and a few scratches here and there, where Julie had attempted to cover it over with leaves and branches from the nearby trees and hedges.

The official police logo and stickers reading 'Northamptonshire Constabulary', could now be seen on the sides, along the word 'Police' written in dark blue letters along the bottom, front and back of the vehicle. "No way" replied Samantha in shock, as Julie grinned from ear to ear at the look on Samantha's face. "Borrowed it from Northampton police stations armed response unit, good isn't it" said Julie, as she began to pull the leaves and branches off of it, so they could make their escape away from the Grey's Pharmaceuticals building. The indicators flashed slightly, as Julie opened the passenger door, allowing Samantha to help Diana into a laying position on the back seat. "Samantha, I want you up the front with me, in case we have to defend ourselves" replied Julie in a commanding voice, as Samantha nodded at her, having just finished aiding Diana to lay down on the back seats.

In the grander scheme of things, this was probably for the best, as Diana wouldn't be able to move fast if they came under attack for any reason. Julie had already climbed into the driver's seat, as Samantha closed her door with a small clicking sound. "Let's get the hell out of here" said Samantha cheerfully, but in her hast to open the window to allow some fresh air in, she had accidently knocked against the controls, which activated the sirens and blue flashing lights. In the immediate seconds following this, Samantha and Julie looked at each other in shock, as the sound of the sirens and flashing lights were bound to tell everyone

311

inside the building exactly where they were. Julie made a sudden dash to turn them all off, but it was too late. "Over there" came a sudden shout, as the air was suddenly filled with the bangs and whizzing sounds of bullets, as Diana let out a small scream from the back seats.

The guards it seemed, had managed to make their way out of the building, and were now fully aware of where exactly their prey was. "Drive, drive, drive" shouted Samantha, as Diana let out a short scream. With a roar of sound, the engine fired into life, as Julie made the wheels spin madly, as they crashed through the hedge, coming face to face with around a dozen men dressed in black special forces uniforms and carrying fully automatic machine guns, who appeared right in front of them. The police car shot towards the soldiers, some of them cried out in shock, before jumping out of the way as the police car came shooting towards them, like a mad bowling ball heading for some bowling pins. Julie turned the steering wheel hard to the right to avoid them, but unfortunately caught one of the soldier's head on, as they heard a load thudding sound, as he yelled out in pain, having been knocked sideways by the impact.

The other soldiers continued to fire at them, as they came off of the wasteland, onto the solid tarmacked road surface, crashing through the closed gates to the car park with a loud bang, sending them flying across the street into the kerb opposite. A loud smashing sound, told them that the rear window had just been blown out, its glass flying everywhere, as the police car took off at top speed, it's sirens and lights now blaring and flashing away. "Don't just stand there, get after them" shouted Edward, who had just emerged from the upper floors, and was now climbing into his own pickup truck within the car park. Helen and Patrick were now standing in the doorway, as Edward's pickup truck and another vehicle full of soldiers, took off after the police vehicle. "I want them back alive Patrick, alive I said" retorted Helen, as Patrick nodded to her, understanding her commands quite clearly.

"Edward is a good man at that, he'll bring them back no problem" replied Patrick, as he too looked angry and frustrated, looking around at his half-destroyed building, where the explosion had ripped through it, caused by Samantha, Julie and Diana during their escape. "And who's going to pay for the repairs on this lot; those three have destroyed my labs and countless of hours of research" snapped back Patrick angrily, as Helen turned to look at him, her chest swelling considerably by anger. "The treasury will compensate you; you'll have three test subjects to experiment on once their caught" retorted Helen in her official tone of voice, thinking that Patrick's small thing of expecting his building to be rebuilt was small fry, considering that Helen wanted Samantha, Diana, and now Julie for terrorism charges, because of the mystery pamphlet, and what it all represented.

After all, Helen claimed that the pamphlet was government property, but it was Patrick who had been sending them out to people, and not her. Helen was now wholly determined to find out exactly who had aided the escape of her suspects, and where they were heading at that moment. Helen's thoughts were hampered somewhat, by the fact that Patrick was still raving about the now half destroyed Grey's Pharmaceuticals building, and how he wasn't exactly going to be able to ask for the insurance to pay for it, and that his staff would have to do it instead. "I used to have cadavers coming in all the time for research, what makes these three any different" snapped Patrick, but Helen held up a finger to him, which made him stare at her in amazement, completely taken aback that Helen had stopped him in his spill about Grey's Pharmaceuticals and the years of research wasted.

"Just remember that you operate here and now because I give you permission too; do not forget who is in charge around here Patrick" retorted Helen, as Patrick snorted and strode away, an angry expression on his face, but realising that he had been outranked, outmanned and outgunned all at the same time. Helen stared back out towards the entrance to the car park, thinking that she had got one over on Patrick, but not wanting to show it on her face. It was a mark really of how badly Helen wanted to find out about what was on the pamphlet, that she been prepared to break multiple international codes of law, just to get her hands on two people, who she thought knew the answers to this one great mystery of the new world. But the one thought that was still playing on Helen's mind was how the mystery pamphlet had ended up in Samantha's possession in the first place.

Helen's smile began to curl around her mouth again, as she slowly ticked over the thoughts in her mind, as it was clear now, that there was a mole in her tightly run ship. Someone who had printed and sent the mystery pamphlet to multiple people behind her back, leaking the covid vaccine programme out to others in the world. "Who else knows about this; who is my spy, one of the soldiers, scientists; is it even Edward or Patrick" thought Helen, as she wrestled with her thoughts, trying to think more clearly. Helen decided to keep her cards close from now on, and not let onto anyone about what she was planning to do, as she turned heel and marched straight back inside, having a very great mess to clean up in the process, as the resulting wall blast was bound to have weakened the entire structure in one way or another. The staff numbers inside the building had certainly been reduced, now that a chase was in motion out on the road.

Back out of the road meanwhile, Samantha, Julie and Diana were speeding away down a dual carriageway, which lead back towards the farm on the outskirts of the city, where the Green Goddess was hidden away under the camouflage sheet. At the last second however, Julie realised that driving in the direction of the Green Goddess was bound to attract attention, so she had chosen to drive the police car in the opposite direction instead, until they felt safe that they were not being followed. This wasn't to last for long however, as within a short period of time, the site of multiple vehicles began to appear behind the police car, there engines revving hard and fast in an attempt to close in on the speeding police car. "We've got company" exclaimed Samantha, as she hauled herself around in her chair, to stare out of the smashed rear window on the police car, catching site of the pursing vehicles.

Julie caught sight of them in the rear-view mirror, as Edward's pickup, which was being flanked by a black four-wheel drive vehicle, was gaining on them with every second. Diana was still breathing heavily in the back seat, and for a second, Samantha was convinced she was going into labour. "Sam, you're going to have to fight them off, I'm sorry, but I can't do it and drive at the same time" shouted back Julie, as Samantha gulped, hearing the seriousness in Julie's voice, and realising that she was going to have to confront her fears head on. Samantha had never been a fan of guns it was true, but under the circumstances, she would have to swallow her pride, and live up to her family's honourable name. "Ok, I'll do it, just don't let them pass us" called back Samantha, as she lowered the passenger side window, and stood up in her chair, resting herself very careful on the door frame, feeling the wind whipping through her hair as she did so.

"Careful Sam" screamed Diana, but Samantha had already pulled out the machine gun that Julie had been using, before taking careful aim at the black four-wheel drive. When the pickup and black four-wheel drive were only around fifty yards away, Samantha pulled the trigger, which was followed by a loud bang as a single bullet flew out of the barrel on the machine gun, followed by a second loud bang a few moments later, as the passenger side tyre on the black four-wheel drive blew out, shedding its tyre all over the road. The black four-wheel drive began to lurch violently from one side of the dual carriageway to the other, narrowly avoiding Edward's pickup truck as he planted his foot on the accelerator to avoid a collision with it, until eventually the black four-wheel drive skidded sideways and began to roll over and over, coming to a stop the right way up, but completely mangled, its occupants badly wounded and fighting for their lives.

"Way to go Sam" screamed out Diana, as she had heard the sounds of a violently crashing vehicle from where she lay on the back seats, whilst Samantha seated herself back down in her passenger seat next to Julie, who gave Samantha a quick pat on the back in gratitude for putting one of the pursing vehicles out of action. It was now only Edward and themselves that remained in the chase, as his pickup truck rammed the back of the police car, making all them judder forward, Diana almost falling into the rear passenger footwell due to the force of the impact. "Oh no you don't Edward Fitzgerald" snarled Julie in a determined voice, as she planted her foot hard onto the accelerator, pushing it all the way to the floor. The police shoot forward by another ten miles per hour or so, but Samantha was suddenly struck with an idea. "Julie, on the count on three, turn sharp left" said Samantha, as Julie looked at Samantha in total shock.

"Are you nuts, at these speeds" exclaimed Julie, as she looked back down at the speedometer on the dashboard. The police car was indeed running at a far higher speed than normal, as it sped along at over ninety miles per hour, its engine revving hard and fast. Even though the police car was capable of going much faster than the ninety miles per hour than it was currently going at, even the slightest change in steering at this speed would have been enough to start a chain reaction which in turn, would have wrecked the police car in seconds. "Just trust me, on three" called back Samantha, as she rested the machine gun on the doorframe, pointing it out towards the forward's position. "Three, two, one, go" screamed Samantha, as on the word 'go', Julie slammed on the brakes making the tyres screech like made, as she spun the wheel hard to the left, applying the handbrake as she went, so as to execute a well performed handbrake turn.

The police car spun around on itself, and in the fraction of a second between the moment that Edward eyes had widened with shock, slamming on his brakes in the pickup truck, and Julie completing the turn, Samantha had taken aim at the pickup truck's passenger side tyre, and pulled the trigger. With another two loud bangs, the tyre blew off its rim, sending the remains of the tyre flying over the opposite carriageway, as the pickup truck spun out of control, only just about staying on its wheels, Edward holding onto the steering wheel for dear life. The pickup truck suddenly veered to the right, as it smashed into the crash barriers, making the pickup come to a dead stop, steam now pouring out from under the bonnet, making the whole vehicle look as though it was on fire. The scene seemed to temporarily freeze in everyone's mind, as if someone was watched a slowed down piece of film, as the effects of shock began to kick in for them all.

As the two vehicles came to a stop, the only sounds that could be heard, was the wailing siren on the police car, which Julie quickly flicked off after a second or so, leaving only the flashing lights on which continued to light up the surrounding countryside. "Erm, a little help here please" came Diana's despairing voice from the back seat, as Samantha turned around to see Diana wedged between her seat, and the rear passenger seats. "Oh sorry Diana, are you ok" replied Samantha, as she helped Diana back up into a sitting position, having surveyed the scene in front of them. Diana's breathing was still rapid, and even Samantha's hands were shaking slightly in shock from the events that had unfolded within the last few minutes. "Do I look alright; I've been in a high-speed pursuit whilst avoiding being heavily pregnant at the same time" replied Diana in an incredibly sarcastic voice, but even Diana couldn't help but crack none the less.

The fact of the matter was, they had all just survived a daring escape attempt right under the noses of what was left of the British Government and what felt like half the armed forces to boot. Diana continued to breath in and out very quickly as if she had just run a mile, although everyone present could tell that this was due to the fact that Diana was pregnant and certainly not equipped to deal with high-speed pursuits in her condition. Julie was the only one who had not spoken since they had stopped; she was sitting there in a state of shock, of how Samantha, who in truth had always had a dislike of guns, could have pulled off two near perfect seamless marksmanship shots, from a moving vehicle, within the space of a few minutes. The scene before them was nothing short of a complete mess it was had to be said, as Samantha, Julie and Diana, all pulled themselves together as they recovered from the chase.

Further down the road lay the black four-wheel drive on its roof;

then there was Edwards's pickup truck, it's front end caved in through the speed of the impact. And then there was the police car, which had a blown out back window, and bullet holes all over it, from where the soldiers had taken pot-shots at them whilst they had made their daring escape from the Grey's Pharmaceuticals car park. "Are you ok Julie" asked Samantha, as Julie still sat there in a state of shock, her hands calming down slightly from the impact. "I am going to have so much paperwork to fill out because of this" came Julie's voice, as Samantha looked at her astounded. "You've just survived a high-speed chase involving a shootout, and you go for 'I'm going to fill in paperwork' as your quote for the day" replied Samantha exasperated, but she soon stopped, as she noticed that Julie had started to laugh out loud, which before long, both Samantha and Diana were doing as well.

The laughter however was short lived, as without warning, there was a sudden crashing sound, as Edward staggered out of his pickup truck, looking like he'd had too much to drink. "You shot out my tyre you bitch" shouted Edward, his speech a little slurred as he advanced on them, blood running down his face from the force of the impact of the pickup truck hitting the crash barriers at speed. The sight of Edward staggering out of his pickup truck, seemed to snap Julie out of her shocked state. Julie threw open her driver's door and marched up to Edward, the old glint in her eye, that Samantha had only seen once before, which was when Julie had arrested Samantha back in Lillington, after they had first met after Covid. Edward laughed at her in a sick way, as without warning, Julie punched Edward squarely in the face, making Edward stop laughing almost immediately.

Edward collapsed back onto the ground, coughing slightly as Julie stood in front of him, teeth bared, looking more like a dog growling at a stranger, as she spoke with a snarl. "Edward Fitzgerald, I am hereby placing you under arrest, for the crimes of sexual assault, possession of an offence weapon, the attempted murders of Samantha Bonham, Diana Gibbs and a police officer, along with dangerous driving; you do not have to say anything, however it may harm your defence when mentioned something you later rely on in court, anything you do say maybe be used in evidence against you" replied Julie, as she placed her hands on her hips, and breathed out slowly, the whole ordeal knocking the wind out of her. Samantha and Diana, who had both climbed out of the police car whilst Julie had been talking, stood there stunned, as even they could tell that this sort of thing would never have happened during the pre-Covid days.

It wasn't worth pointing out that in a normal police chase, the police wouldn't have allowed untrained civilians to operate firearms, or do any of the other crazy things that they'd done that day, including allowing a serving police officer to strike a civilian criminal squarely in the face. Neither Samantha nor Diana thought it prudent to point out that Julie had violated quite a few laws herself in the process of rescuing them, but they thought it best not to mention this to her while Julie was in the zone, so to speak. "Now to fill out the paperwork" replied Julie, as both Diana and Samantha sniggered, and then began to laugh their heads off again, like they had done a few moments earlier. In their glowing moment of success however, none of them had noticed that Edward had managed to stagger back to his feet, and had drawn a knife from his back pocket.

"Look out" cried Samantha suddenly, as Edward advanced on Julie, teeth bared and knife in his hand, as Julie immediately tried to defend herself, scrambling out of the way of Edward as he advanced on them. But Edward had lunged forward, sinking the knife into Julie's stomach as he went, with Julie having no way to defend herself. Julie let out a small scream, as did Diana, on seeing what was happening in front of them. "No; Julie" screamed out Samantha, as Edward leaned into towards Julie, a look of smug satisfaction on his face. "Rot in hell, bitch" snarled Edward, as Samantha stood there frozen in shock, as Edward withdrew, pulling the knife with him as he went. The moment he stood away, Edward began to laugh derisively, as Julie sank onto her knees, a large patch of blood beginning to stain her clothes as it leaked out of the open wound in Julie stomach.

Samantha hurried forward, as she reached Julie a second later, propping Julie up in her arms, as Samantha's eyes began to swim with tears, as Julie's eyes began to flicker. "I win bitches, I win, you are all going" shouted Edward, but he never got the chance to finish his sentence, as at that exact moment, there was an explosion of gunfire, as Edward went flying backwards into his pickup truck, spread eagled in front of it, looking like some pathetic punch and Judy puppet. The ghost of his last laugh was still etched on his face, as his head drooped downwards onto his chest, making small banging noises as his body had hit the pickup trucks bonnet. Edward sank slowly to the floor, his body riddled with machine gun bullets, as Samantha spun around in complete shock at the noise, whilst still kneeing on the ground cradling Julie in her arms, whose life was ebbing away faster than water tricking down a stream.

To everyone's shock, Diana stood there, machine gun raised to her shoulder, the end of the barrel still smoking from where the bullets had left it, a look of rage upon her face. "Diana, what the" started Samantha in a shocked voice, as she was so taken aback by the scene, that Samantha momentary forget that Julie lay dying in her arms. "Never mess with an expecting mother who has just lost her rescuer" snarled Diana, as she stared directly at Edward, who's dead body now looked more like a pound of mince instead of a human being, as it was so riddled with machine gun holes. "Sam" said Julie in a faint voice, as Samantha's attention was turned back to Julie, who's blood soaked hand, was now in Samantha's hand. "It's ok Julie, it's ok, try not to talk; Diana, get over here and help me will you" cried out Samantha, as Diana appeared to snap out of the manic state of mind that she was in.

There as there was a clattering sound, as Diana dropped the machine gun onto the ground, rushing to Samantha's aid as she had requested. "I'll find something to try and stop the bleeding" said Diana, as she raced back to the police car, scrounging a fire blanket from inside the boot, along with a first aid kit, which she rushed back over with, to where Julie lay cradled in Samantha's arms. "I can keep pressure on the wound until the bleeding stops, but it could be internal as well" replied Diana, as she pressed down on Julie's stomach to try and stem the bleeding. "Yeah, that's good babes, that's good" replied Samantha, as she continued to look down into Julie's face. "Whatever happens, it wasn't your fault Sam, please remember that" said Julie, her voice getting fainter and fainter, as Julie's breathing became more rapid and sharp the more spoke.

"You're going to come through this Julie, I know you will, you'll get back to Trevor and the others at Mile End Farm, I know you will" said Samantha, trying to sound encouraging, but Julie looked up into Samantha's eyes, as she shook her head slightly. "I can't go back there, the farm is contaminated; Misim died a few days after you left, and then the others began coming down with Covid as well" gasped Julie, as she was still trying to talk, even though the pain in her stomach was building at an alarming rate. Julie winced slightly from the pain, as Samantha began to stroke her head in a reassuring way, whilst making hissing sounds, so as to not cause Julie anymore pain than what she was already in. "But that means you know that we're both contaminated as well" replied Samantha, making reference to the fact that if everyone else on Mile End Farm had become contaminated, then the three of them were as well.

"No, no that's not the case, we're immune from it for some reason; but Brian told me to go and find you both, as he realised that the farm would have to be made off limits from then on" whimpered Julie, as her voice became a higher pitch than before. The fire blanket which Diana had been using to stem the bleeding, was now caked in Julie's blood, but Diana kept pressure on the wound with all of her strength, determined that Julie was going to pull through this. "Swear to me Samantha that you'll find Greg, swear to me you will be happy" replied Julie, as Samantha nodded, tears rolling down her face, her emotions beginning to get the better of her as she lay crouched on the road surface, cradling Julie in her arms. "I will Julie, of course I will, and you'll be there to see it happen, I'll make sure of it" said Samantha, as Julie laughed slightly, which made her sides hurt even more than they had before.

"You've been a loyal, and wonderful friend Sam, I will never forget it; thank you" replied Julie, who's voice was now getting fainter and fainter with every word she spoke. Even Diana now had tears in her eyes, as she watched Julie's eyes rolling slightly, as her head flopped sideways onto Samantha's arm and her chest stopped moving. "No, no, Julie, don't go, you'll be ok" cried Samantha, but Julie it seemed, had finally given up her fight for life. Julie's eyes had stopped moving, as they looked up into Samantha's face, unblinking and unmoving, as her mouth hung slightly open. Diana reached forward, and closed her eyes with her fingers in silence, as she then looked back at Samantha, unable to stop the silent tears which were now pouring from her eyes. "Sam, I'm so sorry; I'm sure she meant so much to you" replied Diana, but Samantha had begun to scream into the silence, her grieve now beyond tears.

Samantha was screaming so loudly, that even Diana had to cover her ears, due to the noise level of Samantha's screaming, feeling blood pounding in her ears. Within a matter of seconds however, Samantha had stopped screaming, but had instead started sobbing so much, that Diana was worried that her chest might give out due to the strain of her crying. "Sam babes, I feel your pain, I really do" replied Diana, in what she hoped was a reassuring voice, but it didn't appear to have any effect in keeping Samantha calm in any way at all. Samantha had now replaced her crying with a look of anger and pure hatred across her face, as Diana now backed away in alarm, wondering whether Samantha was going to fly at her and attack her in anger. Getting up from the floor, Samantha laid Julie's body careful down upon the floor, but then suddenly dashed towards where the machine gun lay on the ground.

Before Diana could stop her, Samantha had raised the weapon to shoulder height, and fired it straight in the direction of Edward's body, as Samantha emptied an entire magazine of bullets into Edward's body, making it look more deformed and defaced than it had ever been in life. Samantha screamed out again, as Diana attempted to stop her, looking far braver than what she was feeling. "Sam stop this; stop this please" cried out Diana with a whimper, as she attempted to bring Samantha under control. But Samantha was struggling against Diana, trying to get at Edwards body, wanting to kick and punch and stab every inch of it that she could see. "Julie wouldn't have wanted this; she would have wanted us to be the better human beings; we're not monster's babes, we're not" shouted Diana, as Samantha appeared to come to her senses at last, hearing Diana properly for the first time.

Considering that Diana had been the one panicking before all of this, it was surprising how much she now seemed to be taking charge of the situation, never really showing herself or anyone else to be a born leader in any way. "Come on, I need you to help me with Julie's body; we need to bury her properly" replied Diana, as Samantha nodded slightly, whipping away her tears, words failing her for the first time in living memory. Samantha pulled herself back onto her feet, and with Diana's help managed to get Julie's lifeless body laid down in the back seat of the police car, with Diana laying the fire blanket she had found over Julie's face, as a mark of respect to a fallen comrade. "She died the hero of the hour Sam; I'm sure that's how she would have wanted to go" replied Diana, as Samantha helped Diana into the front passenger seat, making sure that Diana was seated comfortably, not wanting to injury her or the unborn baby in any way.

Samantha never spoke again, until she had placed the machine gun into the boot, and then climbed into the driver's seat, closing the door behind her with a light snap. "She always said she wanted to retire to the countryside, so I will take Julie north to bury her, so she can have a good view of the scenery and rest in peace" explained Samantha, as her and Diana sat looking out of the windscreen, at the smashed up pickup truck, and Edwards body, as steam was still issuing from underneath the bonnet. "Wherever you're going, I'm going with you babes; we're both in this now, and we have to finish what you and Julie started on" replied Diana, as Samantha turned to look at Diana, feeling a rush of gratitude and warmth towards one of her best friends. "What do we do about the monster out there" asked Diana suddenly, fearing that this outburst would send Samantha back into a spiralling rage again.

However, Samantha seemed to consider this for a moment, as Diana had made a very good point. Despite trying to kill them all, and succeeding in his mission to murder Julie, Samantha's first thought was just to leave him on the tarmac, rotting away to be eaten by wild dogs, wolves, foxes and the like. But then Samantha remembered that that she and Diana weren't monsters, and needed to show respect regardless. "We'll throw a sheet over him; he doesn't deserve a marked grave, but at least if we cover him, it doesn't violate our humanity" was Samantha's reply, as Diana nodded in agreement. "What about the other soldiers back down there" replied Diana, as she pointed back down the road towards the other four-wheel drive on its roof. "Those who we can get out, we'll bury, those who we can't, we'll just try and cover the car as best as we can" replied Samantha, as Diana again nodded in agreement.

So, they both set about the work, first covering Edward's body with a camp blanket that they had found in the back of the pickup truck, and even managed to extract all of the soldiers from the black four-wheel drive, despite being on its roof and mangled from the speed of its impact. "I could have sworn blind I saw more soldiers in that car" replied Diana, as Samantha dug graves on the narrow strip of grass by the side of the road. "So did I, I'm sure I saw about five soldiers in that car" replied Samantha, as she painted slightly from digging the graves, whilst having to drag and lay the soldier's bodies inside them all on her own. "Maybe some of them got out after all, and decided to try and help the others" replied Diana, who had wondered that at first, but was still thinking of why they hadn't rushed to Edward's aid to help him track her, Samantha and Julie down.

Samantha didn't reply, but was still thinking that herself; maybe after seeing that Edward had lost control of the situation, they'd helped their comrades, and then fled for home, back to Grey's Pharmaceuticals. Samantha finished off the graves by covering the graves with the soil now heaped on either side of the graves, thinking that it wasn't the best way to send off people who were only following orders, but better than just lying rotting out in the open, waiting to be the next meal of a pack of wild dogs or another group of starving animals. "Come on, there's nothing more we can do here now Sam" replied Diana, as Samantha helped her back into the police car's passenger seat, and then fastened her seatbelt, as Samantha then climbed into the driver's seat, closing the door behind her with a snap. Samantha only seemed to be half listening, as dreadful mental images flashed across her mind, as if they were some sort of micro nightmares.

Without saying a word, Samantha started up the police cars engine, before heading away slowly, whilst taking one last look at the crash scene in the rear-view mirror. But they both couldn't help but think that Julie may have made the ultimate sacrifice that day, but it had been Diana, who had taken down; Edward Fitzgerald.

CHAPTER TWENTY ONE

The Geighlon Sisterhood

The drive back to the Green Goddess on the farm was done in complete silence, as Samantha and Diana felt that this was a mark of respect to Julie, who had after all saved both of their lives that day. To their great delight, it appeared that the Green Goddess hadn't been discovered by anyone, as it looked exactly the same as Samantha had left it when she had set out on the scouting trip on the day she had been captured and taken into the Grey's Pharmaceuticals complex. They ditched the police car in one of the farm outbuildings near to where the Green Goddess was parked, throwing a cover over it as they went, hoping that no-one who was trying to track them would discover it sitting in the farms outbuilding. Julie's body meanwhile had been carefully placed inside the container on the back of the trailer behind the tractor unit, having used all of the materials that they could find from the vacant farmhouse to keep Julie's body as respectful as possible.

Having promised to give Julie the proper send-off that She deserved; Samantha managed to find a local funeral directors shop in a small village a few miles north of Leicester. The sign by the side of the road as they drove slowly into the village read, 'welcome to Longhill, circa 1422'. The village of Longhill was home to many Tudor era style buildings and even a slightly shabby looking pub, where they found a handily place well, from where to top up their water bottles and the like. The main high street looked so fresh, that it would have passed more as a costume drama film set, rather than as a deserted village. It was surprising that Samantha and Diana had managed to find a ready-made wooden coffin, and yet as they walked cautiously through the undertaker's shop, there it was, a readymade wooden coffin, sitting on a table in the workshop out the back.

Its golden plaque was completely blank, as the name of the poor departed soul who it had been made for, had still not been inscribed upon it in black letters. Feeling that this was as good a find as Samantha and Diana were going to find, they immediately chose to take the ready finished coffin, carrying it carefully between them as Samantha and Diana both made their way out of the shop, and back to the Green Goddess parked up in the high street, where Samantha was very anxious about leaving the Green Goddess unprotected in the new times. After a short while, Samantha and Diana laid Julie's body inside the coffin, before they driving off down the road in the Green Goddess, until they reached a fuel station on the outskirts of town. The tiny fuel station on the outskirts of Longhill heralded a few surprises as well, as they rolled up to it in the Green Goddess.

The fuel pumps were a bit dusty, and the windows covered in grime and dirt, as if they hadn't been cleaned in decades. The shop seemed to herald just as my surprises as the undertaker's shop, as inside the fuel station, found a whole shelf of bread, and in the back room, Samantha found an updated HGV map of Britain, and papers showing where the petrol station shops suppliers were based. Once outside of the village, they stopped in a layby and carefully placed Julie's body inside the coffin that Samantha and Diana had found inside the undertaker's shop. "I'm really sorry Julie" said Samantha, as both her and Diana nailed the coffin lid down with hammers and nails that they'd found in the undertaker's workshop. The Green Goddess herself, was certainly no horse drawn hearse it was true, but was still quite a respectful ride for a fallen hero in Samantha's opinion.

So, in hindsight, they felt that it wouldn't be too disrespectful to Julie's body, as she would have to travel inside the container on the back of the trailer. Flashing images of Julie laughing smiling and being generally cheerful couldn't help but dart across Samantha's eyes as they drove along, as if they felt like a distant memory of a childhood friend, even though Samantha and Diana had only known each other for such a brief period of time. Samantha remembered giving Julie her wedding dress which Samantha had got from the wedding shop back in Lillington before Covid had struck, and how Julie had said to Samantha that she would never forget her generosity. Considering that Julie had saved both Samantha's and Diana's lives that day, Samantha felt that Julie had well and truly paid back Samantha for her generosity, even if it had come at such a high price.

It suddenly struck Samantha; how pretty Julie had looked on that faithful wedding day when she had married Trevor on Mile End Farm. The Green Goddess cruised past by a point on the motorway, where a sign said 'emergency vehicles only', as Samantha pictured Julie driving them away from danger in the police car, as they had escaped from the Grey's Pharmaceuticals complex. "The labs of death more like" thought Samantha, as she kept her eyes focused solely on the stretch of empty and deserted motorway in front of her. Thinking back to the company, it then occurred to Samantha, that Helen and Patrick still remained at large, and would even now be chasing them across the counties, in an attempt to bring them back to the company to carry on with their sick medical trials. Although Diana had finished off the psychopath, Edward

Fitzgerald; they both couldn't help but feel that this act would not go unnoticed.

It put Samantha in mind of the German and Japanese concentration camps, and it made her shudder with fear to think that her and Diana, would have ended up as corpses on a slab, if Julie hadn't of infiltrated and saved Samantha and Diana from inside the company's labs. "This really is a one-of-a-kind machine isn't it" said Diana, making Samantha snap back to the present-day reality with a sharp jolt. Diana was sat in the passenger seat stroking her stomach, where her unborn baby was giving her a few friendly kicks, completely unaware of what's mother and her friends had been through that day. "It is, she's known as the Green Goddess, because of her power and beauty all at the same time" replied Samantha, as the Green Goddess cruised along the very empty and deserted M1 motorway, between Leicester and Leeds, passing by trees, hedges, and deserted and lifeless buildings.

As Diana felt that truck driving was more of Samantha's department than her own, Diana instead had agreed to take up the role of navigator, using Samantha's new truck map, which listed the many height, weight and width restrictions of the UK's many miles of paved and tarmacked roads. Even as Samantha sat their driving along, she remembered offering Julie the chance to drive, inexperienced as Julie was at driving trucks. "Julie had sat in this very chair once" thought Samantha, as the memory came back to her in a swift moment, firing off a few electrodes inside of her own brain. Despite having witnessed the memory of Julie driving the Green Goddess, Samantha couldn't help but let out a small laugh. "What's the joke" replied Diana, who was a little shocked at Samantha's laugh, making a mental note to realise that there was nothing funny about their current situation.

"Oh, sorry Diana, it's just, I remembered I said I would let Julie drive the Green Goddess for a bit, so I could rest my eyes" replied Samantha, as they passed under a bridge, where a makeshift banner sign made out of a bedsheet, was hanging from it spelled out the message, 'come home Sam babes, the future starts here'. It took Samantha a few seconds to register what she'd just seen, but even Diana had turned white with shock, as she too, registered what the bedsheet sign hanging from the motorway bridge had said. "Hold the phone" came Samantha's shocked voice as all of a sudden, there was a screech of tyres and a scream from Diana, as she was nearly hurled through the cab windscreen, her seatbelt only just holding her back from serious injury. Samantha, it transpired, had stamped on the brakes, making the Green Goddess shudder suddenly to a halt, leaving two perfect symmetrical solid black skid marks on the motorway road surface.

A number of items including crisp packets, charger leads and a first aid box had coming flying out of the compartments, followed by a loud hiss of escaping air, as the Green Goddess had come to a complete halt in the middle lane of the motorway. "What the hell are playing at, are you trying to kill us or something" shouted Diana, as she clutched at her stomach bump, worried that the sudden action of the Green Goddess coming to a sudden stop, had potentially injured her unborn baby. Samantha without looking at Diana, or saying a word, switched off the engine, and hurled herself out of the cab, sprinting away back towards the bridge. "Oi, where are you going, have you completely lost it" shouted Diana after Samantha, as she tried to climb with difficulty, out of the passenger cab door and down from the cab steps, to follow Samantha back up the deserted stretch of motorway.

Samantha, who wasn't pregnant it was true, had reached the sign first, but Diana was considerably out of breath, and red in the face by the time she reached Samantha, who was now staring up at the sign in complete disbelief. "I can't believe it, oh my god, that's his sign, he made that Diana, Greg made that sign" cried out Samantha, grinning from ear to ear, as she jumped up and down on the spot with happiness. "Wow hold up there, Sam babes please slow down; what exactly are you trying to tell me" replied Diana after her breath had returned to her lungs, still clutching a stitch in her chest. "Oh, I've been such an idiot, it's his handwriting babes; that's Greg handwriting; he's leaving me a message" cried out Samantha, gesturing up at the blanket bedsheet sign, which fluttered slightly in the light breeze that had whipped up around them since coming to a complete stop a few moments earlier.

Elation was now flooding through Samantha's body, like she was flying as an eagle in the sky, observing a happy sunny view below her. "But how do you know it's from Greg, I mean, there could be lots of survivors left in the country who could have left that sign there" replied Diana, sounding a little sceptical and exasperated at the same time, but Samantha had her answer ready. "No no, I know it's from Greg, it's the way that he writes; not to mention the fact that it says babes on it, Greg always calls me that". Diana stared open mouthed at Samantha, as if she couldn't believe what she was saying. "What are you talking about Sam, this could be meant for anyone; there's still around two to three percent of the world's population running around out there" exclaimed Diana, as Samantha interrupted her in a rush, feeling that if she didn't say what she was thinking to Diana, she would burst.

"But that would mean if spread equally around the world, the UK would only have around 200,000 people alive inside it's borders; it's a lot I know, but still" cried out Samantha, as she crossed her legs and bit her lip, as if she was fighting the impulse to wet herself. "We've got to take it down" blurted out Samantha, as Diana went wide eyed at Samantha. "We can't take that; we can't even be sure if it's addressed to you, and if you think I'm climbing up there and helping you, you've got another thinking coming" replied Diana, a little hot and bothered by now, but Diana's words appeared to have gone straight over Samantha's head, as Samantha was already formulating a plan in her head. "I'm going to climb up the embankment there, walk along the bridge, and untie the ropes holding up the sign, then you can catch it as it falls" explained Samantha, as she began to move towards the embankment, happiness flowing through her as she did so.

Maybe it was Samantha's happiness and adrenaline that helped her, because she scaled the grassy embankment with surprising ease, considering the fact that she had been sitting down for a while inside the Green Goddess. "Has anyone ever told you this Sam, but your ruddy mental, do you know that" shouted Diana so that Samantha could hear her. Samantha crossed over to the middle of the bridge at a run, before beginning to loosen the ropes, holding the bedsheet to the bridge's railings. "Oh, stop being such a drama queen, you were always like this, do you remember when we at school, and you kept pestering me to find out whether I had grown into my first bra" shouted back Samantha in a jokey type voice. Diana couldn't help but go bright red at this point, when she heard what Samantha had just said, recalling the very memory that Samantha had indicated.

"You had to go and bring that up didn't you; well, you know, I was jealous; you were always the best-looking girl in the class" replied Diana, who sounded a little sheepish as she said this. Samantha, who had never thought of herself as 'the best-looking girl in the class', was so taken aback by this, that she nearly unbalanced herself leaning over to untie the ropes holding the bedsheet to the railings. "Sam be careful up there" replied Diana in a slightly panicked voice, but Samantha managed to recover herself just in time. "Got it" said Samantha in a victorious voice, as the bedsheet banner fell downwards slowly, landing on the road surface with a slight flumping sound, in the same way that a laundrette would drop a bag full of clothing. "You were supposed to catch it Diana" called out Samantha, as Diana had managed to miss the bedsheet banner completely as it fell downwards.

Samantha crossed back over the bridge, and came sliding down the grassy embankment with graceful ease, as she skidded to a stop in the gravel at the bottom. "Now to follow the trail, if Greg had left that up, he must have left others" said Samantha excitedly, as Diana rolled her eyes slightly out of sight of Samantha's gaze, fearing that Samantha wasn't going to let this one go to rest. "Come on Diana, let's get going" replied Samantha excitedly, as Diana attempted to keep up, with a slight look of annoyance on her face, fearing that Samantha wouldn't let go of the whole 'Greg is alive' thing. Samantha had obviously missed this, as they both made their way back towards the Green Goddess, climbing back up into the cab as they went. Once they were both back inside, Samantha pulled out her new HGV map, before flicking madly through the pages, as if she was looking for a particular reference point on the map's pages.

Samantha suddenly came to a stop on the page showing the M1 motorway where they were at that exact moment and began to run her finger along it, muttering to herself as she went. "Erm, aren't I supposed to be the one who's navigating here" said Diana, a little confused, as Samantha grinned slightly, understanding Diana's sarcasm. "Don't worry Diana, I think I've worked out the route we can take" replied Samantha, as she turned the map around so that it faced Diana, as Samantha continued on speaking. "We're here now, and I suspect that Greg would take a good guess to know that I would be driving a big vehicle full of supplies and things; so, my best guess is, he would expect me to stay on the major roads but avoid the cities, so we can't go into Leeds, or any of the other northern cities like Manchester and the like". Diana seemed quite taken aback that Samantha knew so much, but then realised, she had been a lorry driver after all.

"So, where do we plan to go from here" asked Diana, after Samantha had finished speaking and making deductions. "Well, Greg was a trucker as well, so he would know that miles counted as well; so, to avoid burning excess diesel, he would want to go as the crow flies, so we should be looking to travel across the North Yorkshire Moors, and into Northumberland, but via the great north road" replied Samantha, in answer to Diana's question. "I suspect you want to avoid Helen and Patrick as well, as they will be expecting us to use the main roads to get up to Clyde" replied Diana, who had been fully debriefed on everything that had happened to Samantha, ever since she and Julie had left Lillington. Samantha started up the Green Goddesses engine as it began to move slowly forwards gathering speed, away from the bridge where they had found the makeshift bedsheet sign, which was now stowed away safely onboard the Green Goddess.

"I want to reach here by nightfall" said Samantha, as she pointed her finger at the point in the map, which was almost smack bang right in the middle of the North Yorkshire Moors. "According to this, it's a small hamlet called Geighlon" replied Diana, as she looked curiously at where Samantha was pointing on the map. "That's right, it's about the most isolated point in North Yorkshire, so we should be able to hide out there, and give Helen and Patrick the slip" replied Samantha with a slight smile, as Diana gave a nod of understanding, and placed the map back on her lap. The Green Goddess began to gather speed, taking them further away from the bridge where they had both found the bedsheet sign which Samantha was convinced had been left by her fiancée Greg. Diana still felt a slight pang of guilt in her mind that Samantha may have been barking up the wrong tree when interrupting the bedsheet sign.

However, seeing that Samantha was the one driving, and appeared to be the only one with a plan of how to get away from danger, Diana decided that her best course of action was just to do what she was told, and stick as close to Samantha as she possibly could. This course of action was properly for the best, as many miles back down the road, at the crash scene, Edward Fitzgerald's body was being examined by Helen and Patrick's team of scientists, who were all wearing hazmat suits and gas masks. Helen stood a few feet away, staring down at Edward's blood-soaked machine gun bullet riddled body, a look of controlled anger on her face, feeling nothing but hate towards the people who had committed this unspeakable crime. The fact that Samantha, Diana and Julie could have done something like this to one of her own people, was an act of unspeakable evil as far as Helen was concerned.

Even though Helen, Patrick and Edward were the bad guys in all of this, they still couldn't believe that three people could have been responsible for this level of barbarity. "His body is riddled with machine gun bullets; I take it this was done by our escaped prisoners" asked Patrick, who had walked over to Helen to speak to her, after hurriedly conversing with a black uniformed solider a few seconds earlier. Helen didn't speak straight away, but when she spoke, her voice was calm and collected, but Patrick could hear the cool voice of a professional diplomate at work. "This act will not go unpunished; I will not tolerate murder in my country; find them Patrick, and bring them back to justice; this crime deserves capital punishment, and you get to keep the bodies afterwards". Patrick smiled with a slight leer on his face as Helen spoke her words, although unnoticed from Helen, he didn't seem to be as pleased about it as he should have been.

"With pleasure, ma'am" replied Patrick, giving Helen a slight bow, as he proceeded back to his car, before taking off with his car off up the road after Samantha and Diana onboard the Green Goddess. It was true that Helen and Patrick didn't have a lot to go on, other than that Samantha and Diana were heading for the town of Clyde in Scotland. They knew that Samantha had the Green Goddess, so they worked on the assumption, that the Green Goddess would stick to the major roads, and it was this plan that Samantha and Diana had been banking on since they had escaped with Julie. Another advantage that Samantha and Diana had over their pursuers, was the fact that Patrick and Helen believed that Julie was still alive, so at least if Samantha and Diana had to fight their way out of any situations involving Helen or Patrick, they would be able to use Julie's absence to their advantage.

It was true that the Green Goddess had been given a fairly decent head start over them, as the Green Goddess wound her way along the rest of the M1 motorway, finally slowing down slightly on the outskirts of the city of Leeds. Using Samantha's route that she had proposed early on that afternoon, they skirted around Leeds using the ring road, and then began to head deep into the Yorkshire moors, the small winding roads getting tighter and tighter as they went, their speed becoming increasing slower so as to match the changing environment around them. When at last Samantha and Diana reached the small sign that read, 'Welcome to the hamlet of Geighlon, population 34', it was certainly the sort of place that no one in their right mind would think could be housing a huge moving vehicle like the Green Goddess, as the Green Goddess blended perfectly into the surrounding countryside.

It certainly was tiny, as the Green Goddess looked enormous next to the small square timber oaked, dry stoned buildings, lining both sides of the roads, all looking a little run down and lifeless, with their windows covered in grim, as if they had not been lived in for many years. The now ownerless parked cars on both sides of the street didn't help matters either, and at one point, Samantha could have sworn blind that she had heard a crunching noise coming from the rear end, as if the tanker trailer had rubbed against one of them, or even smashed into it as they went past. "There should be a field near here, where we can park up for the night" explained Samantha, as Diana began looking out of the window to see what was around her. As the Green Goddess crawled around the next corner, they saw that there was a field to their left which seemed to be connected to a series of farm building, and what looked like a small church.

As the road was only just about wide enough to allow a single tractor and trailer to come up it, Samantha was forced to widen the road slightly, as she made the mighty Green Goddess mount the pavement in a way to clear a path down the narrow lane. "I love that view you know; I think Julie would have loved to have retired to this place" said Samantha, as she and Diana sat looking out of the cab window for a few minutes, looking out at the now fast setting sun, and the way that it lit the fields and hills up in a golden glow. The small church, which Samantha and Diana had noticed when they first came up the road, now seemed to be prominent amongst the backdrop, it's pein glass windows now glowing with bright multi colours, as the setting sun shone through them. It seemed so beautiful and tranquil somehow, as if the rest of the concrete and human world of the major towns and cities didn't exist around them.

"Let stop here for the night, I'll check out the church yard in the morning" replied Samantha, as she switched off the engine which shuddered to a halt, as there was the usual hiss of air coming from the brake cylinders as the brakes were applied on the Green Goddess. Within an hour or so, they had managed to set up camp, as this was an open field, as the Green Goddess sat half on the road, half mounted on the pavement, as Samantha and Diana sat on the low dry-stone wall which ran along the edge of the field, separating the road from the field. Samantha had managed to smooth it down a little, by breaking out two thick winter survival coats, which were part of her stockpile of supplies onboard the Green Goddess. As the container on the trailer was over forty feet in length and nearly eight feet high, it was surprising how much stuff could be fitted onboard it.

"Good greave Sam, how much stuff have you got on here" replied Diana in a shocked voice, when she had seen for the first time, how much stuff Samantha had got inside the shipping container sitting on the back of the trailer. "Enough to survive in the wilderness for a number of days, weeks, or even months depending on the situation and where the location is" replied Samantha, as Diana tried to take it all in. When Diana failed at coming to terms with this, she instead decided to go back to looking out at the surrounding countryside again. "They obviously don't get a lot of visitors to the village back there" replied Diana, as she tucked into a meal of tinned back beans, which Samantha had been cooking on her mini camping stove. "Yeah true, I bet it would be ten a penny to live in a hamlet like that" said Samantha, who was only really half listening to Diana's words, staring out at the rolling hills of North Yorkshire.

As it was so quiet up on the hill, the only sounds that came to them across the evening air was the whistling wind, which swept across the moors, dropping the temperature slightly as the darkness rolled in. Samantha knew full well, that if anyone was to come along, then they would hear them coming, especially if they were driving a vehicle of any kind. They knew they had to press on at some point, but at least for the moment, they were protected by the remoteness of where they were, and had a good view to go with it to pass the time. The challenge now fell onto Patrick and Helen's shoulders, as being able to track and find even something as large as the Green Goddess without the help of technology, was laughable. Their usual tools that the government or supporting agencies could have used like CCTV, ANPR, or even spy satellite tracking, were all gone.

So the only possible way that Helen and Patrick could now track them down, would be to use mobile patrols, or even by using a helicopter, if any of them still worked through lack of use or repair in the Covid lockdown days, where it was illegal for any commercial or civilian air traffic to be airborne through fear of spreading Covid any further. But even expecting to keep track of two people and a large vehicle within the UK, was a stretch in of itself, even with the help of pre-covid modern technology. "At least I can camouflage the Green Goddess, so it would be hard to spot her from the air, if they did happen to have a helicopter to hand" thought Samantha, as she lay flat on her back, on the lower bunk bed inside the Green Goddesses cab later that night, listening to Diana sleeping above her. "Knowing these guys, they probably would have a helicopter or two" thought Samantha, as she rolled over, in an attempt to get some sleep.

The night heralded no surprises for any of them, as they both managed to sleep peacefully without any interruptions of any kind. The following morning however, Samantha was rather desperate for a wee, not being able to hold it in any longer, not wanting to disturb Diana as she slept. This wouldn't have usually been such a big deal, as Samantha would have just found a plumbed in toilet and then done her business as usual without any fear at all. But since being on the road, and not having access to a plumbed in toilet, she would have to try and squat down somewhere by digging a pit or maybe finding a big enough bush somewhere to cover herself up in. Samantha did hit upon the idea of breaking into one of the houses in the hamlet, and using one of their toilets, but decided against it in the end, as if Diana woke up and saw that Samantha had vanished, would start to worry that something had happened to her.

"In the field it is then" thought Samantha, as she carefully crawled out of her bed, careful not to open and close the cab door too loudly, otherwise she would wake Diana up from her deep sleep. As Diana was heavily pregnant, she would need all of the rest that she could get, as Samantha had been careful not to give Diana anything which would do her and the baby any harm in the future. Samantha vaulted over the dry-stone wall, before walking away from the Green Goddess until she was roughly in the middle of the field, sunlight now pouring across it in the early morning time. But before Samantha had a chance to do anything else, she had stepped forwards onto what she thought had been a pile of wet leaves, when there was a sudden sound of snapping twigs underfoot, and the ground gave way beneath her feet. With a small scream, Samantha fell into a home-made pit trap, which was nearly deep enough to swallow her whole.

It was around three five in diameter, with the soil slightly wet as Samantha landed on it, feeling a slight pain in her ankle as she landed. Samantha tried to stand up again, wincing slightly at the pain, as she brushed leaves and twigs out of her hair. Samantha's first thought was that it was some sort of pit trap to catch a large animal, left over by the owner of the farm buildings before Covid, feeling a little silly that she hadn't seen it beforehand. "That's the last time I go to the loo in a field every again" said Samantha, more to herself than anyone else, as she tried to hoist herself up out of the pit trap. This fact seemed to be tested somewhat, as when Samantha had tried to climb out, she was suddenly aware that a dark-haired woman in her late 40s was standing by the edge of the pit trap, looking down at Samantha from above. From where Samantha was looking up at her, this mystery woman looked like someone out of a church choir.

"Who dares breech our sacred lands then; name yourself, young demon of the world" said the woman, who spoke with a commanding booming voice, whilst brandishing a farm yard pitchfork into Samantha's face as she did so. "Sorry, what" replied Samantha, who was so taken aback, she hadn't registered the fact that the woman standing above her was threatening her with a pitchfork. "Listen, I only just wanted a wee, I didn't realise there was a pit trap here" said Samantha, a little put out, as she tried to grab hold of the end of the pitchfork, so that she could hoist herself out of the hole; but the woman stood firm, refusing to allow Samantha to grab hold of it. "Are you a demon" demanded the woman again in the same commanding booming voice, as Samantha stood there stunned, wondering if the woman was some sort of an escapee from a lunatic asylum.

"Demon, of course I'm not; my name is Samantha Bonham, I'm twenty-six years old from Lillington in Hertfordshire" replied Samantha, as she nearly went cross eyed tried to keep the pitchfork in focus. The dark-haired woman above Samantha spoke with a broad Yorkshire accent, which told Samantha a few things; she would have to be a local if that be the case, or perhaps she was a resident of the Geighlon hamlet. "Well, I am Sister Sophie Everdale, I am the vicar here at the Geighlon chapel, and head of the Geighlon sisterhood" replied the dark-haired woman, as Samantha could now clearly see the white dog collar, which was fixed around Sophie's neck. "Mother, should we not be helping this poor soul, instead of keeping her imprisoned like this" came a second, more lighter sounding voice. Although Samantha couldn't see the person who had spoken a second or so earlier, she could tell that it was a far more friendly one than the first.

This second voice belonged to a far younger woman, with shoulder length gingery hair and an exceptionally pretty face, who suddenly appeared above Samantha, next to Sister Sophie Everdale. She too, spoke with a broad Yorkshire accent as Sister Sophie Everdale had done. "Hello their sweetie, sorry about my mother, she can be a little over the top sometimes". "Your mother" replied Samantha in surprise, as Sophie allowed Samantha to grab hold of the end of the pitchfork, to hoist herself up out of the pit trap. Samantha winced slightly as she clambered up, and placed a hand on her ankle. "Please, we must help, you have injured yourself; we are the sisters of Geighlon and can assist you with your injury" replied the second woman, who immediately shot a look of disgust at Sister Sophie Everdale. "This is Sarah Everdale, my daughter" said Sophie, as Samantha held out a hand to shake both of theirs, who's voice had now become less intimidating.

"I must apologise for the way that you were treated, sometimes we get strangers from the outside attempting to steal our food and livestock, hence why we have set these pit traps everywhere" explained Sophie, as she gestured around to the piles of leaves, scattered all over the field. Now that the sun had properly risen, Samantha could see what Sophie was pointing at, as there were indeed patches of leaves all over the field leading up to the small church, which sat in the middle of the field, surrounded by a small graveyard. On seeing the graveyard, Samantha was reminded of Julie's coffin, which was still in the back of the container, so she quickly looked back at Sarah, who in retrospect, only looked like she was a few years younger than Samantha and Diana were themselves. "Indeed, but it seems you are a traveller from other pastures, and therefore deserve our hospitality" replied Sophie, as Sarah and Samantha grinned at each other.

"It's ok, we are the Geighlon sisterhood, this is a safe place for women, and women only; no men allowed you see" explained Sarah in a sooth caring voice, who in truth did look a little downtrodden when she said this, as if she was missing the company of men very much. "Sam, what's going on, what are you doing" came Diana's voice from where she was standing at the edge of the field. The commotion of Samantha falling into the pit trap, had obviously woken Diana from her slumber. "We did not realise you were travelling with company" said Sophie, as all three of them looked in Diana's direction. "Nor that she was expecting either" said Sarah, who had just noticed Diana's pregnant bump in her stomach. "It's ok Diana, come on over, but tread carefully, there's pit traps where the piles of leaves are" said Samantha, as Diana tried, with difficulty, to enter the field using a lower part of the dry-stone wall to vault over.

"This may be a long stretch, but my friend Julie was sadly killed, and her final wish was to retire on a farm in the countryside" explained Samantha, as Sophie and Sarah both looked very sad and sympathetic to hear this news, as Samantha pressed on. "So, I was wondering, whether she can be buried here, it's sort of a farm by the look of it, with a local graveyard, and I think she would have approved of the view as well". Samantha finished talking, wondering whether she may have gone to far by requesting this great wish on two complete strangers. Samantha looked from Sophie to Sarah, as both of them were a little in shock to hear about Samantha and Diana's very sad and sudden loss of a good friend. "Your right Sam, it is a wonderful view here; and Julie saved our lives, we owe her that" replied Diana, who had just drawn level to where Samantha, Sophie and Sarah all stood by the side of the pit trap.

"Your friend can be buried here, as we always honour good deeds; and saving lives is the highest deed that anyone can accomplish" replied Sophie with a broad smile, as she turned to Sarah. "Wake the other sister's Sarah, we must introduce these two sisters to our brethren" instructed Sophie, as Sarah turned and walked slowly away, her red hair swinging behind her as she went. "Where is your friend's body now" asked Sophie, who was now showing her religious side to her personality, being the head of the mystery Geighlon Sisterhood. "Inside the container, not a hearse I know, but we had to move her somehow" replied Diana, so quickly, that Samantha hadn't even had time to open her mouth to speak; but this was almost word for word, for what Samantha had been thinking, less than twenty-four hours earlier. This wasn't the first time that Samantha had the impression that Diana had the strange physic ability to read minds.

"I believe the other sisters will help us; here they come now" replied Sophie, as around half a dozen ladies, all of mixed height, age and ethic origin, all came walking across the field from out of the small chapel doors on the church in the centre of the field. Sarah, being the youngest and by far the most physically active out of all of them, had reached Samantha, Diana and Sophie first, as the others arrived a few seconds later. "The sisters are assembled" replied Sarah, as Sophie called the group to order, using the same commanding voice that she had done before with Samantha in the pit trap. "I want to welcome you all to our travelling guests; this is Samantha and Diana" said Sophie, as Samantha and Diana gave a small wave to the other women, who were all standing around them, as Sophie continued on. "Samantha, Diana; may we welcome you both to the Geighlon Sisterhood, and we want to honour and remember your friend, Julie".

"Thank you all" said Samantha grinning slightly, as Diana almost stood frozen to the spot, not entirely sure exact what it was that she was supposed to do. Out of all of the places that Samantha had found herself in so far, this was by far the strangest of them all. "I wish to present sisters Salma, Tracey, Penelope and Harriet" replied Sarah, as she pointed out each individual member of the group in turn as she spoke their names. The two youngest, Penelope and Harriet, didn't even look like they were even adults, both looking as if they were still in their teenage years, both with cute smiles, and fair facial complexions. Salma, who was dark skinned, looked as if she was in her early thirties, whilst wearing a hijab head dress, and was by far the most religious out of the whole of the sisterhood. By far the eldest of the group, beside Sophie, was Tracey, who looked like she was in her early fifties, with short blondie hair which only came down to her ears.

She also was the only one out of the group who didn't seem to mind being the one that stuck out in this group, as when the group greeted Samantha and Diana a second later, Tracey was the only one who didn't speak with a broad Yorkshire accent. Tracey instead possessed an Essex accent, which wasn't that far away from where Samantha and Diana had both been from, having just been based over the border from Essex in Hertfordshire. Once the gang was together, the sisterhood seemed to form into a seamless team, as if they were all secret undertakers, that performed funerals and last rights for people all the time. They all trooped across the field, careful to avoid the other pit traps, reaching the Green Goddess a few moments later. The Geighlon Sisters were quite taken aback at the wonder of the Green Goddess, wondering how such a large vehicle had made it into their small remote world.

Samantha opened the container doors with a slight squeak, as she and Diana carefully caried the coffin, containing Julie's body along to the open doorway, as the sisterhood all gathered around, to form a procession around the coffin, in the same way that a coffin would be carried by five or six people at a regular funeral. "Julie can rest in the chapel while we prepare the grave" explained Sarah, as they all moved slowly across the field, careful not to fall into any of the hidden pit traps that they had dug themselves. "Your friend Julie will like it here, the church graveyard has always been home to the previous deceased residences of the Geighlon hamlet, and will continue to be the home for the sisterhood" explained Sophie, in a calmer lower voice than before, as she knew that this was technically a funeral possession, and so needed to show respect for the dead.

It was quite surprising how strong the other ladies of the sisterhood really were, as they carried the coffin containing Julie's body on their shoulders, not a single one of them with bent knees or wincing at all from the strain of it. They all seemed to be as tough as nails, looking the same way as a group of soldiers would, carrying a coffin of a comrade who had been killed in battle. "We can't thank you enough for doing this" said Samantha, as Sophie turned to look directly at her. "Not at all Samantha, we shall care for Julie now, and allow her to be given the send-off that is fitting of a fallen hero" replied Sophie, as they all entered into the small chapel, through its single solid oak door. The sisterhood proceeded up the isle between the chapel pews, before placing the coffin carefully on two wooden trellises, which stood around three feet apart, which supported the weight of the coffin as they placed it down.

The chapel itself was quite a simple one, considering the large oak door on the entrance to the church building. Candles hung in brackets all along the walls, and there was a single praying rug over in one corner, which Samantha suspected was for Salma, as she was the only Muslim in the group. The church pews were very highly polished, as Samantha and Diana could see their reflected faces clearly in some of them as they walked by, heads slightly bowed in respect of Julie's memory. It then struck Samantha where Julie's family would be at this very moment, most likely already deceased themselves because of Covid. The pein glass windows along the walls shone different coloured lights into the room, making the semi dark chapel look more like a disco dance floor then a

345

place of rest, with the only difference being that these light beams were not flashing or moving in any way.

"We must now prepare her for the ground, and an eternal sleep" said Sarah, as she and the others, all proceeded back out of the chapel's doorway, their heads bowed slightly as a mark of respect to Julie; who had paid the ultimate sacrifice; to save her friends, and get them, to safety.

CHAPTER TWENTY TWO

New Life and Old Life

The Geighlon Sisterhood it seemed, was quite a mixed bunch of people to say the least because of their lives before Covid and how they had ended up where they were. Sophie Everdale, had run a shop before Covid, but had also been the Parisian of the small Geighlon hamlet chapel in days gone by before Covid. Sarah Everdale her daughter, had in fact been to university since the age of eighteen, but now at twenty-one years of age, had been working as a bar maid in a local pub for six months before Covid had struck, which had forced her out of work due to the government lockdown that followed the outbreak of the Covid pandemic. Salma Hipla on the other hand, was a thirty-two-year-old accountant originally from the country of Iraq, but had settled in the town of Halifax in Yorkshire a number of years before Covid had struck, where her whole family had been wiped out by the pandemic.

Penelope Sandhill, was a sixteen-year-old, who had been at Wakefield college studying childcare, but she had found the sisterhood instead after Covid. This was also the case with Harriet Cooper, who was fifteen years old and from the town of Wakefield in Yorkshire. Her dream had been to become a Maths teacher, as she had managed to wow them all with her incredible mathematical numeracy skills, showing her to be far more advanced for her age then most people would be of that age group. The last of them was by far the eldest of the group; her name was Tracey Derby, and she was the only one, apart from Samantha and Diana, who hadn't lived or worked in the Yorkshire counties. Tracey was a fifty-one-year-old from the town of Romford in Essex, and had often been referred to be the others as 'The Oracle', because of her wise ways and years of wisdom.

In reality however, Tracey had actually worked in a Bookies shop, but she had picked up many years of wisdom and guidance from her travels in the world. "I'm more of a glorified counsellor really, in an unofficial term" remarked Tracey, as she and the others sat around a long rectangular table, with Sophie sitting at the top of it, and Sarah down the other. They were all tucking into an excellent meal of tomato soup, which had been hand made by the sisterhood, from the local produce all around them on the chapel farm. It put Samantha back in mind of being back on Mile End Farm, sitting around their kitchen table with the Flintstones community. It made Samantha think of how many other communities of people that there were around the country, and how many of those had managed to thrive in the new dystopian world, that had sprung up in the aftermath of Covid-19.

The Geighlon Sisterhood also seemed to have a similar setup to that of the Flintstones community as well on their land. Each member of the sisterhood, had brought a unique set of skills into the group, all overseen by Sophie, who was in doubt the leader of the Geighlon sisterhood. Her years of experience being a shop manager was certainly paying off, as she was displaying natural leadership skills to the others, in the way that she would delegate and manage her coven. It was also tradition every evening for the community to meet for prayers, and afterwards they would tell stories to each other of times gone by, alongside doing farm type jobs and picking grapes from the nearby vineyards across the surrounding fields. That particular evening however, Sophie and the other sisters had instructed Samantha and Diana to tell their stories from before Covid-19.

Diana, who had been very quiet up until this point, seemed to be keen to let people know about her story, which was the one that she had told Samantha back in the prison cell at Grey's Pharmaceuticals, but now with the added twist of telling them of how Julie had died saving them from Edward, Helen and Patrick during their escape from the Grey's Pharmaceuticals complex. Samantha had found that a few tears had started to roll down her face when Julie's name had been mentioned, as it became even harder to explain how her and Julie had ended up on Mile End Farm in the first place. Even Diana seemed to be paying attention at this point, as Samantha explained about surviving the plane crash which had come down on the warehouse where she worked; being involved in the road traffic collision with Edward, and how she had first met Julie at the scene, as Julie had been the first police officer to respond to the road traffic incident.

When Samantha finally got round to telling them all about the pamphlet, and how Grey's Pharmaceuticals had been involved in killing off the world's population, she found that her throat had gone as dry as the Sahara Desert as she struggled to get the words out of her mouth. Samantha had avoided mentioning Greg's name up until this point, but felt that she would have to say something at some point, otherwise Diana would probably steal her thunder by doing it for her. "I'm trying to get back to my fiancée you see; we were engaged to be married and then shortly after Covid hit, we were all forced to lock down in our houses, and that's when he disappeared" explained Samantha, as she finished speaking to the sisterhood, who were all grouped around the table like eager school children listening to a fascinating story being told by the classroom's teacher.

There was a stunned silence for a few seconds, as they all tried to take in what Samantha had told them in both her own and Diana's story. "Wow, and I thought my life had been interesting" replied Tracey in a jokey voice, as the others laughed slightly, breaking the awkward silence, whilst simultaneously lessening the strain on Samantha's nerves. "Love can make us do funny things" replied Salma, as Penelope and Harriet giggled slightly. "I can't even begin to think what you've been through Sam" said Diana in a sympathetic voice, as Samantha bowed her head slightly, both of her arms resting on the table for support, fearing that she was going to slid off the chair and onto the floor. "I'd like to spend some time with Julie, please, excuse me" replied Samantha in a strangely high-pitched voice than normal, as she pushed back her chair, stood up, and then proceeded out of the door.

"Of course, take as long as you need Samantha" replied Sophie in an understanding voice, as she saw Samantha exit through the doorway out into the yard, which was surrounded on all sides by many sheds and barns. It had been another exhausting day, as Samantha and Diana, along with the rest of the sisterhood, had spent most of that day digging a suitable grave in the graveyard for Julie to be laid to rest in. Samantha made her way back across the now twilight yard, towards the small chapel, where she knew Julie to still be laying waiting to be buried. Samantha pushed the door open with a small creak, as she could see that Julie's coffin was surrounded by candles, which burned brightly in their holders keeping Julie illuminated, despite the early evening twilight outside on the moors being darker than the inside of the chapel was. Despite the candles however, Samantha felt that Julie spirit would always burn brighter than any candle ever could.

Closing the chapel door slowly behind her, Samantha walked slowly towards Julie's coffin, making sure not to knock into any of the candles as she went, through fear of accidently knocking them over and starting a fire. "Hey Julie; I thought I'd come and say that we'd finish doing the grave today; it's nice and deep enough for you now, so it will help you sleep" said Samantha, as she drew level to Julie's coffin, resting her hand upon the coffin lid as she spoke. At this point, most people would have pointed out that speaking to a dead corpse in a coffin wouldn't have helped them very much, but Samantha didn't seem to care about this, as she continued to speak, letting her feelings and emotions run ahead of her, like a runaway train with no brakes on it. "I suppose I never really got a chance to say, thank you; thank you for saving our lives; and your one hell of a police driver I'll give you that; you would have been a perfect stunt driver in the movies".

Samantha's voice tailed away, as she left a lonely tear roll down her face, as she seemed to lose track of time and location. "Diana is really grateful for your heroism as well, and we thought that you'd like to be buried here, as you did say you'd want to retire to a farm with a view" recalled Samantha with a slight sob, and a sniffle of her nose, remembering what Julie had said when both her and Samantha had met after Covid had struck. "Diana killed Edward would you believe, right after you were stabbed; at least he's in hell now" cried Samantha, but she felt that she needed to get these things off her chest, before it would burst out of her like compressed air. Samantha's sobs lasted for the next few minutes, when there was a sudden squeak from the door, as Samantha saw Diana come around the door, a little concerned look upon her face, wondering whether Samantha was in some sort of a confession mode at that moment in time.

"The others didn't feel like it was a good idea for you to be here on your own, so I'm here for you Sam" responded Diana, as Samantha sat herself down on the nearest church pew, and whipped her eyes on the back of her hands. Diana sat down next to her, and put an arm around Samantha's shoulder, giving her a small reassuring squeeze. "I miss Julie as well you know, even though, I didn't know her as well as you did" replied Diana, as Samantha gave Diana a very comforting look. "Thanks babes, I should pull myself together really; we'll give Julie the send-off she deserves" replied Samantha, as Diana gave her another little hug. "Of course we will Sam, we always would" replied Diana, as they both looked back at Julie's coffin in complete silence,

351

neither of them saying a word. Samantha nor Diana, knew how long they sat starring at Julie's coffin for, but next thing they knew, Sophie and Sarah were shacking them gently awake.

"Sorry to wake you, but we're ready to proceed with the burial now" explained Sarah, as Samantha and Diana nodded to show they had understood her, as both of them had fallen asleep on the church pews watching Julie until the sun went down the previous evening. The rest of the sisterhood had entered into the chapel at that moment, all wearing identical long black dresses, whilst carrying bouquets of flowers in front of them. "We shall carry her out now; you should both wait by the side of the grave" replied Sophie in a soft reassuring voice, as the rest of the sisterhood gathered around the coffin, placed their bouquets in turn on the lid, in a mark of respect to Julie. Like they had done so when Samantha and Diana had arrived at the chapel the previous day, the sisterhood hoisted Julie's coffin onto their shoulders, before walking slowly outside into the graveyard.

Sophie walking in front of the coffin, and Sarah walked behind it, both of them carrying crosses and wearing the same long black dresses as the others. Samantha and Diana knew that they could not have looked presentable, but even so, they still felt that Julie wouldn't have minded that one little bit. Instead, Samantha and Julie just bowed their heads, as Julie's coffin arrived at the graveside, as it was placed down on the ground beside them. "Police Constable Julie Guard was an example to us all; a brave and courageous officer of the law, a loving daughter and a good friend; she is now to be committed to the ground, to rest in peace, ashes to ashes, dust to dust". Sophie spoke these words loud and sharp to the morning air, as a gentle mist began to roll in, surrounding the chapel and the hill that it sat on. The sisterhood now threaded ropes underneath Julie's coffin, hoisting it back into the air, and began to lower it slowly into the open grave.

When the coffin finally came to a stop with a soft bump at the bottom, they pulled the ropes back up again, as the members of the sisterhood retreated back away from the open grave, all forming a line, whilst keeping their heads bowed and arms together, in a mark of respect towards Julie. Sophie and Sarah now moved forwards and picked up the shovels beside the grave, but Samantha suddenly spoke out. "No, I want to do that, she was my friend after all". Samantha almost took herself by surprise in saying this, and even Diana looked shocked. Sophie and Sarah on the other hand didn't look surprised or jump backwards in alarm; instead, they passed the shovels over to Samantha and Diana and said in a soft calm voice, "of course, it's only right if you want to do that". Over the next ten minutes or so, Samantha and Diana slowly shovelled the earth back into the grave, as the rest of the sisterhood watched on, all muttering some sort of a prayer.

It felt good to be shovelling the earth into the grave, as Samantha finally felt that she been granted the correct chance to do something good in her life, both before and after Covid. Giving Julie the respect that she had deserved in laying her to rest in this peaceful part of the world, was a way of clearing Samantha's conscience slightly. Diana must have felt somewhat the same way, as she too seemed to be doing her best to do the job of burying Julie properly, as they all thought about the millions, even billions of others around the world, who would not be as lucky to receive the correct send-off as Julie was given. As Samantha shovelled away, her burning desire to see Greg again was so powerful, she felt as if a cannon would explode out of her chest at any moment. Diana put down her shovel, breathing heavily, as this large amount of manual labour was more than likely going to be straining her heart to breaking point.

"Are you alright Diana" asked Samantha, as Diana stood up straight, her stomach bump looking bigger than ever. "Yeah, I think I am" replied Diana, as she took a step back, allowing Samantha to finish shovelling the earth back into the grave, which now covered Julie's coffin completely. The sisterhood had all now disappeared, leaving Samantha to finish shovelling the earth into the grave all on her own as she had requested. As the last shovelful of Earth was poured on top, Diana took the wooden cross which lay on the ground a few feet away, and jammed it carefully into the grave's mound of earth, making sure that it was straight, upright, and clean. Written across the top of the wooden cross, in plain black letters were the words, 'Police Constable Julie Guard, 1995-2020'. "Julie is at peace now Sam" said Diana softly, as she took Samantha's arm and lead her away back towards the farm buildings, being as gentle as she could.

The mist started to clear somewhat, as they made their way back across the farm yard, into the main house, which stood alone away from all of the farm buildings and chapel. Inside the main house, the Geighlon sisterhood had prepared what looked like a feast, in the form of a wake for Julie's funeral. There were plates of every type of food you could find, and it made Samantha and Diana's eyes water at how many types of food there was, crammed into one single table space. "Where the dickens did you get this lot from" was Samantha's reply, as she gazed open mouthed at the amount of food, drink and other assorted beverages that sat in front of her. "Julie should be remembered with a celebration, now eat up, it is her wake after all" replied Sarah, in response to Samantha and Diana's stunned looks, wondering if Sarah and the other sisters were taking the whole 'Covid Pandemic' thing seriously or not.

Samantha and Diana really didn't know what to respond in answer to Sarah's words, so instead sat down at the table and began to eat what they could see in front of them. "You'd never think there was an apocalypse going on out there would you, now with all this lot sitting here" replied Diana, through a mouth of chicken leg. As there was no electrical power to the chapel, the farm buildings and the main house; Penelope and Harriet, had both broken out a cello and flute, and begun to play some of the famous classical tunes. It put Samantha in mind of listening to songs being sung around the campfire when she had been a girl guide in her youth. A sudden shouting yell however, made them all look around in alarm, as even Harriet and Penelope stop playing their instruments at the sound of the sudden yell. Everyone seemed to be staring around in confusion, as they were all curious to know where the yell had originated from.

It turned out that it had been Diana who had yelled, as she had stood up in shock, staring down at her dress, where a large wet patch had appeared between her legs, soaking the seat on the chair she was sitting on at the time. Diana took a step back, quickly making a mental note of the puddle of liquid that had appeared beneath her. This could mean only one thing, her waters had finally broken, and the baby, was coming. "Wow, oh my days, the baby's coming" responded Diana, now with panic in her voice, but as one, the sisterhood had come to her aid. "Don't panic now Diana, we need to go you into the dormitory and onto a bed for the birth" replied Sophie, as Sarah marshalled the other sisters into line, looking like some sort of organised medical midwife unit. "Harriet, Penelope, we need fresh towels and hot water immediately; Salma, Tracey, support her head and feet" ordered Sarah in a hurry, as everyone followed their orders.

Diana was hoisted into the air, and quickly carried away into the next room, where she was placed onto a bed, whilst the sisterhood ran around collecting the many different items that they would need to bring a new-born baby into the world. "It's ok Diana, it's ok, just keep hold of my hand now" said Samantha in a reassuring voice, as Diana's breathing became more rapid, as she placed her legs up at right angles and spread apart, so that it was possible to see the baby as it came out. "The screaming will start any second now" responded Sophie, as right on que, Diana began to scream out in pain. Some of the group around the room winced slightly, as Diana screamed again, as they weren't used to being in a hospital, or even aided in the birth of a baby before.

"Nurse, I'll need some peace and quiet to work" ordered Sophie, as Sarah came bustling over to Sophie's side, and jammed a towel into Diana's mouth, preventing her from screaming out again. "What are you doing" shouted out Samantha, as Diana screamed again, which was muffled slightly by the towel, as Samantha winced slightly. It turned out that Diana's grip was a lot tougher than Samantha thought, as she felt her hand go numb as Diana squeezed it again, letting out yet another muffled scream. "Sister Sophie finds it easier to work when the noise level is at a bare minimum, Diana needs to work through the pain, rather than just yelling about it" explained Sarah, in the sort of voice that a tutor would use, as if they were giving a lecture in a classroom. "I bet this wasn't in your birthing plan ah Diana" thought Samantha, as Diana let out another muffled scream, with Samantha's hand going slightly blue due to it being squeezed.

"Ok Diana; I need you to push; now" said Sarah, as she and Sophie kept a close eye on Diana, whilst Samantha tried with all her strength not to scream out herself, due to the fact that Diana was causing her a great deal of pain, due to Samantha's hand being starved of Oxygen and blood. Diana pushed with all of her strength, as Harriet and Penelope appeared in the room through the doorway, carrying the hot water and towels that had been ordered a few moments earlier. "Sorry about the wait, we had to heat the water manually" replied Harriet, who had moved around to behind the bed, just in time to see the baby's head begin to crown. "Baby head is in the crown position nurse, we need a bit more persuasion from the mother" replied Sophie in a commanding voice, as if she was directing troops in battle, rather than delivering a baby into the world.

"You're doing really babes, you're doing so well, babies head is showing so your almost there" said Samantha, trying to sound positive, as she looked back in Sophie's direction. Sophie seemed to be becoming more agitated, the longer the labour went on, almost as if she could sense that something was wrong with the labour. "Nurse, I think we have a baby that's stuck mid-way, we're going to need to operate to save the baby" said Sophie, as Sarah started firing orders at the others again. "Harriet, Penelope, bring the towels and hot water over here, and lay it down by the bed; Salma, Tracey, I need my sowing basket, needle and thread from my office". The others did as they were told, as

Sophie turned to Sarah. "Nurse, prepare the patient for surgery" replied Sophie, as Diana's went wide eyed in shock, but she sadly couldn't speak or put up any form of protest, owing rather unfortunately, to the fact that Sarah had a stuffed towel into her mouth.

"I'm really sorry about this Diana" said Sarah, but Samantha suddenly spoke up, wondering what was going on. "Wait a minute, what exactly are you going to". Whack! With a sound of a fist making contact with flesh, Sarah had raised her arm back to its fullest extent and punched Diana hard in the face, knocking her clean out cold. "What the; how; you" spluttered Samantha, but Sarah had already turned back to Sophie and said, "patient ready for surgery". "Very good nurse, scapple" replied Sophie, holding out a hand for a scapple which Penelope handed to her, as Sophie began to operate on Diana. "Now hang on a minute, you can't just go cutting into another human being like that, and what the hell did you do to Diana" demanded Samantha, as Sarah took hold of her arm and gave it a small squeeze. "That was anastatic love, it's how we doing things here in North Yorkshire" replied Sarah, but Samantha retorted.

"How the ruddy hell was that anastatic, you knocked the poor woman out cold; she's probably got concussion or something now because of that". The others made flapping noises at Samantha, as Sophie called for quiet, so Samantha was forced to bite her lip, watching on as Sophie begun to operate in order to rescue Diana's baby from the womb. As the baby's head had already got to the point where it had crowned, Sophie had to be very careful not to cut anywhere near the baby's head. Hard to do when it was already on its way out; but despite this, Sophie made a quick and small incision right above where the baby's head was. The result of this, was that the baby was now given more room to be carefully pulled out of the womb, and safety into Sophie waiting arms. As the others held their breath, the seconds ticked by, waiting to see if the baby had survived its ordeal.

Suddenly and without warning, there was a wailing sound coming from where Sophie stood, as the happy, healthy baby, popped out onto the bed, covered in amniotic fluid and flecks of blood, but otherwise very much alive. "It's a baby girl" called out Sophie to the room at large, as everyone cheered and clapped in celebration. The baby meanwhile had begun to cry, as it hadn't liked the idea of coming from a warm tummy, into the cold environment of the chapel ward. Salma suddenly rushed forward, as Sophie lifted Diana's baby girl up off the bed, and had placed it carefully into the warm blankets waiting for it, where the little baby girl seemed to stop wailing, and instead began making gurgling noises, with its tiny fingers and hands near to its face. "It's a shame we had to suddenly put baby's mother out for the count, otherwise we would give baby to her" replied Sophie, as she smiled slightly, flushed with success at Diana's birth.

In the sudden aftermath of the baby popping out, Sarah had been forced to quickly run around to Diana's legs with a needle and thread, beginning to stitch up the wound made by Sophie's scalpel, in an attempt to get the baby out. Samantha meanwhile, had momentarily forgotten about the fact that Sarah had socked her best friend in the face; but she had instead decided to come around the bed, and start cooing along with the others, at the sight of the new bundle of joy, which was Diana's baby daughter. "Aww, she's so cute" said Tracey, who had just seen into the eyes of Diana's baby daughter, as Salma held and supported the baby in her arms, stroking her microscopic hands with a fine gentle touch. Diana's baby daughter was tiny in comparison to the size that other babies would have been in the days before Covid, as she was no longer than a loaf of bread, and seemed to be very lightweight.

"I think she's under nourished, she's not the right size or weight for your average baby" replied Sarah, as Sophie looked up at her, half way through putting stitches into Diana's wound. "Give her here, I can breast feed her if you want" replied Samantha, as the others exchanged nervous looks, wondering if this was perhaps a step too far. "It's risky Samantha, have you ever breast feed before" replied Sarah, who looked almost petrified, at the thought of allowing anyone except Diana to breastfeed a new born baby. "What other choice do we have, considering the fact that you've knocked her mother out cold" argued back Samantha, who was still smarting about her best friend being physically assaulted. Sarah seemed to consider her for a moment, but Sophie gave her a stern look. "I know your desperate for a child Sarah, but this won't help, let Samantha do it" replied Sophie, as Sarah, accepting defeat, carefully handed over the baby to Samantha.

"Ok, careful now, the baby's head needs to be tilted slightly downwards, and kept horizontal, so as to keep the airwaves open" said Penelope, who had hurried over to Samantha, and quickly given her a crash course in childcare. "That course in childcare paid off then ah Penelope" said Samantha, as Penelope gave her a quick smile, watching Samantha pull off her top and flick down the right cup of her bra, to expose her right nipple. On catching sight of Samantha's exposed nipple, Diana's baby daughter immediately jumped onto it, as Samantha gave out an involuntary cry of pain, nearly dropping Diana's baby daughter as she did so through the sudden sharp pain. There was a general up-cry from everyone in the room as this happened, as they feared that Samantha may have dropped the baby by accident; but Samantha managed to recover just in time, feeling that her first lesson in motherhood wasn't in the way that she had planned it to go.

"Ahh, cheeky little madam, she bit my breast" replied Samantha, as the others in the room giggled slightly, trying their best to laugh too much. "Welcome to motherhood darling, Sarah did the same to me when she was born" replied Sophie, who had finished sewing up the wound she had been forced to make to get the baby out of Diana's womb. At the sound of these words, Sarah went as bright red as a post box in embarrassment, and went to take a swipe at Sophie, but she missed, and nearly hit Salma in the process, who was standing the closest to her. Salma had the common sense however to duck out of the way just in time, so as to avoid a brain injury by Sarah. Samantha smiled back at them all however, as Diana's baby daughter drank away at Samantha's breast milk. It suddenly dawned on Samantha, that Sarah had a bit of a hungry look in her eye, as if she wanted Diana's baby for herself.

"Aww, I think she's enjoying my milk" said Samantha, a little surprised herself that she even had breast milk in the first place, considering the fact that it had been Diana who was pregnant, and not herself. "Hello there; hello; I guess I'm your Auntie Samantha now" cooed Samantha in a sweet low voice, as she looked directly in Diana's baby daughter's eyes, big and round as they were. As Samantha stood beside the bed, gently rocking the baby backwards and forwards, there came a groan from the bed where Diana lay. Everyone become very quiet, as Diana began to stir from her slumber, after being punched in the face by Sarah during the labour. "What happened; why do I feel sore; did someone punch me in the face or something" asked Diana in a weak voice, as she sat slowly upwards on the bed, wincing slightly from the pain of her injury where Sophie had been forced to do the surgery.

It was hardly surprising, that everyone who was present in the room at that exact moment in time, looked exceptionally embarrassed; although, it was hardly surprising that they did. Sophie had first made Diana lay on a collapsible bed, which was very uncomfortable to say the least. Then been forced to perform a minor virginial operation to get her baby out. Sarah had been made to knock her lights out, so that Diana wouldn't feel anything; and then to cap it all off, caught sight of her best friend Samantha, standing on her left beside the bed, breast feeding Diana's baby daughter. "I bet this wasn't in the birthing plan" replied Harriet, to break the awkward silence, as Diana opened her mouth in the perfect round 'o' shape, taking in the scene all around her. After a second or so, she closed it again, swallowed, and then spoke directly towards Samantha, voicing that very question that Samantha had been fearing that she would ask.

"Sam, babes; is that my baby your breastfeeding"? Samantha swallowed hard and then winced again, as the baby tried to take another bit out of her nipple. "Nah, I borrowed this one from the nursery down the road" said Samantha in a jokey voice, in an attempt to break the tension, as the others around the room sniggered into their hands. Diana fixed Samantha with one of those, 'now I know your lying to me', sort of a looks, showing that she wasn't fooled in the slightest by Samantha's remark. "Oh, alright then, you've got me; yeah, she's your baby daughter, here you go babes" replied Samantha conceiving defeat, as she handed Diana's baby daughter back over, gentling laying her into Diana's arms. Thankfully, Diana's attention was now taken entirely onto her new-born baby daughter, so she didn't feel like throwing insults or criticisms at anyone else for the time being about what had happened during the labour.

"Aww, she looks just like me" replied Diana, as the others around the room all collectively went 'aww' at the same time. "Come on, we're all dying to know, what you going to call her" exclaimed Salma, as Diana went slightly pink, releasing that in all of the excitement that had just been, she hadn't thought about a name for her baby daughter. Samantha decided in that brief moment to quickly cover herself back up again, as she had only just realised that she had been standing there, with her right breast and nipple on show for everyone to see. As Samantha pulled her top back on, she was aware of everyone in the room all looking longingly at Diana, as though waiting for Diana to perform a clever magic trick on them all. "I thought about calling her, well; Julie; after the woman who saved her life" replied Diana, as there was a slight pause in the room, as if Diana thought that this may have been a step too far.

But then, Diana looked around at everyone's faces, and saw that they were all beaming with happiness. "A wise and admirable statement; little baby Julie; long live baby Julie" called Sophie to the room at large, as the call was mirrored on all sides by everyone who was present. "Long live baby Julie" they all said in unison, all except Diana, who beamed around at them all, before turning back to stroke and caress tiny baby Julie in her arms. "Come on everyone, we must leave the mother to rest, it's our tradition you know" replied Sarah, as she walked over to where Samantha was standing and began to lead her away, as they all trooped outside, leaving Diana alone in the room with little baby Julie still in her arms. Diana didn't put up any protest about them leaving, but she gave Samantha a broad smile as they all trooped out of the room, leaving Diana alone on the bed, still cradling baby Julie in her arms.

"You say it's tradition, but exactly how many babies have you had delivered here" enquired Samantha, after they had closed the door to the dormitory, and began to walk back to the table where the food and drink still sat upon it, waiting to be eaten. "In truth, little baby Julie, is the first one" replied Sarah, who at least seemed ready to confess about the fact that none of the Geighlon Sisterhood were trained midwifes or any kind of medical professionals at all. Samantha couldn't help but smile when she heard this, realising that for the first time since escaping from Grey's Pharmaceuticals, both her and Diana were safe, to a point. Diana certainly wouldn't be able to travel for a while, not having just given birth at any rate, so Samantha had decided that she was going to stay put for a while, until Diana was ready to travel of course. Helen and Patrick would still be on their tail, but they hardly had any chance to find them at the Geighlon Sisterhood.

Little did Samantha and Diana know however, that Helen and Patrick had decided to follow the main roads and had discovered the same bridge where Samantha had found the hanging bedsheet sign, swinging by its ropes from the bridge, addressed to Samantha from Greg. "Sir, heavy braking tyres tracks up here, something big has been this way recently" said a black uniformed soldier, as they examined the road surface for vital evidence. "Ah ha, I knew it, they've been this way, I know it" exclaimed Patrick, snapping his fingers in triumph, whilst raising his fists into the air in mock celebration. "Why slam on the brakes here though; they must have been here with people, or seen something to make them stop" replied Helen in a questioning voice, as she stood quite close by to Patrick, looking up at the bridge and its railings, wondering what had happened in their location.

"Wait a minute, that grass on that embankment over there has been flattened down in places; I think someone has climbed up there at some point" replied Patrick, as he hurried over to check the grass, which had indeed been flattened down by Samantha a few days earlier. "Samantha, Diana and Julie have been through here, I'm sure of it" replied Helen, as neither Patrick or Helen was aware of the fact that Julie had been killed by Edward. "This is a bit of a wild-eyed guess, but I suspect that something was hanging from that bridge; there's what looks like rope marks on the railings, as if a sign of some kind was held down pretty tight" replied Patrick, as Helen smiled slightly, a look of eagle-eyed content in her eyes. "We're hunting you down you three, we're hunting you down" thought Helen, as she allowed her thoughts to run wild, feeling that the thrill was in the chase.

"Sir, the results from the skin marks have come back, turns out that the vehicle that made them is nearly a hundred feet in length" responded a second solider, as he came up to Patrick, and handed him a piece of paper, showing a digital readout of the road surface on it. "Good lord, one hundred foot long; there's not a single vehicle on the road like that, not even military ones" exclaimed Patrick, who didn't think that any such vehicle existed from what he knew of. Helen on the other hand was smiling again, as she was starting to piece things together in her mind, realising that Samantha had created a masterpiece of engineering. "The Green Goddess, I suspected that such a vehicle could exist" replied Helen, as Patrick looked at her non plussed, wondering what Helen could be talking about. "What's the Green Goddess" asked Patrick, as Helen explained it to him.

"Some time ago, I got wind of a set of blueprints which had been drawn up by a Corporal Fredrick Loose, a Royal Air Force Engineer; this was where Samantha and Julie had gone too, after leaving Lillington". As Helen finished speaking, Patrick seemed to cotton on to her trail of thought, as he said, "yeah, me and Edward tried to track them until they reached Mile End Farm, but we never saw this Green Goddess herself; although, wait a minute". Patrick trailed off, and then exclaimed, "no, no we did see it, it was in a layby outside a small village in Bedfordshire". "Well then, there's only one thing to do; a vehicle of that size will certainly be easy to spot from the air" replied Helen, as Patrick cut across her. "Don't tell me you've got a helicopter too hand, otherwise that would save a lot of time". But at that very moment, there came a low humming sound, which became louder and louder the longer they stood there.

It suddenly swelled to a roaring sound, as a jet-black painted helicopter, soared over the embankment, hovering around sixty or so feet above them all. "We'll find them in no time, just you see" shouted Helen to Patrick, over the noise of the rota blades, as Helen signalled to the helicopter hovering above them to begin the search for the Green Goddess. The helicopter banked sharply to the left for a second or two and then flew off, flying straight and level as it went, beginning its arduous and near impossible task of searching for the Green Goddess. "Oh, now; that; is just showing off" exclaimed Patrick, gesturing at the black helicopter, which was getting smaller and smaller as they watched it, as it flew further away from them. Helen gave Patrick a smug look that clearly said, 'I've got better toys than you have, just live with it', knowing that Patrick couldn't possibly hope to match Helen's firepower and authority.

Patrick gave one last look of content at Helen, before he walked away back to his car, giving a whistle between his teeth, signalling to everyone to get ready to move out. "We're coming for you girls; you can run, but you can't hide forever" said Helen, more to herself than anyone else, as she watched the now rapidly disappearing helicopter, until it was out of sight over the horizon. Back in the Geighlon Sisterhood dormitory however, Diana had been given a first meal after giving birth to baby Julie, as little baby Julie slept away in a rusted metal cot, which looked as though it hadn't been maintained for centuries. In actually reality, the Geighlon Parish Church Hall, where Julie's coffin had been laid the previous night, had in fact once been an orphanage back in the 1800s, before being closed down in the late 1980s. A church hall in which Sophie herself, had come to as a small child in her youth.

This rusted cot, was one of many that lived on the small church farm where the Geighlon Sisterhood resided, but had been improvised and made more comfortable for little baby Julie, who was wrapped in many warm blankets, and supported by a lovely feather mattress, which separated her from the rusting iron work below. Diana slept peacefully too, having wrapped herself in the warm blankets on her bed, as the temperature outside yo-yoed, between hot and sunny, then foggy and misty in the mornings, as it rolled off the nearby North Yorkshire hills and dales. Samantha meanwhile was outside with the other members of the sisterhood, in a sisterhood ritual which was usually known by those who practiced it as 'Wind Talking'. As it transpired however, Wind Talking, didn't involve learning a code, but was in fact a form of therapy, which was a cross between Yoga, and the Chinese Kung Fu art of 'Inner Peace'.

When Samantha had heard about this rather curious and fascinating artform, she couldn't help but think of a film that her father had watched on the TV, about a group of Second World War American Rangers who had spoken in a code which had never been broken, as they had been nicknamed, 'the wind talkers'. The idea of wind talking had originally been created by Tracey, the Oracle, who had suggested it as a way of dealing with Post Traumatic Stress, loneliness, and any violent urges for action and destruction that had come about as a result of the Covid-19 pandemic. Samantha stood in the middle of the group, which included the entire sisterhood, as they all stood spaced a few meters apart from each other, curving and stretching their bodies, as the entire sisterhood were engaged in the wind talking meditation cycle on a patch of moorland, overlooking the surrounding hills and valleys of the North Yorkshire Moors.

"You must be as one with the wind, let it speak to you, and keep your spirits clean and fresh" spoke Tracey in a mystical voice, as she stood facing the group, all of whom had their eyes closed and were taking slow deep breaths as they did so. "Just remember to keep your mind open and your eyes closed, it takes a few weeks to get into practice with it" was Sarah's words to Samantha, as Samantha had nearly tripped over herself trying to move her body more slowly than she was used to, whilst simultaneously keeping her eyes closed. This had been proved already that day, as when they had started with a warm up exercise of standing on one leg, Samantha had managed to fail this in spectacular fashion, by falling sideways into the now thankfully dry grass. At least no-one laughed when this happened to her, although Samantha could see a few faces go slightly red in an attempt to not laugh too much.

"We are not only speaking to ourselves, but also speaking to each other, by connecting with our thoughts and desires, to those of our fellow sisters" continued Tracey, in the same low and slow mystical voice as before. "You did well today you know Samantha, I'm hoping Diana will be well enough soon to undergo wind talking as well" said Sophie in an encouraging voice, as the group broke up to go about their daily chores and duties around the church farm. "Thanks Sophie, I'm sure she will be fine about it; sorry about falling in the grass again" replied Samantha, who was half way between gratitude and embarrassment at this small little blunder. "Some friendly advice Samantha, but if you're not feeling pain in your first week of doing wind talking, then you're not doing it properly" replied Sophie, with a smile that had started to creep across her face.

When Samantha looked non plussed at Sophie's statement, Sophie continued, "if you're not feeling pain, it's because you cannot feel other people's emotions, and it's about connecting as a group, as you share mental pain and grief to make you a stronger person than you are already". "You could give Greek Philosophers a run for their money you could" thought Samantha, as Sophie was called away by Salma, who was trying to lift a hay bale by herself, who appeared to be struggling badly from the weight of it. "You'll blend into wind talking soon enough; Tracey is a real natural with it, just really gets it you know" replied Sarah to Samantha's silence, as she came and stood next to

Samantha, who was looking in the direction of the dormitory, where she knew Diana was comfortably resting. "I'd love to see Diana do wind talking whilst holding baby Julie in her arms" thought Samantha, as this particular mental image crossed her mind.

"We'll let you spend the day with Diana, she'll need some company when she wakes up, recovering from the stitches you know" replied Sarah, as Samantha smiled at her, but she then immediately remembered what had happened during the labour. "I still haven't forgotten you socking my friend in the face you know" replied Samantha, but Sarah giggled slightly. "Welcome to the North Yorkshire way of life lass, no southern comforts up here you know" replied Sarah, as Sarah clapped Samantha on the back, leaving Samantha a little red in the face as she made her way towards the main house and dormitory, pushing the door open as she reached it. "Sam, babes, nice of you too come and see me; sorry, can you pass me Julie over, I'd like to give her a little feed while I'm here in this position" responded Diana in a cheerful voice, as she saw Samantha enter the dormitory a few minutes later.

"How are you feeling" replied Samantha, as she followed out Diana's request, and scooped up little baby Julie carefully into her arms, before walking baby Julie across the room, to lay her in Diana's cradling arms. "Ah, still got a bit of a headache from being given a taste of the Northern anastatic" replied Diana, who rubbed her jawline in a absent minded sort of way, where Sarah had punched it. Diana's stomach had contracted slightly, as the baby fat which had come on slowly during the pregnancy, slowly retreated back; but it wasn't yet back to normal, as Diana had been very quick to notice, being usually very fit and active with her figure. "What wouldn't I do for a run right now, just to burn this baby fat off" replied Diana, as she suddenly gasped in pain, jerking slightly forwards as she did so. Little baby Julie slipped slightly in her arms, as Samantha was quick to move in to make sure that baby Julie didn't fall out of Diana's arms.

"What, what's wrong, are you ok babes" replied Samantha, quickly rescuing little baby Julie, who was still at risk of falling, as Samantha placed her carefully back into the rusting iron cot, wondering what had caused Diana to suddenly jerk forwards like that. "Ouch, that came from down between my legs" began Diana, as she and Samantha looked down at her legs. But as they both looked down at Diana's leg, a bright red patch began to emerge onto the sheets, growing larger and larger as the seconds ticked by, as they watched it stain a good square foot of the blanket as it went. Diana suddenly went very pale as she lay back on her bed, taking short sharp deep breaths as she did so. "Holy cow, you're bleeding badly babes" replied Samantha in a slightly panicky voice, as Diana's voice became high pitched as she began to hyperventilate into the air, not having access to a paper bag anywhere.

Samantha suddenly sprinted out of the room, into the outside air and screamed for help at the top of her voice. She then raced back inside, where Diana had begun to convulse slightly, whilst her breathing had become deep and shallow. "What's happened" said Sophie in a rush, who had appeared in the doorway, racing into the room at top speed, followed by the rest of the sisterhood, all of whom looked scared and worried. "We were both here talking, then suddenly Diana gasped in pain and started to bleed badly" replied Samantha, who had gone very white and shook slightly, as Sarah took her off to one side, and began a desperate attempt to comfort and reassure her that Diana was going to be ok. For the first time in a long while, Samantha felt that she was in a position where she was unable to help or protect herself from harm, like when Edward had sexual molested her back in the prison cell at Grey's Pharmaceuticals.

Sophie meanwhile had raced around to Diana and lifted up the bedsheet, where she could see that the same stitches that had been used to sew up Diana's wound had ripped apart, and a small stream of blood was slowly and steadily flowing out of the open wound onto the blanket. The smell from the wound was making the noses of those in the immediate vicinity of Diana's legs wrinkle as well, as Sophie had removed the blanket, but she had soon acted quickly, shoving a nearby towel over the wound, and pressing down hard, in an attempt to make the blood clout and seal the wound off from further blood loss. "Everyone remain calm, I need my needles and thread, some new blankets, clean and fresh; I need the rest of you around Diana, holding her steady while I fix the wound" replied Sophie, barking orders at everyone in the room, as they all separated, heading for their different places.

Little baby Julie meanwhile had started to cry at all of the noise, but Penelope, who was the one who had been learning childcare, had quickly swooped in and picked up little baby Julie, rocking her gently to try and get her to settle. "Ok, I need you to keep Diana as still as you can, everyone is to gather around the bed and hold her down; tell her to bite down on this as well" replied Sophie very quickly, as she handed over another towel, which Harriet, who was closest to Diana at the time, stuffed into Diana's mouth to deaden down the noise of her screams. "Ok, go" replied Sophie, as she lifted away the blood-soaked towel which she had used to make Diana's blood clout up, as she moved in with her needle and thread which Salma had in her hands, having just come back racing into the room, skidding to a stop next to Sophie. Samantha meanwhile had acted instinctively, heading straight for Diana's side to hold her hand to try and keep her calm.

As Sophie threaded the needle and thread through Diana's skin attempting to seal the wound back up again, Diana continued to make silent screaming sounds, as she flailed around on the bed, being forcibly restrained by the others, the noise muffled by the towel which was stuffed into Diana's mouth. "She's almost there Samantha, she's almost there" said Sarah, who was speaking to Samantha opposite her, as they stood on either side of Diana, keeping her steady as per Sophie's instructions. "It's ok babes, it's ok, just try and stay calm" replied Samantha, mopped Diana's forehead, with a third towel, which she had found on the bed opposite her, which by now was caked in Diana's sweat. "Done" said Sophie, as Diana stopped thrashing around and slowly sank into the bed, as Sarah removed the towel from inside her mouth. "Breath Diana, you're going to be ok" replied Sarah, as Salma took her hand, placing two fingers just below Diana's wrist.

"She's got a weak pulse, and it's getting weaker, we may need to do CPR Sophie" replied Salma, as Sophie leaned back slightly, having finally stemmed the blood flow by sealing the wound back up again. "Sam" said Diana, in such a low voice that only Samantha could hear her, but the others soon cottoned on, and somehow knew that Diana had spoken at that moment. "You're going to be ok babes, you've just lost a little blood that's all" replied Samantha, as she stroked the side of Diana's face with her hand, slight tears in her eyes at the suddenness of the situation. "There's something I need to tell you Sam" replied Diana, as Samantha spoke the moment Diana had finished speaking. "It can wait babes; you need to rest now". But Diana shook her head slightly, her breathing becoming more rapid and shallow as she spoke, with her eyes flickering slightly as she did so.

"No, this is important, I should have told you a long time ago, and I feel now that I should" replied Diana, as Samantha nodded, to show that she had understood. Diana looked directly into Samantha's eyes, before she spoke again with the words, "me and Greg were having an affair; I'm so sorry". Samantha's eyes widened in shock, but then she recovered quickly be saying, "you're just a little confused Diana, I know you don't mean that". "I do, I was seeing Greg, we were courting for a while, please forgive me" replied Diana, as Samantha began to cry. "You're my friend Diana, I would never think badly of you" replied Samantha, as the others around them looked shocked and horrified, wondering why Samantha was taking things so likely, as it was fair to say if any of them had found out that their partners had been having affairs, they would have not have been as forgiving as Samantha was being.

"You are, and always will be, my best friend Sam" replied Diana, as her voice went so low, that Samantha almost missed the last few words. "And you will always be mine" replied Samantha, as Diana's eyes rolled into the back of her head, as her eyelids closed shut; and she moved no more. There was a collective gasp that went around the room, as they somehow knew, that Diana, was gone. It was all over in a trice; but; Diana couldn't be dead; she just couldn't be. Diana Gibbs; the brainy, the confident, the lady who had been Samantha's best friend ever since her first day at Primary School, lay motionless on the bed, eyes unmoving, with her mouth slightly ajar. "I can't get a pulse" replied Salma, as she laid Diana's now motionless arm back onto the bed, and gave her arm a small squeeze with her hand. There was a complete silence around the room, as they stood frozen for a few seconds, looking at Diana's dead body on the bed.

Even little baby Julie seemed to have fallen silent, as if she somehow knew that her mother had passed away. The only sounds in the room now, were coming from Samantha, who was still staring at Diana's lifeless face, wishing it would move again. "Diana, please, not you too" cried Samantha, but Sophie was already moving slowly around the bed, placing a hand on Samantha's shoulder, as Samantha wept like a small child. "Samantha, I'm so sorry, she's gone now, come on, there's nothing more we can do for her" replied Sophie, who seemed to be the most stable one in the room at that moment. "No" screamed Samantha, who had suddenly leapt up, a look of rage on her face, before running at the nearby wall, and began to punch it with all of her strength, making small holes appear in the plasterboard, whilst small blisters appeared on her fingers from every blow, which was soon followed by small patches of blood.

Everyone had recalled backwards slightly at the sight of Samantha's outburst, fearing that Samantha may fly at them and attack them, as little baby Julie started wailing again. At the sound of little baby Julie's crying, Penelope and Harriet immediately sprang into action, trying to keep her calm. Maybe looking braver than they felt, Sophie and Sarah had closed ranks around Samantha, trying to keep her calm, whilst preventing the entire wall from caving in. "Get away from me" screamed Samantha, as she was suddenly aware of the fact that Sarah and Sophie were around her, knowing full well that Sarah's punches were a guaranteed knock out. "Samantha, we're sorry we're having to do this" replied Sophie, as the others looked on, almost knowing what was going to happen. "Get off me" screamed Samantha again, as she struggled with all of her might against Sarah and Sophie's grip on her.

But next thing Samantha knew, she had felt a sharp pain across her face, and then it had all gone very dark, as lights popped in front of her eyes. Sarah had knocked Samantha out cold, just as she had done too Diana during the labour, as they laid Samantha's unconcise form slowly down onto the floor, the rest of the sisterhood gathered around her, once again looking onto Sophie for guidance. "Take Samantha into confession please everyone, I think it's time Samantha speaks with the Oracle" replied Sophie, as without speaking a word to each other, hoisted Samantha up, and carried her out of the room.

CHAPTER TWENTY THREE

The Oracle

Samantha had no idea how long she had been unconcise for a long time, as when she began to stir, her vision was a little blurry, whilst the room that she was sat in was still lit with a narrow beam of sunlight coming in through the closed curtain above the window, keeping the whole room in semi darkness. The room itself was very small, only around twelve feet of so square, but with comfy arm chairs, and a table in one corner of it. Samantha felt as if she was lying on something, as whatever it was that she was laying on was warm and comfortable, despite the fact that the room didn't look like it had any form of central heating in it at all. Samantha sat up slightly looking around, when a figure in silhouette, who was sat in an armchair opposite to her, suddenly spoke. "Lay down on the sofa Samantha, I am here to help". Samantha jumped out of her skin at the sight of the silhouetted figure in the arm chair, but resisted the urge to shout or scream out.

Without any form of concuss thought, Samantha did as she was told, leaning back on the sofa, resting her head on a pillow behind her, as she starred up at the ceiling unmoving, with only her light fast breathing for company. "Please take slow deep breaths, you are now under the protection of the Oracle" replied the voice, as Samantha recognised it straight away. It was the voice of Tracey, one of the Geighlon sisterhood ladies, the lady who the others referred to as the Oracle. Samantha felt like speaking out, but it was almost as if Tracey had read her mind somehow, being the wise and understanding lady that she was. "Yes, it is Tracey, however I am now your Oracle, and am here to help you" replied Tracey's voice, as it sounded a little calmer and much slower than her usual brash Essex accent was. In some very strange way, considering that Samantha felt a little like she was in pain, she couldn't help but feel very weak and sleepy as Tracey spoke.

You have suffered a trauma; you have suffered, many traumas; but you must stay strong as your spirit has defined you to be" replied Tracey's voice from where she sat in her arm chair. "This feels like hypnosis" thought Samantha, as suddenly, without warning, a sudden number of flashing images raced across her mind, making Samantha feel dizzy and woozy. She was six years old, and her father Richard was showing her how to stand to attention like a solider would. She was eight, and both her and Diana sat in the school playground, laughing at a joke that they had heard. Samantha was now nineteen, and she was being patting on the back by Diana, Rachel and Emily, as Samantha stood next to her new articulated lorry. Greg smiling as he took the photograph of them all as they laughed and smiled at the camera, posing for the shot. "No" screamed Samantha, as she felt a nasty tasting liquid bubbling up her throat that tasted like frogspawn.

"You may now use the bucket" replied Tracey, still in the same mystical voice as before, as Samantha leaned over the side of the sofa, and vomited spectacularly into the bucket which lay on the floor beside the sofa. "What, the, hell, was, that" replied Samantha in a shocked voice, a little out of breath, punctuating every word with a pause, as she struggled to comprehend what had just happened to her. "I have tapped into your sub concuss using a blend of mind techniques and my own abilities" replied Tracey, as Samantha coughed slightly, before then lying flat on her back again, feeling a little weak. "You are focusing on memories of your friend Diana, this is good, you must keep hold of these" replied Tracey, as she too, adjusted herself slightly in the arm chair where she sat. Samantha couldn't put her finger on it, but it was almost as if Tracey the Oracle had somehow hijacked her mind and body.

"You may now close your eyes, and picture a scene in your mind" replied Tracey, as Samantha slowly closed her eyes, not even giving it a second thought as too why she was doing it. Tracey however, had started to speak again, as her voice had become low and soft, as if Samantha was indeed listening to a digital recording of a hypnosis session inside her own head. The room was suddenly filled with a low humming noise, as if someone had just switched on a lightbulb, or even a refrigerator. This did distract Samantha for a second, as she was under the impression that they had both been alone in the room together, however Tracey began to speak, regardless of it. "I want you to picture a young girl, younger than sixteen". Samantha tried to imagine this, having an image of when she was sixteen, and having to listen to her parents bang on about the fact that Samantha should have followed her father Richard into the Army.

Or else become a librarian like her mother Yvette had been, rather than chasing a dream as a truck driver, as Tracey continued to speak. "Her parents died in a car crash, when she was eight years old, and her brother went to different foster homes, with her stepmother being emotionally abusive until she was 13, as she was growing into a young woman". Tracey paused at that moment, allowing Samantha to soak it all up, before she continued on again. "Her stepmother kept criticising and telling her she was not good, useless and plain, of no real value. She left home at 16, as she could no longer stand it any longer" Samantha couldn't help but feel that she was falling into a deep sleep, but then still feeling awake at the same time, as Tracey ploughed on. "Her adopted father could barely look at her, or even sit close to her. She was quite introvert, and had very little confidence, which only made her suffer from insecurity".

Tracey took a breath at this point, and then finished by saying. "In her early adult years, from the age of sixteen until she was twenty-one, she underwent counselling for insecurity. Her life began to move forwards, as she moved into a flat with a friend, who then proceeded to become pregnant shortly afterwards, before leaving with her boyfriend. Alongside her day job at the bookies, she found herself doing some exotic dancing work, which left her very vulnerable to punters within the clubs, so she had a friend teach her some self-defence". "That's incredible, how did she end up here" Samantha suddenly spoke, without even realising that she was doing it, as Tracey's voice stopped speaking, before then continuing again a second or so later, feeling that Samantha's words hadn't heeded or stopped Tracey in any way, as it slowly dawned on Samantha that this was Tracey's life that was being explained, and not Samantha's one.

"She found the sisterhood by travelling for days on foot, scrounging food and drink where she could, and occasionally running into other survivors, until she found a home amongst the Geighlon sisterhood" Tracey replied, as Samantha took long slow deep breaths, as she felt her worries leaving her slightly at Tracey's washed over her, as if Samantha were laying in a nice warm bath at home. "This definitely feels like hypnosis to me" thought Samantha, who for some reason wasn't feeling any pain at all. Samantha should have felt as if she was in considerable pain, but now she came to think of it, she felt guilty about the fact that she wasn't, as if Samantha was somehow in some sort of an emotions trial. Samantha should have been feeling an urge to scream and cry out, as after all, her best friend that she had known almost from birth, had died through a massive loss of blood.

But yet when Samantha went to open her mouth to scream, she felt that she couldn't, as if her breath had been taken out of her somehow.

"You must control yourself Samantha, the Oracle has the way to heal, she is trained in the counselling and Autism reading arts" replied Tracey. Samantha suddenly widened her eyes slightly on hearing the word 'Autism', as it did seem like such a weird thing to say at a time like this. "I don't follow you" replied Samantha, as she felt another wave of the soft warm feeling hit her, working its way from her feet, up to her head. "The Oracle is wise in the ways of the learning difficulty and the mental mind box, as she herself, is one such creature" replied Tracey, still in the same mystical voice, making Samantha think for a second about this. Samantha had after all seen every type of person from the generous to the psychopaths, so those with disabilities and difficulties would have survived as well.

"You're kidding, I honestly thought that those sorts of people wouldn't have survived Covid" replied Samantha, but Tracey immediately responded with, "that is where you are mistaken my dear, the creatures who know themselves as the Aspie race, continue to make progress to this day; and now, we have the task of rebuilding the society that once existed on this planet, using our own breed of logical thinking, and combined practical and mental skills to do so". Samantha honestly thought at that very moment that she had walked into the land of the fairy tale, as the Oracles way of thinking was to suggest that the whole world was going to be populated by Autistic people. Samantha suddenly had a fleeting image of a boy she knew at school called Duncan, who had been on the Autism spectrum, who had always craved a soft spot for Samantha, making her feel even more guilty that she hadn't helped him out somehow.

Samantha had found Duncan really cute it had to be said, but not the sort of person she would have wanted to spend the rest of her life with, as Duncan was a little bit of a recluse, and absolutely hated socialising with other people, as it made him very nervous when he did so. "We have strayed from our original thought process, and we must return to it as soon as possible" replied Tracey, as Samantha blinked slightly, feeling her eyes becoming heavy again, whilst they started to drop, lower and lower, as Tracey continued speaking. "Tell me about your adventure coming here, tell me about Julie, tell me about Diana, tell me about, Greg". The last two names of Greg and Diana made Samantha twitch slightly as she lay on the sofa, trying not to let the events of the last few days cloud her judgement. Samantha did the best that she could, recalling everything that had happened to her since leaving Lillington.

Trying to find Diana and Greg, both of whom had disappeared right after Covid had flushed through the country. Then Samantha explained how she had come to her workplace, broken Betsie out of the warehouse, and then narrowly escaped death by missing the ghost plane by a matter of seconds as it had crash landed, destroying both the nearby warehouse buildings, and her father's army jeep. Samantha felt a slight bone get stuck in her throat, as she told Tracey the Oracle about meeting up with Julie, and then finding out that they were being stalked, as they proceeded to RAF North Lakes, before converting Betsie into the infamous Green Goddess. Her actions in helping Misim undergo gender reassignment surgery at Mile End Farm, felt like they had been a lifetime away, whereas in truth, it had only been less than a week earlier when it had all happened.

It made Samantha think about them all, isolated by Covid on the farm, unable to go anywhere or see anyone at all. Julie had escaped to warn Samantha about it, but then paid the ultimate price with her life, and now so had Diana. "No more" spoke Samantha defiantly, after she had finished telling her story to Tracey the Oracle. "How do you mean" asked Tracey, as Samantha replied again, "no more, no more death I mean, I've lost enough friends, I don't want to lose anymore". Samantha felt her voice starting to crack, as she tried to hold her nerves. "Your pain is felt by us all Samantha; you will always be strong and kind, and your friends knew this" replied Tracey. "Thank you, I wish to bury my friend here; but little baby Julie doesn't have a mother now" replied Samantha, as she was suddenly aware that she and Tracey weren't the only people in the room.

"Baby Julie will be given a home here in the sisterhood; she will be loved and cherished above all else" came Sarah's voice floating throughout the small room, as Sarah herself suddenly came forward very slightly, dressed in a black cloak with a hood, which she had lowered as she stepped forward into Samantha's eyeline. Samantha gave a little start when she saw Sarah, as after all, it had been Sarah who had delivered a knockout punch to her, to bring her here to this strange place in the first instance. As Samantha tried to keep her breathing under control, a new voice sprang up, which floated through the air towards her. "Baby Julie is one of a few children to be born here; she's most likely the only child to be born in this new world" came Sophie's voice, as she too stepped forward out of the shadows, wearing the same black hood and cloak as Sarah was.

"I feel guilty to be leaving her here, but I suppose I have to press on" replied Samantha, more out of determination, rather than sorrow; although this decision seemed to go against every single mothering instinct that Samantha possessed. "We believe this is what Julie and Diana would have wanted, after all, you were all reunited in the same quest" replied Tracey, as Samantha sat up slightly, rubbing her eyes. "I think Samantha's counselling here is complete, we may now show her to Diana" replied Tracey, as both Sarah and Sophie stretching out their arms ready to take Samantha's, to lead her back outside to where Diana's body was most likely being prepared for burial. Many miles away however, the jet-black painted helicopter which had been sent by Helen and Patrick, continued to search the surrounding countryside, determined to find the Green Goddess.

As it did so, it maintained a constant link to its ground units, which were made up of a convoy of official looking four-wheel drives and four door saloon cars, closely monitored by Helen and Patrick, who were part of the convoy themselves. "Sir, ma'am; urgent update from Skyhawk one" said a black uniformed soldier, who had just walked over with an official looking folder, which contained a number of aerial photographs. Skyhawk One was the official callsign of the jet-black painted helicopter, that was searching for the Green Goddess, having just delivered its intel back to the convoy group. "Thank you" replied Helen, as she took the folder containing the aerial photographs from the soldier. The soldier then hurried away to join the others, who were examining a nearby tree, which looked as if some of its branches had been snapped clean off by a large vehicle.

"That's the beauty with big vehicles I suppose, they always leave a trail to follow" said Patrick, as Helen opened up the folder and examined the aerial photograph's inside of it. "It seems that Skyhawk One hasn't located the Green Goddess, its searched most of the upper half of the country and there's no sign of it" replied Helen, as Patrick looked a little put out that Helen hadn't even seemed to acknowledge the fact that he had just spoken to her. "Well, the Green Goddess is painted green after all, if it was going to be anywhere, it would be where it would blend in the easiest" said Patrick, who felt as if he was clutching at straws as he said it. "We know the Green Goddess isn't in any of the cities, we've checked; Manchester, Leeds, Liverpool, Blackpool, Newcastle, we've checked them all" replied Helen, as Patrick cut over the end of her sentence.

"Exactly, so something that big would stand out in a city, so now we can start to comb the countryside; a dirty big thing like the Green Goddess would most likely be in the undergrowth, and probably have some sort of heat shielding technology on it". Helen seemed to shake her head slightly, as she flicked through the aerial photograph's, still not looking at Patrick. "You do remember Patrick, that I am in charge around here" replied Helen, in a cool calm voice, but with all of the authority that she could muster, now turning to look Patrick dead in the eye. "Of course, I know you're in charge, ma'am" replied Patrick, as he put a slight emphasis of sarcasm on the last word. "Then you will remember, that I give the orders around here, and I say what happens" replied Helen, as Patrick looked a little murderous. "I was under the impression, that Operation Flower was my idea, not yours, ma'am" replied Patrick, as Helen too seemed to square up to him.

It seemed at the mention of the mysterious 'Operation Flower',

Helen went very stony, whilst suddenly looked around very nervously, fearing that maybe other people would have heard him. "Go and give Skyhawk One orders to search the Yorkshire Moors area, I have reason to believe the Green Goddess is hiding in there" replied Helen after a short pause, but she made it very clear in her tone of voice, that the conversation was over. Patrick scowled slightly, but recognised defeat, as he strolled away, back towards the convoy vehicles. "Mount up, we have a new target area to search" called Patrick to everyone who was present, as the group of soldiers and scientists rushed back to their vehicles, starting the engines with a new spring in their step. Helen, Patrick and the others were closing in on Samantha now, as they were confident that they were going to get what they wanted, despite still working on theory alone.

The followed day, after a restless night's sleep, Samantha had found herself once again at the graveside, this time with Diana's coffin in front of her, rather than Julie's. Going through a second funeral in the space of two days, wasn't what Samantha had ever dreamed would happen. First Julie, now Diana; and again, Samantha found herself shovelling earth soil into a grave which she felt deep down, should have been hers, as a manic form of survivor's guilt took hold of Samantha, as if she was suffering from Post-Traumatic Stress Disorder. After everything Samantha had been through, she never would have thought in a million years that it would end up like this, having to bury her long standing school friend so early in life. It almost felt as though a large chapter in Samantha's life had defiantly closed, leaving behind it a large hole where beforehand, there had been friendship and love.

It even felt ten times worse than when the Covid pandemic had flashed around the world, finishing off the society that Samantha and indeed everyone else had grown up in and become accustomed too. After the burial had finished, Sophie, Sarah, Salma, Tracey, Penelope and Harriet, had all taken it in turns to hug and wish Samantha farewell, as Samantha began a solitary trip back into the Green Goddess, as she was to continue on her journey to find Greg. Samantha however, was now so fixed with a determination, that she felt it bubbling around inside her like hot wax. She would help anyone she encountered now; if it meant bringing her closer to Greg, then so be it, she would do it. It had been her wishes to lie low at the sisterhood for a while, so that maybe Helen and Patrick would pass her by, thinking that Samantha was heading straight for Clyde in Scotland.

But it then slowly dawned on Samantha that maybe lying low, wasn't her best plan after all. Helen and Patrick by the sounds of it had a building full of people under their control, so they could easily splint into groups and search on the ground, covering a larger distance than just two people. Samantha of course had no idea that Skyhawk One was looking for her as well, so she felt that travelling through the countryside was her best way out of it to throw Helen and Patrick off of the cent. But one small thing kept holding her back, and that was little baby Julie. Sophie, Sarah and the other sisters had agreed that she could be raised in the sisterhood, but even so, Samantha still felt that she had to perform her duties as baby Julie's unofficial Auntie and godmother. "Your Auntie Samantha is going to have to go away now" couped Samantha to little baby Julie, who lay inside her cot in the dormitory, staring up at Samantha through her big round eyes.

Little baby Julie wasn't crying or wailing, but instead was laughing slightly as Samantha's hair tickled her face and nose. Samantha did her best to smile at down at little baby Julie, knowing that she would have to leave her behind, perhaps even forever. "I'll treat her like she's my own daughter, she will have the best care that we can give her" replied Sarah, who had come into the room at that moment, and was looking longingly at little baby Julie in her cot, doing a very poor job of hiding her desire to become little baby Julie's new mother. "I suppose in the old days Diana would have probably put her into my care; or into the care of one of my friend's, if they were still alive" replied Samantha, who hadn't really noticed Sarah's last comment, trying not to focus on the journey that lay ahead of her. Little baby Julie meanwhile had started making small gurgling noises again, not being able to understand any of them.

382

Sarah smiled slightly without speaking, as Samantha carefully picked up little baby Julie, and whilst supporting her as best as she could, carried her over to Sarah, who looked a little surprised at what Samantha was doing. Samantha stood up ramrod straight, and in her most official like voice, spoke out; "As an unofficial godparent to baby Julie, and because this is the new world, where laws are being made and enforced by those who live in their own communities; I am hereby charging baby Julie into your care, Sarah Everdale". Sarah's face lite up faster than a set of Christmas tree lights display at that very moment, as Samantha carefully handed over little baby Julie to Sarah. "Thank you, I really don't know what to say" said Sarah, as Samantha smiled, as little baby Julie was rocked gently in Sarah's arms, as Sarah starred down into her big round eyes.

"I never planned to have a baby with me on my travels, and you have always wanted a child; it seems only fitting that you become the parents to this beautiful bundle of joy" replied Samantha, as she looked at little baby Julie, now cradled in Sarah's arms. "Aww" they both couped, as little baby Julie gave out a small cry at being taken out of Samantha's gaze, and into Sarah's gaze instead. But little baby Julie soon seemed to settle, as Sarah began to run caress her finger over her soft skin, whilst little baby Julie dozed off in her arms. It was amazing to see that a small number of hairs had begun to appear on the top of her tiny little head, but they both knew that within a few years a full head of hair would be there, as baby Julie would become a young woman in this new world. "I can't thank you enough Samantha, you've made my world today, you really have; what can I do in return" asked Sarah, catching Samantha off balance slightly.

"Just remember to tell her, how brave and courageous her mother and Auntie were; remember to tell her about the way that she was named after a brave and exceptional police officer, who gave her life, so that she could live" replied Samantha, as both tears appeared in Sarah's and Samantha's eyes at the same time. But somehow, Samantha suspected that Sarah's tears were both tears of joy and of sadness at the same time.

"What are you going to do now then" replied Sarah, as Samantha paused to think about what she was going to say. "There's one more life than needs to be saved, and I have to be the one to save it" replied Samantha, as Sarah gave her a small smile. "Your Greg is a very lucky man to have you fighting for him" replied Sarah, as it was now Samantha's turn to go a shade of pink, feeling her ears burning slightly, as it looked like Sarah was doing her, 'is he a fit guy' look on Samantha.

"He's my world; I mean, I'm going to kill him when I see him for sleeping with my best friend; but then I'm going to forgive him because he was still prepared to leave me a message to come and find him" replied Samantha, as she remembered the scene in where she found the bedsheet sign hanging from the bridge, which had indicated that it had been left there by Greg, which was still folded neatly on the cab bunk inside the Green Goddess. "I think he regrets his mistake too, but I think you and him will make up from it all the same" replied Sarah, as the pair of them giggled slightly. "Time to fire up the Goddess I think" said Sophie, who had just walked into the room, and seen the pair of them standing there; Sarah holding little baby Julie as if she was cradling a long-lost treasure in her arms. "Of course, I'll be starting her up and leaving with the Goddess shortly" replied Samantha, as she rummaged around in her jeans pocket for the ignition keys.

Samantha located them safe and sound in her pocket, as Sophie came over to them both, looking down at little baby Julie in Sarah's arms. "Mum, you've got a granddaughter" replied Sarah, as she gestured with her head to little baby Julie in her arms. Sophie's face also lite up as Sarah's had done a few moments earlier, on the news that she was getting a granddaughter, feeling as though she was being promised a real treat. "I think it's for the best, she'll be happy and contented here, as I know that you, Sarah, and the rest of the sisterhood will treat her as if she is your own" replied Samantha, as Sarah and Sophie both beamed at Samantha, feeling that this act of kindness would not go unrewarded. Then without warning, Sophie threw open her arms, and embraced Samantha in a hug. If Samantha had thought that Sarah had been powerful with her knock out punches, it was nothing compared to Sophie's hugs.

Samantha felt that she was being crushed to death, as Sophie squeezed her so tightly, that her eyes bulged in her sockets, and her breaths became sharper and more rapid, as she tried to get as much oxygen into them as she could. When Sophie finally let go, Samantha nearly doubled up in pain, as Sophie issued a hurried apology on Sophie's behalf, fearing that crushing Samantha wasn't the best way to reward her for allowing them to mother and raise little baby Julie. "Sorry hunni, you know what we North Yorkshire folk are like, family people through and through" replied Sophie, as Samantha managed to recover herself slightly after Sophie's rib cracking hug. "Aww, bless you" said Samantha, as she stood there momentary staring at little baby Julie. It was an awkward moment; though Samantha had only known them all, including baby Julie, for a very short period of time, she somehow felt that she belonged there.

After all, Samantha, Diana and Julie had all been running from the new world's power to be, if you could call them that; but even so, they'd still risked a hell of a lot; hiding so called criminals for one thing. Samantha looked down again into little baby Julie's face, but felt at that moment, that she had to be strong for her; put aside her feelings, and just go for it. "I'm ready, I'm ready to move on" replied Samantha, as Sophie led her outside, Samantha taking one last look at Sarah and little baby Julie as she went. "Good bye Samantha, I hope we meet again" replied Sarah, as she went back to cuddling little baby Julie, as Samantha disappeared around the doorway and out of sight. Outside of the dormitory, Samantha saw that the other members of the sisterhood had gathered around her, to wish her goodbye. One by one, they all hugged and wished Samantha well on her journey, as they knew that her path forwards was uncertain and full of danger.

"We fear there maybe be other groups of survivors knocking around in small pockets across the county, so please take care" said Sophie, as she led Samantha back across the field towards where the Green Goddess was parked on the road on the other side of the low dry-stone wall. "I will, I'm planning to stay in the countryside for a bit, in case there are any city gangs or anything out there that might want to attack me" replied Samantha, as she turned back to speak to Sophie, after opening the Green Goddesses cab door. "You will be welcome back here at any time Samantha, you and Greg could live happily here for the rest of your lives" replied Sophie, as Samantha looked back at her a little curiously, wondering what Sophie could mean by what she had said. "But I thought you said that no men were allowed here" replied Samantha, but Sophie waved a hand in front of her.

"I would make an exception with you two, as you would be a married couple, from what you were kind enough to tell the Oracle about yourself" explained Sophie, as she was referring to Samantha's counselling treatment within Tracey's tiny counselling room. "That is kind of you; thank you; and I shall try to return, I promise" said Samantha, as she swung herself into the Green Goddesses cab, once again placing the infamous keys into the ignition, and turning them all the way forwards. As per usual, the lights lit up on the dashboard, which was followed by the low thumping noise, which told them all, that the mighty Green Goddess engine had roared into life. "Happy trails Samantha, and good luck" was the general cry on all fronts from the other members of the sisterhood, as Samantha smiled and realised the air brakes using the handbrake lever.

There was the usual hiss of air from the brake cylinders, as the Green Goddess rolled slowly forwards, bumping slightly from side to side due to the rough road surface. Samantha waved back at them all, until the small Geighlon church hall was out of sight, before returning to the job at hand, on her quest to find Greg.

CHAPTER TWENTY FOUR

Operation Flower

Samantha had decided that for the best protection, she would try to stay in the surrounding hills and valleys, as hopefully they would provide her with adequate protection, should Helen or Patrick be across a valley from her, looking through a pair of binoculars or a similar piece of spyware technology. Samantha's next choice of destination that she had decided on, was to be the Lake District in Cumbria, as she had decided that this was going to be her next best place to stop for a night or two, as well as placing her on the right side of the country in order to get to into the harsh Scottish Highland wilderness. Apart from anything else, Samantha enjoyed being out in the countryside, as it was such a massive breath of fresh air, then being near the major towns and cities, where most survivors were likely to congregate, having thought that they would benefit from the resources and things that the city would have.

"But even they must be running down by now" thought Samantha, as she chanced a visit into a fuel station along the A66 just outside of the town of Darlington, the afternoon after she had left the Geighlon Sisterhood. Samantha was not surprised to learn that there was no fuel at the fuel station, so she was glad to known that she had made the decision to keep the fuel tanker trailer that she was towing, topped up with petrol and diesel. Samantha had suspected that she may have run into another group of survivors, having being this close to a major town like Darlington, and could have sworn blind that she had seen some bushes rustling with multiple pairs of eyes staring at her through them, fearful maybe to show themselves because of the size of the Green Goddess. Although Samantha hadn't bargained on it, the Green Goddesses size was certainly being of great help to keep wannabe scroungers at bay.

The rustling bushes on the other side of the road however, turned out to be nothing more than a pack of stray dogs, which took fright at the sight of the Green Goddess, scampering in all directions like small moving darts of fur, some of them the size of Great Danes, where as one or two of them looked so small, they could have easily fitted into a large lady's handbag. As she saw these types of dogs, Samantha was reminded of the same Chikwawa dogs, which would have been carried around by their owners in large handbags, or else walked around on a lead, looking microscopic next to their owners. Samantha fortunately had the common sense to not go and try to comfort the dogs, as she suspected that they were wild ones, who would have most likely taken her hand off or even a chunk out of her leg, if she had attempted anything to try and help them in any way.

Instead, Samantha allowed herself a grin, before using the fuel line attached to the tanker trailer to pump fuel into the Green Goddess main fuel tank from the storage tank areas, which would have been able to get Samantha another six hundred miles or so further on her journey. After completing this task, Samantha chanced a bit of driving on the A66, around Darlington, and then onto the A67, which wound through hills and valleys. The scenery was quite spectacular, and it felt weird to look up into the sky and not see any of the vapour trails from the aeroplanes or helicopters flying around, as they would have been doing in the pre-covid times. Samantha chanced a stop at a local pub an hour or so later, and found it too be completely deserted, just to have a quick rest from driving, knowing full well that she wouldn't be able to stay there for too long, through fear of attracting unwanted attention.

The pub itself looked so run down, that it might have fallen over even if Samantha had blown on it with a small breath of wind, as this was a building which had obviously not had love or care put into it, even before Covid had reared its ugly head. Samantha travelled a little further up the road, before finally stopping for the night on what looked like a village green of some kind, where the sign over the entrance read 'welcome to Askham', which sat right on the northern edge of the Lake District. It was a risk being in an open area such as this one it had to be said, but Samantha felt somehow, that she was doing the right thing. Samantha felt weird bedding down for the night completely on her own, as she had always been in company since leaving Lillington, apart from the few days that Samantha had spent doing observations on the Grey's Pharmaceuticals complex after leaving Mile End Farm.

As night fell around her, Samantha could hear the sounds of birds singing in the trees, and once or twice, saw a bat or two fly in and out of a few roofs nearby to her. But what was making Samantha's hairs stand on end most of all, was the funny feeling, that she was being watched. And even once or two, could have sworn she saw a curtain twitch in one of the dry stoned built houses that lined either side of the village green. There was also a funny smell coming from a few of the houses, as Samantha must have known that there would be dead bodies inside of them of those who had caught Covid and died, becoming yet another statistic of the fatal virus. "These places must be haunted" said Samantha to herself, as she almost felt like a ghost herself, sat alone in the middle of the village green, with it all silent and deserted around her. Once upon a time, this would have been a thriving village, with local residence greeting each other as they went about their lives.

But now, it was just deserted as everywhere else was in the world, an echo of an age gone by. Putting this scary but reality spinechilling thought to the back of her mind, Samantha pulled the cab curtains closed, and laid back on the bunk, not even bothering to get underdressed, as she slowly drifted off to sleep. She was suddenly awoken by of all things, a banging noise, which seemed to echo through to the cab where she lay, half asleep, and a little confused as to what was going on. At first, it sounded as if the container doors were being forced on the back of the Green Goddess. Samantha always had the common sense to lock them with a padlock that only she knew the code for, but that still wouldn't have stopped people having a go at trying to break the lock anyhow. Peeling back the curtain slightly, she gazed around at the now lite up village, as the sunlight of another clear sunny morning shone in through the cab windows, through the gap in the curtains.

Careful not to make too much movement, so as not to rock the cab and alert those that there was someone inside it, Samantha careful reached up and opened the sun roof. "What's wrong with this dam thing, this container must be full of stuff". The voice was rough and didn't sound a friendly one at all, but Samantha knew full well that if she just sat there, they were soon likely to try and target her at any rate. "Hey, did you feel something" said the voice, as Samantha accidently knocked into the seat as she climbed down onto the floor off of the bunk, which made the who cab rock slightly. The voice swore loudly, and then said, "there's someone in the cab, come on, lets whack them". Samantha's eyes widened in shock as she realised in horror, that the person who had spoken was not alone. Samantha crept to the window, and pulled back the curtain just an inch, so she could look in the passenger's side wingmirror.

Sure enough, she could see what looked like a teenage boy, no older than sixteen, slowly creeping along the side of the Green Goddess towards the cab, brandishing some sort of a Swiss army penknife in front of him. A second later, Samantha looked out of the driver's side wingmirror and saw an older man, probably in and around his mid thirty's, doing the same thing, forming a sort of pincer movement on Samantha within the cab. "These guys are clever" thought Samantha, as she looked upwards towards the sunroof. Even with her fit and petite figure, Samantha was still far too large to fit out of the sunroof, and these two men would be on her and dragging her out at any minute. From what Samantha could see, neither man had a gun, but they could still be carrying knifes or some sort of a sharp implement of some kind, as she had seen the teenage boy holding a few seconds earlier.

Thinking quickly, Samantha worked out that the older man would be the tougher of the two, and far more likely to hurt Samantha, whilst the younger man would be more hesitant. So, in a daring and unpredictable gamble, Samantha made the decision that she would tackle the older man first, hopefully injuring him enough so that he couldn't fight back, and then hopefully bringing the younger man under control afterwards. It was a bit of a risky move it had to be said, but under the circumstances, Samantha felt that this was the only way forward. Carefully removing the keys from the ignition, she pocketed them, and then slowly and carefully unlocked the driver's door, whilst keeping the passenger door locked. Hopefully the younger man would be stupid enough to try and keep opening the passenger door for long enough, that Samantha would have time to subdue the older man.

Within seconds, they were both at the cab doors, as Samantha prepared herself to jump out, hoping to flatten the older man to the ground using her bodyweight. The door clicked, as the older man flung the driver's door open, which was followed by a look of shock that came over his face less than a second later, as he saw Samantha crouched on the driver's seat, ready to jump out at him. "What the" shouted the older man, as Samantha screamed; "bonsai". Even though Samantha was barely half the man's weight, they both still fell to the ground in spectacular fashion, landing spread eagled on the grass below them. There was a sudden cracking sound like a whip being used, as they both landed on the grass, as the older man screamed out in pain. By the sounds of it, his back had fractured due to the weight of Samantha landing on him from where she had jumped out of the Green Goddesses cab.

The teenage boy meanwhile had done exactly what Samantha had predicted and tried to open the passenger door on the side of the cab, but on hearing the screaming noises of pain from his fellow, had come running around the Green Goddess, just in time to see Samantha rolling off the older man, as he lay on the grass crying out in pain. "Kill her son, do it" screamed the older man, as the younger man brandished his knife at Samantha, but still couldn't believe that a woman like Samantha could have injured the man now lying on the grass in agony. "You're going to pay for that you" began the younger man, but stopped mid-sentence, as the air was suddenly ripped by a whooshing sound, as an arrow came flying through the air, slamming into the teenager's shoulder. The teenage man screamed out in pain, as the arrow went right through his shoulder whilst Samantha jumped about a foot in the air, as saw the arrowhead come through his shoulder blade.

Samantha whirled around in a rush, keeping herself as low as possible to the ground, in case the mystery shooter fired again, although in hindsight, the mystery shooter had just saved her life. The older man however had recovered a bit of his strength, as he lunged at Samantha pinning her to the floor, a look of malice in his eyes, their faces less than six inches apart from each other. The older man's hands however had now found their way around Samantha's throat, as Samantha herself was struggling for breath due to the grip. "You would both attack a defenceless woman; shame on you sir" came a deep voice with a strong Scottish accent. Having a rough guess from where she lay on the ground, Samantha would have said that the new voice was a resident of Glasgow, having her face obscured by the older man on top of her. The older man whirled around at the sound of the new voice, still keeping his hand clamped around Samantha's throat.

The newcomer was wearing what looked like a Karki army smock, with matching trousers and hat, which had been coated in leaves and twigs too help blend into the local woodland nearby. Samantha managed to look sideways slightly and could see the newcomer for the first time. He had a slight beard, which was black in colour, and only around an inch long. From his looks, and the way that he was standing, Samantha wouldn't have put him any older than his mid-thirties. The newcomer had a bow and arrow drawn in front of him, as he pointed it straight into the older man's face. "She's mine now, if I can't have food" said the older man, who was still pinning Samantha to the ground. Samantha almost knew what was coming, and she prayed that the older man was not about to rape her like Edward Fitzgerald had tried to do back in the prison cell at Grey's Pharmaceuticals.

"I'm telling you now; leave her alone; or I will open fire on you" replied the newcomer, as Samantha tried to keep her breathing under control, having it still being restricted by the man pinning her to the ground. The older man considered him for a moment, and then decided against it, as he realised that he wasn't going to win this argument. The older man may have had Samantha pinned to the ground, but the newcomer was armed, and ready to shoot; meanwhile he suspected that his spine had been badly injured, and the younger man lay on the grass several feet away, moaning and groaning at the arrow, which had penetrated his shoulder, making his shoulder look dark and wet through the blood which was leaking from the wound made by the arrow now sticking out of it. The scene seemed to be frozen for a second, as the newcomer was still pointing his bow and arrow at the two men, in a bid to help Samantha.

"Come on son, we're leaving" said the older man, who tried to stand up, gave another cry of pain, and then staggered slowly over to the younger man, helping him up as well. With a nasty glare back at Samantha and the newcomer, the two men slowly staggered away, limping slightly as they went. "Are you alright lass" said the newcomer, as he shouldered his bow and arrow, and held out a hand to pull

Samantha up. Samantha held out her hand in return, as he gripped hers, and pulled her upright with such force, that she almost fell into him, still feeling a little winded because of her near suffocation at the hands of the two men a few moments earlier. "Thank you, sir, I think you might have just saved my life" replied Samantha, as the newcomer smiled, showing that he seemed to be in very good health, considering the fact that this man looked like he had been living in the wild.

It suddenly struck Samantha, how much bigger this man was compared to Samantha, and she could have sworn that in the pre-covid times, this man would have worked out in a gym. "That's what happens when these people cross into my patch and attack vulnerable ladies like yourself" said the newcomer, who now seemed to be far more relaxed, now that the other two men had disappeared. "Your patch" replied Samantha in a curious voice, as the newcomer smiled slightly, understanding that this was Samantha's way of saying thank you. "Aye, this is my patch, I control this village you see; I hunt deer, sheep, even wolves sometimes if they try and take a snap at me" replied the newcomer, as he stuck out a hand. "What do they call you then lass" asked the newcomer, as Samantha stuck out her hand in response to his hand. "I'm Samantha, Samantha Bonham, most people call me Sam" replied Samantha, as they both shook hands.

"Pleasure to meet you Sam, you're in safe hands with me; I'm Lieutenant Andrew Hawkins, number four squadron, Special Air Service, from Glasgow". "Wow, your S.A.S, and from Glasgow" replied Samantha, as Andrew responded, "that's right, well, former special forces I suppose you should say, when the whole world came crashing down; I saw your vehicle parked here, and I thought that you might be ex-military too". "Well, yes and no, my father was an engineer in the Army, and I was a lorry driver before Covid, so I was given this; she's called the Green Goddess" replied Samantha, as Andrew took in the Green Goddesses twin container and tanker trailer, all linked up together to form one whole vehicle. "This is some vehicle you've got yourself here Sam, I've never seen anything like it before" replied

Andrew, as Samantha explained to Andrew about the Green Goddess, and the conditions around its construction.

"You have been busy" replied Andrew, as Samantha moved in to ask Andrew a question of her own. "So, what brings you down here Andrew, if you're originally from Glasgow" asked Samantha, as Andrew smiled slightly. "Well, I've always wanted to live in the countryside personally, I found that modern living was starting to get me down; to be honest, I'm a little surprised that Covid didn't see off everyone before this year". As Andrew finished talking, Samantha looked shocked that he would say that, but then pressed on, "why look at me like that for, it's a fact of life Sam; we as a society became too lazy for our own good; technology, computers, modern living, it was destroying the planet we live on; now that the human race has been cut down to a smaller size than before Covid struck, the Earth can get back on its feet, and things for everyone will be easier again".

It struck Samantha how confident Andrew sounded in his ways, but then again, he had been an officer in one of the world's most elite special forces units. "I'm sorry, I just never expected anyone to say that the world would be a better place with no humans in it" replied Samantha, who seemed a little silly even just voicing her views. "Oh, I didn't say that Sam, what I meant was that if there's less human being's around, we'd be far better people towards each other; the world was becoming too crowded, why do you think there were so many wars being fought; it's because people were fighting over resources and land that was never meant for us in the first place" replied Andrew, as he beckoned Samantha to follow him. Samantha had to confess to herself that following a stranger wasn't the best idea in the world, but after all, Andrew had come to her rescue, so he can't have been as bad as Samantha thought.

They walked a short way up the road into the village itself, Samantha taking in all of the abandoned buildings and dirty cars, which stood stationary with their fuel filler caps open, as if people had been syphering fuel from them. Samantha shivered slightly too, as she hadn't put a coat on, and a light breeze had started to pick up within the surrounding area. "I bet it's been really peaceful up here, no aircraft, no traffic coming through" began Samantha, but she was stopped by Andrew, who had held up a hand to suddenly silence her. "What, what's wrong" said Samantha, in a rushed voice, but Andrew made flapping noises in a desperate bid to get her to shut up. Samantha did look a little hurt at being told to be quiet by a complete stranger, but then she heard it too, a low whirring sound, which was becoming louder and louder as they both stood there listening hard.

"Well I'll be blowed, it can't be them surely" said Andrew, as suddenly to their left, a small black dot appeared on the horizon, creeping slowly towards them like a large angry insect. The small black dot was Skyhawk One, as it had started to patrol the Lake District area by now, having covered everywhere else in the northern half of the country. "That's not possible, I think I know who that is, but how could they have found me" replied Samantha, as it was now Andrew's turn to look puzzled. As there were plenty of buildings to shelter them, it would appear that they would both remain hidden for a time. However, with a shock of horror, Samantha realised that the Green Goddess was still very much in the open, and exposed for the helicopter to see. "Oh no, the Goddess, she's in the open, they will see it" exclaimed Samantha in a hurry to Andrew, as they heard the helicopter zoom over their heads.

By some miracle, it had managed to miss them, and the Green Goddess, as it carried on flying in a straight line over the top of the other buildings in the village. "Well I'll be blowed, that's a special forces helicopter that is; I recognised it from my S.A.S days; why did you think you knew who they were" asked Andrew, as Samantha was forced to take a few slow deep breaths, before she spoke again. "There's something I haven't told you, there are some people who are after me, as they accused me of terrorism charges and think that I'm now a criminal on the run". Andrew's face went pale at that moment, but

396

he seemed to steady himself all the same. "Why do they think you're a terrorist, you don't strike me as a dangerous person" asked Andrew, as Samantha beckoned him back towards the Green Goddess, parked on the village green, as they were sure that the black helicopter was out of range by now to spot them.

"They're coming after me because of this" replied Samantha a few minutes later, as she climbed up into the Green Goddesses cab and pulled down the pamphlet, which had been dominating her life since the start of the Covid pandemic. Samantha handed the pamphlet over to Andrew, who read it over once, and then stood there as his eyes widened in shock. "Where did you get this" he asked, as he looked at Samantha in amazement, not daring to believe that Samantha could be in possession of such a document. "Erm, well, it was sent to my fiancée Greg before Covid, but he never really knew what it was, so he gave it to me to try and work it out" replied Samantha, but Andrew had a look on his face of complete and utter amazement, as if someone had just pranked him on a comedy TV show. Samantha didn't know what to think when she had seen Andrew's reaction, although she wouldn't have to wait long to find out the answer.

"This is an Operation Flower document; I recognise this from when I was given a patrol duty once before Covid" replied Andrew, as Samantha gapped at him in shock. "You know about this, and what's Operation Flower, and where did you patrol" asked Samantha, the words in a rush to tumble out of her mouth, as if she felt worried that she would never speak ever again. "Grey's Pharmaceuticals were behind this; they had a section in their building which I knew about, and everyone who worked in their were known as the Flower operatives, hence why the project was given the name Operation Flower" replied Andrew, but wild thoughts were suddenly chasing themselves around Samantha's mind as Andrew made his explanation to her. Samantha knew that Grey's Pharmaceuticals had been the site where experiments had been done on people, as herself and Diana had almost become victims to the same experiments themselves.

It was only thanks to Julie's bravery, swooping in to save them both when she did, that Helen, Patrick or even the now deceased Edward, couldn't carry on with their sick and twisted experiments. "In around August 2019 time, I was given an assignment by my commanding officer to head up a security detachment in a company where it's public name was Grey's Pharmaceuticals, although in the official documents it was just known as, 'the company'" replied Andrew, but Samantha spoke to add onto the end of his sentence. "I know, I had a friend called Diana who worked at Grey's for a while, before the boss of that place rapped her, and then escaped justice" replied Samantha, feeling her anger towards Patrick boiling back to the surface again, images of Diana's gravestone still fresh in her mind. "Sorry, you've lost me; how could the boss of Grey's Pharmaceuticals have raped your friend, the boss is a woman" replied Andrew, a little puzzled.

If this piece of information didn't shock Samantha, then she didn't know what would, as the mystery only appeared to become more deeper and make less sense as it went along. "No, no, you must be mistaken, Patrick Devises is the head of Grey Pharmaceuticals" said Samantha, as Andrew pulled a confused face at her, wondering if Samantha was going slightly mad. "No, Helen Dukes is the head of Grey Pharmaceuticals" replied Andrew, as Samantha gasped in horror again, as the picture started to become clear all around her, realising that she had been looking at things the wrong way around. "So that's why Helen was interrogating me about this pamphlet; this wasn't of her design at all; this was done by someone outside of Grey's Pharmaceuticals" replied Samantha, a sudden blister of truth popping right in front of her eyes as she spoke.

"Patrick Devises, he was the man who was saw sitting in the C.E.O's office every day; he's an MI5 intelligence officer" replied Andrew, as Samantha gasped again, releasing that Patrick Devises may not be one of the bad guy after all, but instead an intelligence service mole, trying to bring down a corrupt government official. "MI5 are involved; but; that must mean that" began Samantha in an amazed voice; but

Andrew finished her sentence for her. "He's one of the good guy's Sam, he did a random selection of people to determine who would go on his programme, your fiancée Greg must have been one of the people selected; he's been working against Helen Dukes all this time". "So that's why Greg was giving the pamphlet to me; he knew what it meant; but he couldn't say anything to me because of national security" replied Samantha, as Andrew nodded his head in agreement.

Samantha pressed on, now being able to think more clearly than she had been since the start of the Covid pandemic. "So, Greg couldn't tell me directly about the programme, so he had to tell me in another way; so, he gave me this pamphlet and left me a trail of breadcrumbs to follow him, all the way to Clyde" replied Samantha, the words again tumbling out of her mouth, as if they had just been spun at top speed inside of a washing machine. "I think I remember seeing Greg one day; I'm pretty sure he went into a meeting with Patrick at Grey's headquarters building near Leicester" replied Andrew, but Samantha was already ahead of him on that one, having been told this information by Diana herself back in the prison cell at the Grey's Pharmaceuticals complex. "This is all fitting in with Diana's story that she told me, but it still doesn't explain why Patrick raped her" replied Samantha, still at a loss of what to think anymore.

On one hand, Samantha hated the fact that her best friend had been sexually assaulted; but on the other hand, she wanted to be grateful that Patrick had in some sense, attempted to save Greg's live by including him in the programme, whilst Greg had used his incitive to then give the pamphlet to Samantha, in order to save her life as well. "That I think we will never know; but I tell you this, we all do stupid things in our lives" replied Andrew, but Samantha glared at him, as if Andrew had just committed an unspeakable crime. Even Andrew, with his superhuman soldier like toughness, couldn't help but recall slightly at the look that Samantha now gave him, wondering whether Samantha was about to launch at him and attack without warning. "My best friend Diana is dead because of him, and he has a baby daughter which

I had to leave behind at a sisterhood in Geighlon, North Yorkshire" snapped back Samantha, feeling her anger boil to the surface again.

Andrew, it seemed, didn't attempt to argue back or reason with Samantha, but instead issued a hurried apology for mentioning about Patrick and the rape incident, unaware of the fact that one of Samantha's school friends had paid the ultimate price for Patrick's unspeakable actions. "I'm probably guessing that if Patrick made your friend pregnant, he would somehow been able to help her onto the Operation Flower programme, otherwise some would ask questions as to why she was on it" replied Andrew, as Samantha's anger seemed to abate slightly. Andrew had inadvertently made Samantha aware that maybe Patrick's intentions hadn't been the best in the world, but if he had tried to get Diana onto his Operation Flower programme, then Patrick could have tried to find another way of doing it, rather than resorting to an act of rape and sexual assault.

Either way, Samantha's anger towards Patrick wasn't abating anytime soon, and maybe she would be tested if her and Patrick ever came face to face; so, in hindsight, Samantha was of the opinion that the jury was out on this particular matter. "Your right; I shouldn't be so stupid" replied Samantha, as she hung her head slightly, feeling that continuing to drag up recent history wasn't what she had planned to do in that exact moment. "We all make mistakes, but even so, it sounds as if Helen is after you, and Patrick maybe alongside her, still acting the spy; and now they've got a special forces helicopter team on their side as well" replied Andrew, as Samantha seemed to give an understanding nod of the head, realising that some sort of a battle plan needed to be formed, rather than wasting time worrying about the past. "Good thing I'm standing next to an elite soldier then" thought Samantha, as she steadied her nerves.

"So, what's the plan now, how do we alert Patrick to the fact that we're here, unless you think that I should go straight to Clyde and see what's there" asked Samantha, as Andrew shock his head slightly, feeling that Samantha may have not been thinking along the right lines. "I think this maybe a hunch, but I'm guessing that helicopter saw the Green Goddess from the air, and it's maybe either taking photographs or video footage of these areas, just so they can see the Green Goddess, and plot its position" replied Andrew, as Samantha had a sudden steely glint in her eye, as if an adrenaline rush has suddenly overtaken her entire soul and bodily motor functions. "You have a plan don't you" said Samantha, as Andrew smiled at her, as Samantha wondered whether the same level of excitement had just overtaken him, as it had done with Samantha a few moments earlier.

"Indeed, I do Sam, but it would be tricky and dangerous; we would have to get that helicopter to go exactly where we wanted it" replied Andrew, beginning to formulate a plan in his head which would be paramount in helping him and Samantha to stop Helen in her tracks. Unknowing to Andrew and Samantha's knowledge however, Skyhawk One had indeed spotted the Green Goddess, and as Andrew had predicted, it had been taking photographs of the surround area, as it flew overhead. Helen and Patrick had also picked up the photograph's as well, which had been beamed back to the ground convoy they were travelling in. "We have located the Green Goddess, I repeat, we have located the Green Goddess; it's position is in the village of Askham, Lake District National Park, Cumbria" were the triumphant words of the Skyhawk One pilot, as they radioed back to Helen and Patrick's vehicle convoy.

The convoy had then given orders back to Skyhawk One to refuel at a nearby Royal Air Force base, before getting back into the air, to make sure that the Green Goddess didn't move from its position. This was exactly what Andrew had been banking on, as he and Samantha stepped up their plan to ambush Skyhawk One as it returned to do an observation run for Helen and Patrick. As it transpired, there was an army base a few miles to the north of Askham village, where Andrew had managed to find a few weapons of choice in the armaments and quartermaster stores, powerful enough to bring down Skyhawk One.

"Wow, where did you get all of those from" was Samantha's response, as Andrew returned an hour or so later in an Army jeep, carrying what looked like half an armoury with him. "The A-Team didn't even have all of this lot to hand" thought Samantha, as she was reminded on the 1980s TV series of the same name.

There were enough explosives to be able knock out multiple buildings and vehicles, alongside ammunition boxes, some water bottles, a few machine guns, and the largest box of all contained a javelin rocket launcher, along with around half a dozen rocket propelled grenade rounds to go with it. "Managed to find it all in the stores, combined with what you have onboard the Green Goddess, should keep us going here for weeks; but the main thing will be to rig up a ring of traps around the village, so if Helen and her gang of thugs makes a move on us, we'll be ready for them" replied Andrew in response to Samantha's stunned look. "Thank god for the army, where would we be without them" replied Samantha, as Andrew let out a small laugh, understanding full well that equipment like this in the days before Covid wouldn't have been readily available to them.

"True, and this will come in handy as well" replied Andrew, as he gestured to the javelin rocket launcher inside its metal case. Samantha secretly thought that she had to give Andrew his due on that particular point; after all, he had been a member of one of the world's most elite special forces units, so knew a thing or two about weapons, weaknesses of enemies, and the like. "A helicopter's weakest point is its tail rota; hit the chopper with one of those, and it's goodnight Vienna; the chopper then can't control itself and it crashes all on its own, which is then a huge advantage to us, as that will prevent the chopper from giving away our location in the village through aerial observations" explained Andrew, as he pointed to the rockets that were designed to be loaded into and fired out of the javelin rocket launcher. The Javelin rocket launcher itself was quite a sizeable lump, as Samantha attempted to try and pick it up, whilst nearly dropped it due to its weight.

"Wow, careful, those things are worth a lot of money you know" came Andrew's voice, as Samantha attempted to lift it onto her shoulder. Andrew thankfully came to Samantha's rescue, resting it from her shoulder before she did any major damage with it, or accidently pulled the firing trigger. "I think it's probably best if I use that weapon there Samantha; I know a great place of where to set it up for the perfect ambush" replied Andrew, as Samantha without speaking, secretly agreed with Andrew about the distribution and handling of what weapon to use and who would use it. Samantha didn't want to be the one responsible for accidently hitting something that she shouldn't, as she felt that knowing her, that was exactly what was bound to happen. "So, how do we draw Skyhawk One away to where we want it" asked Samantha, as a little tingle went up her spine, feeling that she now going to be getting justice for losing Julie and Diana.

Andrew smiled slightly, as he responded to Samantha's eagerness with the answer, "well, our best chance is to light a fire, say in the grounds of Askham Hall over there". Andrew gestured to the tall dry-stoned wall which ran along one edge of the village green, before he continued to speak again. "Those types of eurocopter choppers like the one we saw earlier have night vision and thermal imagining technology on them; it means they will first see smoke rising up from a distance, then its camera's will pick up the heat signature from the fire". "And then what will happen" asked Samantha, as Andrew pressed on. "Then the chopper will hopefully fly low into the grounds to investigate it, and that's when I take a well-aimed shot at the tail rota from behind; they will have barely a second to respond, by which point it's found it's mark, and been taken down" finished Andrew, as Samantha looked determined.

"Let's do this" she said, with a determined air in her voice, as Andrew chuckled slightly. Taking out Skyhawk One was one thing, but they would then need to repel a possible ground attack from Helen's troops as well, should Helen choose to take the fight straight to them. Andrew was banking on the fact that Patrick would hopefully see sense, and choose to change sides before too long, but these chances were slim if not at all. Patrick's allegiance could have changed after all, as he could have chosen to take Helen's side, even when it was clear that the old world was gone forever. Samantha had hoped that she could have remained untraceable and invisible to Helen and Patrick during her trip, but it seemed that Helen, Patrick, and Helen's gang of thugs had the ways and means of tracking her down. The convoy had already paid a visit to the Geighlon sisterhood, and discovered Julie's and Diana's graves together in the churchyard.

Sophie and the other sisterhood members had all tried in vain to protect Samantha, but Helen had managed to find out about Samantha from them anyhow. "This is a place of holiness, not a free for all" was Sophie's surprise, as she was pushed aside at gunpoint by a black uniformed armed soldier wearing a gas mask, Helen and Patrick looking on with smug looks on their faces. As the Geighlon sisterhood were not armed in any way, it was difficult for them to try and stop Helen and the others, but they still put up a brave vow of silence, as Helen and her gang of thug's tore the place apart, looking for evidence that Samantha had been there. They found little baby Julie curdled up in her cot in the dormitory, and were quite puzzled by it, until Sarah lied, and explained that little baby Julie was in fact her baby, and not Diana's. Helen didn't appear to be phased by this, as she brushed the members of the sisterhood aside, having no care for any of them at all.

Patrick. who had seen little baby Julie without knowing the full facts, had managed to put two and two together, trying his absolute best to hide his emotions from the others that he was in fact, the biological father of little baby Julie. It didn't take Helen very long however to find the graves with Julie's and Diana's names on them, meaning that Samantha had now lost the element of surprise for the upcoming battle, as Helen was now sure Samantha was travelling alone, and much more of an easier target to track down and destroy friendless and alone. The Geighlon Sisterhood had been shaken up by Helen's fury at the fact that Samantha had been there and escaped, as the convoy proceeded northwards towards the town of Darlington, past the very fuel station and pub where Samantha had stopped and taken a rest at, before proceeding to the town of Askham.

These were made possible by the fact that on some occasions, the Green Goddess had widened the road with her huge size, leaving rather obvious and unmissable signs that it had been through certain parts of the country. The convoy also came across a group of teenage boys, who were looting the same petrol station that Samantha had been into a few days earlier. The boys couldn't possibly hope to win as they were bullied and tortured about what Samantha had been doing there at the time, only knowing that the Green Goddess had been through their part of the world. "There was a big army truck or something here a few days ago, we saw it, but didn't want to go near it as we thought it was dangerous" was one of the boy's responses, as one of the black uniformed soldiers held him roughly by the scruff of the neck, whilst at the same time directing the barrel of his machine gun into the square of his back.

"You boys are useless" was Helen's response after the teenage boy had told her what he had seen, as his friends all gasped, and the boy began to cry, fearing that he was going to be killed at any moment. But before Helen or the soldiers had the chance to do anything else, a loud shout came from one of the other vehicles. "The Green Goddess has been located, we have a location for it, Lake District, North Cumbria". "Leave him, we have work to do" replied Helen, as she nodded to the black uniformed soldier, who pushed the teenage boy away back towards his group of friends, as Helen and the other members of the convoy all saddled up and moved out, squealing a few tyres behind them as they went. It seemed that Helen, Patrick and the convoy were hot on Samantha's heels now, and now they knew that Samantha was all on her own, and completely defenceless against them.

As the convoy closed in on Askham as fast as they could go, Skyhawk One had landed at the airbase a few miles away from Askham, and was beginning its refuelling process to get back into the air again. Skyhawk One's crew suddenly noticed a long straight smoke cloud, rising rapidly into the air in front of them. "Hey, look over there" shouted the observer, as the other crew members came hurrying over, whilst Skyhawk One was taking on fuel from the now abandoned air bases fuel tankers. "It looks like a fire over in the village; get Skyhawk One airborne, now" barked the pilot, who looked through a pair of binoculars over the tree line, to where the smoke was still rising up slowly and steadily. The sounds of the helicopter rota blades began to spin faster and faster, and a few seconds later, Skyhawk One lifted back up into the sky. This was it; the battle of Askham; was about to begin.

CHAPTER TWENTY FIVE

The Battle of Askham

Back over in the grounds of Askham Hall, inside the Askham village boundaries, Andrew had started the fiery blaze that he proposed to Samantha, by setting fire to one of the trees in the Askham Hall grounds. The flames had quickly taken hold, as the top half of the tree just become a solid mass of flames within a matter of minutes. "The dry wood is helping to keep the fire going, the chopper should be with us soon" explained Andrew, as he directed Samantha to crawl underneath the Green Goddess and wait for Andrew's signal to come out again. Andrew meanwhile had taken the Javelin rocket launcher, and set up a good firing position inside one of the rooms on the top floor in Askham Hall itself. Sure enough; minutes after Andrew had ordered Samantha to take cover, Skyhawk One appeared, loaming low over the tops of the house, like a big black bird of prey.

Samantha felt the grass under her rippling slightly as her hair blew into her face, whilst Skyhawk One hoovered for a few seconds close by, around sixty or so feet off the ground. Samantha reached a hand forward to brush the hair out of her face, but as she did so, there was a sudden whoosh and a whistling sound, as a small Javelin rocket flew from one of the top floor windows of Askham Hall fired by Andrew, which went flying through the air. It struck bang on target with a loud explosion, taking Skyhawk One's tail rota blade clean off, like a knife through butter. Immediately as the rocket hit, Skyhawk One began to spin out of control, its crew cursing, swearing and crying out in anger, as they tried in desperation to stay airborne. Andrew swore loudly at that moment, before picking up the Javelin, and running as fast as he could out of the room, and down the stairs inside Askham Hall.

Andrew's sudden flight out of the room and down the stairs, had been due partially to him making a terrible miscalculation. Andrew hadn't realised until it was too late, that Skyhawk One was going to crash into the very building that he was standing in, as the noise of its rota blades become louder and louder with each passing second. Realising his mistake just in time, Andrew made it out of the front door and began to sprint at top speed towards the main gates, just as Skyhawk One crashed spectacularly into the back of Askham Hall. The following explosion that followed was so violent, that it ripped a hole in the boundary dry-stone wall, sending lumps of stone the size of footballs flying through the air, smashing windows, and a few of them even striking the container and tanker trailers on the back of the Green Goddess, each blow followed by a large banging noise as they went.

But all that Samantha could hear was the eye deafening explosion, which had nearly made Samantha clamp her hands over her eyes, fearing that a large piece of flying dry stone wall was going to come through the container above her at any second, and serious injury her where she lay. Other pieces of dry-stone wall landed in the village green, making small craters as they landed, as one of them landed inches away from where Samantha lay, making her scream slightly. As the sound died, a large mushroom smoke cloud rose up from where Skyhawk One had crashed, as Samantha felt a slight ringing in her ears, feeling the same way as when the ghost plane had crashed back in Lillington. As Samantha's hearing begin to recede back to normal, she could hear running footsteps coming towards her, and then a hand pulling her roughly out from under the Green Goddess, as she lay on the ground panting, feeling as if she had just run a marathon.

"Samantha, Samantha, are you ok" asked Andrew, as Samantha pulled herself up, her hearing properly returned to normal by now. "Yeah, yeah, I think I'm ok; that must have been heard from miles away" replied Samantha, as she brushed herself down, looking over in the direction of the remains of Skyhawk One, which was now just a twisted lump of metal, all of its crew sadly killed as a result of the crash. It had also made a sizeable hole in the boundary wall too, as lumps of dry-stone wall lay everywhere around them, looking more like moon rocks on a village green backdrop. "Come on, we could have hours at most before they get here, we need to prepare for battle, and take the fight to them" replied Andrew, as Samantha regained herself back again. "Yes, let's do this, I'm tired of running away; time to fight back" replied Samantha, as Andrew clapped her on the back, pleased to hear that Samantha wasn't seriously hurt.

"We'll make a soldier out of yet Samantha" replied Andrew, as he and Samantha walked back to the army jeep, to begin the preparations for the next attack. The sound of Skyhawk One's explosion did indeed carry on for miles, like a giant airwave on the still country air. As there were no ambient sounds of the towns, cities or even a hum of electricity from the pylons any more, the sound of explosion reached the ears of the convoy, who at that time were around fifty or so miles away. "What was that" replied Helen to Patrick, as they were both riding in the same car together, the convoy coming to a sudden stop, as everyone strained their ears to listen more carefully. "Skyhawk One is down; I repeat, Skyhawk One is down" came a voice from the handheld radio, situated in the front of the car. Patrick banged his hand against the back of the driver's seat in front of him in frustration, realising that they had just lost their aerial lookout.

"I knew it, I knew it; they'd set a trap for Skyhawk One, and now it's flown right into it and been destroyed; that's our eyes in the sky gone now" exclaimed Patrick, as he picked up the radio set, before promptly throwing the radio down onto the floor in anger. "You are forgetting who is in charge around here, I should have never left you in charge of this; it's been one complete disaster after another with you" replied Helen, who was speaking with a little malice in her voice. "And what's that's supposed to mean, Skyhawk One was your property after all; you ordered it in to search for the Green Goddess" snapped back Patrick with a slight snarl in his voice. "I was made aware by you that Samantha Bonham did not have military training, as according to her file, her father was in the Royal Army Engineers, but has never been trained by the M.O.D" argued back Helen, as Patrick changed tact at the speed of light.

"Your files Helen; your files; or should I say, the illegal government operation that was set up to monitor her fiancée Greg when he agreed to take part in Operation Flower". Helen balled her hands into fists where she stood; for a moment it looked like she was going to hit Patrick, but a look of steely determined cunning had just come across her face as Patrick finished speaking, feeling that her thoughts about a spy in the camp were starting to come true. "If she hasn't had military training, how do you explain how she took down Skyhawk One" replied Helen in a cool calm voice, but still with an air of grim satisfaction across her face, as if a sudden understanding had just hit her. "Skyhawk One was flying low, it could have hit a tree or a power line, or anything low lined, it could have even accidently hit a building or something" argued back Patrick, now gesturing with hands in the air.

"We both know that's not true, according to the pilot's last message, Skyhawk One had seen smoke rising up into the air around the area of Askham village before we heard the explosion" replied Helen, as Patrick looked at her a little confused. As Helen said this, she pressed play on an audio file which was up on the laptop screen she had in front of her. The audio began to play, where the pilot and observers voices could be heard quite clearly over the rota blades. Then suddenly there was a loud whooshing sound, followed by a bang on the recording, as the voices began to scream that Skyhawk One was being fired upon, which was followed by a second loud bang, as the audio come to a complete stop. "That was the last recording that came from Skyhawk One; at exactly the same time that audio stopped, we heard a loud explosion through the air" replied Helen, as Patrick regained his voice.

"That sounded like a rocket propelled grenade device of some kind, Bonham wouldn't know how to operate one of those" replied Patrick, as Helen replied. "Well then, she's obviously not alone in that village; she must have recruited someone to help her, who knows how to handle and fire weapons like that". Patrick responded with a mumbled word, which Helen didn't catch, as she was distracted by a black uniformed soldier, who had just come over to her to hand over a report; but the word that Patrick had mumbled had sounded much like, 'Hawkins'. Patrick shook himself slightly; no, it couldn't be Hawkins surely; Hawkins had disappeared before Covid had struck, he couldn't have survived; or could he? Patrick was distracted again by Helen, who turned to him with triumph in her voice, as she replied, "we're ready to move in within the hour, ready yourself for a battle like no other, Patrick".

"I hope you know what you're doing" responded Patrick, as Helen shot him a look of loathing, before giving the order to the other convoy vehicles to move out. Back in Askham village however, Andrew had taken Samantha to his living space, inside the village's Black Swan pub, which was located a little further up the high street from where the Green Goddess was parked, having survived the barrage of dry-stone wall pieces which had rained down on it during the Skyhawk One crash. "Erm, I don't know if anyone ever told you this, but I'm really not that great with guns" replied Samantha, as she watched Andrew offloading the equipment from the army jeep into the bar area at the front of the pub. "Well, you're going to shape up now Samantha; in this game it's kill

411

or be killed; we're at war now" responded Andrew, as Samantha couldn't help but secretly agree with Andrew that he had a fair point.

Samantha meanwhile looked terrified at the thought that she would have to take on what could be dozens of training soldiers and the like, but Andrew smiled slightly, and rested a hand on her shoulder. "You'll be fine; just remember, you pull the trigger at one end, and the bullets come out of the other end" replied Andrew, as Samantha gave him a bit of a sarcastic look. "I had worked out that much for myself thanks" replied Samantha in a sarcastic voice, as Andrew handed her one of his machine guns and a few spare ammunition clips, all full of shinny brand new bullets. "I just have two rules; one, don't shoot me if you can help it; and two, try your best" replied Andrew with a slight chuckle. Samantha did think at that very moment that it probably wasn't a good idea to mention about the fact that all she had taken shots at in her entire life was car tyres; and even then, it was during the heat of the moment in a high-speed pursuit.

"Come on, follow me" replied Andrew suddenly, as Samantha was loaded up with what felt like a tonne load of equipment, which made her knees buckle slightly under the weight of it all, as she followed Andrew outside through the pub's front door and into the main high street, which was now bathed in early afternoon sunlight. "This pub here is our fallback point, in case either one of us is killed or injured" began Andrew, as he gestured up to the Black Swan pub sign, Samantha only just being able to lift her head up due to the weight of the equipment which was pushing down on her shoulders, as if she was trying to carry a car on them. "I'm going to set myself up here in this position, so I'm looking down the main road into the start of the hill down there" continued Andrew, as he pointed down the main high street towards the perimeter blown-out wall of Askham Hall.

Because of the way things had been when Skyhawk One had come down, it had created a nice bottleneck where only a single file column of vehicles could come up the street at any one time. Andrew seemed to realise this, as he responded, "as you know, they will try and bring a vehicle up that road to block your escape, should you try and make one; but they will also come up the other roads as well in an attempt to try and cut you off, so our plan should be to try and filter them into this village green, and then pin them down with rapid continuous fire and everything else we have in our armoury". Andrew spoke with such confidence on these matters, that it made Samantha feel even smaller than she already was, but this may have had something to do with the mountains of equipment that Andrew was making her carry, her spine now feeling as if it was going to snap in half under the strain of it all.

Andrew had decided that the best way to prevent any other vehicles from entering the village, was to block up all the other remained entrances in and out of the village itself. As the Green Goddess was going to be acting as bait for them to bring in the convoy, it had to remain where it was. Fortunately, the now deceased owners of the houses in the village all drove nice big four-wheel drive cars and big high sided panelled vans, which meant that there was no shortage of big vehicles to block up the roads with to prevent anything else from getting past them. Within half an hour or so, every entrance and exit to the village was blocked, all except for the narrow one which came up the hill next to the perimeter wall to Askham Hall. As the road was only just about wide enough to allow a single file movement of traffic to go up and down it, it would make it easier to plan and execute an ambush.

While Samantha had taken up the task of blocking up all of the roads with abandoned vehicles, Andrew had rigged up the army jeep so it would now roll in a straight line down the hill between the narrow walls, creating a block to prevent Helen and Patrick getting their vehicles into the village. "Government vehicles are always armour plated, so the less of them that can get into the village, the better, as chances are they will use them like tanks for protection against us" explained Andrew, as he showed Samantha the Centex plastic explosives which had been rigged to the army jeep and the very cleverly disguised land mines, which Andrew had very cleverly disguised to look like cow-pats, which now lay on the road, smoking slightly as if they'd only just been left there by a heard of cows. This cover would be especially reinforced by the fact that there were a couple of farm shed nearby in the village, where a few cows stood munching on some grass.

"Oh wow, I've heard of that, my dad told me about it once; they used to do that during the war to stop vehicles and things" said Samantha, as she gestured to the cow-pat land mines, remembering what her father had told her about such cleverly thought up devices such as these land mines. "Quite right, it's still quite the trick to this day; I was in Northern Island during the troubles, and the I.R.A would use the very same trick to destroy UK military vehicles" replied Andrew, who was quite impressed with Samantha's knowledge of military hardware. "I don't suppose you know how many vehicles are in this convoy their bringing in do you" asked Andrew suddenly, catching Samantha off guard slightly. "Erm, no, sorry; we made such a quick getaway from Grey's Pharmaceuticals, that I didn't have time to see how many followed us; all I did was made two vehicles crash, and my friend Diana killed the driver of the third" replied Samantha.

"That's pretty good going for a civilian, I'm impressed you know Samantha" replied Andrew, as Samantha couldn't help but blush slightly at his words. "Thanks; I always did wonder what it would be like to be a part of the UK's most elite unit, the action men as my father used to call them" replied Samantha, as Andrew let out a small laugh. "Well, I shouldn't really be telling you any of this strictly speaking, but we're all just ordinary people really, not like you see us in the films at all" replied Andrew, as Samantha sat down on the grass to listen, whilst Andrew busied himself with cleaning his machine gun, having finished laying the explosives down onto the road surface. "We were all on a call reserve list you see, only called in when we were needed for missions and the like" explained Andrew, as Samantha leaned back slightly on her hands, allowing herself to be more comfortable sat on the grass to listen.

"By day, I was a motor mechanic you see, but the company I worked for knew that I was a military reservist, but not in the S.A.S, so my cover was still pretty much intact; then when it came to it, I would be expected to get to my nearest barracks, where I would then be flown out to wherever I was needed" said Andrew, as he finished explaining his life up until Covid had struck. "I'd always wonder what life was like in the special forces, I wonder" began Samantha, but Andrew suddenly held up a hand to silence her. Samantha stopped talking at once, listening hard, as Andrew's and Samantha's senses had suddenly perked up. Through the very still country air, they both heard the unmistakable sounds of vehicle engines running at a faster pace than usual, which then slowed, as the sounds of tyres on leaves and tarmac reached their ears, appearing to come from the general direction of the single lane hill road they were looking down.

This was it; the convoy had finally arrived in the village; the battle of Askham, was about to begin. "Positions" said Andrew in a rush, as he leapt to his feet and sprinted for the open pub door, making his way up to the top floor of the Black Swan pub, where Andrew kicked out a window which made a shattering sound as it hit the ground below. Samantha meanwhile had run straight across the village green, slinging a machine gun over her shoulder as she went, to a point behind the Askham Hall blown-out wall, where Samantha was easily hidden from sight, whilst still being able to see the convoy enter the village. Samantha only just had time to duct out of sight, when the first convoy vehicle entered the village, moving slowly forwards, it's passengers looking around slowly, catching sight of the Green Goddess parked up on the village green.

It was Helen and Patrick's car, which came a halt less than a few feet away from the cow pat land mines, as Andrew silently swore to himself up in the top window of the Black Swan pub, watching as Helen and Patrick climbed out of the car, standing in the middle of the high street looking around them, taking in the scenery and surrounding buildings. "Dam, just a little further forward" said Andrew to himself, as he raised the Javelin rocket launcher to shoulder height, ready to fire it at the convoy. Helen and Patrick meanwhile looked a little confused, as they could see the army jeep sitting dead in the middle of the road at the top of the hill, with no one in sight. "Where is she, the Green Goddess is empty" said Patrick, as he looked at the Green Goddess's cab, which was empty, whilst wrinkling his nose slightly at the smell of the cow-pats lying on the road.

"Disgusting" replied Helen, as she too wrinkled her nose at the smell of the cow-pat, wondering which one of the offending cows had left it on the road surface, little realising that a cleverly concealed land mine was just out of site under the smell of it. "Search the village, I want Bonham alive" barked Helen at the other convoy vehicles, which were still down parked down the lane, as there came a number of shouts from the other soldiers, as they all spread out searching for Samantha. Samantha meanwhile, had been told what to do if this scenario occurred, as she readied herself for the oncoming battle. "Err, boss, what's that" asked Patrick, as suddenly without warning, the army jeep slowly started to roll down the hill towards them, gathering speed as it went. Little did they know, that Andrew had rigged a fuse to burn through the hand brake cable, which had now snapped the cable, allowing the army jeep to roll away down the hill.

Helen and Patrick looked at the army jeep open mouthed, as it veered off course, mounting the village green, crashing into a park bench at it went with a small crunching noise as the bumper made contact with the park bench. Helen sniggered slightly, as Patrick looked on a little confused at the fact that an army jeep had just rolled down and hill and crashed with no driver inside of it. "Is that supposed to be scary" Helen called into the still air, obviously thinking that people could hear her. Patrick whistled, and signalled for his scientists and soldiers to follow him, as Helen's car was reversed backwards out of the way. "Come on, just a little nearer now" said Andrew to himself, as he steadied himself ready to fire, watching the lead convoy vehicle creep slowly forwards towards the cow-pat land mines. The other soldiers had now spread out, marching in equal distance apart, keeping their eyes peeled for any signs of movement from the nearby buildings.

Then just as Patrick placed his hand on the cab door handle to open the cab door on the Green Goddess, one of the black uniformed soldiers inadvertently stepped on the cow-pat land mine, as it clicked underfoot. The resulting explosion that followed blasted them all off their feet, killing three of the black uniformed soldiers instantly. Helen was knocked sideways onto the grass, banging her head as she went, meanwhile Patrick had hit thrown himself to the ground and crawled underneath the Green Goddess for protection. Andrew took this as a signal to start the attack as he pulled the Javelin's trigger, adrenaline now surging through his system, feeling the blood pounding in his ears. A small long thin rocket came flying out of the end of the Javelin's barrel, whizzing through the air until it slammed into the lead convoy vehicle with another almighty blast.

A few soldiers screamed in pain, as the four-wheel drive car exploded, sending flaming shrapnel flying in every direction, which burnt and blistered everything it touched. "Over there" came a shout, as the soldiers began firing in the direction where the rocket had come from, narrowly missing Andrew by inches, who ducted out of the way just in time. Small thudding and whistling noises could be heard, as the bullets peppered the walls of the pub, but Andrew managed to miss them as he ducted and sprinted down the stairs, towards the main bar area, ready and waiting to face the soldiers head on as they came. In the confusion, Helen had managed to duct out of the way, getting back into her car, which had managed to avoid the two blasts from the explosions. The scientists however, who weren't trained soldier's, seemed to stand momentary stunned, as the battle started in earnest all around them.

"Well, don't just stand there; get after them; stop them" shouted Helen at the scientists, who seemed to be stuck, wondering which way to go, whether to fight as Helen had ordered, or to take cover, as none of them were armed with weapons to fight with. "But we have no weapons" bravely spoke up one of the scientists after a few seconds; but Helen had already reached for a small pistol which was hidden in the driver's side door, as she then proceeded to point the pistol out of the window at the group of scientists, who backed away nervously at the sight of it. The group of scientists all seemed to be too scared to move, but Helen was looking so menacing at that moment, that none of them felt that they could disobey her, even though there were more of them, than there was of her. As they stood there, the continuing sounds of gunfire and shouts continued to reach everyone's ears, unsure about who was winning or who was losing the battle.

"Either you fight, or I will have you shot" snarled Helen, as the scientists, hands raised slightly into the air in a mock surrender gesture, seemed to realise that there was no way out of this. "Charge" shouted one of the scientists, as they all ran, not even armed with so much as a pen knife, towards the Black Swan pub, where the main concentration of machine gun fire was being firing towards at that very moment. "Come out now Samantha, there's no escape" came Helen's magnified voice, through a megaphone which she was holding in one hand, over the noise of the bullets that were flying through the air. "Like hell I will" came Samantha's voice, as she came out from behind the wall, took careful aim at the army jeep with the machine gun and then pulling the trigger. The scene suddenly changed, as if the whole world was in slow motion somehow; it was almost as if someone had turned off the sound, being replaced by a low ringing sound instead.

Helen spun around, as a single bullet flew from the barrel of Samantha's machine gun, whizzing through the air, as it hit the army jeep squarely in the front radiator grill, from where Samantha knew the fuse to the rest of the explosives was housed. "Ha, you missed Bonham" replied Helen in her usual smug voice, a thin curling grin appearing on her face. "Have I" replied Samantha, a look of pure malice on her face, as there was a second's pause, as the air was ripped with the loudest bang so far. The sound was so loud in fact, that for the second time that day, it knocked everyone off their feet, as yet again, Samantha's ears were filled with the ringing sound that followed such loud noises. The air too was transformed; the resulting fireball which had completely obliterated the army jeep tore in every direction, as Patrick felt his face burning whilst he hid underneath the Green Goddess.

The scientists who had charged at the Black Swan pub, also collapsed to the ground, covering their ears with their hands, yelling at the pain that the second explosion had done to their eardrums. The other soldiers meanwhile had been knocked to the ground as well, but they soon recovered as scattered yells of retreat filled the air. In all of the confusion however, Helen had vanished into the smoke from the explosion, as her car had disappeared out of sight whilst Samantha had got back onto her feet, her face and hands blackened, whilst flicking her hair to get bits of hot metal out of it. Then there was the sudden sound of a war cry, as Andrew came running into view down the high street, looking like some demented zombie on an attacking spree, his face blackened by the pace of the unfolding battle. He'd fixed a bandana around his head, throwing his smock jacket as he went, so that his six pack was visible on his incredibly well-built body.

"Ahh, that's how we do things S.A.S style suckers" shouted Andrew, who seemed, if it was even possible under the circumstances, to be enjoying being back in the thick of battle again, like in the olden days. "The testosterone is certainly flowing now that's for sure" thought Samantha, as she caught site of Andrew with his bulging six pack, feeling her face going slightly red as she blushed. It was true that she'd always had a bit of a thing for hunky sweety men, like Andrew looked at that moment in time, covered head to foot in his own sweat. Clouds of smoke billowed up from everywhere, making the surrounding area somehow a little less dark than before, as it partially blocked out the sun for a few minutes afterwards. Some of the smoke was coming from the exploded land mines; other plumes of smoke were coming from the nearby buildings were the bullets fired out of all of the machine guns had started small fires inside the houses.

The village green was littered with debris, small pieces of metal, wood and other singed material lay on fire all over the place, adding to the already smoke-filled sky. As Samantha surveyed the scene, she was strongly reminded of the war films on the TV, where soldiers would be fighting in house-to-house combat, in streets that now looked incredibly similar to the one that she was now standing in. Amazingly, the Green Goddess had managed to escape the flying debris, the bullets flying in all direction, and even managed to shield Patrick, who had rather cowardly still remained underneath the Green Goddess even after the battle had been won. But Patrick soon steadied himself, as he crawled out from underneath the Green Goddess, clutching his ears slightly, where he was experiencing a ringing noise in them. The fighting appeared to have come to a sudden and abrupt halt, as everyone seemed confused about what was going on.

"All troops stand down, we must regroup, that is an order" called Patrick to the rest of the black uniformed soldiers, who's usually clean and trim suit and tie, were now blackened and dirty from laying on the grass underneath the Green Goddess. "Sir" questioned one of the black uniformed soldiers, as he stood there transfixed at Patrick, thinking that he had not heard Patrick correctly. "That is an order soldier, do it; and someone help put out these fires out as well, they'll be all over the place if we don't stop them" shouted Patrick, as the soldier nodded, and then started barking orders at the other soldiers and scientists who had recovered the quickest from the battle. As Patrick turned however, he was greeted by a sight that he had been half expecting all along, but that didn't make the sight of Samantha pointing a machine gun into his face, any more reassuring than Patrick had realised.

"Say something nice to me, so I don't have an excuse to blow your head off" snarled Samantha, as she cocked the fingering trigger back on the machine with a loud clicking sound. Patrick slowly raised his hands into the air, as the other soldiers and scientists who had survived the battle began attempting to beat out the fires with blankets, mops and even running backwards and forwards with buckets from the nearby lake, using the lake water to quench them. "Samantha please, don't do this, I'm not who you think I am; and I'm sorry for what happened to Diana" began Patrick, but he quelled at the look Samantha gave him,

420

fearing that at any second, Samantha was going to blast him out of this world for good. Samantha's face was set, her anger seemed to be beyond words, as she took slow heavy breaths, bringing herself to do what she knew had to be done.

The very man responsible for her two best friend's deaths, maybe even everyone's deaths across the planet, was standing right in front of her, at her mercy. Samantha's finger shook slightly on the trigger, but yet she still didn't pull it, feeling some strange impulse not to shoot Patrick, whilst every nerve in Samantha's body was ordering her to do so. "You don't want to kill him Samantha, I know you don't" came Andrew's calm voice from behind Samantha, which made her jump about a foot into the air, as Samantha hadn't seen Andrew come around behind her, after the battle had finished. Samantha didn't look around at Andrew, but instead she kept her eyes focused on Patrick, the glint of rage still very much present in her tiny pupils. "I'm on your side Sam, I'm one of the good guys; I've been helping you and your friend's all this time" replied Patrick, a note of pleading in his voice, as Samantha contemplated Patrick for a second or two.

"Julie and Diana are dead because of you; you raped my best friend, and she died giving birth to her daughter" snarled Samantha, now brandishing the machine gun so close to Patrick's face, that he went cross eyed just to keep it in view. "I know, and I'm sorry; I only raped her as it would make her marry me, and then I could save her from Helen" replied Patrick, now close to tears, as Samantha gritted her teeth and shoved the machine gun into Patrick's head, so it was now smack bang between his eyebrows. Patrick closed his eyes, as he felt the cold hard metal pressed to his skin, knowing that at any second, he was going to be leaving this world for good. "Operation Flower was your programme, you could have just taken Diana on it without molesting and raping her" snarled Samantha, but Patrick replied back quickly; "you know about flower, but how".

The revelation that Samantha had known what the name of the

programme was called, took Patrick aback so much, that he opened his eyes wide in shock, temporarily forgetting somewhat that he was potentially seconds away from death. "I told her; I'm sorry boss, but I thought she had a right to know, as her fiancée was on the programme too" replied Andrew, who was still hopeful that Samantha wouldn't act stupidly by killing Patrick. "His name was Greg, and you know where he is; where is he" demanded Samantha, as Patrick closed his eyes again, waiting for the inevitable fatal shot that would take him out of this godforsaken world that he had found himself in, along with other survivors. "Greg Stent was selected at random; we sent out thousands of pamphlets, alongside those people who I could trust and would be crucial for the rebuilding plan" replied Patrick, as Samantha's look of anger, turned to that of confusion.

This certainly didn't tie in with what Andrew had told to her, as Samantha suspected that Patrick wasn't being as completely open with her about the whole situation. "But Greg never worked it out, I was the one who worked it out; Greg gave it to me as a prank joke to solve, it was only after Covid hit that I started to think that the pamphlet was somehow connected to it all" replied Samantha, as even her voice trailed off, not sounding remotely menacing anymore. "Come on Samantha, he's not the enemy now, we need him to find out where to send you next" replied Andrew in a softer voice than his usual deep soldiering one, as even Patrick still stood there taking short sharp breaths. Samantha seemed to be fixed to the spot, not knowing which way to turn next, as if a furious battle was raging inside her head, seeming to make up her mind on what to do next.

"Killing him won't bring Diana or the others back" said Andrew after a short pause, as Samantha closed her eyes, trying to fight back tears, before admitting to herself that Andrew was right; she needed to set aside her fears and worries, to focus on the job in hand. Samantha lowered the machine gun and turned away slightly, letting it drop to her side; but then suddenly without warning, turned back towards Patrick raising the machine gun upwards slightly before smacking Patrick hard in the jaw with it. Patrick fell backwards onto the grass, having just been knocked out by the force of the impact. Andrew had let out a sudden exclamation as Samantha had done this, as Samantha threw away the machine gun onto the ground. Recovering slightly, Andrew quickly moved forwards and carefully picked up the machine gun, as Samantha stood a few feet away, not speaking or moving a muscle.

There was a long silence between them now, only punctuated by the sounds of the soldiers and scientists running backwards and forwards with any implement that they could to put out the fires, which were trying to take hold in the nearby houses and shops. "Ahh, what did you do that for" replied Patrick, who had come round after being knocked out by Samantha minutes earlier. "I honestly don't know, I think it's a lady thing" was Andrew's response, as Patrick sat up slightly on the grass, rubbing his head slightly as he went. "Where's Helen's gone, she fled right in front of me, after I'd shown myself to her" responded Samantha, who didn't seem to be directing the question towards anyone in particular, but instead seemed to pose it towards the nearest people in the vicinity. "Helen fled" replied Andrew and Patrick in unison, as Samantha turned back to face them both.

Patrick seemed to recover first, as he said, "Helen fled, that sounds just like her now I come to think of it; always letting her minions do the work for her, rather than getting her hands dirty herself". It was now Andrew's turn to speak up, as he slung the machine gun he was holding over his shoulder. "If Helen has fled, that will make her more dangerous than ever; she'll be looking for revenge for losing this battle". "She'll be heading for Clyde now, but she's now lost her armed protection, so she'll have to fight with her bare hands if she wants to get through" replied Samantha, as Andrew nodded in agreement, reaching inside his military yoke belt he was wearing for a small first aid kit. "We'll need these men to get through to Clyde, you don't mind if I give them medical attention, as some will need it" replied Andrew, as Samantha nodded her approval at the sound of Andrew's suggestion.

"Can I help, these men will still take orders from me after all" asked Patrick, who looked a little sheepish, wondering what was to become of him. "I've no objection, what do you think then boss" replied Andrew, as he directed his question towards Samantha. Samantha felt a bit strange being called the boss, but she soon recovered quickly, snapping herself into line as a soldier would do when given orders. "You can, but if he tries to sabotage you or the Green Goddess in any way, shoot him" replied Samantha, as Patrick went wide eyed, but then nodded to say that he understood. "Understood boss, what are you going to do now" asked Andrew, as Samantha turned to move away, but looked back at Andrew before saying, "I'm going for a bath, there's a small lake over there I'm going to use as a bathroom, and I don't want any peeping tom's following me either".

Patrick and Andrew looked confused, but then realised what Samantha meant, as they both suppressed grins realising that Samantha was still body concuss, even in this strange new world. Samantha hadn't properly cleaned herself since leaving Mile End Farm, and now she looked as if she'd just climbed out of a coal mine, with her hair, skin and clothing, as black as a midnight sky. "Ok, I'll make sure no one bothers you while your over there Samantha" replied Andrew, as he and Patrick made their way across the village green to where some of the soldier's and scientists lay injured, whilst the others were still tackling the small fires inside the neighbouring buildings. Samantha walked slowly across the village green and through the pub car park, pushing open a kissing gate at the back of the pub car park, which marked the boundary edge of the Askham forest area.

Samantha also stuck her nose under her armpit, before immediately retreating her head back out of it again, as she was hit by the exceptionally strong smell of body odour and sweat. "Ok, that answers that question, I stink" said Samantha, more to herself than anyone else, as the surround forest seemed to come alive with animals, with the birds tweeting in the branches of the trees, whilst catching sight of a deer of some kind, sculking several meters away between the trees. As the lake itself was in the forest, it didn't take Samantha that long to reach it, where she stopped by the side of the lake bank, gazing at the open flat still water within it. She knew that no one was likely to come across her, so Samantha began to strip off, until she stood dressed only in her underwear in front of the lake, her clothes hanging from some of the branches of a low hanging tree by the lakes edge.

Samantha then strode over to a small jetty which stuck out into the lake, as she took in how surprisingly mild it was in the air for the time of year. Samantha could see her reflection in the lake water's surface, realising how rugged her appearance now looked, having been tamed by nature and living in the new world, realising that the lake water wasn't going to stay smooth for very long. Samantha took a deep breath; closed her eyes; and then leapt forwards; into the water.

CHAPTER TWENTY SIX

The Convoy

Almost at once, Samantha wished she hadn't jumped into the water. Even though it was around ten degrees Celsius or so in the forest air around her, the water itself couldn't have been any warmer than about three degrees Celsius, as Samantha had found out to her cost when she had jumped in. "Stupid thing to do really" thought Samantha, as she wondered what her parents would have said if they knew she had jumped into a lake without thinking first. Samantha immediately let out a short sharp scream, as she felt how cold the water was around her through the shock of it, as the cold seemed to bite at her from every angle, like someone had suddenly dumped a bucket full of ice over her, just like in the insane and crazy ice bucket challenges Samantha had seen people doing on internet websites such as YouTube, Facebook and other social media platforms.

Samantha hoped that her small scream hadn't carried through the still air back towards the village, as Andrew, Patrick, or one of the soldiers or scientists would have certainly come running to see what was going on. The water however had done one good thing for her, as Samantha felt the muck and dust from the last few days falling away from her body as she rubbed herself vigorously with her hands, in an attempt to try and keep warm, even as the water bit and scratched at her like some demented pet would do, trying to escape from a sealed car on a very hot day. "Note to self, don't ever do that again" said Samantha to herself, as she proceeded to rub her hands through her hair, only stupidly realising now after she'd jumped into the lake, whilst being soaking wet in the process, that she hadn't brought any shampoo, soap, or any other cleansing products to wash herself with from the Askham village.

"Great, think before you act Sam, come on" thought Samantha in an annoyed state of mind, as she swam around for a little bit, making her muscles ache slightly. It had been a little while since she had been for swimming lessons, and the fact that she hadn't had a proper square meal since before Covid; living only on army ration packs and the fried breakfasts at Mile End Farm. When Samantha next whipped the water out of her eyes a few minutes later, she suddenly noticed a small bright object laying on the riverbank. Being quite a sophisticated and incredibly able-bodied swimmer in her youth, Samantha had no problem whatsoever swimming around the lake, to investigate what this small object was, after slowly feeling the aching feeling in her limbs start to fade away. As Samantha got closer to the object, she could see that it was a bar of soap, which made Samantha jump backwards in alarm when she saw it my clearly.

After getting as close to the lake edge without climbing out, Samantha grabbed the object, which she could now see was an up-market brand of soap. Written on it, in small red letters was a message which read, 'This isn't over, Samantha Bonham'. Samantha guessed almost immediately who had left the message, as she whirled around quickly, sending water from her hair flying in all directions, whilst the water splashed and rippled away from her as she did so. Helen had left that message, Samantha was sure of it; and Helen had to still be nearby, as she would have had to have known that Samantha would come this way and go for a swim in the lake. It made Samantha shiver even more than she was already doing, as it was the sort of message that a demented stalker would leave their victim, taking pleasure in seeing there would be victim living in fear for their lives.

From what Samantha could see, there was no sign of Helen anywhere, and as Samantha remained in the lake treading water, she strained her ears to listen for a tell-tale sign of twigs and branches snapping, or leaves rustling; but no sounds came her way. After a few minutes, no sounds came to her, except for those of the nearby birds in the surround trees in the woodland. Feeling that Helen was not in the immediate vicinity, Samantha finished washing herself with the soap, which made the immediate water around her bubble slightly, as the soap suds washed off into the surrounding lake water. Samantha had done many things in her twenty-six years that she had spent on the planet, however washing in a lake was certainly a new one to add to her new list of life experiences. The water soon started to feel warmer, as Samantha swam up and down the lake, creating ripples behind her as she went, until she was ready to climb out half an hour later.

The water splashed slightly as she swam to the shore and climbed out, shaking herself like a dog would do to remove all of the water off of her body, and out of her hair. Picking up the clothes she had been wearing before, Samantha gave them a quick rinse in the lake, rung the water out of them, and then proceeded to slip them back on again, as she had fresh clothes in her suitcase onboard the Green Goddess. It was just so she did not have to injure the other survivors staring at her, like she was an extra-terrestrial creature from out of this world. As Samantha made her way over to the pub car park, she could see that all of the fires had been extinguished, as the soldier's, scientists and Patrick all sat on the grass, some talking to each other, others looking up at the sky with relaxing looks on their faces. It suddenly occurred to Samantha, that these people had been through just as much as she had, although maybe under the protection of Grey's Pharmaceuticals.

Their boss Helen Dukes had fled, and they had been left wandering and confused about what to do next, relying on Patrick for their instructions and orders. "That should be fixed up no problem at all, any problems, let me know" came Andrew's voice from nearby, as he spoke to a black uniformed soldier, who was having a bandage fixed to his arm, where a piece of shrapnel had pierced it during the battle, staining a small patch of his uniform a little darker than it had been before. The soldier thanked Andrew, as Samantha drew level with them both, having first returned to the Green Goddess to change into fresh new pair of jeans and a top. "How's it going Andrew" asked Samantha, as Andrew turned to face her, a pleased look on his face, not yet aware of what Samantha had seen and delt with at the lake's edge in the Askham woodland area after going for a wash.

"Sam, I'm glad your back with us; looks like everything is under control here; Patrick's been helping me patch up the injured, and there's been a few interesting details come to life too" replied Andrew, as Samantha held out the bar of soap she had been using, showing Helen's message on it. "I found this by the lakes edge in the forest, I think Helen's been back here after the battle" replied Samantha in a determined voice, as Andrew looked a little sheepish, as he replied, "ah, that confirms a bit of suspicion that I had; one of the scientists reckoned he'd seen a figure stalking behind one of the bushes at the edge of the village, around towards the forest where you'd gone to the lake". Samantha looked worried and confused, as she responded with, "what can Helen possibly do though; these guys here will take orders from us and Patrick now, not Helen".

Samantha gestured around at the soldiers at scientists as she said this, as Patrick walked over to them both, still looking a little scared that Samantha hated him for what had happened with Diana. "Sam, I meant to say, I'm really sorry for what happened to Diana; I was impulsive, and it was wrong; you can imagine how deeply sorry I feel" replied Patrick, swallowing hard, as he tried to apologise for past events. Samantha considered him for a few seconds, before letting out a weak smile. Then without warning, Samantha let rip, punching Patrick as hard she could squarely in the face with a smacking noise which was so loud, that several of the soldier's and scientists looked around in alarm, wondering what the noise was. Patrick let out a cry of pain, and even Andrew jumped backwards in shock, as Samantha lowered her fist back down to her side, breathing heavily.

"That's for raping my friend" replied Samantha, who didn't shout, but instead brandished a finger into Patrick's face, feeling her anger boiling back up again as she spoke, watching a winded Patrick straighten back up blinking slightly, as small white stars popped in front of his eyes. "I have to admit, I deserved that" said Patrick, as Andrew looked backwards and forwards between Samantha and Patrick, as if he'd never seen another human being before. "And this is for coming over to the right side" said Samantha, who lunged forwards and embraced Patrick in a tear bear style hug. If being hit in the face didn't shock Patrick, being forcibly half crushed to death by Samantha certainly was. Samantha broke away from him, whipping her mouth as she went, as Patrick and Andrew stood there stunning at Samantha's actions. After a few seconds of silence Patrick replied, "ok; I probably deserved that as well".

Samantha let out a small giggle of laughter, as Andrew looked so shocked and confused, that he replied with the words, "Sam, has anyone ever told you this, but you're completely crazy". "Welcome to the apocalypse" replied Samantha, as there was a stunning silence all around them from the onlookers. "What just happened" asked one of the scientists, as a black uniformed soldier replied, "your guess is as good as mine". Samantha laughed, as she could see how bizarre the situation looked to everyone else around them. "Permission to debrief the team, ah, boss" asked Patrick, as Samantha looked directly at him now, fixing Patrick with an understanding look. "Be my guess" Samantha replied, as Patrick stood up straight and addressed the small group of soldiers and scientists all around them, many of them still looking a little tired and run down after the battle and its aftermath.

"We now have a new mission, Helen Dukes has been relieved of command; this is for the simple reason, that Helen has fled the field of battle like the coward that she is; she would gladly let you all go to your deaths, knowing it to be a pointless exercise" exclaimed Patrick, as he spoke in a speech like fashion, feeling like he was rallying around for moral and support. As Patrick essentially had been a member of the intelligence services once, public relations should have been his number one skill, having to work in close proximity to hostile agents of other foreign government organisations. Patrick was certainly showing his skills now however, as he addressed the rag tag group of soldiers and scientists, by speaking out, "I only have one question for you, a damsel in distress is searching for her true love; will you help me, in helping her, to find him".

There was a general roar from the soldiers and scientists, as the scientists waved their arms into the air and the soldiers waved their guns into the air, firing off a few bullets as they went, making the still air around ring out with gunfire. "I guess that's settled then, we're coming with you Sam" replied Patrick, as Andrew clapped him on the back. "Welcome to the good guy side Patrick, glad to be working together again" said Andrew, as even Samantha leaned forward and hugged Andrew, though not as tightly as she had hugged Patrick a few moments earlier. As Samantha broke away, Patrick had a look of steely determination on his face, as he said to Samantha, "so, what do we do now". "Get me a map and a table, and I'll show you" replied Samantha, as Andrew started to bark orders at everyone in the group in turn, relishing in the adrenaline rush that he was once again on another lifesaving mission.

"Alright everyone, you heard the chief, let's get a table and some maps, there's bound to be some around here somewhere" replied Andrew, as the crowd before them dispersed, roaming all over the village, gathering whatever they could find to aid and help Samantha in her quest. "You know Helen better than anyone, what is she likely to do next" asked Samantha, directing this question towards Patrick, as she watched Patrick's eyes widened slightly, as he run a hand through his hair in deep concentration. "At a best guess, she was after you, so wherever you go, she's bound to follow" replied Patrick, as a few black uniformed soldiers ran over to them, carrying a table between them, which they set down on the grass in front of Samantha, Patrick and Andrew. A few seconds after that, a shedload stack of maps appeared before them all, showing Askham village and the surrounding countryside.

In turned out that Askham village was practically a whole treasure trove of information, which the soldiers and scientists had scrounged from the nearby houses, shops and pubs in the village. Samantha thanked them all as they arrived in turn, as the group of soldiers and scientists all gathered around her along with Patrick and Andrew, to listen to what Samantha was planning. "I'm proposing a convoy, one vehicle in front, one behind; with the Green Goddess in the centre" explained Samantha, as she gestured with her hands over the maps, showing a route out of the village, using the main M6 motorway to cut across the country, right the way up to the town of Clyde, where she was hoping all of her answers would be solved. Samantha felt a little tingle of excitement as she spoke to the crowd, as it had been a while since she had been in a convoy of vehicles, like when Samantha ran convoy with other trucks on the motorways before Covid.

"If that be the case, we will need a scout and a tail" replied Andrew, as he made a line with his finger on the map in front of them, pointing his finger at either end of the line while he spoke. "A scout and tail" replied Samantha in a curious voice, as Patrick elaborated, watching the soldiers around him nodding to show that they understood him. "One vehicle will go ahead of the Green Goddess to make sure of no booby traps and the like, whilst the tail vehicle will lag behind, making sure that no one is following you, a.k.a Helen and the like". As Patrick spoke, he too pointed at the vehicles around him, showing how it would all work in theory and practice. "I second that; but how do we stay in touch" asked Samantha, as Patrick showed her a radio earpiece, lodged in his ear. "We have radios Sam; this lets the vehicles stay in contact; all you have to do is drive the Green Goddess" replied Patrick, who was doing his best to stay in Samantha's good books.

For Samantha, it felt just like breaking into Grey's and planning the battle of Askham all over again; how weird it felt to Samantha to be doing it at that time, especially in the company of those who were tasked with tracking her down, rather than assisting Samantha to reach her goal of Clyde, and maybe even Greg if she was lucky. "Didn't Helen have an eyepiece just like yours" asked Samantha, but Patrick quickly shook his head. "No, she didn't thank heavens, nor did her vehicle have a radio in it, so she would be completely blind to us, and not have a clue what was happening" replied Patrick, as Andrew also nodded his head in agreement, realising that this put the group ahead of the game. "All the same, we should have a code that we use, just so that only we know what it means" explained Andrew, who would have been familiar with all of these things, thanks to his days as a member of the elite S.A.S unit.

"I agree" replied Samantha, as placed her hands up to her face in a thinker type pose, pondering what to do next. After a short pause however, Samantha spoke again. "I think the codewords for the lead and tail vehicle should be Alpha and Bravo, and the Green Goddess should be Princess". Samantha expected this to be met with nods of approval from the others, but she could see Andrew shaking his head slightly as she suggested her idea to everyone. "I like the idea of calling the Green Goddess as the Princess, but Alpha and Bravo are too obvious to an outsider who could be listening in" replied Andrew, as Samantha went into a thinking pose again, feeling a little silly that she'd come up with that idea. Patrick seemed to come to her rescue however, when he suddenly spoke up, "I think two better codewords would be north and south, it's still a direction as such, but they don't know what direction you're travelling in as such".

"Aye, nice one Patrick, Helen probably already knows where we're going anyhow, but as long as we keep moving, we should be ok; major roads only I should think too" replied Andrew, as Samantha definitely looked more confused this time. "Isn't that a bit exposed, why not stick to the back roads" asked Samantha, but Andrew already had his answer ready for her. "Because Helen knows that your modus operandi; if you go on the back roads, it's easier to set up an ambush". "But Helen will be operating alone surely, she's lost her fighting force" replied Samantha in a curious voice, as Patrick spoke up. "You don't know Helen as I do, people will remember her face and voice from the TV and the news programmes; if there are any other survivors out there, she will most certainly try and sweet talk them into joining her and make them do what she wants".

"If that be the case, then we'll have to move fast, if we want to avoid another battle like the one that happened earlier" replied Andrew, as the others nodded in agreement. "It's getting late, we won't be able to do anything later in the evening, and if we left now, it would be dark before we reached Clyde" said Samantha, who seemed to now feel her eyes starting to drop slightly at all of the action that had happened that day. "Alright, we move out at first light, dismissed" replied Andrew, as the others around them broke up, heading for resting places and the like. As so many houses lay vacant and unoccupied around the village, the soldiers and scientists in the rag tag group had no problem finding places where they could sleep comfortably that night. Andrew had retreated to his usual resting places inside the Black Swan pub along the high street, as he had agreed to keep his eyes on Patrick, as per his and Samantha's agreement.

Samantha meanwhile had decided to rest up in the Black Swan pub as well in the downstairs bar area, as she felt that a sofa would have been more comfortable sleeping place then the bunk bed inside the cab of the Green Goddess. Although as Andrew pointed out to Samantha earlier in the evening; if Patrick had of wanted to sabotage their operation, he would have done so by now, and he had the men behind him to do it. This thought was certainly a comfort to Samantha, as she drifted off that night wrapped in a warm blanket, but this thought wouldn't distract her for very long. Helen was still out there somewhere, and Samantha had a shroud suspicion that Helen hadn't gone that far from the village, having been able to sneak back unnoticed by anyone else, to leave a message for Samantha on a bar of soap. Helen could even be watching them all right now, crouched in some bush somewhere, stalking them all as they slept.

Samantha somehow found the idea of the former Prime Minister of Great Britain crouching in a bush quite ludicrous, although in the new world, anything was possible. Samantha soon found that her dreams were full of images of Helen wearing a red catsuit and horns, cackling like some demented witch, while Samantha remained imprisoned by a ring of fire, listening to her saying, "you'll never see Greg again my dear, you have lost your battle". Samantha suddenly awoke, sitting bolt upright, feeling light headed from the speed of her ascent. Samantha felt a drop of something run into her eye, as she realised that she had woken up drenched in sweat. It was a few seconds before Samantha realised that Andrew was standing close by too her, where a familiar smell wafted towards her through the air from the open downstairs window, which appeared to be originating from the village green.

"Rise and shine Sam, breakfast is served, and then we can move out" came Andrew's voice, as Samantha quickly whipped her forehead with her sleeve, and then proceeded to make her way out of the Black Swan pub, towards the Green Goddess still parked on the village green from the day before. As Samantha slept fully clothed these days, she wasn't worried about people walking in on her, as she may have been before Covid. "This is Bonham's mobile all you can eat café, how may I serve you sir" replied Samantha, in a jokey type voice, as Andrew let out a short laugh, understanding Samantha's little joke. "You're the only one around here with food onboard Sam, and I suspect you may be flooded with customers fairly soon" replied Andrew, as low and behold, the soldiers and scientists began to emerge from there respected houses where they had been sleeping, looking forward to a good breakfast.

Up until now, Samantha's ration packs that she had been given from

RAF North Lakes had only been designed to feed herself and maybe a few other people. Now Samantha was faced with feeding at least half a dozen people, which would mean that her supplies would be stretched quite badly to its lowest point. By Samantha's guesses, if she would be expected to keep this team alive, she would only have around a week's worth of supplies left onboard, so they would need to reach Clyde quickly if salvation really was there, as it appeared the pamphlet was showing it to be. Within the next few minutes or so, Andrew, Patrick and the others had managed to help Samantha offload all of the supplies that they needed for breakfast, as it was going to be a difficult day ahead of them. Samantha expected that it would be a few days before they reached Clyde, but was still prepared for a hard slog all the same.

Patrick, it later transpired, had been given many of the field training skills as Andrew had received, as Samantha didn't know that the special forces and the intelligence services were people who worked together on a regular basis. This meant that Patrick was able to get a small camp fire started in the road, which he used to boil water for everyone could use to wash, clean and keep themselves fresh. "The trick is that none of the electric showers work inside the houses, and the pump cleaning station which used to supply this village is run off of mains power, so that went offline after Covid" explained Andrew, as Samantha served out fried eggs from the saucepan that she was handing around. "So how have you been getting water here, as I noticed that you seemed to be pretty clean here" replied Samantha, with a single look at Andrew, as the question of hygiene was one that had made her quite curious since arriving in Askham.

It had occurred to Samantha that Andrew had been living wild here for weeks on end, and yet he still seemed to look presentable and fresh all the same. "Simple, I rigged up a system of pipes and found a beer pump in the pub cellar; rig that up to a hot water tank with a small gas fire underneath it, whilst hanging a bucket overhead, and; well; bob's your uncle, you have yourself a wild shower" explained Andrew, as he waved his hands in the air, describing how his wonder contraption worked.

"Shame you'll have to leave it behind though Andrew" replied Patrick, who was enjoying Samantha fried eggs, as he tried to pinch another one off of her frying pan as Samantha passed him, frying pan in hand. Samantha took a small jokey swipe at Patrick as she said, "oi, behave you, otherwise I won't have any left". There were a few sniggering faces around everyone in the group, which Samantha seemed not to notice.

Patrick let out a small laugh, as he straightened up, placing his plate down on the ground next to the large cooking pot, where Samantha was using the warm water inside it to clean off the plates with a dishcloth, she'd borrowed out of one of the houses. It wasn't what you'd call the most hygienic way of cleaning, but even so, it was far better than nothing, as the old saying went. It did seem strange, watching each member of the group come back in turn with an empty plate, thanking Samantha as they went for the meal, being strongly reminded of the play Oliver Twist, where little Oliver held up his plate saying, 'please sir, I'd like some more'. In some sort of ironic truth, looking at the wider scheme of things, everyone in the group were some sort of orphans now, as they would have all lost someone or even whole families to Covid. It made Samantha think about those in other countries, and how they were coping with the aftermath of Covid.

Maybe these people had known this all along, and maybe the reason they had survived, was that somehow, they had all been shielded from the effects of Covid by some unknown vaccine, that Grey's Pharmaceuticals, or a partner agency somewhere had been working on. If that had been the case, then surely Patrick, or one of the others would have told her about it by now, or whether maybe there was another higher power somewhere controlling Patrick, based on the theory's told to her by Doctor Victor back at Mile End Farm. Some of the rag tag group sat out in front of Samantha on the village green, were scientists with degrees and higher scientific qualifications after all; they all weren't completely stupid it had to be said. But it did make Samantha think what exactly it was that they were doing, that day that she, Diana and Julie were inside the Grey's Pharmaceuticals building.

"Ok guys, briefing in five minutes" called Patrick to the group as a whole, whilst simultaneously holding up all of the fingers on his right hand. There was a general mummer of acknowledgement from the group at large, as Patrick walked away slowly towards the Black Swan pub, keeping his eyes moving all around him, as if he half expected someone to jump out from behind a doorway and shout boo at him. Five minutes later, Samantha, Patrick and Andrew along the rag tag group of soldiers and scientists, all gathered around the table in the middle of the village green alongside the Green Goddess, casting a shadow over them all in the early morning sunlight. It was a surprisingly warm day for the time of the year, as the leaves on the trees blew around in the small breeze that had whipped up around them suddenly as they stood there, listening hard to what Patrick and Andrew had to say.

Patrick led the briefing, as Andrew and Samantha watched on, ready to jump in should they have needed too to fill in any gaps. "We know our enemy is battle hardened and determined; we know that they will go to any lengths, to get what they want". Patrick took a short breath, before pointing to the other half of the group, and then continuing to speak. "North team, which will be headed by Lieutenant Hawkins, will act as the lead scout vehicle, moving ahead of the group, but will stay in sight of the Green Goddess at all times; meanwhile South team, will take up the rear six o clock position behind the Green Goddess, to ensure that both angles are protected". "How can we protect against an attack from the side in case the South team is compromised" replied one of the black uniformed soldiers, who was the on the far side of the table they were all standing at listening to the briefing.

"I'll just have to protect myself; I've done it so far up until this point" replied Samantha, in what she hoped sounded like a confident voice, realising that she had always had company when travelling and only been alone in the time between the Geighlon Sisterhood and Askham village itself. But something must have showed on her face, as the same black uniformed soldier that had spoken before, then replied, "well, no offence ma'am; but you don't exactly look or act like a soldier". Samantha

439

considered this for a second, as she felt all of the eyes of the group turn towards her. After a second's silence, Samantha replied, "my father was in the army; he was an engineer and taught me a few survival techniques when I was a child; it's helped me to survive so far, and I think it will help me to the end" replied Samantha in a calm relaxed voice, as she didn't want to show any fear, even though she could feel the fear creeping up inside her like ice-cold water.

"That's good enough for me ma'am, I'm in" replied the black uniformed soldier, as the others spoke out in turn saying, 'I'm in, I'm in' over and over again. After a second or so of this, Patrick held a hand up, as the group fell silent in anticipation, wondering what was going to be said next. "You have your orders team, to your stations, dismissed" ordered Patrick, as the message was repeated on all fronts with replies of 'yes sir' all around them. The soldier's and scientists broke up, heading back to their usual places, preparing equipment and supplies for the journey ahead. A few soldiers were even making adjustments to their vehicles that they had brough with them, as the one's that hadn't been completely destroyed by the battle, had to be serviced and maintained, for the journey ahead of them.

Samantha stood and watched the hive of activity going on around her, not being able to help but feel slightly energised by what was happening. "One step closer; one step closer to Greg" Samantha kept thinking, over and over again, until a sudden tap on her shoulder, made her jump backwards and spine around in alarm, as Andrew came over with a cup of tea. "Here, I think you've earned this" said Andrew, as Samantha thanked Andrew for the tea, before clasping it firmly in her hands. "Yeah, I think so" replied Samantha, as she took a quick sip of the tea, and then shuddered slightly, as the hot water hit her mouth and tongue, feeling the burning sensation in here throat. "Oh, sorry Sam, did I make it a bit strong for you" asked Andrew, as he looked a little worried and concerned that he may have just allowed Samantha to come to harm, by nearly scolding her with his own brand of tea.

"No, it's not that, it's just, I've never tasted tea like that before" replied Samantha, with a slight grin, as she tried to cover up the fact that the tea tasted a little different than normal. "Ahh, my mother's own recipe that is; home brewed Scottish Glaswegian tea, made without milk you see, as I haven't had any fresh milk for months now" replied Andrew, as Samantha looked curious about Andrew's interesting brand of tea. "Ah I see, surely you've been able to get milk from somewhere, after all, there are farms all over the country" said Samantha, as she remembered seeing a few farms on her way to Askham village in the last few days. "Aye, that's true that, trouble is if it's not fresh, then you can get food poisoning from it; plus, I did find a local farm near to here, but sadly all of the cows had died because of the lack of milking, so getting milk from there wasn't an option" replied Andrew.

Samantha suddenly had a fleeting image of the Flintstone community back at Mile End Farm as Andrew spoke about cows and farms, remembering that they would often go and milk the cows that Brian had owned for fresh milk every day. Even then, the milk had tasted slightly different from what Samantha had been used to in the past on her cereals and in her every day cups of tea. But as Brian had explained to her back at Mile End Farm, the milk that they purchased at the supermarkets would have been through a processing plant first, before reaching the average family kitchen table. "It's almost a bit like, trying to hold in the fact that you really need a pee, but you can't go, and the pain you're in when that happens" explained Andrew suddenly out the blue, snapping Samantha out of her temporary day dream, where she had been thinking about what almost felt like a previous life.

So much had happened in a short space of time since leaving Lillington, that Samantha almost felt like she had lived a whole other life, to the one that she had been living before Covid. "Oh yeah I know that feeling; that's happened to me many times when I've been stuck in a traffic que, nearly wetting myself because I've not been able to get to a loo anywhere" couped Samantha, thinking of how awkward it had been in the past, even to visit a place where she could go and be a civilised

441

human being, rather than having to live wild, resorting to doing her business in bushes and makeshift small holes dug in the ground. "Well, it's exactly the same with a farm yard cow, if you don't milk it, it dies" replied Andrew, sounding a little sad at that point, as he spoke in a way which told Samantha, that he would have found it handy to have a cow or two walking around the village for some fresh milk.

As milk would have been quite an important drink to keep bones healthy and strong, having the lack of some breeds of animals like farm yard cows, would certainly be a major drawback in a post-apocalyptic world like the one they were in now. "Well, I'm glad that I don't need to be milked, just a nice soft lavatory seat would do for me thanks" replied Samantha, as Andrew let out a small laugh, however, they were suddenly both interrupted by the arrival of Patrick, who had been overseeing the preparation work for the journey ahead. "We're pretty much ready to go guys; the work's been completed in record time, with the vehicles being modified to suit any terrain, so we're just waiting for the go signal" explained Patrick, as Samantha looked between Andrew and Patrick, a grin beginning to unfold on her face, as Samantha felt that she was finally closing in on Greg and maybe even salvation.

"Gentlemen, let's go and get my fiancée" replied Samantha, as she turned around and headed straight for the Green Goddess, climbing into the cab and closing the door behind her with a clunking sound. Andrew whistled into the air, as he waved his hand in the air, gesturing to the group as a whole. "Mount up, we're moving out" shouted Andrew to the group, as the soldier's and scientists began climbing into their respected four-wheel drive convoy vehicles. As the original convoy under the command of Helen Dukes had been six vehicles, and as Edward's pickup had been destroyed, Helen's car used by Helen to flee the battle, and the other two vehicles destroyed during the battle itself, only two vehicles remained in active service. This meant that the group who had come in were a little cramped in like sardines, as they all packed themselves in to the convoy vehicles.

As this was proved to be quite dangerous before the convoy had even left the village, Samantha had offered up a space to ride in the back of the container behind the Green Goddess, making sure to pack plenty of water inside it, as the metal container was still very much exposed to the sun for the trip ahead, meaning that temperatures inside could skyrocket even at the slightest ultra violet ray exposure. "Ok, wagons roll" shouted Patrick, as he climbed into the South team's four-wheel drive, and waved his arm in a circular movement out of the window, before retracted it, and winding up the window. Samantha started up the Green Goddesses engine which rumbled into life, as it had done so many times before, shifting into gear with a giant clunking sound from the gearbox. "North to all units, ready to move out" came Andrew's voice over the military type radio which Samantha had in the cab with her.

"Princess to North, ready to move out" replied Samantha, picking up the radio receiver, whilst speaking into the mouthpiece. As saying the words Green Goddess over the radio would have been a bad idea in case anyone was listening in for any reason, they had decided as a group that the Green Goddesses codename was to be, princess. "If that isn't as obvious as it gets, I don't know what is" said Samantha to herself, as she listened carefully for the order to move out. "South to North, ready to move out" came Patrick's voice through the radio, as Andrew's voice spoke after Patrick had finished. "All call signs, advance forward and proceed to exit route". Samantha watched, as the four-wheel drive ahead of her, moved slowly forwards onto the road, and turned right at the end of the street, making sure to do so slowly in case anyone had been waiting to ambush them.

The Green Goddess began to move slowly forwards, and only just about made the sharp right turn at the end of the street, despite a few parked cars on either side of the road. Samantha looked in her wingmirror, and could just about see the South team in their four-wheel drive, trailing slightly behind to ensure. The cars which had been used to block the roads before the battle, were soon rammed out of the way, owing to the new bull bar modifications which had been fitted to the front of the four-wheel drives. The Green Goddess had of course been fitted with its own bull bar modifications, but Samantha was being a little cautious of late. If the Green Goddess was knocked out of action, they were all stuffed, as it was the main carrier of equipment and supplies; so, if the Green Goddess became stuck, damaged, or sabotaged in any way, the entire convoy would be in jeopardy.

Samantha was pleased when the road began to open up and became a dual carriageway, as a few times along the winding Cumbrian roads, she had feared that she would get stuck. However, the Green Goddess seemed to deal with everything that Samantha threw at her, as they made their way slowly and steadily towards the motorway, and the legendary Scottish boarder. A couple of times along the trip the convoy was brought to a standstill, as Andrew could have sworn, he had seen something or someone move close by too them. Fortunately, it had turned out to be a cat, foxes, and even at one point, a pack of wild dogs, which fled in fright when they saw the sight of the convoy approaching them. Every so often, they would come across a dead body or two, where they had been either killed by other survivors, or died through a lack of drinking water or starvation.

"We need to keep moving as much as possible, and never when it's dark, otherwise, it's not just Helen we will have to think about attacking us" replied Andrew, when the convoy had pulled up to the outside of a service station on the deserted stretch of motorway. The service station itself had been stripped of most of the items on the shelves, however a decaying body of a young women hung from the ceiling by a length of rope, with a cardboard sign around their neck which read 'criminal' on it, in big black letters. Samantha couldn't help but let out a small cry when she saw the young woman hanging from the ceiling, as the young woman couldn't have been any older than Samantha was herself. This was clearly the work of some sort of thuggish gang, who had resorted to killing other survivors to get what they wanted, all in the name of self-preservation.

It then suddenly occurred to Samantha, that this unspeakable crime could well have been Helen's doing, but that would have been near impossible to prove, due to a lack of evidence. It felt wrong to leave the woman hanging from the ceiling, so they all helped to take her down, before laying her carefully on the floor, and then throwing a sheet over her, as a mark of respect. "Come on Sam, there's little we can do for her now" replied Patrick, a look of hopelessness on his face, as he took Samantha by the hand, and led her back outside, where the convoy moved off on its way again a few minutes later. They had all been thinking as a group, that it was only a matter of time before the other remaining survivors of Covid would start to kill each other off, in order to survive in this new and rather unusual world, knowing that they wouldn't face any form of justice for doing these sorts of things to themselves.

Up until now, Samantha had only met people who were willing to help her, it was only when she had met people with the likes of Helen and Edward, that this dreadful thought started to creep into her mind. The convoy made good progress throughout the day, only having to stop to dissemble what looked like a vehicle snare, which had been strung across the road, along with a police stinger strip, which had been laid across the road by a fellow group of survivors. It hadn't been a complete shock to them however that they were ambushed by a gang of rugged looking survivors, who then promptly all scarpered, when the soldiers in the convoy took aim and fired at them, managing to shoot one of them in the leg. The middle-aged man who had been shot in the leg let out a cry of pain, as he limped away into the trees by the side of the motorway, dragging his wounded leg behind him as if it had gone numb.

"I should have expected this, things are starting to get desperate now for people like that; they'll likely ambush anything that comes along now, hence why this is here" replied Andrew, as he and Samantha stood by the road side, watching the other soldiers dismantle the booby traps that had been left by the gang of survivors who had ambushed them when they had come to a stop. It was relatively easy travelling after the

445

action of the booby traps, finding themselves hiding out in the Scottish mountains, where they all stopped and rested for a night in the shadow of a large hill, on the edge of a still flat calm Locke. They were all up at cockcrow the very next day, but their speed had been reduced somewhat as the landscape had presented a perfect opportunity to be ambushed again, which left progress down to the very minimum throughout the whole of that days travelling.

They spent a second night in the mountains, where rain battered them for half of the night, as even the inside of the Green Goddesses container wasn't the warmest of places, where the wind rattled the sides, making howling noises which kept everyone awake for hours. When they set off the next morning, they were pleased to see that none of the vehicles had been tampered with, and the rain had kept away any would be scavengers who were bound to be hidden in the surrounding hills, like some of the native tribes of the Amazon rainforest, or Indian islands would be. They passed through a small remote village in the mountains, as Andrew had ordered them to stop, so they could check their map positions, as even their government issue state of the art satellite equipment didn't work in these sorts of places, due to the lack of signal and power usage.

When they finally came to a stop that night, they were parked by the side of a narrow winding road, on the only passing point for miles around. As the clouds had closed in, they couldn't see much, but by the time they rose the following morning, they were looking down at a stunning scene. The town of Clyde, was nestled between what looked a Scottish Locke on one side, and a huge mountain on the other. The familiar coastline Samantha had on her pamphlet, was now directly in front of her, as if the photographer had only taken the photo a few minutes earlier.

CHAPTER TWENTY SEVEN

A Town called Clyde

"There it is; Clyde; all we have to do now, is get down to it, and wait for this date" said Patrick in an excited voice, as Samantha looked through a pair of binoculars down towards the town nestled in the valley. As Patrick spoke, he gestured to the pamphlet in his hand, which showed a date only two day's time from the current time and place. "Why do things always sound like it's easier said than done" replied Samantha, continuing to look through the binoculars at the town of Clyde. There was a single road leading up to the edge of the town, and the familiar cliffs in the pamphlet's picture stood out on the opposite side of the river. From where they stood up on the hill, they could also see a number of Royal Naval Trident class nuclear submarines moored at the jetties, as if they had just docked into the harbour to be made ready for their next mission out to sea.

The once mighty Royal Navy's continual at sea deterrent Clyde Dockyard looked a little strange with no one inside it, but then again, during the days before Covid, it would have been a thriving Royal Navy dockyard, with military staff and boats sailing in and around it, all doing the vital job of defending the mighty United Kingdom. Now however, all that the submarines were doing were just floating large lumps of scrap metal in the water, completely deserted and abandoned, as no sailors would ever sail in them ever again. There enormous black metal bulk and coning towers stood out amongst the background, as everything else around them was so brightly coloured. This did catch Samantha out a little, as she always had the impression that military bases were designed to blend into the background, rather than stand out a mile away to any potential attacking enemy forces.

"This doesn't make any sense, the town and dockyards look deserted from here; surely, if there was a plan to get people out, it would be bustling, and there would be transport out of there" replied Samantha, as the horrible thought hit her, that they might have just come all this way for nothing at all. "Well, we know they can't fly people out because there's no airstrip, unless there is some sort of aircraft carrier out at sea that a helicopter would fly in and out from to here; so, my best guess is that it will be some sort of boat we're looking out for, to sail up the Locke into the harbour" explained Andrew, who had joined both Samantha and Patrick, after hearing Samantha's comment. "Clyde was to be the meeting point, but even I don't know who was pulling the strings higher up" replied Patrick, as Samantha and Andrew both looked at him with raised eyebrows, wondering if this statement was entirely truthful.

"Do you mean to tell us that you were the one trying to save everyone, and you didn't know who was organising it" replied Andrew in amazement, as Patrick looked a little scared that he might get shot again for being a traitor. Patrick hadn't quite forgotten about being punched in the face by Samantha, as his face did seem to feel sore at times as a result of it. "His voice was always scrambled and he never gave a name, but that's how it worked in the secret service game" replied Patrick, hoping that this answer was satisfactory enough to not get him smacked in the jaw again. "Well, it looks like your mystery mate might have sold us a dummy, it doesn't look like anyone has been in that town for weeks on end" retorted Andrew, being just as disappointed by Patrick's lack of help in this situation; but Patrick had his answer ready before Andrew had finished speaking.

"That's because the town isn't a real living town; it was sold to the Ministry of Defence for training and living accommodation for the Trident crewman and their families; it was also the only base that wasn't used by the M.O.D to house victims of Covid, because of the nature of the equipment being stored there". "What about the people on your programme, surely they will be still be hold up in the town waiting for transport" asked Samantha, as Patrick looked hopeful after this suggestion came up. "If they managed to work out the pamphlet, then yes, they would all be here, providing that they survived Covid of course" replied Patrick, as Samantha placed the binoculars back up to her eyes again to scan the town of Clyde below, after lowering them to briefly look at Patrick when he was speaking to them. It did seem quite bizarre that those on the programme weren't still hold up in the town, if this was the place that the pamphlet had indicated.

"If only we had Skyhawk One; it could have done a flyover of the town to find out who was there" replied Patrick, as his voice tailed off slightly. "Well, these things happen ah Pat" replied Andrew, as they remembered Skyhawk One crashing into Askham Hall, after it had been lured into a trap by Samantha and Andrew, whilst Helen pursued them to Askham village. "Even so, we need to get down there before sundown, and then hopefully wait for this date to see what happens" replied Samantha, as the others seemed to take this as an order. "As you wish boss" was Andrew's joyful reply, as they all formed back up into a convoy again, before making their way down the long winding hill road, towards the outskirts of Clyde. The sun was starting to set a little as they crawled along the open stretch of flat road leading up to the foreboding barbed wire high metal fence which ran around the town.

There was a guard post, and a closed gate, along with a sign saying 'HMS Clyde, Ministry of Defence Property, Keep Out'. This was followed by a second sign which read, 'Photography is Prohibited'. Followed by a third sign which said, 'Trespassers will be prosecuted, fined, or face lethal force if found trespassing on this base'. All of these signs came with many different warning stickers, with red backgrounds and white writing, along with the logo of the British Royal Navy and Royal British crown attached to each of them. The convoy rolled to a stop at the gate, as Andrew hopped out to try and open the gate, which was the only obstacle between themselves and the town itself. It remained solid, but this was no problem, as the lead convoy vehicle reversed slightly, before driving towards the close gate at top speed a second or so later, smashing it open with a loud crashing sound.

Usually, this sort of sound would have rung out for miles around them, alerting people for miles around; but in truth, there was unlikely to be anyone for miles or even hundreds of miles around them, considering the remoteness of their location. The gate went flying through the air, landing a few feet away, as Andrew dragged it out of the way, before climbing back into the four-wheel drive lead convoy vehicle. "Nothing's going to stand in my way today, not some pointless gate anyhow" Andrew said to himself under his breath, as he barely noticed the weight of the gate as he dragged it out of the way onto the grass nearby, to make way for the others. "Never mess with a rogue warrior" Samantha said to herself, as she followed the lead convoy vehicle through the now open gateway, only just about making it through the gateway with the Green Goddess.

It was true that the Green Goddess was slightly wider, and considerably longer than any other post-apocalyptic vehicle in existence, probably even throughout the world. Then again, the Green Goddess put Samantha in mind of the Australian road trains, which blasted and powered their way across the great Australian outback, which could be towing multiple trailers at a time, maybe more, as they took vital goods and cargo from coast to coast, or even to remote settlements in the vast outback. It suddenly struck Samantha what life would have been like in this aging military base, being one of the most heavily guarded bases in the country, even more than places like Buckingham Palace, or number ten Downing Street would have been. Samantha even wondered whether there were still active nuclear weapons nearby, stored onboard the nuclear submarines moored up in the dockyards.

They slowly crawled through the street, only just about making it between the lines of buildings, and military vehicles, which stood abandoned here and there, their doors wide open, as if their occupants had only just climbed out of them. They figured out, by Andrew's incredible soldiering abilities, that their best way of defending themselves from attack, and to be seen by anyone approaching by sea or by air, was on the small beech area on the outskirts of the town beside the Locke. They would be able to hear anyone coming through the town, because the town's abandoned buildings, would act like giant amplifiers, channelling the noise in their direction, like being standing in the middle of a strange open air rock concert at somewhere like Glastonbury or Stone Henge. If this strange spectacle wasn't weird enough, it had to be said that what said next, was even stranger still.

"We've got a good view of the surrounding hills here too, so on a clear day, we can see any vehicles coming a mile away" replied Andrew, as they all set up camp on the beech outside of the town, where the pamphlets picture of the coastline was reflected in the glass on the Green Goddess and other surrounding vehicles. "What happens if they approach in the dark, or if it's foggy, or we can't see further than our own hands" replied Samantha, but Patrick was already ahead of Samantha in his answer, as he replied, "ahh, well, we do have an upper hand on that one; thermal imaging cameras; and we've got a sonar listening device as well, which we can place in the water, so if we hear any splashing or propeller noises, it will give us an early warning whilst giving us time to prepare". Patrick showed Samantha the settings on her binoculars which allowed them to be set to night vision, which made Samantha feel a little more relaxed than before.

Samantha relaxation however turned quickly to surprise, as she was a little freaked out when a few of the soldiers began chuckling as they unpacked the thermal imaging camera and started to set it up in the direction of the towns abandoned buildings. "What's so funny" asked Samantha, a little confused as one of the black uniformed soldiers said, "sorry ma'am, it's just that you look really hot in this". Even Samantha couldn't help but crack a smile when she heard them say it, understanding that though this would have been seen normally as sexual harassment, but that a bit of office-based banter wouldn't have hurt anyone. "It's thermal imaging, not x-ray, otherwise you'd be able to see my bra" laughed Samantha as she said this, hiding her face a little in embarrassment. Leaving the soldiers setting up the thermal imagining camera's, Samantha proceeded towards the edge of the dockyard, where Andrew was keeping himself busy.

"Is that a sonar device, it looks really small if it is" asked Samantha, directing her question towards Andrew, who had walked to the end of a small wooden jetty and lowered a microphone which was about the length of Samantha's arm into the water. The microphone in question was attached to a cable, which ran back to south team's convoy vehicle parked over on the beach area besides the Locke. Inside the vehicle was a small laptop, where a sonar software programme was showing on the screen, showing sound waves just like on an oscilloscope. "Testing" called Andrew suddenly, as he stuck his hand into the water, and tapped the end of the microphone was his hand. A few short pings came through on the laptop, and through the headset which was being worn by Patrick, to test the system. "Check, it's coming through loud and clear Andrew, should hear a pin drop a mile away with this lot" called back Patrick, from the south team's convoy vehicle.

Andrew gave Patrick a quick thumbs up in the air, before turning to Samantha and saying, "it is indeed a sonar system, but it's a powerful one at that; sound travels faster in the water than in the air you see, so we should hear anything like a boat coming a long way off". Samantha had to confess, that she had been quite good at science when she was at school, achieving a C grade during her GCSE exams, so she was fully aware of how a sonar system and other systems worked. This wonderful science knowledge however, still filled Samantha with a little dread. There had always been an ever-present danger that they were being followed to Clyde by Helen, or maybe others, but the fact that Helen hadn't tried to stop them from reaching Clyde was a little concerning to say the least. For one thing, what was so important that other survivors had been forced to pay with their lives for?

What possible motive could Helen have to stop Samantha from reaching her goal of finding Greg, and finding out was going to happen the day after tomorrow? Why had Helen not attacked them, surely, she knew full well where they were going? All of these questions raced themselves around Samantha's mind, and when Patrick called to the group at large that they should turn in for the night hours later, she still felt as if something was coming for them, whether they were ready for it, or not. Whatever it was, the town of Clyde held the answer, and Samantha was going to find out the truth; even; if it killed her. The following morning sunlight seemed to blind them all, as they all began to stir from their slumbers, looking forward to another tasty breakfast, courtesy of the Green Goddesses supply of military grade rations, which even Samantha had to admit were rather filling.

"Nothing to report sir; couple of whales humping by the sounds of it on the sonar, and nothing on the thermal imaging cameras" replied one of the black uniformed soldiers, who had been posted on guard duty throughout the night, to watch over them all as they slept. "Good work Halt, keep me informed if there are any changes" replied Patrick, as the black uniformed soldier named Halt, gave Patrick a small salute, and then returned to the screen, sliding a pair of headphones back onto his head. As the groups supplies had been run down slightly, they choose to go raiding for more within the town itself, as the Royal Navy had turned this town into a thriving sailing community before Covid. "I'd go and check out those Trident submarines you know, to see if any of the food supplies have survived" suggested Andrew to Samantha, who had looked a little lost, as she watched the other soldiers and scientists split up to go hunting in groups.

"Oh ok, I suppose I could always get a chance to look around a submarine; but won't any food onboard have gone off" replied Samantha, having to confess that shed wasn't the greatest expect on the workings of Trident nuclear submarines. "Nah are you kidding, if the reactors onboard the submarines haven't been switched off, there'll still be running even now, and the fridges will still be on as well, so probably fresh food inside them as well" replied Andrew, as Samantha still looked a little puzzled at this. "How could food still be fresh after all of this time" thought Samantha, as Andrew busied himself with looking through a set of binoculars, towards the submarines moored in the dockyards, their big black bulks standing out against the backdrop, despite the fact that at least half to three quarters of the submarines remained hidden below the water line.

Andrew suddenly replied, "Uranium and Plutonium which make up nuclear reactor fuel has a half-life of well past a submarines life span, you could run a Trident submarine for decades without needing to refuel it, and the reaction process onboard produces pure Oxygen and pure water, both of which are used to run the modern submarines". "Got you, ok, yeah sure, I'll go and have a poke around for you" replied Samantha, as she went to walk away, but Andrew stuck out his arm to stop here, lowering the binoculars for the first time. "Are you crazy lassi, you're going to walk in their unprotected" exclaimed Andrew, as he reached down to his trousers pockets, and pulled out a Glock pistol, where he then proceeded to cock back the firing pin on it, before sliding a magazine cartridge full of bullets into it, allowing the slider to retract back into place, a bullet now loaded into the chamber ready to fire.

"I'm not good with those, I hope you know that Andrew" replied Samantha, as she seemed to back away slightly at the sight of the pistol. "You'll be fine, it's for your protection rather than ours" replied Andrew in an encouraging voice with a slight smile on his face, as he handed the pistol over to Samantha. "Thanks, I'll take your word for it" replied Samantha, as she took the pistol, and slotted into her jacket pocket that she was wearing, keeping her protected from the sea breeze, which was coming in off the coastline. Andrew chuckled slightly at Samantha latest remark, as he watched her walk slowly away towards the silent stationary submarines, moored up in the harbour at the other end of the town. It was only when Samantha was walking along the jetty next to them around ten minutes later, it suddenly struck her how big these submarines really were.

Each one was painted a blackish grey sort of colour, and seemed to sit half and half in the water, so that half of the submarine remained visible above the waterline. Samantha was amazed to see that a walkway was strung across to the submarine, and that the hatch wasn't locked when she tried it a second or so after crossing the walkway. The hatch felt heavy and weighty, as Samantha lifted it open with a long-drawn-out creaking sound as it went, followed by a bang when it was fully opened. Andrew had been right about one thing; the submarine was indeed still switched on and running, as Samantha saw lights on below her in the corridor at the bottom of the conning towers steps. Making her way slowly down the ladder, Samantha began to creep forwards slowly, trying to make as little noise as possible, not fully knowing what to expect inside the submarine.

There appeared to be a low-level hum coming from somewhere, as if a giant electrical power unit was running inside the submarine. It made the floor vibrate slightly as Samantha walked over it, feeling the vibrations through her feet as she walked through the different compartments onboard the submarine. "That must be the reactor" said Samantha, more to herself than anyone else a few minutes later, as she reached a large yellow and black painted heavy hatch type door, which had a sign showing a nuclear radioactive warning symbol on it. Samantha may not have known much about boats, sailing or nuclear submarines, but she knew that going into a room where a nuclear reactor was, wasn't the most sensible of ideas. Samantha chose that her best option was to turn back, this time heading down another corridor, where a sign hanging on one wall read, 'HMS Stinger, Trident Class'.

At least Samantha now knew what the name of the submarine was called; it may not have been much to go on, but at least it was a good start. It suddenly struck Samantha, that there were no bodies onboard; it was almost as if the crew had suddenly decided to abandon ship. "Hello, anyone here" called out Samantha, her voice echoing through the corridor and the compartments leading off of it, but no reply came her way. After a few minutes walking around, she came to the larder and the galley's giant walk in fridge. It was indeed sealed, and when Samantha opened it, the sudden drop in temperature made her shiver violently where she stood. Leaving the door ajar, she walked inside, and saw shelves upon shelves of food, everything from tinned baked beans, to full joints of meat, strung up from the ceiling, swinging slightly to the motion as the submarine bobbed in the water.

Fearing that there was a far too likely chance of getting shut in here by accident, Samantha chose to retreat back out again, closing the fridge door behind her as she went. Samantha wished that she'd brought some sort of walkie talkie with her so she could tell the others what she had found, along with a bag to carry the supplies out with her. Samantha knew full well that she would have to go back to the others, and then return later on to collect this complete treasure trove of goodies, as there was enough food in the galley to fill an entire supermarket. It was then as Samantha walked back down the corridor, that she heard it, a small clatter right behind her from the other end of the corridor. Samantha spun around at the noise, nearly jumping out of her skin as she went, trying to locate the source of the noise. Someone was inside the corridor with her alright, maybe a hermit or something, that had its home here amongst the silent and deserted corridors.

It certainly sounded like a spanner, or other tool which had fallen from a height to land on the floor with a clattering sound. "Who's there, show yourself, I'm armed" called out Samantha, pulling out the pistol, and directing it forwards, towards the direction of the noise. Samantha slowly walked forwards, still keeping the pistol outstretched, when she suddenly tripped up, landing smack on the floor, as she had felt someone grab her legs from behind. The pistol spun away across the floor away from Samantha, as she was turned over, and felt a man's heavy breathing on her. "Get off me" shouted Samantha at the stranger, as she managed to roll herself over, before looking up into the face of a young man, with a long black beard and wild looking black hair. On catching site of Samantha, the young man suddenly froze where he stood, a look of complete shock and amazement on his face.

A few long and lengthy seconds filled the gap where the man had stopped trying to struggle with Samantha and let her go. Samantha had also frozen, wondering why the young man had stopped struggling with her, realising that she was still out of range to reach for her pistol, which had spun away across the floor. "Oh my god; it's you; it's really you; Samantha Bonham" came the voice of the man, who was now able to look at Samantha properly for the first time since their encounter. "How the hell do you know my name" shouted Samantha, who was still shaking slightly in shock, wondering who this stranger could be with such knowledge of knowing Samantha's name. "Samantha Bonham, from Lillington, Hertfordshire, known to her friends as Sam, due to be married to Greg, and one hell of a stunning lady if I should ever say so" recounted the man, leaving Samantha even more stunned than she had been before.

"How did you" began Samantha, but then she suddenly froze, as the shock of realising who was standing in front of her, hit Samantha with the equivalent power of a bolt of lightning. Greg Stent stood before Samantha, a little worse for wear it had to be said, not the clean presentable man who she had once known what felt like a lifetime ago, still in shock that it had only been a matter of weeks since they had last seen each other. There was a sudden clang, as Samantha's head made contact with the floor, as she had fainted due to the shook of seeing Greg again after all of this time. When Samantha next awoke, she saw herself surrounded by a large group of people, as it took her a few seconds to figure out where she was. Samantha was back at the campsite, having been laid on one of the camp beds surrounding the tents around the campsite, the Green Goddess easily the biggest and most noticeable thing on the campsite.

Samantha felt as though she must have been out cold for hours, as it was morning when she had climbed onboard the submarine, and now the sun was beginning to set around them. "How you feeling babes" asked Greg, as he sat beside the camp bed where Samantha lay, still a little dazed and confused from her encounter onboard HMS Stinger. Greg looked like his usual self now, having been given the change to have a shave and a wash after being stuck onboard HMS Stinger for weeks on end. "Greg" cried out Samantha, as she reached up and flung her arms around Greg, nearly knocking him backwards onto his back. "It's good to see you too Sam babes" replied Greg, but he suddenly started to groan and cry out in pain, as Samantha suddenly began to hit every part of him that she could reach. "Ouch, what the, what are you" spluttered Greg, as every painful blow hit him.

"You left me to die out there you bastard, and I searched for weeks trying to find you" cried Samantha through sobs of tears, which no-one could tell whether they were tears of sadness, or joy. Greg remained speechless, and everyone else had looked up from what they were doing, unsure whether to get involved, or to stay away, as this seemed like the sort of situation that either scenario was possible. After a second or so of this onslaught, Samantha stood up, and then pulled Greg into a vice like hug, as Greg stood there shocked and aching all at the same time, after being physically assaulted by his own fiancée, to the point that he felt like a championship wrestler, who had just walked out of the ring after a bout with an opponent that was far stronger than he was. Once again, everyone in the group seemed to be transfixed on Samantha and Greg, but none of them were brave enough to approach and inquire what was going on.

"I was worried about you babe, and you were having it off with

Diana behind my back as well" sobbed Samantha into Greg's shoulder, as the little colour left in Greg's face disappeared completely, as Greg learnt about the fact that Samantha knew this little secret that Greg had hoped would never come up. Patrick and Andrew, along with the other soldiers and scientists had started to creep closer to them both, but Patrick looked the most confused out of all of them. "Hang on, you were having a fling with Diana, when was this" asked Patrick, who's eyes had gone wide in shock, as he realised that Samantha could give away his crime at any moment. "I was stupid, I shouldn't have done it; she was drunk, and I helped her home one night after a night out, then she started coming onto me" replied Greg, who was trying to fight back tears himself, realising the pain that he had put Samantha through by hooking up with her best friend.

"We all do stupid things mate" replied Patrick, but Greg still looked confused. "But she's here isn't she, I mean, Diana survived Covid, I know she did because I saw her at Grey's Pharmaceuticals" replied Greg, as Samantha continued to sob. "Diana's dead babes, she died giving birth to a baby girl we called Julie" sobbed Samantha, as Greg looked around in shock at the rest of the group, hoping that someone was going to shout, 'April fool' at him. When no-one did, Greg looked sad, shocked and even slightly annoyed at the same time, which was hardly surprising. Greg had after all been very close to Diana, even without the awkward affair lark hanging over his head, and even officially down to be the chief bridesmaid at Samantha's and Greg's wedding. "Aww Sam babes, I'm so sorry" replied Greg in the most sympathetic voice that he could muster, his throat very dry, as Samantha pulled away, her face splashed with tears.

Samantha quickly wiped her eyes with her hands in an attempt to get rid of the tears, but her eyes were still very red and sore from where she had been sobbing into Greg's shoulder, whilst her head dropped downwards slightly, feeling a little embarrassed by the situation. Greg placed a hand on her shoulder, whilst using the other to lift her head upwards to look Samantha directly into her eyes. "Babes, I'm so sorry, but I want you to know that I love you, and I know that you do too; I'm so glad you found me, I've been so worried" replied Greg, as Samantha sniffed slightly, due to her running nose. "I knew you weren't dead, but I swore to myself that was the first thing I would do the moment I saw you again" replied Samantha, her voice beginning to return to normal after her sobbing. "What, beat ten bells out of me" responded Greg in shock, as Samantha laughed slightly; Greg on the other hand continued.

"I knew I couldn't leave you messages digitally, as the internet was being watched, and then Covid shut it all down forever; but I knew somehow that you would come to me via road". As Greg said this, he gestured in the direction of the Green Goddess, which stood out in the semi darkness, her container and tanker trailers looking large and impressive against the beach coastline backdrop. "I saw your message on the motorway bridge, and I thought that it had to be from you" replied Samantha, who's anger had started to abate by now, and her love and affection for Greg only increased with every passing second. "Ah of course, the bed sheet" replied Greg, who only seemed to be half paying attention, as he'd been finding it difficult to keep his focus away from the Green Goddess, feeling that it was a work of art of how Samantha had managed to use what resources she could find to build such a machine as the Green Goddess.

"Bed sheet" replied Andrew in a puzzled voice, as he hadn't quite understood what Greg had meant. The memory of finding the bedsheet sign hanging on the motorway bridge, suddenly swam before Samantha's eyes as she spoke. It had been the first real sign that Greg had been alive, after hearing it first hand from Diana back at Grey's Pharmaceuticals. "I left messages for Sam all over the place, it's been quite a challenge trying to think from a female perspective for the whole time I've been on the move" replied Greg, in answer to Andrew's puzzled statement. "You didn't come straight here then" replied Samantha, in a puzzled voice, thinking that Greg would have either come first to Samantha's home in Lillington, or gone straight to Clyde itself after Covid had destroyed life as they knew it, unsure as to whether Greg was aware of the pamphlet's secret by this point.

Greg as it transpired, had been on just as big of an adventure as Samantha had been, as he sat next to Samantha on the camp bed, talking late into the night about what had happened to him since leaving Lillington. As Greg recounted his adventurous tail to Samantha, it transpired that Patrick hadn't been entirely as truthful with Samantha and Andrew than what he was letting on. For one thing, Greg had in fact been selected to take part in a medical trial to find a cure to Covid-19, that was the Operation Flower side of things as Greg explained this to Samantha in great deal. Greg had been ordered by Patrick to come directly to the Grey's Pharmaceuticals complex, as he had heard it from Helen Dukes that the roads would be clear of any traffic, and that Greg wouldn't meet any resistance or be challenged whilst being outside of his house against lockdown regulations.

So, it came as a complete shock to Greg to hear about Samantha's encounter with the ghost plane, which had exploded whilst crash landing in Lillington's industrial estate, destroying half a dozen warehouses in the process, including the one where both himself and Samantha had both worked before Covid, with Samantha being a first-hand eye witness to the whole event. However, Greg had been ordered by Patrick to flee after Helen had come up from Whitehall in London, as Helen knew about their connection, and would have easily used Greg as a hostage to bring Samantha to where Helen wanted her. "I'm sorry babes, if I knew any other way of contacting you; the trouble was, everything was being watched you see; I couldn't just send you a text, or call you, or even leave you WhatsApp or Facebook messages, as they could all be seen by Helen and the others" replied Greg, as Samantha seemed to nod slightly as Greg told his story to her.

"It was important that Greg looked like he'd gotten cold feet about Operation Flower, and run away from it all; that way Helen would leave us alone to complete our life saving work" replied Patrick, but he quailed slightly at the look Samantha gave him. "My friends died because Helen came after us; I watched Edward Fitzgerald stab Julie Guard to death, then watched as Diana emptied a machine gun magazine into his body;

she then later died giving birth to your baby Patrick; baby Julie; and you're telling me, that all of that, was so that you could use my fiancée as bate, to lur Helen away, so you could finish some lifesaving work you still can't show me proof of" shouted Samantha, as Patrick recalled slightly, whilst the soldiers and scientists looked up from where they were gathered around a large camp fire in front of them. "I'm sorry Sam, but I have proof, I can show it to you right now" replied Patrick, as everyone looked at him in shock.

"What; proof; proof of what Samantha has just said, there is a cure to Covid-19" exclaimed Andrew in surprise. This complete revelation had taken everyone aback, as Greg, Andrew and Samantha all remained where they were, staring open mouthed at Patrick, as Patrick continued, "me and Edward knew where the cure to Covid was all along; it's inside you, Sam; you're the Covid-19 cure". If the revelation of a Covid cure had been amazing enough, this latest revelation nearly made Samantha pass out again, as she had done so after seeing Greg onboard HMS Stinger. Samantha clapped her hands over her mouth; Greg jumped backwards so much in surprise that he nearly tripped over the camp bed that Samantha had been lying on; and Andrew's eyes widened so much, that his eyebrows were in danger of disappeared out of sight under his hair line.

Around ten whole seconds of silence followed Patrick's statement, as the others tried to settle themselves back down again. "That why you were being stalked Samantha, so we could get you on your own, so as to bring you to Grey's Pharmaceuticals; you were protected all along; if we saw you, we would of course have told you everything, and you would have been safe" replied Patrick, feeling a great weight lifting off of his shoulders, as everyone could tell that Patrick had been dying to tell them all this from the get-go. It certainly sounded like Patrick had been dying to say all of this for a very long time; but Samantha's shock still hadn't abated, and instead had filled her head with even more questions than ever before. Prominent among them was the fact that if Samantha had been stalked since leaving Lillington, then why not come to her and summon her away to Grey's Pharmaceuticals before she had been given a chance to leave.

"The Coventry conundrum" said Greg suddenly, as all of the eyes around him seemed to focus in Greg's general direction. "The what" asked Samantha in surprise, having never heard of the Coventry conundrum before. "The Covent conundrum was the name that was used to describe the Blitz bombing raid on Coventry during the second world war; British codebreakers had decoded that the town of Coventry was going to be bombed, but instead of telling people and risk revealing that the German enigma code had been broken, they had to let people die" explained Greg, as Patrick took up the story from there. "Exactly Greg, you need to understand that we had evils to choose from; risk revealing the future start here programme, or bring Samantha in to roll out a cure". Samantha still looked from one face to another, still at a complete loss as to why Patrick and Edward hadn't tried to bring Samantha to Grey's Pharmaceuticals before Covid had struck.

"But; how can I be the cure to Covid; I mean" stuttered Samantha, before she finished with, "I never contracted Covid in the first place; how can I be the cure to it, if I never got it in the first place; my body wouldn't have the right antibodies to make a cure". Patrick seemed to consider Samantha for a second, but yet again, Andrew stepped in to cover for the awkward silence that had sprung up within the group. "Sam's got a point their Pat, if she never contracted Covid in the first place, how can she be the cure for it" asked Andrew, as he too, looked interested rather than concerned. "Samantha, I believe, is what we call a super spreader; she contracts Covid, but doesn't show any symptoms of it; this is quite a rare situation obviously, but it can still happen" explained Patrick, sounding exactly the same as a university lecturer, giving a lecturer to a hall full of eager eyed students.

"So, let me get this straight, Samantha is a super spreader, and she has been carrying Covid for all of this time" replied Greg, as Samantha stood rooted to the spot, still trying to take in what Patrick was saying about her anatomy. So now Samantha had the truth; the truth; which had been hidden from her, since the start of the Covid pandemic near to the beginning of the year itself. This was the very reason why the others had got sick on Mile End Farm; it wasn't Misim who had been the Covid carrier, Samantha herself had been the source of it. They must have all been infected when both her and Julie had arrived there, meanwhile Misim was the first to show any symptoms of Covid. As this thought crossed her mind, Samantha suddenly begun to back away, carefully stepping over the camp bed as she went. "Wow, Sam babes, where are you going" asked Greg, as the group as a whole were looking worried that Samantha may have finally cracked.

"I can't, I can't stay here; I'm exposing myself to you, you'll all get sick and die, and I can't do that" replied Samantha in a panicky voice, holding out her arms to stop Andrew, Patrick and Greg from approaching her; but Patrick was shaking his head at Samantha, a reassuring look upon his face, as this was some form of technicality that could be swept out of harm's way. "You're not putting anyone in danger Sam, not at all; myself, Andrew and Greg, along with the rest of the team have all been vaccinated against Covid using this cure that we have been researching and developing since the outbreak of the pandemic; but it's all down to Greg here, he's the man to thank" explained Patrick, now with a slight grin beginning to appear on his face. On hearing this piece of news, Samantha seemed to change her tune, as she went from an air of panic, to that of wonderous delight.

"What, Greg's already been vaccinated against Covid, and Andrew too" replied Samantha, hoping against hope, that Patrick wasn't leading her down the garden path again. However, by the look on Greg's face, Samantha somehow secretly knew, that this was not another deception away from the truth like so many of her trips into unknown territory had been. "It's true babes, they managed to get a blood sample from you before Covid; do you remember that blood donation you made to the hospital; that's when they found it in your blood samples, and then worked at it from then" replied Greg, as Samantha suddenly without warning, walked back up to Greg, and threw her arms around him, embracing him in another one of her teddy-bear like hugs. Greg seemed to be a bit abashed by what Samantha was doing, but he put an arm around her all the same.

"I knew you'd never let me down babes" replied Samantha, as Greg looked around at Andrew and Patrick, who had both sniggered at the sight of Greg being put in this embarrassing situation, as apart from anything else, it just come to show that true love still existed in a post-apocalyptic world, Samantha and Greg being a good example of this fact.

CHAPTER TWENTY EIGHT

Showdown

"Trouble is, most of our research was destroyed at Grey's Pharmaceuticals during the rescue mission, so we have lost all of our research on it, and any that was left was too badly damaged to be interpreted" replied Patrick, but he still seemed to have a slight grin on his face, as if he knew something good that the others did not. "Why do I sense there's a 'but' coming" replied Andrew, as he turned to look at Samantha and Greg, who had now broken apart to look at Patrick. "Well, isn't it obvious; some of my team is here with us now, and we have a regenerating amount of anti-covid genes standing right in front of us" exclaimed Patrick, as if he was trying to make them all understand that a cure could be generated right in front of their very eyes. A sudden flickering of truth had crept across Andrew's face, and it seemed Greg had understood as well, although it did Samantha a few moments to recognise what was going on.

"No way, Sam has been through enough already" exclaimed Greg in a stubborn voice, as he threw his hands in front of Samantha in a noble and gallant way to defend her, which made Samantha almost melt in support of Greg as he did so. It was only after Greg had thrown himself in front of her like that, that it dawned on Samantha what Patrick was implying. They were intending to take blood samples from her again, and use it to recreate the Covid cure that they had all been vaccinated with back at Grey's Pharmaceuticals. "Greg babes, please; I've just stayed alive for weeks in a post-apocalyptic world; I've been sexually molested by a psychopath, lost my friends and family, fought in a battle, aided in a surgical operation, been a farmer and many other things besides; if I can't manage to have a blood sample taken after all of that, then I don't know what I can do" replied Samantha, ticking each item off on her fingers as she spoke.

"Oh, and I narrowly avoided being killed by a falling plane too, and designed, created, and helped build a super truck" finished Samantha, as Samantha swallowed after not stopping for breath until she had finished speaking. Greg had taken a step back from her, as even he was shocked at how resilient his fiancée had been in this new dangerous world. "Blimey babes" replied Greg, after another minute's awkward silence amongst them all. But Samantha looked determined that if action needed to be taken, then now was the time to do it, as Samantha had always been a big believer in helping anyone who needed help the most. "Will this help; will this save lives Patrick" asked Samantha, in a determined voice, guessing what the answer was going to be, before it was even spoken. "If we make it properly and everything goes to plan, then yes; we can create a formula for others to follow" replied Patrick, as Samantha seemed to swell up with pride in front of Patrick.

"Then do what you have to do, I want to save some lives; let's do this" replied Samantha, as there was a general up cry, not just from Greg, Andrew and Patrick, but from the rest of the group as a whole, who all begun to applaud Samantha in a standing ovation, as if she'd just won a marathon. It just come to show that even if the old world had disappeared forever, the new one that they were living in, didn't have to be a bad one; and that good people still existed within it. Samantha certainly went to bed that night feeling a lot better than she had done over the last few days; in fact, she hadn't slept this soundly since before she had left Lillington. And so, when the sun rose on the following morning, they all set to work, having been up since before cockcrow preparing a surgery room in the town's military hospital, for the lifechanging work ahead of them.

The night beforehand had been a clear calm one, as they had all gone to sleep, only being able to hear the sounds of the water splashing up on the shoreline from the Locke estuary that led out to the North Atlantic Ocean. The soldier who had been on monitor duty throughout the night, had spoken about a disturbance within the town, which had been picked up by the sonar and sound equipment during the night. "It might just be stray animals, but we'll check it out anyway" replied Andrew, as the others gathered around for that day's hard work. Andrew had decided to lead a team into Clyde itself, to check out what the disturbance had been, whilst Patrick, Greg, Samantha and the rest of the team, would be going to the town's hospital, to perform the scientific studies to replicate the cure that had been injected into them. It seemed that Samantha hadn't been the only excited about the upcoming science tests and medical experimentation.

"What's going to happen to Sam if they do things to her" replied Greg, as the team entered the local hospital, trying to locate the nearest science lab in order to conduct their experiments. "Sam's blood is full of antibodies which appear to help her fight off Covid" replied Patrick, but Greg looked confused as he replied, "but, I survived, you survived, everyone here survived Covid, surely our blood is just as good as hers". Patrick considered Greg for a second, before he responded, "Samantha told us about how a new strain of Covid had been found at Mile End Farm, and our research appears to back that up; there could be a second, third, fourth or even fifth waves of Covid yet to come, maybe more". "So, by harvesting her blood, you plan to stop any future waves" asked Greg, who now seemed to understand the importance of what they were doing, and that history could even be in the making within the walls of the Clyde hospital.

"Exactly, Samantha is a perfect scientific specimen to test this out on, she could save countless lives and protect future generations for years to come" replied Patrick, as Greg held a finger up to him. "Alright, but just remember, she's still a human being, and not a lab rat; if anything happens to her, I'm coming after you and finishing you off myself" replied Greg, in a sterner voice than before, but Patrick was ready with an answer to that. "If Samantha dies during these tests Greg, then I will forefeet my own life in her place" replied Patrick, as he turned away from Greg and walked into a room to his left, leaving Greg standing out in the corridor alone, placing his hands on his hips, whilst breathing out very slowly and running a hand through his hair. "What's going on, where's Greg" asked Samantha to Patrick, as Patrick entered in through the double doors into the laboratory area.

Samantha had been ushered into the science lab inside the hospital, and was now laying herself on an operating table, her head being supported by a pillow, from the large stockpile inside the laundry room. The pillow itself was a little dusty and stuffy, and made Samantha cough a little as she lay her head on it where it had been gathering dust for weeks on end. To prevent this, another scientist within the group had quickly lifted her head up, removed the pillow, given it a dam good beating to get rid of the dust and then inserted it back underneath Samantha's head, before carefully lowering her head down onto it again. "You need to relax now Samantha, don't worry, Greg is right here with you" replied Patrick, as Greg walked in through the double doors, appearing to Samantha's right. "Don't worry babes, I'm here for you" replied Greg, who had begun to stroke her hair with his hand in order to comfort her.

Samantha suddenly felt a weird squeezing sensation down by her feet and hands, as if someone was wrapping something around them very tightly. "Why are you strapping me down" Samantha suddenly exclaimed, feeling that she'd things weren't going to be as painless as she had first imagined. "It's just a precaution, where going to be taking a lot of blood from you to produce and research vaccinations, so it may hurt a bit I'm afraid" replied Patrick, as all around them, the group of scientists began to move around making notes on clipboards. Samantha winced slightly, as she felt a needle prickling sensation go into her arm, as she had never been the greatest fan of needles, even before Covid. "Ok, began extraction" replied Patrick, as Samantha suddenly felt a strange tingling sensation rising up her arm, and then to her shoulder, then felt her neck go numb.

Suddenly without warning, Samantha began to twitch and convulse, feeling as if electric sparks were arching inside of her. "Greg, I'm scared, I'm scared, help me" screamed Samantha, as Patrick called over from the monitor a few feet away; "it's working, the neutrons are firing in her blood stream, it's generating anti-bodies". "Shut it off Patrick, shut it off, she's in a lot of pain from it" shouted Greg across the room, as he went back to stroking Samantha's head, as Samantha screamed again. "Kill me Greg, kill me, I can't stand it anymore" screamed out Samantha again, as tears welled up in her eyes, watching as Greg advanced on Patrick, snarling with his teeth bared. "Shut it down, it's killing her" shouted Greg, as he made a lunge for Patrick to stop the process in its tracks, but Patrick beat him away as Greg landed on the floor.

"Don't be a fool Greg, if we don't do this, the antibodies in Samantha's blood won't activate, and we won't get the right cure for everyone" replied Patrick, as Greg picked himself up from the floor, a small trickle of blood running from his lip, as he rounded on Patrick again. "She's still flesh and blood to me, and you're torturing her right now, shut it down". "Don't you see, this is going to save the world Greg, Samantha's pain maybe a lot now, but she can give her life knowing that she saved the world; she'll be famous, a legend" argued back Patrick, but Greg already had his answer ready. "She's already those things in my book; always has been;

always will be; now stop this process; now"! Patrick seemed to faulter for a second, considering his options, but before he could fully make up his mind, one of the other scientists said, "Sir, we've collected enough blood, if we don't stop now, she could die on us".

In the brief pause between the scientist speaking, and Patrick faltering, Greg had suddenly lunged forward out of Patrick's control, slamming his fist into a big red shut down button on the monitor. Samantha's body stop twitching at once, as she began to breath very heavily, still shaking all over from feeling as if she had been electrocuted. "I'm sorry, I had to do that, it's important, for all of us; but you know that it" began Patrick, but he never finished the rest of his sentence, as Greg had struck Patrick squarely on the jaw with his fist, knocking him over onto the floor. "Sam, you ok babes" asked Greg in a caring voice, as he rushed back over to Samantha's side, seeing Samantha looking up at him. "What was that" cried Samantha, as she managed to regain herself slightly, whilst Greg thrust a glass of water into her hands, as Samantha watched Patrick pick himself up off the floor, rubbing his jaw slightly from where Greg had hit him.

"In order to make antibodies, we first have to subject the body to a form of pain, in this case, electronic stimulus" replied one of the scientists who was nearby to them. "It was an idea we had been developing back at Grey's Pharmaceuticals, that using electronic stimulus would energise the antibodies, and generate more of them for use in medical development" replied another scientist, as they carefully took the blood samples which had been extracted from Samantha during the experiment, placing them under a microscope for analysis, as all around them multiple computer screens showed facts, figures and formulars being analysed in vast qualities. "Why does my head feel like it's on fire" replied Samantha, as she vigorously rubbed her forehead, hoping that this would stop the pain from hurting here. When this didn't help, Samantha instead just placed a hand on her forehead, and shut her eyes tight, as if suffering from the effect of brain freeze.

472

After the experiment had stopped, Samantha had suddenly developed a very stiff headache, as she gulped down the water Greg had given to her in one go, as if Samantha was somehow involved in some sort of weird pint drinking contest at a bar. The water itself felt fresh and clean, and seemed to help immensely with Samantha's recovery from her latest trauma. "I will be honest, I did expect that to happen" replied Patrick, as he pointed to his rather red jaw, where Greg had punched it a few minutes earlier. This was shortly followed by an uproar a few seconds later, as one of the scientists pointed at the screen and said, "look, Samantha's blood is producing antibodies against Covid; the experiment worked; we have enough here to replicate a cure". The room as a whole immediately began to clap and cheer, as Samantha was patted on the back over and over again, which made her feel even weaker than she had been beforehand.

The happiness however was short lived, as sudden banging sounds and mixed shouting were coming from the direction of outside in the street, beyond the hospital doors, making Samantha's eyes jerked open suddenly in surprise. They all fell suddenly silent, as Greg went to open the door to the science lab, to find out what was going on. They all didn't have long to wait however, as the walkie talkie that Patrick had clipped to his belt suddenly crackled into life, as Andrew's voice came out of it, sounding sharp and desperate like in nature. "Science team from ground protection, ambush in progress, all units withdraw to base immediately"! Even as Andrew spoke, they could all hear the unmistakable sounds of gun fire in the background. Everyone in the room seemed to have frozen where they stood, as they all tried to take in what was happening; however, it was Patrick that spoke first.

"Team, move out; secure those samples now, and then get the hell out of here" exclaimed Patrick to the room at large, as everyone seemed to act on his words at once. "Sam, you're with me" replied Greg, as he raced back to Samantha, pulled her up onto her feet, and began to half carry, half walk her towards the exit, pushing the door open with his hand. "Get Samantha to safety Greg, I'm counting on you" replied Patrick, as

Greg nodded at Patrick to show that he had understood him, as Patrick helped the other scientists quickly parcel the blood samples into solid protective metal cases with foam interiors. Outside in the corridor, the gun fire could now be heard more clearly, as Greg helped Samantha limp along, as she still felt very weak from the experiment inside the science lab. Both Greg and Samantha got as far as the hospital doors, before a sight of carnage met their eyes, as they both could see what was going on in the street outside.

Outside the hospital in the street, chaos reigned supreme; the squad of soldiers lead by Andrew, had managed to form a protective ring around the hospital, but were now fighting tooth and nail, against what looked like an entire army of people, young and old. They were all wearing what looked like caveman type outfits, most of their skin was exposed, with only their private parts being covered up. They were all caring speers, and some even had bows and arrows which they were firing at the soldiers in Andrew's team with scaringly pinpoint accuracy. "What took you so long, come on" shouted Andrew over the noise of the gunfire, as he helped Greg hoist Samantha onto his shoulders, and then run with her at full speed down a side street, back towards the beach front, where Samantha was in no position to complain about Andrew carrying her down the street like a sack of potatoes.

"My god, I've never seen so many" replied Greg, as he sprinted after Andrew down the alleyway, trying to keep up with him, keeping a close eye on Samantha in the process. "So many of those guys, who the hell are they anyway" replied Andrew, as he rounded another corner, down a back row of houses, where they could still clearly hear the gun fire from where the hospital was, followed by the other soldier's shouting orders at each other. "I've seen them in the town before; I always used to call them the cavemen, because they looked like tribes of some kind living in the hills around the town" replied Greg, as he panted slightly in an attempt to keep up with Andrew, who despite being older than Greg, was still a lot more active, owing to his Special Air Service training. "What about the other soldiers, we can't just leave them" replied Greg, as both he and

Andrew made it to the edge of the town, the Green Goddess coming into view by the beach front.

"There under orders to retreat back to here, there up against men who have bows and arrows, and they are armed with fully automatic weapons; it's no one's guess who's going to win the battle" replied Andrew, as they reached the Green Goddess, Greg clutching a stitch in his chest. "Crickey, I've carried sacks of potatoes that are heavier than Samantha" joked Andrew, as he set her down carefully on the ground, making sure not to bang her head as he propped Samantha up against the Green Goddesses fuel tank. Greg didn't entirely understand how Andrew could be cracking jokes at a time like this, but even so, he couldn't help but crack a small laugh all the same. "Look, here comes the science team" replied Greg, as he pointed over to the row of house on the beach front, as half a dozen people in white lab coats flanked by Patrick, came sprinting across the beech towards them, some of them carrying metal cases, which contained Samantha's blood samples.

Then over the sudden blast of sound, action and adrenaline rushes they were all having, came a new sound; a sudden loud ping sound, echoed from the sonar machine onboard one of the four-wheel drive vehicles. It sounded again; this time clear and precise; as if someone had dropped a stone into the water by the beach front. "No way; no way" responded Andrew, as Greg suddenly realised what the sound from the sonar machine was. "That can't be a" started Greg, but Andrew finished his sentence for him; "Submarine". With dramatic suddenness, there was an almighty roar, followed by a large spray of water, which washed up the shoreline in a mini tsunami style wave, as a jet black coloured American Navy Los Angeles class submarine broke the surface, its conning tower rising high above the waterline. Everyone immediately covered their arms over there's heads and faces, fearing that a wall of water was going to slam into them where they were.

The submarine floated slowly to a stop, as Greg and Andrew stared at it, not daring to believe that an American submarine had just popped up out of the Locke in front of them, looking as if it was too big to be allowed. Greg swore at the top of his voice, which caused Samantha to regain conciseness and scream out in alarm on catching sight of the submarine floating in the middle of the Locke. "Wow, that's a submarine, what's that doing here" asked Samantha, as Patrick and the other scientists reached them, all stopping suddenly at the sight of the submarine. "Bang on queue" called out Patrick, who didn't seem to be bothered by the fact that an American submarine had just popped up out of the water right in front of them all. There was a sudden clanging noise, and then a thud of metal, as a man's head popped up above the conning tower on the submarine.

The man on top of the conning tower had a clean-shaven face with short cropped hair under his cap, which made him look as though he was a man in his late forty's. "Patrick, is that you down there" called the man, who looked as if he was the captain of the submarine, speaking with a broad American accent. "Yes sir, glad you can make it; we have it; we have the vaccine we've been working towards for months" called back Patrick, waving the metal case he was carrying above his head, so that the submarine captain could see it from where he was standing. "That's awesome Patrick, let's get you all onboard, you all look like death warmed up" replied the captain, as they all looked tired and weary from what they had all been through. From behind them came a sudden hammering of footfalls, as the rest of the soldiers came running to meet them, some of them covered in blood and the like, as they all came level to Samantha, Patrick and Andrew.

"Sir, all enemies have been neutralised, but we may have encountered a problem" replied one of the soldiers, as Patrick looked back at them, curious to know what exactly this problem was that the soldiers spoke of. "Good work team, who were those guys" asked Patrick, as Greg looked up from where he had been sitting next to Samantha, who was still looking a little shaken from her ordeal. "The cavemen, I've been trying to fight them off for weeks now, but they've never been out in these numbers before; someone must be leading them" replied Greg, but he was cut off by the suddenness of the situation. A loud bang ripped through the air, followed by a sudden whistling sound, as a bullet flew with lightning speed into Patrick's shoulder, knocking him to the ground. Patrick began to gasp and yell in pain, whilst clutching his arm for support, as everyone spun wildly around, looking to see what had happened.

And to their complete horror, they all saw Helen Dukes standing a few feet away by one of the four-wheel drive vehicles, a machine gun raised to her shoulder, having just fired the bullet that had knocked Patrick to the ground. Helen's face had streaks of blood running down it, and her usual smart blouse and skirt were splashed with dirt and mud, as if she'd just been on a physical assault course. "Stay where you are traitor; hands in the air, all of you; and you" Helen barked at everyone, including the submarine Captain, as they all raised their hands up above their heads, all except Samantha, who was still very weak, but still looked terrified all the same. "So, you thought you would go behind my back did you, Patrick" snarled Helen, slowly and deliberately, as if she was enjoying the situation very much, but with cold hearted malice in her voice as she spoke.

"You were vent on destroying this world, I was vent on saving it; that's why I came up with my plan; the future starts here" replied Patrick, as he gasped on every word, trying to conceal the fact of how much pain he was really in. "Idiot man, my plan was to keep this country in check; I knew all along what you were doing, but you've led me right to what I want" replied Helen, as she slowly walked forwards, still making sure that she had the entire group where she wanted them, and thoroughly enjoying the power play over them all. "Place the blood samples case at my feet, don't try anything smart now" replied Helen, as one of the scientists broke away from the group, and carefully laid the samples at Helen's feet, before backing away, keeping his hands in the air as he did so. "And I think I'll take Samantha as well, just for a bit of insurance; get up Samantha, and stand over here next to me"!

Helen said this last part with a slight bark in her voice, as she raised the machine gun menacingly towards the others. "No, she can't, she's not strong enough" yelled out Greg, but Andrew threw up a hand up to stop Greg in mid-sentence. "Let her go son, there's nothing you can do; we'll get her back for you, I promise" replied Andrew, as Samantha, still feeling very weak, struggled to her feet, as Greg suddenly observed Samantha do a very strange thing. The set of keys to the Green Goddess suddenly fell out of her pocket onto the floor, as she turned to look at Greg with a small smile on her face. "Ten four, good buddy" said Samantha, as Greg's eyes suddenly widened in shock, as he realised what Samantha was telling him to do, and from what he could tell, Helen had no idea what Samantha was telling Greg to do. "No talking; walk towards me; slowly" commanded Helen, keeping the machine gun trained on Samantha as she went.

Whilst Helen's soul attention was focused completely on Samantha, Greg seized his chance, lunging forwards and then retreating back again quickly, with the fallen keys in his hands. Ten four good buddy, was a term used in the trucking world as a way of saying, 'I'm ok'. Samantha hadn't given a wink or a nudge, but knowing what his fiancée was like, Greg now had a solid plan formulated in his head. "What was that all about" asked Andrew under his breath to Greg, but Greg only answered under his breath with the response, "when I say the word fingers, stuff your fingers in your ears". Patrick and Andrew quickly tried to pass this message around to the others, without trying to alert Helen to what they were doing. However, Helen's attention was focused entirely on Samantha, so she didn't seem to notice the low-level resistance that was popping up right under her nose.

"You must be so afraid right now Samantha, unable to do anything, and with no help from your friends either" replied Helen, as Samantha drew level to her, a look of ill content now etched all over her face. "Hardly, I've been through a lot in this new world, and I don't think much of your new empire" replied Samantha, as Helen laughed, but it sounded more like an evil cackle than anything else. "Oh, I have great plans for this new world, this country will be great again, but in a new image, a better image; democracy never worked in this country anyway" replied Helen, as Samantha bit back, "I'd never follow you, you're just sick; you wiped out billions of people, just so you could have your own little world". It was a mark of how much Samantha hated every bone in Helen's body, and Helen feeling that she could walk all over humanity, which made both women feel like goddesses amongst insects.

"This world was never anyone's, with less humans, the planet will repair; climate change will be a thing of the past; wars will never be fought; and humanity can start anew, with me as their leader" replied Helen, as this time, it was Samantha's return to laugh. "You're just mental, we were already on our way to achieving those things" replied Samantha, remembering seeing news articles on climate and peace summits being broadcast in private homes through television sets. Helen suddenly looked angry and jabbed the machine gun straight into Samantha's forehead, as the two women faced each other. Samantha felt the cold metal against her skin, but she stood her ground all the same, feeling that showing fear to Helen would never be an option. Samantha felt that if she was going to die here and now after all that she'd been through, then she was safe in the knowledge that her blood would cure future generations to come.

"You're nothing to me, you stuck up little bitch, if you were anyone else I would" replied Helen, but she suddenly stopped as a loud cry rent the air. "Fingers" shouted Greg, as he placed his elbow against one ear, and his finger in the other, pressing the lock button on the Green Goddess set of keys. Samantha only just had enough time to raise her own hands to her ears, as Helen suddenly looked at Greg, and saw them all with their hands over their ears. "What the" exclaimed Helen, but the air was suddenly full of a gut wrenching, ear-splitting noise, as the Green Goddesses air horn, which Samantha had remembered nearly going deaf from back at RAF North Lakes, rang through the empty silent air, echoing off the nearby buildings. Helen screamed loudly, as she dropped the machine gun into the sand on the beach, staggering backwards in pain from the sound of the noise.

Greg let go of the button, as everyone reacted at the same time. "Come on, get moving, everyone onboard now" shouted the submarine captain from the top of the conning tower, as he too had been watching the situation, and had the common sense to place his hands over his ears. With all of her remaining strength, Samantha turned and sprinted for the open water, as the others followed suit. Helen hadn't taken long to recover from the shock however, but Andrew had got there first. Smack! With a sound like a whip crack, Andrew punched Helen squarely in the face, knocking her to the ground again, as he stood on the machine gun to prevent Helen from picking it up, whilst the others scattered for the open loch water, swimming towards the submarine in the middle of the loch before them. The air was now filled the sounds of splashing, as they all tried to escape, helped along by the submarines captain calling encouragement to them all.

"Andrew; get on the submarine; get the others out of here now; go" shouted Patrick, who had managed to stagger to his feet, still clutching his arm where Helen had fired a bullet into it, as blood stained his suit and blazer from the wound it had made. "I'm not leaving you behind Pat, your injured" yelled back Andrew, but Patrick shook his head at Andrew in defiance. "No, someone has to take care of Helen; now go" shouted Patrick, as Andrew seemed to be puzzled for a few seconds about what Patrick was trying to do; but he soon realised, that arguing with Patrick wasn't an option. "Don't dawdle, I'll see you onboard" replied Andrew, as he gripped Patrick's arm, to show that he understood, as Andrew sprinted for the water's edge, helping a struggling Samantha, who was still very weak. Wincing slightly, Patrick began to limp away, not towards the water, but instead towards the Green Goddess, a look of understanding in his eyes.

It must have made sense to Patrick, as Helen soon recovered from being punched a few seconds later, catching sight of Patrick as he scrambled towards the Green Goddess. With her face full of malice, and the air of an angry lioness ready to attack, Helen scrambled to her feet, grabbing the machine gun as she went. Patrick was less than a foot away from the Green Goddesses full tank, when there was a loud bang, as Helen fired another bullet, this time hitting Patrick in the leg. Patrick yelled out again, as he fell to the ground, felling the blood now flowing out his leg, as well as his shoulder. "You are a traitor; a liar; and you have betrayed me, Patrick Devises" replied Helen, as she drew level with him, as Patrick painfully turned himself over onto his back, now with his head propped up against the Green Goddesses fuel tank, panting heavily and coughing slightly, as he felt blood pounding in his ears.

"Don't worry, I resign" choked Patrick, as Helen raised the machine gun to her shoulder, directing the barrel straight at Patrick's forehead. "Does the condemned have anything to say before his sentence is carried out" asked Helen in a sickly-sweet voice, as Patrick suddenly raised a hand upwards and grabbed a small black pipe to the side of the fuel tank. "Ka-boom" replied Patrick, as he gave it a sharp tug, whilst at exactly the same time, Helen pulled the trigger on the machine gun. The small black pipe in question, was the fuel line that connected the fuel tank to the engine on the Green Goddess, as thick yellow coloured diesel came spraying out, soaking both Patrick and Helen all over with diesel, as Helen's bullet made contact with Patrick's head, killing his instantly. Helen had only a fraction of a second to swear out loud, before there was an almighty explosion, as she was first incinerated and then blasted into atoms.

The resulting explosion, caused one of the loudest bangs any of them had heard so far, as everyone who was now in the water swimming towards the submarine, saw the flash of light and the large mushroom cloud originating from where the Green Goddess had been, as it went soaring up high into the air, looking as if a small nuclear bomb had just detonated on the shoreline. Debris of all shapes and sizes now began to rain down on them, as they were forced to dive under the water, to prevent the items from striking them from the air. Andrew, who was the fittest out of all of them, managed to reach the submarine first, and was the first one to see what was really happening on the shoreline. The smouldering remains of the Green Goddess now sat on fire, burning away, knowing that they would never be extinguished, acting as a permanent memorial to the Green Goddess, and Patrick's legacy.

The force of the explosion had also been felt onboard the submarine, as the shockwave from the explosion, made the submarine sink downwards slightly in the water, and then bob back up again a second or so later. "Everyone out of the water, quickly" shouted Andrew and the submarine Captain in unison, as they began to see large chunks of debris falling from the sky, making whistling noises as they descended, followed by loud splashes, as the items of debris splashed down into the water, before sinking below the surface. Most of them had chosen to dive under the water, but one of the scientists hadn't heard the warning in time, and was struck by a section of burning fuel tank, as he cried out in pain, disappearing below the waterline. "Where's Samantha, can you see her" asked Andrew in a hurry, as he scanned the water in front of him for a sign of a head full of brunette hair.

As soon as Andrew had spoken, Samantha suddenly broke the surface, gasping for air and coughing at the same time, as she spurted out a long spout of water from her mouth. "Sam, grab the line, here" shouted Andrew, as he threw a length of rope into the water, which struck Samantha as it landed in the water. "Sorry" shouted Andrew, as Samantha managed to grab hold of it, as she was dragged through the water towards Andrew, who proceeded to pull her up the side of the submarine, where she finally collapsed on the submarines deck coughing up water, whilst being soaked to the skin at the same time. "What happened" spluttered Samantha, as Andrew and Greg helped her to her feet, whilst the submarine captain wrapped a warm dry blanket around her, as Samantha felt as if she was suddenly inside a tumble dryer from the verrucosity of the blanket that was now being rubbed up and down her body.

"Patrick blew up the Green Goddess, looks like he took Helen with him, brave sod" replied Greg, as Samantha seemed unabashed, glad and hopeful that once again she had survived another traumatic experience. "I'm sorry, I know he was a friend" replied Samantha, who knew that Patrick had been a friend of Andrew's for a long time, but Andrew seemed to understand Samantha completely. "It's ok; he's a hero in my book, and that is what matters; plus, Helen is gone now; she can't hurt anyone else anymore" replied Andrew, as Samantha stood there for a second, watching the burning remains of what had been her mobile home away from home for months, and a reliable and trusty steed before that in the old world. "I'm sorry he's gone, he did so much for us" replied Samantha, as Andrew placed a hand on her shoulder, in what he hoped was a comforting sort of way.

"I know Sam, but what matters is that he stopped Helen for us, and now the country can pick itself up and hopefully get better again" replied Andrew, as he watched the other surviving soldiers and scientists being fished out of the water by submariners wearing US Navy uniforms. "Captain, permission to get underway as soon as possible" called Andrew to the submarine Captain, who had begun to climb up the ladder on the conning tower. "Once all souls are onboard and settled, I shall give the order" replied the submarines Captain, as Andrew nodded to show that he'd understood him. "We've got a quarantine chamber onboard, you'll all need to be kept confined to it for the duration of the journey" said the captain, as the last of the soldier's and scientist were helped onboard, being wrapped into warm blankets. "I wonder where there taking us" asked Samantha curiously, aiming this question more to herself than anyone else.

"Well, I'm no expect, but I'm guessing that the American's must have something to do with it" replied Greg, in a slightly jokey type voice. Samantha sniggered slightly at Greg's little joke, before allowing him to help her to her feet, as they all began to descend in through a hatch on the deck of the submarine. Samantha took one last look around her, wondering when she would next see daylight again, before then climbing down the ladder, allowing Andrew to close it behind her, having just come through it himself. "All main hatch's secure sir, ready for diving stations" said one of the submariners into a radio set on the wall, as the captain's voice came back on the submarines loud speaker system. "Diving stations, diving stations" came the captain's voice, as Samantha was suddenly jolted by the sound of the claxon alarm, and the fact that other submariners were now hurrying around them.

Outside in the open air, the submarine began to dive, slowly disappearing into the water, as it moved slowly forwards in a wide arc, turning itself around to head back out up the estuary towards the open sea. Back onboard the submarine, Samantha, Andrew, Greg and the others, were all directed towards what looked like a large compression tank with a heavy round thick door, which was so bulky, that it needed two submariners to open and shut it. "Standard practice, but you'll be in here for the next two weeks, as we need to make sure you're not carrying anything like Covid" explained the submariner, who had helped Samantha down the conning tower ladder into the submarine. "Two weeks in here" exclaimed Samantha in shock, but the others around them didn't seem to be bothered by this, as even though with all of the soldiers and scientists, plus Andrew, Greg and Samantha inside the chamber, there was still enough room to move around comfortably.

The chamber itself was quite comfortable, with bunk beds, chairs, and with a hatch in the wall where food and drink could be inserted into the chamber, without coming into contact with the outside crew. "Don't worry, it's standard practice; the trip itself is about fourteen days long, but you won't miss much, being under water and the like" replied the submariner, cracking a little smile. Even Andrew couldn't help but crack a smile at this as well, even though he had been more used to working on the ground, rather than at sea. "We really appreciate it guys, thanks for coming up for us" replied Greg, as the submariner gave him the thumbs up, before closing the chamber door on them, locking it tight, just to make sure that it was completely contaminant free. "Just when I thought things couldn't get any stranger" replied Samantha, as she turned back to face the others, having watched the submariners walk away into the next room.

There were now only eight of them in that room, but still not feeling squashed in the slightest, but at least for once on their journey, they were as safe as they could possibly be. "Oh, and I meant to say Sam, try not to pass wind in a place like this, it travels quicker through the air in one of these chambers you know" replied Andrew, giving Samantha a small wink, as the others roared with laughter. Samantha giggled slightly too, but then felt that the one thing that she really needed right now, was a good night's sleep. "You sleep soundly now little lady" were the last words that Samantha heard, as her head rested gently on the floor, and her eyes began to droop. Samantha would sleep soundly now, as she knew that for the first time in weeks, she was properly safe. No one was going to hurt her, or try and do anything too her at all now; and as she slept, flashing images kept flashing across her mind.

Leaving Lillington, the plane crash, finding Julie, finding Diana, killing Edward Fitzgerald, escaping from Grey's Pharmaceuticals, along with seeing Brian's face and the others on Mile End Farm. Then Samantha's mind wandered to Fredrick, and whether he'd managed to fly to the Isle of Wight, to set up a new home there. Realising she owed Fredrick a lot, not just for the Green Goddess, but also for pointing her onto the right track in the first place. Positive and negative thoughts kept Samantha sane over the next few weeks, but she also would chat to the others as well, wondering what lay ahead of them all. "Of course, I'm guessing it's some kind of island somewhere" replied Andrew, bringing Samantha out of a daydream she had been having, eight days into their quarantine onboard the submarine. "What makes you say that" asked Samantha, as Andrew continued on with his speech.

"Glad you asked me that Sam; well, you'd have to be separated away from everyone else, so doing it on a mainland continent landmass would be a bit difficult, and it could be a combination of different governments with different agents and groups of people with skills and the like, so it would be like rebuilding society anew". The others all seemed to nod in agreement to this, as Samantha thought through would Andrew had said, before replying, "but I'm a trucker driver, you wouldn't need those sorts of skills on islands or in small groups". "Well, you never know Sam, you never know" replied Andrew, as an announcement, came over the loudspeaker, echoing slightly within the inside the isolation chamber, as though they were all sat inside a giant church bell tower. "Attention all personal, shift change in three hours; attention all personal, shift change in three hours".

"Usual drill, you could set your watch by this lot" replied Andrew, as the others chuckled again, whilst Andrew reached over to the wall and crossed off another day on the calendar he'd pinned up on the side of the chamber. "Six more days in here, getting through it" replied Samantha, rubbing her forehead, hoping that the day's couldn't come fast enough, wanting to be out of the chamber once and for all. But the fact still remained that Samantha's next great adventure, was only just around the corner, Greg always being there beside her for moral support, giving encouragement when Samantha felt as if things were getting too much for her. "Attention all crew members, docking in two minutes, repeat, docking at T.C in two minutes" came the loudspeakers voice over the intercom system, as Samantha woke with a start, having been dozing on one of the bunkbeds, a blanket wrapped up around her as she slept.

She looked over at the calendar on the wall, and saw that it was now day fourteen inside the chamber, and that there was a steady vibration coming from all around her, as if the submarine was floating on the surface, dealing with heavy waves that were smashing against the sides of the submarine. "Looks like it's going to be a bit rough" replied Andrew, showing that he had guts of steel, as Samantha felt her insides squirm slightly from the rocking motion of the waves. Samantha had sadly never been the best on boats it had to be said, and it had not been this rough since the start of the journey fourteen days ago, when they were moored on the loch outside Clyde. "I need a bag" suddenly blurted out Samantha, as in gentlemen style fashion, Greg immediately presented one in front of her. "Thanks" was about the only word that Samantha got out, before she chucked up inside the bag, feeling her gut ease a little as she did so, whilst her mouth felt wet and sickly.

"Better out than in eh lass" replied Andrew, cuffing her on the shoulder, making Samantha chuck up into the bag again. "Get it all up now Sam, you're going to ok" replied Greg, who looked a little green himself, as the others wrinkled their noses slightly at the sight of Samantha chucking up into the sick bag. It was fortunate that none of the others had chucked up, as owing to the strict quarantine rules onboard the submarine, all items had to be kept inside the chamber itself, unless it could be flushed down the toilet of course. "You're sealing that bag yourself mind, I maybe a gentleman, but I'm not a nursemaid" joked Greg, who was hoping that he wouldn't smell of sick when they disembarked. "Don't worry babe, I hear you" replied Samantha, as she wiped her mouth with a towel, before sealing the sick bag up by folding it over and over, until it could be placed in the palm of her hand.

The order to dive the submarine a few minutes later, couldn't have been a more welcome sound to Samantha's ears, as the rocking motion finally stopped, and everything become still again. Feeling quite weak because of her sickness episode, Samantha had laid back down on the bunk bed, and closed her eyes, little realising that she had fallen asleep again due to her incredibly frail state. To her great surprise however, when she woke up again, it wasn't to the inside of a quarantine chamber onboard the submarine, but instead to what looked like a Chinese massage parlour, with a slight breeze blowing in through the open door, with the soundtrack of gentle waves washing up on a sandy beach.

CHAPTER TWENTY NINE

Tremon

Both the floor and the ceiling were decorated with the most beautiful and striking artwork that Samantha had ever seen in her life, whilst a strong smell of sea air was wafting in from the open-door way. It put Samantha in mind of a Caribbean or tropical island beach somewhere in world, with brightly coloured sand and crystal-clear blue water; like the sort of advertisement, you would see pinned up on a local bus stop in the ordinary town centre for a quick holiday getaway. Samantha lay on the bed, feeling so warm and comfortable, that she could very easily drifted back off to sleep again. Now however, she felt wide awake, feeling a burning desire to investigate and explore this strange new place. Pulled herself to her feet with ease, Samantha suddenly became aware of the fact that she only wearing her underwear, which made her jump backwards in alarm.

Fearing that some sort of foul play was at work here, she looked around for her clothes she had been wearing on the submarine, but couldn't find them anywhere. As if by a stroke of luck however, she suddenly saw what looked like a fluffy dark green dressing gown, which was hanging on the wall besides the open door. Samantha raced over to it and slipped it on, hoping against hope, that she could use it to get to another building where there would be better clothes to wear, but still thinking that it would be a little strange walking along a street wearing nothing but a fluffy dark green dressing gown. Walking slowly out of the doorway, Samantha found herself on a small veranda, overlooking the most beautiful and sunny background she had ever seen in her life. It was so picture perfect, it was almost as if someone had just taken a photo of it, and then printed it out on all of the holiday pamphlets throughout the world.

"They don't make them like that in Britain" Samantha said out loud to herself, feeling the slight humidity hit her, as she soaked up the view all around her. "No, I suspect they probably don't in the United Kingdom" came a sudden voice to Samantha's right, which sounded very friendly and welcoming. Samantha let out a small scream and jumped out of her skin, clutching at her chest for support, whilst nervously pulling at the dressing gown, hoping that it hadn't come undone when she had jumped backwards in alarm at the sound of the stranger's voice. "Hello Samantha, why don't you come and sit down, I've made you some tea" said the strangers voice again, as Samantha spun around, fixing her eyes on a man sitting to her right who had just spoken to her. He was an older looking man, by far looking a lot older than anyone else Samantha had seen so far after Covid had struck.

The strange man put Samantha in mind of Brian Fields back on Mile End Farm, except much more smartly dressed, with an air about him of a man who was very highly educated. If Samantha would have had to made a rough guess, she would have suspected that this man was in his seventies at the very least, as a number of winkles covered this man's face and hands. He was dressed in a smart suit and tie, almost in the same way as a company C.E.O would look, as he spoke with a slow upper-class accent, like someone from a posh well to do society would. The man sitting before her on the chair beside an outdoors coffee table, put Samantha in mind of a senior hospital practitioner, or a posh professor of some kind, although Samantha was at a loss as too what made her made her think about this. "Please, come and sit down" said the man, as he gestured to the chair opposite him at the coffee table between himself and where Samantha was standing.

Samantha was a little wary at first, but slowly moved forwards and took a seat, as the old man pushed a cup of tea in her direction. "You need to drink up, you will get heat exhaustion and dehydration if not" said the old man, as Samantha took a sip of the tea. It wasn't too hot or too cold, but just perfect. It was certainly true, as Samantha had started to sweat under the dressing gown, even though she was in the shade on the veranda. "Sorry, who are you, what is this place" replied Samantha, as the old man chuckled slightly. "My apologies Samantha, where are my manners these days; my name is Professor Quinton Tremon, Head of The Company, T.C for short you know" replied the old man, as Samantha suddenly had a flashback to when she had been on Mile End Farm of Doctor Victor saying about there being a higher power involved, when it came to the company branding itself as Grey's Pharmaceuticals.

Professor Tremon held out his wrinkled hand at that moment, offering it to Samantha, as she nervously took it, and gave it a quick shake. "Ah, you're wondering where here is; well, let me tell you, this is the company island" replied Professor Tremon, as Samantha still looked a little non plussed at this, wondering if perhaps this was some sort of a dream she was having, or maybe Samantha had managed to go into some sort of comatose state whilst onboard the submarine. Professor Tremon continued to look at Samantha, as Samantha continued to stare back at Professor Tremon, not daring to believe that he was even real, or even possible. "I see you have had a long journey, and your friends are anxious to see you again; but I must give you the orientation talk first, before we continue" explained Professor Tremon, as he cleared his throat, before continuing on with his explanation.

"Some time ago now, the company received intelligence reports that something very large and very dangerous was loaming just over the horizon; you see, a pharmaceutical company in Wuhan, China, had begun medical research trials to find a cure for the common cold. As you know, so many people have been forced to take sick days every year because of it, so having a cure for it would have been the answer to all of our prayers; unfortunately, a rogue scientist weaponised it, and instead succeeded in turning it into a killer virus, which as you know turned into a pandemic and wiped out ninety eight percent on the world's population. So, the company had to act on this new information; we had agents inside every major secret service on the planet, the C.I.A, MI5, G.R.U and so forth. Our contact in MI5 was the man you knew as Patrick, and he had recruited your fiancée Greg as well, knowing of your rather special abilities".

At the mention of Greg's name, Samantha sat bolt upright, realising that for the first time that she hadn't seen him anywhere since waking up on the island. "Is he ok; I mean, he was recruited to MI5" replied Samantha, as Professor Tremon smiled slightly, understanding Samantha's curiosity to her new surroundings and willingness to learn the whole truth of the old world's demise. "Greg did say that you were a smart one when he first came onto the programme; and yes, it was our duty to save as many lives as possible, but without arousing suspicion; as you suspected when you thought that Greg had abandoned you after Covid had struck and begun to take effect on the people all around you". Professor Tremon finished speaking, before taking another swig of tea, as it was now Samantha's turn to speak, questions exploding inside of her like brightly coloured fireworks.

"So, if you were trying to save people, what was Helen Dukes doing" asked Samantha, as Professor Tremon let out another chuckle, but it was a friendly chuckle, rather than a cackle. "A greedy public servant to say the least; Helen Dukes was nothing more than a power grabber, nothing more; Helen Dukes was no more of a threat to our plans, than an ant would be to a flamethrower" explained Professor Tremon, treating Samantha's question as more of a throwaway one, rather than one to be taken seriously. "What you have to understand Samantha, is that I was Patrick's boss; I ordered Patrick to allow Helen into the programme, letting her believe that she was really in charge of it all, whilst Patrick could save as many lives as he could" replied Professor Tremon, whilst Samantha remembered back to seeing the inside of Grey's Pharmaceuticals and its human experimentations that they were conducting within its walls.

"But Grey's Pharmaceuticals was torturing people, using them as lab rats and all sorts; that's not human, that's barbaric" said Samantha, feeling her anger boiling to the surface, as Professor Tremon took a deep breath, knowing that Samantha had clearly developed a form of post-traumatic stress from her experiences. "Samantha, what if I told you know, that every scientific advancement over the last fifty years has been done to us as humans; evolution Samantha, that is what's key here; humanity has survived; we have won against nature" explained Professor Tremon, in the same air as someone would explain the inner workings of a kitchen whisk to an over excited nine-year-old child. "But people died, my family died; my father, mother, best friends, they all died from Covid" exclaimed Samantha, feeling a little bubbling anger boiling to the surface, feeling her face turn a little red from the pain of it.

Professor Tremon appeared not react to Samantha's outburst, or change his facial expression in any way at all. Instead, he leaned back in his chair and said, "we did not create Covid Samantha, your family and friends died at the hands of something that had been a supercharged virus from nature itself; pandemics have been going on around this planet for millions of years; I'm sorry your family is dead, but you're not, and your anatomy is fuelling our research into the future in ways no one could have ever believed possible before" explained Professor Tremon, again becoming both excited and saddened in the sound of his voice, as he tried to imagine what Samantha could have been through in her time back in the UK after Covid. It was certainly true that Samantha's emotions were all over the place since leaving Lillington many weeks ago, but the pain of loss hadn't quite fully sunk in with her.

"You don't know what you have done Samantha, you're not just a survivor, you're a thriver too; after you'd landed on the island, we sent the blood samples that were collected from you for analysis, and as you know, we have now managed to create a cure, which we will now be shipping out to every country, whilst undergoing a vaccination programme for other survivors against Covid; you saved the world Samantha; you; you did that" exclaimed Professor Tremon sounding almost buoyant as he said it, like a scientist who had just solved an age old mystery. "You know nothing about me, I mean, I'm a truck driver from Hertfordshire, not some superhero" replied Samantha a little hot and bothered, feeling that a big deal was being made about her for no reason whatsoever. Professor Tremon sat back slightly, allowing Samantha to vent her emotions to him, looking more like a professional counsellor than a professor of medicine.

"We know everything about you; your Samantha Bonham, twenty-six years old from Lillington in Hertfordshire, United Kingdom; you worked as a lorry driver where you had a truck called Betsie, which later become known as the Green Goddess" replied Professor Tremon, as if he was reading Samantha's details from a file pulled out of a filling cabinet. At the sound of the words 'Green Goddess', Samantha spat out a bit of her tea that she was trying to drink at that very moment. "What, how, when; how did you know about the Green Goddess" replied Samantha, as she spluttered on every word that she spoke, the tea having gone down the wrong way. Professor Tremon had in fact coped some of the spilt tea on his smart suit, but had found a way of either masking it, or else wasn't fazed by the fact that the contents of Samantha's mouth were now on his nice clean suit.

"We interviewed Greg and Andrew when they arrived, and they told us all about you, and about how you found them, fighting in the Battle of Askham, whilst also being on Mile End Farm with Brian and the others, and how you built the Green Goddess alongside Police Constable Julie Guard and Corporal Fredrick Loose". As Professor Tremon spoke, Samantha seemed to deflate slightly, as she remembered what had happened to Julie and the others, as if the bottom had suddenly fallen out of her stomach. "You need sleep and rest, this is your new home now Samantha, you and Greg can easily get married here, as we have jobs and work for you all; we have our own economy, a school, a hospital, a small police service who is fair and incorrupt; plus, I think you would fit in quite well moving goods around the island on our small railway line, and also we are looking into getting trucks as well".

Professor Tremon again spoke with positivity in his voice, as he placed down his cup of tea, before finishing by saying, "the future starts here Samantha, as it said so on the pamphlet that Greg was given, so he knew where to come; but he gave it to you, knowing you would do whatever it took to work it out, and you did; you did". There was a brief silence, which was followed by Samantha looking all around her, wondering what to do next, a little lost by her surroundings. Samantha eventually sighed, thinking of what she had been through, and then gulped her tea done in one gulp. "If this is where the future starts, what role do you play in it, if you don't mind me asking that" asked Samantha in what she hoped was a polite and unoffending voice, as Professor Tremon waved a finger in the air, as he had been wondering when Samantha was going to ask this particular question.

"That Samantha my dear, is a jolly good question; well, I suppose you could say, I'm the president of this island, but my board of directors make the rules that the rest of the island live by, just like a democratic parliament; and the people always vote to say who is on the board of directors, and who is not; we have no corruption here, everyone is family". Professor Tremon finished speaking, as Samantha's mood seemed to brighten, with the thought of somewhere away from danger and suffering, knowing that the people around them had been handpicked to help rebuild the world as a whole. "And; we live here; we don't leave the island" asked Samantha in a curious voice, wondering where the catch was going to be. This has been the burning question that she had longed to ask, after all, Samantha didn't want to think that she had travelled all the way here, just to find out that she was a prisoner on the island.

"Leave, why would you want to leave my dear; the world out there is dangerous as you know, but it will heal, and we can start all over again; and we can start to do that, right here" explained Professor Tremon, pointing his finger out to the wider view around them. Samantha considered this point very carefully, before she replied, "but what about the other waves of Covid, surely there will be others to contend with". "Well, that I can safely say, is something that is already being researched into right now, as your blood will provide the answer to that problem" replied Professor Tremon, as Samantha seemed to relax a little, knowing that she wasn't about to subjected to inhuman practices. Professor Tremon meanwhile had suddenly noticed a group of people who were coming towards them along the beach front. At their head was Andrew, who waved as he approached, catching sight of Samantha and Professor Tremon as he went.

"Good afternoon, Professor, glad to see your awake Sam" said Andrew happily, as Professor Tremon gave Andrew a small bow in acknowledgement. "A very good afternoon to you Andrew, I was hoping you would show up soon, as it's time for you to take Samantha on her tour of the island" replied Professor Tremon, as Andrew smiled at them both. "Erm, if it's all the same to everyone, I think I shall be doing that task, seeing as that's my fiancée you're talking about" came Greg's comical voice from behind Andrew. Without pausing to think, Samantha leapt up out of her seat and locked both of her arms around Greg, as if she had never seen him before. "Welcome to paradise babes; I did say I would get you a honeymoon somewhere, and it looks like we've found it" replied Greg, who had taken a quick step backwards after Samantha had locked her arms around him.

"I'm so glad to see you" replied Samantha, who began snogging Greg on the lips, with the others looking on a little embarrassed. Professor Tremon however, was the first to break the awkward silence between them all, as he stood up and said in a cheerful voice, "well, I shall leave you all too it; I have things I must be getting on with, but I hope to see you all again soon". "Thank you, Professor, I don't know how we could have thanked you enough for bringing us here" replied Greg, as Professor Tremon waved a hand in front of his face. "Not at all Greg, not at all, you are welcome here, as this is where the future will start after all" replied Professor Tremon, as Samantha, Greg and Andrew all trooped away down the steps of the veranda, onto the paved street before them, the Caribbean style beach front before laid before them as they set off on a slow walk up the street.

It really did look like the sort of background that you would expect to see on a Caribbean holiday destination, with its palm trees on the beach front, bright white sands and crystal blue water. Samantha caught site of the infamous Los Angeles class Submarine which had brought them all to the island, moored up on a jetty in the background, further around the island's coastline. But the most shocking and amazing thing of all, was the hive of activity that was going on all around them. The whole island itself was around the same size as the Scottish Shetland islands were, but it was still incredible how many people seemed to be here, nestled within its confines. Professor Tremon was right; the community on the island was just like a holiday island would be, which filled them all with a positive type vibe, almost as if the islands residences were gearing up for a holiday season.

Other people of all ages and nationalities, walked up and down the streets as they went, greeting them, wishing them well, and busying themselves with their daily tasks. There were shops, a school building, even a small hospital, and all of the other buildings and recourses that Professor Tremon had mentioned to Samantha when she had spoken with him. "What do you think babes, new home for us, better than Lillington at any rate" asked Greg, as he put an arm around Samantha's shoulder, whilst giving it a little squeeze at the same time. "It's defiantly better, I always dreamed of coming to a place like this" replied Samantha, as even Andrew pipped up at this point, "so did I funny enough; here, let me help you with that". Andrew suddenly darted away, as he saw a middle-aged woman in front of a nearby shop front, struggling with a heavy box.

The woman Andrew had helped with the heavy box issued a hurried thank you, as Andrew called over that he would stay there and help out in front of the shop, allowing Greg and Samantha to carry on walking slowly along the main high street. It was almost as if they had never left Lillington, as the high street thrived with activity, just like Lillington had done so back in England. "This is the main high street Sam, and Professor Tremon has even said that we can have a home of our own in the hills around the island" replied Greg, as Samantha looked at him, excitement all over her face. The prospect of owing her own home back in Lillington before Covid had been one where Samantha hadn't had a hope on achieving. Now however, the prospect of having her own home along with Greg, was quite exciting, especially one they could have to whatever they wanted it to be.

"Can we" Samantha smiled, as Greg pulled a funny face at her in mock surprise. "Of course we can babes; well, we just have to build it first" replied Greg, as Samantha giggled slightly, getting the joke. Her face muscles ached slightly, as if felt like Samantha hadn't laughed or smiled within the last million years or so. "We're living down by the bay at the moment in one of the beech huts, while they continue building up resources on the island" explained Greg, as Samantha suddenly pointed out to sea, to a series of buildings on a small neighbouring island to the one they were currently on. "What are all of those buildings over there" asked Samantha, as Greg realised what Samantha was pointing at, as he replied, "ah, that's the Covid research centre, they keep it separated from the rest of us here on the island, as that's where they do medical research and the like".

"It must be off limits to everyone" replied Samantha, as she couldn't see anyone at the windows, or any patrolling guards around the perimeter. "Yeah, it's protected by the sea, no one is allowed to go there unless by direct permission of Professor Tremon" replied Greg, as Samantha nodded to show that she had understood him, feeling that anywhere to do with Covid would have been completely off limits to everyone. "Oh, I almost forgot, I've got a present for you back at the beech hut, when we've finished touring the island" suddenly exclaimed Greg, making Samantha nearly jump out of her skin in shock, wondering what Greg had got for her. They continued to tour the island for the rest of the day, Greg showing Samantha all of the sites, which included a spectacular view out across the ocean, where Samantha could see for miles out to sea under the warm sunny evenings.

Then back down into the town, where Samantha was invited to another meeting with Professor Tremon, to discuss with her about taking part in a medical trial for his Covid research programme on the opposite island, which the locals had come to know as 'Covid Island'. It was also a place where people were sent if they showed any signs of infection, where they would hopefully be cured of their ailments, whilst being kept in isolation to stop other infections which may have presented themselves. "No prizes for guessing how that name come about" Samantha jokingly thought to herself, as she strolled away from the meeting a few hours later, agreeing to be escorted over to the island by boat the following day, where she would begin the medical trials for Professor Tremon and the company. But by far the biggest surprise of the day, came after Samantha had gone back to the beach hut with Greg that evening.

As Greg pushed open the beach hut door, Samantha couldn't help but let out a small scream of delight, whilst clasping her hands over her mouth in the process. Hanging up on the far wall of the beach hut, was a bright white wedding gown, that was almost identical to the one that Samantha had originally been given when she had gone shopping before Covid. "You won't believe how much trouble I had to go to try and get one that was near identical babes, you really don't" replied Greg, in response to Samantha's reaction to her new wedding gown. But

Samantha never even gave Greg a chance to say another word, as she had once again locked her arms around him in a teddy bear like hug, whilst kissing him all over at the same time. Greg did look slightly embarrassed by this, but soon recovered, as her released that there was no one around them at that moment in time.

"Hey, save it for the ceremony will you" jokingly retorted Greg, but it didn't seem to stop Samantha anyhow, as her kissing suddenly turned to tears, as it brought back memories of donating her original dress to Julie in the leadup to Julie's own wedding to Trevor. "Ah babes, I'm so sorry, did it affect you or anything, I know it's a bit much" began Greg, but Samantha cut across him. "No, it's ok babes, it just brought back a few memories from when I was in England". "Mile End Farm, I remember you telling me about giving the dress to Julie for her wedding" replied Greg, as he recalled Samantha telling him about this, whilst they had both been locked inside the isolation chamber onboard the submarine, while on their way to the island. Samantha broke away from Greg, before walking forwards to examine the wedding gown, letting it run through her hands, feeling the softness of the material slipping through her fingers.

It was amazing how clean and fresh it was, considering that it must have been shipped in from elsewhere outside of the island, feeling slightly guilt but yet elated at the same time, about the fact that people had risked their lives to bring Samantha such an amazing gift. "Incredible isn't it, turns out that the captain of the submarine put into another port on the way down here to the island, and the crew went ashore and found a store with one of these gowns inside it" explained Greg, as all that Samantha, Greg, Andrew, along with the surviving soldiers and scientists had remembered was just being locked inside the isolation chamber, with no connection to the outside world at all for the duration of their journey by sea. Then again, Samantha had to admit to herself that she had been out for the count for a matter of days, as her body had tried to heal itself from shock, trauma and the many other things that she and the others had been through getting to the island.

"Aww babes, it's perfect" replied Samantha, who had only seemed to have been half listening, as the vast majority of her attention had been taken up examining her new wedding gown. "I do spoil a girl rotten don't I" replied Greg, as Samantha strode back to him, and gave Greg a bone crushing hug, making Greg slightly worried that Samantha was going to be making him spend the rest of his life seeing an Osteopath, due to Samantha teddy bear style hugs. "Yes, you do babes; you do spoil me rotten" replied Samantha, as she let go of Greg, looking like she was floating on thin air, walking dreamlike on tip toes out of the open doorway, laying herself down on the beach in the early evening sunshine. Greg followed Samantha outside, closing the beach hut door behind him as he went, before then laying himself down next to Samantha on the sand, feeling the water splash up against his toes as the tide washed in and out.

"I've always dreamed on coming to a place like this, ever since I was a child" said Samantha, as she looked up into the sky, which had turned a golden-brown colour due to the late setting sun. "Yes, I thought about maybe retiring out here someday, back in the old days you know" replied Greg, as they both stared up at the sky, as there was suddenly a streak that went across it like a slow-moving shooting star. "What was that" replied Samantha, as she caught site of the shooting star, fearing that another Lillington style plane crash was about to happen on the island. Greg must have sensed the fear in Samantha's voice, as he responded in a reassuring voice, "it's ok, it's only a satellite burning up on re-entry". "But wouldn't we" began Samantha, before she realised that the satellites and space stations floating around the planet did lose their orbit at the end of their lifecycle.

"That's the trouble now after Covid, with no computers or humans left at the control centres to guide them, they'll just keeping dropping out the sky like flies until there's none left" explained Greg, as he pointed up at the trail of light in the sky, which they guessed was the remains of one of the worlds thousands of orbital crafts circling the planet. Greg suddenly felt a smooth sensation down by his hand, and realised that

Samantha was squeezing in a compassionate sort of way. "I wonder if the International Space Station has still got people onboard it" replied Samantha, as they both remembered seeing the news broadcasts on television of the word famous astronauts, embarking and disembarking from the Kennedy space centre onboard the space shuttles and other spacecraft. It put them both in mind of the many thousands of museums across the planet, where the achievements on humanity would live on for decades to come.

"Oh they got them out ok, I remember the news broadcasts saying on the TV about how NASA sent a rocket up to get them all out just before Covid hit" replied Greg, who recalled seeing the news bulletins reporting on the many activates going on around the world. "I'm glad they got out; I couldn't think of a more hellish situation than being stuck up there for the rest of their lives" replied Samantha in a reassured voice, feeling Greg lying beside her on the beach, feeling the soft sand underneath them. As they both watched the sky, the trail of light disappeared across the horizon, glowing fainter and fainter as it went, before disappearing completely. "Another one down eh, mind you, it's giving the atmosphere a good clean up because of all the junk that's falling to earth" replied Greg, who didn't seem worried about the facts that large lumps of metal from space were dropping out the sky all around them.

"I remember my mother was always worried about the bins not being collected on a Friday because the neighbours used to throw out half a street worth of stuff every week" replied Samantha with a slight giggle, not being too worried herself about the possibility of being hit by potentially hostile space junk. For the rest of the evening until darkness fell, Samantha and Greg lay on the sandy beach until it was too dark to see anything, before making their way back to the beach hut, falling asleep the moment their heads hit the pillows on the bed. Greg continued to do his duty as a caring fiancée, thinking about the following weeks ahead, as he had a little time ahead to plan the wedding ceremony, while Samantha had been recovering on the island. The trip to Covid Island was set for the following morning, so both Greg and Samantha knew it was important to be completely rested for the day ahead of them.

Samantha was quite surprised in herself that she didn't feel any fear whilst she strolled along the jetty the following morning, to where a small boat was moored beside her, manned by two heavily built security guards, who ran metal detectors over Samantha over before she boarded the boat to Covid Island. Ever bone in her body however seemed to be a drumroll, as Samantha allowed the two security guards to sail the boat over to Covid Island, Samantha's gaze fixed solely on the island's buildings, which appeared clean and fresh against the background. The boat began to slow down a few minutes later, bumping gently into the harbour jetty as it went, whilst allowing Samantha to disembark the boat, flanked by the two stern looking security guards who escorted Samantha into the main reception area. Once inside the main reception hall, the two security guards exited back out through the main sliding doors, taking positions either side of it as they went.

The main reception area itself was very brightly lit from the early morning sunlight, now streaming in through the glass windows and doors. It put Samantha in mind of being inside a posh private clinic, as there were abstract artwork paintings on the walls, whilst being surrounded by clean tables and chairs. It was also deadly silent inside as well, as Samantha sat all alone in the empty room, wondering what was going to happen next. Suddenly to her left, came the sounds of footsteps, as one of the scientists that Samantha had seen from Grey's Pharmaceuticals came through a double set of doors, carrying a clipboard. "Hello Samantha, we're ready for you now, please come this way" said the scientists, as Samantha gingerly followed the scientist through the double set of doors down a corridor to where a white sign with black letters on it read 'operating theatre' above the door.

"Please, after you Samantha" replied the scientist, as Samantha swallowed hard before then proceeding into the room beyond the door, followed by the scientist. The medical staff on the island were exceptionally friendly towards Samantha, although Samantha still felt a little fear being inside this strange new room without Greg by her side. Greg had sadly been instructed to remain on the main island, due to an island wide fear of any cross contamination in case any of the experiments went wrong and generated another virus strain. "Ah here she is, the superhero lady to save the world; don't be scared now Samantha" said Professor Tremon, who was standing a few feet away, dressed from head to foot in protective medical clothing, which was mirrored on all front by the other medical staff. "Proceed behind the screens Samantha, and put on the medical robe" explained one of the scientists across the room from where Samantha stood in the room.

The room itself was a half operating theatre, half laboratory, which was lit on all side by large surgical spotlights, which made Samantha feel like she had suddenly been ushered on stage as some sort of star attraction in a theatre show. Without speaking, Samantha did as she was told, making her way to behind the medical screens, where she had been ordered to strip out of her clothes, when just above her head, a warm shower kicked into action, hosing her down with warm water. Samantha let out a small scream of shock as the water hit her, as she had not been expecting to be soaked in water; although in hindsight, it made her feel privileged that she was getting the first proper cleansing wash in a very long time. Before Samantha had a chance to cover herself up however, a group of men in full hazmat body suited were upon her, rubbing her down with stiff brushes and strong-smelling soap suds.

Samantha was starting to feel quite uncoverable by this point, as she was being forced to stand complete stark naked in front of a team of hazmat suited men, who were rubbing her down so vigorously, it was if Samantha had just come out from a radioactive fallout site like Chernobyl. After this quite sensitive and very awkward scene, Samantha was immediately handed a hospital gown, and told to put it on. Samantha did as she was told, and no sooner had she slipped on the hospital gown, she was led away into what looked like a decontamination chamber, which was surrounded on all sides by large glass windows and thick walls. "What's going on" cried out Samantha suddenly, but the hazmat suited men had now exited the room, closing the large steel door behind them, locking Samantha inside it. "Excuse me" said Samantha, but as she finished speaking, Professor Tremon's voice came over the intercom system inside the chamber itself.

"Samantha, I'm sorry for how we've had to go about our work, but it's important that you're as sterile as we can make you before the medical trails; please, lay back on the couch for me". "You could have told me about the shower Professor" replied Samantha, as she lay down on the couch which sat in the middle of the chamber. Suddenly to Samantha's left, a small hatch opened up, revealing a number of activities including a colouring book and a stack of old newspapers. "Erm, pardon me Professor, but what are all of these for" asked Samantha, wondering if this was the islands idea of a laughable joke. "Don't worry Samantha, these are tasks for you to complete as part of our medical trials here" explained Professor Tremon, his voice still coming over the public announcement system. It suddenly dawned on Samantha that this was exactly the sort of thing that scientists would do, as she took out the old newspapers and colouring book from the tray.

"One thing that our research centres were unable to pick up was how the Covid virus was spreading; we still need to investigate this more carefully, whereas to hopefully prevent it from spreading again as part of our recolonise programme" explained Professor Tremon, as a look of understanding came across Samantha's face. "I understand Professor, but I still don't understand what these are for" replied Samantha, as Professor Tremon let out a small noise of understanding. "Ahh, well you see, the items in front of you will allow us to monitor your life signals and body motor functions while we conduct our experiments; this should help to determine what the effects of long Covid might be" explained Professor Tremon, as Samantha looked puzzled again. "What's long Covid" asked Samantha, picking up the colouring book and some colouring pencils on the table next to her, before laying back on the couch.

"Long Covid is a theory that our scientists have devised would most likely be stage two of the Covid virus, rather than killing people, it would deform or weaken them in some way" explained Professor Tremon, as Samantha opened up the colouring book to the first page. On the first page of the colouring book, was a picture of your average family home, with its slanted roof and rectangle bricks, along with double glazed windows. "We'd like you to colour in the house for us; please take your time Sam, and we shall be monitoring you to see when you have finished" explained Professor Tremon, as Samantha without speaking, picking up her first colouring pencil and began to colour in the house. Samantha had to admit that she hadn't done colouring in since she was a small child, but found the art quite therapeutic all the same, realising that in a busy lifestyle, when did people ever get a chance to do this sort of thing.

Samantha certainly had a keen eye for detail, as after ten minutes or so, she had coloured in a quarter of the picture, without missing a single line or putting the wrong colour in the wrong place. It was only after this, that Samantha suddenly started to feel a little strange, as a slight headache had started to fog up her brain. Samantha rubbed her eyes slightly, wondering why she was suddenly feeling so tired, as one of her lines that she was colouring in curved away, rather than keeping it on the straight line it was supposed to be on. "Samantha, are you alright" asked Professor Tremon's voice over the speakers inside the chamber, as Samantha rubbed her eyes again, wondering what was going on. "Yeah, I think so; I just feel really light headed all of a sudden" replied Samantha, as her eyes began to go in and out of focus. Little did Samantha know at that moment, but the entire chamber was being filled with a form of the Covid virus in gas form.

Samantha had been unknowingly breathing it in from the moment she had been locked inside the chamber, as the effects of the Covid gas began to take hold of her. "Sir, Samantha's heartbeat is fluctuating, she may pass out from the effects" replied one of the scientists back in the other room, as Professor Tremon kept watch on Samantha inside the chamber via a series of screens inside the lab, using a state-of-the-art

CCTV system to keep tabs on Samantha. "Good work everyone, so we know that the virus can spread through the air, ok, let's stop pumping the gas in and allow it to circulate in the room" replied Professor Tremon, as a scientist standing by a control panel pushed a few buttons, as they watched Samantha cough slightly from the effects of the gas cloud. As Samantha could nether see or taste the gas within the chamber, she was still under the impression that maybe she was dehydrating somehow.

Sitting up slightly, Samantha took a sip of water from the bottle left on the table next to her, instantly feeling much better. "Sorry Professor, looks like I was a little dehydrated" replied Samantha, as she placed the bottle down on the table, feeling her eyesight returning to normal again. Without warning however, Samantha suddenly felt her vision go white again, as her head fell backwards onto the couch's headrest, as she felt her body become weaker and weaker. Although being immune to the effects of the Covid gas, it had still made her pass out as a result.

CHAPTER THIRTY

The Future Starts Here

When Samantha next awoke, she felt incredibly warm and sleepy, as if someone had wrapped her in an electric blanket. Samantha slowly opened her eyes just enough so that she could see what was around her, before suddenly sitting bolt upright in shock to what greeted her. She was lying in a hospital bed, in what looked like a hospital wing dormitory, with rows and rows of empty beds inside it. It was only after a few minutes of being concuss again, that Samantha realised that Professor Tremon was sitting on a chair next to her, glasses on his nose, staring down at some kind of a report in his hands. "Ah, Samantha, glad to have you back with us; you've been asleep for a while now" replied Professor Tremon, as Samantha did her best not to jump backwards or scream in alarm. "How are you feeling" asked Professor Tremon, as Samantha rubbed her eyes, yawning as she did so.

"I think I'm ok Professor, how long was I out for" asked Samantha, as Professor Tremon smiled at her. "Almost three days now; our last experiment that we were performing within the lab was exposing you to a gas form of the Covid virus" explained Professor Tremon, as a look of understanding came across Samantha's face. "So that's why I felt light headed while in the chamber" replied Samantha, as Professor Tremon smiled at her. "Correct; and I have to say that the result we have managed to collect from that test have been fantastic, we now know that Covid could have easily been sprayed on a person or persons in certain places, little realising they were carrying a deadly pathogen" explained Professor Tremon, as Samantha looked surprised. "That's amazing Professor, I'm glad I was able to help; have I really been unconcise for nearly three days" asked Samantha, working out that she had passed out in the chamber.

"Aye, she's a tough nut Samantha Bonham, makes me proud to see her saving the world" came a familiar voice, as Samantha saw Andrew walk in through the doorway, drawing level with them both a few seconds later. "Andrew, hi, thanks for coming to see me; what are you doing here on the island" asked Samantha, as Andrew smiled broadly. "Professor Tremon offered me a job as head of security here on the island, so I get the honour of protecting you every day" replied Andrew, as Samantha smiled broadly. "Aww that's wonderful Andrew, congratulations" couped Samantha, as Professor Tremon nodded to a scientist, who proceeded over to Samantha, who placed a thermometer Samantha's her mouth, in order to check her temperature. "Ah, full bill of health Professor, Samantha is completely clear of the effects of the Covid gas" responded the scientist.

Professor Tremon thanked the scientist, who then removed the thermometer from Samantha's mouth and strode away up between the beds and out of sight. As the scientist disappeared from view however, a new figure emerged, walking quickly towards the bed where Samantha lay, a glass of water in his hand. It was Greg, and for the first time since arriving on Covid island, Samantha was shocked to see him. "Don't look too surprised Samantha, I'll explain it all in a moment, here" replied Greg, who handed over the glass of water. Samantha thanked Greg for the glass of water, as she took a gulp of it, and then replied, "I feel quite light headed and dehydrated". "That might be because of the heat, your back on the main island as well, so the humidity might be starting to get to you" replied Greg, as he took a step back from Samantha, whilst Professor Tremon and Andrew looked on.

This was certainly very true, as Samantha now began to feel hot and light headed after her treatment on Covid Island, but Professor Tremon had warned her about this before they had started. "How long have I been here" asked Samantha, knowing that she had asked this question before, but still feeling that she needed to ask it, just to make sure she wasn't in some sort of a coma. "Three days now at least, the test zapped nearly all of your strength, and it put you into a sort of mini coma in the process" replied Andrew, as Professor Tremon nodded to him in acknowledgement. "Indeed Samantha, I am pleased to say you have made a remarkable recovery, despite being part of the experiment in the chamber; please excuse me everyone, I have things to attend to" replied Professor Tremon, as he got up, thanked Samantha for her time, before then proceeding up the ward and out of site though the doorway.

"They were worried you wouldn't come out of it; so was I to be honest, seeing as if we're getting married the day after tomorrow" replied Greg, as Samantha jumped so much, that she nearly spilled the rest of her water all over the bedsheet. "The day after tomorrow, but I don't know if I can walk, let alone stand up in heels at a wedding" exclaimed Samantha, as Greg and Andrew chuckled slightly. "It's ok Sam, we checked with the Professor, and he says there are no side effects, so you'll be perfectly ok" replied Greg, as he placed a reassuring hand on Samantha's shoulder. "You better make yourself scarce you know Greg, being tradition and all that" suddenly spoke out Andrew, as this time it was Greg's turn to jump in surprise. "Oh heck, yes, I nearly forget, love you Samantha babes" exclaimed Greg, as he suddenly sprinted from the room, the door banged shut behind him as he went.

Andrew chuckled again, as he replied, "bless him, you're a lucky girl to have someone like him you know Sam". Samantha smiled in appreciation, as a few nurses entered the room, to check on Samantha. "Best be off Sam, let the nurses do their stuff, speak soon I suspect" replied Andrew, as Samantha wished Andrew well, as he too exited the room through the far door as Greg had done a few moments earlier. The nurses helped Samantha to her feet, as she managed to stand up on her feet with surprising ease, as if her strength had suddenly come back to her all at once in one swift movement. This wonderful euphoria was short lived however, as Samantha nearly collapsed back into the hospital bed again, realising that she was getting married the day after tomorrow. "Greg must have done all of the planning while I was away" thought Samantha to herself, thinking that Greg must have done everything in record time.

The usual pre-Covid wedding ceremonies often took months to plan and put together, but Greg had managed to do it in a matter of days, possibly being aided and abetted by Andrew or Professor Tremon no doubt. "You must take it easy over the next few days dear, you're recovering from the effects of a nasty virus, and your body needs to regenerate it in order for you to function properly" replied the matron, who was part of the small group of nurses who were now giving Samantha a check-up. "I feel fine now, I just can't believe I'm going down the aisle within the next forty-eight hours" replied Samantha, as the matron frowned slightly. "Hmm, yes; not what I would recommend after being a medical Guinea pig, but Professor Tremon says that you should be fine in a few days, so that's good enough for me" replied the matron, as she walked with Samantha up the hospital ward and out into the corridor, which was flooded with bright sunlight.

As Samantha stepped outside, she had no problem at all adjusting to the brightness of the sunshine outside, as it was again another clear sunny day; far more different, than it had been back in England. This new island paradise, made the British Isles look small fry in comparison to it, as Samantha remembered the rain, wind and cold that would have usually have been associated with the Great British weather. "Your fiancée has drawn up a list for you of things and places he has organised for the wedding" replied the matron, as she handed Samantha a piece of paper, which was half of a to do list, and a list of requests that Greg had written down for Samantha to look at. Samantha could clearly see that the list involved a series of names and businesses, which Samantha guessed were shops and people on the island who were specialists and skilled in certain fields.

The very top of this list said just one word; hairdresser; which Samantha knew was a must, not knowing exactly what form of style she would go for herself. Taking a little walk across town, Samantha soon located the hairdresser's salon, with its barber's stripes spinning around and around by the front door. The hairdresser herself was a very charming lady, which put Samantha back in mind of Melissia back at Mile End Farm, who had styled Julie's hair before her wedding to Trevor only a matter of weeks ago. She was a youngish looking lady by the name of Rebecca, with shoulder length blondie hair, and a heart shaped face. As Samantha listened to Rebecca's voice, she made a rough guess that Rebecca was a native of one of the Eastern European countries, as her accent put Samantha in mind of a Polish truck driver, she had known thought her works back in the days before Covid.

"Ah, this hair is a mess darling, what have you been doing, dragging yourself through a hedge backwards" sighed Rebecca, as she flicked and played around with Samantha's hair, Samantha looking a little guilty as sat in the hairdresser's chair. "If I told you about what has been happening to me, I suspect it would never make a good story, otherwise they'd think I was lying" replied Samantha, as she giggled slightly, feeling slight twinges every so often, as Rebecca flicked, curled, and ran a comb through Samantha's hair, Samantha feeling every single tug and knot in her hair. "What makes you say that Samantha my darling" replied Rebecca, as a curious expression crossed over onto her face. Feel that she didn't have much of a choice in the matter, Samantha soon launched into her story from when she had left Lillington, right up to being rescued from the town of Clyde and coming to the island on the submarine.

"You've certainly had a traumatic and scary adventure to say the least" replied Rebecca, as Samantha watched Rebecca roll and twist her hair up into a bun at the back of her head. "There, do you think that will work for you" asked Rebecca, taking a step backwards, as Samantha admired her hair in the mirror. It took Samantha a few seconds to properly see how her reflection looked, but she certainly didn't look like the same well-groomed lady that she had been when she had left Lillington, many months beforehand. In the time they had been talking, Rebecca had washed, combed, trimmed and styled Samantha's hair so much, that she hadn't recognised it from what it looked like before. It was truly a nice feeling to have, as Samantha had been practically living out of a cardboard box for so many weeks, deprived of her usual access to the hair and beauty products that the pre-Covid world sold by the bucket load.

Samantha's face didn't look too pretty either, as her eyes carried small bags underneath them through poor nourishment, alongside a great lack of looking after her skin, like she always had done before Covid. Samantha's improvised bath that she had chosen to take in Askham lake, hadn't cleansed her as much as she would have liked, but at least now on the island, Samantha seemed like she was back in some form of normal society, like it had been before Covid. "Aww, I think it's lovely, thank you" replied Samantha, grinning from ear to ear, which made her face light up a little, taking aware some of the features that Samantha wasn't proud of, like the small bags under her eyes. "Aww, your welcome darling; it's just a taster of course, but I shall do that for your big day" replied Rebecca, as she began to unclip Samantha's hair, so that it dropped down into the normal wavey form that it took on a day-to-day basis.

Something in Samantha's face must have given her thoughts away however, as Rebecca suddenly pulled a funny face at Samantha and said, "your worried about the eyes aren't you". "Yes, well, I've just been so far away from my usual treatments" began Samantha, but Rebecca had cut her off mid-sentence with a wave of her hand, before beckoning Samantha to follow her. Puzzled, Samantha followed Rebecca through the shop into a back room, where there was a massage parlour table and assorted cosmetic tools. "Lay down here, and when I'm finished with my treatment here, you will look like a princess" said Rebecca, as she gestured to the massage table, watching Samantha do as she was instructed, laying down upon it. It felt weird to Samantha laying down on the table, like she was back in the chamber on Covid Island again, being a part of the medical trials.

Samantha lay flat on her back, staring up at the ceiling where the small ceiling lights shone down at her, making the room just as bright as the street outside the shop. "Just take slow deep breaths Samantha, close your eyes, and relax" came Rebecca's voice, as Samantha did as she was told, closing her eyes and doing her best to relax. Samantha had no idea what Rebecca was doing, but she could feel Rebecca's hands running over her face in a massaging effect, with some sort of cream like substance. This was then followed by a vigorous cleansing of her face with what felt like cotton wool. "Ok, that should do it perfectly" finally spoke Rebecca after an hour or so, with Samantha feeling so relaxed, she had nearly fallen asleep laying on the table. Whatever it was that Rebecca had done, certainly seemed to be having an effect, as Samantha felt refreshed and more awake than ever before.

"See you in a few days" replied Rebecca, as Samantha departed the salon around ten minutes, wishing Rebecca a good day as she went. According to what Professor Tremon had said, Samantha wasn't due to start her new job on the island's railway line until a few days after the wedding itself, so she had a bit of a chance to relax, and take in the views around her. Samantha did miss Greg not being there however, but then again, it was always the tradition that the bride and groom were never together before the wedding. It did suddenly occur to Samantha, as she took a trip around the islands many shops, that she didn't have any bridesmaids for the wedding itself. Her natural bridesmaids of choice, were all now sadly deceased back in England, so what exactly was Samantha supposed to do about this particular sticky situation, knowing that she didn't have anyone at all.

Samantha almost had a fleeting image of going around the island, picking ladies up at random, and asking them to be bridesmaids. Even as Samantha sat there thinking this very thought, she immediately dismissed it, as the idea just sounded plain stupid; or was it? After all, they were in a post-apocalyptic Covid society, so in Samantha's book, anything was possible. This too went for the same as the guests, both Samantha and Greg's families were dead and gone, so how would they go about it all. "A private ceremony perhaps" thought Samantha, but even that didn't sound possible. What was the point in having a wedding, if no one was there to see it, other than her and Greg of course? Samantha stopped walking for a moment, resting her body up against the side of a building, listening to the sounds of the waves crashing up on the beachfront, when suddenly, she was aware of someone standing quite close by.

Samantha carefully looked around to see Professor Tremon standing there, leaning up against the same building as Samantha was. "You look like a lady who is pondering a great problem my dear" he replied, as he approached Samantha, looking at her directly in the eye. Samantha didn't flinch or spin around this time, but instead turned her head towards Professor Tremon and said, "you can say that again Professor". "Ah, well, I have helped a great number of people in my many decades on this planet Samantha my dear, so I'm sure that whatever your troubles are, you can share them with me" replied Professor Tremon, as Samantha turned her head, hoping that Professor Tremon wasn't going to expect Samantha to pull miracles out of a hat, as she had often demonstrated in his science lab. Samantha couldn't help but think that Professor Tremon struck her as being more like a psychologist, rather than a man of medicine.

However, in hindsight, Samantha felt that if anyone could help her, Professor Tremon was most certainly the man for the job, with all of his connections and the islands entire population listening to his every word. "Me and Greg have been lovers for years now; we'd planned our wedding down to a tee during the Covid lockdown, but neither of us predicted that we'd be getting married on a tropical island in the Caribbean with no family or friends" replied Samantha, after she'd taken a small intake of breath, along with a small sigh. "You are worried that no-one will see it; please remember my dear, that you and Greg are the first wedding we will have on this island, so I want to make it as memorable as possible for you" replied Professor Tremon, scratching his chin slightly with his fingers, pondering his answer. "Aww thank you Professor, I don't know how to thank you for this" couped Samantha, as Professor Tremon waved a hand at her.

"Ah that should never be a problem at all; in fact, I thought that being the man who is the elected leader of this community, that I would have the honour to walk you down the aisle, your family sadly not being able to do it themselves" replied Professor Tremon, as Samantha's eyes widened in shock. "You would really do that Professor" said Samantha, as Professor Tremon smiled at her in a fatherly sort of way. "I would consider it as the greatest gesture of welcome that I could bestow Samantha; a number of the lovely ladies on the island have been practically queueing up to be your bridesmaids, and even Greg has his best man lined up while you were on Covid Island" replied Professor Tremon, in a reassuring voice. "Wow, I didn't know I was as popular as that, considering I've only just arrived on the island" replied Samantha, thinking of how quickly the news had spread on the island.

"On an island as small as this one, it's hardly surprising that news travels fast; the islands people are more than aware of your daring do and survival as a refugee" replied Professor Tremon with a small chuckle, as even Samantha giggled slightly, feeling as if a huge weight had lifted from her shoulders at the sound of Professor Tremon's words. If the lovely ladies of the island were practically queuing up for the bridesmaid's positions, Samantha felt that she might have to start interviewing them all, so she that she didn't become overcrowded with overly keen fans and admirers. "I think also, that a break from tradition is what is needed; we shouldn't become too bogged down in things from days gone by" replied Professor Tremon, as he leaned in towards Samantha a little, snapping Samantha out of her temporary day dream that she had been having about sitting down behind a desk to interview the islands ladies for bridesmaid's positions.

"I maybe an old man around here, but that doesn't mean to say that I don't like a good old fashioned beach party" replied Professor Tremon, as he winked slightly, making Samantha giggle, and then blush bright red, having a sudden fleeting image of Professor Tremon in a Hawaiian beach shirt and shorts, rather his usual smart suit and tie. "Thank you, Professor, you're very kind for allowing this" replied Samantha, as Professor Tremon waved a hand in front of his face. "Oh, not at all Samantha, it would be a great shame if we didn't let our hair down every once in a while" said Professor Tremon, as he gave Samantha shoulder a quick squeeze, before strolling away, back towards the buildings in the background. Feeling that leaning up against a wall wasn't the most comfortable of places to be, Samantha instead proceeded down to the beach, resting herself up against a palm tree, watching the sun sink below the horizon.

Her small chat with Professor Tremon, had certainly lifted Samantha's spirits considerably since she had propped herself up against the palm tree on the beach. When darkness had finally fallen around Samantha, and she could hear the sounds of parrots and other birdlife slowly dying away all around her, Samantha stood up off the sand, and turned back towards the town, making her way back into a small villa, where she was to spend the next few days undergoing counselling, and preparing for the wedding. It did seem strange to Samantha that she had to undergo counselling, but Professor Tremon had explained to her the following day that it was a compulsory requirement for everyone who arrived on the island, as many, if not all of the islanders, had been through some form of trauma in order to get to the island, having been trapped and isolated within each of their own countries due to Covid.

With what Samantha had been through to get to the island, it was hardly surprising that Professor Tremon had insisted upon Samantha undergoing this treatment, and at least she would have a clear head going forwards from then on. Samantha wasn't sure what was more painful;

thinking back on her time in England after Covid, or talking about it to a complete stranger. "But then again, Andrew, Patrick and the others had all been complete strangers, and I'd told them about my story" thought Samantha, as she woke the following morning inside the villa's master bedroom, feeling a little sad that Greg wasn't with her. Samantha's voice was so croaky and horse after completing the counselling session that morning, that Samantha had been forced to drink three whole litres of water in the space of five minutes, after speaking to the councillor for what felt like hours.

Samantha had also done a little bit of crying as well, which according to the councillor, was to be expected in the cases of victims dealing with post-traumatic stress disorder, which Samantha had been diagnosed with by the island's main counsellor. The afternoon however was considerably a lot more enjoyable than the morning was, as this was where Samantha was helped in getting ready for the following day, as she was moved from room to room on a weird sort of production line, being treated from everything from spa and massage treatments, to her dress fitting and makeup. By the time Samantha went to bed that evening, she was so tired from the day's activities, that she felt as if she could have slept for the next thousand years, but knew her wedding the following day was going to be quite the show. Samantha had to allow herself a giggle however, as she pictured Greg on his stag night, most likely the victim of a silly prank of some kind.

Samantha's own hen party that evening hadn't been a very long one, but it had at least granted Samantha the opportunity to meet her bridesmaids for the following day, who came in all shapes and sizes from the youngest who was fifteen, to the oldest who was nearly sixty, and even included Rebecca in their numbers as well. Even though Samantha felt as light as a feather in what was undoubtably the most comfortable bed on the island, she was still fully awake before the sun had fully risen, despite the feeling of tiredness that was still lingering around her from the previous day. As Samantha rolled over in bed, she felt a soft gentle breeze blowing in through the open windows around her bedroom. The light breeze was making the net curtains around her bed twitch slightly, as if an invisible hand was pulling them backwards and forwards. It was surprising how cold it could really get on a Caribbean Island during the night time hours.

Samantha shivered slightly, pulling the bed clothes over her, as she drifted slowly back off to sleep again, her eyes feeling heavy again after she had awoken. When Samantha awoke again a few hours later, she was suddenly given the shock of her life, as she saw every single one of her bridesmaids, which included Rebecca the salon owner, all huddled around her bed, looking a little tired themselves, because of the hen do the previous evening. Samantha could see them very clearly this time, owing to the fact that the sun had now risen, and was pouring beams of sunlight in through the windows around her. "Come on Princess, you can't lie around here all day" said Rebecca, as Samantha felt many hands pulling her to her feet, making the bed clothes fall away onto the floor. Samantha was then forced into a silky dressing gown, before being frogmarched out of her bedroom, into the makeup and styling room.

The chair that had been set out for her was so comfortable, that Samantha could have quite easily gone back to sleep in it again, but pressing hands and nibble fingers were prying and pocking their way around her as she lay there, surrounded by her loyal bridesmaids. The odd occasional flick of the makeup brush was also enough to make Samantha jump slightly, as she had closed her eyes, so as not to spoil the final result when she had the opportunity to see herself standing in the mirror as the blushing bride. Instead, Samantha contented herself to listen with wrapped interest to the talk of her bridesmaid around her, listening to the crushes the other ladies had on other islanders, and how Greg was a really lucky guy to have Samantha by his side. Samantha couldn't help but crack a small grin at the sound of this comment, but couldn't move too much, because of the makeup artist, now applying lip gloss to Samantha's lips.

Eventually, Samantha found herself gingerly stepping into the bridal gown, her feet twitching slightly as she went, worried about how it was all going to work out, as the wedding dress was laced up at the back, sitting so comfortably around Samantha, that she felt as if she was floating along rather than walking. "I hope those bags don't show too much" thought Samantha, worrying of how they would come out under her makeup, remembering Rebecca's work that she had performed on Samantha's face in a bid to repair the damage. It was quite a challenge to not look in any of the mirrors around the room, as Rebecca made up Samantha's hair using all of the tools that she had at her disposal around her. Tongs, hair clips and scissors littered the bench in front of them, as Samantha sat ramrod straight in her chair, eyes closed, not daring to peek even for a second in fear of revealing herself too early.

"There, you're ready for the reveal" came Rebecca's voice, after a good hour or so, as Samantha let out a short sharp breath, bracing herself for the greatest moment of her life. "Are you ready my darling" replied Rebecca in an excited voice, as Samantha cracked a wide smile, not daring to open her eyes. "Ok, I'm ready" replied Samantha, her nerves almost at breaking point, as she was helped over to the big tall mirror, eyes still clamped tight shut, not wanting to spoil anything sooner than what it had to be. "Ok, open them up wide my darling" replied Rebecca, as Samantha, now on her feet, threw her eyes wide open; and what she saw, nearly made her pass out in shock. She was Samantha the bride, looking every bit as beautiful and fabulous as she had dreamed it would be; but somehow maybe by chance, Samantha couldn't see the same lady from England looking back at her.

Her makeup was so perfect, that the small bags under her eyes had disappeared completely, to be replaced with flawless features. Her hair was tied back into a smart bun at the back of her head, with a small parting at the front, where a few hairs hung down past her ears. Her floral bouquet was full of white and red rose flowers, which in of themselves, seemed to brighten Samantha's appearance tenfold. Two flawless diamond earrings hung from her ears, glinting in the sunlight as Samantha turned her head slightly to admire them, whilst the mermaid style dress she wore hugged her body shape so well, it was almost as if it had been custom made to her exact size and figure. "Wow" was the only word that escaped Samantha's lips, as she felt tears welling up behind her eyes, staring at her reflection, hardly daring to believe that she was the woman looking back at her in the mirror.

"Of all the things you could have said, and you had to go for 'wow'; honestly" replied Rebecca with a small sighing sound, putting a small emphasis on the word 'wow'. Samantha couldn't help but crack a laugh as Rebecca stopped speaking, but Samantha got what she meant all the same, just about coping with the shock of seeing herself as the bride in the mirror. "Sorry Rebecca, I just; I just can't believe that's me" replied Samantha, still trying to fight back the tears of joy, as Rebecca smiled at her sympathetically. "Well, you better believe it princess, as that is you; you look amazing darling" couped Rebecca, as all of the other bridesmaids stood around behind Samantha, all wearing strapless floor length dresses in a scarlet red colour, made out of a soft satin silky material, all with broad smiles on their faces as they admired Samantha the blushing bride.

"Just remember that this is your day today, Samantha; you've been through so much to be here, and now you have a chance to be happy" replied Rebecca, as Samantha straightened her gown slightly, still not daring to believe that she really was the bride on her big day. Professor Tremon arrived a few minutes later, asking if Samantha was ready, wearing a crisp new light grey suit and red tie, along with a rosette in his blazer jacket button hole. He too, was amazed at how Samantha had turned out, and even went as far as to offer Samantha a kiss on her hand, which made Samantha giggle and blush bright red at the same time, which was powerful enough to show through her makeup. As the ceremony was due to take place out on the beach itself, a small metal archway had been constructed on the sand, which was followed by rows and rows of seats, all leading up to it.

These seats were already occupied by what looked like most of the island's residence, as Greg, and his best man Andrew, stood nervously in front of the rows of seats under the archway. The archway had been painted bright white in honour of the occasion, and was covered in flowers, which snaked their way up and down the archway, bringing out all sorts of different vibrant colours as they went. It had to be said, that even though Greg was the one who was getting married, it was Andrew that seemed to be shaking slightly with anxiety. Greg was wearing a smart white suit and tie, while Andrew had gone all out with a scarlet red number one dress uniform accompanied with ceremonial sword, which made him look more like a member of the Queen's Grenadier Guards, rather than a member of the special forces. Samantha meanwhile, had still not appeared behind the rows of seats, although that didn't stop Greg from nervously twitching his hands.

"What are you so nervous about, wrong uniform or something, or are you going to poke me with the sword" joked Greg, giving Andrew a quick nudge in the ribs as he spoke, noticing Andrew's fear in his posture. Andrew didn't seem to notice the dig in his ribs that Greg had given him, but quickly replied, "no it's not that, it's just; I haven't done ring bearing duty in a while, or been a best man for that matter". Greg couldn't help but stifle a snigger, as he replied, "you are joking me aren't you; you've been in the world's most elite military force, and yet you get the shivers in the simple task of giving a pair of rings to me". "Give me a behind enemy lines operation any day, but this is something else" replied Andrew, as Greg looked at Andrew in a sarcastic look as if he was going to say, 'really'. It took Greg a few seconds to take in this incredible knowledge about his best man Andrew, but realised that he hadn't known Andrew that long at all.

Before Greg had time to give this anymore thought however, the music had started up, as Samantha suddenly appeared behind the rows of seats alongside Professor Tremon, ready to walk up the aisle between the seats, towards the archway where Greg and Andrew stood, along with the vicar. It immediately dawned on Samantha, that the day was starting to warm up, being on an island somewhere near the Equator as this one was. Beads of sweat had already begun to build up on her forehead, and even her armpits had sweat in them already, maybe more out of nerves rather than the warmth of the day. "As long as it doesn't show through on the dress" thought Samantha, but it was too late to do anything about it, even if had she wanted to. A collective sigh seemed to go right the way around the crowd seated in the rows of chairs, as Greg and Andrew clocked Samantha, standing at the far end of the aisle.

Every head seated within the rows of seats had turned towards her, as Professor Tremon had taken Samantha's arm and slowly began to walk her up the aisle to the music being played from a grand piano, which was nearby to them, standing to the left of the archway. Back at the front under the archway, Greg and Andrew had turned their heads towards Samantha, and even their facial expressions were a picture in of themselves. They had both opened their mouths wide at the sight of Samantha and her radiate beauty, as Samantha drew level too them, ascending the few small steps in front of her, so that herself, Greg and Andrew were all grouped together under the archway. Professor Tremon released Samantha's arm, taking a seat on the very front row along with Rebecca and the rest of Samantha's bridesmaids, as Greg took Samantha's arm in his own.

"You look amazing babes" was Greg's response, as Samantha looked into his eyes, blushing all over as she did so. "Aye, brush up well don't you lassie" was Andrew's response, as Samantha couldn't help but place a hand on her chest and say, "aww, thank you guys" in response to their compliments. Greg now reached his hands forward and carefully lifted up Samantha's bridal veil, seeing her face properly for the first time since they had last seen each other a few days earlier. A man in his early forties, now approached the archway, standing in front of Samantha and Greg, wearing a black vicar's uniform with white collar. "Do you have the rings" was the vicar's response, as Andrew held out two boxes in his hand. "Ah, very good, then we can begin" replied the vicar, as he cleared his throat, as a deadly silence now fell across the crowd of onlookers seated in the rows of seat behind them.

The only sounds that could be heard now, were the waves crashing into the beach shoreline, and a gentle sea breeze whipping around them, making the hem of Samantha's dress blow against her legs slightly. It was also quite a while since she'd worn any kind of shoes with heels on them, as Samantha stood there balancing herself whilst wearing a pair of three-inch-high heels, which matched her dress perfectly. "Dearly beloved, we gathered here today in the site of god, to marry together this man, and this woman, in holy matrimony" began the vicar, after clearing his throat a second or so earlier. As the vicar carried on with his religious vows for the wedding, Samantha was briefly reminded of another post Covid wedding she had been too in the past, and how that had been completely different to how a normal wedding would have been performed in the days before Covid had struck.

But when the sound of Greg's name was mentioned, Samantha seemed to snap out of her daydream, remembering that this was her and Greg's wedding, and not Julie and Trevor's one back on Mile End Farm. "Greg, will you take Samantha to be your lawfully wedded wife, to cherish and hold, so long as you both shall live" recited the vicar, as Greg looked directly into Samantha's eyes, seeing the love in them properly for the first time. "I do sir" replied Greg, as the vicar turned to Samantha and said, "do you Samantha, take Greg to be your lawfully wedded husband, to cherish and hold, so as you both shall live". "I do" replied Samantha, as she couldn't help but grin from ear to ear. Greg took Samantha's hand, and slid one of the diamond rings onto it, as Samantha then repeated the process onto Greg's hand, before they both looked into each other's eyes, smiling broadly at each other, as if they were the happiest people on earth.

"By the power vestured in me, and in the sight of the lord, I declare you both as husband and wife; you may kiss your bride" replied the vicar, but Samantha had beaten him too it. "Hold these will you" replied Samantha, as she thrust her floral bouquet into the vicar's hands with such force, that she nearly knocked him over, before then wrapping herself around Greg, kissing him squarely on the lips. The seated crowd laughed slightly at the sight of Samantha disposing of her bouquet on the vicar, before a collective sigh went up, followed by everyone clapping and applauding them, as Samantha and Greg both turned to face the crowd, beaming so broadly, that they could easily eclipsed the sun out of the sky with happiness. "I won't forget this babe, I really won't" replied Greg, as he kissed Samantha again, Samantha blushing deeply as he did so, feeling butterflies rising in her stomach.

"I'll never forget this Greg, I really won't" was Samantha's reply, as they both cuddled close to each other for the photographer, who was snapping pictures away like mad, the camera flashes clearly visible over the bright sunlight from where they stood underneath the flowery archway. It was not like any celebration they had ever attended in their lives, and it seemed to fly past so quickly, if was almost as if someone had tampered with the clocks to make them travel at twice their usual speed. Everything was all being done down on the beach, so that by the time the evening came around, they were all very sweaty indeed from the heat of the day. Even Samantha could have sworn blind that she had dropped two whole dress sizes just through sweating alone, even though the reception meal after the ceremony was quite filling with the many meals and deserts that were being served.

The speeches at the meal were quite interesting as well, as Professor Tremon was doing Samantha's speech, and Andrew had been elected to read out the best man's speech. As neither person had known Samantha and Greg that long at all, the comments and stories about them were varied to say the least. Both Greg and Samantha felt that their lungs might well have exploded under the pressure, due to the amount of laughter that they were doing. As there was a fully working electrical supply on the island for the houses and other facilities, there was no shortage of music and lighting to keep them all dancing late into the night. And by the time that Greg and Samantha collapsed in the honeymoon suite, which had been set aside for them on the island, they felt like they couldn't have moved an inch further than the bed that they were now laying on, still chuckling and reminiscing at how great the day had been.

"I'm glad I might never have to wear this thing again, I must have lost twelve stone in sweat today" said Greg, as he unstuck his shirt from his back, feeling it drenched in sweat due to the humidity of the day. "Same, I'm surprised this gown isn't yellow with the amount I've lost" giggled back Samantha, as she run her hand up and down her wedding gown, trying to check for any sign of sweat patches on it. It seemed to feel quite dry, which defiantly shocked Samantha at first, but she then realised that the gown itself was probably designed with that in mind. "Well, I can always give you a helping hand, to get it off" replied Greg, in quite a sexy, seductive voice. Samantha giggled again, realising what Greg was after, and after the wonders of that day's brilliance, she wasn't going to refuse him anything at all. "You never have to ask me babe, just dive straight in" replied Samantha, in her most seductive and sweetest voice that she could muster.

Samantha then reached back, and started pulling the hair pins out of her hair, which had kept her hair in the tight bun that it had been in since first thing that morning. Samantha's hair fell gracefully downwards onto the sheets, as Samantha lay on her side on the bed, looking directly into Greg's eyes, as they started kissing again. But Samantha couldn't help but notice the feel of Greg's hands, which had found their way up to her back, where they slowly began to loosen the lace straps holding up Samantha's wedding gown. It was fair to say, that the rest of the night passed with a passion for Samantha and Greg, and they both awoke late the following morning, having indulged in romantic activities the previous evening. "Morning babe, how are you feeling" said Greg in a sleepy voice, as he yawned and stretched slightly, gently stroking Samantha's hair as he did so.

Samantha lay curled up beside Greg, as she smiled, her eyes still closed, thinking how lovely it was to be here, married at last to the man she had gone so far to find and save back in England. "I'm feeling; ecstatic" replied Samantha, after a short pause, finally turning over to look at Greg directly, her eyes now wide open and pretty. "So, you should be Sam; we're married; we did it" replied Greg, as he threw his arms up into the air in triumph. "Yeah, we did, and we're going to be that way forever" replied Samantha as she reached over and kissed Greg on the cheek. "I was going to go for a walk on the beach, get some air into my lungs" said Samantha, as Greg returned her kiss, this time on her forehead. "You do whatever you like babe, I'll try and get us some breakfast" replied Greg, as Samantha smiled back at him, before she pulled herself out of the bed, slipping on a dressing gown as she went.

Greg exited the room shortly after this, as Samantha walked out onto the ground floor balcony, looking out over the perfect sea view laid out before her from the ground floor balcony. "I'm in paradise" said Samantha to herself, as she walked down the small set of steps in front of her, towards the white sandy beach, sitting herself down on the white beach sand underneath the shade of a palm tree. The early morning sun had only just begun to rise, as it bathed the surrounding buildings in a yellow glow from where the sun had just started to poke itself up from out of the sea in front of her on the horizon. Samantha had only been sat on the sand for a few short minutes, when she was suddenly aware of a small group of around half a dozen young children standing just to her right. The oldest of the group being around twelve years old, and the youngest being no older than six, all looking quite reserved, as though they were waiting for something.

They all seemed to be a little nervous at first, and didn't feel like they wanted to approach Samantha through fear of some unknown terror. Samantha wasn't surprised to see children on the island, as she had seen so many weird and wonderful things on this island, that nothing seemed to surprise her much these days. "Hello there, don't be afraid, I mean you no harm" said Samantha, in her most mother like of voices, holding out a hand in a gesture of welcome. The group of children seem to hesitate for a few moments, before Samantha replied, "I'm going for my breakfast soon, would you like that"? Around four of five of them nodded their heads enthusiastically, as Samantha gave them a friendly smile, and watched as the group of children sat themselves down on the sand next to Samantha underneath the palm tree. "You must all really like me, I'm honoured" giggled Samantha, as one of the children suddenly spoke up.

"Excuse me miss, are you Samantha". "Yes, I am, how did you know that" asked Samantha in a kind voice, as if she was a school teacher in a class room, teaching young children a valuable life lesson. "Professor Tremon told us who you were, and he said that you had a good story to tell, an adventure he said" said a second child in the group. "Ah did he now; well; did he also tell you, that I'm also a highly skilled and talented lady as well" replied Samantha, in her most story time type of voice that she could muster. "Oh please Miss Samantha, please tell us about your adventures" pleaded a few of the children, as there was a sudden sound of footsteps behind Samantha, as Professor Tremon came into view again. "Ah Samantha my dear, I hope your well today" asked Professor Tremon, as he suddenly caught site of the group of children huddled around Samantha.

"Ahh, I see our young generation has found our islands newlywed; well, don't let me hold you up Samantha, there dying to know about your adventures" replied Professor Tremon, as Samantha beamed at him in appreciation, as Professor Tremon hadn't allowed Samantha time to answer his question. "Thank you, Professor, your most kind" replied Samantha, as Professor Tremon gave her a short bow, and then proceeded back up the beach, becoming smaller and smaller the further he walked away. "Well, I guess if the professor is happy for you to be told, then I suppose hearing about my adventures won't harm you one little bit" replied Samantha, as the children in the group cheered at the sound of Samantha's voice. They quickly fell silent however, as Samantha began to speak again, her voice turned over again to the tone of story time, tails and adventures.

"Once upon a time, there was the nearly ordinary girl; she was a truck driver, and she had a loving friend and partner called Greg". Samantha allowed herself a breath, before continuing on, as all of the children were now listening with rapt attention, their ears wide open and alert with interest. "This girls name, was Samantha; and Samantha would have some of the strangest and craziest moments of her life; she would defeat supervillains, build and drive a super truck, work on a farm and even fight in a great battle". As Samantha sat telling her story to the kids, Greg suddenly appeared at her shoulder, laden with what looked like half of a family kitchen upon it in food. "I didn't know we were having a breakfast picnic" Greg chuckled, as the children all looked up at Greg this time. "Everyone, I'd like you to meet my husband, this is Greg everyone".

"Hi Greg" chorused the group of children, as Greg said 'hi' in return to them all, giving his hand a little wave in the air as he did so. Greg was carrying a tray in his arms, which was laden food, it was almost impossible for Greg to carry it, at which Samantha couped at the sight of it, and insisted that Greg join her, as she told the story to the group of children. "I do love a good story time, has she got to any of the good bits yet" chuckled Greg, as some of the children tittered and laughed at Greg's joke. Even Samantha couldn't help but crack a grin, as she took a bite out of a piece of toast, and then insisted that the other children tuck into the breakfast meal as well, which the children did with great gusto. "So, where are we up to in the story" asked Greg, as Samantha took a deep breath, and continued on with her speech, carefully to make it sound as adventurous and exciting as possible.

"My name kids; is Samantha Bonham, from England; this is my story; and this; is where it begins" replied Samantha, as she looked around her at the young eager faces, just waiting to hear the adventures of Samantha and her friends. Time; it seemed; would come to serve the island well in the many years to come. The old world may have been dead, but a new one, was rising from the ashes, faster and greater than anyone could have seen possible. Mother nature had certainly won this round; but despite its raw fire power and strength, it had not beaten Samantha Bonham; the Survivor. The next few weeks past by with no incidents whatsoever, as Samantha balanced both her new job as a train driver on the island, along with her dedication to the Covid research on Covid Island. Professor Tremon was always present at the sessions, making sure that Samantha never came to any harm during the medical trials she was undergoing for the company.

Samantha had reported to the Covid Island, and been placed under a cat scanner to check for any medical problems which may have aroused in the past. To everyone in the room however, the scientist looking at the screen monitoring Samantha's x-rays was taken aback by what he saw. "Professor, you may want to come and look at this" said the scientist, as Professor Tremon came over to the computer screen, staring the strange anomaly on the x-rays. "Well, I'll be blowed, her and Greg have been having a good time together as our married couple" joked Professor Tremon, as he pointed to the screen. "Shall I tell her the good news Professor" said the scientist, but Professor Tremon held up a hand to stop the scientist. "I'm going through to her now, so I'll tell her for you; she will be pleased to hear about the medical trials" replied Professor Tremon, as he exited the room into the room next door, where Samantha lay on the operating table.

"Hello Professor, is everything ok" asked Samantha, as Professor Tremon smiled at Samantha in a way which told Samantha that she was about to receive good news. "Samantha, I can safely say, that you have a bundle of joy on the way; your pregnant; congratulations" replied Professor Tremon, as he waited for Samantha's response. What Samantha thought about this however, Professor Tremon never really found out; as Samantha had chosen that particular moment to pass out in shock; onto the floor.

THE END

Lightning Source UK Ltd.
Milton Keynes UK
UKHW041501130223
416719UK00001BA/104